The Third Life
of Grange Copeland

Meridian

The Color Purple

The Third Life
of Grange Copeland

Meridian

The Color Purple

Alice Walker

BLACK EXPRESSIONS REDISCOVERIES

The Third Life
of Grange Copeland

For my mother,

who made a way out of no way

And for Mel, my husband

Sometimes I had an intense desire to cry because of something my father said, but instead, because life, cynicism, had taught me to put on a mask, I laughed. For him, I did not suffer, I felt nothing, I was a shameless cynic, I had no soul . . . because of the mask I showed. But inside, I felt every word he said.

MANUEL, IN *The Children of Sanchez*
—BY OSCAR LEWIS

O, my clansmen
Let us all cry together!
Come,
Let us mourn the death of my husband,
The death of a Prince
The Ash that was produced
By a great Fire!
O this homestead is utterly dead,
Close the gates
With *lacari* thorns,
For the Prince
The heir to the Stool is lost!
And all the young men
Have perished in the wilderness!

"SONG OF LAWINO"
—A LAMENT BY OKOT P'BITEK

"The great danger," Richard told Sartre, "in the world today is that the very feeling and conception of what is a human being might well be lost."

RICHARD WRIGHT TO JEAN-PAUL
SARTRE, IN *Richard Wright*
—BY CONSTANCE WEBB

The Third Life
of Grange Copeland

PART I

1

Brownfield stood close to his mother in the yard, not taking his eyes off the back of the receding automobile. His Uncle Silas slowed the car as it got to a place where a pointed rock jutted up out of the road: a week before he had busted an oil pan there. Once past this spot, which he had cursed as he passed to and fro over it during the week, he stuck out his arm and waved jauntily back at them. Brownfield waved sadly, his eyes blurred with tears. His Aunt Marilyn, not visible through the rear window of the car, waved a dainty blue handkerchief from her front window. It fluttered merrily like a pennant. Brownfield's cousins had their faces pressed to the rear window, and their delicate, hard-to-see hands flopped monotonously up and down. They were tired of waving, for they had been waving good-bye since they finished breakfast.

The automobile was a new 1920 Buick, long and high and

3

shiny green with great popping headlights like the eyes of a frog. Inside the car it was all blue, with seats that were fuzzy and soft. Slender silver handles opened the doors and rolled the astonishingly clear windows up and down. As it bumped over the road its canvas top was scratched by low elm branches. Brownfield felt embarrassed about the bad road and the damage it did to his uncle's car. Uncle Silas loved his car and had spent all morning washing it, polishing the wheel spokes and dusting off the running board. Now it bounced over gullies and potholes in the road, tossing Uncle Silas and his wife and children up in the air and slamming them down again. Brownfield sighed as the sound of metal against rock reached his ears. The road was for mules, wagons and bare feet only.

"A wagon'd be easier," said his father.

"But not nearly 'bout as grand as that." His mother looked after the car without envy, but wistfully.

Brownfield watched the automobile as it turned a curve and was finally out of sight. Then he watched the last of the dust settle. Already he missed his cousins, although they made him feel dumb for never having seen a picture show and for never having seen houses stacked one on top of the other until they nearly reached the sky. They had stayed a week and got over being impressed by his small knowledge of farming the first day. He showed them how to milk the cow, how to feed the pigs, how to find chickens' eggs; but the next day they had bombarded him with talk about automobiles and street lights and paved walks and trash collectors and about something they had ridden in once in a department store that went up, up, up from one floor to the next without anybody walking a step. He had been dazzled by this information and at last overwhelmed. They taunted him because he lived in the country and never saw anything or went anywhere. They told him that his father worked for a cracker and that the cracker owned him. They told him that their own daddy, his Uncle Silas, had gone to Philadelphia to be his own boss. They told him that his mother wanted to leave his father and go North to Philadelphia with them. They said that his mother wanted him, Brownfield, to go to school,

4

and that she was tired of his father and wanted to leave him anyway. His cousins told Brownfield this and much more. They bewildered, excited and hurt him. Still, he missed them; they were from a world he had never seen. Now that they were gone he felt the way he usually felt only in winter, never in June; as if he were waiting for something to happen that would take a very long time to come.

"I wish we lived in Philydelphia," he said.

"Well, we don't." That was his father.

Brownfield looked at Grange with surprise. His father almost never spoke to him unless they had company. Even then he acted as if talking to his son was a strain, a burdensome requirement.

"Uncle Silas like to talk about his automobile," said Brownfield, his lips bumbling over the word. It was his uncle's word, a city word. In the country they always said car. Some people still called them buggies, as if they could not get used to a conveyance that did not use horses.

"I wish we had a automobile like that!"

"Well, we don't."

"No, we don't," said Margaret.

Brownfield frowned. His mother agreed with his father whenever possible. And though he was only ten Brownfield wondered about this. He thought his mother was like their dog in some ways. She didn't have a thing to say that did not in some way show her submission to his father.

"We ought to be thankful we got a roof over our heads and three meals a day."

It was actually more like one meal a day. His mother smiled at Brownfield, one of her rare sudden smiles that lit up her smooth, heart-shaped face. Her skin was rich brown with a creamy reddish sheen. Her teeth were small and regular and her breath was always sweet with a milky cleanness. Brownfield had hands like hers, long, thin aristocratic hands, with fingers meant for jewels. His mother had no wedding ring, however.

Brownfield listened to the familiar silence around him. Their

5

house was at the end of the long rugged road that gave his uncle's car so much trouble. This road looked to be no more than a track where it branched off from the main road, which was of smoothly scraped dirt. The road scraper, a man on a big yellow machine like a tank, never scraped their road, which was why it was so rough and pitted with mud holes when it rained. The house was in a clearing and at the edge of the clearing was forest. Forest full of animals and birds. But they were not large animals or noisy birds and days passed sometimes without a sound and the sky seemed a round blue muffler made of wool.

Brownfield had been born here, in the vast cotton flats of southern Georgia, and had been conscious first of the stifling heat in summer, and then of the long periods of uninterrupted quiet. As a very small child he had scrambled around the clearing alone, chasing lizards and snakes, bearing his cuts and bruises with solemnity until his mother came home at night.

His mother left him each morning with a hasty hug and a sugartit, on which he sucked through wet weather and dry, across the dusty clearing or miry, until she returned. She worked all day pulling baits for ready money. Her legs were always clean when she left home and always coated with mud and slime of baits when she came back. The baits she "pulled" were packed in cans and sold in town to gentlemen who went fishing for the sport of it. His mother had taken Brownfield with her to the bait factory when he was a baby, but he was in the way, and the piles of squirming baits, which were dumped first for sorting on a long table, terrified him. They had looked like a part of the table until one day his mother sat him down near them and he rolled over and became entangled in them. It seemed to him the baits moved with a perfectly horrifying blind wriggling. He had screamed and screamed. His mother was ordered to take him out of there at once and never to bring him back.

At first she left him home in a basket, with his sugartit pressed against his face. He sucked on it all day until it was nothing but a tasteless rag. Then, when he could walk, she left him on the porch steps. In moments of idle sitting he shared the steps with their lean mangy dog. And as the flies buzzed around the

6

whiskered snout of the dog they buzzed around his face. No one was there to shoo them away, or to change the sodden rag that attracted them, and which he wore brownish and damp around his distended waist. For hours he was lost in a dull, weak stupor. His hunger made him move in a daze, his heavy eyes unnaturally bright.

When he was four he was covered with sores. Tetter sores covered his head, eating out his hair in patches the size of quarters. Tomato sores covered his legs up to the knee—when the tomatoes in his mother's garden were ripe he ate nothing but tomatoes all day long—and pus ran from boils that burst under his armpits. His mother washed the sores in bluestone water. Suddenly, out of his days of sitting and of picking the scabs from his sores, there evolved a languid slow order of jobs he had to do. He fed the pigs, brought in wood and led the cow all over the clearing looking for fresh grass. When he was six his mother taught him how to feed and milk the cow. Then he became fond of the calm, slow patience of the cow and loved to catch her rich milk in a tin syrup pail and drink it warm and dribbling down his chin.

His father worked: planting, chopping, poisoning and picking in the cotton field, which ran for half a mile along the main road. Brownfield had worked there too now, for four years, since he was six, in the company of other child workers. His father worked with men and women in another part of the field. The cotton field too was generally silent. The children were too tired to play and were encouraged not to play because of the cotton. The grownups talked softly, intermittently, like the sporadic humming of wasps. The buzz of their conversations became part of the silence, for nothing they said came clearly across the field to where the children worked.

At the end of the day all the workers stopped. There were close to twenty grownups, and each had several children who worked in the children's section of the field. The children's job was to go over the rows their parents had gone over the week before—"scrapping cotton" it was called. When the children

7

saw their parents put down their sacks they came and stood beside them at the edge of the field as all of them waited for the truck to come. Brownfield waited for the truck along with his father. His father never looked at him or acknowledged him in any way, except to lift his sack of cotton to the back of the truck when it arrived. Brownfield was afraid of his father's silence, and his fear reached its peak when the truck came. For when the truck came his father's face froze into an unnaturally bland mask, curious and unsettling to see. It was as if his father became a stone or a robot. A grim stillness settled over his eyes and he became an object, a cipher, something that moved in tense jerks if it moved at all. While the truck stood backed up in the field the workers held their breath. A family of five or six workers would wonder uneasily if they would take home, together, a whole dollar. Some of the workers laughed and joked with the man who drove the truck, but they looked at his shoes and at his pants legs or at his hands, never into his eyes, and their looks were a combination of small sly smiles and cowed, embarrassed desperation.

Brownfield's father had no smiles about him at all. He merely froze; his movements when he had to move to place sacks on the truck were rigid as a machine's. At first Brownfield thought his father was turned to stone by the truck itself. The truck was big and noisy and coldly, militarily gray. Its big wheels flattened the cotton stalks and made deep ruts in the soft dirt of the field. But after watching the loading of the truck for several weeks he realized it was the man who drove the truck who caused his father to don a mask that was more impenetrable than his usual silence. Brownfield looked closely at the man and made a startling discovery; the man was a man, but entirely different from his own father. When he noticed this difference, one of odor and sound and movement and laughter, as well as of color, he wondered how he had not seen it before. But as a small child all men had seemed to merge into one. They were exactly alike, all of them having the same smell, the same feel of muscled hardness when they held him against their bodies, the same dis-

8

regard for smallness. They took pride only in their own bigness, when they laughed and opened their cavernous mouths, or when they walked in their long fearsome strides or when they stooped from their great height and tossed him about in their arms. Brownfield's immediate horrified reaction to the man who froze his father was that the man had the smooth brownish hair of an animal. Thinking this discovery was the key to his father's icy withdrawal from the man, Brownfield acquired a cold nervousness around him of his own.

Once the man touched him on the hand with the handle of his cane, not hard, and said, with a smell of mint on his breath, "You're Grange Copeland's boy, ain't you?" And Brownfield had answered, "Uh huh," chewing on his lip and recoiling from the enormous pile of gray-black hair that lay matted on the man's upper chest and throat. While he stared at the hair one of the workers—not his father who was standing beside him as if he didn't know he was there—said to him softly, "Say 'Yessir' to Mr. Shipley," and Brownfield looked up before he said anything and scanned his father's face. The mask was as tight and still as if his father had coated himself with wax. And Brownfield smelled for the first time an odor of sweat, fear and something indefinite. Something smothered and tense (which was of his father and of the other workers and not of mint) that came from his father's body. His father said nothing. Brownfield, trembling, said "Yessir," filled with terror of this man who could, by his presence alone, turn his father into something that might as well have been a pebble or a post or a piece of dirt, except for the sharp bitter odor of something whose source was forcibly contained in flesh.

One day not long afterward Grange was drinking quietly at home, stretched out on the porch. Brownfield sat on the porch steps gazing at him, mesmerized by the movement of the bottle going up and down in his father's hand. Grange noticed him looking, and Brownfield was afraid to move away and afraid to stay. When he was drinking his father took every action as a personal affront. He looked at Brownfield and started to speak.

9

His eyes had little yellow and red lines in them like the veins of a leaf. Brownfield leaned nearer. But all his father said was, "I ought to throw you down the goddam well."

Brownfield drew back in alarm, though there was no anger or determination in his father's voice; there was only a rough drunken wistfulness and a weary tremor of pity and regret.

Brownfield had told his cousins about the man, and it was then that they told him how his father was owned and of how their father escaped being owned by moving North. And now they had a nice new car every other year and beautiful plush furniture and their mother didn't pull nasty baits but worked instead for people who owned two houses and a long black car with a man in it dressed in green with gold braid. That man being their father, who had taken them one day for a ride in the car, so they knew what they were talking about. They had played with rich children, and, talking about them to Brownfield, who lived in a house that leaked, they sounded rich as well.

Angeline, his girl cousin, who eavesdropped as a matter of habit, told Brownfield impatiently that she and her brother Lincoln had heard their mother say that Brownfield's family would never amount to anything because they didn't have sense enough to leave Green County, Georgia. It was Angeline who told him that her mother said that Grange was no good; that he had tried to get his wife to "sell herself" to get them out of debt. Brownfield's mother and Angeline's were sisters.

"He even wanted her to sell herself to the man who drives the truck," Angeline lied.

"Or anybody else who'd buy her!" Lincoln said.

Lincoln began to dance around Brownfield. "You all are in debt twelve hundred dollars! And you'll never pay it!"

Angeline sniffed primly with her nose in the air. "My daddy says you'll never pay it 'cause you ain't got no money and your daddy drinks up everything he can get his hands on."

What did "sell" mean when it applied to his mama, Brownfield had wanted to know, but his cousins only giggled and nudged each other gravely but in apparent delight.

For Brownfield his cousins' information was peculiarly omi-

10

nous. He tried to remember when his father's silence began, for surely there had been a time when his father cooed hopefully to him as he fondled him on his knee. Perhaps, he thought, his father's silence was part of the reason his mother was always submissive to him and why his father was jealous of her and angry if she spoke, just "how're you?" to other men. Maybe he had tried to sell her and she wouldn't be sold—which could be why they were still poor and in debt and would die that way. And maybe his father, who surely would feel bad about trying to sell his wife, became silent and jealous of her, not because of anything she had done, but because of what he had tried to do! Maybe his mother was as scared of Grange as he was, terrified by Grange's tense composure. Perhaps she was afraid he would sell her anyway, whether she wanted to be sold or not. That could be why she jumped to please him.

Brownfield got a headache trying to grasp the meaning of what his cousins told him. The need to comprehend his parents' actions seeped into him with his cousins' laughter. The blood rushed to his head and he was sick. He thought feverishly of how their weeks were spent. Of the heat, the cold, the work, the feeling of desperation behind all the sly small smiles. The feeling of hunger in winter, of bleak unsmiling faces, of eating bark when he was left alone before his mother returned home smelling of baits and manure. Of his mother's soft skin and clean milky breath; of his father's brooding, and of the feeling of an onrushing inevitable knowledge, like a summer storm that comes with high wind and flash flooding, that would smash the silence finally and flatten them all mercilessly to the ground. One day he would know everything and be equal to his cousins and to his father and perhaps even to God.

Their life followed a kind of cycle that depended almost totally on Grange's moods. On Monday, suffering from a hangover and the aftereffects of a violent quarrel with his wife the night before, Grange was morose, sullen, reserved, deeply in pain under the hot early morning sun. Margaret was tense and hard, exceedingly nervous. Brownfield moved about the house

11

like a mouse. On Tuesday, Grange was merely quiet. His wife and son began to relax. On Wednesday, as the day stretched out and the cotton rows stretched out even longer, Grange muttered and sighed. He sat outside in the night air longer before going to bed; he would speak of moving away, of going North. He might even try to figure out how much he owed the man who owned the fields. The man who drove the truck and who owned the shack they occupied. But these activities depressed him, and he said things on Wednesday nights that made his wife cry. By Thursday, Grange's gloominess reached its peak and he grimaced respectfully, with veiled eyes, at the jokes told by the man who drove the truck. On Thursday nights he stalked the house from room to room and pulled himself up and swung from the rafters of the porch. Brownfield could hear his joints creaking against the sounds of the porch, for the whole porch shook when his father swung. By Friday Grange was so stupefied with the work and the sun he wanted nothing but rest the next two days before it started all over again.

On Saturday afternoon Grange shaved, bathed, put on clean overalls and a shirt and took the wagon into town to buy groceries. While he was away his wife washed and straightened her hair. She dressed up and sat, all shining and pretty, in the open door, hoping anxiously for visitors who never came.

Brownfield too was washed and cleanly dressed. He played contentedly in the silent woods and in the clearing. Late Saturday night Grange would come home lurching drunk, threatening to kill his wife and Brownfield, stumbling and shooting off his shotgun. He threatened Margaret and she ran and hid in the woods with Brownfield huddled at her feet. Then Grange would roll out the door and into the yard, crying like a child in big wrenching sobs and rubbing his whole head in the dirt. He would lie there until Sunday morning, when the chickens pecked around him, and the dog sniffed at him and neither his wife nor Brownfield went near him. Brownfield played instead on the other side of the house. Steady on his feet but still ashen by noon, Grange would make his way across the pasture and through the woods, headlong, like a blind man, to the Baptist church, where

12

his voice above all the others was raised in song and prayer. Margaret would be there too, Brownfield asleep on the bench beside her. Back home again after church Grange and Margaret would begin a supper quarrel which launched them into another week just about like the one before.

Brownfield turned from watching the road and looked with hateful scrutiny at the house they lived in. It was a cabin of two rooms with a brick chimney at one end. The roof was of rotting gray wood shingles; the sides of the house were gray vertical slabs; the whole aspect of the house was gray. It was lower in the middle than at its ends, and resembled a sway-backed animal turned out to pasture. A stone-based well sat functionally in the middle of the yard, its mossy wooden bucket dangling above it from some rusty chain and frazzled lengths of rope. Where water was dashed behind the well, wild morning-glories bloomed, their tendrils reaching as far as the woodpile, which was a litter of tree trunks, slivers of carcass bones deposited by the dog and discarded braces and bits that had pained the jaws and teeth of many a hard-driven mule.

From the corner of his eye Brownfield noticed that his father was also surveying the house. Grange stood with an arm across the small of his back, soldier fashion, and with the other hand made gestures toward this and that of the house, as if pointing out necessary repairs. There were very many. He was a tall, thin, brooding man, slightly stooped from plowing, with skin the deep glossy brown of pecans. He was thirty-five but seemed much older. His face and eyes had a dispassionate vacancy and sadness, as if a great fire had been extinguished within him and was just recently missed. He seemed devoid of any emotion, while Brownfield watched him, except that of bewilderment. A bewilderment so complete he did not really appear to know what he saw, although his hand continued to gesture, more or less aimlessly, and his lips moved, shaping unintelligible words. While his son watched, Grange lifted his shoulders and let them fall. Brownfield knew this movement well; it was the fatal shrug. It meant that his father saw nothing about the house that he

13

could change and would therefore give up gesturing about it and he would never again think of repairing it.

When Brownfield's mother had wanted him to go to school Grange had assessed the possibility with the same inaudible gesticulation accorded the house. Knowing nothing of schools, but knowing he was broke, he had shrugged; the shrug being the end of that particular dream. It was the same when Margaret needed a dress and there was no way Grange could afford to buy it. He merely shrugged, never saying a word about it again. After each shrug he was more silent than before, as if each of these shrugs cut him off from one more topic of conversation.

Brownfield turned from looking at his father and the house to see his mother brush a hand across her eyes. He sat glumly, full of a newly discovered discontent. He was sad for her and felt bitterly small. How could he ever bear to lose her, to his father or to death or to age? How would he ever survive without her pliant strength and the floating fragrance of her body which was sweet and inviting and delicate, yet full of the concretely comforting odors of cooking and soap and milk.

"You could've gone," said Grange softly, to his wife.

"I don't know nothing about up Norse."

"You could learn."

"Naw, I don't believe I could." There was a sigh in her voice.

Brownfield came alive. So his cousins had been right; there had been talk about him and his mother going back with them to Philadelphia. Why hadn't they gone? He felt peeved and in the dark.

"I didn't know nobody *asked* us to go. *I* want to go up Norse." His cousins said only the greenest hicks from Georgia said "Norse" like that.

His mother smiled at him. "And wear your hair pressed down like a woman's? Get away from here, boy!"

Brownfield, an admirer of Uncle Silas, was not dissuaded. "I just wouldn't wear the headrag at night," he said.

"My poor sister Marilyn," his mother muttered sadly, "all bleached up like a streetwalker. The Lawd keep *me* from ever wanting to brush another woman's hair out of *my* face. To tell

14

you the truth," she continued to Grange over Brownfield's head, "I don't even think it *was* real hair. I felt it when she took it off for me to try on. Just like the hair on the end of a cow's tail, and when you pulled a strand it stretched."

"I like it 'cause it swooshes," said Brownfield rhapsodically.

"That's 'cause you ain't got no sense," said Grange.

2

Five years after his cousins' visit, Brownfield stood on the same spot in the yard watching the approach of another vehicle. This time it was a big, gray high-bodied truck that he knew well. It rolled heavily over the road, blasting the misty quiet of the Sunday morning. The man driving the truck was not the one who usually drove it. As it came nearer Brownfield saw a brown arm dangling from the window. It was Johnny Johnson, a man who worked for Mr. Shipley. The truck stopped at the edge of the clearing and Brownfield's mother descended. She stood for a moment talking to the driver, then turned and came slowly and quietly toward the house. The truck made a noisy turnabout and disappeared back up the road. His mother took off her shoes and carried them in her hand. She walked gingerly and reluctantly over the dew. So intently was she peering at the ground she did not see Brownfield until she nearly bumped against him. He was taller than she, and bigger, and when she noticed him she jumped.

" 'Morning," he said coolly.

His mother carried her shoes guiltily to her bosom, clutching them with both hands. Her beautiful rough hair was loose about her shoulders like a wayward thundercloud, with here and there a crinkly and shiny silver thread. Her dress was mussed, and the golden cross that usually nestled inside her dress lay jutting up atop her collar. Her eyes were haggard and blinked foggily at her son. She gave off a stale smoky odor. With nervous fingers she sought to thrust rumpled stockings farther inside her shoes.

"Oh," she said, looking toward the house, "I didn't see you standing there."

Brownfield stood aside, saying nothing.

"The baby all right?" she asked quickly, her knuckles sharp against her shoes.

"He all right," said Brownfield. He followed her into the house and watched as she stood over his little half-brother. The baby was sleeping peacefully, his tiny behind stuck up in the air. The baby was a product of his mother's new personality and went with her new painted good looks and new fragrance of beds, of store-bought perfume and of gin.

"Your daddy and me had another fight," she said, sinking down on the bed. "Oh, we had us a rip-rowing, knock-down, drag-out fight. With that fat yellow bitch of his calling the punches." She was very matter of fact. They had been fighting this way for years. Gone were the times she waited alone on Saturday afternoons for people who never came. Now when her husband left her at home and went into town she followed. At first she had determinedly walked the distance, or hitchhiked. Lately she had switched to riding, often in the big gray truck.

"I see he ain't back yet," she said.

Brownfield lounged in the doorway, hoping his job as baby-sitter was over.

"Said he wouldn't be back no more," his mother said, pulling her dress over her head and shaking it out. She chuckled spitefully. "How many times we done heard *that*. You'd think he'd be satisfied, me feeding him and her fucking him!"

Brownfield carefully closed his ears when his mother cursed. He knew his father was seeing another woman, and had been seeing one, or several, for a long time. It did not affect him the way it did his mother. He watched her roll down her slip and did not think to look away when it touched the floor. She turned to face him, eyes weary but defiant.

"What the hell you staring at?" she asked.

"Nothing," said Brownfield, and turned away.

16

His mother located the cross at the end of its chain around her neck and fingered it solemnly.

"I was just thinkin' about Uncle Silas and Aunt Marilyn," he said with his back to her.

"What you thinkin' about them for? I ain't heard from Marilyn since Silas was killed. Just think, tryin' to rob a liquor store in broad daylight! Marilyn always had a lot to say about her new icebox and clothes and her children's fancy learnin', but never did she breathe one word about Silas being on dope. All the time coming down here in they fancy cars and makin' out like *we* so out of fashion—I bet the Norse is just as much a mess as down here." She knelt by the side of the bed. "Give the baby a bottle of milk when he wakes up," she said from the floor. Within minutes after saying her prayers she was sound asleep.

Brownfield looked at the baby with disgust. Always it was his duty to look after the baby. It made him feel like a sissy. Fortunately the baby was sleeping deeply, for if he had awakened then Brownfield would have felt like giving him a pinch that would bring his mother flying from her bed, her curses and blows falling first on his, then on the baby's, head.

He was too big to play in the clearing, so instead he went to his box at the foot of his bed and brought out his new shoes, bought with money earned from spare-time work at the bait factory, and carried them outside. He sat on the porch steps polishing them with a piece of one of his father's old shirts.

As he stroked his shoes caressingly with the rag, Brownfield sank into a favorite daydream. He saw himself grown-up, twenty-one or so, arriving home at sunset in the snow. In this daydream there was always snow. He had seen snow only once, when he was seven and there had been a small flurry at Christmas, and it had made a cold, sharp impression on him. In his daydream snow fell to the earth like chicken feathers dumped out of a tick, and gave the feeling of walking through a quiet wall of weightless and suspended raindrops, clear and cold on the eyelids and nose. In his daydream he pulled up to his house, a stately mansion with cherry-red brick chimneys and matching brick porch and steps, in a long chauffeur-driven car. The chauffeur glided out of the car first and opened the back door, where Brownfield sat puffing on a cigar. Then the chauffeur vanished around the back of the house, where his wife waited for him on the kitchen steps. She was the beloved and very respected cook and had been with the house and the chauffeur and Brownfield's family for many years. Brownfield's wife and children—two children, a girl and a boy—waited anxiously for him just inside the door in the foyer. They jumped all over him, showering him with kisses. While he told his wife of the big deals he'd pushed through that day she fixed him a mint julep. After a splendid dinner, presided over by the cook, dressed in black uniform and white starched cap, he and his wife, their arms around each other, tucked the children in bed and spent the rest of the evening discussing her day (which she had spent walking in her garden), and making love.

There was one thing that was odd about the daydream. The face of Brownfield's wife and that of the cook constantly interchanged. So that his wife was first black and glistening from cooking and then white and powdery to his touch; his dreaming self could not make up its mind. His children's faces were never in focus. He recognized them by their angelic presence alone, two bright spots of warmth; they hovered about calling him "Daddy" endearingly, while he stroked the empty air, assuming it to be their heads.

Brownfield had first had this daydream the week after his cousins told him about the North. Each year it had grown longer and more intensely real; at times it possessed him. While he dreamed of the life he would live as a man no other considerations entered his head. He dreamed alone and was quiet; which was why his mother thought baby-sitting an ideal occupation for him. But with the baby near, capable of shattering the quiet at any moment, Brownfield was cut off from deep involvement in the snow, in the cozy comfort of his luxuriously warm limousine, and in the faithful ministrations of his loving

18

imaginary wife. He harbored a deep resentment against his mother for making it so hard for him to dream.

He finished his shoes. Piercing the silence now was the cry of his baby brother. Without hurrying, partially in his dream's afterglow, he stood, his hands holding the shoes carefully, palms up, so as not to smudge the shiny leather, and walked toward the box by his bed. It was a cardboard box and, like a small trunk, complete with cardboard shelves. He lifted the flap that was its top and placed his shoes with care a distance from his other possessions. There were a pair of new denim pants, a new green shirt with birds and Indians and deer on it, and a soft yellow neckerchief made of satin. He had bought the neckerchief from the rolling-store man. It cost a quarter and he was very proud of it.

The baby was still crying. Brownfield looked for a moment at his mother in the bed, who had pulled the quilt over her head. The wall around her bed was aflutter with funeral-home calendars, magazine pictures and bits of newsprint which she had cut out of the 1st Colored Baptist Christian Crusade. The baby looked hopefully toward the bed and then pathetically at Brownfield. With a harsh push of his fingers Brownfield thrust the bottle into the baby's mouth. The baby lay on its side, intently sucking, and looked at his big brother with swollen distrustful eyes. The baby was almost two years old but refused to learn to walk. Instead it allowed itself to be dragged about, propped up and ignored, until something caused it to scream. The baby's name was Star, but it was never called anything. It was treated indifferently most of the time and seemed resigned to not belonging. It had grayish eyes and reddish hair and was shadowed pale gold and chocolate like a little animal. From its odd coloration its father might have been every one of its mother's many lovers.

Margaret had not been impressed, ever, by her sister's Northern existence, or so she had repeatedly said to Brownfield. But she had grown restless about her own life, a life that was as predictably unexciting as last year's cotton field. Somewhere along the line she had changed. Slowly, imperceptibly. Until it was too late for Brownfield to recall exactly how she had been when he had loved her. It seemed to Brownfield that one day she was as he had always known her; kind, submissive, smelling faintly of milk; and the next day she was a wild woman looking for frivolous things, her heart's good times, in the transient embraces of strangers.

Brownfield blamed his father for his mother's change. For it was Grange she followed at first. It was Grange who led her to the rituals of song and dance and drink, which he had always rushed to at the end of the week, every Saturday night. It was Grange who had first turned to someone else. On some Saturday nights Grange and Margaret left home excitedly together, looking for Brownfield knew not what, except that it must be something strong and powerful and something they had thought lost. For they grew frenzied in pursuit of whatever it was. Often they came home together, still bright, flushed from fighting or from good times, but with the glow gradually dying out of their eyes as they faced the creaking floorboards of their unpainted house. Depression always gave way to fighting, as if fighting preserved some part of the feeling of being alive. It was confusing to realize but not hard to know that they loved each other. And even when Margaret found relief from her cares in the arms of her fellow bait-pullers and church members, or with the man who drove the truck and who turned her husband to stone, there was a deference in her eyes that spoke of her love for Grange. On weekdays when, sober and wifely, she struggled to make food out of plants that grew wild and game caught solely in traps, she was submissive still. It was on weekends only that she became a huntress of soft touches, gentle voices and sex without the arguments over the constant and compelling pressures of everyday life. She had sincerely regretted the baby. And now, humbly respecting her husband's feelings, she ignored it. What Brownfield could not forgive was that in the drama of their lives his father and mother forgot they were not alone.

When Brownfield woke in the night his mother was gone. From his bed in the kitchen he could see his father sitting on the bed, cradling something in his arms. It was long and dark, like a steel rod, and glinted in the light from the kerosene lamp. Grange's face was impassive, its lines brooding. Placing the rifle on the bed he picked up his dusty black-green hat. He stood looking at the floor, his shoulders slumped, motionless. He looked very old. Ploddingly he moved about the room. He waited indecisively for his wife to return. He gazed at the baby asleep in its makeshift crib, a crate that had once been filled with oranges. He shrugged. Then he lifted his eyes toward where Brownfield's bed was, at one side of the kitchen, between the table and the stove. Slowly he walked into the kitchen, which was chilly and smelled of old biscuits, and which changed to a new rhythm of night with his entrance into it. The air was gently agitated by his movements. The sounds of the floor shifted with each step he took.

Brownfield pretended to be asleep, though his heart was pounding so loudly he was sure his father would hear it. He saw Grange bend over him to inspect his head and face. He saw him reach down to touch him. He saw his hand stop, just before it reached his cheek. Brownfield was crying silently and wanted his father to touch the tears. He moved toward his father's hand, as if moving unconsciously in his sleep. He saw his father's hand draw back, without touching him. He saw him turn sharply and leave the room. He heard him leave the house. And he knew, even before he realized his father would never be back, that he hated him for everything and always would. And he most hated him because even in private and in the dark and with Brownfield presumably asleep, Grange could not bear to touch his son with his hand.

"Well. He's gone," his mother said without anger at the end of the third week. But the following week she and her poisoned baby went out into the dark of the clearing and in the morning Brownfield found them there. She was curled up in a lonely sort of way, away from her child, as if she had spent the last moments on her knees.

3

"You can get yourself a wife," said Shipley confidentially, "and settle down here in the same house. It might need a little fixing up, but I could lend you enough for that, and with a few licks here and there it ought to be good as new."

Shipley's hair was still like that of a sleek greasy animal, but now it was dingy white and thin. He looked at Brownfield from under brows that had faded from blond to yellowish-gray. His pale blue eyes struggled to convey kindness and largesse. Brownfield slid down from the truck knowing his face was the mask his father's had been. Because this frightened him and because he did not know why he should have inherited this fear, he studiedly brushed imaginary dust from the shoulders of a worn black suit Shipley had given him.

He had been shocked to see Shipley at the funeral, but soon guessed he had come hoping to catch Grange. Shipley did not take kindly to people running off owing him money, no matter that they had paid off whatever debts they might have owed many times over. Nobody had whispered a word against him while he stood looking down on the bloatedly sleeping mother and child. To most of the people at the funeral Shipley's presence was a status symbol and an insult, though they were not used to thinking in those terms and would not have expressed such a mixed feeling. Shipley squeezed out a tear for the benefit of the other mourners, and Brownfield had chuckled bitterly to himself. The tear wasn't necessary: pity was scarce at his mother's funeral; most of the people there thought she had got what she deserved. Shipley's crocodile tear was the only one shed.

Brownfield himself had sat, limp and clammy, wishing he were a million miles away. His mother as she was in the last years got none of his love, none of his sympathy and hardly any of his thoughts. The idea that he might continue to live in her house

22

aroused nothing but revulsion. He knew too that the minute he accepted money from Shipley he was done for. If he borrowed from Shipley, Shipley would make sure he never finished paying it back.

"Don't know but what we might can build you a new house," said Shipley, thinking that with Brownfield's muscles he could do a grown man's work. Shipley believed with a mixture of awe and contempt that blacks developed earlier than whites, especially in the biceps. He thought too that as long as he had Brownfield there was a chance of getting Grange. Believing that Brownfield was choked up from grief and from his generous offer Shipley continued speaking to him on an encouraging plane.

"After all, if you marry one of these little fillies on my place she's going to want to smell some new wood. Why, I can't stop by a house on the place without the womenfolks waylayin' me; talking about me fixing up the house they already got or wanting me to build 'em a new one."

He fished about for sympathy, while Brownfield stood looking at the ground.

"But the main thing is"—Shipley smiled kindly—"we want you to stay here with us. And we don't hold it against you what your daddy done. We'll just wipe that off the books." He continued to smile but eyed Brownfield shrewdly from under his brows. "Of course, I believe you said you didn't know which way he was headed?"

"No, sir," said Brownfield, from a great hollow distance.

"Well," said Shipley sadly, as if a great wrong were being done him but one which he would not allow to dissuade him from future acts of kindness, "you think about all we discussed. And take the day off and get yourself straightened out. I tell you this much, I think we going to work out fine; and I know my boys will be glad to have somebody they already know to work with them when they take over Shipley's Farm and Bait." He leaned out of the truck, the hand dangling from the end of his coat sleeve like a papery autumn leaf. "You and me will start out fresh," he said, "and remember, the North ain't all people say it is. Just remember that."

When Brownfield looked up, Shipley and his truck were gone. He was left in the familiar clearing. Scornfully, shaking the ice from his gut, he spat on Shipley's ground. His mind raced headlong into the realm of his dream. The fear of Shipley that had tied his tongue disappeared as the urge to sample his new freedom grew. He would be his own boss. From the forlorn and empty house he took only his box. As he left the clearing a thousand birds began wildly singing good luck.

PART III

PART II

4

He walked in the direction the sun was going. He walked all day without stopping, except to throw a rock into a stream and to watch squirrels play across the tops of trees, twisting and flying among the branches as if they had wings. Under his feet the earth, being moist with spring, became sunken; he stopped to watch as the print of his foot sprang back to smoothness on the moss along the streams. Rivers and creeks crisscrossed his route, and everything he saw in the woods delighted him. When it became dark he made himself a bed in a shed in a big field, a shed used for storing cotton to keep it dry after picking. The shed was empty now, but he found a few discarded croker sacks outside. On these he lay down and went to sleep.

After walking a few miles next morning he was very hungry. He walked past farmhouses that were big and painted white, with shrubs and flowering trees around them. When he saw a baked gray two-room shack he quickened his pace and walked for its flat dry yard.

There was a woman standing in the back yard over a rusty black pot. Her fire was kept going with rubber tires and refuse. The air around her was smelly and smoky. She was stirring her boiling clothes with a long lye-eaten stick. She took the stick out of the water and shook it as Brownfield came up to her. She looked about quickly to locate three small children, who were playing with car tires all over the yard, and didn't say a word or even seem to notice him until he spoke.

" 'Morning," he said.

"All right . . . how're you?" she answered in a low, singsong voice.

"Nice bright morning, ain't it?"

"Shore is," she said and stopped.

"My name Brownfield—Brownfield Copeland—and what might yourn be?"

"My name Mizes Mamie Lou Banks glad to know you." She stuck out a bleached and puckered white palm and they shook hands.

"I wonder if a starving man might ax a lady for a little somethin' to eat?" said Brownfield, looking sideways at her as if she were not the lady he meant.

"Why," she said, putting down the stick, placing it across the pot, "you is just a boy, ain't you?"

"Yessem, I reckon," he said, unconsciously hanging his head.

"You runnin' from any white peoples? If you is," she continued, not looking at him but down at her pot, "you best to go on in the house where can't none of them see you if they's a mind to pass. They's some grits on the stove 'n some eggs if you knows how to cook. I got my washin' to do, 'n if you *is* runnin' from the white folks I ain't seen nothing but potash 'n lye this morning, 'n that's the truth." She smiled very slightly, at least her mouth quivered about the corners. There was a chunky bulge in her bottom lip.

"Thank you kindly, ma'am, I ain't runnin' but I shore is hongry. Fact of the matter is, I'm kinda lookin' for my daddy."

28

"Was the white folks after him too?" she asked. "Or did he just run off?"

"It was both."

"Well, I can't picture nobody runnin' *back* this way."

Brownfield nodded and walked to the door she shook her fingers at and went in. While he was cooking the eggs she came through the house to get more dirty clothes. He thought she must be a washerwoman, she was washing so many clothes.

"Hep yourself now," she said. There was something stern in her kindness. He thought that if she had ever been good-looking it must have been when she was no more than eleven or twelve.

"Oh, I got plenty."

"I tell you, a growin' boy can eat it up like a brand-new stove."

"You got children bigger'n them outdoors?"

"Oh, five more, but they all be gone up Norse." She said it proudly, as if she were saying she sent them off to Harvard. "They says they couldn't just hang round here and hang round here." She paused a minute, going to the china closet for butter and putting it down next to his plate. "Don't know if I blames them neither." She was a very thin woman with knobby cheekbones and dark circles under her eyes. She had no more figure than a stick, and wore a man's pair of overalls and a tight checkered headrag. "For all I know somebody just might be feeding my old hongry younguns up there in Chicago. I swear, they could eat up yere 'bout a whole hog at one dinner." She sighed and walked outside with the clothes.

Brownfield thought perhaps he would go to Chicago, or maybe even New York City. Maybe he would just keep walking and walking and then hop a freight and wake up in the morning in a place where people were nice and had manners. He wouldn't even care if they didn't have manners, if they didn't try to lure him into debt and then cause him to turn into stone whenever they came around. He stopped chewing a moment to think about what his mother had said about up Norse; and he remembered that his cousins said that up Norse was cold and people never spoke to one another on the street or anything. His father had once said that being up Norse ruined Uncle Silas and Aunt Marilyn, being so cold and unfeeling and full of concrete, but even while Grange said this his eyes had shown a fascination with the idea of going there himself.

"Say, you know. I done heard some things about up Norse," Brownfield said, after he had eaten and come outdoors again. "They say it ain't as good as folks make it out to be."

"Maybe not, maybe 'tis," she said, stirring her pot, spitting snuff juice into the fire. "I wouldn't be saying I knows. But I *declare* it so out of fashion round here you'd think most any other place would be better."

"Yessem," he said, thinking what was so confounded bad about people not speaking to you if there was no Shipley around to see that you never made any money of your own. "Yessem." He looked about the bleak yard and at the house that seemed about to cave in. "You just might have somethin' there."

She continued to stir the pot, stoke up the fire and bustle about the yard.

"They daddy work round here?" he asked, pointing to the three small children, who were busy rolling car tires.

"Well, I tell you," she said, standing up from putting more rubber around the pot and resting her back by swaying it, "one of they daddies is dead from being in the war, although he only got as far as Fort Bennet. The other one of they daddies is now married to the woman what lives in the next house down the road. If you stands up on your tippy toes you can jest about see her roof, sort of green colored. I thought she was helpin' me get another husband and all the time she was lookin' out for herself. But I am still her friend. The other one of they daddies was my last husband, by common law, but he dead too now, shot by the old man he was working for for taking the chitlins out of a hog they kill." She looked at the children and frowned. "But they is so much alike, just to look at; they git along right well together."

"Reckon they going to grow up and go on up Norse too?" he

30

asked, looking at the children. They had bad colds and snot ran down their lips like glue.

"I don't know," she said, stirring her pot. "The Lawd knows I loves them, but when they does grow up I hope they has sense enough to git away from round here."

"Well, I thank you kindly for that good breakfast."

"Aw, don't mention it. 'N if you gets hongry runnin' back the other way drop in again." She gave him a grave, boastful, wry and conspiratorial smile. "I also hope you finds your daddy."

"Bye, you all," he said, waving to the children, who stopped playing to stare at him.

"Bye-bye! Bye-bye!" they piped like birds, running after him to the edge of the highway, and yelling "Bye-bye!" long after he had turned the curve and was out of sight. He heard their mother call "Y'all *come* back here before you hit by a car!" and the voices stopped abruptly; then the only sound was his footsteps against the grainy damp shoulder of the road.

5

After weeks of indecisive wandering, of worrying that Shipley might be following him, of breakfasting with dozens of secluded families in hollows and clearings deep in trees, Brownfield abandoned all hope, for the present, of reaching Chicago or New York. He had spent several days looking for a slow freight to hop but had not even found railroad tracks. He had no idea which direction he should follow to go North; unlike thousands of his ancestors he had never heard of the North Star. Often at night he gazed at the sky, searching for an omen. To gaze hopefully at the sky was in his blood, but nothing came of it.

On the last morning of wandering he breakfasted with a family of women, whose various husbands and boy friends were off hunting. With their own men away the women lavished attention on Brownfield. They drew water for his bath, pressed his new shirt and yellow satin tie, and gave him a shoe box for his things, which they said would be easier to carry than the trunklike box he had. Brownfield watched as the youngest girls tore the old box to bits. Then he felt truly that it was time to quit, that he had come far enough, and that where he was by nightfall he would stay. At least for a while. As he told the women shyly, he "needed a little chance to catch his breath."

Resplendent in his new Indian-bird-and-animal-decorated shirt, daring in the yellow satin necktie, awkward in stiffly starched denims and highly lustered shoes, Brownfield set out in the new direction the women showed him. He mumbled, almost inaudibly, that he was "kinda" looking for his daddy. That made parting gayer somehow, his walking away less bleak. He liked the women, all temporarily menless, without cares; he liked commanding their uninhibited attention.

When he described Grange to them they looked at one another and smiled and smiled; but they would not say if they had seen him. They only insisted that Brownfield take a certain road, and no other, which ran a certain way, and which would bring him by dusk to a certain peaceful town.

⑥

He reached the town when the sun was setting. There were two streets, lightly graveled, which formed the upper corner of a square. To Brownfield's right, within the square, off the main street, rose the solid brick dimensions of the county courthouse. Directly ahead of him, in a circle of grass in the middle of the street, stood a stone soldier, his bayoneted rifle lifted, his intrepid but motionless foot raised to advance northward. On both sides of the street there were stores. Brownfield met buggies and two cars and a few storekeepers on foot. Raucous boys from the blacksmith's shop rushed past in leather aprons; one of them looked with fleeting envy at Brownfield's tie. Except for this glance Brownfield entered the town unnoticed.

He had never seen more than thirty people at once before, unless they were working in a cotton field, and he was amazed at the diversity of clothing people wore. There were storekeepers in black suits, their helpers in threadbare blue. He saw a few white women leaning on the arms of their husbands, fussy-looking in frills and wide hats. He saw black women trudging home from the day's nannying, their uniforms remarkably starched and ironed, their aprons still on. He saw a mixed group of black people walking determinedly, eyes down, heads down, for the very end of the second street. On a hunch, Brownfield followed them.

Soon losing sight of this group, Brownfield turned left off the street in the direction of some shacks. In a few minutes he stood in front of the local Negro bar and grill. It was a small wooden structure with a bare, hard, cleanly swept yard. Its sides were covered with tin and wooden posters, some of them advertising Brown Mule tobacco, Red Cherry snuff and laxatives; the rest advertising Cajun whiskey, Old Joe and Grape Beer.

He could tell what each thing was because he was thoroughly familiar, as was every black person in the county, with all of these products. No father came to town on Saturday evening without bringing home at least one. If tobacco, on him; if whiskey, mostly inside him.

The juke joint, when he imagined how it must jump with light and life at night, fascinated Brownfield, and he thought he would try to get a job there. He had no money, and knew he would need some if he decided later to push on to Chicago.

His mother and father had come to such places, perhaps this same one, and when they had fought and argued in public it was usually among the kind of people who would frequent such a place. But this thought only heightened Brownfield's interest in the night spot, which, in the dull gray dusk, held all the latent tension of an important club. Sighing and feeling young and incapable, he squared his shoulders and walked in.

There were twelve small tables with black-flowered oilcloth covers on them arranged neatly around a potbellied stove, in which a fire was burning low. The smell of chitlins, pig's feet and collard greens was strong and thick coming from somewhere in back behind the counter. There was a box in the corner for keeping beer cold, and kerosene lamps around the walls. A gramophone, like those he had seen in catalogues, was pushed against one side of the counter, its big horn turned outward like a gourd that had been cut off at one end. A murky silence with a near-undercurrent of voices that went with the cooking food, enveloped him; he was overwhelmed already by the gracious aspects of town living that he saw.

A heavy cantaloupe-colored woman with freckled cheeks and gray-green eyes looked him up and down and said, "You kinda *young,* aincha, cutie?" She eyed him in a way that made his palms sweat, and he was sure she had no intention of hiring him.

"But I can do your cleaning, and help move things around. I'm strong," Brownfield said, rubbing his hands on his pants. "I can do your chopping."

At that the woman looked interested and smiled a sly little smile.

"Does good choppin', does you?" she asked.

"Yessem."

"No need to yessem me," she said lazily. "The name is Josie. *Fat* Josie." She looked at Brownfield as if she expected him to have heard the name before. During the pause a thin, very black young woman slid by.

"This here's my daughter, Lorene." Josie reached out abruptly, arrested the woman, and pulled her unwilling and muscled arm close beside her, holding it in a pinch. The woman, darting her eyes at Brownfield, snatched her arm from her mother's grip, then looked from one to the other of them with baleful scorn. She was cursed with the beginnings of a thick mustache and beard. Her hard, malevolent eyes were a yellowish flash in her dark hairy face. She was sinewy as a man. Only her odor and breasts were female. She reeked of a fishy, oniony smell.

"Yep," said Josie, chuckling at the look on Brownfield's face

34

and watching her daughter slouch off, "that's the pride of her mama's heart."

Lorene turned and hissed something vile, her tongue showing through her lips like a snake's. With one hand she yanked at her waistband. Brownfield looked down with astonishment as her slip disappeared under her short tight skirt. Her legs were even more hairy than her face.

When he looked at Josie she was running her tongue over her teeth, her eyes small brassy points between the fat.

"You sort of gets a thrill from the thought of plowin' through all that hair, don't you?" she asked, shamelessly grinning while Brownfield stammered.

Confounded by her, Brownfield pushed his shoe box farther under his arm and turned away.

"*Wait* a minute," the woman wheezed. "What's your name?"

"Brownfield."

"Brown*field?*" the woman cackled. "Shit. Brownfield what?"

"Copeland," said Brownfield weakly.

Josie was fingering his tie. She was so close he could feel her breath. Suddenly she drew back.

"Where you *from?*" she asked suspiciously.

"Green County," said Brownfield. "What county's this?"

"Baker." She took the shoe box from him and pushed him to a table in the back.

"Now," she said, "tell me just how you happened to turn up *here.*"

"What's the matter with here?" he asked.

"I don't know. Maybe that's what you come to tell me," she said.

By nine o'clock that night he was installed washing dishes and chopping wood, scarcely believing his luck, and listening to the thoroughly arousing music that came from the magic gramophone. Josie had clucked sympathetically as he told of his unfortunate life with Margaret and Grange. She was deeply interested in what he had to say about Grange and when Brownfield spoke of him Josie fidgeted with her hands and nibbled her lips.

After his story she fixed him a supper and pulled him along behind her upstairs to her room. There she fitted him with an apron, standing behind him and reaching around and under his shoulders to get at the halter.

"How come you so curious about the Copelands?" Brownfield had asked.

"Oh," Josie had said, "it just seem like to me I had done heard that name before." Then—looking down the front of his trousers—"But on a heap *bigger* man."

And he said "Ma'am?" In his excitement over having the job, he did not think that his father might indeed have passed exactly this way; through the town, through the tavern, and even through Josie. And then she had laid her arm on his, her skin like dry cracked honey, and said in a sporty way, "Never you mind, Sugar, I'm just talkin' *to* myself."

In the weeks to follow he found her a devouring cat, voracious and sly, wanting to eat him up, swallow him down alive. Thoughts of his father ceased to come to him as he was led into her incredible softness; thoughts of moving northward melted from him in the snug forgetfulness of her experienced warmth. What she had said about the much bigger man with the same name didn't begin to haunt him until it was too late. His contented existence could not have anticipated a day when he would see Grange once more, not in New York or Chicago, but in the very room in which the majority of his nights were to be spent. Grange, not bewildered or rich in the North but crazy and well-to-do in the South, in Baker, in Josie's room, in Josie's arms, disgusted with everything, caring for nothing, but for some reason wanting to take the great lusty insatiable cat up to the altar.

7

Josie had violent dreams. Once she had gone to Sister Madelaine for help. Sister Madelaine said her dreams had to be told, and Josie could never do that.

"They just embarrasses me so bad, Sister," she said. "When I prays in church the other womens laugh at me. They don't know how I've suffered; if they did they wouldn't laugh at me."

"That's your feelings about it anyhow. But listen, they say you should lay your burdens at the feet of the Lord. They say He'll listen." Sister Madelaine stifled a yawn. "But you have to tell *Him* the truth; that's the only catch there. Else, even *He* can't help you."

"I have laid them everywhere, believe me that is the truth. Starting years ago I went to everybody that would listen. Including Him. But the more I lays them down the heavier they gets. All around me is a great big hush, like before a storm, and when I dream it is just to let witches ride me."

Sister Madelaine raised an eyebrow. "My colleged son will tell you there is no such thing as witches riding people. From Morehouse he learns it is· indigestion. Something you ate, the way you are laying in the bed. The circulation of your blood stops and you can't move. While you lay there sweating and not able to move you have nightmares, and when you wake up you think a witch has been riding you. According to my son you wouldn't need a fortuneteller, you'd need a dose of salts."

"He rides me," Josie cried, pleading for belief. "I seen him do it."

"Who?"

"Now," said Josie, "I can't tell you that."

"Well," said Sister Madelaine, handing Josie a cup of tea, "you wouldn't go to a doctor with a pain in the behind without telling him a mule kicked you, would you? I am a fortuneteller, but I ain't God. I got limits. Also a boy in college."

Josie took a sip of tea and handed over some bills.

Sister Madelaine paced, her Indian-chief profile to Josie.

"That theory about witch-riding belongs wholly to my educated child. I don't argue with him to keep peace in the family. But I ask you, what kind of business could I have built up if I *didn't* believe in witches? I know they are real because I have had to shed a few of my own. My son has learned they are *not* real in college, where everybody believes in a man called Freud who uses old couches. Well, *I* don't believe in couches! But what do youngsters know about anything?"

She stopped pacing and looked down at Josie. There was never pity in Sister Madelaine's eyes, just a steady, beady waiting. This unnerved Josie, who thought of the fortuneteller as of another species than herself. She could not bear to look Sister Madelaine straight in the eye.

"Everyone who is straddled by a witch knows the identity of the witch," Sister Madelaine said with her back to Josie. "If you can call his name," she said, as Josie was leaving, "you will be cured."

After Josie was gone, Sister Madelaine scribbled a short note to her son, put it in an envelope, together with the money Josie had paid her, and then sat back reflectively in her chair, savoring the last drops of her tea.

8

Josie had not been able to say his name. She even told herself she did not remember him. She did not know why he came to her while she slept, drenching her in perspiration, racing her heart with fear, holding her immobile with his weight, like judgment, across her chest. For her father had been a heavy man, and it was her father who rode Josie, stifled through the night.

Her father. How did she remember him? A question asked slowly, always in bewilderment, to dull the unforgotten impression of one cruel night over thirty years ago. Her last night in her father's house as a young girl. The night that was to have changed her life of sin back to its original country righteousness.

She had thought her father agreed to let her back into his house. He had not refused her gifts to his other children or to himself or to Josie's mother. And Josie had worked hard to buy them. She had thought, *at last* I will go home to stay, to be again a child, be again sixteen, and near his heart and hand.

It happened on her father's birthday. Josie came walking down the road, dusty-shoed, into the hard swept yard. Her father was on the porch, a shabby dais of power, not knowing about the party she planned for him. She carried small bundles, but had hidden away larger ones the night before. His deep solemn eyes followed her up the steps and into the house. He did not speak. But his eyes seemed to glow with promise and there was a bemused smile on his lips. She thought she was about to be forgiven.

"Do you think he'll let me come back?" she asked her mother, who, like her daughter, was big with child. The money Josie put into the party for her father would be the last she would earn before she delivered. Her mother's answer was a prayer in silence, a frightened and hopeful *cautious* nod of the head. Her mother was a meek woman, and though she rarely agreed with Josie's father she never argued with him.

Josie had come early to prepare the food, mix the drinks— corn liquor, sugared water, crushed mint leaves—and to greet her father's guests. They knew her shame but would come, fearing her father in his stiff sobriety and decency, but depending on his abundant Christianity, the same that he preached to them, to help him forgive. Not only Josie, but them.

For themselves, those who had fucked his daughter, they had paid when possible and felt only a very limited twinge of conscience when they knew she used that money to try to buy back her father's love. And he took the new pipe, the slippers, the big brass watch, and they watched him wear them, and listened to his thoughts on crops and the weather, and saw the amused yet baffled horror in his eyes.

At the party they sat in a semicircle around him and watched him ignore her.

"You want some of this, Pa?" "You want some of that?" And the big questioning eyes over the big thrusting stomach that none of them owned. Josie took more of the liquor for herself and moved out from them on its floating haze, and when she fell clumsily on her back within the curve of the all-male semicircle (the wives of the men had, of course, not come) it was then and only then that her father rose from his chair, from the garish cushion of war, with birds and cannon and horses and red roses, that she had bought him with the money, that he rose and, standing over her, forbade anyone to pick her up.

Her mother stood outside the ringed pack of men, how many of them knowledgeable of her daughter's swollen body she did not know, crying. The tears and the moans of the continually repentant were hers, as if she had caused the first love-making between her daughter and her daughter's teen-age beau, and the scarcely disguised rape of her child that followed from everyone else. Such were her cries that the men, as if caught standing naked, were embarrassed and they stooped, still in the ring of the pack, to lift up the frightened girl, whose whiskied mind had cleared and who now lay like an exhausted, overturned pregnant turtle underneath her father's foot. He pressed his foot into her shoulder and dared them to touch her. It seemed to them that Josie's stomach moved and they were afraid of their guilt suddenly falling on the floor before them wailing out their names. But it was only that she was heaving and vomiting and choking on her own puke.

"Please, sir," someone said from the intimate circle, "let her *up*. She in a *bad* way."

They saw that Josie had seemed to faint, her dark dress pulled up above her knees. Knees turned out. Arms outstretched. She was like a spider, deformed and grotesque beneath the panicked stares of the gathered men. Stares that were only collectively horrified and singly aroused. They had seen her so stretched out before.

"Let 'er be," growled her father. "I hear she can do *tricks* on her back like that."

Such was the benediction of Josie's father, the witch who rode her breathless in her middle age. Lorene had almost been born beneath his foot. As it was she was born into a world peopled by her grandfather's male friends, all of whom frequented the little shack on Poontang Street where "fat Josie" (she grew large after the baby) did her job with a gusto that denied shame, and demanded her money with an authority that squelched all pity. And from these old men, her father's friends, Josie obtained the wherewithal to dress herself well, and to eat well, and to own the Dew Drop Inn. When they became too old to "cut the mustard" any more, she treated them with jolly cruelty and a sadistic kind of concern. She often did a strip tease in the center of their eagerly constructed semicircle, bumping and grinding, moaning to herself, charging them the last pennies of their meager old-age savings to watch her, but daring them to touch.

⑨

A wet gurgle came from Josie's throat. An alien force seemed to be pressing her into the mattress. She drew her breath shudderingly, her body rigid. She was building up pressure for a scream. Brownfield poked her dutifully and after a minute she opened her eyes. She lay breathing heavily, trembling.

"You all right?" he asked. "You want some water or something?"

"God help," said Josie.

"What *is* this dream you keep having?" asked Brownfield. "You gets just as stiff and hard as a dead person. Except you sweat. You kind of vibrates too, like there's a motor on right there where people say the heart is."

41

For a year Brownfield had been asking about the dream. Josie never talked. They lay in bed between crisp white sheets. On Josie's side the crispness had become moist and limp with sweat. Brownfield lit the lamp and placed it on the table near her head. He stood, naked and concerned, gazing down on her face. Josie's face was heavy and doughy, lumpy and creased from sleep, wet from her dream. She had the stolid, anonymous face of a cook in a big house, the face of a tired waitress. The face of a woman too fat, too greedy, too *unrelentless* to be loved. She could grin with her face or laugh out of it or leer through it, but she had forgotten the simple subtle mechanics of the smile. Her eyes never lost their bold rapacious look, even when she woke from sleep terrified, as she was now.

Josie, Brownfield was sure, had never been young, had never smelled of milk or of flowers, but only of a sweet decay that one might root out only if one took the trouble to expose inch after inch of her to the bright consuming fire of blind adoration and love. Then she might be made clean. But Brownfield did not love Josie. He did not really wonder, therefore, that she told him almost nothing about herself, although she constantly pumped him for details of his own life. To shock him once she had told him a strange tale about how his father had stopped at the Dew Drop Inn on his way North, and stayed with her, and loved her. Brownfield had laughed.

"If he love you so much why ain't he here with you right now?"

Josie had retreated in tears, and the next day pretended she'd made her story up.

"Thank *God* I ain't poor," Josie murmured from the bed. "And thank the good Lord I takes care of myself without the help of strangers, *which,* in a matter of plain speaking, ain't got a pot to piss in nor a window to throw it out of." She took the liberty occasionally of reminding Brownfield of his penury. Now she took his pillow from his side of the bed and cradled it in her arms like a lover.

"Listen," she said, "my side of the bed's wet."

Brownfield stumbled next door without a word, into Lorene's

42

room and, not caring to sleep on the floor, he climbed unhesitatingly into Lorene's bed.

10

The first time Brownfield saw Mem, Josie's "adopted" daughter, he had been balling Josie and Lorene for over two years. Mem had been away at school in Atlanta, an errant father paying her bills. She was Josie's sister's child. Her mother was dead.

"She died and left me the *sweetest* li'l burden," Josie occasionally allowed as how to impressionable friends.

"That girl have to buy *books* that cost as much as a many of us pays for dresses!" Josie would smile proudly and with malicious aforethought at some of her less well-off acquaintances. For her "business" in the lounge paid off, and she didn't mind letting people think she was putting Mem through high school.

Mem's father, Brownfield learned, was a big Northern preacher with a large legitimate family. He had met Josie's sister one summer when he came South to preach revival services in Josie's father's church. They had fallen in love and Mem was conceived. The preacher went back North to his family and Mem's mother was put out of her father's house. Josie took her in until Mem was born, and shortly afterward she died.

"Of course, my sister sort of snatch that preacher from me on the rebound, you understand." Josie smiled coyly, insistently, at Brownfield. "But it were really *me* he actually love."

According to Josie, the only reason Lorene didn't go to school ("of course, I were anxious and well off enough to send her") was because she was too stubborn to go. However, by the time she was fifteen Lorene was the mother of two baby boys. Living in the lounge with her mother's boy friends always after her, she was tripped up from the start by the men underfoot, and was the fastest thing going, next to her mother, in town. It had not taken Brownfield long to see that Lorene had her kind of

43

crush on him (anything her mother tried appealed to her), and that Josie more than liked him. At seventeen he was well set up between the two of them and the lounge was as much his as theirs. Or so they were quick to assure him.

He got along well with them both and turned his back when they fought over him. Lorene, a smoke-cured slattern who doused herself with cheap perfume and wore her hair a bright new penny red, was as flattering a lay as her mother. For although she looked more like somebody's brother than anybody's girl, she had a reputation for toughness that earned her an abundance of respect from youngsters who hoped to grow up to be like her. She was noted for her expert use of the razor, and it was said that she had once cut up a customer's wife and then run the customer out of the room while his wife almost bled to death. Brownfield enjoyed her also for her language, as when she said of the customer and his bleeding wife, "I was just tryin' to *catch* that nigger and tell him to get that bleeding brood sow off my floor. I ain't gonna kill *my* ass mopping up after these nasty folks." Brownfield was happy until he got his first look at Mem.

Mem was cherry brown, not yellow like Josie or dark and hairy like Lorene. She was plump and quiet, with demure slant eyes. When she came home from school she was barely noticed. She stayed upstairs when the lounge was rocking, and when she did come down she kept right on out of the house and out walking, just walking, in the woods. Brownfield tried to talk to her but she answered him shyly, her eyes on the ground, without interest, it seemed to him, and went her way, with him more and more turning to look after her. He had never known anybody to go walking, "just walking," in the woods, unless they expected to walk up on a good stick.

"Who the hell she think she *is?*" he asked Josie, frowning at what he couldn't understand. "I can't stand for women to go away for two weeks and come back talking proper!"

Part of what he meant was "walking proper," for Mem certainly had a proper walk. For a while her walk alone mystified him, intrigued him, and in every way set his inquisitive itch on edge. He was not averse to making his person available to all members of the family.

"Aw, quit your going on and get on in this bed," Josie purred, looking more like a fat caterpillar every day. "Ain't no need for you looking at *that* one, she ain't got no real itch in her pussy. She can't do for you what I can do."

Brownfield responded to her soft, sinful old hands by taking her to bed.

"When's you and me going to get married, lover?" Josie asked, while Brownfield realized that Mem's bed was just on the other side of the wall, about a foot from her benevolent "mother's."

In moments of spitefulness, Lorene tried to tell Brownfield that what Josie had said about Grange and her was true. It didn't make any sense to Brownfield that his father and Josie might have been lovers. Besides, what did he care if he now plowed a furrow his father had laid? Josie's old field had never lain fallow. And after Mem came, what Lorene or Josie told him about anything didn't matter. He was interested only in Mem. How to penetrate her quiet strangeness occupied his whole mind.

11

What he felt always when he thought of Mem was guilt. Shame that he was no better than he was. Grime. Dirt. He thought of her as of another mother, the kind his own had not been. Someone to be loved and spoken to softly, someone never to frighten with his rough, coarse ways. But he could never successfully communicate his feelings to her; he did not know the words she knew, and even if he could learn them he had no faith that they would fit the emotions he had. She could read magazines and books, and he could only look at the pictures in them and

45

hazard a guess at what the print meant. Often, when they were thrown together in the house and she walked outside on the porch to keep from being inside alone with him, he followed and tried to talk to her. She would smile and speak a few words, never harsh, about his carryings on with Josie and Lorene. He expressed an interest in wanting to read and write, and she offered to teach him. He caught on quickly to small things, and they spent many afternoons, before the Dew Drop Inn opened, on the steps outside with her old school books. When she began teaching grade school in the fall she took him along with her class. Or tried.

"In the first place," she would begin, in an intense prim way Lorene and Josie scoffed at, "if you have two or three words to say and don't know which word means two or more, it is better to just not use 's' on the end of any of the words. This is so because the verb takes on the same number as the subject. You understand? Well, all I'm saying is 'I *have* some cake,' *sounds* better than 'I *haves* some cake.' Or, 'We have a friendship,' is better than 'We *haves* a friendship.' Now is that clear?" And she would look at him, properly doubtful, wrinkling her brow. And he would nod, yes, and say over and over happily in his mind, We haves a friendship! *We,* Mem and me, haves us a friendship! and he would smile so that she would stop her frowning and smile too.

She was a good teacher. He had never had one. He learned to write his own name, to recite the ABC's, and to write his name and her name linked together, all in a flourish, without lifting his hand from the paper. When she began to teach at school he sometimes sat on the porch by the open door and listened to her clear voice directing the small children, and he concentrated on what she said, as much for the subject matter (which taught him how to spell chicken, goat, cow, hog) as for the pleasure of hearing her speak. She did not sound at all like Josie and Lorene, who talked like toothless old women from plain indifference. Mem put some attention to what she was saying in it, and some warmth from her own self, and so much concern for

46

the person she was speaking to that it made Brownfield want to cry.

In his own mind he considered himself perfect for Mem, if only because he loved her. But much of the town saw things differently, including Josie and Lorene, who were so jealous of their Cinderella that Brownfield became afraid for her (although he was hardly royalty, unless they considered him Prince Stud). Besides, Mem had never told him she cared for him.

But what really began to bother Brownfield was that since he became the man of the establishment, he had not felt it necessary to draw a salary. He was constantly dependent on Josie or Lorene for money, which they gave him readily enough, but with the understanding that he must work for his living and in exactly the ways they specified. And so he stood it around the house as long as he could, screwing Josie and Lorene like the animal he felt himself to be, especially when he stood next day in the same room with Mem, whose heart, pained, was becoming readable in her eyes. There was no longer any joy in his conquest of the two women, for he had long since realized that *he* wasn't using them, *they* were using him. He was a pawn in a game that Josie and Lorene enjoyed. Sometimes he felt he was the link they used to prove themselves mother and daughter. Otherwise they might have been strangers. They existed for the simple pleasure of flirting with each other's men, and then of fighting it out in the street in front of the lounge, where every man in the district soon learned that if you wanted a piece of pussy you had only to make up to one of them to have the other one fall in your lap.

For a while it was grand being prize pawn; for both women, fast breaking from the strain of liquor, whoredom, money-making and battle, thought they truly loved him—but as a clean young animal they had not finished soiling. Their lives infinitely lacked freshness. They were as stale as the two-dollar rooms upstairs. Innocence continued to exist in him for them, since they were not able to see anything wrong in what they did with him. He enjoyed it and after all he was nobody's husband.

47

And if guilt feeling did exist, as perhaps it did on Sunday mornings in the Baptist church, when they outdressed all the women in town and outshouted half of them, it was a minimal and momentary uneasiness, fanned into a pleasurable passion of repentance by inflamed readings from the Scripture. They shouted out their sins in paroxysms of enjoyable grief. The righteous cleanliness of their souls hardly outlasted the service.

12

Matters came to a head for Brownfield when he saw Mem walking for the first time with a man, a teacher like herself. Suddenly he felt he might be passing up a great chance. He felt injured by her choice. Had Mem bypassed him because he was not a well-taught man? His pride was hurt. Gloomily he thought of his poverty and his dependence on Josie and Lorene. All he owned were the clothes on his back and they were none too new.

One night he spied on Mem and her upright, clean-living beau and knew he must have her for his wife. And coming in that night, with him standing in the unlit doorway gazing out at them, Mem brushed past him with tears in her eyes. That was the first time he knew she loved him, and that she was forcing him out of her life by womanly design, and that if he didn't do something soon she would be lost to him. He caught her in his arms as she was going up the stairs and vowed in words and kisses never to let her go.

The next day he went out into the country, to a plantation not far from where he was born, to a man he had heard was fair. They talked of farming on shares for two years, or until Brownfield could make enough money to take his bride northward.

The next week Mem and Brownfield left Josie and Lorene still fighting each other over him, each claiming the other had pushed Mem on to "ketch" him. Brownfield borrowed a wagon from the man he was now working for, and Mem sat beside him on the splintery wooden seat.

"We ain't always going to be stuck down here, honey. Don't you worry," he promised her while she sat quietly, holding her veil in her warm brown hands, and looking and smiling at him with gay believing eyes, full of love.

13

Three years later when he was working the same farm and in debt up to his hatbrim and Mem was big with their second child, he could still look back on their wedding day as the pinnacle of his achievement in extricating himself from evil and the devil and aligning himself with love. Even the shadow of eternal bondage, which plagued him constantly those first years, could not destroy his faith in a choice well made. For Mem was the kind of woman who sang while she cooked breakfast in the morning and sang when getting ready for bed at night. And sang when she nursed her babies, and sang to him when he crawled in weariness and dejection into the warm life-giving circle of her breast. He did not care what anybody thought about it, but she was so good to him, so much what he needed, that her body became his shrine and he kissed it endlessly, shamelessly, lovingly, and celebrated its magic with flowers and dancing; and, as the babies, knowing their places beside her as well as life, sucked and nursed at her bosom, so did he, and grew big and grew firm with love, and grew strong.

They were passionate and careless, he and Mem, making love in the woods after the first leaves fell, making love high in the corncrib to the clucking of hens and the blasting of cocks, making love and babies urgently and with purest fire at the shady ends of cotton rows, when she brought him water to the field and stood watching with that look in her eyes while he drank and leaned an itching palm against the sweaty handle of his

49

plow. As the water, cooling, life-giving, ran down his chin and neck, so did her love run down, bathing him in cool fire and oblivion, bathing him in forgetfulness, as another link in the chain that held him to the land and to a responsibility for her and her children, was forged.

PART III

114

It was a year when endless sunup to sundown work on fifty rich bottom acres of cotton land and a good crop brought them two diseased shoats for winter meat, some dried potatoes and apples from the boss's cellar, and some cast-off clothes for his children from his boss's family. It was the summer that he watched, that he had to teach, his frail five-year-old daughter the tricky, dangerous and disgusting business of handmopping the cotton bushes with arsenic to keep off boll weevils. His heart had actually started to hurt him, like an ache in the bones, when he watched her swinging the mop, stumbling over the clumps of hard clay, the hot tin bucket full of arsenic making a bloodied scrape against her small short leg. She stumbled and almost fell with her bucket, so much too large for her, and each time he saw it his stomach flinched. She was drenched with sweat, her tattered dress wringing wet with perspiration and arsenic; her large eyes reddened by the poison. She breathed with difficulty through the deadly smell. At the end of the day she trembled and vomited and looked beaten down like a tiny, asthmatic old lady; but she did not complain to her father, as afraid of him as she was of the white boss who occasionally deigned to drive by with friends to watch the lone little pickaninny, so tired she barely saw them, poisoning his cotton.

That pickaninny was Brownfield's oldest child, Daphne, and that year of awakening roused him not from sleep but from hope that someday she would be a fine lady and carry parasols and wear light silks. That was the year he first saw how his own life was becoming a repetition of his father's. He could not save his children from slavery; they did not even belong to him.

His indebtedness depressed him. Year after year the amount he owed continued to climb. He thought of suicide and never forgot it, even in Mem's arms. He prayed for help, for a caring President, for a listening Jesus. He prayed for a decent job in Mem's arms. But like all prayers sent up from there, it turned into another mouth to feed, another body to enslave to pay his debts. He felt himself destined to become no more than overseer, on the white man's plantation, of his own children.

That was the year he accused Mem of being unfaithful to him, of being used by white men, his oppressors; a charge she tearfully and truthfully denied. And when he took her in his drunkenness and in the midst of his own foul accusations she wilted and accepted him in total passivity and blankness, like a church. She was too pure to know how sanctified was his soul by her silence. He determined at such times to treat her like a nigger and a whore, which he knew she was not, and if she made no complaint, to find her guilty. Soft words could not turn away his wrath, they could only condone it.

He was expected to raise himself up on air, which was all that was left over after his work for others. Others who were always within their rights to pay him practically nothing for his labor. He was never able to do more than exist on air; he was never able to build on it, and was never to have any land of his own; and was never able to set his woman up in style, which more than anything else he wanted to do. It was as if the white men said his woman needed no style, deserved no style, and therefore would get no style, and that they would always reserve the right to work the life out of him and to fuck her.

His crushed pride, his battered ego, made him drag Mem away from schoolteaching. Her knowledge reflected badly on a husband who could scarcely read and write. It was his great ignorance that sent her into white homes as a domestic, his need to bring her down to his level! It was his rage at himself, and his life and his world that made him beat her for an imaginary attraction she aroused in other men, crackers, although she was no party to any of it. His rage and his anger and his frustration ruled. His rage could and did blame everything, *everything* on her. And she accepted all his burdens along with her own and dealt with them from her own greater heart and greater knowledge. He did not begrudge her the greater heart, but he could not forgive her the greater knowledge. It put her closer, in power, to *them,* than he could ever be.

His dreams to go North, to see the world, to give Mem even the smallest things she wanted from life died early. And in his depression he saw in his submissive, accepting wife a snare and a pitfall. He returned to Josie for comfort after his "mistake" and for money to pay his rent, leaving Mem to carry on the struggle for domestic survival any way she chose and was able to manage. He moved them about from shack to shack, wherever he could get work. When cotton declined in Georgia and dairying rose, he tried dairying. They lived somehow.

Over the years they reached, what they would have called when they were married, an impossible, and *unbelievable* decline. Brownfield beat his once lovely wife now, regularly, because it made him feel, briefly, good. Every Saturday night he beat her, trying to pin the blame for his failure on her by imprinting it on her face; and she, inevitably, repaid him by becoming a haggard automatous witch, beside whom even Josie looked well-preserved.

■■■■■■

55

The tender woman he married he set out to destroy. And before he destroyed her he was determined to change her. And change her he did. He was her Pygmalion in reverse. The first thing he started on was her speech. They had begun their marriage with her correcting him, but after a very short while this began to wear on him. He could not stand to be belittled at home after coming from a job that required him to respond to all orders from a stooped position. When she kindly replaced an "is" for an "are" he threw her correction in her face.

"Why don't you talk like the *rest* of us poor niggers?" he said to her. "Why do *you* always have to be so damn proper? Whether I says "is" or "ain't" ain't no damn humping off *your* butt."

In company he embarrassed her. When she opened her mouth to speak he turned with a bow to their friends, who thankfully spoke a language a man could understand, and said, "Hark, mah *lady* speaks, lets us dumb niggers listen!" Mem would turn ashen with shame, and tried to keep her mouth closed thereafter. But silence was not what Brownfield was after, either. He wanted her to talk, but to talk like what she was, a hopeless nigger woman who got her ass beat every Saturday night. He wanted her to sound like a woman who deserved him.

He could not stand having his men friends imply she was too good for him.

"Man, how did you git hold of that *school*teacher?" they asked him enviously, looking at his bleached and starched clothing and admiring the great quantities of liquor he could drink.

"Give this old blacksnake to her," he said, rubbing himself indecently, exposing his secret life to the streets, "and then I beats her ass. Only way to treat a *nigger* woman!"

For a woman like Mem, who had so barely escaped the "culture of poverty," a slip back into that culture was the easiest thing in the world. First to please her husband, and then because she honestly could not recall her nouns and verbs, her plurals and singulars, Mem began speaking once more in her old dialect. The starch of her speech simply went out of her and what came out of her mouth sagged, just as what had come out of her ancestors sagged. Except that where their speech had been beautiful because it was all they knew and a part of them without thinking about it, hers came out flat and ugly, like a tongue broken and trying to mend itself from desperation.

"Where all them books and things from the schoolhouse?" Brownfield asked one day when he wanted to see if she'd learned her place.

"I done burned 'em up," she said, without turning from a large rat hole she was fixing in the bedroom floor.

For a moment he felt a pang of something bitter, as if he had tasted the bottom of something black and vile, but to cover this feeling he chuckled.

"I were just lookin' for something to start up a fire with."

"Take these here magazines," she said tonelessly, pulling some battered *True Confessions* from under her dress. She thought he had seen the bulge of them under her arm, but he hadn't. He reached out a hand for them and with a sigh she relinquished all that she had been to all she would become now.

Everything about her he changed, not to suit him, for she had suited him when they were married. He changed her to something he did not want, could not want, and that made it easier for him to treat her in the way he felt she deserved. He had never had sympathy for ugly women. A fellow with an ugly wife can ignore her, he reasoned. It helped when he had to beat her too.

There was a time when she saved every cent she was allowed to keep from her wages as a domestic because she wanted, someday, to buy a house. That was her big dream. When she was teaching school they both had saved pennies to buy the house, but when he was angry and drunk he stole the money and bought a pig from some friends of his who promised him the pig was a registered boar and would be his start in making money as a pig breeder. Mem cried when he came home broke, with the pig. Then the pig died. The second time she saved money to buy the house he used it for the down payment on a little red car. She was furious, but more than furious, unable to comprehend that

57

all her moves upward and toward something of their own would be checked by him. In the end, as with the pig, his luck was bad and the finance company took the car.

The children—there were two living, three had died—did not get anything for Christmas that year. On Christmas Eve they sat around and watched him until he ran out of the house to see if Josie would give him money for a drink. When he got home he woke the children and cried over them, but when he saw they were afraid of him he blamed Mem. When she tried to defend herself by telling him the children were just frightened of him because he was drunk he beat her senseless. That was the first time he knocked out a tooth. He knocked out one and loosened one or two more.

She wanted to leave him, but there was no place to go. She had no one but Josie and Josie despised her. She wrote to her father, whom she had never seen, and he never bothered to answer the letter. From a plump woman she became skinny. To Brownfield she didn't look like a woman at all. Even her wonderful breasts dried up and shrank; her hair fell out and the only good thing he could say for her was that she kept herself clean. He berated her for her cleanliness, but, because it was a small thing, and because at times she did seem to have so little, he did not hit her for it.

"I ain't hurting you none," she said, pleading with something in him he kept almost suppressed, and he let the matter drop.

"Just remember you ain't white," he said, even while hating with all his heart the women he wanted and did not want his wife to imitate. He liked to sling the perfection of white women at her because color was something she could not change and as his own colored skin annoyed him he meant for hers to humble her.

He did not make her ashamed of being black though, no matter what he said. She had a simple view of that part of life. Color was something the ground did to flowers, and that was an end to it.

Being forced to move from one sharecropper's cabin to an-

58

other was something she hated. She hated the arrogance of the white men who put them out, for one reason or another, without warning or explanation. She hated leaving a home she'd already made and fixed up with her own hands. She hated leaving her flowers, which she always planted whenever she got her hands on flower seeds. Each time she stepped into a new place, with its new, and usually bigger rat holes, she wept. Each time she had to clean cow manure out of a room to make it habitable for her children, she looked as if she had been dealt a death blow. Each time she was forced to live in a house that was enclosed in a pasture with cows and animals eager to eat her flowers before they were planted, she became like a woman walking through a dream, but a woman who had forgotten what it is to wake up. She slogged along, ploddingly, like a cow herself, for the sake of the children. Her mildness became stupor; then her stupor became horror, desolation and, at last, hatred.

Strangely, Brownfield could bear her hatred less than her desolation. In fact, he rather enjoyed her desolation because in it she had no hopes. She was weak, totally without view, without a sky. He was annoyed when she despised him because out of her hatred she fought back, with words, never with blows, and always for the children. But coming from her, even words disrupted the harmony of despair in which they lived.

For Brownfield, moving about at the whim of a white boss was just another example of the fact that his life, as it was destined, had "gone haywire," and he could do nothing about it. He jumped when the crackers said jump, and left his welfare up to them. He no longer had, as his father had maintained, even the desire to run away from them. He had no faith that any other place would be better. He fitted himself to the slot in which he found himself; for fun he poured oil into streams to kill the fish and tickled his vanity by drowning cats.

15

Each Saturday evening Brownfield was at the Dew Drop Inn lounge. Josie welcomed him; it was like home. Having been lovers they were now much more. They were comrades. They shared confidences. Lorene had migrated North, and Josie ran the lounge alone, except for two very young and talented girls who had Lorene's old room.

Brownfield and Josie spent a great deal of time talking. About Mem and her self-righteousness, about Brownfield's error in marrying her, and about Josie and her fears and dreams and the cruel tricks fate had played on her. They talked of Josie's driving will to survive and to overcome. Her need to avenge herself on those who wronged her. They talked about Brownfield, about how numb he felt when he allowed himself a fleeting remembrance of his mother. They talked about Margaret and her bastard baby, Star. They talked for hours and hours about Grange.

"Your mammy was a *fool*, boy. Thinkin' she could keep Grange by making him jealous of other mens." Josie's chin shook the slightest bit.

"You tried the same thing," said Brownfield, "in his *absence*. Or do you plan to tell me I got the job here just 'cause you liked my face?"

"Oh, but I weren't *tryin'* to make Grange *jealous,*" said Josie.

"No?"

"No." Josie's chin fairly quivered. "I were tryin' to *kill* the son of a bitch!"

For some reason Brownfield laughed. "It wouldn't have killed him, seeing you with me. He never cared no more for me than a stranger."

"You don't understand yet how the thing go, do you?"

"I know enough."

"Ain't you the lucky one, then," said Josie. "Now set down and listen."

Brownfield sat down in a familiar blue chair, facing Josie, who was propped up in bed.

"It was some weeks before *you* come," said Josie, "that me and Grange made all our plans to leave Georgia. We was goin' up to New York. To Harlem, the black folks' city, where we owns *every*thing! Ain't that something? We was goin' to go away and never come back. You may wonder what I was planning to do with Lorene," she said, looking at Brownfield. "Well, just between you and me, I was goin' to *dump* Lorene. She been a chain round my neck long enough. If it hadn't been for her me and your daddy would have *been* together in the first place. Grange and me started goin' to church them weeks he was here. And I want you to know he *promised* me he was goin' to take me with him; and then he sneaked off and I ain't seen him from that day to this one!"

Josie leaned her head back against the pillows, her eyes on the ceiling. In a minute, in a lower, more careless voice, she continued.

"Oh, Grange and me goes back a long ways. Since *way* before you was born. Way before he even met your mama."

Brownfield was not surprised. He had waited to know this part of his father's life.

"Where you keep yourself all that time?" he asked. "I never heard nobody at home talk about no Josie."

"You remember tellin' me 'bout that fat yellow *bitch* your mammy use to mention?"

"You don't *mean* . . ." said Brownfield, still not very surprised.

"Nobody else but." Josie wore a red silk kimono with blue and purple dragons on the sleeves. She ran a pudgy hand down into the cleavage of her dress.

"Lemme tell you," she said, "Grange never would have married Margaret if he hadn't been pushed into it by his damn 'respectable' family. His African Methodist Episcopal brothers and they mealy-bosomed wives couldn't stand the thoughts of

61

having me in the family; I weren't *good* enough for him. Never mind I built up a establishment with my own hands and figured out how to git rich with my own brain. I still wasn't good enough. Nothing would do the family but that your daddy marry Margaret. The only thing she had that I didn't have was a unused pussy. But it didn't stop me and Grange from being together. He didn't have the heart to leave your mammy outright. But every Saturday evening, by the *clock,* you could find Grange Copeland right where you is now."

"So he come here, and you took . . . *care* of him?" The chair he was sitting in felt uncomfortable. Brownfield got up and paced.

"Yes," said Josie, proudly. "I took care of him, 'cause he was *mine.* I didn't pity your mammy *one* bit."

"Mama was okay," said Brownfield. "At least she put herself out of the way. I wondered why she done it like that. Looked like to me at the time she knowed something I didn't."

"She knowed plenty," Josie sneered. "Knowed she wouldn't do for your daddy what Fat Josie would do. You think she could come up with any idees of how to git Grange out of debt? And with half the men in the county after her tail? The *thought* never crossed her mind! Then, when it *did* strike her, *she forgot to charge!* Shit."

"Well," said Brownfield, embarrassed, "it been ten years almost since he left here. Long enough for me to done run up *on* you, run away *from* you, and run back *to* you." He turned to face her, seeing the new gray hair she had not had time to blacken, seeing the deepened wrinkles everywhere.

"You might as well stop sleepin' with me," he said softly, feeling so grown up and knowledgeable he could hardly bear it. "Grange ain't coming back. If you still want to give him a little shock you got to go all the way up Norse to do it. I ain't no good to you."

Josie read the sickness in his eyes.

"But, *lover*"—she smiled maternally, loosening her robe and coming to hold him—"ain't you found out *yet* that I also likes you for your*self?*"

16

As the years passed, Brownfield got in the habit of thinking of Grange as someone he had never closely known. He didn't refer to him as Father, but as Grange. This made Josie seem not such a burden and lessened the feeling Brownfield often had that Josie had made a fool of him, pretending she cared for him, a boy whose manhood meant only one thing and went easily to his head, when all the time she was eating her heart out for Grange.

He would never forget Josie's face the night Grange returned to Baker County. How fear, self-condemnation, guilt and *joy* flushed through her as she hastily pushed Brownfield away; pushed him away as if he were as odious as a toad, as inconsequential as some kind of harmless lizard. For all her boasting that she wanted to "kill" Grange, she would have spared him that moment if it cost her her life. Brownfield wanted one day to see her damned for that stricken and guilty look on her face.

They had been lolling on the bed, rubbing and feeling each other, Josie in her slip. They were speaking of their insatiable passion for each other, a subject they brought up whenever he became impotent with her. He was often unable, after Mem, to make love to Josie; the thought of Mem and her perpetual tired grayness shriveled him up. He and Josie talked about their passion, about the old days, and Josie made up lies to tell him about Mem. And sometimes, by pretending to believe something nasty about his wife, something low-down enough to go home and beat her about, he could succeed in making love to Josie. Josie didn't care how she got his passion up, she just wanted it up. With him covering her she released her mind from its memories of betrayals; she forgot the terrors of her recurring dream, and she entered a world of gentleness and contentment. Her face

63

became that of a pure and guileless fat girl; she was innocent, uncomplaining, real.

Even so, Brownfield never really shared sex with Josie, not in the complete, sustaining way he had with Mem. Josie took and he took. She was either stirred to a single-minded vileness, when she swore at him and used foul descriptive words, or she passed into a safe solitude. A solitude to which Brownfield was genuinely happy to send her, for then he thought of his screwing as an act of kindness, and he wanted to be kind. Josie's nightmares, witnessed over the years, had moved him. The least he could do, he thought, was help her sleep.

But that night he had had no chance to help her sleep. Grange, graying, bushy-haired, and lean as a wolf, came through the bedroom door. Curses erupted from Brownfield. His first impulse was to knock his father down. But he realized immediately, and it made him sob, that he was still afraid of him. He might still have been a child from the fear he felt. So instead of fighting his father, Brownfield cursed him and cried and left one of his socks near Josie's bed. Grange stood against the wall near the door gazing from Brownfield to Josie and finally resting his eyes on Josie.

Brownfield put his arms around Josie's neck. His tears dripped onto her bosom. But Josie looked beyond him, over his shoulder; for the final time she pushed him away.

Forgetting about Brownfield, Grange and Josie shut him out. Josie wriggled into a somber wrapper, dabbed at her neck and throat with moist hands, and looked at Grange with eyes that said she'd die on the spot if he wanted her to. As Brownfield staggered away, angry and shaken, heading for a drunk, they hardly moved, frozen by some strange commitment to each other that Brownfield had not even been aware of. They did not fear him, for all his threats. Nor did he seem to matter to them in any way at all. In two weeks Grange and Josie were married.

PART IV

17

Very early on the morning of Ruth's arrival into the world, at about five o'clock in the morning on a gray drizzly Thursday in November, Mem awakened Brownfield and asked him to get the midwife, who lived some eight miles away. Brownfield was sleeping off a drunk and could not rouse himself, although he tried, before seven o'clock, and by then Ruth had popped out by herself. Brownfield woke finally, groggy, with a sense of something new having been added, to find his wife surrounding a small bundle, shivering on the bed. His own cot, nearer to the fire than Mem's bed, blocked the little heat that came from a smoldering hickory log in the fireplace. He was apologetic and sorry for his neglect and tried to make up for it with various cooing pleasantries directed at his small daughter, but Mem was in no mood to have Ruth subjected so soon to the foul after-aromas of puke-smelling brew.

"Git out of my sight," she whispered, turning from him to warm the baby with what heat she could call her own.

It was toward this charged atmosphere that Grange walked, laden with meat, collards, candy and oranges. Brownfield, embarrassed, uneasy and fuzzy, got up and walked out to meet him. Grange was stepping briskly down the road freshly and neatly dressed, bashfully smiling.

"Aw, *Grange,*" Brownfield stammered in greeting, as his father came up to the edge of the yard.

Brownfield was angered to see the packages in his father's arms. This intrusion of goods—Grange never set foot in his son's house without a load of eatables and wearables—made Brownfield wish more than ever to see him someday on the rack.

"*You* shouldn't have did that, Grange," he said sheepishly, smiling but gritting his teeth; hating himself for wanting to see what was inside the bundles Grange thrust into his hands. He realized self-pityingly that he was ravenous and hadn't eaten a meal in two days.

"That's all right," Grange mumbled, patiently waiting for his son to lead him into the house. Brownfield sniffed at one of the bags in his hands. It contained fruit, a treat the children would love, another reason for adoring their grandfather. It was only at Christmas that Brownfield's children got apples and oranges and grapes. As a child Brownfield had never seen a grape. He clutched the bags in a confusion of feeling. He was hungry, he was suffering from a malaise of the spirit, he was jealous of his children's good fortune. He wished he did not have children down whose gullets the good fruit would go; he wished he were a child himself.

Brownfield was not as tall as Grange, who had to bend his head to his chest to enter the room where Mem and Brownfield slept. In winter, usually, they all slept in the same room. Brownfield, Mem, Daphne and Ornette; because it was impossible to heat two rooms in such a hole-filled house. It was impossible, really, to heat one room; but when four people slept together in

68

one small room and kept a fire going they could manage not to freeze to death before summer.

To see his wife and children through his father's eyes—knowing of the farm and the snug house Grange and Josie owned—made Brownfield eager for his family to appear warm and happy and well-cared for. One look at the walls of the room they were in made it clear no one could ever be warm in it. The walls had been covered, probably neatly at one time, with paper bags. Bags cut open along one side and flattened out, sides overlapping. But the bags hung down now, here and there, in rustling flaps; the wind had pushed them loose. Where the flaps hung down from the ceiling one could look directly up into the loft and in several places straight through the loft into the sky. In the window frames without panes someone had tried to put in neat square pieces of cardboard, but the rain, coming down against these squares at a slant, made the bottom half of them wet and the same wind that pushed the flaps aside to reveal the holes in the roof forced aside these pieces of cardboard, and puddles of icy water were collected on the bare gray floor.

Grange, as he entered, took in the sorry condition of the room in a glance and could not withhold a sigh. A sigh Brownfield heard and understood immediately as condemnation. Brownfield thought of the money his father had brought back from the North—enough to buy a farm, enough to marry Josie, enough to lend Brownfield some on the condition that he stop drinking! —and thought maybe now was his chance to get more of what his father seemed so willing to give his family. Money. Accordingly, Brownfield whined, "Just poor folks, that's us." He wiped the hardened matter from the corners of his eyes and bade his father sit down on the little cot which was his bed, now that Mem used all of the double one.

Grange looked about him silently. The fire sputtered and went out. Brownfield made no move to relight it. Grange took off his coat and started to work over the fire. He was outraged to find there was no more wood.

"*How* can you not have *wood* and your *wife* 'bout to pop?" he asked.

Brownfield looked over his shoulder at his wife's folded pallet. Not wanting the children to see the blood she had folded it as neatly as a newspaper and had tied it with string. There was a sheet hanging before Mem's bed. It formed a curtain which would have protected her children from the sight of childbirth. Brownfield thought what a blessing it must have been to Mem that the baby was born at night while Daphne and Ornette slept and wind and rain muffled her sounds of struggle.

Brownfield could not, dared not, tell his father that Mem had already had the baby, and without help from him or from anybody. He only hoped his father would soon leave and not try once more to "explain," as he so often tried to do, his reasons for deserting his own family. Grange felt guilty about his son's condition and assuaged his guilt by giving food and money to Brownfield's family. He never gave money directly to Brownfield, who had drunk up the first sum Grange had given him. After that there was no second chance. Grange had no faith in him, Brownfield correctly assumed. But, having laid aside his bundles, Grange was in no mood to leave. He wanted to talk to Mem, see if she needed anything for the baby, whose birth, Grange thought, was so near.

"Why, she *sleep*ing," Brownfield said, hoping his father would hurry out. But Grange, looking into the fireplace, rubbing his hands, spoke of unimportant things like the weather and then of what was pressing on his heart.

"Like I been trying to tell you, ever since I come back, there's a lot I *done* I didn't a*gree* with. It was the times, I reckon. You could work so *hard,* for nothing. And as tight as times was they started tightenin' up some more. I was worked so hard, I tell you the truth, my days had done all run together. There wa'n't no beginning nor no end."

Brownfield stared bitterly at the floor.

"Margaret's days all run together *too,* after *you* left." He said his mother's name thickly, with abundant emotion, though he disliked the memory of her last days as much as ever. Brownfield felt he had been abandoned by Grange's desertion to whatever wolves would take him; not at the time of his leaving, nor

70

while Brownfield was living at the Dew Drop Inn, but in married retrospect, seen through Brownfield's own miserableness in the life he convinced himself he was courageous enough to *accept*. He did not really care what his mother had felt at all.

Grange looked at Brownfield, Brownfield looked at him. Josie's shadow came between them. She kept them from becoming what they had never really been anyhow, father and son. That was her revenge.

"That'll have to be a strong chile to be born in here. And it'll have to be kin to the Eskimos or it'll freeze to death. Well," Grange said, rising finally, "when Mem wake up tell her I'll send Josie over to help out, or maybe I might just come back myself." Grange stood, looking toward the bed. "Lawd knows the *whole* business is somethin' of a miraculous event. Out of all kinds of shit comes something clean, soft and sweet smellin'."

"If you think it so *sweet smellin'*, you *take* it," said Brownfield, seeing his baby with entirely different, unenchanted and closely economic eyes.

Behind the muslin sheet Mem lay, huddled against her baby. The baby, unwashed, was moist and sticky against the soft cloth that was wrapped around her. Mem had been drying the film of wetness from her when Grange came in. Fearing the sharpness of the cold she stopped, and now, instead, rubbed the baby softly up and down its hardly moving body. The window near her bed let in sporadic bursts of damp air. In the middle of the night she had asked Brownfield to cover it with a quilt, but the only quilt he could use, he said, was the one on his bed, or the one on hers.

The wind came through the window, moving the newspapers under the bed. Weakly Mem called out to her husband.

"What you say you want, honey?" he asked, coming to peer at her from around the curtain. Grange also came. Mem heard the intake of Grange's breath as he stood beside Brownfield, looking down on her, seeing the bundle, rooted in disbelief.

"You no-good, *sorry*, good-for-nothing *tramp*," he said, pushing Brownfield aside and impatiently bending to move Mem's bed closer to the fire.

"It won't move," said Mem, glancing fearfully at her husband. "It just set up on some blocks."

Her eyes were sunken and hazy from her long night. Meekly her eyes pleaded with Grange to go away, to leave them alone. She watched him anxiously as he moved about the room, burning the pallet, which, made of newspapers and old clean rags, burned well, despite its spots of slimed wet, and then taking out the slop jar that was so filled with the proof of how her night was spent.

Grange took down the makeshift curtain, ordered Brownfield to make up his bed and go out for wood, and prepared the baby for the eyes of her two sisters.

"I'm all right, I'm just fine," Mem said, when Grange reached for the thin quilted covers of her bed.

With a great show of control, Grange took the wood Brownfield brought in and put it on the fire. Thankfully he watched it begin to burn.

"At least you got sense enough to know wet wood won't burn," he said. Brownfield stood at his elbow with an amused and belligerent smirk.

"Got it off the barn," he said.

"Brownfield, git me a little warm water to drink or maybe a little coffee," said Mem. Grange had raised her head and placed his own coat across her shoulders.

Grange had always liked Mem. He had known her when she was a child, playing behind the lounge. Lorene was always making her cry and run and hide in the woods. Grange had been glad when Josie told him that Brownfield had married her. He thought a good wife would mellow Brownfield, even if she was kin to Josie. Though Mem had none of Josie's hardness.

On the night he had returned to the Dew Drop Inn and found Josie with Brownfield he discovered the bitterness his son felt toward him, the resentment, the hate; but he had hoped Brownfield's own experience as a family man and sharecropper would change that. But now, looking at Mem after eight years with Brownfield was like seeing some old mangy aunt of the

72

girl Brownfield had married. Mem's hair, which had been so thick and black, now pressed against her pillow gray as charcoal. Much of it had fallen out. Grange felt, among all the other reasons for her being laid so low, his own guilt. That was why he spent so much time with her and his grandchildren, and brought them meat and vegetables, and gave them money on the sly, and reaped in full the anger of his wife and the unflagging bitterness of his son.

Brownfield was handing Mem a cup of barely warm coffee.

"I know that's what she asked for," said Grange, "but surely there's somethin' to *eat* in this house. I mean like some *soup* or something."

Brownfield walked calmly to the door, his face set, and tossed the coffee out into the yard.

"I give her what she ask for, what more you want?" He sat down solidly in front of the fire, not willing now to give her anything. His face was as sulky as a child's.

From the provisions he'd brought Grange made a stew. When Daphne and Ornette crawled out of their damp covers in the next room it was to the hot spicy smell of the stew and to the warming leaps of a good fire. At first Brownfield would not touch the stew. He grudgingly watched his children fall all over their grandfather. Soon, though, he began to eat, his hunger caring nothing for his pride.

"My trouble is," he told his father, "I always *could* do *without* childrens." He watched Daphne and Ornette take turns examining the baby's tiny fists. "I didn't like having to baby-sit that brat *you all* dumped on me." Brownfield looked his father in the eye.

"I never liked my brother—*you* know that—'cause *you* didn't like him neither. I seen you pinch him when you thought nobody was looking. Looks like back then the whole *business* just about made you puke—takin' care of Margaret's bastard, and *me* too."

Grange hung his head and endured in silence.

18

To his three daughters Brownfield gave the dregs of his attention only when he was half drunk. To him they were not really human children, although his heart at times broke for them. He could not see them as innocent or even as children. He scolded Ornette, who had come a year after Daphne, with the language he would use on a whore. And the baby, Ruth, he never touched.

As they grew older, Daphne, the only one who could remember the scanty "good old days" before Brownfield began to despise them, took the baby and Ornette out under the trees and told them of how good a daddy Brownfield had once been. Brownfield overheard her whispering her stories into the baby's ear, as if she wanted her little sister to grow up believing that the few greedily cherished good times with Brownfield had also been her own.

PART V

19

Brownfield did not believe Mem would be able to find a house. He had not found a decent house the first and only time he had looked for one. What was more, he did not believe she had been looking for one.

"You get through telling all them old dried-up friends of yours that I just got kicked out on my ass and you already out looking for a *mansion* to live in—for a change?"

He reached out an arm and grabbed her quickly around one wrist.

"Ow, Brownfield," she said, dropping her shoes.

"I ought to make you call me Mister," he said, slowly twisting the wrist he held and bringing her to her knees beside his feet. "A woman as black and ugly as you ought to call a man Mister."

"I didn't find no house today," she whimpered dryly, because she was so tired and her feet hurt. "And I didn't see *no*-body but people that was renting."

He shoved her and she knocked over her flower boxes, spilling flowers and dirt. She scrambled shakily to her knees, then to her blistered and callused feet, sniffling and putting a wrinkled hard hand to her head. Her daughters stood at the battered screen watching, their baby sister in their arms.

We ought to jump on him and kill him dead, Mem thought, as she avoided her children's eyes, took the baby, Ruth, into her arms, and went into the house.

"Goddam rib-ridden *plow*horse," Brownfield muttered spitefully, propping his legs against the rotten railing of his sagging front porch.

20

At the end of the second feeding, when he was putting the scoops back into the feed bags, Captain Davis came in and stood in the doorway chewing and spitting, acting half-interested in what Brownfield was doing and half-interested in emphasizing that he owned the cows and the barn and everything else in sight. He just stood there, with his shirt sleeves pinned up and his bald head mottled, being boss man.

"I told Mr. J. L. you was going to be looking for a place right soon," he said. He turned his head down at a slant and watched Brownfield tie up the feed bags. His lips pursed tightly when a few grains of feed spilled on the concrete.

"I told him he could probably do worse than you if he's in the market for a field and dairyman."

Brownfield's hands stopped momentarily tying the bags.

"Yassur?"

He made as if to straighten all the way up but managed to stand stooped a little so that he felt small and black and bug-like, and Captain Davis, with his sparse white hair, seemed a white giant that could step on him.

"Yassur?" he said again, while Captain Davis's eyes swept the ceiling and roamed over the rumps of his cows. Slowly.

Damned one-arm son of a bitch, Brownfield thought, as he stooped motionless, looking up at the tall white man and waiting to shift his eyes the moment the captain turned his face to him.

Why don't he say what he going to say, 'stead of acting like I got all goddam *day* to hear 'bout his slave-driving son. Let him get his own motherfucking help 'stead of trading *me* off! As the captain turned, Brownfield averted his eyes. A vacant obliging smile wavered on his face.

"'Course you won't be living as easy as you do here," Captain Davis said as his eyes came down to the level of Brownfield's and Brownfield dropped his own, being careful to maintain a smile that was both alert and respectful.

"You interested in this, Brown?" the old man asked, clearing his throat and spitting between them, not bothering to turn his head. "I already told Mr. J. L. you was."

"Yassur!" Brownfield said, taking out a large print handkerchief and wiping his hands. Paying special attention to between the fingers. He thought about what Mr. J. L. was like; stingy and mean, not to be trusted around black womenfolk, and shuddered. He did not want to work for him. He remembered how he and Mem had come to work for Captain Davis. Captain Davis's brother had sent them after he had finished with Brownfield and his wife had died and there was no further need for Mem. In return Captain Davis had let his tractor go for a season. The swap had been made exactly as if he and his family were a string of workhorses.

"I be much obliged to you for putting in a word for me." Brownfield nodded up and down still smiling but with his eyes carefully averted. He thought about turning down the offer but when the words of refusal came to his lips he found they would not come out. He cleared his throat and prodded the ground in front of him with his foot as if he would speak, but no words came out, only a hesitant grunt that sounded like further strangled acceptance.

"What you say, Brown?" Captain Davis asked in impatiently severe tones. He turned his tall frame in the doorway so that the sun made a halo of his thin ring of white hair. Looking for a brief second into his light blue eyes Brownfield stood speechless.

"Yassur," he said finally, hypnotized by the old man standing in the sun.

Captain Davis shrugged his gaunt white shoulders and walked away toward his white house with the bright red chimneys.

Pity how you got to look after 'em, he thought, as he wrapped his good hand round his stub.

21

He was late and had not told her he would be; still they had not dared to begin supper without him. Daphne was looking at a page full of bathroom fixtures, staring nearly cross-eyed in the light of the kerosene lamp that hung from a cord over the table.

"Is this the kinder toilet we going to have, Ma?" Ornette asked, looking dazzled over Daphne's sharp elbow at all the sparkling fixtures.

"Look at them shiny *toilets!*" she whispered urgently, her spread fingers touching four commodes, excitement making her voice rough and burpy. Daphne nudged her playfully with the elbow she kept between the Sears, Roebuck catalogue and her sister.

"Why don't you get on out the way, girl!" she said, and tried to hog the book, but Ornette clamped a grubby fist on a corner of the book, covering, except for a bright corner, a deep white bathtub filled with greenish blue water like that in the white swimming pool in town.

Mem, her knees spread under the table and her battered hungry face cracking every once in a while in a grin, supervised the turning of the pages.

"Wait a minute, Daphne, I ain't through looking at these sinks and dishracks!" she said sharply, when Daphne wanted to race on ahead to the warming glowing pictures of multicolored light bulbs and fancy lamps.

"Is us going to have 'lectric lights in our new house?" Ornette asked breathlessly, caressing the slick pages of the catalogue. The yellow glow of the lamp encircled Mem and her homely children in soft kindly light, making them look good to one another. The baby, Ruth, too small to be interested in home furnishings, gurgled and cooed in her box by the stove. In vain did she compete for her mother's attention.

"I ain't promising nothing," Mem said, laughing at Ornette's big serious eyes and running one rough hand over her head. "I ain't saying what's going to be," she continued, "but the Lord *wills* we going to have 'em!" She said the last flatly, almost to herself, hearing the back door open and shut and feeling the draft caused by Brownfield's entry and seeing the lamp flicker and almost go out.

"Why ain't supper on the table?" Brownfield demanded as soon as he walked in.

"We didn't know *when* you was coming, Brownfield," Mem said softly, pulling herself out of her chair so fast she scraped her bony knees. Meekly she hovered over the stove stirring and taking up peas and ham hocks. She placed a heaping plate in front of Brownfield and backed into the stove, getting food for herself and the children. Brownfield saw she had burned herself turning around clumsily, and he smiled as he plowed into his peas, sending them scattering across the table, down his shirt front, and down his throat.

Ornette sat dazed, watching her father pick up his meat with his hands and tear at it, sending the juice flying over the tablecloth Mem was proud to make white. When her father was eating Ornette could not think of him as anything but a hog. She blinked her eyes as he said to her over a mouthful of peas and bread, "What you looking at me for?"

Her eyes quickly riveted to her own plate and she began slowly to eat, trying very hard not to hear the whistling noise her father made as he sucked at the meat and gobbled the peas.

Mem ate with her head down, passing the food up to her husband the moment she thought he might like some more. Daphne sat completely squelched, nervously chewing and beading her dress under the table, as close to her mother's side as possible. She hallucinated vividly that Brownfield ate so many peas he swoll up and burst. She saw herself helping gleefully to bury him and then watched in horror as the huge twisting and congested pea vines began to come up. Aloud, she began a strange blank-eyed whimper.

"What's the matter with *you, stup*id?" Her father's eyes were on her, intense and hard, like the eyes of a big rat.

I wish he'd get swoll up and die! she thought behind her alerted but sad and empty face. I wish he'd just *do* that for us so we could *bury* him!

"What's this I hear about some *new* house?" Brownfield asked, finally, chewing noisily and sweating from eating so vigorously. He grunted slyly as if choking back a laugh. "We going to move over on Mr. J. L.'s place."

He was pleased to feel the weight of their tense and silent response.

"I ain't," Mem said. "I ain't, and these children ain't." She stiffened her thin tough neck for his blow. But he only laughed and kept eating, stabbing at stray peas with round wads of cornbread.

"Get me some water," he grunted to Ornette, who pretended she was fetching slop for a hog.

"Yassur," she mumbled with her head down, going to the icebox.

"You should have got some ice from the iceman yesterday," Mem said, smelling the reek from the box.

"You ought to have stayed at home yesterday instead of traipsing off all over creation looking for a mansion to live in. If you acted like a woman with some sense we'd a had ice." He rolled his eyes to indicate her foolishness and coughed in her face without turning his head.

A shiver of revulsion ran through his wife. "He's just like a old dog," she thought, guiltily urging her nervous children to eat their fill.

He had once been a handsome man, slender and tall with narrow, beautiful hands. From trying to see in kerosene lamplight his once clear eyes were now red-veined and yellowed, with a permanent squint. From running after white folks' cows, he never tended much to his own, when he had any, and he'd developed severe athlete's foot that caused him to limp when the weather was hot or wet. From working in fields and with cows in all kinds of weather he developed a serious bronchitis aggravated by rashes and allergies.

He was not a healthy man. When he first started working with cows his hands broke out and the skin itched so that he almost scratched it off. It was only after years of working every day milking cows that the itch gave up, and by then his hands were like gray leather on the outside, the inside scaly and softly cracked, too deformed for any work except that done to and for animals. The harder and more unfeeling the elephant-hide skin on his hands became the more often he planted his fists against his wife's head.

I ain't never going to marry nobody like him, Daphne swore to herself, watching the big ugly hands that smelled always of cows and sour milk.

"It's all settled," said Brownfield, belching loudly and digging under the table between his legs. "We going to move over to Mr. J. L.'s come next Monday and," he spoke menacingly to Mem, "I don't want any lip from you!"

"I already told you," she said, "you ain't dragging me and these children through no more pigpens. We have put up with mud long enough. I want Daphne to be a young lady where there is other decent folks around, not out here in the sticks on some white man's property like in slavery times. I want Ornette to have a chance at a decent school. And little baby Ruth," she said wistfully, "I don't even want her to *know* there's such a thing as outdoor toilets."

"You better git all that foolishness out your head before I knock it out!"

"I ain't scared of you," his wife lied.

"When the time comes, you'll see what you do, Miss Ugly," he said, and pinched her tense worn cheek. Even as he did it he knew dull impossible visions of a time when that cheek was warm and smoothly rounded, highlighted and sleek. It was rare now when it curved itself in a smile.

"Me and these children got a *right* to live in a house where it don't rain and there's no holes in the floor," she said, snatching her cheek away. From long wrestles in the night he knew she despised his hands. He held one gigantic hand in front of her eyes so she could see it and smell it, then rammed it clawingly down her dress front.

If I was a man, she thought, frowning later, scrubbing the dishes, if I was a man I'd give every man in sight and that I ever met up with a beating, maybe even chop up a few with my knife, they so pig-headed and mean.

22

" 'Evening, Brown," she said solemnly the following afternoon, Wednesday.

" 'Evening, Ugly," Brownfield said, crossing the porch and eying her with suspicion. He detected a sad meager smile beginning to work itself across her broad lips. The sun across her hair made him notice how nearly gray it was. She was hanging there in the doorway, her ugly face straining between deep solemnity and sudden merriment. It had been years since he'd seen her look anything near this excited.

"What you turning that idiot look on me for?" he asked, facing her, his hand on the screen door. He had never despised her as much. Was she looking like she was going to be this ugly when I married her? he asked himself, as the face in front of him spread itself out in a funny-shaped pie and Mem laughed soft and deep, as she used to laugh when they were first married and not one day passed without some word of deepest love.

"We got us a new house," she said, as if she were dropping something precious that would send up delightful bright explosions. "We got us a new house in *town!*" she whispered joyously.

He looked around to see the children also with wide spreading mouths, looking just like their mother.

"I know we got a new house," he said patiently, "but it's going to be over on Mr. J. L.'s place, and nowhere else!"

"Oh, nooo," she said gaily, still laughing in her rough, unused-to-laughing way. "This house has got sinks and a toilet inside the house and it's got 'lectric lights and even garden space for flowers and greens. You told me yourself," she said, laughing harder than ever, "that old man J. L.'s place done fell down on one side and is anyhow all full of hay." Talking about the house seemed to make her dizzy. She fell into a chair, placing her hands to her eyes as if to clear her head. "Besides," she said, suddenly sobered, "it don't cost but twenty dollars a month to rent and you can make enough at a factory in town to pay that much: factory work'll keep you out of the *rain*. A school is close by for the children and the neighbors look like nice people. And on top of that . . ." She started to list assets of the house again. Her eyes lit up, then went dull and tired. She had spent all day looking for the house. "Besides all them things," she said tonelessly, and resigned as she stood up, "I told the man we'd be there to start living in that house Monday morning. I signed the lease."

"You *signed* the lease?" He was furious. He could not, even after she'd tried to teach him, read or write. It had gone in with the courting and out with the marriage. "I ought to chop your goddam fingers off!"

"I'm real sorry about it, Brownfield," said Mem, whose decision to let him be man of the house for nine years had cost her and him nine years of unrelenting misery. He had never admitted to her that he couldn't read well enough to sign a lease and she had been content to let him keep that small grain of pride. But now he was old and sick beyond his years and she had grown old and evil, wishing every day he'd just fall down and die. Her generosity had shackled them both.

"*Some*body had to sign the lease, Brownfield," she said gently, looking up into his angry eyes. "I just done got sick and tired of being dragged around from dump to dump, traded off by white folks like I'm a piece of machinery." She straightened her shoulders and drew her children to her side, the baby, Ruth, in her arms. "You just tell that old white bastard—Stop up Your Ears, Children!—that we can make our own arrangements. We might be poor and black, but we ain't dumb." There was a pause. "At least *I* ain't," she said cruelly, burying her face in her baby's hair.

"I guess you know that up there in town you wouldn't be able to just go out in the field when you're hungry and full up a sack with stuff to eat. I hope you know what you doing too, going out there pulling up all the greens and things just when we leaving the place."

"They sell food in the grocery stores there in town," said Mem, not slackening her work. "And I planted these greens myself and worked them myself, and I be damn if I'm going to let some sad-headed old cracker that don't care if I starve scare me out of taking them!"

"If you had any sense you'd know it don't look right," said Brownfield, raising himself up on an elbow. "Here we is moving off to Mr. J. L.'s place next Monday and you goes out and strips the fields on Thursday." He turned his gaze on her callused feet. "My ma always told me not to git myself mixed up with no ugly colored woman that ain't got no sense of pro*prid*y."

86

"I reckon if your ma was black, Brownfield," Mem said, putting a hand on her hip, "she found out a long *time* ago that you can't *eat* none of that."

"You don't surely think that I intends to move to town," Brownfield said slowly, turning his back as if he were about to fall off to sleep. He smiled at the wall. "I'm a *man,* and I don't intend working in *no*body's damn factory."

Daphne and Ornette looked at their parents through a sudden darkening blur. They came and stood in the kitchen door behind their mother, silently watching.

"You hear that, Woman!" Brownfield swung up and placed his feet with a stamp on the floor. "We moving exactly when and where I say we moving. Long as I'm supporting this fucking family we go where I says go." He bullied his thin wife murderously with his muddy eyes. "I may not be able to read and write but I'm still the man that wears the pants in this outfit!" He towered over her in a rage, his spittle spraying her forehead.

I don't have to stand here and let this nigger spit in my face, she thought more or less calmly, and for the first time very seriously. Who the hell he think he is, the President or somethin'.

"You do what you want to, Brownfield," she said, swiftly stepping out of range of his fist. "You do exactly what you want and go precisely where you please. But me and these children going to live in that house I leased. We ain't living in no more dog patches; we going to have toilets and baths and 'lectric lights like other people!"

"I reckon you think you ain't going to need somebody to *pay* for all them toilets and baths and 'lectric lights, you chewed-up-looking bitch!" Brownfield broke past his defensive children and grabbed Mem by the shoulder, spinning her round.

"Let me tell you something, man," Mem said evenly, though breathing hard, "I have worked hard all my life, first trying to be something and then just trying to be. It's over for me now, but if you think I won't work harder than ever before to support these children you ain't only mean and evil and lazy as the devil, but you're a fool!"

"Who the hell you think'd hire a snaggle-toothed old *plow*

87

mule like you?" He was sweating and felt his hands beginning to itch. "You ought to look in the glass sometime," he said, clenching his fists. "You ain't just ugly and beat-up looking, you's old!"

I ain't thirty, she wanted to say, but instead she said, "I know what I look like and I know how old I am." It seemed impossible that she could face him and not weep. "And neither one of them knowledges is going to keep me from getting me a job so we can move on in that house Monday morning."

"I'd like to see you *try,* Bitch," he cried on his way out, shoving her and pushing against his daughters. Ruth woke from her nap with a yowl from the noise. Mem dried her and lifted her high along her shoulder.

"And this one is going to grow *up* in 'lectricity and gas heat!" she said tremblingly, giving her baby small tearful kisses all around her fuzzy head.

23

"How's Mem?" Captain Davis asked pleasantly Friday noon when Brownfield was on his way home for lunch. "How she feel about moving over to Mr. J. L.'s? I told J. L.'s wife about her shortbread. Ummm Um," he said magnanimously, "she sure can cook!"

"Oh, she fine!" Brownfield said with enthusiasm. "She fine, and she all ready for the big move over to Mr. J. L.'s." He could not breathe normally and felt black and greasy under the man's cool gaze.

Ought to pick up a rock and beat it into his old bald head that hell naw me and Mem don't want to go work for his crazy motherfucking son! What the hell he think, we both of us crazy or somethin'! He smiled broadly at Captain Davis and clasped his hands together behind his back. His knees under his overalls leaned shakily against each other.

"We both right sure it going to work out fine," he said hopelessly, making his face as pleasant as possible and bland, "just fine."

"See you do your work good," the old man said sharply, clearing his throat and turning in the direction of his house. "You and Mem ain't bad hands," he said almost as an afterthought. "Glad to be keeping you in the family!"

But this is 1944! Brownfield wanted to scream; instead he said "Yassur," and waited until Captain Davis was three yards away before he moved. "I ought to stick my feed knife up in him to the gizzard!" he whispered, nervous sweat running down his sides. He walked home slowly, kicking rocks and bushes.

24

"Brownfield, I got me a job in town," Mem said, sitting herself down on the porch railing and dangling her hard skinny legs. Brownfield sat in silence; behind his head he could feel the two children standing there hiding big grins behind their eager apish faces.

"I got me a job in town that pays twelve dollars a week!" Mem spoke softly but with excitement in her voice. She said it like a bird might talk about first flying.

He continued to say nothing, but his hands gripped the bottom of his chair so hard his fingers ached.

"Twelve dollars a week is more than *you* makes, ain't it, Brownfield?" asked Mem, who had never been told her husband's wages. Her ugly mouth crinkled happily at the corners. Slowly she let the crinkling go and watched him silently for a while. Her children came to stand beside her, all of them looking at Brownfield.

"You coming with us or no?" she asked, without much caring in her voice. "If you is," she went on, "you got to get a job and pull your weight. If you ain't, we going on ahead anyhow."

They left him sitting there with his feet up on the railing, looking every one of his relatively few sick old years, with another dozen added on.

25

Saturday night found Brownfield, as usual, liberally prepared for his weekly fight with Mem. He stumbled home full of whiskey, cursing at the top of his voice. Mem lay with her face to the wall pretending to be asleep.

"You think you better than me," he cried. "Don't you? DON'T YOU! You ugly pig!" He reached beneath the bedclothes to grab her stiffly resistant shoulder.

"You wake up and *look* at me when I talk to you!" he said, slurring the words, bending close enough to kiss her with his foul whiskey-soaked mouth.

"You and them goddam sad-looking high and mighty brats of yours, that you done turned against me!" He said the last with an angry sob in his throat. As if he cared. Mem said nothing, lay so silent it was as if she were not breathing or thinking or even being, but her tired eyes rested directly on him with the tense heated waiting that many years of Saturday-night beatings had brought.

"I'm sick and tired of this mess," she said, rising abruptly, waiting for the first blow to head or side or breasts. "Shit!" she said, flinging the covers back, looking frail as a wire in her shabby nightgown. "I'm sick of *you!*"

No sooner had the words fallen out in a little explosive heap than Brownfield's big elephant-hide fist hit her square in the mouth.

"Don't you interrupt me when I'm doing the talking, Bitch!" he said, shaking her until blood dribbled from her stinging lips. The one blow had reduced her to nothing; she just hung there

90

from his hands until he finished giving her half-a-dozen slaps, then she just fell down limp like she always did.

"You going to move where I says move, you *hear* me?" Brownfield yelled at her, giving her a kick in the side with his foot. "We going to move to Mr. J. L.'s place or we ain't going nowhere at all!" He was hysterical. Mem lay with her eyes closed.

"You listening to me, Bitch!" Mem opened her eyes like someone opening up the lid of a coffin. "I ain't *going* to Mr. J. L.'s place," she said quietly. "I done told you that, Brownfield." Hesitantly she moved her hand up to wipe blood from her chin. "I have just about let you play man long enough to find out you ain't one," she said slowly and more quietly still. "You can beat me to death and I still ain't going to say I'm going with you!"

"You goddam wrankly faced black nigger slut!" Brownfield said, beside himself. "You say one more word, just one more little goddam *peep* and I'll cut your goddam throat!" He fumbled in his pocket for his knife and reached down and grabbed Mem in a loose drunken hug. Mem closed her eyes as he dropped her abruptly against the bedpost and gave her a resounding kick in the side of the head. She saw a number of blurred pale stars, then nothing else.

In the next room, with tears trickling so slowly they made them want to sneeze, Daphne and Ornette held their trembling skinny arms around each other and licked their warm red tongues over each other's salty homely eyes and wished nothing so hard as that their father would trip over his own stumbling feet, fall on his open knife and manage somehow to jab his heart out.

There was a restless whimper from Ruth. "You reckon he going to come in here?" Ornette asked her sister, thinking of ways to run and also of ways to be a man and protect her.

"He come in here," Daphne whispered with a grown-up coldness in her voice, "he come in here, you let him grab you for a minute while I run in the kitchen and get the butcher knife." She ran her tongue carefully down her sister's cheeks tracing her tears. "If by time I get back he done hit you just one time—I'm going to cut his stanking *guts* out!"

Huddled there under the bed they heard the birds begin chirping at dawn. They fell asleep dreaming in chilly exactness of killing that would set them free.

Brownfield did not dream. He just dropped out of his mind, and the late Sunday morning sun stabbed at his eyelids as if it were a gangman's pickax. Stretching his body, he felt he had been undressed. He spread his body leisurely over the bed and reached out a hand to grab his woman for the morning.

"Open your eyes!" Mem's voice was as even as a dammed-up river. Slowly he stopped turning and opened his eyes, squinting them stickily to keep out the light. Mem was propped up against the wall on her side of the bed, holding a shotgun. At first he saw only the handle, smooth and black and big, close to his head like that. One of Mem's long wrinkled fingers pressed against the trigger. He made a jump, half toward her, half away from her. He felt a sharp jab on his body down below the covers, the shooting pain caused him to wince and thrash on the bed.

"Don't you move a inch," Mem said lazily, controlling the cool hard gun barrel down between his thighs. He broke out in a quick cold sweat, and his eyes rambled frantically and dizzyingly over the room.

"What's the matter with you, Mem?" he asked hoarsely, his mouth tasting like somebody'd died up in it. Weeks ago. "What in the Lawd's name is troubling you this Sunday morning?" He looked around the room. "Where is the children, Woman?" he asked, expecting to see them. "Ain't you got no sense of what's decent?" Mem began to chuckle low in her throat. Oh, my Lawd, Brownfield thought, and began to tremble underneath the sheet, that kick in the head I give her last night done run her crazy! Mem gave a light jab at him with the gun, her whole hand wrapped around the stock. Brownfield cried out in pain and moved his big thick hands slowly downward.

"You move one more one hundred per cent of a half of a *half* inch," Mem said, putting her other hand lower down on the gun, "you move just a teeny weeny little bit more *Mr.* Brownfield, and you ain't going to have nary a ball left to play catch with."

"Aw, Mem." He began to whine. "Honey, you ain't got no cause . . ."

"Shet up," Mem said, staring at him with purple-circled eyes. "The children is out to church for the day. They grandpa came by and I even let him take the baby. Ain't nobody here but us chickens. Ain't nobody round to know or care whether one of us gits fried."

"Oh, Lawd," Brownfield began to moan in prayer.

"Call on the one you serves, boy!" Mem said, chuckling drily at his terror. "Call on the one you serves."

Brownfield thought irresistibly of Captain Davis; the tall old cracker just popped into his mind like he was God or somebody.

"Captain Davis won't let you git away with nothing." He began to babble and to throw up.

"Don't you let none of that mess drop on this bed!" Mem said when she saw his hand going to his mouth. He leaned his head over the side of the bed and let it all out on the floor. He was a long time vomiting the dead-smelling stuff and fell back worn out and weak. He almost forgot Mem and the gun, his head was spinning so.

"Now you can just git on down there with it," Mem said, wrinkling her nose from the smell. "I don't want you laying up here with me! Go on, git down there!" she said, jabbing him again with the gun. Brownfield slid down onto the floor, slipping on the rotten vomit and falling wetly on his naked behind on the outskirts of the stagnant yellow pool. He'd never felt this sick in his life. Mem watched him from the bed with a cold and level eye. She uncovered the full length of the big gun and pointed it where she had before. Brownfield lay back for a moment, then quickly crouched over his groin, shielding himself from her. She was grinning mirthlessly. Like a skinny balding gorilla, he thought.

93

"To think I put myself to the trouble of wanting to git married to you," she said. "And to think that I put myself to the trouble of having all these babies for you and you didn't even go out but once to git the midwife, *you was too drunk* or the weather was too *cold!*" Her left hand stroked the long barrel of the gun.

"You reckon Captain Davis really would give a good goddam if I shot you, Brownfield?" she asked. "What you reckon he'd *say?* Now Mem, I bet he would say, whoever heard of anybody going around shooting somebody else's *balls* off? Why, you *colored* people—you never heard tell of any *white* people going around shooting each other's balls off. Shame! Shame! He'd be thinking, *I always said niggers is crazy!* And this here Mem Copeland proves me right, going around shooting her husband's balls off, for Lawd's sake. 'Course, he'd go on, spitting on the ground like he created the dirt himself, far as I'm concerned with that Brownfield Copeland, I never knowed he *had* any!" Mem carried on her talk with her eyes opening and almost shutting like she'd seen Captain Davis do when he didn't want to look at her or Brownfield. Which was every time he had to talk to them.

"Nobody ever give a shit about you but me, you mean old fool! Don't you know that yet!"

"You ugly black hound!" Brownfield whispered weakly, trying to pull himself back in control. Mem swung the stock of the gun with both hands and laid a gash an inch wide right across his forehead. Dark red blood began dripping down over Brownfield's naked stomach, trickling down on the floor, making the weathered floorboards deep red and yellow. He began to cry.

"Long as you live—and that won't be long the rate you going—don't never call me 'out my name!" Mem sat calmly, watching the blood drip. "To think I let you drag me round from one corncrib to another just cause I didn't want to hurt your feelings," she said softly, almost in amazement. "And just think of how many times I done got my head beat by you just so you could feel a little bit like a man, Brownfield Copeland." She squinted her eyes almost shut staring at him. "And just think how much like an old no-count *dog* you done treated me for

94

nine years." She tightened her grip on the gun. Brownfield's body began to tremble in deep convulsive shudders. "Woman ugly as you ought to call a man Mister, you been telling me since you *beat* the ugly into me!" his wife said, and moaned.

"Mem," he whined, assuming weakness from her altered face, "you know how hard it is to be a black man down here." Tears and blood and vomit ran together down his shaking legs. "You knows I never wanted to be nothing but a man! Mem, baby, the white folks just don't let nobody *feel* like doing right."

"You can't stand up to them is what you mean, ain't it?" asked Mem, regaining her composure and propping up her chin with her right palm, holding the gun in her left hand. "Look at you now, crying like a little baby that's going to be whipped for peeing in his pants."

"Lawd, Mem, you knows how hard I try to do the right thing. I don't make much money, you knows that. And the white folks don't give us no decent houses to live in, you knows that. What can a man *do?*" he asked, holding his head up like a whipped hound. "What can a man do!"—planning to reach up and snatch the gun. Mem put both hands back on the gun-stock and crossed her bony knees.

"He can quit wailing like a old seedy jackass!" she said, hitting him over the head with the gun. Brownfield skidded in the mess on the floor and lay too weak to move.

"The thing I done noticed about you a long time ago is that you acts like you is right where you belongs. *All* the time!" She climbed from the bed and stood on the floor at his feet.

"Now I'm going to say this here just one more time; I realize at last that you is just a weezy little bit hard at understanding anything. But you best to git this straight. Me and my children is moving to town to the house I signed that lease on. We is moving in with you or without you." She kicked a clean spot on his limp left leg. "You hear me, boy?" Brownfield groaned and nodded his head.

Serves me right for gitting mixed up with a crazy woman! he thought weakly, feeling pain shoot through the calf of his leg.

"If you intend to come along I done made out me some rules

for you, for make no mistake it's going to be my house and in my house what the white man expects us to act like ain't going to git no consideration! Now, first off you going to call me Mem, Mrs. Copeland, or *Mrs. Mem R. Copeland.* Take your pick. And second, you is going to call our children Daphne, Ornette and baby Ruth. Although you can call any one of them 'honey' if you got a mind to. Third, if you ever lays a hand on me again I'm going to blow your goddam brains out—after I shoots off your balls, which is all the manhood you act like you *sure* you got. Fourth, you tetch a hair on one of my children's heads and I'm going to crucify you—stick a blade in you, just like they did the Lawd; if it was good enough for him it's good enough for you. Fifth, you going to learn to eat your meals like a gentleman, you ain't going to eat like no pig at my table. You going to use spoons and knifes and forks like everybody else that got some sense. Sixth, I don't care about your whoring round town, but don't you never wake me up on Sunday morning grabbing on me when you been out all Saturday night swinging your dick. Seventh, if you ever use a cuss word in my new house I'm going to cut out your goddam tongue. Eighth, you going to take the blame for every wrong thing you do and stop blaming it on me and Captain Davis and Daphne and Ornette and Ruth and everybody else for fifty miles around. Ninth, you going to respect my house by never coming in it drunk. And tenth, you ain't never going to call me ugly or black or nigger or bitch again, 'cause you done seen just what this black ugly nigger bitch can do when she gits mad!" Mem backed off a step. "Now git your ass up," she growled, "and wash yourself off!"

Brownfield started slowly to his feet, head hanging, body slick with sweat and blood and vomit, eyes bleary with fear. He was still crying forcefully, his nose dripping all over him. "And when you've cleaned yourself off you come back here and git up this mess. When my children come back from church with their granddaddy they going to find a model daddy, and if they don't you and me is going to know the reason why! You hear me, Brownfield?" Mem said, keeping the gun leveled at him. Brownfield's throat was too choked to speak. He stumbled toward the kitchen.

"You hear me, I say, *Boy!?*" Mem ran up behind him catching him across the back of the head with the gun barrel. His knees buckled, but he caught hold of the door casing. He could not raise his bloodied eyes to her steely yellow ones.

"Yes, ma'am," he mumbled, cowering against the door, not looking up. "Yes, ma'am," he said again, sobbing, as Mem set the gun down in a corner with a weary hand.

PART VI

26

Brownfield lay in wait for the return of Mem's weakness. The cycles of her months and years brought it. The first early morning heavings were a good sign. Her body would do to her what he could not, without the support of his former bravado. The swelling of the womb, again and again pushing the backbone inward, the belly outward. He surveyed with sly interest the bleaching out of every crease on her wrinkled stomach. Waiting. She could not hold out against him with nausea, aching feet and teeth, swollen legs, bursting veins and head; or the grim and dizzying reality of her trapped self and her children's despair. He could bring her back to lowness she had not even guessed at before.

27

In the city house, a "mansion" of four sheet-rocked rooms, no holes, a grassy yard and a mailbox on the porch, he lay low in his role. He played his conversion by terror long after the terror was gone and was replaced by a great design to express his rage, his humiliation, his deep hatred.

During the day at his job in a frozen pie factory, he was in a rage against his own contentment. It did not seem fair to him that the new work should actually be easier than dairying or raising cotton or corn. True, there was the boring placing of trays of peach pies on the assembly line, but after tramping for years after white folks' cows, the monotony soothed him. The even coolness of the building almost made him forget the stifling heat of the fields. His hands were drier now, for he could and did wear rubber gloves whenever there was wet work to do. He enjoyed pouring the mixture for the pies into the big vats, and liked regulating the hoses for water into the pressure cookers, and looked forward every day to washing up the big shiny, always new, utensils.

At the new house too there was a feeling of progress. An indoor toilet with a white tub, a face bowl, mirror and white commode. Now he could shit, and rising, look at himself, at the way his eyes had cleared themselves of the hateful veins and yellow tigerish lines, without much odor or rain, and much like a gentleman; or, as he invariably thought of it, like a white man.

He was cowed into wielding a paintbrush against dingy walls, planting bushes, attempting to fix the faulty wiring. For there were electric lights, and he was sometimes moved to read (look through the pictures of) the catalogues his wife got in the mail. The pictures of the new clothes and the guns and the boats and everything looked extra good in the clear light. He woke in the mornings now to the warmth of an almost noiseless gas heater;

and the refrigerator, another example of Mem's earning power, although not new by some years, had nothing to do with melted ice or spoiled food.

If he had done any of it himself, if he had insisted on the move, he might not have resisted the comfort, the feeling of doing better-ness with all his heart. As it was, he could not seem to give up his bitterness against his wife, who had proved herself smarter, more resourceful than he, and he complained about everything often and loudly, secretly savoring thoughts of how his wife would "come down" when he placed her once more in a shack.

And when they became reconciled again in a happiness similar to but not very near in depth to what they had known as newlyweds, it was only Mem who looked forward to a less destructive and less inhuman future. He could not see beyond his emotion. He held himself back and, even when desperately—for there was a passion in them that often served as affection—still making babies, he planned ahead. Planting a seed to grow that would bring her down in weakness and dependence and to her ultimate destruction. Like the nonfighter she essentially was, Mem thought her battle soon over. She was not evil and he would profit from it.

What replaced the desire to heal old wounds was the desire to wipe them out as if they had never been.

When he considered his wife's poor health, which he did in some tight lonely hours, her boniness, her rotted teeth (and those knocked out by him and the two coated in gold by a dentist who assumed she wanted glittering gold), he could not face what he could remember of how she had been. Round and plump, a mouth of pure white when open—he and they had robbed her of her smile. Now, when she guffawed hoarsely at some tiny joke, corralling the slight intensity of the funny to her innermost heart, he could see himself reflected in the twin mirrors of her eyeteeth; and he wanted one dark gigantic stroke, from himself and not the sky, to blot her out.

28

What a sly and triumphant *joy* he felt when she could no longer keep her job. She was ill; the two pregnancies he forced on her in the new house, although they did not bear live fruit, almost completely destroyed what was left of her health. Yet, how sad he was somewhere inside that he should still be strong and free to rove about while she spent so much time nursing her feet, attending her children's colds, trying to reassure them they would not have to move back to the country because she could still find work in town. But it was hopeless, her dream for herself and for them was slipping away. She had tried so hard, and even her husband, she thought, had started to respect her again. She didn't ask herself if she loved him. They were at a kind of peace; in the house in town he no longer struck her. The children went to school with happy faces. The baby was trained on an indoor commode.

All of her confidence wore away with her health as Brownfield watched, gloating and waiting. She could not believe he had planned it. She thought he had behaved well, considering everything, which was what he wanted her to think, until he was ready to reveal the plot to her. And then there came the day when she could not even get out of bed to look for work.

It had been raining for several days. Mem had tried every day to find something, anything, in factory, shop or kitchen. But perhaps the employers thought she looked too thin, probably tuberculous, and would not hire her. Each day she had come home beat.

The children took their cue from her silence, and they, sooner than she, knew the danger of their father's rising to rule them again now that their mother was sick. And sure enough, on this day, while Mem coughed and shivered, the blow fell.

"Why ain't the heat on?" she wheezed, when Brownfield came home from work.

" 'Cause ain't nobody paid the bill."

"Well, why ain't *you* paid it?"

" 'Cause it's your house, you pay the damn bills."

Mem groaned and turned her face to the wall. Ruth walked over to her and tried to play patti-cake with her face, but her mother pushed her away. She had turned the color of ashes, as if she'd seen a ghost.

"But you got a duty too," she told her husband. "You can't just let these children freeze to death."

"The rent ain't paid either." He began taking all his clothes from the chifforobe behind his wife's bed.

"How long?" All of their eyes were upon him, frightened, frozen as if he held the lungs that controlled their breathing.

"Since you bought all that medicine and spent all that money that you ought not have on you and the kids. I reckon that been two months ago." And then he pulled his trump. From his pocket he drew an eviction notice, flung it on the bed. "You read so damn good maybe you can tell me what all this here's about."

His wife picked up the eviction notice and read it through, trembling. Horrified, pale, weak, she looked at her husband packing his clothes.

"What you doing?"

"Gitting ready to move out."

"But—*move!*" She looked around at their smart little house and the things she was buying on time. She looked at the clean blue walls, the polished wood floor, the window sills full of evergreens.

"But where can we move? We ain't made no plans. Why didn't you pay the rent? You make enough money." Then, "We was *sick,* we all had flu; that's how come I spent all the money last month." She was becoming hysterical; the girls sat along the side of the bed, in a cloud of her VapoRub, but she was not mindful of them. "Where in the *world* do you expect us to move now?" she asked again, weakly, pathetically, trying to show strength she no longer had.

"Why," he said, and sniggered in spite of himself, "can't you make one of your eddicated guesses? *We* going to move over on *Mr. J. L.'s place!*"

It was like an overwhelmingly bad dream, and Mem fainted and was loaded half conscious into the cab of the truck that came to move them. She had no chance to pack, to cover her things from the weather, to say good-bye to her house. She was too weak to argue when the friends he got to help him move broke her treasured dishes, tore her curtains, dragged the girls' dresses through the mud.

They arrived at the house he had reserved for her "come down" in the middle of the night, and even his skin prickled at the sight of it. Mr. J. L. had promised that someone would clean it out, but it was still half full of wet hay. There were no panes in the windows, only wooden shutters. Rain poured into all three of the small rooms, and there was no real floor, only tin, like old roofing, spread out to keep the bottom of the hay bales from getting soggy.

"Git out, git out, this is your new home!" Brownfield shouted. They acted afraid to touch the ground. The house was not far from the highway, but there was a darkness about it, a crippled abandoned look.

"No—I can't." Mem drew back from his hands but fainted again. When she awoke she found herself stretched out between her girls on the hay, with all her newly acquired furniture stacked haphazardly around her. Brownfield had gone back to town with his friends and the girls said they had had to struggle hard to make the friends give them all the furniture. Brownfield had been intent on giving it away, they said.

29

"I done waited a long time for you to come down, Missy," he said when he came home, reeking of alcohol for the first time in almost three years. "This is what I can afford and this is what you going to have to make do with. See how you like *me* holding the upper hand!" He was enjoying himself in a sort of lunatic way.

"You was going to have your house, straight and narrow and painted and scrubbed, like white folks. You was going to do this, you was going to do that. Shit," he said, "you thought I fucked you 'cause I wanted it? Josie better than you ever been. Your trouble is you just never learned how not to git pregnant. How long did you think you could keep going with your belly full of childrens?" He stood glowering down at her. There was no electricity in the house, but it was nearly morning and they could see enough of each other to know that Brownfield's mask was decidedly off.

"Miss high-'n-mighty, you come down off your high horse now," he could not help giggling, she was so incapable of doing anything.

"You come down off your high horse now," he said again, laughing out loud, thinking how she looked like she was going to die.

"Brownfield, I'm sick," said Mem, "but I ain't going to ask you for mercy and I ain't going to die and leave my children. Even in this weather you brought me out in I ain't going to catch pneumonia. I'm going to git well again, and git work again, and when I do I'm going to leave you."

"Ain't no stopping you, is it? You a real red-hot ball of fire, ain't you!" He continued to laugh. "You *skeleton*," he said, stopping in the middle of a laugh and gazing at her from under his hat, "you can't do nothing but lay up there and *moan*. And if you could get your ugly ass up I wouldn't let you go nowhere, make a fool out of me, have people laughing at me!"

"You really think you can stop me?" she asked, knowing her children trembled at her saying anything that might provoke him.

"I'll stop you," he said, looking over at something that was covered in plastic.

"You can't stop much with a gun."

"I can stop *every*thing for you, Bitch. I can stop *you!*"

Daphne whimpered, Ornette cried, Ruth alone merely looked on with all the bewilderment and disgust of a small child. The three girls did not know their father. They too thought him capable of change. They thought he had changed. They thought it had been a matter of less work, fewer worries, gas heat and electric lighting. They had misjudged him because they were so young and because they knew nothing of most of his persistent memories. They saw now only that they had made a mistake; and knew their father was not so much changed as changeable. He could put on a front to fool the trusting.

"You know what," piped Ruth seriously from behind her blanket-covered bale of hay. Her father turned away from them; Daphne tried to shush her. "Hey, I say do you know what," she said again loudly, in her best fearless voice, though the pit of her stomach quivered. Her father turned toward her. She was his youngest, barely four. "You nothing but a sonnabit," she said, and quickly covered herself with her blanket so she wouldn't feel the first really hard blows Brownfield ever gave her.

30

At this house, the only one of her father's choices she would ever recall with any degree of clarity, Ruth saw the comings and goings of her fourth and fifth and sixth birthdays. When she was five she began school, tagging along each morning with Daphne and Ornette. J. L.'s house—her mother always said to friends who had never visited them at their new location, "We haves that old house of Mr. J. L.'s"—was a place of icy kitchen water buckets in winter, and in summer flashing rainstorms uncovered sharp bits of colored glass in the back yard along with pieces of rusty tin and fragments of scarred linoleum. In the summer the house gave off a quiet hot musty smell and *hum,* like droning flies, and the air around it was full of motes thrown up from the trampled dust of dung and rotting hay.

There was a spring down the hill behind the house where they got their water; a little beyond it was a pigpen. The wild grass grew high beside the woodpile, near which leaned an ancient corncrib gray with weather and full of old plowshares and funnels and dried horse liniment in motley green bottles with tattered rag stoppers. Dozens of sharecropping families had lived in the house and had left their various odors of sweat, hogslop and discomfort deep in its rotting wood.

Daphne and Ornette found J. L.'s house unbearable and complained all the time with their eyes. It was a great fall for them, after the house in town, to have to tote water up to the house from the spring and suffer through muddy trips to the odorous outhouse when it rained. They had thought such days gone forever. Being little more than a baby, Ruth was less stricken by the move, although she knew it made her mother unhappy and therefore hated it. But there was much in the straw field behind the house to occupy her. And she enjoyed the cool greenness of the ferns and water lilies that grew beside the crayfish-inhabited spring.

Daphne was nine when they moved into J. L.'s house and Ornette was eight. The big gap between Ornette's age and Ruth's was because of the babies that had died. When Ruth was four Mem became pregnant again, and for a brief time afterward there was a baby in the house. Daphne and Ornette liked to hold him in their arms for Ruth to see. Daphne, always the inventive one, made up stories about the baby's future. He would be a doctor, she said, and run a big hospital in town, and marry one, maybe two (if the first one didn't work out) of his nurses. He was small and still and gray. Ruth thought he looked more like a possum than a child. He curled himself in sleep and, with his grayish red-rimmed eyes and the yellowish fuzz of his hair, which was more white than yellowish, he seemed a phantom baby, not the real thing. Ruth could never imagine him becoming anything. She could not even imagine that he would eventually grow on the food he was fed, much as she herself had grown. His cry was a thin pitiful thing. Nevertheless, in moments of small loneliness, when Daphne and Ornette claimed she was too much a baby to play with them, Ruth contemplated having a tough bouncy little brother to play with and perhaps to boss around. In the main, though, it was hard to tell he was in the house he was so quiet. He slept a great deal. They did not miss him very much when he died. Daphne and Ornette cried and whispered between themselves that somehow the baby had frozen to death because when they saw him lying dead he was all blue. But with school and play and the routine of living in J. L.'s house, the pale little brother was rapidly forgotten.

After his death Mem took a job that kept her away from home all day. She became a maid in a house in town. Ruth could not really understand why her mother left her again. When they had lived in town she had had her fill of being left with strange women, big snuff users with dusty bosoms and thin nervous girls with no prospects who were short with her. Daphne told her that Mem worked so that one day they would be able to leave the county, leave Georgia and leave Brownfield. Ruth did not know about the first two, but the idea of leaving her father pleased her.

Daphne knew more than Ornette. She called herself the Copeland Family Secret Keeper. What this meant was that at every opportunity she talked about how Brownfield had played with her when she was little. How he had bought her candy. How he had swung her up in his arms. How he had sung and danced for her. Ornette and Ruth were jealous of her memories and appropriated them for themselves. Daphne's memories of Brownfield as doting father became theirs, although the Brownfield they pretended to remember had no relation (except for Daphne) to the one they knew. To "remember" Daddy when he was good became their favorite game. When Brownfield overheard Ornette babbling to Ruth about some extraordinary kindness he had done her ("he bought me a dress" or "he fixed my dolly") he did not think anything of it except that Ornette was going to turn out to be an incorrigible liar. They knew he did not understand their game and that made it all the more fun; their "good" daddy would have understood, they said, which proved Brownfield was nothing compared with him.

Daphne was more forgiving than Ornette. Her temper became murderous only when Brownfield abused Mem. When Brownfield beat Daphne she tried to endure it by keeping her mind a perfect though burning blank. She tried so hard to retain some love for him, perhaps because of her memories of an earlier time, that she became very nervous. She jumped at the slightest noise or movement. Because she was so jumpy Brownfield teased her and called her names. He told her she was stupid and crazy. He swore at her, called her Daffy instead of Daphne, and pinched her sides until they bruised. Through it all she bravely stood, seeking to hide her trembling as best she could. She despised the house because it was impossible to clean and because she, more than Ruth or Ornette, had some idea of the struggle Brownfield had forced upon Mem. She hated it because it was cold in winter and she could never get warm; she must tremble summer and winter. Somehow she kept her feeling for her father separate from her hatred of the house. How she did it Ruth and Ornette never knew. They saw Brownfield less charitably than Daphne because they saw him only as a human devil and felt wherever he placed them would naturally be hell. They were as afraid of him as Daphne was, but in a more distant, impersonal way. He was like bad weather, a toothache, daily bad news.

Ornette was jolly most of the time. A loud, boisterous girl, sassy and full of darting rebellion. She was fat and glossy. Her skin had a luscious orange smoothness and felt like a waxed fruit. Of the three children Brownfield appeared to like her least. He thought she would grow up to be a plump, easygoing tramp and was telling her so constantly by the time she was eight. Ornette learned to toss her head at him. When she was seven she refused to go to church or to say her bedtime prayers. She had a flexible sexual vocabulary at eight and a decided interest in pussies and bowwows at nine. Her opinion of the house was that it was a barn and that only the stupidest cows lived in worse. She could not be depended upon to sweep the floor or even to pull the proper kind of straw with which to make a broom. She liked to sit in the middle of the straw field and sing rhythm-and-blues tunes she'd heard on the radio. Mem, pulling straw and binding it into brooms as she moved across the field, would listen to Ornette's songs almost dreamily. She did not scold her. Ornette was bold with her mother, thought her a hag and of little account. She thought Mem had married beneath her and should have married instead a teacher or a mason or anybody with land of his own and a fine house. She did not respect Mem. Occasionally she stole pennies from Mem's purse.

Mem's grief over losing the "decent house" was not a sign around her neck. She recovered from the illness that had caused her to lose it and with grim determination attended to roof leaks and rat holes in this house. She fixed sagging shutters and cleared away the rubbish that choked the weeds in the front yard. She did not do as much work on this house as she had on the ones before it. She tried to see that it was fairly clean, or as clean as she and Daphne could make it, that it did not leak overmuch, that the rats did not stay in control of it, as they had when she and her family moved in, and dispiritedly she threw a few flower seeds in the moist rich soil around the woodpile. Never again did she intend to plant flowers in boxes or beds.

PART VII

31

When Ruth struggled sleepily to open her eyes the morning of her first day at Grange's house, the big grandfather clock on the mantel made a last clinking echo across the chilly bed and sitting room. She sniffed, for her nose felt stuffy, and snuggled into the long warm back in front of her, but that back slid gradually away from her and stood stretching by the side of the bed. She heard footsteps shuffling up to the front of the room. She sighed, blinked her eyes, and turned over. The person on the other side of her was lying snoring with her face turned toward her and her breath was onions and dandelion weeds. Ruth turned over and lay drowsily in the warmth vacated by the person who had got up. She was aware of a feeling of oddness and insecurity, as if she had been on a long journey during the night; the morning air smelled different to her somehow, and when she opened her eyes to peer over the covers she could not recall having fallen asleep in this room. She looked around. There was a chif-forobe in the corner, brown wood around yellow-glazed drawers, with cut-glass handles, a stuffed sofa the color of fuchsia gerani-ums under the window opposite the bed; and on the wall there were several old-fashioned pictures of people in top hats with waxed mustaches and kinky though slickly pomaded hair worn with a part in the middle. One of the pictures was of an ashen, sickly looking woman who might already have been dead when her picture was made. This was a tinted drawing of Ruth's grandmother, Grange's first wife, Margaret.

Ruth's mind, reluctantly becoming alert, was unwilling to set her straight about where she was, but it finally came to her in a prickly little rush that she was at her grandfather's house and that it was his wife, Josie, who slept beside her. She tried to re-member having gone to bed here the night before but could not.

From the front of the room she heard the swift flare of flame as her grandfather put kerosene on the fire, and the sound of her stepgrandmother's snores was an abandoned droning in her ears. Without rustling the covers or making any sounds of being awake, she began to remember.

The night before had been Christmas Eve. Ruth had been going to get a tricycle for Christmas, or she had thought she was. But her mother had kept saying that this whole year had been a very hard one for Mr. Santa Claus, mainly because Mrs. Santa Claus had died (or run away) and Mr. Santa Claus didn't feel much like making anything, especially not toys; for it would hurt him to see everybody else making merry while he sat in a corner at the North Pole just crying his eyes out. The most it was best to look for, she had said to Ruth and Ornette and Daphne, was oranges and maybe some peppermint sticks.

Brownfield had come in from town that night very drunk. He was raving so badly that Daphne had taken Ruth and Ornette and they had hidden in the chicken house. Ruth remembered how all the chickens began to squawk and how they all smelled so fresh, not good-fresh, but fresh in the way raw meat smells. They had got dodo all over their hands and faces crawling around in the chicken house, but Daphne made them sit down in a rotten-smelling corner while she peeked out at the house through a crack. Once they had begun to giggle loudly because Ornette, who was in the fifth grade, said that a boy at school was always trying to pull her bloomers down during recess. But Daphne slapped them both hard across the face. She was trembling violently. She never cut up like they did because she had some kind of fits once in a while and was always serious. Until she slapped them they had thought the whole thing something of a joke. A rough one, but with some fun in it. It seemed to them that Brownfield was nearly always mean and unruly and drunk.

Usually, though, he didn't come home but would spend the night fighting in the juke joints in town. Most of the time he would get beaten up by whomever he picked a fight with and then they would take pity on him and force him to let them drive him home, with him shouting, slurring, "I got my goddam *pride, I is!*" then falling asleep on the way. They would dump him lifeless and foul-smelling or sometimes singing onto the porch. Thump! He would land on the porch, and if it woke them up Ruth and Ornette would laugh at him under the covers.

Daphne felt strongly tensions in the house to which Ruth and Ornette were oblivious. She was always having to look out for them, because Brownfield, even when sober, would beat and kick them. They hated him while he was doing it, but not between times, and spent whole days playing contentedly under the trees behind the house where not even the vaguest consideration of him followed.

Mem tried hard to control him when he beat them. She always said, "Brownfield, you ought not to carry on this a-way. You *know* you won't be able to look yourself in the face when you gets old and the children done gone." To which he would answer with a lick against her head or a kick against her legs.

Only Mem was working. He had been fired from his job with J. L. They rented the house. The rent money came from Mem's salary. She made seventeen dollars a week, which seemed like a fortune to them, in its lump sum. What she made from six days of work was far more than Brownfield had made as J. L.'s

117

dairyman and cotton farmer. Brownfield hinted to his drinking buddies that he made Mem go out and work for him, but she never left the house in the morning without him trying to pull her back. Sometimes he would be lying in bed watching her get ready for work, and just as it was time for her to step out of the house he would reach out and grab her arm and try to get her to lie down with him.

"Aw, come on, honey," he would say, "how about laying down here with your pore ol' man?" His mattering yellowed eyes would be still and deadly.

And Mem would say, furrowing her brow and looking around at the children, who immediately stopped whatever they were doing whenever he put his hands on her ("Why he want her to git in the bed," they'd ask themselves suspiciously, "can't he tell it *day*time?"), "You ought to turn loose my arm, Brownfield, you know I got to get to work." She would be looking down at her shoes, which were white, like nurses' shoes. Then she would pull herself loose and disappear almost running down the road.

And Brownfield would say, "Shit. All these fucking womens can think about is they goddam *jobs*. One of these days I'm going on over to Jay-*pan,* where the womens know what they *real* job is!" And he would spit at the cold fireplace or throw a shoe at one of them, usually knocking over a jar of leaves or a picture from a magazine which Mem had put up against the bare cracked walls.

The three of them would dress hurriedly, grab the pieces of bread that were in the warmer on the stove, biscuits from last night's supper, and run out the door to the school.

"You ain't going to learn nothing *use*ful," he would say, lounging on the bed with his hands behind his head, "not unless they teaching *plow*ing!" His words had hurt Ruth at first, unbearably hurt her. But one day she surprised him trying to mouth some of the simpler words in her speller. When Brownfield saw her looking at him he threw the book at her. She dodged it and, though feeling somehow sad, she ran laughing out the door. In the first grade she knew envy when she saw it.

The dustiness of the hen house made them sneeze, and their father staggered onto the porch and looked out at the bushes around the house. He cursed, holding his shotgun in the air, and hobbled back into the house.

It became apparent to Ruth and Ornette, finally, that they were not engaged in a game. Fear at last hit them and, seeing the gun in his hand and knowing without being told that he was waiting for their mother, they began to cry.

Daphne, always brooding and nervous so that if you walked into a room behind her and said "Hey!" she was likely to go into convulsions, was holding her stomach. She did this whenever she was upset or confused. She had bad sickness once a month and would cry and cry, and one time, when she was holding her stomach and crying, with sweat popping out like grease bubbles on her face, Brownfield had kicked her right where her hands were. He was trying to sleep, and couldn't because of the noise, he said.

Mem had taken Daphne to the clinic, but the nurse said she didn't see anything wrong with her, except that she was nervous. Mem had said that she knew the child was nervous and wanted the nurse to tell her what to do about it, but the nurse was busy talking to another nurse about changing her hair color, and both nurses ignored Mem, who was standing there exasperated, holding a quivering Daphne by the hand. Daphne was particularly frightened of white people; she did not fear them because she found them to be particularly cruel, she had very limited dealings with them; she was afraid, childishly enough, of their ghostliness, the shadowless lightness of their faces, the twinkling vacuity of their marble eyes. She could believe they were pure, free of passion, odor or blood, and that they belonged, as she did not, to a horrible God. Her fear encompassed the world and included darkness, buildings, ancient trees and flowers with animal names. She was afraid of the world; but it was she who protected her sisters; she who stood trembling and barely able to stand underneath her father's fist, while Ornette and Ruth ran yelling and crying from Brownfield, out through the back yard and into the woods.

119

Now she told them, with her voice shaking, that she was going to walk to town to try to head Mem off. She said maybe she could keep her from coming home while Brownfield was drunk. They wanted to go with her but she said she could go faster if they stayed behind. They watched her sneak out, ashy and dark, without a sweater. It was hailing lightly. She skittered out and down the highway like a lean brown rabbit. The black night, grayed down with white hailstones, soaked her in against the wet highway.

Left in the hen house Ornette cried silently and Ruth sat shivering with cold, looking out through a crack at the yard. The hen house was to the front of the front yard, a leaning musty building made of slabs and pieced out with scraps of rusty tin. In summer sparse patches of green grass grew in front of the door, but now in winter the whole area was slushy and wet and slippery with ice. The house sat back from the highway about thirty yards; a narrow road filled with sharp gravel turned off the highway, ran risingly up, and stopped abruptly in front of the door. The outside of the house had changed little since they moved in. There was an old weather-beaten bush with purple flowers in summer and nothing but thorns in winter that stood misshapen by the wind on the far side of the yard. The porch sank heavily at one end and rose off its foundation on the other. Around the porch on the end next to the hen house there were bits of old rusty screen with great jagged holes punched in. The steps were two logs that Mem had cut from a stout tree, then halved and pushed into the dirt. The house was made of thin gray boards with no reinforcement on the inside. Mem had lined the inside with cardboard boxes, and when the wind rose and came through the cracks outside it caused the cardboard to strain and throb as if it were alive.

Ruth could see a light on in the room where her parents slept, the room that was also the living room. The house had three rooms altogether, one of these a kitchen. They were better off than some people, for they did not have to share a bedroom with their parents, and though their room was small it was private. That is, you could hear through the walls, but at least you

120

couldn't see through them. Sometimes the shadow of her father loomed against the window as he looked out into the night. Ruth shrank down in the dust. She and Ornette were not completely knowledgeable about why they were sitting there nearly frozen in the hen house, but they knew they were afraid and too afraid to trust being anywhere else.

Occasionally Mem walked or hitchhiked to and from town, but sometimes the husband of the woman she worked for would drive her in his long blue Chrysler. He was a strange sort of man, according to Mem, for he insisted on paying her seventeen dollars a week, which was five dollars more than the usual rate of pay for domestics. He was from the North and was dying, it was said, from cancer of the mouth. Some said he was a Jew, but they did not know quite what it was that made him different —his eyes didn't make you look at your feet like the eyes of other men—and they did not very much care. Mem was fond of him because he let her take home magazines and sent books to Daphne and Ornette. She did not like his wife, however, who was a Southern belle and whose father owned a big plantation outside of town. She was all the time mentioning how "cute" colored children were and giving them pennies. Ruth hated her because she called Mem, "Mem, my colored girl."

Ruth was startled to hear the sound of a car stopping down by the highway. She heard the low murmuring of her mother's voice—she would be thanking him for the ride—and then she heard her heavy footsteps trudging up the drive. She looked out the crack to see if Daphne was with her but did not hear her mother talking to anyone as she came up, and she thought that in the car her mother and the white man had not seen her on the road. Soon Ruth was able to see the outline of Mem's figure.

Mem did not quit work until six o'clock and then it was dark. She was carrying several packages, which she held in the crook of both arms, looking down at the ground to secure her footing. Ruth wanted to dash out of the chicken house to her, but she and Ornette sat frozen in their seats. They stared at her as she passed, hardly breathing as the light on the porch clicked on and the long shadow of Brownfield lurched out onto the porch waving his shotgun. Mem looked up at the porch and called a greeting. It was a cheerful greeting, although she sounded very tired, tired and out of breath. Brownfield began to curse and came and stood on the steps until Mem got within the circle of the light. Then he aimed the gun with drunken accuracy right into her face and fired.

What Ruth remembered now with nausea and a feeling of cold dying, was Mem lying faceless among a scattering of gravel in a pool of blood, in which were scattered around her head like a halo, a dozen bright yellow oranges that glistened on one side from the light. She and Ornette were there beside her in an instant, not minding their father, who had already turned away, still cursing, into the house. They were there looking at the oranges and at the peppermint sticks and at everything. It occurred to Ruth sadly that there really was no Santa Claus. She was Santa Claus. Mem. And she noticed for the first time, that even though it was the middle of winter, there were large frayed holes in the bottom of her mother's shoes. On Mem's right foot the shoe lay almost off and a flat packet of newspaper stuck halfway out. Daphne ran up screaming and threw herself across her mother's legs. She began to rub Mem's feet to make them warm.

What happened after that Ruth did not know, and now she did not want to know. She buried her face in the pillow and began to whimper. Why had her mother walked on after she saw the gun? That's what she couldn't understand. Could she have run away or not? But Mem had not even slowed her steps as she approached her husband. After her first cheerful, tired greeting she had not even said a word, and her bloody repose had struck them instantly as a grotesque attitude of profound, inevitable rest.

"She sleeping, Ruth, ain't she?" Ornette had asked, trying to see closed eyes where there were none at all.

"Hyar, hyar," her grandfather said, coming to her and sitting beside her on the bed, "we don't want to wake up the old lady, now does us?" She shook her head, sobbing softly with her arms

122

around his neck. He had been drinking already and smelled of corn liquor, but his strong tobacco-and-corn-smell was soothing, and he patted her thoughtfully on the back.

"I might could tell you a right interestin' story 'bout old Br'er Fox. But you wouldn't listen. . . ." He looked sadly down at her. "Naw, I knows you wouldn't listen, and ain't no need of me saying nothing *no*how. I don't know what I'm talking about. Shit, baby gal, we just got troubles on top of troubles, and there ain't no trouble like losing your ma." He shook his head. "Lawd, and that's the truth, and"—looking at his wife—"say, I shore do wish my wife would shet her goddam mouth, her snores about to drive me crazy."

Ruth looked at him carefully and long. His eyes were moist and his cheeks quivered.

"Don't look at *me*," he said sourly. "I don't know no more about *any* of it"—throwing his arm up indicating everything in the world—"then you!" And she was never to hear him seriously claim, even in a boast, that he did.

32

Grange was a tall, gaunt man with a thick forest of iron-gray hair that whitened shade by shade over the next few years until it was completely white, completely pure, like snow. His mouth was unusually clean-looking, although he chewed tobacco, smoked, used snuff, drank anything strong, and rarely brushed his teeth. Sometimes he would go after them with the end of his nightshirt, but Ruth could never see how that could keep them so sound and white. For the longest time after she saw them grinning at her from a jar on the back porch, bubbling, she thought he just took them all out once in a while for a boiling. She knew her own cavity-weakened baby teeth only came out one at a time.

He was immensely sick at times. There were days of depression when he spoke of doing away with himself. There were times when she could tell he needed her to tell him to pull himself together. He would lie immobile on the floor, dead, and she would be drawn to him to try the magic of her hugs and kisses. She soon learned to overlook the differences between them. They got along well for grandfather and child and trivial complications in their relationship did not develop. Grange never spanked her and would probably have beaten up anyone who tried to do so. Even Josie was not allowed to touch her. Poor Josie, she was never even allowed to scold.

"You don't know nothing about raising no child," Grange said when Josie tried to make her do anything. "Look what a mess you did on your own young 'un!" Josie would sulk, but Grange's was the final word.

At the beginning Ruth was jealous of Josie, for she thought maybe Grange found her pretty. But Grange also thought his wife was not very nice, and he said so, often and loudly. He said she lived like a cat, stayed away from home too much. Josie was one of those fat yellow women with freckles and light-colored eyes, and most people would have said she was good-looking, *handsome,* without even looking closely. But Ruth looked closely indeed, and what she saw was a fat yellow woman with sour breath, too much purple lipstick, and a voice that was wheedling and complaining; the voice of a spoiled little fat girl who always wanted to pee after the car got moving.

Ruth sensed that Josie was none too happy to have her with them. "What do I know about plaiting hair on a eight-year-old kid?" Josie had asked Grange one day when Grange wanted her to wash and braid Ruth's hair. "I notice you cut Lorene's hair rather than take up time over it," Grange had replied, "but this my *grand* girl, you do hers up or I pulls yours off." Ruth had snickered that day while Josie, fuming, braided her hair. She and Josie were not to be friends, it seemed.

Before she moved in with them, Grange had spent his days fishing, sunning, whittling. After she came he began to grow cotton. Ruth could play in the fields beside him all day during the summer, though she was not allowed to pick the cotton. She wanted to, because it was so soft and light and looked so pretty early in the morning with the dew glistening on it. Why Grange forbade her she could not understand. Josie, who was asked to pick, said she would not if Ruth did not. "You may have talked me into helping you buy this damn *farm*," Josie sneered, "but if I ever picks another boll of cotton I hope somebody rush up and have me committed." With one long sack and his own two hands Grange was left to manage his cotton. Ruth was allowed to ride on the back of the truck when the cotton was taken to the gin. That is, she was allowed to ride on the back of the truck while they were on the dirt road which led to the highway. Each time, as they approached the highway, Grange stopped the truck and either sent her back home or put her inside on the seat next to him.

"You not some kind of field hand!" he muttered sharply when she said she'd love to ride on top of the cotton all the way to town.

"But Grange, my goodness, can't I ride as far as the *bridge?*" she asked the first time. He seemed too annoyed at the thought to answer her. She began to get the feeling she was very special. At school she avoided the children whose parents let them ride on the back of trucks—"Grinning niggers for the white folks to laugh at!" she scoffed. And the children in turn quickly learned what hurt her most. They called her "Miss Stuck-up" and when that produced no effect, *"Mrs.* Grange."

The time she did manage to spend atop the truck was supremely happy. From that high perch she could see, it seemed to her, miles and miles across fields and forests and on into the sky. A sky which was benign and cloudless in those days. More often than not she and Grange left Josie at home. Ruth rarely thought about Brownfield; when she did, Grange was quick to assure her that Georgia jails were among the best.

Grange also raised vegetables in his garden in front of the house. You could sit on the front porch and watch the tomatoes grow. He would cut big coarse cabbages at the stem with a flat dull knife and balance one like a crown on her head. He raised carrots and tomatoes and peas, and in fall, after the peas had dried in the sun, they sat up late at night gossiping and shelling them. Josie, who hated all kinds of work, farm or otherwise, would get up reluctantly from telling long tales about the "olden days" or her younger days and wash fruit jars so that in the morning Grange could help her can, "put up" the peas.

It was at times of such domesticity that Ruth felt keenly Josie's objection to her and mourned the loss of her mother. Memories that might have been tossed aside by a child more innocently brought into a new home with new sources of play, came rushing back at odd moments of wakefulness, more usually in dreams. The long fall days, languid and slow and heavy, of gathering in, and then of putting up, brought to mind the good memories she had of her mother, when they had seemed to prosper in the hot summers, canning and making potato hills, and winter held no fear for them.

Other grownups she saw never mentioned her parents. They acted as if they did not, or had not, existed. Josie was a clam when she was asked a simple question about them, or asked simply to remember. But Grange was drawn to discuss them. He said they should not be forgotten, especially Mem, who was a saint. He liked to use some reference to Mem's thriftiness or her hard-working goodness as a beginning to a list of comparisons he made between her and Josie. He would be carried away by his vivid recollections of Mem and reproach his wife viciously because she was not the kind of woman his son's wife had been. Josie would begin to cry, or pretend to suffer.

"You lazy yaller heifer!" he would start out, "and don't you come saying nothing defending to me. You no-good slanderous trollop, you near-white strumpet out of tallment, you motherless child, you pig, you bloated and painted cow! Look to your flopping udders hanging out in mass offense! You lustful she-goat! Close up your spreaded knees before this innocent child and my gray head!" But he became unsure of himself when she began to cry. "Shit," he would mutter, finally. "What you standing over there with your damn mouth hanging open for *any*way. Come here and set on my goddam *knee* when I'm talking to

126

you!" At first such scenes of forgiveness were frequent and at times they were very happy. Josie would come placidly over to him, chewing her gum, wetting her purple lipstick with her sly little tongue, her tears vanished. And Grange would mumble from deep in her dress front, "Ah, me oh my, here I is. *Lost* again."

Ruth did not always sleep with them. Grange was gentle but firm.

"It ain't healthy for a heap of peoples to sleep in the same bed, don't you know. Anyways, it all right for just two. If they be grown."

Shut away from them, turning restlessly on her bed, Ruth tried to fathom the mystery of her grandfather's contempt for and inevitable capitulation to Josie. When she could not fall asleep Mem came back to confront her; Mem, whose hands were callused and warm, whose lips were chapped and soft, and whose eyes were restored to their look of tough, gentle sadness and pain.

33

Gradually, sulkily, Josie faded into the background, and Ruth and her grandfather became inseparable. They did not plan it this way; but always they were together; where Grange went, Ruth went, what he did, Ruth did. Josie, having sold her lounge to help Grange pay for the farm, had no place to go and none of her old friends came to see her. Ruth and Grange halfheartedly tried to interest her in their pursuits, but the farm held no attractions for Josie; she thought of herself as a city woman. She brushed them off, and they were happy to be brushed off. They left her muttering and pacing the floor, filing her purple nails.

In the wintertime, a few days before each Christmas Eve, Grange began his preparations for making ambrosia. He was an uneducated man, but he still remembered that somebody, some old white lady's daughter no doubt, had once told him that ambrosia was what all the gods used to eat before there just came to be one God, which they had now, that never did eat anything. "That's 'cause He done got stocked up while He was creating Hisself," was Grange's short explanation.

To make ambrosia you needed fresh, hand-shredded coconut and pineapples and oranges. Probably something else went in, a shot of whiskey or wine, but Ruth remembered mostly the oranges and coconuts. Grange's sister, who lived in Florida, would send these in one large and one small crate, along with so many grapefruits the whole house looked like a fruit stand. Grange liked to put out every piece of fruit on a "high place," like the mantel or the tops of dressers and chifforobes, and when children came to visit—and they were allowed to come only at Christmas—he had a generous way of reaching behind him or over his head and producing a bright orange or grapefruit. Then he would grin at the small bewildered visitor and say, as if he had forgotten the words at the beginning, "Hocus-pocus on *you*, boy!"

The next thing you needed to make ambrosia was a big churn. Grange had two, one milk-white with a lovely faded drawing of a blue bull near the top, and a brown earthen one. They had belonged to Josie's mother, and Grange said that she had liked to use the white one during the week and the brown one on Sunday. In remembrance of her—her wide-eyed picture was among those in the front room—they used the brown churn for the Christmas ambrosia.

Grange and Ruth and Josie would sit around peeling oranges and shredding coconut until two o'clock in the morning. Of course, the whole business could have been finished in an hour, but Grange would stop ten or fifteen times during the process to tell a story, or the truth about something or somebody. He knew all the Uncle Remus stories by heart, although he could make up better ones about a smart plantation man named John. John became Ruth's hero because he could talk himself out of any situation and reminded her of Grange.

128

Grange thought that Uncle Remus was a fool, because if he was so smart that he could make animals smart too, then why the hell, asked Grange, didn't he dump the little white boy (or tie him up and hold him for ransom) and go to Congress and see what he could do about smartening up the country, which, in Grange's view, was passing dumb. "Instead of making the white folks let go of the stuff that's rightfully ours, he setting around on his big flat black ass explaining to some stupid white feller how too much butter in the diet make you run off at the be-hind! We needs us a goddam statesman and all he can do is act like some old shag-assed *min*strel!"

He would reminisce about his boyhood, which was filled with all sorts of encounters with dead folks and spirits and occasionally the Holy Ghost, which he said was the same thing as a sort of chill, and which, if you didn't watch out, could turn into the soul's pneumonia.

He told stories about two-heads and conjurers; strange men and women more sensitive than the average spook. He said they could give you something to wear under your hat that'd make your wife come back (if she ran away), or make her run away if you were sick of her. He told about how one old juju man who, people claimed, could turn into a bat, had actually cured him of a bad case of piles by giving him a little bag of powder to dust down in the stool. "What's piles?" Ruth asked. "A serious grown-up disease," he answered.

He said there was a two-headed lady in town named Sister Madelaine. She had changed herself from a white colored woman to a gypsy fortuneteller. "Why she do that?" asked Ruth. " 'Cause she didn't want to be nobody's cook," said Grange. She was a powerful woman, according to Grange, but not as good as the two-heads he had known when he was a boy. Two-heading was dying out, he lamented. "Folks what can look at things in more than one way is done got rare."

Ruth's favorite story was about how he came to join the church.

It had happened one spring when he was seven or eight years old. And it was during a revival. He had already begun getting

129

into fights with the white children who lived down the road, usually "beating the stuffing out of them" to let him tell it. His mother, a pious and diligent house servant for most of her life, never seriously attempted to make him stop fighting (she would say gently that she didn't want to break his spirit), but instead urged him more and more toward the "bosom" of the church. Grange could never say bosom without looking down the front of Josie's dress. Anyway, he had resisted with everything in him, for he hated revivals, hated church, and most of all hated preachers. His mother, gently persuasive and getting nowhere with him, was trying to convince him to join the church one night when her brother, Grange's Uncle Buster, came to visit. He was built like a keg around the chest, and mean. Grange didn't like him because he had seen him knock his wife, Grange's aunt, through a plate-glass window. Hearing his sister's mild, obviously ineffectual pleadings, the uncle grabbed Grange roughly by the shoulder and gave him a long lecture on receiving the Holy Ghost, and about how good it was to be saved and how if he would just open up his heart the "pue" light would just come aflying and aflooding in. In short, he said that if Grange didn't get religion that same night he would get a horsewhipping when he got home.

Grange punctuated his tales with mirthful explosive laughs, which startled them, though they were expected. He was very good at these stories and liked to watch their eyes fasten on him, lit to glowing points of light from the crackling fire, which from time to time he spat into with unusual delicacy and accuracy. Ruth even liked the spitting, the pursing of the slick, finely molded dark brown lips against, for a minute, the clean white of his teeth, then the stinging buzz of the irons in the fire as they were hit, the momentary halting of the fire, the sound of steam rising quickly, and the sputtering consummation of the spit by the flames, for which they all waited, staring into the fire without letting out their breaths.

Grange had been placed harshly, or as he put it, "sheved down," on the mourner's bench. All around him the revival spirit was evident. In the first place, around the "brothers"—

130

every one of them saved—there hung the heady aroma of spirits; mostly corn liquor or home-made wine. At the beginning of the service all these brothers were sitting as stiff as ramrods, and that evening all of them, in order to keep from falling off their benches, fastened their eyes on Grange, who was sitting dejectedly on the hard wooden bench. His Uncle Buster was one of them, and Grange fancied he could smell his breath of peach-peel brandy clear across the church.

The sisters were all got up in their best. "They wore these long-tailed dresses then," said Grange. "In them days you could break your *neck* trying to see a little leg." They wore lots of red and yellow and green, and their hair was straightened to a "fare-thee-well." Grange grinned. "If a lizard had fell on one of them heads he was bound to slip off and break a claw!" Before the preacher started to preach they sat around gossiping like so many peacocks. "Lawd, how *you*, Sister So-an'-so! Chile, you shore does look good enough to eat!" Or, "You hush your mouth, girl, you ain't got no 'leven chilren. You looks jest like a sprang chicken!" They'd be spitting out of windows and into the stove, each one trying to show some ankle under her dress tail. But as soon as the preacher got up in the pulpit they started right in with "O Sinner!" which they did mournful things to, all the while looking at Grange and looking sad.

At the end of the sermon the preacher started calling for converts. ("Calling for what, convicts?" quizzed Ruth. "Same thing," Grange said, without stopping his story.) Two or three formerly unsaved and happy teen-agers filed up front with their heads bowed. They'd probably stole something the night before, Grange said. The church began to rock with song, the sisters were shouting and the preacher stood in the pulpit dripping with sweat. Every once in a while he swiped at the top of his bald head with his handkerchief. The same handkerchief, Grange had noticed, that he was spitting into all during the service. He could feel his mother looking piteously at him, for he knew she wanted him safely enchurched more than she wanted anything in the world. He wanted to get the Holy Ghost too, for he was deathly afraid of the whipping Uncle Buster had promised him.

131

Looking at his mother, he thought about his uncle, and looked over in the amen corner for him. He was still there, but while the church throbbed with life and the spirit of the Lord had everybody else almost climbing the walls, Uncle Buster was fast asleep. Well! There he snored, with a long sliver of saliva collecting on his vest pocket. Grange looked, enthralled; for intently digging around in the trash that had collected around Uncle Buster's mouth was a huge fat housefly. The kerosene lights made the fly's wings shine like amber gems. His busy activity around Uncle Buster's mouth was like that of a housewife sweeping out a corner, or of a greedy little boy eating stolen pie. It was then that Grange made his bargain with the God of the AME church.

Watching Uncle Buster's wide-open mouth, around which the big fly played, he said to himself that if the fly got inside Uncle Buster's mouth, *and if Uncle Buster swallowed it,* he would jump right up, claim he had found the Holy Ghost and join the church. He had decided the Holy Ghost was never coming on its own. As soon as he had done this, said Grange, the fly very cautiously sneaked into Uncle Buster's mouth, and Uncle Buster, waking to find everybody in the church gazing in his direction, or so it must have seemed to him, snapped together his ponderous whiskered jaws, and in a pious self-righteous gulp, downed the fly! He immediately began to heave and turn a sickly color; and when Grange, at that moment, rose and started up to shake the preacher's hand, Uncle Buster passed him with one hand clapped most firmly over his mouth. Grange said his mother had cried and shouted and was in general happy from then on.

And that was how come, Grange said, he was a member of the church but did not believe in God. For how could any God with self-respect, he wanted to know, bargain with a boy of seven or eight, who proposed such a nasty deal and meal.

During the latter part of the story Ruth bounced in her chair with laughter. And when she and Grange sat in church together they quite often giggled like silly girls over their own conventional absurdities, one of which was going to church. To preachers and church-going dandies alike, they were the dreaded incarnation of blasphemy. But it was funny, what they witnessed every Sunday—the placid, Christ-deferential self-righteousness of men who tortured their children and on Saturday nights beat their wives.

34

Josie saw them dancing together once, in the small log cabin Grange had built Ruth as a playhouse. It was on Ruth's tenth birthday and she was dressed from head to toe in brand-new clothes. Josie was furious. Grange had not bought clothes for her since they'd been married. And he had never, after Ruth came to stay with them, taken the trouble to dance with her.

"It ain't decent!" she cried, while Grange and Ruth danced breathlessly all around her. "And with your heart already full of holes!" They continued to dance, the music coming bluesy and hoarse from Grange's straining throat. When he sang he seemed to be in pain. But Ruth knew nothing of the physical condition of his heart. She knew she was in it, and that seemed enough.

"What's she talking about your heart?" she asked. But Grange was caught up in his lament. Ruth thought her grandfather a very sexy sort of old guy. He was tall and lean and had a jutting hip. When he danced you couldn't tell if his day had been bad or good. He closed his eyes and grunted music. His songs were always his own; she never heard them sung over the radio. His songs moved her; watching him dance made her feel kin to something very old. Grange danced like he walked, with a sort of spring in his knees. When he was drinking his dance paced a thin line between hilarity and vulgarity. He had a good time. His heart, to Ruth, was not an organ in his body, it was the tremor in his voice when he sang.

They danced best when they danced alone. And dancing taught Ruth she had a body. And she could see that her grandfather had one too and she could respect what he was able to do with it. Grange taught her untaught history through his dance; she glimpsed a homeland she had never known and felt the pattering of the drums. Dancing was a warm electricity that stretched, connecting them with other dancers moving across the seas. Through her grandfather's old and beautifully supple limbs she learned how marvelous was the grace with which she moved.

Josie began to leave them every Sunday. She went into town to visit the jail where Brownfield was kept. Grange did nothing to detain her, or if he did Ruth knew nothing of it. Ruth, however, was startled by this turn in events. She could not imagine anyone being fearless enough to see her father. Josie had brought them word that Brownfield had changed since he was in prison, and that they would hardly believe it was him when they saw him. Ruth had assumed she would never see him again; she had even hoped he would be done away with. Josie made her afraid that her father would be out of prison very soon. However, as week followed week and Josie's visits became less extraordinary to her, Ruth began to relax and to enjoy her grandfather, who, now that Josie spent her time cooking chickens and baking pies for Brownfield, was all her own.

"Do you ever think how selfish and spoiled you is?" Josie asked her one day, her face oddly contorted.

"I don't know what you mean," said Ruth. Grange had promised to take her to the picture show, and she was in a hurry to get dressed. She honestly did not realize that she never thought of Josie as her grandmother, and never, never thought of her as Grange's wife.

"You didn't want to go to the show with me and Grange?" asked Ruth, flying out the door. "Did you?" she called, as they were driving off.

134

35

Summer and fall found Ruth and Grange dedicated to the earthy, good-smelling task of making wine. They could name a long list of wines they knew how to make with maximum success. There was a short list of others that always soured. During the peach season peach stones and peels were gathered and dropped into the brown churn with water and allowed to set. This would make strong peach wine by September. Or, nearing the end of summer, big Alberta clings were halved and pushed into the churn and left in water, treated occasionally, and peeked into at least once a week. Grange did the "treating"—he drank some—and at Christmas time they had brandy, with shreds of peach sticking to the sides of the glass. In summer too they made corn-cob wine, white and sweet and cold when they left the jars outside in the spring; and blackberry wine and muscadine and scuppernong wine and sometimes plum wine. Ruth liked wine almost as much as Grange, and once in company she got sick and threw up, and it became quite apparent to everyone that Grange wasn't the only one drunk at the gathering. By the time she was nine, even Grange was astounded by her capacity to drink wine. She would try to pretend she was unaffected by it because she liked the taste of it so much she wanted to drink it by the glassful, like milk. But he knew how, momentarily, to keep her from starting. He would move the jar from where they hid it last, and hide it somewhere else. But this precaution worked badly for him, because then he would forget where he hid it, and would have to ask her to help him find it.

He was an unembarrassed drinker, a regular heathen. Throughout the day he nursed at a half-gallon jug, wine or corn liquor, he did not seem to care which. On weekends he doubled his usual intake and would sometimes find himself unable to come home. Twice he was lying beside the highway where their own road began, unable to make it any farther. These times when they found him he went into long exhaustive monologues on the merits of freedom.

"Just leave me hyar to die like a goddam dog!" he bluffed. "A black man is better off dead and in hell!" They took him, Josie supporting him on one shoulder, and Ruth walking behind him with a switch, and carried him home. Each time he threatened to sink onto the road Ruth cut him across the back of his legs with her switch. She always felt older than Grange when he was feeling bad. When he sobered up she lectured him, wouldn't acknowledge his headache, made him get his tobacco for himself and in general ignored him so that by Monday night he was not only sober and ashamed but also a wreck, and scared stiff that he had at last pushed her too far. (After all, she was only a *little* thing, and didn't understand, and might get the wrong idee!) He thought she might at last be turned against him. He would curse himself for being the father of his son and in danger of being thought just like him by his son's daughter.

Ruth was reminded of Brownfield when Grange got drunk; it was as if the closed parts of her mind were painfully forced open, and again she saw the demon of hate and destruction in someone close to her. But she believed Grange drank because of his murderous son and because of Josie. Grange and his wife now rarely spoke to each other; the house was often miserable because of their coldness. There was always in the air something of Josie's feeling of Ruth's intrusion. Ruth also knew that Grange had had another wife, Margaret, whom he had never got over. He cried whenever he talked about her (only when he was drunk) and Ruth hated her (dead though she was and had been for many years) with all her heart.

But Grange's crimes, she believed, were never aimed at anyone but himself, and his total triumph over his life's failures was the joy in him that drew her to him. He was a sinner, which he readily admitted, but he gave of himself. (She did not then notice that what he had to give he gave only to her.) The passion he lavished on living she could never quite condemn.

136

When he was sober and feeling guilty and ashamed, and when Josie lambasted him prior to dressing up and "visiting" somebody else (usually Brownfield), and they were in the house alone, there was a pall hanging over the house, thickest around Grange's bowed gray head, which only lifted when she stationed herself close to him, or raised his head by shoving her own pigtails sharply, abruptly, sometimes even painfully, under his lowered chin. Then they embraced.

And of that other life of father and son, between the old man she loved and the younger one she feared, what could she know? And how could she judge? And what of Josie and the life of marital intimacy that was not there for Ruth to see, to understand? For all she knew her grandfather might never have been a father, her own father notwithstanding. Brownfield and Grange cursed each other, neither respecting the other's age or youth. Maybe Grange's love contained a gap. Like his life. Or where and when had the violence started? And what secrets did Josie know? How could one so young comprehend the crops of fraternity blighted, and hatred like stone, the ground between hearts scorched, and vengeance a cry in the souls of those concerned?

36

The beginning of her life with Grange was the beginning of her initiation into a world of perplexity, and a knowledge of impersonal cruelty beyond what she had known in her own home. After her long depression and sadness had passed, except for fleeting moments when she felt tears on her cheeks for no easily discernible reason, there were casual but emphatic talks about Indians, and yellow people who lived in houses with roofs like upside-down umbrellas. Ruth learned for the first time that there was a sea and that its waters were larger than the whole of Baker County. She listened to sketches of places with foreign names,

Paris, London, New York. In addition to the full and joyous days of wine-making and dancing, there were days devoted to talk about big bombs, the forced slavery of her ancestors, the rapid demise of the red man; and the natural predatory tendencies of the whites, the people who had caused many horrors.

There were days of detailed description of black history. Grange recited from memory speeches he'd heard, newscasts, lectures from street corners when he was in the North, everything he had ever heard. There was impassioned rhetoric against a vague country of wealthy mobsters called America. And, when she was old enough to carry a gun, she was taught to shoot birds and rabbits. She would rather have done almost anything else. But rabbit was good cooked with potatoes, and birds were like chicken. Still, her heart was scarcely in it.

Ruth could not understand Grange's aversion to white people. Mem had let her play with white children, and now, at her grandfather's, there were wonderful ones, she thought, down the road. Playing with them, however, was strictly forbidden. Apparently they were not, at six and seven, as completely wholesome as they looked.

"Why?" she asked, rebelling and beginning nervously to chew her nails.

"One," Grange said, "they stole you from Africa."

"Me?" she asked.

"Be quiet," he said. "Two. They brought you here in chains."

"Hummm?" she murmured. Looking at her slightly rusty but otherwise unmarked ankles.

"Three. They beat you every day in slavery and didn't feed you nothing but weeds. . . ."

"Like we give Dilsey?" she interrupted.

"Collards," he said. "And guts."

"Chitlins? I like them. I like collards too."

They did nasty things to women. (She was only nine then.)

"What, what!" she asked, excited.

They are evil.

They are blue-eyed devils.

They are your natural enemy.

"Stay away from them hypocrites or they will destroy you."

"They didn't do nothing to me, I think you making a mistake," she said, fingering her buttons.

"They killed your father and mother," he said.

As far as she was concerned her father still lived, although at times she wished he wouldn't.

"No, they didn't," she said, for she just couldn't see it.

37

To Grange his son was as dead as his son's murdered wife. If he had stopped long enough to consider that his son still lived, his opinion would not have been much different: he would have said he was a member of the living dead, one of the many who had lost their souls in the American wilderness. The cesspool of Brownfield's life was an approximation of nothingness. In prison now for the murder of his wife, Brownfield continued to plot evil. He spent every moment he could in the presence of vileness. His only confidante was his father's wife. Grange considered the possibility of Josie, aided by Brownfield, turning against him, trying to make him suffer for his neglect of her in favor of his granddaughter. But he did not concern himself long with such wonderings; Ruth needed him to teach her the realities of life. What plotters might do to him, his wife and son, or otherwise, was something he could confront when the time came. In the meantime, he watched Josie coming and going, he heard Brownfield's name often on her lips. He was not unmoved, but as Josie was one day to learn, he was by nature the most unjealous of men.

It disturbed Grange that Ruth appeared drawn to Brownfield at times, attracted to the same qualities that he knew repulsed and frightened her. It seemed to him that Ruth turned her father's image over and over in her mind as if he were a great conundrum. When she was thinking about him her look was confounded, as if she knew a door very well but found it lacked a key. He did not like to recall the night he had rushed to Mem's house to find Mem and her children piled in a heap in the middle of the yard. The other girls, Daphne and Ornette, were whisked away by a smooth-talking Northern preacher (Mem's father), and his wife, who were all quivering chins and amazement. The old guy was sadder than his wife, so moved by the tragedy that he wanted to take all the children, though he had not, so long ago, wanted their mother. Ruth alone could not be pried loose from her grandfather's arms. And he had wanted her so much he could not believe himself capable of such strong emotion. Not after everything. Josie had at first found his attachment to the small frightened child amusing. He'd never wanted *her* like that, she said. And it was true. His motives for marrying Josie in the first place were suspect, and she rightfully suspected them. Her weakness was that she cared for him and had waited for him a long time. She foolishly believed that having her he could do no wrong.

When he had come back from the North, knowing that even if she had not remained faithful to him she would be waiting, there was no way for her to understand the changes he felt. When he had gone through Baker County on his way North he was a baby in his knowledge of the world. Although he knew the world was hard. He had not even comprehended what he was running to. He was simply moving on to where people said it was better. Josie had had no way of knowing how revulsed he was by what he found in that world, how much he needed to bury himself out of sight of everything. She could not understand, as so many people like her (small, untraveled, thoughtless), how he loathed the thought of being dependent on a white person or persons again, how he would almost rather be blind than have to see, even occasionally, a white face. He had found that wherever he went whites were in control; they ruled New York as they did Georgia; Harlem as they did Poontang Street. If he had taken Josie with him as they had planned, perhaps she would have understood. Two things and two only he wanted

140

when he came back to Baker County. Independence from the whites, complete and unrestricted, and obscurity from those parts of the world he chose. For this security he needed Josie's money. Josie had thought it was love for her that made him such a seeker of privacy. She thought he needed to own a secluded farm so as to enjoy her charms the better. Her vanity at all times was both provincial and great.

He had tried countless times to initiate her into the hatreds of the world, the irrepressible hatreds he contained, barely, in himself. Once he had told her of a murder (or suicide) which he had caused, and she had been horrified. As horrified that the victim was white as she would have been if she had been black. He could not make her understand there was a difference.

"One life is worth any other," she said religiously, his fat whorish wife who was raped at sixteen and never avenged.

"What about what they have done to us?"

"How could *you* do such a thing?"

"An eye for an eye—anyway, you knowed I walked out on my wife and child. They could have starved. You never made no complaints about that!"

Josie ducked her head. "That were a little different," she said.

"Why?" he asked. "Because by leaving them it meant you would end up with *both* of us?"

She began to cry. "The Lord *help* you," she blurted, her chins shaking.

" 'Bout time he did," he said to her, "just about time he did!"

Now, as he sought to teach the ways of the world to his granddaughter and she resisted him, he was reminded of his own education in foreign parts of the world. For though he hated it as much as any place else, where he was born would always be home. Georgia would be home for him, every other place foreign.

"If you don't like 'em, Grange," said his Ruth, "if you don't like 'em, seems like to me you'd a shot five or six of 'em in the head!" Her imagination beyond her warped reality was fixed by TV westerns. According to them, if you didn't like the guys on

141

the white horse you challenged them to a draw. You always won, of course, and a child of ten is very strict at applying the rules.

"There are more of them than me."

"How many more?"

"Billions."

"Wyatt Earp one time shot five men that were gunning for him. One was on the roof over the saloon, one was in the saloon door, one was in the middle of the street behind a wagon, and the other one was behind him hiding behind his wife. How many is that?"

"Too many in real life."

"But you're a good man, Grange, *all things considered,* and you'd be all right."

Beside such faith his acts against injustice seemed not just puny and ineffectual and selfish but *cowardly* as well.

"I wonder if *He* don't like them too?" She looked perplexed. Always she spoke of her father as He with a capital H, as if she were speaking of God. At times like now she both hated and respected him.

"Did you know I run away from your grandmother once a long time ago?" he asked her another time.

"Was she *funny* acting, like Josie?"

"What you mean?" He was surprised to know a child so young could be so *un*blind.

"Aw, you know. I would have run away from her too. She was trashy!"

"She wasn't trashy," he said gently. "She was a pretty woman and wanted nice things like any pretty woman and when she couldn't get them, well, she wanted something exciting to keep happening to her to take her mind off them. I wanted them things too, so after a long spell of not getting no pretty things nor no excitement neither we couldn't seem to get no thrills from nothing but fighting each other." Grange looked off over his granddaughter's head.

"I worked for a old white man that would have stole the skin right off my back, if black hides'd bring a good price."

"Ah!" she said, taking a step away from him.

He knew what was wrong. "Wait 'til you're grown. You'll see. They can be hated to the very bottom of your guts, can the white folks!"

"You put it *all* on them!" she said, starting up. "You just as bad as Him! He killed . . . !" She could not go on; furious tears filled her eyes.

"Let us go look at our traps," he said, pretending not to see. He reached for his gun.

"The white folks didn't kill my mother," she said at last. "He did!"

"I won't say you're entirely wrong," said Grange, putting an arm around her shoulder. "If there's one snake that'd kill my theory it's your pa."

"Tell me something real mean that you did." Ruth was soothed somewhat by their slow walking through the woods looking at the traps.

He was afraid all their arguments would end this way, and as he could not risk losing her he could never tell her. If he could never back up his words of fighting with actual deeds done and battles won, how could he teach her the necessary hate? The hate that would mean her survival. He was ashamed of himself. It was his weakness, this certainty that she thought him good. She honestly thought him incapable of real evil, of murder, which to her would always be the unthinkable crime. She would have no sympathy for anyone who took the life of another human being. And yet, he was not innocent, he had, once he had learned it, lived his code. The resistance of his choosing was all around her. Even she was part of it. He had lost his innocence, his naïveté, all the better qualities of himself. He had discovered, as Ruth must, that innocence and naïveté are worthless assets in a wilderness, as strong teeth and claws are not.

"Well . . . ?" she began.

"There was a time—" he said, and stopped. Slowly he shook his head. All his years of violence and hardness swirled through

143

his mind, like bits of dirty paper with dates and pictures. Alone, from the vast sea of criminal debris, there arose the memory of a night many years ago.

It was in the spring of 1926 that he had left his wife and Brownfield and the baby, Star, to go North. He had stayed with Josie for several weeks at the Dew Drop Inn until her possessive "love" and jubilation over Margaret's death began to get on his nerves. Yes, he had known about Margaret's death the day after it happened, but he had not returned home. It had hit him hard though, and he had wondered and worried about Brownfield. But he had felt he must continue North. He had his mind on living free, and that meant that even Josie, especially Josie, could not come with him.

By the middle of that summer he had worked, begged, stolen his way North, to New York. Among the frozen faces and immobile buildings he had been just another hungry nobody headed for Harlem. For some months he existed on a variety of hustles. He soon found himself doing things he'd never dreamed he'd do; he sold bootleg whiskey and drugs and stolen goods; he sold black women to white men, the only men at that time who seemed to have money for such pleasures. All of his hustles were difficult for him at first because, as his partners in crime declared, he was just a small dog from the backwoods. Luckily, his backwoodsness did not rule out the possibility of his learning new tricks. Unlike some unfortunate Southern migrants, he did not starve, though he was often close enough to it.

He had come North expecting those streets paved with that gold, which had already become a cliché to the black people who had come before him and knew better, but who still went down home every summer spreading the same old rumors. He had come expecting to be welcomed and shown his way about. No golden streets he was soon used to. But no friendliness, no people talking to one another on the street? Never. He was, perhaps, no longer regarded as merely a "thing"; what was even more cruel to him was that to the people he met and passed daily he was not even in existence! The South had made him miserable, with nerve endings raw from continual surveillance

144

from contemptuous eyes, but they *knew he was there*. Their very disdain proved it. The North put him in solitary confinement where he had to manufacture his own hostile stares in order to see himself. For why were they pretending he was not there? Each day he had to say his name to himself over and over again to shut out the silence.

"Grange. My name Grange. Grange Copeland is my name."

He had killed a woman with child on a day when he was in excruciating pain from hunger. He had been begging in Central Park, barely escaping arrest from mounted police. Evening was falling after a bright winter day. He crouched underneath some shrubbery, waiting for the park to empty of cyclists and walkers and the old people, who, forgotten by their children but at least well-dressed and fed, spent their days as long as there was any bit of sun in the lively park.

He had been in New York three and a half years then and was wearing the one warm suit of clothes he had managed to steal. He had become a good thief and, beyond a few beatings "on suspicion" (never for things he had done) by the police, had never been caught. There had been times when he hoped to be caught and sentenced, if only to be fed and kept bathed and warm, but his luck, like his need to run about unhampered, took him out of danger of that "safety" into another kind which suited his spirit to some degree but wreaked havoc in his mind.

Crouching in the weeds, silently kneading his fingers to keep them from becoming and staying stiff, he kept his eyes on a frail, hugely pregnant woman who was sitting on a bench by the pond. She had been sitting there a long time, obviously waiting for someone. He could discern no ring on her finger. From minute to minute she seemed to shudder, whether from cold or exhaustion he could not tell. She wore a heavy blue coat, somewhat faded, and black boots probably lined with fur. Her hair was cut very short and was blonde almost to whiteness. Her face was broad and from what he could see, very pale and drawn, though her lips, against her white face, seemed incredibly red. When he saw her closer he saw they were painted red, with the lipstick going far out over the edges of her natural lips, so that it was

145

hard to tell where her natural mouth was, and they were bitten red, puffy and swollen, and seemingly inflamed.

He was fascinated by pregnancy, and this woman's big belly brought forth a mixture of sweet and painful recollections. The creative process was tremendous, he thought. A miracle. But when he thought of Margaret's belly, bitter grimaces forced themselves to his lips.

While he crouched tremblingly, blowing on his hands, a tall muscular soldier, also very blond, strode up to the woman and they embraced. They walked up and down the length of the pond for several minutes, with him chafing her hands and blowing against her ears. The park was nearly deserted. A park policeman rode by and smiled when he saw the lovers. Grange thought that to the policeman too they must have looked *so real,* so remindfully like somebody that might have been yourself.

Soon they sat down upon the bench by the pond. The soldier, after looking carefully all around, gingerly touched the top of the large stomach and the young woman smiled. Grange crept close beside their bench, he did not know why, except that he was drawn to this life that was starting, and drawn to the look of love on the faces of the couple. At least he thought it looked like love. He forgot his hunger for a while watching them kiss in the gathering dusk. Chaste kisses they exchanged, as befitted soon-to-be parents perhaps never-to-be-wed. But the young man, with the light from the park lamps above shining on his gold hair, took from his pocket a silver object. He held it flashing briefly in the light. The young woman sat with her face glowing, calmly, joyously, but, Grange felt, with tears, while he slipped the ring on her finger. He said a few tense words still clutching both her hands and she turned just her shortcropped head on her heavy body and stared incredulously. "Why?" she cried. And the sharp, stricken hurt sound of a woman betrayed touched his ear. He watched them arguing now, the girl trying to throw the silver ring into the pond. The young man prevented her, and finally, woodenly, she dropped the ring to the ground between their feet. They sat in silence making no move to pick it up. From what Grange had managed to hear it appeared the

146

young man already had a wife. Soon, glancing at his watch, the soldier rose to leave and tried to brush his lips across her brow. She ducked her head.

He looked tall and brave and honorable in his uniform. Perhaps that was why the girl's face set itself in such a sneer of contempt. Grange saw the sneer when she turned her face from the young man. He saw her battered and cruel and shuttered profile. The man poked at the ring with his shoe, muttered something (perhaps concerning its value) and reluctantly took out his wallet. (Had she said she would throw any ring of his into the pond?) Grange had never seen such money; the young man pressed a fat wad of it into the girl's lifeless hand. On the profile that was turned to Grange a tear must have fallen, for a small thin white hand quickly brushed the area near her eye, down to her chin.

And now he was turning away, and she was not looking at anything, just vacant. Her eyes turned away from the pond and back into the trees and the high hard rocks. When he was out of sight she looked in the direction he had gone, but then the dusk had made empty air of the last sliver of shadow from his strong frame. She began, silently, to cry. Then she sniffled, then the sobs came hard and fast as if she wanted and believed she could, if she tried, cry herself to death, and if not to death, to a long forgetful sleep.

Grange had watched the scene deteriorate from the peak of happiness to the bottom of despair. It was the first honestly human episode he had witnessed between white folks, when they were not putting on airs to misinform the help. His heart ached with pity for the young woman as well as for the soldier, whose face, those last seconds, had not been without its own misery. And now the perhaps normally proud woman sat crying shamelessly—but only because she thought herself alone. There she sat, naked, her big belly her own tomb. Or at least it must have seemed so to her, for from cry to cry she pressed with both hands against her stomach as if she would push it away from her and into the pond.

Grange had about made up his mind to speak to her and offer what help he could, for he feared she would harm herself with her crying and staying out so long in the freezing weather. But abruptly, when she apparently considered she had cried enough, the young woman stopped, blew her nose and wiped her eyes. Quite containedly. He could almost see the features settle into a kind of haughty rigidity that belied the past half-hour. Her face became one that refused to mark itself with suffering. He knew, even before he saw them, that her eyes would be without vital expression, and that her lips and cheeks and old once-used laugh wrinkles would have to do all her smiling from then on. He did not even feel she would regret it.

Somehow this settling into impenetrability, into a sanctuary from further pain, seemed more pathetic to him than her tears. At the same time her icy fortitude in the face of love's desertion struck him as peculiarly white American. No blues would ever come from such a saving of face. It showed a lack of self-pity (and Grange believed firmly that one's self was often in need of a little sympathetic pity) that also meant less sympathy for the basic tragedies that occurred in the human situation. She appeared to him to be the kind of woman who could raise ten sons to be killed in war, sending them off with a minimum of tears one at a time, collecting a stack of flags to prove her own bravery.

How did he expect her to act? He really didn't know. Shivering, he stepped over the low green fence and skirted the edge of the shrubbery. She was just rising to leave. The silver ring still lay in the worn dirt before the bench. The money she had let drop, carelessly, from her fingers. Bills fluttered, folded in half, in a small bright green pile. Grange had a hard time noticing anything else once he saw that the money was about to be abandoned and that it was not counterfeit. (Such tantalizingly green bills could not be!)

He had stolen so much and from so many sources in New York that stealing had become a useful and ready tool to be used at will, not unlike a second language. He knew tricks and he knew sob stories (unfortunately more true than not) to melt his victims' hearts (if caught) and he knew cunning and he

148

knew violence. He had had few qualms about stealing before, but now, when it was simply a matter of taking, he felt a totally unprecedented hesitation.

The woman had walked some distance along the pond when he picked up both the ring and the money and counted it. His breath came in a joyful gasp of disbelief when he counted seven hundred dollars in one-hundred-dollar bills and twenties. In his excitement he dropped down upon the bench and rested his head against the back. He was lightheaded from hunger and his body could barely sustain the excitement without making him black out. He struggled with dizziness and nausea, clamping his teeth hard together and gripping his left hand with his right. The money, like a heavy paper frog, seemed to jump in his inside coat pocket, but it was his heart thumping against it and drowning out everything else. He darted up briefly to look after the woman; when he was sitting down he couldn't see her, but standing he could see that she had stopped some distance away beside the deep end of the pond and that she stood, seeming to blow in the wind—perhaps his tired eyes made her waver. His first thought was to run away as fast as he could, to get out of the park as quickly as his shaking legs would carry him. Already he thought he could hear a couple of park policemen on horses patrolling nearby. But there had been something so poignant, so sad, and so infinitely pathetic about the scene he had witnessed that he found himself unable simply to disappear. Instead, in a matter of seconds, his feet turned themselves in the direction of the young woman.

All thought of his shaggy, unkempt appearance, his bushy beard and stinking underarms and breath, had ceased with his first acquaintance with starvation. He did not consider the possibility that the young woman might find cause to object to foul body odor, or to a black tramp appearing out of nowhere to solace her. He should have thought of those things, he thought later on, when the woman and her baby were dead. But he did not really then; in fact, at the time, he could think of no matterable difference between them. Misery leveled all beings, he reasoned, going after her.

149

Hastily he divided the money; he would give her three hundred, he would keep four hundred. She could also have the ring.

He approached her cautiously, looking over his shoulder each few steps to be sure the police were not around. He stopped four feet from her, and like her, began to stare into the pond. Gradually, for he had begun to feel unsure of what he planned to do, he moved closer, inch by studiedly nonchalant inch.

At that time of the year only the center of the pond was free from ice, the sides near the banks were white with it. It was a dismal sight; the fallen leaves had drifted down to the edge of the water and turned into a sort of patterned slime, the ice keeping them from disintegrating altogether. There was not much to look at that was not depressing. The night was grayish and cold; the park lights offered only brightness, no warmth or cheerfulness.

As she stood downwind from him she quickly sensed his presence. Putting her hand gently against the end of her nose, and looking at him with a typical New York, not-seeing look, she moved.

"Ma'am?" he said, pursuing her, holding out his hand.

She pretended not to hear him, but went to stand on a small platform that jutted out over the pond. He stood below her, watching her, holding the money and the ring in his hand.

" 'Scuse me, ma'am," he said, and as if by rote his arm took his hat from his head. "I found this here back yonder by the bench and I was just wondering if . . . ?" She had turned a truly paper-white and her eyes held the cold tenseness of a prepared learned scream.

"No!" she cried shortly, holding a thin arm back and up as if to ward him off and strike him. "It's not mine." Abruptly she turned her back to him, waiting for him to leave.

"It yours all right," he said patiently, with one foot raised on the steps to the platform, the fistful of money clenched at his knee. "I seen that young solyer give it to you."

The small back stiffened. If it had not been so cold Grange would have sworn he saw, in the fleeting moment she turned

150

to look at him, a crimson blush. He stood shivering quietly behind her.

"Give it to me!" she said sharply, turning and looking him up and down in fury. He handed it to her, along with the ring. The ring she laid on the railing, the money she counted.

"This ain't all of it," she said. "I want all of it! *You* ain't going to have any of it; before I let *you* sneak off with it I'll throw it all into the pond!" She threw one of the twenties into the pond, her painted lips smiling archly as she watched Grange go down instinctively to retrieve it from the ice. When he rose up empty-handed her mouth laughed. "Look at the big burlyhead," she said, and laughed again.

Grange swallowed. He hated her entire race while she stood before him, pregnant, having learned nothing from her own pain, helpless except before someone more weak than herself, enjoying a revenge that severed all possible bonds of sympathy between them.

She stood there like a great blonde pregnant deified cow. She was not pretty, but only a copy of a standardly praised copy of prettiness. She was abandoned, but believed herself infinitely cared for and wanted. By somebody. She was without superiority, but believed herself far above him.

"Give me that money, nigger," she said, menacingly, moving toward him. His tongue would not work he was so angry.

If she put her hands on me I'm going to knock that white brat right out of her stomach! he thought grimly, watching the almost transparent white face come closer to his own. He felt, as if asleep, a sharp pain in his leg above the ankle. He had to look up into her twisted face and pitiless eyes to believe she had kicked him.

A thousand drums pounded behind his temples. His throat was dry. His eyes, bleary from hunger and fatigue, were red and wolfish as with a lunge he fell on her, bearing her to the stone floor of the platform. She began to scream as he held her by the shoulders and shook her, dragging her finally to her feet. His hunger made his rage shortlived and he could not hit her. He relived his old plantation frustrations as she stood there before

151

him stoically calling him names. She was not afraid of him. It seemed unreal to him that she could persist in calling him nigger when he might have been challenging her to fight for her very life.

Steady on her feet again the woman tried to jump from the platform to the grass. He was standing in front of the steps and she did not "care" to order him to move. She knew his weakness before a single scream from her, and did not fear him as much as she despised him. She would get the police and they would get the money from him, teaching him a lesson in the meantime. Misjudging the distance and the weight of her heavy body, she fell through the ice into the pond. Grange had been standing mute and still, but immediately he raced down the shallow steps to try to reach her from the bank. In a split second he recalled how he had laughed when his grandfather admitted helping white "masters" and "mistresses" out of burning houses. Now he realized that to save and preserve life was an instinct, no matter whose life you were trying to save. He stretched out his arm and nearly touched her. She reached up and out with a small white hand that grabbed his hand but let go when she felt it was *his* hand. Grange drew back his dirty brown hand and looked at it. The woman struggled to climb the bank against the ice, but the ice snagged her clothes, and she stuck in the deep sucking mud near the steep shore. When she had given him back his hand and he had looked at it thoughtfully, he turned away, gathering the scattered money in a hurry. Finally she sank. She called him "nigger" with her last disgusted breath.

On his way out of the park he saw the mounted police headed in the direction of the pond.

"Git out of the park, *you!*"

"Don't you know better than to be here this time of night?"

"Yassur," said Grange, pulling an imaginary forelock. "Jest now leavin', boss."

The two men laughed scornfully.

He often thought about that woman; in fact, she and her big belly haunted him. Probably any other woman (or even preg-

152

nant bitch) he would have pulled to safety no matter how much she feared him or despised him or hated him or *whatever* that woman had felt so strongly against him. But he faced his refusal to save her squarely. Her contempt for him had been the last straw; never again would he care what happened to any of them. She was perhaps the only one of them he would ever sentence to death. He had killed a thousand, ten thousand, a whole country of them in his mind. She was the first, and would probably be the only real one.

The death of the woman was simple murder, he thought, and soul condemning; but in a strange way, a bizarre way, it liberated him. He felt in some way repaid for his own unfortunate life. It was the taking of that white woman's life—and the denying of the life of her child—the taking of her life, not the taking of her money, that forced him to want to try to live again. He believed that, against his will, he had stumbled on the necessary act that black men must commit to regain, or to manufacture their manhood, their self-respect. They must kill their oppressors.

He never ceased to believe this, adding only to this belief, in later years, that if one kills he must not shun death in his turn. And this, he had found, was the hardest part, since after freeing your suppressed manhood by killing whatever suppressed it you were then taken with the most passionate desire to live!

After leaving the park that night he had waited for an end to come to him. He was both ready and not ready. He felt alive and liberated for the first time in his life. He wanted to see a thousand tomorrows! For, perhaps because he had both killed and not killed the woman (it was her decision not to take his offered help, he reasoned), he did not know if his own life was required. But his exaltation had been part readiness to die. As a sinner, after seeing the face of God, is ready then immediately to meet him, not wanting a continuation of his sordid past to reverse his faith.

"Teach them to hate!" he shouted up and down the Harlem streets, his eyes glazed with his new religion. "Teach them to *hate,* if you wants them to survive!"

Mothers, shuffling along Lenox Avenue with dozens of black

children in tow turned to look at him with hopeless eyes. The children giggled at him as if they already understood the amusing complexity of it all.

At store-front churches he disrupted services.

"Don't teach 'em to *love them!*" he cried. "Teach them to hate 'em!"

The black, oily-voiced preachers and the beige and powdered (and elaborately wigged) sisters looked at him in horrified pre-eminence.

"Git that drunk sinner *out* of here, deacons!" the preachers shouted. The parasites!

The overworked deacons, with rough pious hands that beat their women to death when they couldn't feed them, would come up to him apologetically.

"You *drunk,* brother?" they asked him gently.

"Betta *sleep* it off!"

Not one of them earned enough to feed his children meat for Sunday dinner.

"*Love* thy neighbor," they whispered to him. "Do *good* to them that despitefully use you."

"We *have* loved them," Grange whispered back, his voice rising to compete with the melancholy notes of the church's organ. "We loves 'em now. And by God it *killing* us! It already done killed *you.*"

The kindly deacons walked him to the street, urging him with soothing words to see reason. Grange hated them with great frustration. Loving their white neighbors in the North as in the South got them nothing but more broken heads and contemptuous children. But did they dare to learn why they had no love for themselves and only anger for their children? No, they did not.

"Hatred for them will someday unite us," he shouted from the corner of Seventh Avenue. "It will be the only thing that can do it. Deep in our hearts we hates them anyhow. What I say is brang it out in the open and teach it to the young 'uns. If you teach it to them young, they won't have to learn it in the school of the hard knock."

154

"Hatred is bad for a man's mind," someone told him.

"Man don't live with his mind alone," said Grange. "He live with his mouth and with his stomach. He live with his pride and with his heart. That man's got to eat. That man's got to sleep. That man got to be able to take care of his own life. I say if love can git man all this, then go 'head and let it; but it ain't done nothin' all these years *for us*. If love can do so much good to the minds of all these here *dope* addicts an' cutthroats hangin' round this here street it mighty late startin'—on account they is so *many* dope addicts and cutthroats, and they ain't all children!

"You wants to keep on teachin' your children Christian stuff from a white-headed Christ you go right on—but *me*, an' later on *you*—is goin' to have to switch to somethin' new! And since hatred is what's got to be growin' inside of you that's exactly what has to come out, and in the right direction this time!"

He was like a tamed lion who at last tasted blood. There was no longer any reason not to rebel against people who were not gods. His aggressiveness, which he had vented only on his wife, and his child, and his closest friends, now asserted itself in the real hostile world. For weeks after the incident at the pond he fought more Italians, Poles, Jews (all white; he did not understand differences in their cultures, and if they "acted white" he punched them in the nose!), in and around Harlem than he had been aware lived there. And in this fighting too he tasted the sweet surge of blood rightfully directed in its wrath that proclaimed his freedom, his manhood. Every white face he cracked, he cracked in his sweet wife's name.

But soon he realized he could not fight all the whites he met. Nor was he interested in it any longer. Each man would have to free himself, he thought, and the best way he could. For the time being, he would withdraw completely from them, find a sanctuary, make a life that need not acknowledge them, and be always prepared, with his life, to defend it, to protect it, to keep it from whites, inviolate.

And so he had come back to Baker County, because it was

155

home, and to Josie, because she was the only person in the world who loved him, and because he needed even more money than he had to buy the rock of his refuge.

Josie, who had lived so long in the hope of his love, was persuaded, out of her own love for him, to sell her cherished livelihood, the Dew Drop Inn. With his money and hers he bought a farm. A farm far from town, off the main road, deep behind pines and oaks. He raised his own bread, fermented his own wine, cured his own meat. At last, he was free.

But his freedom had cost him. There was Josie, learning each day that once again she had been used by a man and discarded when his satisfaction was secured. He had done her wrong, and the thought nagged at him and had finally begun to make him appreciate her for the first time. She was big-hearted, generous; she could love in spite of all that had gone wrong in her life. But then there had been Ruth, breaking in on his growing love for Josie, his acceptance of her genuine goodness and adoration. Ruth, who needed him and who was completely fresh and irresistibly innocent, as alas, Josie was not. He had felt himself divided, wanting to comfort the old but feeling responsible for the new. And then there had been Brownfield, again. And though he had forgiven Josie once (true, not out of love but greed and expediency) for her attachment to his son, he did not know if he could forgive her a second time. Josie and Brownfield sought to retaliate against his indifference to them; but even for this was he not to blame?

"You are not selfish," Ruth was saying as she bent over to lift a small rabbit from a trap. "You would never steal. Even your cussing is harmless." She laughed as her grandfather took the rabbit from her, felt its smallness and let it go. "I know you don't like killing things, even things to eat."

"It ought never to be necessary to kill nobody to assert nothing," he said. "But some mens, in order to live, can't be innocent."

Ruth was still laughing. "You so tall and rough-looking with your big boots and your long gun." Impulsively she hugged his arm. "But *we* know you got a heart, don't we?"

156

And Grange knew he would never tell her of his past, of the pregnant woman and his lectures of hate; he would never tell her that he'd mugged old women and weak-limbed students to buy his food. He would never tell her that he was guilty of every sin, including selfishness, or that Josie's heart was purer than his had ever been. He would never tell her that the land she stood on, which would be hers someday, was bought with blood and tears. He would never tell her because she might believe him, and because with Ruth he had learned an invaluable lesson about hate; he could only teach hate by inspiring it. And how could he spoil her innocence, kill the freshness of her look, becloud the brightness of her too inquisitive eyes?

At least love was something that left a man proud that he *had* loved. Hate left a man shamed, as he was now, before the trust and faith of the young.

"The mean things I've done," he began. "Think of me, when I'm gone, as a big, rough-looking coward. Who learned to love hisself only after thirty-odd years. And then overdone it."

She was not to know until another time, that her grandfather, as she knew him, was a reborn man. She did not know fully, even after he was dead, what cruelties and blood fostered his tolerance and his strength. And his love.

PART VIII

PART VIII

38

After Mem's funeral, to which he was allowed to go, though chained to a red-faced warden in dirty boots, Brownfield had thought uncomfortably but not regretfully of what he had done. But he had never been able to think himself very far. *He liked plump women.* That was the end-all of his moral debates. *Ergo,* he had murdered his wife because she had become skinny and had not, with much irritation to him, reverted, even when well-fed, to her former plumpness. He was not a fool to ask himself whether there was logic in his nerves. He knew what he liked.

The days of her plumpness haunted him as blackberry pie had done when he was a growing boy and pies of any kind were few and far between. He longed for a now over-and-done with lushness. His time of plenty, when he could provide.

Plumpness and freedom from the land, from cows and skinniness, went all together in his mind, and her face as it had been when he first knew her at the Dew Drop Inn took on for him the same one-dimensional quality as his memory of pies and a whiskey bottle. He could forget her basic reality, convert it into comparisons. She had been like good pie, or good whiskey, but there had never been a self to her because one no longer existed in him. Dead, Mem became a myth of herself, a beautiful plump girl with whom he had fallen in love, but who had changed before his eyes into an ugly hag, screeching at him and making him feel small.

If she had been able to maintain her dominance over him perhaps she would not stand now so finished, a miniature statue, in his mind, but her inherent weakness, covered over momentarily by the wretched muscular hag, had made her ashamed of her own seeming strength. And without this strength, the strength to kill his ass, to make him wallow continually in his own puke, she was lost. Her weakness was forgiveness, a stupid belief that kindness can convert the enemy. The logical next step from hitting him so magnificently over the head with the gun was for one of them to use it. That was where her staunch ten-point resolution had failed her. And he, without resolutions, but with the memory of his humiliation, could, and did, at last regain what she had stolen that Sunday morning when he lay in vomit at her feet. The punishment he had devised for her "come down" had not been enough. She had thought she could best him again by leaving him. And he had warned her, if she tried, what he would do. A man of his word, as he thought of himself, he had kept his word. His word had even become his duty.

But she was not a plump woman and he did not like them skinny. When they were like that something was wrong, and you weren't doing them right. And he did not want to know about it.

39

Josie told him that Ruth now lived, and happily, with Grange. It maddened Brownfield that his father should presume to try to raise his child. Ornette and Daphne, taken up North by Mem's father, did not concern Brownfield as much as Ruth, because when they went North he relinquished claim to them, knowing quite well he would never go North after them. In prison, condemned for ten years to cut lawns and plant trees for jailers, judges, and prominent citizens of Baker County (though he was to be paroled after seven years), he realized an extraordinary emotion. He loved the South. And he knew he loved it because he had never seriously considered leaving it. He felt he had a real understanding of it. Its ways did not mystify him in the least. It was a sweet, violent, peculiarly accommodating land. It bent itself to fit its own laws. One's life, underneath the rigidity of caste, was essentially one of invisibility and luck. One did not feel alone in one's guilt. Guilt dripped and moved all over and around and about one like the moss that clung to the trees. A man's punishment was never written up somewhere in a book before his crime was committed—it was not even the same as someone else's punishment for the same crime. The punishment was made to fit the man and not the crime. It was individual punishment. One felt unique in one's punishment if not in one's crime. This appealed to Brownfield. It meant to him that one could punish one's own enemies with a torture of one's own choosing. One could make up the punishment and no one had the right to interfere.

In the prison with Brownfield were murderers, pimps, car thieves, drunkards and innocents, and their sentences bore no set relation to their crimes. A young boy of seventeen was in for stealing hubcaps and his sentence was five years. A hatchet murderer whom Brownfield came to know quite well, who had

163

dispatched not only his wife but his wife's mother and aunt, was paroled after three years. Before he was paroled he was a trustee. Before that he had been able to go out of the prison to attend church every Sunday and to spend a few minutes with his woman whenever the desire arose. He had played poker on weekends with the jailers. There was no order about this, which was why it appealed to Brownfield.

Brownfield brooded, while he worked—setting out dogwoods, magnolias and mimosas on spacious well-tended lawns—on his father's audacity at taking his daughter. He brooded on Grange's serenity and on his prosperity. Although he did not love Grange, he was very often depressed by the thought that his father had never really loved him.

Brownfield learned to read and write rather well while in prison. One day he was looking through the account, on the colored page, of Mem's murder, and he saw his own name. Without knowing what was happening he read the whole article and went on to read other articles. The hatchet murderer, who became his friend, told him that the same thing had happened to him. On the day he was brought to trial, he said, his woman had thrust some newspapers into his hands. Look, she had said, there's your picture! She wanted to cheer him up because she was afraid he was going to be electrocuted. The jailers had taken the papers away before he had a chance to examine them, but later, in jail, his woman brought him some more, to celebrate, she had said, his light sentence. They were both very pleased that there was a picture of him in the paper! He had sat a long time marveling at his big ugly picture in the paper, he said, and then, interested in what the paper might say about him, he began to read it. He could not recall where he learned the ABC's; when he was a child he had owned a tiny children's prayer book, from which his mother had read to him over and over. That had been his entire education, as far as he knew.

The boy who stole the hubcaps had been in high school and read well. Brownfield and the hatchet murderer took lessons from him and called him professor. One day, as Brownfield was writing his name, age and prison number on the margins of a

164

newspaper it struck him suddenly that Mem had actually succeeded in teaching him to read and write and that somehow he had not only forgotten those days with her but had also forgotten what she'd taught him. He wondered about this, staring the while at his hands, then he burst into terrible sobs that tore his chest and brought him to the floor.

But his tears did not soften him, did not make him analyze his life or his crime. His crying was just a part of the life that produced his crime. It only made him feel lonely. Introspection came hard to Brownfield and was therefore given up before he became interested in it. The least deep thinking and he was sure he would be lost. As it was, while in prison, he wanted Josie, he wanted his father, he even wanted his mother. He wanted Ruth. He had a great fear of being alone. He thought he could understand better than any of the other prisoners why God had created the universe when He found himself alone, and fixed it so man had two warm arms and a tongue.

"My daughter," he wrote, in crude spellbound letters. And, "I wish I had got Grange too." He did not hide these words, written on candy wrappers, newspapers and bits of paper from the trash. He left them lying around, clear marks of his existence and his plan.

Brownfield and the hatchet murderer talked sometimes about their motives in life. They watched television every Saturday evening and motives was a new word picked up from the television series, "Dragnet." The motive that got him into prison, said Brownfield, was a keen desire to see if he had any control over himself. No matter which way he wanted to go, he said, some unseen force pushed him in the opposite direction.

"I never did want to be no sharecropper, never did want to work for nobody else, never did want to have white folks where they could poke themselves right into my life and me not have nothing to do with it."

"Yeah, Lawd, and I know what you mean," said the hatchet murderer, who had been a minister before he married one of his converts and started a family. He had discovered too late that he couldn't feed his wife and her kin on what he made off the gospel. Marriage had stripped his nice black suit from him and in its place he had had to make do with overalls caked with sweat and dust he got in fields that would never be his. He knew what his friend was talking about because he had himself struggled against the unseen force. But he had decided the unseen force was God and so killed his wife and her kin. It was his way of leaving God's company.

"I felt just like these words here in the newspaper must feel, all printed up. The line already decided. No moving to the left or the right, like a mule wearing blinders. These words just run one word right behind the other to the end of the page." Brownfield looked at his friend with some small exhilaration in his eyes as he continued, stabbing at the paper with his finger. "Just think how this word here'd feel if it could move right out of this line and set itself down over here!" The two men pondered the power of the mobile, self-determined word. The hatchet murderer nodded.

"I often felt more like a shoe," he said; "a pair of farted-over brogans, just for feets to stand on. I used to put my shoes up on a shelf in the wardrobe to show how I felt. Wouldn't let my wife or her crabby snot-picking ma move 'em down on the floor."

"Yeah," said Brownfield, "you'd think more peoples would think about how they ain't got no more say about what goes on with 'em than a pair of shoes or a little black piece of writing in a newspaper that can't move no matter what it stands for. How come we the only ones that knowed we was men?"

Leaning heavily on his pencil Brownfield wrote m-e-n, then waited glumly for the word to rise and beat its chest.

"Well, that was us," he said. He looked at the hatchet murderer and smiled.

40

It was not difficult for Brownfield to take advantage of Josie's pain. He had been surprised the first time she visited him at the jail, but had soon become able to read her like a book. Josie had given up taking her burdens to the Lord; she no longer sought to confess her sins in church; she no longer said prayers or told her troubles to fortunetellers. But all of this she could do at the jail.

She would come on Sunday afternoons when the prisoners were allowed out under the trees. She would sit on one side of a small table, Brownfield on the other. Over the months and years she poured out the anguish of her heart for Brownfield to hear. And he listened sympathetically, craftily, with a priest's show of concern.

He listened to her complaints of his father's indifference, Grange's total infatuation with the idea of preserving innocence, his blind acceptance of Ruth as something of a miracle, something of immense value to him, to his pride, to his will to live, to his soul.

"He don't even know I'm *alive*," said Josie, wringing her hands. "All day long the two of 'em is together. I just set round, praying for a *word* from him. . . ."

Brownfield listened with a pitying expression on his face. He took one of her hands in his.

"When I get out of here I'll take her off your hands," he promised. But Josie sat up, startled.

"If you took that gal away from him it'd be the same as if you took the air. He wouldn't live out the week! I tell you he *love* her!"

"Josie," he said, "you recognize that you a *fool* for giving a shit whether he live or die?"

"Don't you say that!" she said, drawing her hand from his.

"All right, okay," he said, "don't git your back up." But he was thinking of his father's attachment to Ruth and of how perfect a revenge it would be if he could break it.

Josie was looking at him cautiously. "If you going to talk about your daddy in any mean way, I ain't coming here no more. He *love* me, your daddy do, I *know* he do. This thing with Ruth is something he can't help. But one day he coming to his senses and when he do I'm going to be right there waiting. It ain't like it was *impossible* for him to love us both!"

" 'Spose he don't never come to his senses?" asked Brownfield. *"Then* where will you be?"

Josie looked bleakly out across the yard. "He got to come to me," she said. "He *got* to come."

The months went by. One day Brownfield asked about her love life. Josie, sixtyish, had always felt there would be no end to it. She began to cry.

"Which mean he don't come *near* you no more, even for that?"

Josie nodded.

"You mean to tell me," said Brownfield, "that after all you have did for him he don't show *no* kind of 'preshation?"

He began to smile. A flush came to Josie's cheeks. Before she rushed out of the room she slapped him.

After that it was easy.

"After all I done for him!" Josie began to fume when she talked with him. "He don't pay me the mind you'd pay a *dog.*"

"And you sold everything you owned and worked so *hard* for to buy him his precious *farm!* Uh, uh, uh," said Brownfield. "Some peoples are just not grateful. Now, if *I* had had a woman like that to do all you done for him, I wouldn't be here today." He was elated when Josie, forgetful of everything but her anger, agreed with him. Soon he had brought her back to his original idea.

"When I gets out I can take Ruth off your hands," he said. "An' then, just think, you and Grange'll be alone just like you

168

was before she come. Things'll be *just* the same." Josie nodded eagerly. "I won't even let them *near* one 'nother."

"But how can you 'complish that?" she asked. "Grange'd shoot to kill if you laid a hand on Ruth."

"Grange may think he above all the rest of the white folks," said Brownfield, "but he ain't above the white folks' law. Maybe the law will be on our side for a change. Anyhow, you let *me* worry 'bout that."

"So glad to!" said Josie, smiling happily. Planning as she'd done for years just how to win for good the man she loved.

PART IX

41

"Good fences don't make neighbors," said Grange. "Which is why we's putting this here one up."

Ruth stood beside him holding the hammer. She was barefoot and wearing a pink dress with ruffles at the hem. As Grange stretched the top strand of barbed wire from one post to the next and secured it with a nail, she tiptoed behind him with round watchful eyes befuddled by his activity. She had never seen anyone put up a fence before.

"You finds your stakes—they marks your propity—and going by the deed, you puts your fence square on the line. Then you tightens all your wires," he said, tightening the top wire, "and you be sure all your bobs is good and sharp."

She pricked one finger on a small barb of wire, then gazed intently while the blood welled up. Quickly she stuck the drop of blood against her new dress and her eyes sobered to an ex-

173

pression of remembrance, horror and pain. They appeared to darken, much as the sky, which is open enough until a single cloud puts out the sun.

Grange stopped his work abruptly, not noticing the girl, one might have thought, and placed his own callused finger against a barb, pressing the wire until his finger bled.

"I never did git round to tellin' you 'bout how the Injuns got to be blood brothers with us black peoples," he said, reaching casually for her finger (at which she stared in panic), and which she gave him after first looking to see if she had wiped all the blood away. It was no longer there on her finger tip, but when her grandfather squeezed her finger the dot of blood came back. He drew her down beside him on the grass and stuck their two bleeding fingers together.

"But, Grange," she said scornfully for so young a girl, "they didn't stick *fingers* together. It was *arms,* right here"—she pointed—"they stuck this part of the *arm.*" She placed her tenderer forearm next to his darker, more sinewy one.

"Of course," said Grange, *"that* was the way they become blood brothers with the white folks. But see, they didn't *mean* that. Next thing them white brothers knowed they was scalped —which give 'em some of they own medicine. Now, take with us, they was more au*then*tic. That's on account of us all gitting put in such a pass by the white folks. But with one another and with black folks they only press fingers, not arms, and not no lying wrists never!"

"Are you sure?" she asked. "Or are you lying to me?"

"Don't say words like 'lie' to me in company," Grange said pleasantly. "Folks might think you ain't being raised good."

"Well, nobody's here but me and you. Besides, I don't care what folks think. Anyhow, I don't embarrass you nearly as much 'in company' as you embarrass me with your drinking and gambling away all our money all the time."

"Um, yes," said Grange. "Like I was saying. The Injuns is ever to be your friend. We has just performed the ceremony. . . ."

"But we aren't Injuns, we . . ."

"NO, INDEED. No matter what anybody tells you 'bout the Injuns—I mean I don't care if it is a Injun hisself—don't you believe nothing but that they's friendly Injuns. Even if they don't act friendly. Them that don't act friendly just don't know no better. You can sort of keep your gun trained on them while you explain all this I'm telling you to 'em."

"I don't want to get scalped." She giggled.

"Just remember neither does they. Besides, this here is serious." The old man frowned. "The black man must be friends to every other of the downtrod, especially if he's a man of color."

"There's those poor folks down the road and you putting up a fence to keep them away. Ain't they downtrod? They eat dirt," she said, grimacing. "They ought to be. I don't see what their white has to do with it."

"We has tried with them. They is the onliest group of peoples you can't be blood brothers to. They don't want it and we don't want it either after all these years. They is the reason fences was invented. I mean, take before they come here with all they Bibles, do you think the Injuns had done hogged propity from one another and fenced it all off? No, ma'am. They hadn't. They didn't mind letting folks use the grass and the good earth like the Lawd intended it should be used. Those people over there, you give 'em a chance, they try to take our land, never mind it belong to us. They want hit, they take hit. They been that way since hist'ry. They the cause the fence was invented. Now. Far as we concerned they going to have to learn to live with it . . . and I mean with the sharp bobs turned toward them!"

Grange returned determinedly to his fencing, Ruth watching from under her long grapes. They were bleached brownish by the sun with a yellow lion-colored edge. The rest of her hair had been botchily braided and the grapes had not been worked in and caught up. She thought when she got older she would straighten her hair with combs, if Grange let her. She would convince him that her grapes were too nappy to put up with. The finer points of hair care mystified her almost as much as they did her grandfather, whose only advice to her when she mentioned her hair was to wash it and grease it a little. Sometimes she even wished Josie would help her out. But just to fix her hair, not to talk and lie around the house with her titties hanging out.

"You're a mean 'un, if you ask me," she said lazily, leaning back on her elbows, turning her face to the sun. "Just a mean, mean old man. Without good home training, or somethin'," she murmured, closing her eyes.

He did not look at her, he concentrated on the fence, thrusting the post-hole diggers deeper and deeper into the hard red soil, stringing the wire tighter and tighter, raising the fence higher and higher.

Not far from where he stood there existed still, it seemed to him, at least the shadows of his first life. He was on his third or fourth and final. The first life of Grange Copeland. The glow of the sun enclosed him in a gone but never-to-be forgotten landscape with its immediate sealing-off heat. And again, as in a stifling nightmare, he saw the long rows and wide acres of cotton rising before him. He felt the sun beating down on his bent back, exploding, pounding, bursting against the back of his head through the wide straw hat. He saw Margaret (first life, first wife!) as she had been when they married, seductive and gay, a whimsical girl-lady, acting strong and stoical out of love for him. While the love lasted. He saw the change come as it had occurred in Margaret's face. Gradually the lines had come, the perplexed lines between the eyes, placed as if against and in spite of the young, smooth and carefree brow. Actually she had had a gay but somnolent face then, as if she existed in a dream. Misery had wakened her, and he had not needed to tell her she had married not into ecstasy, but into dread. Not into freedom, but into bondage; not into perpetual love, but into deepening despair. And he had not needed to tell her who was behind their misery—she knew and then he did not—for someone, *something* did stand behind his cruelty to her (he made himself believe), pushing him on to desert her, and driving her down and to the purgation of suicide for herself and murder for her bastard child.

176

What could he tell his granddaughter about her sadly loving, bravely raging and revengeful grandmother?

Could he tell her that the sweaty, unkind years plastered themselves across her lovely face like layers of dull paint put on every year? That sometime, in that hopelessness, when cotton production was all that mattered in their world (and not ever their cotton!), even love had stopped and that soon they had not been able even to *remember* love? Could he tell her of his own degradation, his belief in a manhood devoid of truth and honor; of the way he had kept Josie always tucked away for himself, as men tuck a bottle away against despair or snake bite? Could he tell her that Margaret had thought a marriage finished whoredom for a man; that she had thought Grange's respect for his marriage would put an end to his visits to Josie, the whore of his lusting youth? Could he tell Ruth of her grandmother's bewilderment when she learned he still saw Josie once a week, rarely missing a Saturday night? Could he tell her of how Margaret grappled with his explanation that Josie was necessary for his self-respect, necessary for his feeling of manliness? If I can never own nothing, he had told her, I will have women. I love you, he had assured her, because I trust you to bear and raise my sons; I love Josie because she can have no sons.

He could see Margaret sitting alone in the doorway of their cabin. She would watch him leave in the wagon, rolling determinedly, toward the Dew Drop Inn. Her bewilderment had changed to a feeling of inadequacy and she had tried to play her husband's game. She threw away on other men what she felt her husband did not want. And she had finally bedded down with Shipley, the man who had caused everything. This Grange had not been able to bear. His choice was either kill her or leave her. In the end he had done both.

The strangely calm eyes of the old man looked across the fence to rest on his granddaughter. He marveled that, knowing him so well, she knew nothing of that other life. Or even of the dismal birth of her own father. That gray day of retribution in sorrow when the newly born was sentenced to a familiar death.

177

"And what's *his* name going to be?" he had asked Margaret, feeling no elation at the birth of his son.

In her depression, carelessly she asked him, "What's the first damn thing you see?"

And he, standing before the door, saw the autumnal shades of Georgia cotton fields. "Sort of brownish colored fields," he had answered. And he had wondered, without hope, if that was what covered also the rest of the universe.

"Brownish color," she had said, pushing the sleeping baby from the warm resting at her breast. "Brownish field. Brownfield." There was not even pity in her for her child. "That'll do about as well as King Albert," she said. "It won't make a bit of difference what we name him."

Already she was giving him up to what stood ready to take his life. After only two years of marriage she knew that in her plantation world the mother was second in command, the father having no command at all.

"Grange, save me! Grange, *help* me!" she had cried the first time she had been taken by the first in command. He had plugged his ears with whiskey, telling himself as he ignored her, that he was not to blame for his wife's unforgivable sin. He had blamed Margaret and he had blamed Shipley, all the Shipleys in the world. In Josie's arms he had no longer heard Margaret's cries, no longer considered his wife's lovers who were black; his hatred of Shipley's whiteness had absolved Grange of his own guilt, and his blackness protected him from any feelings of shame that threatened within himself.

His wife had died believing what she had done was sinful and required death, and that what he had done required nothing but that she get out of his life. And now Grange thought with tears in his eyes of what a fool he had been. For, he said to himself, suppose I turned my back on that little motherless girl over there and spent my time with somebody else, some other little girl; would she understand that something *beyond* myself caused it? No, she would not. "And I could parade Shipleys before her from now till doomsday and she'd still want to know what's done happened to her granddaddy's love!" Grange mumbled to

178

himself, his eyes moist and his hands trembling over the wires.

"Looks like some old sad story, from the way you standing there frowning. Wake up!" The child stood beside him with her hand over his arm. "You looking sort of sick from all this heat. I think you better sit down." She pulled him by the suspender strap, like pulling a horse to drink. "Too much sun is not good for old men your age."

"Shet up. What you know 'bout old age? 'Too much sunshine ain't good for ol' men your age!'" he mimicked her, but seated himself in the shade by the fence. "By the time you git ol' enough to have mouthy grandchildren, you know what's good for you. Only by then it seem like too late to do much about it!" Quickly he rolled up his past and lay back on it, obliterating the keen spots, completely erasing the edges. "I never in my life seen such a womanish gal," he said, stretching out with his back to a tree and taking out his pipe. She lit a match, held his fingers while he lit the pipe, then blew it out.

"I ain't any more sassy than you," she said smartly, pushing him over roughly so she could also prop herself against the tree. He almost fell down.

"You ain't supposed to say ain't," he said, looking at her solemnly. ("Her eddication," he was known to declare to odd colleagues and peers, "is where I draws the line!") "And don't say you say hit because *I* say hit. I say hit 'cause I don't know no better. I mean, I *know* hit ain't correct, but I can't always remember what to replace hit with."

"A perfect score of hits!" Ruth shouted, clapping her hands. "You ain't—aren't—supposed to say 'hit' for 'it,' neither. 'It' ain't got no h *in* 'hit.'" She giggled.

"I just wanted to check if you was noticing," he said, fussing with his pipe. "You know the *good* part about owning a fence around propity you also owns is that you gits to shoot down any man or beast that sets foot over your boundaries. They is a law what says you can do that."

"You sure are in a bloodthirsty mood," she said tolerantly, "you *sure* you didn't get too much sun?" She lay drowsily, with her chin against her chest. Idly she thwacked him across the leg with a weed. Her new dress had grass stains on it. She inspected them with concerned attention, then turned humming, blissfully, on her stomach.

"Did I ever thank you properly for this dress?" she asked, looking up into his eyes. Reluctantly, he smiled.

"I winned that dress at the poker game last Saddity. I winned near to twenty dollars, then, dang it, I lost fifteen, and I figured I'd get that dress. I spoke to some of the womens there. I say, what size reckon do my grand girl wear?—and they say, they don't know sizes too good (they mostly steals clothes of all sizes), but they thought a twelve. So I pick that there which are a twelve, and I figured them frills round the tail made hit—it—grown up enough for you. I told the white woman what sold it to me. (She act like she didn't want me to say nothing to her, but I did.) I say, you want you one grown-up adolescent-acting, *spoiled* young 'un, you take my granddaughter. She take all my money to deck herself out. I say, she shore is spoiled all right. I say, she see this dress, and the first thing you know she done got grease on it and out setting round in the dirt in it, then she like to wind up tearing it rat down the mittle if the spirit move her to it. Yes, ma'am, I say, she *rough* stuff! I says to the woman what sold it to me." Grange laughed. "She must didn't '*pre-shate* your fine qualities," he said. "She just stood there looking at me like she thought I'd bite, kind of holding onto her teeth like this." He clamped his lips together and made them prune up.

"You ought to call me by my name instead of 'my grand girl.' No wonder nobody knows what you talking about." She laughed nonchalantly. "Anyway, I ain't any more spoiled than you. *However,* I do thank you for this dress." She decided to use other words she'd learned at school. Grange was a glutton for them. "It is so *pleasant*." She smiled. "It *certainly* is. You know, you have real *excellent* taste!" she deliberately spoke from the back of her mouth, so she would sound like an actress on radio. Her grandfather beamed.

Confusedly, he searched around behind some bushes on his

180

hands and knees, and brought out a pint bottle. "I would offer you some . . ." he began.

". . . but, no thank you," Ruth added. "I'm only ten, and there are some who are concerned about their liver."

"Don't you go upsetting yourself 'bout my liver, it'll keep," the old man said, drinking his whiskey through a chuckle. When the whiskey spilled down his chin, Ruth, who had been flexing her injured finger, and thinking vaguely about Indians, swiped the droplets for her wound. "Antisepsis." She smiled loftily, licking her whole hand.

"Ruth ain't no kind of name for you! Maybe that's why I don't like to use it. . . . You rat out the Bible though, I can guarantee you that much, but it probably one of the parts I ain't read."

"God knows I ain't if you ain't," she said, collecting several whiskey droplets on her tongue.

One day they watched the people who lived on the adjoining property. There was a man who had lank, neck-length hair the color of greasy pine bark. There were half a dozen little cracker children around him. They grew in stairsteps, looked hungry and rusty, and kept straws and pine needles in their teeth. Ruth and Grange lay concealed behind some bushes on their side of the fence. It was Grange's idea that they inspect some "white people" for Ruth's further education. What Ruth noticed was that they were not exactly white, not like a refrigerator, but rather a combination of gray and yellow and pink, with the youngest ones being the pinkest.

"What they doing?" she wanted to know. The daddy of the bunch and two of the older boys lay under a tree, smoking and chewing.

"They probably plotting how to git our land," said Grange.

"Why do you think that?"

"Well, what else do you think they'd be doing, laying over there in the weeds, hiding out from they womenfolks?"

"Well, they could just be trying to get shut of the women's yapping," said Ruth.

"That's just what they'd like for you to believe," said Grange, glowering at the group.

"Do you mean to tell me that that's all they have to do—*all* of them, *all* the time—just lay around and think up ways to take this farm?"

"Yup," said Grange, momentarily peevish.

"Well, when do they talk about the weather, then, and the price of cotton and all like that?" Ruth sat upright and Grange quickly pulled her down again out of sight of the group. "I mean, what I want to know, is did anybody ever try to find out if they's real *people*."

"Nope," said Grange. " 'Course the rumor is that they *is* peoples, but the funny part is why they don't act human."

"Well, when I get big I'm going to find out," Ruth said as they crawled away from the fence. "I want to see and hear them face to face; I don't see no sense in them being looked at like buzzards in a cage."

"All I seem able to teach you is that you want to know," said Grange. "I never seen such a gal as you for looking underneath revealed truth."

Later in the day he asked her, "What would you say if I told you I knows of that family we saw, and that I happens to know the womenfolks don't 'low no smoking nor chewing in they house an' parlor?"

"And that's the reason they sit ganged up in the woods?" Ruth pondered over it a minute. "Well, it makes more sense to me than the other reason did," she said simply, and her grandfather stood exasperated in his truth.

42

One day at school something happened that said more about white people than anything Grange had ever told her. Her day had started out, as usual, reluctantly. She hated getting up in the morning, especially when she woke up in the house: "Josie's house," she called it, instead of in the cabin, which she considered hers and Grange's, but mostly hers. She and Grange had their breakfast, oatmeal and wine for him, oatmeal and milk for her. Then they walked along the highway to the school. The school was only about half a mile from their house, even nearer through the woods, and they could walk it in a few minutes. Grange left her at the steps of the school as he always did, with the other children standing around staring, as *they* always did. It was a bright March day, warm and balmy, and the sun made light shadows on Grange's blue shirt as he disappeared around the back of the school and into the woods. Both of them loved to walk home through the woods, not only because Grange kept a still between the schoolhouse and his house, but because the woods offered the privacy and quiet they both enjoyed.

The school had three rooms. One room on the end near the well was for the first, second and third grades. The middle room was for the fourth, fifth, sixth and seventh grades, and the one on the other end was for the rest of the grades, including the twelfth. The building was raised off the ground on a foundation of cement blocks and underneath was a cellar of sorts where some of the older boys took some of the older girls. There were tall steps at each end of the building as if the schoolrooms formed a second story. Ruth climbed the steps to the platform-porch which led to the middle room with a mixture of anticipation and dread. She was in the sixth grade and her classroom contained classes four through seven. Her teacher was Mrs. Grayson. Mrs. Grayson would also be her teacher for another year until she passed into the room next door and to a teacher named Mrs. Little. Mrs. Grayson was a handsome, dark brown woman with meticulously manicured nails, and processed hair. She was in the habit of wearing everything gray, and of straightening the seams of her Red Foxx stockings with a spit-daubed finger when she thought no one was looking.

The first subject for the four classes was Health, and Mrs. Grayson walked from one group of desks to another lecturing about the care of "our clean minds and bodies." The next subject was Citizenship, and Mrs. Grayson lectured back and forth about the importance of having "forthright patriotic minds for use in service to your country." By ten o'clock, above the bored humming of the other three classes, she was talking about the importance of studying history. History, Mrs. Grayson said loudly and with great precision and straining of her vocal cords, taught you what had gone on in the world. Eli Whitney, the cotton gin, Thomas Jefferson and the Declaration of Independence, George Washington and the Minutemen. American History was more important than any other kind, she said. And why was that? she asked. Then she answered herself: "Because it is the history of you and I, the proud history of a free people! We have fought to remain free," she shouted, her shrill voice reverberating off the pasteboard walls. "Our history teaches us what has been done for us, as Negroes, and what we have done for ourselves." Pearl Harbor, she said, rhetorically, and the Civil War. History, she beamed, struggling to rise above the noise in her room and the noise from the rooms on each side of her, tells us where we are and shows us how we got there and how important history is to the total enlightenment of the world!

She had to leave from in front of their class for a few minutes because someone in the fourth grade raised his hand from the back of the room and said he couldn't hear what she had said. Ruth heard her, like a recording, ask the small boy personally, "Why is it important to study history?" The boy said sullenly, "I don't know." Then Mrs. Grayson said, clapping her hands in time to her words, "Because history lets you know what has gone on in the world!" The boy said, "Oh, yes, ma'am." And Mrs. Grayson was called across the room to someone in the fifth grade who asked wasn't it also true that George Washington was the father of our country. When last Ruth listened Mrs. Grayson was congratulating the child for having already read this from his new history book.

To Ruth, Mrs. Grayson never made sense. She mouthed all the words in the textbooks but they did not come out coherently as they appeared on the page. When she interpreted a paragraph to the class you could never tell how any of it fit together. Between the few words you were able to catch over the noise and Mrs. Grayson's own abstraction there was little that could be gleaned and put to use. However, having had Mrs. Grayson the year before, Ruth feared her for her ability to keep track of who was shutting her out. She could pounce on an unsuspecting dreamer the minute his mind strayed. And then it was a beating or you were sent to the principal for discipline. The principal always sent you home for a week, usually without looking up from his desk or without interrupting a pupil's recitation in his classes.

As she always did when Mrs. Grayson turned her back for a minute, Ruth put on a look of concentration and fiddled intently with the books on her desk. This was her cover while she began to dream. Today she looked at the new world history book the classes had been given that morning. The new book was the main cause of Mrs. Grayson's history lecture. Before they got it from the white school they hadn't had a history book. Only a speller, a geography and a reader. Ruth had read these months before and could recite every one of them by heart because she had read them so many times. Now she looked through the new book, at the pictures, some in color but most in black and white, and at the worn brown cover which had a pretty city scene on it with blond round-eyed children crossing a street under a bridge and across from a towered clock. In small lettering to one side was written "London." But then she opened the cover, not the pages of the book, but the cover, before the pages began. On the righthand side of the book there was another girl's name, Jacqueline Paine, and under her name was written, Baker County Elementary School, the name of the white school. All their books came from there so this did not surprise her. But then she looked down at the rest of the page and gasped. For on this page and across the entire front inside covering of the book was a huge spread drawing called at the top in big green letters, "The Tree of the Family of Man." And on this tree there were all kinds of people. At the top, in pale blue and yellow, there were the white people. Their picture showed them doing something with test tubes, the lettering on one of their jackets said "Scientist." Behind them were drawings of huge tall buildings and cars and trains and airplanes. Jacqueline Paine had written underneath their picture: *Note: Americans, Germans, People who live in the extreme Northern part of Europe.* In parentheses she had written *(England)*. Below the "Americans" were people drawn in yellow, and they were wearing funny little straw hats and were driving huge water buffalo. Behind them were a lot of pretty small objects made of jade and bamboo. Under their picture Jacqueline Paine had written in her round script: *Note: The Yellow Race. Chinese, Japanese, etc., and people who live far away from us, in the Far East.* Beneath them was a drawing in red of American Indians. They were sitting placidly, one old man smoking a long feather-covered pipe. Some women were sitting next to him making beautiful rugs and pottery and baskets. Underneath their picture Jacqueline Paine had written: *Note: Our own American Indians. We saved from disease and wild primitive life. Taught them useful activities as pictured above. They have also been known to make beads.* But it was the last picture she saw on the page that made her gasp. For at the very bottom of the tree, not actually joined to it but emanating from a kind of rootless branch, there was the drawing of a man, in black, with fuzzy hair, fat grinning lips, and a bone sticking through his nose. He was wearing a grass skirt and standing over a pot of boiling water as if he expected, at any moment, a visiting missionary. Underneath his picture Jacqueline Paine, in her neat note-taking script, had written just one descriptive word. She did not even say whether he had made his own grass skirt. It leaped out at Ruth like a slap in the face. *Note: A nigger.*

When she could pull herself out of her daze, dreaming no longer, she knew something was wrong. All the children from all the classes around her were looking at her. Looking at her and snickering. Before her eyes they turned into ugly grinning savages and she gave them her most disdainful scowl. But then she looked up just in time to see the strap coming down across her shoulders. It came down again and again and the snickering was quieted by the strap's thick whistling. They knew what it

186

felt like. Slowly, in a rage, Ruth stood up, flinging the book to the floor. Mrs. Grayson's voice sounded hysterically in her ears. "You're just like the rest of them," she shouted. "You'll never be anybody because you don't pay any attention to anything worthwhile!" Ruth walked slowly toward the front of the room. "Where do you think you're going?" yelled Mrs. Grayson, picking up the history book and dusting it off. "All people like you do is tear up other people's property! You come right back here and sit down!" But Ruth's hand was already on the door. She turned to see Mrs. Grayson advancing with the strap; over her shoulder the delicious excitement of her classmates rose so thick it could be tasted. A pure and simple lust for diversion. A pure and simple lust for blood. Her blood. "You goddam mean evil *stupid* motherfucker!" Ruth hurled at her from her huge stock of Grange-inherited words. Mrs. Grayson and the classes stopped together and took a long indignant breath. "What did you *say,* young lady?" Mrs. Grayson finally demanded, advancing more menacingly than before. "You heard me," Ruth said, trembling. "And if you touch me just one more damn time, my granddaddy and me will pull this piece of junk right down on your head and cram planks and bricks down your lying *dumb* motherfucking throat!" Quickly she pulled open the door and fled down the steps. It was not until she reached the woods that she began to cry, the tears hurting her so much she thought she'd never survive them. "Was this what Grange meant?" she asked herself over and over, wishing she were dead.

The summers offered her shelter. From May until October she was free. Free to play in the cabin they built far back in the woods, free to read comics and books Grange cunningly stole from the white library; and for confusion, she was free to read the Bible's "wherefore, hereat, thereto—lo, lo, lo!" The winters were cold and cruel, and although she loved learning she hated school. When she had lived with Mem it had not been bad at all. It had even been fun. She and Ornette and Daphne had walked to school together, laughing and gossiping, sometimes throwing sand at the white school buses that passed them. But now her mother was dead and her father was in prison. Where exactly "in the North" her sisters were remained a mystery. She could not imagine the North except as an enormous cold place full of buildings and people where birds had no place to move their bowels. This picture she got from Grange who said you could take the North and make the Southerners eat it without sauce for all he cared.

As painful as it was to her to have to admit it, she was considered a curiosity after her mother's death and though all the children at the school were poor she was considered the poorest because her father was a murderer and she had no mother. Mothers, she learned very soon, were a premium commodity among her classmates, many of whom had never known a father and if they had could no longer even remember him. She got no consideration either for living with her grandfather, who was believed to be a strange, "funny" old man. Good at cards he was, the children admitted, but too quiet to be trusted, they said. Had anybody ever heard Grange Copeland laugh at one of their fathers' jokes? they asked. Nobody had, except Ruth, and her classmates did not admire her for it. At times she was sorry she giggled in church with Grange, the community being such a pious, scorekeeping one.

Snubbed and teased she was from the month she went to live with Grange, and it became almost like a game. Children would be playing "Sally Go Round the Sunshine" or "Hey, Miss Liza Jane" and she had only to show her composed melancholy face for all merriment to cease and a harsh silence to fall. There was a rumor going around the school when she was eleven that if she ever got anybody to walk with her in the woods (she was often seen walking in the woods and talking to bushes and that was certainly odd) he would never be seen alive again. They said she had a gun that she kept hidden in the woods and that she used to shoot people's heads off so she wouldn't have to see their eyes. Eyes, they said, reminded her of her mother. Ruth knew, when she overheard this rumor, that whoever started it must have been at Mem's funeral and seen the botched up job of the undertaker. But what could she say? Her only delightful times were when new children who didn't know the story came to the school or when she discovered by accident old ones who had either missed the gossip or not been able to attend the funeral. She was not the only one gossiped about. Josie came in for heavy slander too, as did everyone in the family. By the time she was in the fourth grade Ruth had begun to walk with her head down; she brought it up gradually during the fifth grade, and by the time she reached the sixth grade it was said of her that she didn't even know she had a head, it was stuck so far up in the clouds.

As she grew older, she was even more ostracized and neglected. By the time she was thirteen everybody knew she was the daughter of a murderer (and it was not just that he was a murderer that they minded—many of their own relatives had killed—but for a father to kill a mother was a thought that shook them) and although the overt harassment had gone— nobody taunted her any more—the tension remained. Then her father was released from prison, and was seen in town. The same week he was released Josie left the house she shared with Ruth and Grange and went to live with him. A fresh wave of gossip and ridicule swept through the school. Before they had teased her and shunned her for being the daughter of a murderer, now they taunted her for being the "wife" of her grandfather, who was so different from their own palsied and placid progenitors. The day after Josie left she must have done a lot of blabbing in curious ears, for the rumor was that Grange preferred his granddaughter to his wife and so she had left the two of them to the uninterrupted enjoyment of each other. Josie made their cabin, which Grange had built only as a playhouse for Ruth, sound indecent. She just had no idea what *really* went on down there between them, Josie was heard to say. Her classmates shied away from Ruth more obviously than ever, in a derisive, suspicious way.

Rossel Pascal was the only person at school she liked, and Rossel had never spoken to her. A brooding, beautiful girl with satiny skin and dark curly hair, Rossel was the only child of an

189

alcoholic father. He never recovered from his wife's death, people said, and, unfortunately, they also whispered, his wife had not been worth such bother. The teachers regarded Rossel with a distinct chilliness, which aroused Ruth's fury and compassion, though Rossel herself never seemed to notice.

Rossel was in the twelfth grade when Ruth learned she planned to marry Walt Terrell. Walt was the richest black man in the county. He had returned a hero from World War II, with the remains of bullets in his legs and a chest full of carefully polished medals which he wore, at the drop of a hat, on any auspicious occasion, and even to Sunday School barbecues. The school was named after him, as it stood on his property, and everybody respected him. The schoolteachers fawned on him. Still, he was old, as old as her father, Ruth thought. Why would Rossel, who was no more than sixteen, marry him?

At the graduation ceremonies Ruth watched as Rossel stood beside her future husband. Rossel's father stood close by, pale and abstracted, clearly not sober. Other people walked about and spoke, but he seemed to drift, like a chip, through the bright stream of Sunday dresses and children's voices. When his daughter's name was called his eyes brightened for a moment. Sitting beside Walt, who towered over him with his thick head and great shoulders, in that instant Rossel's father came alive. When Rossel sat down again with them she looked as if she might like to fling herself into her father's arms. Father and daughter gazed at each other with eyes like closing doors.

"Rossel," Ruth said impulsively, as they walked carefully down the high school steps, "can I talk to you?"

"Sure you can," said Rossel, deliberately careless and cool.

They walked away from the men as if disengaging themselves from a battalion of soldiers. Ruth looked behind her and saw Grange holding forth with some of the men. Whenever she walked away from him and looked at him like a stranger he seemed grotesque, his long frame gangly, his hair bushy in a style that went out with Frederick Douglass, his hands doing a wild emphatic dance in the air between him and whomever he spoke to.

190

"You're Mrs. Grange," Rossel said, and immediately Ruth felt an unbearable hurt, as if she had taken her cares to the Lord and he had asked if she was bringing his laundry. Rossel was smiling brightly, as if at her own drawl, which was an amusing one. Ruth herself spoke without an accent, at least she thought she spoke without one, even though she'd heard nobody talk in real life but Southerners. She did not know why she didn't sound more like them. It was true her mind tended to blot out or change to something fine and imaginative whatever Southerners said. That included everybody, except Grange, whose speech she found colorful and strong. But Rossel spoke just like a Southern white woman, with the same careless softness. And on her too the accent sounded charming and dumb. When the other children called her "Mrs. Grange," Ruth got angry, but with Rossel she felt only hurt.

"My name's Ruth," she said.

"I know," said Rossel.

They stood under some trees at the edge of the schoolyard. Behind them was the girls' outhouse, at the far side of the yard was the well. Several small children were waiting their turn for the dipper that was being passed around. A bigger boy stood by patiently, his hand holding the rope that held the big wooden bucket from which droplets of water fell and spattered on the ground.

"By the time you're old as me," said Rossel, "you won't have to drink water from that dirty old well. You all can throw away that mossy bucket and that *slith*ery communal dipper! That's gonna be progress—an' just a scant fifteen years behind the white folks."

Ruth did not know what to say. She hated drinking from the dipper too, but hadn't heard anybody say one day they wouldn't have to. Rossel's face was grim as she looked out toward the highway. Cars full of white people passed by without slowing down. There was no sign indicating that a school was near, and children who had to cross the highway did so at a run. A boy had been killed trying to get across the road, and the state of

191

Georgia had put up a white wooden cross as a "death" marker for motorists, but had not thought to put up a warning sign.

Rossel was plainly bored; she looked questioningly at Ruth. It took all Ruth's courage to ask her what she had drawn her aside to ask.

"Why you going to marry *him?*" she managed to blurt out finally.

"Why not?" Rossel asked indifferently. "I'd rather marry the devil than get stuck with any of the stinking jobs they give you round this town."

"Jobs?" asked Ruth. Her idea of marriage romantically included love. But she tried to imagine Rossel as a short-order cook in a hash house. Rossel was too lovely. She tried to see her as some woman's maid. Rossel was too close to needing a maid herself. Rossel was not meant to be among the wretched of the earth, and Rossel apparently knew it.

She wanted very much to hug Rossel. But how could she hug somebody so cold, so indifferent, so unfeelingly beautiful, such a *grim* girl? Instead Ruth burst into tears, and it was Rossel who hugged her.

"Don't cry over it," Rossel said, her voice strange and thin and bleak. "Maybe someday we'll both understand why marrying him is supposed to be so much better." For a moment they clung together and then Rossel was gone, her face calm, set, resolute; the face, Ruth thought, of a doll. A face without anything but confidence in its own empty perfection.

It was a long time before she saw Rossel again, a whole year. It was at the funeral of Rossel's father, who had frozen to death in the cemetery on top of his wife's grave slab. Rossel was richly robed in black and looked like a stricken queen. She had grown older in that year, and, apparently, more devoted to her husband, for she leaned within the protection of his arms with the abandoned dependency of a child. And Walt, through his perpetually dull and military exterior, seemed to beam with pride and accomplishment.

43

One day the question of what her future was to be loomed very large. It was the day her body decided it was ready for a future and she knew she was not. She felt tightened and compressed by panic. Grange had bought her napkins, a belt, and a lovely talc that smelled like a warm rose. He was excited and troubled over what he would say to her about such an unplanned for, though not unexpected, development. However, she was too well read to make him struggle with her enlightenment. What scared her was that she felt her woman's body made her defenseless. She felt it could now be had and made to conceive something she didn't want, against her will, and her mind could do nothing to stop it. She was deathly afraid of being, as she put it, "had," as young girls were every day, and trapped in a condition that could only worsen. She was not yet at a stage where the prospect of a man and marriage could be contemplated with equanimity.

"What *am* I going to do when I get grown?" she asked her grandfather with some alarm.

"What you mean? We got this farm. We can stay here till kingdom come."

She looked at Grange's patch of cotton that was so lovely under the moon. There was a garden and chickens and pigs. The life would be perfect for a recluse.

"I'm not going to be a hermit," she said. "I want to get away from here someday. Meaning no offense to your farm, of course. You know, I think maybe I'll go North, like you did; I want to see New York, 125th Street, all those night clubs and people standing around cussin' in public."

"I won't let you," said Grange sternly.

"I wouldn't try to go while *you* were here," she said, as if he should be ashamed to imagine such a thing.

"I still don't want you to go up there, it's cold as a witch's titty, and nasty, and the people speak to you funny."

"You told me all that. But what would I do down here? I *could* take over Sister Madelaine's job, except she's still on it, old as she is. As a matter of fact, I suspect that's what you'd want me to do, turn myself into a fortuneteller and scare the hell out of unbelieving white ladies. But I don't think I'm cut out for digging up roots and nailing feces into trees! Ugh! Maybe I could teach down the road with Mrs. Grayson; two dumdums together. But I wouldn't have the nerve to stand in front of those children knowing they can't hear a word I'm saying. Besides, I despise Mrs. Grayson too much to subject her to the pleasure of my company."

"You smarter than her," said Grange. "You read enough stuff to know what to teach anybody."

"Being smarter than Mrs. Grayson would be my greatest liability. She'd come up behind me one day and push me in the well. Mean old bitch!"

"You don't need to get excited. She got her orders from me not to get rough with you no more. I told her I'd wring her neck till her eyes wall. Her husband's too."

Ruth sighed. "What is left!" She ran into her room and brought out the newspaper. Turning to the want ads she read: " 'Wanted: Beautiful Southern Belle type with charming, winning manner for job as receptionist in law firm.' " There was only one law firm in town and it was white. "My charm probably wouldn't be up to it anyway," muttered Ruth, continuing to read: " 'Wanted: WHITE LADIES—to fill vacancies in sewing plant. New plant recently revitalized and under new management needs seamstresses to make overalls. Will train.' Blah," she said. In the colored section of the want ads there was only one opening for "middle-aged colored woman to do light domestic work evenings with some light ironing and cooking. $6.00 per week." Ruth put down the paper and looked at Grange.

"You know I ain't going to be nobody's cook, don't you?"

"You ain't," he agreed.

"Well, what do you suggest I do when I'm grown? There

wasn't but one Walt Terrell," she added bitterly, "and Rossel got him!"

"You won't sell yourself; don't even get that thought in your head. Maybe something'll turn up. Things change," he said, without much conviction. "Presidents change—we get some that help us sometime. Roosevelt, you don't remember him, but he once had Booker T. Washington to lunch in the White House. The rest of us was starving, but it seemed to help us some then. And today there's Eisenhower, as wishy-washy a lookin' rattler as ever was, but the court been tellin' everybody that the black schools ain't up to the white 'n they say he's back of it."

"Meantime our school is hanging together by sheer inadequacy."

"Don't interrup' me. What I know, and I reckon the *most* I know is that people change. That is the main reason not to give up on them. Why, if you had knowed me when I was a young blade, drinking and fighting and beating your grandma, you'd a give up on me. Sure, you would. You ain't long on patience. *But,* now, you didn't give up (mainly because you wa'n't born or thought of then) and here you see me tamed and fairly civilized, taking my drinks for stomach's sake, like a gentleman, toiling in the fields for just one gal, and bringing home all my money. And don't you forget, there have always been black folks fighting for better. Maybe their ranks will swell till they include everybody. I don't know how it can be done—I never *seen* such a sorry passel of niggers as in your daddy's generation —but with the right change and some kind of leader it can be.

"There was a time I didn't own my life and then there was a time I didn't care if I lost it when I had it, long as I took a dozen or so white folks with me. I'm still inclined to believe that that *was* my finest hour. But then I came back here, sick of feeling that way and seeing all the rest of our folks standing around praying. And the Lord or something dropped you in my lap. A voice said to me you stop that cuttin' up, Nig, here is a reason to get yourself together and hold on.

"When I die this farm ain't going to be nobody's but yours. I done paid for it with every trick I had. The fence we put up

195

around it will enclose freedom you can be sure of, long as you ain't scared of holding the gun. The gun is important. For I don't know that love works on everybody. A little love, a little buckshot, that's how I'd say handle yourself.

"Anyway, you might as well know I don't care much for nobody except you. I 'member when I was a churchgoer proper, I tried to feel something real big, something that would make me love the whole world. But I just couldn't come at that feeling no kind of way. Your grandma and me was fighting a heap then over one thing and another; and I think we scrappled so much because she *could* love all sorts of folks she didn't have no business.

"The white folks hated me and I hated myself until I started hating them in return and loving myself. Then I tried just loving me, and then you, and *ignoring* them much as I could. You're special to me because you're a part of me; a part of me I didn't even used to want. I want you to go on a long time, have a heap of children. Let them know what you made me see, that it ain't no use in seeing at all, if you don't see *straight!*"

"And all from behind a fence?" Ruth looked doubtful. "I'd be bored stiff waiting for black folks to rise up so I could join them. Since I'm already ready to rise up and they ain't, it seems to me I should rise up first and let them follow me."

"What that takes I'm afraid you ain't ready yet to give. How many black folks would you say you really know—I mean that would rise without squawking?" he asked. "And how many white?"

She counted the black ones on three fingers, only one an old warrior, the white ones not at all.

44

After Josie left, the house gradually took on the charm of the cabin, the charm of peace, of quiet and of the pursuit of interesting contentment thoroughly enjoyed. Together Grange and Ruth experimented with the beautiful in rugs, curtains, pictures and pillow covers. Ruth's room was a veritable sun of brightness and yellow and white. For her bed she made a quilt of yellow-and-white cotton and her curtains were white-dotted Swiss which she could just see through. Her desk, facing the woods, was littered with books. She liked mythology, the Brontë sisters, Thomas Hardy, any romantic writer. If she had been shipwrecked on a deserted island she would have taken *Jane Eyre,* a pocket thesaurus she had, all her books about Africa. She would have taken her maps of the continents, everything she owned by Charles Dickens, plenty of paper and a stock of pencils. She would have left on her desk her red-covered Bible, which Grange had lifted from a cart that stood outside a motel room, her big dictionary, which he got for her she knew not how, and which would have been too heavy, and her copy of Miss Vanderbilt's *Etiquette,* which she ignored as much as she could without making her grandfather feel like a fool for getting it for her. Of her clothes she would have taken her two pairs of dungarees and plaid shirts, her winter boots, her red woollen jacket and probably one dress. She would have taken her locket picture of Mem, which had been a present from Grange on her fourteenth birthday. In the picture Mem was a harried hopeful young wife with one child. She looked out of the little locket with calm, disbelieving eyes.

Grange's room was all in brown and red and blue and black. His room was a part of him and was filled with his smell, of tobacco and hay and, lightly, orange wine. When he was seated by the fire, his brown brogans rested against the brown stones of his fireplace, and his red flannel underwear, as it hung over his rocker, complemented the red among the blue in the quilt on his bed. During three-fourths of the year there were flowers in every room of the house, in the two bedrooms as well as the kitchen, and of course in the "front" room, where their few visitors were allowed to sit themselves down and partake of a sip of iris root or sassafras tea.

"What *is* this stuff?" the boldest of their guests would ask, recalling perhaps some uncharitable comment made by himself or others regarding the oddness of his hosts.

"This is the tea of survival," Ruth would say, with a wink at her grandfather, who sat silently smoking, ignoring the guest except to comment, "She give it to you, you better drink it," and seeming entirely comfortable before ill-at-ease company who invariably visited out of curiosity.

"How you know?" they sometimes asked defensively.

"I told her," would come the indifferent assertion from Grange, with whom no one ever gathered up the nerve to argue.

The older Grange got the more serene and flatly sure of his mission he became. His one duty in the world was to prepare Ruth for some great and herculean task, some magnificent and deadly struggle, some harsh and foreboding reality. Nothing moved him to repent of his independent method of raising her. In vain did deacons of the church admonish him for teaching Ruth to avoid the caresses of pious sisters and to shun the embraces of baptizing brothers. In vain did preachers and missionaries warn him of the heathenism of her young soul. It was commonly supposed that Ruth was even taught to bite the hand that would spiritually feed her, and this supposition was correct.

"Before you let 'em baptize you in they muddy creeks an' waterholes, after I'm gone, you kick the legs out from under 'em and leave 'em drown." To that purpose he hired a poor white lad to teach her to swim.

"The shackles of the slave have one end tied to every rock and bush," he said to her. "Before you let some angel-distracted

198

deacon put his mitts on you, you git you a good grip on his evangelical ear and you stretch it till his nose slides."

And if the various congregations believed the spirit of the devil had already entered young Ruth Copeland, her ready adoption of Grange's teachings more than proved their point. They noted with shock that her greatest delight, along with her grandfather, when they came to church, was to giggle in serious places.

PART X

45

Several times after Josie began living with Brownfield, Ruth saw them loitering in the woods behind the school. Her classmates ran from her father, some of them jeered. Josie, whitely powdered and haphazardly wigged, would stand beside him supporting his drunken weight with a patient, long-suffering look that totally mystified Ruth. It was Grange's custom, particularly on overcast days, to pick her up at the school well, and if not there at the small wooden powerhouse on the edge of the playground. One day they faced a confrontation with Brownfield and Josie. On that day they had indeed strolled along the edge of the school grounds like lovers, Grange carefully tucking her scarf around her neck every few steps. They were murmuring and giggling about the black janitor at the white library in town, whom Grange managed to get drunk each time he went to the library to steal books for her. They did not see Brownfield and Josie until they almost bumped into them.

"Well, if it ain't the Gold Dust Twins," said Josie, insolently, eying their closely knit fingers. For the first time Ruth was chilled by the naked jealousy she read in her stepgrandmother's eyes.

"Yeah," said Brownfield, who kept a proprietary hand on his stepmother's shoulder, "goddam Gold Dust Twins. Out just taking the goddam air!" He rubbed the palm of one hand boldly down the front of his pants.

Ruth was startled and became hysterically baffled, pressing herself into her grandfather's side and trying to walk past without seeing them. For although she had glimpsed her father's profile from her classroom window she had been able to convince herself that he was not real, that he was at most a shadow from a very painful past and a shadow that could never gain flesh and speak to her. The drunken tones of his voice brought back a terror she had tried hard to forget.

"Well, well," said Grange. "My wife and my son." His eyes when Ruth looked up at him were a kind of flinty brown, almost black, and his skin seemed to have aged and become ashen and papery. It was one of the few times she thought of him as being old, one of the few times she thought it might be possible after all for him to declare he'd had enough of everything and die. That day he was wearing his overalls and brogans but with his old Sunday gabardine overcoat. It was very soft against her face, and it surprised her that her face reached all the way to his shoulder. "What do you want?" he asked the leering pair, a slight quaver in his voice.

"I want my goddam daughter!" said Brownfield. "She don't belong to you. She belong to me and I want her."

"Yes," said Josie, pushing out her still incredible bosom, "she's his child and he wants her. It ain't decent for just a old man like you to try to take care of a little girl." She turned to Brownfield for support, but he, while staring at Ruth, seemed to lapse into a trance. His daughter shivered under his dull incredulous stare. She had never considered that as a big girl she might look more than a little like her mother.

"I don't know why they give you only seven years," her grandfather said in a firm voice, drawing himself up. "They ought to have kept you in the pen."

"But she *are* his child!" said Josie, trying to laugh but seeming frantically close to tears.

"Shet up," Grange said, without looking at her. "I guess you intend to be a good mother to her?"

"Well, no," said Josie, nervously reaching out to touch her husband and then succumbing to coyness. "If she go back to her daddy I'll come back to you." This jerked Brownfield out of his trance and he gave her a dangerous smirk. Ruth thought she saw Josie wince as if preparing to move away from a blow. That tremor was too much for her and Ruth began to cry. She threw herself into her grandfather's arms, trembling uncontrollably.

"I don't want you back, you distant strumpet, let the evil that men do go before them, which is what happened in your case. I wish I never had laid eyes on you." Then he turned fiery eyes on his son.

"I took this child when you had made her an orphan. You killed her ma. Where was you all these years when she needed a daddy? Nowhere to be found! You wasn't to be found even when you lived under the same roof with her, except in a whiskey bottle. And then you was in the pen for killing the only decent thing you ever had. I don't know how you prevailed on the white folks to let you out so quick, for you ain't repented; although we know they don't give a damn *no*how as long as all we kill is another nigger! You made a bargain," he said, turning to Josie, who had begun to weep, streaking her face powder, "you stick to it. If you thought you could humble me by running off with my son you was wrong. You're two of a kind; wallow in the mud together!"

"Don't be so *hard*, Grange," wept Josie. *"Don't be so hard!"*

"He thinks I ought not have run out on him a long time ago," said Grange, ignoring Josie, "and he's right. But I tried to make up and he wouldn't let me. And *he* run out on this child. Now he won't get her back, I don't care what he do. He won't!"

"Grange, I *tried*—" Josie began, but Brownfield cut her off.

"Don't beg for nothing from him, he so damn righteous he ain't going to hear you. But *you was no daddy to me!*" he said to Grange, "and I ain't going to let you keep my child to make up for it!"

"You no-good rascal!" said Grange, pushing Ruth away from him, lifting his fists. "You say one more word—"

"You wasn't no daddy to *me!*" Brownfield shouted, but made no move to get nearer his father's fists.

"Grange," said Josie, "your son *love* you. He done told me all about how it was. You walked out on him and then look like everywhere he turn the white folks was just pushing him down in the mud. You know how it is," she pleaded. "They just made him do things when he didn't *mean* them."

For a moment Grange was too choked with disgust to speak. When he did, he turned to Ruth. "Your daddy's done taught me something I didn't know about blame and guilt," he said. "You see, I figured he could blame a good part of his life on me; I didn't offer him no directions and, he thought, no love. But when he become a man himself, with his own opportunity to righten the wrong I done him by being good to his own children, he had a chance to become a real man, a daddy in his own right. That was the time he should of just forgot about what I done to him—and to his ma. But he messed up with his children, his wife and his home, and never yet blamed hisself. And never blaming hisself done made him *weak*. He no longer have to think beyond me and the white folks to get to the root of *all* his problems. Damn, if thinking like that ain't made *noodles* out of his brains."

"Why," said Brownfield, "you old bastard!"

Josie had pulled out a handkerchief too small for her. She soon watered it through with tears. "Grange," she said, dabbing at her eyes with the small wet ball, "you know you got some blame; which, actually, you always did admit—"

"Shut up," said Brownfield.

206

"—and you know you used to blame the white folks too. For they *is* the cause of all the dirt we have to swallow. . . ."

"Every bit," said Brownfield.

Grange continued to speak to Ruth, his shoulder to Brownfield and Josie. He spoke rapidly, breathlessly, his hands doing their jabbing dance.

"By George, I *know* the danger of putting all the blame on somebody else for the mess you make out of your life. I fell into the trap myself! And I'm bound to believe that that's the way the white folks can corrupt you even when you done held up before. 'Cause when they got you thinking that they're to blame for *every*thing they have you thinking they's some kind of gods! You can't do nothing wrong without them being behind it. You gits just as weak as water, no feeling of doing *nothing* yourself. Then you begins to think up evil and begins to destroy everybody around you, and you blames it on the crackers. *Shit!* Nobody's as powerful as we make them out to be. We got our own *souls,* don't we?"

"For a old man what could eat ten of 'em for breakfast, from what Josie tells me, you sure done turned into a cracker lover!" said Brownfield.

"I don't love but one somebody, black *or* white," said Grange, turning briefly to his son. "An' what I'm talking about ain't love but being a man!" He turned once more to Ruth. "I mean," he said, "the crackers could make me run away from my wife, but where was the *man* in me that let me sneak off, never telling her nothing about where I was going, never telling her I forgave her, never telling her how wrong I was myself?"

"You never cared nothing for my ma!" said Brownfield.

"And the white folks could have forced me to believe fuck-ing a hundred strumpets was a sign of my manhood," said Grange, "but where was the *man* in me that let me take Josie here for such a cheap and low-down ride, when I didn't never care whether she lived or died, long as she did what I told her and I got me my farm!"

"Ah, Grange, baby," said Josie, reaching out to him, "it not too late for us now, don't say that."

"Will you shut your slutty trap!" said Brownfield, pushing at her hand.

"And with your pa," Grange continued, "the white folks could have forced him to live in shacks; they might have even forced him to beat his wife and children like they was dogs, so he could keep on feeling something less than shit. But where was the *man* in him that let Brownfield *kill* his wife? What cracker pulled the trigger? And if a cracker did cause him to kill his wife, Brownfield should have turned the gun on himself, for he wasn't no man. He *let* the cracker hold the gun, because he was too weak to distinguish that cracker's will from his! The same was true of me. We both of us jumped our responsibility, and without facing up to at least *some* of his wrong a man loses his muscle."

Grange's eyes were misty now; he turned to face his son. "If I had my life to live over," he said, "your ma and me would maybe have starved to death in some cracker's gutter, but she would have *died* with me holding her hand! For that much I *could* have done—and I believe she would have seen the man in me."

Grange was shaking as much as his granddaughter, and this unsteadiness where he had always seen strength, emboldened Brownfield.

"You kinky-haired son of a bitch," said Brownfield, who was annoyed that his father wore his hair long, "a heap of good it would have done my ma for you to hold her hand when she was dying! When a man's starving he don't *need* none of that *hand*-holding shit."

"But my answering for everything had to be to her, don't you understand yet how it go? Nobody give a damn for me but your ma, and I messed her up trying to be a big man! After two years of never gitting nothing on the plantation I turned my back on what I did have. I just couldn't face up to never making no progress. All I'm saying, Brownfield," said Grange, his voice sinking to a whisper, "is that one day I had to look back on my life and see where *I* went wrong, and when I did look back I found out your ma'd be alive today if I hadn't just as good as shot her to death, same as you done your wife. We *guilty*, Brownfield, and neither one of us is going to move a step in the right direction until we admit it."

"I don't have to admit a damn thing to you," said Brownfield, "and I ain't about to let the crackers off the hook for what they done to my life!"

"I'm talking to *you*, Brownfield," said Grange, "and most of what I'm saying is *you got to hold tight a place in you where they can't come.* You can't take this young girl here and make her wish she was dead just to git back at some white folks that you don't even *know*. We keep killing ourselves for peoples that don't even mean nothing *to* us!"

"The court say I can have her back. Old man, I'll fight you on it! I wanted to give you a chance at a fair exchange, your old lady for her." He reached out to touch Ruth and she shied miserably away. "Too good for me, is you?" he wanted to know, scowling at her. Throughout this ghastly interview she had not been able to say a word. She wanted to tell Brownfield how she despised him for killing Mem and for making her suffer by being shunned and friendless, but nothing came out. She was too terrified that somehow he would make good his threat and she would be forced to leave Grange and go live with him.

"He'll never have you again," Grange said, as Josie and Brownfield stalked away. But he was holding his heart as if it hurt him, and the look he gave her was unsure.

In tears they stumbled home through the woods, where they collapsed momentarily together. They sobbed as if they knew already what was to come; and just as Ruth could finally envision a time when Grange would not be with her, she knew Grange was imagining a time when his powers of protection and love would be no more and she would be left again an orphan with a beast for a father—a beast Grange himself had created.

That night Grange pored over Ruth's Bible for hours before he went to bed. He had great admiration for the Hebrew children who fled from Egypt land. For perhaps the hundredth time he told Ruth the story of the Hebrew exodus.

"They done the right thing," he said.

"Did they?"

"Got out while they still had some sense and cared what happened to they spirit. Also to one 'nother. I may be wrong, but nothing ain't proved it yet." He looked thoughtfully over the book at the fire.

"What?" asked Ruth.

"We can't live here free and easy and at home. We going crazy."

"Here?"

"I don't mean this farm; I mean in this country, the U.S. I believe we got to leave this place if we 'spect to survive. All this struggle to keep human where for years nobody knowed what human was but you. It's killing us. They's more ways to git rid of people than with guns. We make good songs and asylum cases."

"Maybe it would be better if something happened to change everything; made everything equal; made us feel *at home,*" said Ruth.

"They can't undo what they done and we can't forget it or forgive."

"Is it so hard to forgive 'em if they don't do bad things no more?"

"I honestly don't believe they *can* stop," said Grange, "not as a group anyhow." He lounged back in his chair and stuck a hand in his pocket. "Even if they could," he said slowly, "it'd be too late. I look in my heart for forgiveness and it just ain't there. The close as I can come to it is a kind of numbness where they concerned. So that I wouldn't add kindling to a fire that was roasting them, but I wouldn't hear 'em calling me neither."

Ruth chuckled.

"That ain't no feeling to be proud of," Grange said sternly, "not if you going to call yourself a human." He leaned forward, looking sadly into the fire.

"When I was a child," he said, "I used to cry if somebody killed a ant. As I look back on it now, I *liked* feeling that way. I don't *want* to set here now *numb* to half the peoples in the

210

world. I feel like something soft and warm an' delicate an' sort of *shy* has just been burned right out of me."

"Numbness is probably better than hate," said Ruth gently. She had never seen her grandfather so anguished.

"The trouble with numbness," said Grange, as if he'd thought over it for a long time, "is that it spreads to all your organs, mainly the heart. Pretty soon after I don't hear the white folks crying for help I don't hear the black." He looked at Ruth. "Maybe I don't even hear you."

"You'd hear me all right!" said Ruth.

"Your daddy don't, do he?" asked Grange, returning to the story of the Hebrew children.

"*'If the foundations be destroyed,'*" he read after a few minutes, "*'what can the righteous do?'*"

"Rebuild 'em?" asked Ruth.

"Too late to rebuild," said Grange, "for the righteous was there when they was destroyed." He turned to another part of the Bible and read: "*'Thou hath repaid me evil for good to the spoiling of my soul.'*" He looked up at Ruth. "The Lord knowed that you could dump shit on a fellow for just so long before he begin to stink from with*in*. It's the spoiling of the soul that make forgiveness impossible. It just ain't *in* us no more," he said with a sigh. "How can the young 'uns stay fresh here? *That's* what got *me* bothered."

"It'll be okay," said Ruth, taking the Bible from him and putting it away. "For a man who don't like church, you sure like to thumb this book."

"This is serious business, though," said Grange, looking steadily at her. "You been protected on this farm. . . . You don't know how *tired* you be after years of strugglin'. I want you to fight 'em every step of the way when they tries to abuse you. An' they *will*, 'cause you'll be a nigger to 'em. Damn! I hates they guts already for making you feel bad! But I don't want you to fight 'em until you gits completely fagged so that you turns into a black cracker yourself! For then they bondage over you is complete. I'd want you to git out before that happened to you!"

211

"Why didn't *you* get out?" asked Ruth.

"The world wasn't as big then as it is now. I thought the U.S. covered the whole shebang. Besides," said Grange, grimly, I wouldn't give the mothers the satisfaction!"

"Aw," said Ruth, standing behind him and tugging playfully at his big ears, "you know you caught your soul in the nick of time, before it spoilt completely."

"I wish I *did* know that," said Grange, rising to wind the clock, "but I look at Brownfield and Josie an' I know I was *way* too slow."

In the middle of the night Ruth was awakened by a noise.

"You 'sleep?" her grandfather asked. He was standing over the bed. "I couldn't git off to sleep. I just kept thinkin' about what happened today."

Ruth sat up and turned on the light. Grange was standing in his long nightshirt, with a stocking cap on his head. "What's the matter?" she asked sleepily.

"I wanted to give you this," said Grange, handing her a small booklet.

"What is it?"

"A bankbook. I put away a few dollars for you to go to college on. Your daddy's up to something an' I don't know how long I can keep 'im away from you."

Ruth rubbed her eyes and opened the bankbook. Her name and Grange's were on the inside. There were nine hundred dollars.

"That's just from the bootlegging," he said. He went back into his room and returned with a battered cigar box that rattled and clinked. He opened it and began to count the bills and quarters, half dollars and dimes, nickels and pennies. He counted out four hundred dollars and then took twenty dollars and some change for himself. "An' this much I winned at poker." He'd gambled almost every week since she came to live with him. Ruth took the cigar box and eased it down under her bed.

"You put it in the bank tomorrow," Grange said.

212

"Okay," she promised lightly, though she felt tears rising in her throat.

"I beat all my old gambling partners so bad I made 'em make over they straight life policies to you too," said Grange, holding his little bit of money in one hand and shyly holding his nightshirt away from his body with the other. "I figure if they starts to die at the rate of one a year after the next few years they money can keep you comfortable. I know a girl in college need things."

"I couldn't do that!" said Ruth. "What about their own children? They going to need things too!"

"Well, that's left up to you. If you needs the money it yours, I winned it." He was silent for a minute, looking at the floor. "You don't think I done wrong to do that, do you?" he asked. He looked down at the bills in his hand. "I s'pose it *wasn't* too *hu*man of me."

"I don't blame you," she said quickly. "I know you did it for me. But I won't need it with all this you already gave me! Don't be so worried about anything happening," she added, reaching out to touch his hand. "Brownfield's probably so drunk by now he can't even remember I *am* his daughter!"

"You go to the bank first thing in the morning," he said again, turning away. "I'll git up and drive you."

"You go to sleep," she ordered.

"You too," he said. But for hours the house was tense and awake, and neither of them slept.

The running of the house acquired a certain orderliness it lacked before. Bills were paid in full and Grange's bookkeeping explained to Ruth. Old acquaintances were hunted and found and made to cough up monies owed. Ruth's bank account grew in tiny bounds. Two dollars from Fred Hill, five from Manuel Stokes, sixteen from Davis Jones for that pig he ran over three years ago. The fence was inspected with care, rotting posts replaced, the wire restrung to make it more taut. Even the wine crocks were taken out of hiding and reburied under Ruth's direction. Two stills were closed down, the small remaining one,

213

not very productive, easily destroyed. For her sixteenth birthday, when her fear of Brownfield had abated somewhat, Grange made her sole owner of their old car. He had already taught her to drive, and now it became her duty to drive into town to do the shopping, confronting for the first time, alone, the whites who owned and ran the town. Grange's plan was to teach her everything he knew. Already, he liked to boast, "Your aim's a heap better than mine!"

For all that he liked to see her self-sufficient, he was against her acting boyish. He grumbled when she spoke of cutting her hair, an unruly, rebellious cloud that weighted down her head. He insisted she trade her jeans for dresses, at least on weekends, and placed jars of Noxzema and Pond's hand cream on her dresser. He became softer than Ruth had ever known him, reflectively puffing on his pipe for hours without saying a word. He spent evenings examining maps, wondering about the places in the world he would never see, and gradually what he was groping for became almost tangible. Believing unshakably that his granddaughter's purity and open-eyedness and humor and compassion were more important than any country, people or place, he must prepare her to protect them. Assured, by his own life, that America would kill her innocence and eventually put out the two big eyes that searched for the seed of truth in everything, he must make her unhesitant to leave it.

And still, in all her living there must be joy, laughter, contentment in being a woman; someday there must be happiness in enjoying a man, and children. Each day must be spent, in a sense, apart from any other; on each day there would be sun and cheerfulness or rain and sorrow or quiet contemplation cf life. Each day must be past, present and future, with dancing and wine-making and drinking and as few regrets as possible. Her future must be the day she lived in. These were the thoughts he thought, sitting before the fire, pulling on his pipe, or hunched up on his bed clipping his toenails. Survival was not everything. *He* had survived. But to survive *whole* was what he wanted for Ruth.

46

One day on her way to school Ruth saw her father alone. He was waiting beside the road, squatting near the asphalt like a hobo over his fire, his face brightened and cleared by the clean softness of the eight-thirty sun. When Ruth saw him her heart jumped, and a nervous habit she had acquired recently, of pressing her hand against her forehead, was repeated several times before she found herself abreast of him. She quickened her pace and averted her head. She imagined herself treading cautiously around a bull in a pasture and would soon have been in a trot, but Brownfield stopped her; not by reaching out to touch her, which she could not have stood, but by simply standing alone and mute there beside the road.

Against the high green shoulder of the road he looked smaller than when she'd last seen him. She felt herself larger, because at sixteen she was no longer a child, but smaller somehow too, because she faced him alone. Brownfield was sober and that surprised her. He wore a clean shirt that fitted him loosely, as if he had lost weight or wore someone else's, and she noticed for the first time knotted coils of gray-black hair growing up from his chest to the base of his creased and dry-looking neck. As her eyes traveled up and down his face she wondered at this hair on her father's chest; she latched onto this discovery to save for a moment the shock of looking into his eyes. His eyes, which frightened her, and which she always avoided, were full of a pained sadness, which surprised her, and she felt they were trying to speak to her. Her answer was to shudder and to hug her books to her bosom with both arms. Seeing her confusion he looked down at his shoes. The air around them was filled with the sweet motey smell of hay and red dust and flowers that is Georgia's in the spring. There was the timeless sound of birds and the noise of children from the direction of the school.

215

"What do you want?" she asked, feeling fear and anger and hope all at once. She could not understand the hope. Surely there had never been any reason for it that her father had provided. There is something about my father that makes me pity him today, she thought, and knew a momentary wariness and more surprise. Brownfield wet his lips with his tongue. So wet with whiskey he was usually, so dry he seemed today!

"You—" he began, and faltered, "you looks just like your mama."

"Yes?" Ruth said sharply, "but what do you *want?*"

"I wants to see you, if you don't mind," he said humbly, and slowly, as if afraid of her.

In the silence, punctuated only by the birds and the distant ringing of the school bell, Brownfield kept his daughter before him and looked and looked at her. It was disconcerting and almost eerie. She felt he had never looked at her before.

"I have to go now," she said faintly, after a few minutes of his greedy staring, for if she had been an oasis in the desert he could not have gazed more longingly at her. "I'm already late for school," she murmured further, feeling hot and cold. But he said, "Wait!" and though he did not touch her or stand in her way she could not move. His close scrutiny of her continued. On the ground near his feet was a gaily wrapped package that looked as if it might be candy. She did not allow herself more than a glance at it for she wanted no part of him, but he noticed her glance and said, she thought, slyly, "A present for you. They tells me you pretty big on reading books."

Slowly Ruth recovered the indignation that came to her whenever she thought of him. After all these years of nothing he had the nerve to think he could get her to like him by offering her one lousy book!

"What is it?" she asked coolly, though a great scathing heat had started behind her eyes.

"Why, er, well, I don't recall the name, but Josie thought you might like it."

"Well, you just tell Josie I *don't* like it and I wouldn't like it as long as either of you had anything to do with it!" As she

216

spoke she rudely kicked a film of dust over it. After she did it she became afraid but Brownfield barely noticed it. He continued to stare and almost to marvel at the size of her, the sound of her, the whole reality of her.

"Oh, shit," she muttered under her breath. What is he looking at? Is he trying to decide whether I'm worth the fuss he wants to make to get me? she wondered. And then she thought, Good God, don't let him touch me with those hands that still and always will look like weapons! Her strong indignation began to lose its heat, and she started again to tremble and to press her forehead and her cheeks. She felt all red and sweaty, as if the dust of the ground were sticking to her.

"You don't even remember your mama, do you?" Brownfield asked after a while, accusingly, his eyes full of a sudden remembrance and a fiery reclaimed jealousy.

"She . . . she *died* before I was very old," said Ruth. "But—" and she looked him in the eye—"I remember her. You don't forget your mama, or anybody that you've loved."

"But you forgets your daddy?" he asked in a gruff, argumentative tone. But then, "You don't act like you remember me. A child what's got respect for her daddy'd run up and give him a hug!" His voice, a moment ago so charged with scorn, was empty of it now. It was old and lonely and pleading. For a moment Ruth could see how much he resembled Grange. She thought of what Grange had told her about people being capable of changing, although lately he'd changed his views about that. But she did not want to hear about the change Brownfield was undergoing, for she could never believe it.

"You never cared for us," said Ruth. "You never cared for mama or Daphne or Ornette, or for me." I don't want any of your damn changes now, she thought, and hated and liked herself for this lack of charity. She glimpsed for the first time what Grange had known, the nature of unforgiveness and the finality of a misdeed done. She saw herself as one both with her father and with Grange, with Josie thrown in to boot.

Her father turned away from her for some private reflections of his own. His hands plucked nervously at a chipped button on his big shirt.

"Daphne's in—I wanted to get them back, and be their daddy—but Daphne's in a crazy house up North. And Ornette"—his mouth, usually so vile and slack with whiskey or foul words, was tight and grieving—"Ornette's a—*a lady of pleasure!*" He remembered that phrase from the letter from the old guy, the preacher, Mem's father. Brownfield had written for word of Daphne and Ornette, planning somewhere in the back of his head to entice them home again. How Josie had cackled with delight to see his sickness at what had become of his daughters! The news of their downfall, especially of Ornette's, had made her jolly throughout one entire day! Though later he had surprised her weeping into her soapsuds, squeezing his overalls and singing about feeling like a motherless child. It had unnerved him to see her so maudlin, but when he had moved to touch her, thinking they might comfort each other, she had turned away, shutting him out, forcing him back into his role of instrument and tormentor.

Brownfield's large shoulders sagged and his hands, hands Ruth had felt in fury against her own young ears, fumbled loosely with some bits of straw tugged up from the banks of the road. His mumbled, embarrassed, prudish "lady of pleasure," almost made her laugh out loud, but she was too near to bursting into tears and perhaps beating her head against the closest tree.

"You were the one who *said* Ornette would *be* a woman of pleasure, a tramp! That's all you used to call her. Just 'tramp.' 'Come here, tramp,' you used to say. *I remember that almost as well as I remember my mama.*"

The past rose up between them like a movie on a screen. The last dilapidated, freezing house which he had forced on them, the sickness of Daphne, her strange fits of which Brownfield had taken no notice, the waywardness of Ornette, whose every act was done to make someone notice her. The murder of Mem.

"You think I don't remember," said Ruth. "The trouble is I can't forget!"

"You don't remember nothing," he said. "You been *fed* on all the hatred you have for me since the time you was this high!" He turned one heavy palm down toward the ground. "You don't know what it *like* for a man to live down here. You don't know what I been through!"

A tremor of pity shot through her at his anguish, for it was real, although it changed nothing.

"I couldn't ever even ex*press* my *love!*" he said.

Considering the past, the word was false, a bribe, meaningless. Ruth tossed her head to dismiss it. Although it made an impression on her. She had not known he even *thought* of affection, except to make fun of it.

"Don't you *shake* your head; I loves you and you mine!"

"Yours!"

"Mine," he said, holding her with possessive eyes.

"What do you want with me *now?*" she asked. "I don't know you and you don't know me!"

"An' I know who to thank for that! Grange won't never let you forgive me. Long as you're with *him*. That sly old cooter! If he so damn good to you, why wasn't he a proper daddy to *me?*"

For all she knew it was an honest enough question. "I told you, you don't know me. If you did you'd know I'm not just a pitcher to be filled by someone else. I have a mind, I have a memory," she said.

"I loved my childrens," said Brownfield, sweating now. "I loved your mama."

These tortured words, and they did sound as if they escaped from a close dungeon in his soul, hung on the air as a kind of passionate gibberish. Ruth shook her head once more to clear it; truly she could not even understand him when he spoke of loving. It was odd, and she said nothing.

"I mean to have what's mine," her father said, much in the way she was used to hearing him speak. He had the curt swagger and roughness of a robber.

"I'm not yours," Ruth said humbly, for she felt, momentarily, a great dam about to fly open inside her, and when and if it broke she wanted it to be soft and gentle and not hurtful to him, although whatever she said, since she could never forgive him, or even agree with him, would have to hurt some. But suddenly he reached out for the first time to touch her. And his touch was not, as some of his words had been, either pathetic or kind. He grasped the flesh of her upper arm between thumb and forefinger and began to twist it. Her defenses went up again, higher than before, and bitter tears came to her eyes. He don't know his own strength, she remembered Mem had said time after time, rubbing her own bruises.

"You belongs to me, just like my chickens or my hogs," he said. "Tell that to your precious grandpa. Tell him *he* can't keep you; and before I let him I'll see you both in hell!"

"You said you loved me," she said, crying. "If you love me, *leave me alone!*"

"No," he said, pushing her away. "I can't do that. I'm a *man*. And a *man's* got to have *some*thing of his own!"

"A *man* takes care of his own when he's got it!"

"Aw, Grange been messing with your mind. I would have took care of my own had the white folks let me!"

"I don't like you, I don't like you, I don't like you!" she cried, stamping her foot. Her arm felt as if a plug had been pressed out of it.

"You going to like me better when I gets you in *my* house!" he said.

"You need shooting," she said, and trembled. Making herself move very slowly she walked away from him. She held her books tightly and wondered what new thing under the sun she might learn in school that day.

When Brownfield returned to the small linoleum-and-tin-patched house he shared with Josie, he found Josie up to her elbows in soapsuds, muttering against him. Her existence with him since she left Grange, always so fraught with trials, had now reached its nadir with Brownfield's crazy desire to capture one of his family to live with him. He did not want them out of love, Josie knew; he wanted them (or at least *one* of them) because

220

having his family with him was a man's prerogative. Josie called distrustfully on God to deliver her from evil, as she heard Brownfield walking up behind her. Two neighboring women stood by sympathetically. They took up their patent-leather pocketbooks as Brownfield came in. They never stayed in his house after he got there. Brownfield heard the thin pursy-mouthed one say to Josie that her husband didn't like her to be around so *no*torious a man, and laughed to think she imagined he could be attracted to her, a woman so thin and juiceless she made a papery rattle when she walked. As he approached her she lowered her grayish head in a vain nod of virginal piety. Her fatter, bolder friend, whom Brownfield had occasionally and casually screwed, and who was never seen without her fan, vigorously fanned herself past him as if his presence in the room had upped the temperature a hundred degrees.

"*Bye*, Baby! Bye, *Honey!* Bye, *Sweet*ness!" Brownfield said merrily as they left, switching their cheaply dressed rumps down the road, hoping he'd be interested. He knew women! A swine of a man was more interesting to them and far more intriguing than a gentleman and a prince. Pigs, he thought, liars and hypocrites!

"Say, Josie, you ever sleep with Judge Harry?"

"Naw," said Josie, with the unquestioning honesty of a woman whose self-respect has ceased to be a matter of moment to anyone, including herself.

"I thought you might have, when you was young. When me and Judge Harry was boys—actually when I were at the lounge with you and Lorene—I used to get him a little bit of pussy now and then. Guess I never ask you. 'Course I don't mean if he'd slept with you lately. Ain't nobody that hard up no more. When I was up before him and he give me ten years I spent four of the seven I did as his gardener. I didn't know nothing 'bout no damn garden, and I told him so, but he just sort of winked at me and said, 'Boy, you always did know more about gardening than anybody I ever met!' The old son of a gun, he hadn't changed a bit! And you would have thought he would, him being the judge and all. But he used to say all the time when folks came to the house and ask him why he have a prisoner hanging round, 'Brownfield and me grew up together, we understands one 'nother.' He, he, he."

Josie said nothing. Her face was puffy and sad. Her dress was ripped along the seams under the arms and her yellow flesh poked out wet and slack. She was very fat and tired.

"You know, I *bet* Judge Harry'd make Grange give me back my child!" said Brownfield, still chuckling.

Josie laid down her washing and looked at him. "I really would do anything to keep you from doing this dirt to my husband," she said grimly. Her smallish eyes were red-rimmed and bleak, inexpressibly hopeless and dull. All the impudence of self-determination was gone. She washed clothes for white and black to buy their bread.

"Would you kill me?" asked Brownfield recklessly, as his old lumpy woman began to cry.

Brownfield took out his pocket knife and picked up a branch and began to cut small twigs from it. He began to chuckle.

"Josie, Josie," he said, "what the matter is with you is that you so easy to take in, you so easy to feel sorry for folks; no matter if they deserves it or no. Just like, supposing you *could* sneak back into Grange's house and git back on the good side of him. And suppose he started to plot somethin' against *me*." Brownfield's chuckle was becoming a laugh. "Do you know what you'd do?" he asked. "You'd feel sorry for *me,* an' you'd probably hightail it over here to *warn* me that somethin' was afoot! You never growed up, Josie, you never learned to pick one side an' stay on it. You're a fat, stupid whore, Josie, and never learned to think with your head instead of your tail."

"What you going to do?" she asked. "You don't want Ruth back! I know you don't!"

Brownfield looked at her with a subtle half-smile. "I don't know quite yet *what* I'll do. Maybe I'll just keep the waters stirred. You told me once that the ol' man had a bad heart . . . well, maybe we ought to sorta *worry* him now 'n then, a little bit. I bet we could even bring the old sinner to God," said Brownfield, and doubled over laughing.

222

Josie leaned over her washing and closed her eyes. She felt she was of no use to anyone. She was reminded of a night several years before when a young sailor had come into the Dew Drop Inn and she had taken him upstairs to her room. She had been especially good to him, and when he spoke of paying she had told him to forget it; she knew he was almost broke and that he was on his way home to a wife and small children. To express his gratitude, the young sailor had wanted to take her again but she refused because she had other customers waiting. When she refused he beat her black and blue and the people downstairs had to come up and pull him off her. Thinking of the incident now, after over twenty years, Josie began to cry afresh for all the love she'd never had. She felt she was somehow the biggest curse of her life and that it was her fate to be an everlasting blunderer into misery.

"If I *do* take her back," said Brownfield, "it'll be just to make Grange sweat. But right now I like having him right where he is. We got him *scared*, Josie!"

"You can kill him, Brownfield," said Josie. "You can worry him to a heart attack and he still going to come out on top."

"How you figure that?" Brownfield asked, scowling.

" 'Cause he know which side he on. And it ain't your side and it ain't even just his own. He *bigger* than us, Brownfield. We going to die and go to hell and ain't nobody going to give a damn one way or the other, 'cause we ain't made no kind of plan for what happens after we gone. But Grange thinks about the world, and Ruth's place in it. And when he dies Ruth's going to *know* he gone. I got grandchildren too, somewhere," she said forlornly, "but I don't know where."

That night he became furious with Josie when she mumbled what had become for her, the answer to everything: "the white folks is the cause of everything." Brownfield did not know why, but suddenly this thought repelled him, just as before he had found support for the failure of his life in it. He felt an indescribable worthlessness, a certain ineffectual *small*ness, a pygmy's frustration in a world of giants.

"Ah, what do *you* know?" he sneered. "Nothing. You don't know the half of what you *think* you know." He chuckled with his usual omnipotent disdain. Josie was so dumb. "Did you know, f'instance, that one of my wife's children was white? That's right, one of Mem's children was white. The one that come after Ruth. The *last* one." He laughed at the expression on Josie's face. "Naw," he said, "don't go looking sick like that and green around the gills. He wasn't a *real* white baby. She never did fool around with white men, though they tried to fool around with her and I accused her of it often enough. She was stupid enough to be faithful to me if it meant fighting her goddam head off. Naw, I mean it was one of them babies without color, *any* color, with the light eyes without color and the whitish hair without color, and everything without color. Soon's I seen it, for all that it looked jest like my daddy, I hated it. It were a white Grange though, jest the same as my daddy is a black one."

"Was it what they calls an albino?" asked Josie, beginning to tremble. "Is that what you mean by without any color?"

"Yeah, I reckon that's what you'd like to call it. Curious looking, just *all over white.* Well, you know what I did to my wife when that baby was born? I beat the hell out of her a minute after I seen that baby's peculiar-looking eyes. She was just a-laying up there moaning, she were too weak to holler, and I beat her so she fell right out the bed. I 'cused her of all *kinds* of conniving with white mens round and about, and she jest kept saying she didn't do nothing with no white mens. 'I swears to *God* I didn't!' She says. And I axed her, 'How come this baby ain't got no brown color on him?' and she says, '*Lawd knows I don't know, Brownfield,* but he yours!' and I said, 'Don't you go lying to me, woman . . . if he ain't black he ain't mine!' Well, I told her that if that child didn't darken up real soon she'd better git prepared to get 'long without him. And she cried and begged and cried and begged, and she started leaving him close to the fire and in the sun when it come out, but that baby stayed like he was, not a ounce of color nowhere on him. An' one night when that baby was 'bout three months old, and it was in Janu-

224

ary and there was ice on the ground, I takes 'im up by the arm when he was sleeping, and like putting out the cat I jest set 'im outdoors on the do'steps. Then I turned in and went to sleep. 'Fore I dropped off, Mem set up and said she thought she heard the baby but I told her I had done looked at him and for her to go back to sleep. I kept her so wore out them days that she couldn't even argue; she was so tired she didn't fall asleep like folks—she just fell into a coma.

"I never slept so soundly before in my life—and when I woke up it was because of her moaning and carrying on in front of the fire. She was jest rubbing that baby what wasn't no more then than a block of ice. Dark as he'd *ever* been though, sorta *blue* looking.

"Now, 'cording to you I done that 'cause I thought that baby was by a white man. But I knowed the whole time that he wasn't. For one thing, although it were white, it looked jest like me—or rather like my daddy, as it had a right to since it was a grandson. It looked like the two of us. Ugly. For another thing, I had talked to old Dr. Taylor in town about it, and he said these things happen. Then, when the baby's hair begin to grow it was stone nappy. I knowed he was my child all right. Mem knowed I would have broke her neck if she so much as let a white man *look* at her. If some white man had knocked her in the head and raped her she still would have caught hell from me! She knowed the score. You should have seen her when she was young and pretty and turning heads, putting on veils and acting like a cripple or something when white mens was around. They used to ax me how come I was to marry something so ugly, but they jest didn't know what all your sister's child *had* under all them veils!"

Oddly, it was the first time Josie felt genuine pity for Mem. She stared at Brownfield with horror, seeing for the first time that he was, as a human being, completely destroyed. She was shocked that what he was telling her went beyond the meanness to which, by now, she was thoroughly accustomed, into insanity, the merest hint of which always unnerved her.

"I know what you think," he said to Josie. "You sitting there

225

saying to yourself, he crazy! That's why all this is. But I *ain't* crazy, no more'n anybody else. All it was was that I jest didn't *feel* like trying to like nobody else. I jest didn't *feel* like going on over my own baby, who didn't have a chance in the world whether I went on over him or no. It too *much* to ask a man to lie and say he love what he don't want. I had got sick of keeping up the strain."

"If you had kept up the strain," said Josie, with a rare combination of logic and courage, "you'd a had a son now."

"Little white bastard!" said Brownfield, waving her away.

Oh, no. He wouldn't repent. None of what he had done mattered any more. It was over. What had to happen happened: the beautiful faded, the pretty became ugly, the sweetness soured. He had never believed it could turn out any other way. But what had *she* thought, his quiet wife, when he proved to be more cruel to her than any white man, or twenty? She was not a fighter, and rage had horrified her. Her one act of violence against him, which she must have considered an act of survival, brought her lower than before. Instead of rage she had had an inner sovereignty, a core of self, a rock, which, alas, her husband had not had. She had possessed an embedded strength that Brownfield could not match. He had been, at the best times, scornful of it, and at the worst, jealous.

"It's done, *done!*" he muttered to himself as he drifted near sleep. But now Ruth's face floated before him and her eyes glared accusingly at him. *Ruth,* with her thin legs and startled eyes, always running from him, her mind behind the eyes always in flight. She still ran *toward* something. This annoyed Brownfield. What did she see in the world that made her even wish to grow up? he wondered. He had to make her see that there was nothing, *nothing,* no matter what Grange promised her. He had seen the nothingness himself. And if she hated him more than ever, what did it matter? That was what the real world was all about.

But what about *love?* he asked himself, and a great hollow emptiness answered.

"It's a lie!" he cried into the dark, causing Josie to jump in her sleep. For Brownfield felt he *had* loved. But, as he lay thrashing about, knowing the rigidity of his belief in misery, knowing he could never renew or change himself, for this changelessness was now all he had, he could not clarify what was the duty of love; whether to prepare for the best of life, or for the worst. Instinctively, with his own life as example, he had denied the possibility of a better life for his children. He had enslaved his own family, given them weakness when they needed strength, made them powerless before any enemy that stood beyond him. Now when they thought of "the enemy," their own father would straddle their vision.

Brownfield ground his teeth under the pressure of his error, though too much thought about it would make it impossible to sleep. It occurred to him, as an irrelevancy, that Ruth might never believe "conditions" caused his indifference to her. He wished, momentarily, that he *could* call out to someone, perhaps to Mem, and say he was sorry. But what could he give as proof of his regret? He must continue hard, as he had begun. He would take his daughter from her grandfather, not because he wanted her, but because he didn't want Grange to have her. He gave no thought whatsoever of how he might attempt, once he had Ruth under his roof, to treat her kindly.

PART XI

47

The months they waited to see what Brownfield planned to do, the world moved in on Ruth. She found it not nearly so lovely as she had occasionally dreamed, nor quite as unbearable as she had been prepared to accept. She found it a deeply fascinating study, a subject for enthusiasm, a moving school. It all happened with the news and the Huntley-Brinkley Report.

It was her last year in school and each afternoon she hurried home to watch the news on television. She became almost fond of Chet Huntley and David Brinkley, especially David Brinkley, who was younger than Chet and whose mouth curved up in a pleasingly sardonic way. The only black faces she saw on TV were those in the news. Every day Chet and David discussed the Civil Rights movement and talked of integration in schools, restaurants and picture shows. Integration appealed to Ruth in a shivery, fearful kind of way. Her grandfather thought it negligible. Ruth often wondered if she would have liked the news-casters as much were they not discussing black people. She thought not; for though she had listened to them before, only now did they become real to her; she could look at David's smirk-smile and often cheer the bit of news that caused it. Each day there were pictures of students marching, singing, praying, led by each other and by Dr. Martin Luther King. She accepted the students and the doctor as her heroes, and each night she and Grange discussed them.

"Do you think he's got something going?" she asked Grange one night, pointing to Dr. King's haggard, oriental eyes which looked out impassively and without depth from the TV screen.

"I'd feel better about 'im if I thought he could be the President some day," Grange said. "Knowing he ain't never *going* to be somehow take the *sweet* out of watching him. He a *man*, though," he said. " 'Course," he had continued, "I believe I would handle myself different, if I was him. Then again, I ain't handling myself at all, setting here on my dusty, so I ain't the one to talk. The thing about him that stands in my mind is that even with them crackers spitting all over him, he gentle with his wife and childrens."

"Why do they have to *sing* like that?" she asked one night, moved to tears without realizing it.

"For the same reason folks whistle in a graveyard," Grange answered.

"They don't believe what you do," she said another evening, seeing black hands clasp white hands, marching solemnly down an Atlanta street. "They think they can change those crackers' hearts."

"I'm glad," said Grange. "On the other hand, they might be trying to learn in two weeks what it took me twenty years; that singing and praying won't do it. If that is the case I'm still glad. No need for them to stay all murked up in fog the way I was an' the way your daddy is yit." He leaned closer to the TV, his face contorted. "Look at them ugly cracker faces," he said. "What kind of 'heart' is anybody going to rouse from behind them faces? The thing done gone on too *long;* them folks you see

232

right there before you now, chasing that nigger down the street, they is wearing what heart they *got* on they sleeves. Naw, better than that. They is wearing they *tiny* hearts on they *faces*. Which is why they faces is so ugly. If any amount of singing and praying can git the meanness out of them eyes you let me know 'bout it. Crackers been singing and praying for years, they been hearing darkies singing and praying for years, an' it ain't helped 'em. They set round grinning at theyselves, floodin' the market with electric can openers! Ugh!"

"I think I believe like the students," Ruth declared. "Ain't nothing wrong with *trying* to change crackers."

"What I want is somebody to change folks like your daddy, and somebody to thaw the numbness in *me*." He looked at his granddaughter and smiled. " 'Course," he said, "you done thawed me some."

One evening, as she was watching the Huntley-Brinkley Report, Grange came home looking sick.

"What's the matter with you?" Ruth asked, looking up. She thought their time had come, that Brownfield had done his worst.

Grange didn't answer. He turned his chair from the TV and toward the fireplace. He took out his pipe and knife and scraped out the pipe bowl. Then he filled the pipe with fresh tobacco. Ruth turned off the television and sat beside him. Soon the two of them were engulfed in thick, aromatic smoke.

"You 'member my old gambling buddy, Fred Hill?" Grange spat into the fireplace. "They found 'im yestiddy face down in a ditch."

"Too drunk to move?" asked Ruth.

"Naw, not no *more* drunk, he wasn't. Half his head was blowed off."

"What?"

"From here to here," said Grange, running his finger from ear to chin.

"Well, who done it?"

"Them as has the last word say he done it hisself."

Ruth was stunned.

233

" 'Course, wasn't no gun nowhere *near* the ditch," said Grange.

"How did he manage to shoot half his head off without a gun?" she asked.

"A neat nigger trick," said Grange.

He stared into the fireplace for ten minutes without speaking. "I once seed a woman," he said, "had been strung up, slit open and burned just about up." He thought for five more minutes, Ruth waiting impatiently for him to speak. "They said she was one of them people *bent* on suicide. Kill herself three ways." He smoked, pulling on his pipe as if to jerk it from between his teeth. "Do you know, they writ it up in the paper just that way. Said she was *one* nigger with determination!"

Ruth sat thinking about Fred Hill. She'd heard about the "suicide" case before. Fred Hill was a short, pudgy, tan-skinned man with boyish bowlegs; when he walked he seemed to be swinging. His head was very round and he had had no neck. She had watched him play poker with Grange around the kitchen table. He had taught her how to shoot marbles when she was nine. Now he was dead.

"What was you watching on TV?" asked Grange.

"News."

"Fred Hill's grandson is making news. Tried to get into one of them cracker schools."

"And did he make it?"

Grange leaned his head back and looked at the ceiling, his chair tilted back on two legs. "Naw," he said, "he didn't make it. How you going to study in a cracker school with half your granddaddy's head missin'?"

"Well," said Ruth, attempting to see a bright side, "you don't need your granddaddy's head to study. You just need your own."

"Everything going to prove you wrong, girl," he said, getting up and walking heavily out into the dark.

And then it was spring and school was over and the student

234

marchers were in Baker County. Ruth saw a long line of them parading up and down the streets when she went into town. Their signs were strange and striking. I AM AN AMERICAN TOO! said one. THIS IS MY COUNTRY TOO! said another. I WANT FREEDOM TOO! said still another. Although she had seen marchers before on television she was amazed to see real blacks and whites marching together in her home town! There were trim white girls in jeans and sneakers with clean flowered blouses marching next to intense black girls in high heels and somber Sunday dresses. There were dozens of young black and white male marchers; it looked peculiar to Ruth to see them whispering confidences to one another, curious that she could detect no sign of mutual disgust. "Are they for real?" she wondered. She watched wide-eyed, her glances moving from the marchers to the residents of Baker County. Baker County had been so surprised by the students' arrival it had not done anything yet. Even the sheriff stood on a street corner and stared with his mouth slightly open. His deputies hung around him, so closely it looked as if they needed protection, or at best, minute instructions on how to handle the demonstrators. Local blacks and whites stood under the trees on the courthouse lawn and gawked at the white girls. Some of the men sneered and called them dirty names. Of all the people marching the white girls got the most abuse. One of them carried a sign that said BLACK AND WHITE TOGETHER and each time she passed a group of whites they spat at her and hissed "I'll *bet!*" One of them added, aiming a Coke bottle at her, "You nigger-fuckin' whore!" Ruth passed close beside this girl and noticed her right ear, the one next to the bystanders, was bleeding, and that she marched with stiff wooden steps as if to a chilling inner music. Tears slipped quietly and endlessly down her pale cheeks and the sign in her hand had begun to waver.

As Ruth was leaving town someone pushed a piece of paper into her hands. At the top of the page she saw a white man and woman chained to a rock. The rock was called "racism"; underneath was written "You Will Not Be Free Until We Are

Free." She looked back to see who had given it to her and saw a tall, thin young man in overalls like her grandfather's. He was trying to hand the leaflet to whites who passed, but none took it. She looked back a couple of times and one of the times he was watching her. She felt her heart give a kind of bump against her ribs, such as she'd never felt before. The young man continued handing out leaflets, though only black people took them. The sun on his skin made him all aglow in different shadings of brown, like autumn leaves late falling from the tree.

On her way home she drove the car with her left hand and with her right she touched the paper, then her face and hair, then the paper again, and its message meant less to her than the young man who'd given it to her. Drawing close to their white neighbor's mailbox, she stuffed the leaflet in, then drove pensively onto her grandfather's farm.

Three days later Ruth and Grange were sitting on the front porch. They had just learned that Brownfield, in order to get Ruth, had decided to take them to court. To calm their rather severe case of jitters, Ruth was eating watermelon compulsively and reading *Bulfinch's Mythology,* and Grange was just as compulsively polishing shoes. When they saw the dust in the distance Grange went inside and got his shotgun and leaned it against the banister in front of him, then sat down and continued polishing shoes. The car turned into the yard, made a half-circle around the trees and came to a stop. It was a dark blue car, covered with layers of red dust, as if it had traveled hundreds of miles over Georgia's back roads. The thin young man from town got out on the driver's side. A white girl and boy were in the back seat and a black girl got out of the front seat on the side of the car near the porch. Ruth looked the black girl up and down almost hostilely. It surprised her that she felt a small tug of jealousy. After all, she knew nothing about the young man who'd given her the leaflet and who now stood before her —not even his name.

"So this is where you live!" the young man said, looking up

236

at her from the yard. He was beginning to grow a beard and it made his shapely lips very rosy and well-defined.

Grange looked over at Ruth. She was standing at the edge of the porch with one arm around a roof support. Her eyes were shining! He could almost feel the hot current that flowed through her, making her soft young body taut and electric with waiting. He would not have admitted that he was slightly shocked, but he was.

"This is where I live," Ruth answered the young man. "Anybody could have told you!" She was laughing a shy but bubbly delighted laugh; forgotten completely was the fact that nobody ever visited the farm without her grandfather's permission.

"Where you know him from?" asked Grange, who at that moment decided he didn't like young men with beards.

The young man made long strides up the steps and across the porch to Grange. "How do you do, Mr. Copeland," he said, smiling. He was thinking how much Grange reminded him of Bayard Rustin, except Grange was more leggy and stuck his thumb in his belt like a cowboy. He held out his hand for Grange to shake. Grange scowled up at his smile and looked at his granddaughter, whose eyes had never left the young man, and whose eyes also roamed up and down the young man's body. She was a Copeland, he thought. Sighing and putting down his polishing cloth he shook hands with the young man. His handshake was warm and firm and he was taller than Grange. Grange felt old and gray and as if his hand couldn't squeeze hard.

"How you?" he mumbled. Something about the young man seemed familiar to him. He looked up at him quickly. "Say, don't I know you from somewhere?" he asked, cocking his head to one side. The young man's smile turned into a chuckle.

"I was the little joker used to trail along behind Sister Madelaine," he said. He had spent much of his childhood ashamed that his mother was a fortuneteller, but by the time he left Morehouse and joined the Movement he was as proud of how she earned her living as his best friend was that his father was a surgeon. His mother had faced life with a certain *inventiveness*, he thought, and for this he greatly respected her.

237

"Yass . . ." said Grange, thawing, "I can see the resemblance." He had no remembrance of the young man as a child, but he had known and admired his mother for years. He hadn't ever believed in her magic powers much though.

The black girl had come and stood beside the young man. The two whites had not come closer than the steps.

"My name is Quincy," the young man said, "and this is my wife, Helen."

Grange shook the young woman's hand, then looked over her head at Ruth. Ruth's arms had dropped to her sides and the corners of her mouth sagged. Not only was Helen the young man's wife, but she was pregnant. Ruth saw her grandfather's look and shrugged her shoulders. She pushed a chair behind Helen and mumbled for her to sit down. Quincy had settled himself on the banister.

"Who them?" asked Grange, pointing with his chin. "Is they white, or do they just *look* white?" His whisper could be heard for yards.

"This is Bill and this is Carol," said Helen. "They're working with us." Bill and Carol nodded, but made no move to climb the steps. Bill was dark and muscular with brown eyes. Carol was small with freckles like a second skin.

"They've heard, as have we all, about how you feel about white folks. We had planned to leave them outside the gate near the highway, but we were being followed," said Helen. She sat solidly in the chair, her hands on top of her rounded stomach. She laughed suddenly, looking down at Bill. "He's already been shot at once."

Grange looked down at the young man who looked back at him with nothing in particular in his eyes. Bill took Carol's arm and they walked slowly back to the car. Grange wanted to invite them up to the porch but the urge lasted only a moment. He could not bring himself to admit a white woman under his roof. He said nothing, however, to Ruth, who traipsed out to them with cool water, and he watched her chatting with them for a minute or two.

238

"Mr. Copeland," said Quincy, "do you vote?" Ruth had given him water too and he sipped it, looking very relaxed on the banister, with one leg dangling over the side.

"Vote for what?" asked Grange.

"For sheriff and governor and police chief and county commissioner."

"Nope," said Grange.

"Why not?" asked Helen. She had finished half her glass of water and now rubbed the bottom of the glass over the top of her belly as if to cool it.

" 'Cause every one of 'em is crackers," said Grange, "an' there ain't a teaspoon of difference between one cracker and another."

Quincy laughed. Helen laughed too, but then said firmly, "That's not what we found out in Green County."

Grange snorted. "I used to live there," he said with authority, "an' I don't know what you found, but it wasn't that crackers'd let niggers vote. Last hanging they had was some nigger trying to cast his vote for the cracker of his choice."

"Well," said Quincy, "they voting for the cracker of they choice *now*."

"They voting now?" asked Grange.

"Yep!" said Quincy. "We worked there last summer. They're voting in droves."

"Ain't a cracker in Green County worth the bother," said Grange.

"What about black folks?" asked Helen.

"The black folks wasn't shit neither when I was there," said Grange. "Everyone that wanted to try somethin' to help his people got knifed in the back by 'em." He took out his pipe and began pulling on it, chewing the stem. "You don't mean to tell me that some fool of *ours* is trying to run for office in Green County, do you?" he asked.

"Not *this* year," said Helen.

"Where you *from*, girl?" Grange asked sharply.

"Green County," she answered sweetly, laughing at him.

"Well, I be damned," said Grange. He felt he had been caught sleeping, and that his nap had lasted twenty or forty years.

"Who your peoples?" he asked, thinking that perhaps she was lying.

"My mother's name is Katie Brown. My father's name was Henry. They lived on old man Thomas's place."

Grange remembered the Thomases, but not the Browns. "You say your pa's name *was* Henry?" he asked.

"He was killed in '55," she said. "Shot down right in front of the voting booth."

"Where's your ma at?" he asked.

"She couldn't be dragged away from Green County."

"She ain't still on the white man's place?"

Helen laughed. She laughed a lot. She seemed as carefree as a bird. "She was until we got there last summer," she said. "We moved in with her. All of us. Me and Quincy and Bill and Carol. But that was too much for the Thomases. They had said how sorry they were that old Henry was shot down thataway and had helped me when I went away to college, but when they saw me with Bill and Carol they kicked Ma off the place."

"And then?" asked Grange, leaning forward in his chair. He wanted to reach out and touch Helen, she was so calm. He felt her calmness *meant* something, and he wanted desperately to know what.

"And *den,*" Helen said, chuckling, "*den,* Ma hauled off and cussed old man Thomas out and his ancestors back through the Civil War and spit on his wife and they had her locked up."

"She got out," said Quincy. "We had some smart lawyers come down from New York. When she got out she moved to a little house just down the road from the Thomases. She browbeat the preacher who owned it into letting her set up a center for us. It was full of all kinds of people all summer long. She's there still."

"That woman's plainly done lost her mind," said Grange. "You all ought to go get her."

"She loves it there," said Helen, shrugging her shoulders. "If

240

anything she wants us to come 'home' and settle down beside her."

"And one day we might," said Quincy.

"Quincy's going to run for Mayor," said Helen. "I'm going to be first lady of Green County."

"You're all crazy," said Grange. "You best be spending your energy in getting yourselves out of here. How long you think you going to be able to laugh like you do?" he asked Helen.

"I ain't going to let *them* make me stop!" she said.

And Grange thought, You may keep being able to laugh when other peoples is around, but when you and your husband and the baby is all alone dodging bullets and jumping out of your skin at every noise, will you be able to laugh *then?* He imagined Helen in ten years, her young husband maybe buried in some swampy unmarked grave, her child hounded by grownups and children who hated niggers. He saw her at the mercy of some white town whose every gesture would mean she was worthless, an intruder, an American on good behavior. Suppose she couldn't ever become "first lady" of anything. Then where would her laughter be?

"We want you to register," said Quincy. "I even got my mother to register, though she swears she's been hexing the *bad* crackers all along!"

"I can't promise you," said Grange. He felt a deep tenderness for the young couple. He felt about them as he felt about Dr. King; that if they'd just stay with him on his farm he'd shoot the first cracker that tried to bother them. He wanted to protect them, from themselves and from their dreams, as much as from the crackers. He would not let anybody hurt them, but at the same time he didn't believe in what they were doing. Not because it wasn't worthy and noble and inspiring and good, but because it was impossible.

"What I'm scared of, children, is the bitterness; the taste of bile thrown up by the liver when you finds out the fight can't be won."

Quincy put his arm around his wife, his hand moving up and down her side. He held her loosely yet completely, as if she

241

meant everything to him, and the glow in her eyes was pure worship when she looked up at him. Grange was touched almost to tears by the simplicity and directness of their love and he shuddered with fear for them.

"If you fight," she said, placing soft black fingers on Grange's arm, "if you fight with all you got, you don't have to *be* bitter."

Grange walked out to the car with them and opened the door for Helen. "Wait a minute," he said. He turned and went into the house and pulled a watermelon from under the bed. It was cool and green and heavy. He took it out to the car and handed it into the back seat. Helen was laughing again and all of them thanked him profusely. Grange still couldn't quite look at the white girl but he gave a short nod to the boy. And when he waved good-bye he waved to all of them.

He turned, smiling, and saw Ruth sitting dejectedly on the steps.

"I bet *all* the *good* ones have got taken!" she moaned, frowning at him.

"You really got a kick out of him, didn't you, girl?" asked Grange. "One day another one'll come and he won't have a wife and you can grab him before he starts looking for one."

"I don't expect a whole stream of 'em to come passing by *here*," she said with dismay. "I think I'm going to have to go out an' *find* the one I want."

"What about this farm?" Grange asked.

"Oh, good grief!" she said, and stormed into her room, slamming the door and throwing herself across her bed.

48

On the morning they were to confront Brownfield in court, Grange helped Ruth tidy up the house with a reserved concentration. Both found it difficult to speak. Grange's hair, as white as any snow but more silvery and of course crinkled and bristly electric, was combed in the fashion Ruth so loved, brushed straight back on the top and sides, neat but bold. Combed back this way, flatly, his hair would rise again slowly, crinkle by crinkle, so that soon, with the sun making it shine, he would look like Ruth's idea of God. He was wearing his best and only dark suit with vest to match and his coat flared over his hips, emphasizing the leanness of his long legs and the tense long strides that somehow reminded Ruth of Randolph Scott.

They had an old 1947 Packard, black, chromeless, which they parked on the street near the courthouse. The courthouse was in the center of the square in the middle of town. It was red brick, made something like a big dusty box. Its corners were decorated with concrete cornices full of ornate scrolls; the steps were tall and wide, though hopelessly unimpressive. They were beginning to crack.

Because it was a Saturday morning few people were in town. The cotton farmers and dairymen would come in later. On the top of the steps Ruth turned for a last look at the town.

"I wish they'd move their damn stone soldier," she said, glaring at the Southern soldier facing his old and by now indifferent enemy of the North. "I can't see what time it is." There was a new electric clock the size of a stop sign across the street in the window of the drugstore, but the stone soldier's meager hips were enough to cover it.

"But I got my watch," Grange said with some surprise, drawing out a heavy gold watch on a chain. Then he took her elbow firmly, too firmly for her to pull away. "Don't you worry," he said, shaking her gently. "I wouldn't be worth nothing if I couldn't take care of my own. And I want you to always remember—you is my own." Grange kissed her on the top of her hair, lightly, and they walked together into the house of justice.

The judge was a kindly eyed, sallow-faced condescending water sportsman. A picture of him holding a fat glistening string of fish was the "in color" photograph that graced the front of the Baker County *Messenger* the week before. His face was the alert, watchful and yet benign face of a man who had started out in life with nothing and who had added positions as he added

243

weight until he came to rest with heavy jowls and a judgeship in the same county where he was born penniless fifty years before. Behind his benign look was a door, never publicly opened, which led back into a soul so empty of charity and so full of dusty conceits that his townspeople could hardly have stood the sight. Not that their own souls' doors were securely fastened enough to allow them to wonder about someone else's. Even that of their judge. All in all, however, he was not a bad man, as bad men in the South go. He had never personally trafficked in violence; he had not even strenuously condoned it. He had, however, meted out unjust sentences and had been the benificiary of much yard labor and housework which the city paid for and which he was able to secure from his position on the bench. In short, he was a petty person, with all the smallness of mind that went with being so. He was capable of stealing the labor of innocent people, almost always black, sometimes poor white, but was not capable of stealing large sums of money. Because of this honesty his townspeople respected him and made him a deacon in the First Presbyterian Church. Among the black boys for whom he felt responsible he was affectionately known as "Judge Harry." His relationship with the "nigras" was generally good.

It was over so quickly! The judge showed them to his colored chambers. He and Brownfield exchanged jovialities. Grange stared beyond them, his face pale.

"How old are you, Ruth?" the judge asked.

"Sixteen."

"You won't be a grown woman in the state of Georgia till you're two years older," the judge said.

The room was quiet, except for Josie's breathing. She wheezed.

"You want to be with your *real* daddy, don't you, Ruth?" the judge asked kindly, looking at her with eyes that neither asked questions nor cared about answers.

"No, sir," she said firmly.

Grange started to speak of his son's criminal record, of his neglect of his children, of his threats.

"This man killed his wife, your Honor!" said Grange, out of order.

"Now, I didn't ask you nothing yet," the judge said pleasantly, hurt. "You don't have no right to go making unsolicited speeches in my chambers." He looked at Brownfield solemnly and winked. Ruth knew it was over for her and Grange; she held tightly to her grandfather's hand. She could not look up into his face for she could feel the tremors running through his body and knew he was crying.

"Hush," she whispered under her breath, "hush, old baby." His breath caught in a sob; she knew it was from helplessness. Ruth was so angry she couldn't cry.

What the judge and Brownfield and Josie were doing was not important to Ruth. Not while she leaned her soul toward Grange and encouraged him to share her resignation. When she looked at the judge again he was taking a pair of tall slick boots from a closet near his desk.

"But no rough stuff now, Brown, you hear me?" He was smiling in that way Southern white men smile when they control everything—birth, life and death. Ruth hated him forever. She had been given in all speedy "justice" to a father who'd never wanted her by a man who knew and cared nothing about them. Any of them. Just a man who was allowed to play God. Ruth felt something hot standing in front of her. It was Josie, flushed and vermillion.

"You got to go with your daddy now," she said, relieved, and Ruth was annoyed to see a pitying tear in Josie's eyes.

"But don't worry," Josie continued, venturing to sit on the bench next to Grange, "I'll take care of him."

Brownfield came toward them grinning. "Got you this time," he said, gloating.

Grange slowly raised his head and slowly stood. He looked down coldly at his son. One thumb strayed to and fro under his belt.

"Touch her and I lay you out," he said; with one long arm he pushed Ruth behind him. Brownfield looked around for Judge Harry, who was just going toward the door.

"Judge Harry!" Brownfield called confidently. Judge Harry glanced back, took in the situation and walked purposefully to the door. Grange's next words were like a cold blast against his back.

"Halt, *Justice!*" said Grange. The contempt in his voice was as tangible as the floor on which the judge stood.

Brownfield made a lunge for Ruth and managed to catch her arm for half a second. Then he felt himself thrown back as if by a great gush of wind. He saw lightning and thought he smelled a bitter smoke. He sank limply to the floor and did not manage to get a word out before he died. Underneath his flared tail coat Grange had carried his blue steel Colt .45. With it he had shot down his son.

"You can't do this in a court of law," the judge began to babble; he was still holding his fishing boots. His eyes bulged when he saw Brownfield's blood spreading along the floor.

"Shet up, *Justice,*" said Grange, "or you sure 'nough going to be deaf, dumb and blind." He grabbed Ruth by the arm, stepped around Josie, who was sobbing over Brownfield, and headed for the door.

"We'll catch you, Copeland," said the judge. "You can't run away."

"I ain't running away," said Grange, briefly, "I'm going *home,* and the first one of you crackers that visit me is going to get the rest of what I got in this gun."

"We don't have a chance," said Ruth, as they raced home, sirens already sounding behind them.

"I ain't," said Grange, "but you do." He ran his hand over his eyes. "A man what'd do what I just did don't deserve to live. When you do something like that you give up your claim." He slumped on the seat. "And what about that judge?" he asked bitterly. "Who will take care of him?"

Out of the car and into the house they ran. Police cars were racing down the dirt road to the house. Grange combed the house for guns and took off in a trot through the woods toward the cabin. Immediately cars circled the house; Ruth waited

246

quietly on the bed. Grange had not even left her gun, knowing as she knew that she would live longer without it, at least in this battle. Ruth heard the men begin the sweep toward the house and then she heard a shot from far back in the woods. Grange leading the police away from her. Suddenly the air rang with the rush of bullets and a few minutes later, just as suddenly, everything was still.

To a person peeking it would have seemed that Grange prayed, sitting there dying outside the cabin that had been Ruth's "house," with the sun across his knees, and his back against a tree. But if it was a prayer, how strange it was; for it was all about himself, and his deliverance to and from, and his belief in and out. Actually it was a curse.

It is true he opened his mouth wide in a determined attempt to pray. So near the end of the journey it seemed appropriate, as a drink is an appropriate end to a long dry poker game. But it was not, in fact, to be the case with Grange. He could not pray, therefore he did not.

He had been shot and felt the blood spreading under his shirt. He did not want Ruth to see. Other than that he was not afraid. He did not even hear the rustle of footsteps creeping nearer.

"Oh, you poor thing, you poor thing," he murmured finally, desolate, but also for the sound of a human voice, bending over to the ground and then rearing back, rocking himself in his own arms to a final sleep.

Meridian

For Staughton Lynd and Mar*yam* L.
and for John Lewis the unsung

CONTENTS

Ending

I wish to thank the Radcliffe Institute, the MacDowell Colony and the Yaddo Corporation for their support during the writing of this book. I also thank Mel Leventhal and Rebecca Leventhal.

I did not know then how much was ended. When I look back now . . . I can still see the butchered women and children lying heaped and scattered all along the crooked gulch as plain as when I saw them with eyes still young. And I can see that something else died there in the bloody mud, and was buried in the blizzard. A people's dream died there. It was a beautiful dream . . . the nation's hoop is broken and scattered. There is no center any longer, and the sacred tree is dead.

—Black Elk, *Black Elk Speaks*

me • rid i • an, *n.* [L. *meridianus*, pertaining to midday, or to the south, from *meridies,* midday, the south; *medius,* middle, and *dies,* day.]

1. the highest apparent point reached by a heavenly body in its course.

2. (a) the highest point of power, prosperity, splendor, etc.; zenith; apex; culmination; (b) the middle period of one's life, regarded as the highest point of health, vigor, etc.; prime.

3. noon. [*Obs.*]

4. in astronomy, an imaginary great circle of the celestial sphere passing through the poles of the heavens and the zenith and nadir of any given point, and cutting the equator at right angles.

5. in geography, (a) a great circle of the earth passing through the geographical poles and any given point on the earth's surface; (b) the half of such a circle between the poles; (c) any of the lines of longitude running north and south on a globe or map, representing such a circle or half-circle.

6. (a) a place or situation with its own distinctive character; (b) distinctive character.

7. a graduated ring of brass, in which a globe is suspended and revolves.

first meridian: see *prime meridian* under *prime.*

magnetic meridian: a carefully located meridian from which secondary or guide meridians may be constructed.

me • rid i • an, *a.*

1. of or at noon or, especially, of the position or power of the sun at noon.

2. of or passing through the highest point in the daily course of any heavenly body.

3. of or along a meridian.

4. of or at the highest point of prosperity, splendor, power, etc.

5. southern. [Rare.]

Meridian

The Last Return

Truman Held drove slowly into the small town of Chicokema as the two black men who worked at the station where he stopped for gas were breaking for lunch. They looked at him as he got out of his car and lifted their Coca-Colas in a slight salute. They were seated on two boxes in the garage, out of the sun, and talked in low, unhurried voices while Truman chewed on a candy bar and supervised the young white boy, who had come scowling out of the station office to fill up the car with gas. Truman had driven all night from New York City, and his green Volvo was covered with grease and dust; crushed insects blackened the silver slash across the grill.

"Know where I can get this thing washed?" he called, walking toward the garage.

"Sure do," one of the men said, and rose slowly, letting the last swallow of Coke leave the bottle into his mouth. He had just lifted a crooked forefinger to point when a small boy dressed in tattered jeans bounded up to him, the momentum of his flight almost knocking the older man down.

"Here, wait a minute," said the man, straightening up. "Where's the fire?"

"Ain't no fire," said the boy, breathlessly. "It's that woman in the cap. She's staring down the tank!"

"Goodness gracious," said the other man, who had been on the point of putting half a doughnut into his mouth. He and the

3

other man wiped their hands quickly on their orange monkey suits and glanced at the clock over the garage. "We've got time," said the man with the doughnut.

"I reckon," said the other one.

"What's the matter?" asked Truman. "Where are you going?"

The boy who had brought the news had now somehow obtained the half-doughnut and was chewing it very fast, with one eye cocked on the soda that was left in one of the bottles.

"This town's got a big old army tank," he muttered, his mouth full, "and now they going to have to aim it on the woman in the cap, 'cause she act like she don't even know they got it."

He had swallowed the doughnut and also polished off the drink. "Gotta go," he said, taking off after the two service station men who were already running around the corner out of sight.

The town of Chicokema did indeed own a tank. It had been bought during the sixties when the townspeople who were white felt under attack from "outside agitators"—those members of the black community who thought equal rights for all should extend to blacks. They had painted it white, decked it with ribbons (red, white, and of course blue) and parked it in the public square. Beside it was a statue of a Confederate soldier facing north whose right leg, while the tank was being parked, was permanently crushed.

The first thing Truman noticed was that although the streets around the square were lined with people, no one was saying anything. There was such a deep silence they did not even seem to be breathing; his own footsteps sounded loud on the sidewalk. Except for the unnatural quiet it was a square exactly like that in hundreds of small Southern towns. There was an expanse of patchy sunburned lawn surrounding a brick courthouse, a fringe of towering pine and magnolia trees, and concrete walks that were hot and clean, except for an occasional wad of discarded chewing gum that stuck to the bottoms of one's shoes.

On the side of the square where Truman now was, the stores

4

were run-down, their signs advertising tobacco and Olde Milwaukee beer faded from too many years under a hot sun. Across the square the stores were better kept. There were newly dressed manikins behind sparkling glass panes and window boxes filled with red impatiens.

"What's happening?" he asked, walking up to an old man who was bent carefully and still as a bird over his wide broom.

"Well," said the sweeper, giving Truman a guarded look as he clutched his broom, supporting himself on it, "some of the children wanted to get in to see the dead lady, you know, the mummy woman, in the trailer over there, and our day for seeing her ain't till Thursday."

"*Your* day?"

"That's what I said."

"But the Civil Rights Movement changed all that!"

"I seen rights come and I seen 'em go," said the sweeper sullenly, as if daring Truman to disagree. "You're a stranger here or you'd know this is for the folks that work in that guano plant outside town. *Po'* folks.

"The people who don't have to work in that plant claim the folks that do smells so bad they can't stand to be in the same place with 'em. But you know what guano is made out of. Whew. You'd smell worse than a dead fish, too!"

"But you don't work there, do you?"

"Used to. Laid off for being too old."

Across the square to their left was a red and gold circus wagon that glittered in the sun. In tall, ornate gold letters over the side were the words, outlined in silver, "Marilene O'Shay, One of the Twelve Human Wonders of the World: Dead for Twenty-Five Years, Preserved in Life-Like Condition." Below this, a smaller legend was scrawled in red paint on four large stars: "Obedient Daughter," read one, "Devoted Wife," said another. The third was "Adoring Mother" and the fourth was "Gone Wrong." Over the fourth a vertical line of progressively flickering light bulbs moved continually downward like a perpetually cascading tear.

5

Truman laughed. "That's got to be a rip-off," he said.

"Course it is," said the sweeper, and spat. "But you know how childrens is, love to see anything that's weird."

The children were on the opposite side of the square from the circus wagon, the army tank partially blocking their view of it. They were dressed in black and yellow school uniforms and surrounded somebody or something like so many bees. Talking and gesticulating all at once, they raised a busy, humming sound.

The sweeper dug into his back pocket and produced a pink flier. He handed it to Truman to read. It was "The True Story of Marilene O'Shay."

According to the writer, Marilene's husband, Henry, Marilene had been an ideal woman, a "goddess," who had been given "everything she *thought* she wanted." She had owned a washing machine, furs, her own car and a full-time housekeeper-cook. All she had to do, wrote Henry, was "lay back and be pleasured." But she, "corrupted by the honeyed tongues of evildoers that dwell in high places far away," had gone outside the home to seek her "pleasuring," while still expecting him to foot the bills.

The oddest thing about her dried-up body, according to Henry's flier, and the one that—though it only reflected her sinfulness—bothered him most, was that its exposure to salt had caused it to darken. And, though he had attempted to paint her her original color from time to time, the paint always discolored. Viewers of her remains should be convinced of his wife's race, therefore, by the straightness and reddish color of her hair.

Truman returned the flier with a disgusted grunt. Across the square the children had begun to shuffle and dart about as if trying to get in line. Something about the composition of the group bothered him.

"They *are* all black," he said after a while, looking back at the sweeper. "Besides, they're too small to work in a plant."

"In the first place," said the sweeper, pointing, "there is some white kids in the bunch. They sort of overpowered by all the color. And in the second place, the folks who don't work in the guano plant don't draw the line at the mamas and papas, they throw in the childrens, too. Claim the smell of guano don't wash off.

"That mummy lady's husband, he got on the good side of the upper crust real quick: When the plant workers' children come round trying to get a peek at his old salty broad while some of *them* was over there, he called'em dirty little bastards and shoo'em away. That's when this weird gal that strolled into town last year come in. She started to round up every one of the po' kids she could get her hands on. She look so burnt out and weird in that old cap she wear you'd think they'd be afraid of her—they too young to 'member when black folks marched a lot—but they not."

Catching his breath, Truman stood on tiptoe and squinted across the square. Standing with the children, directly opposite both the circus wagon and the tank, was Meridian, dressed in dungarees and wearing a light-colored, visored cap, of the sort worn by motormen on trains. On one side of them, along the line of bright stores, stood a growing crowd of white people. Along the shabby stores where Truman and the sweeper stood was a still-as-death crowd of blacks. A white woman flew out of the white crowd and snatched one of the white children, slapping the child's shoulders as she hustled it out of sight. With alarm, Truman glanced at the tank in the center of the square. At that moment, two men were crawling into it, and a phalanx of police, their rifles pointing upward, rushed to defend the circus wagon.

It was as if Meridian waited for them to get themselves nicely arranged. When the two were in the tank and swinging its muzzle in her direction, and the others were making a line across the front of the wagon, she raised her hand once and marched off the curb. The children fell into line behind her, their heads held high and their feet scraping the pavement.

"Now they will burst into song," muttered Truman, but they did not.

Meridian did not look to the right or to the left. She passed the people watching her as if she didn't know it was on her account they were there. As she approached the tank the blast of its engine starting sent a cloud of pigeons fluttering, with the sound of rapid, distant shelling, through the air, and the muzzle of the tank swung tantalizingly side to side—as if to tease her—before it settled directly toward her chest. As she drew nearer the tank, it seemed to grow larger and whiter than ever and she seemed smaller and blacker than ever. And then, when she reached the tank she stepped lightly, deliberately, right in front of it, rapped smartly on its carapace—as if knocking on a door—then raised her arm again. The children pressed onward, through the ranks of the arrayed riflemen and up to the circus car door. The silence, as Meridian kicked open the door, exploded in a mass exhalation of breaths, and the men who were in the tank crawled sheepishly out again to stare.

"God!" said Truman without thinking. "How can you not love somebody like that!"

"Because she thinks *she's* God," said the old sweeper, "or else she just ain't all there. *I* think she ain't all there, myself."

"What do you mean?" asked Truman.

"Listen," said the man, "as far as I'm concerned, this stuff she do don't make no sense. One of my buddies already done told me about this mummified white woman. He says she ain't nothing but a skeleton. She just got long hair that her ol' man claims is still growing. That fool sets up breshin' it every night." He snorted and sucked his two remaining side teeth.

"Just because he caught her giving some away, he shot the man, strangled the wife. Throwed'em both into Salt Lake. Explained everthing to the 'thorities up there and they forgive him, preacher forgive him, everybody forgive him. Even her ma. 'Cause this bitch was doing him wrong, and that ain't right!"

He poked Truman in the ribs. "That ain't right, is it?"

"No," said Truman, who was watching Meridian.

"Well sir, years later she washed up on shore, and he claimed he recognized her by her long red hair. He'd done forgive her by then and felt like he wouldn't mind having her with him again. Thought since she was so generous herself she wouldn't mind the notion of him sharing her with the Amurican public. He saw it was a way to make a little spare change in his ol' age.''

Another poke in the ribs. A giggle.

"He drags her around from town to town, charging a quarter to see her. Course we don't have to pay but a dime, being po' and smelly and all. I wouldn't pay nothing to see her, myself. The hussy wasn't worth a dime.''

The schoolchildren were passing in and out of the wagon. Some adult blacks had joined the line. Then some poor whites.

"Her casket though!" said the old sweeper. "They tell me it is great. One of those big jobs made of metal, with pink velvet upholstery and gold and silver handles. Cost upwards of a thousand dollars!''

The crowd, by now, had begun to disperse. The last of the children were leaving the wagon. Meridian stood at the bottom step, watching the children and the adults come down. She rested one foot on the rail that ran under the wagon and placed one hand in her pocket. Truman, who knew so well the features of her face, imagined her slightly frowning from the effort to stand erect and casually, just that way.

"Her name's Meridian," Truman said to the sweeper.

"You don't know her personally?" asked the sweeper in sympathy.

"Believe it or not," he said.

The door to Meridian's house was not locked, so Truman went in and walked around. In the room that contained her sleeping bag he paused to read her wallpaper—letters she had stuck up side by side, neatly, at eye level. The first contained Bible verses and was written by Meridian's mother, the gist of which was that Meridian had failed to honor not just her parents, but anyone. The others were signed "Anne-Marion" (whom Truman knew had been Meridian's friend and roommate in college) and were a

9

litany of accusations, written with much viciousness and condescension. They all began: "Of course you are misguided . . ." and "Those, like yourself, who do not admit the truth . . ." and "You have never, being weak and insensitive to History, had any sense of priorities . . . ," etc. Why should Meridian have bothered to keep them? On some she had gamely scribbled: "Yes, yes. No. Some of the above.   No, no. Yes. *All* of the above."

Above and below this strip of letters the walls were of decaying sheetrock, with uneven patches of dried glue as if the original wallpaper had been hastily removed. The sun through a tattered gray window shade cast the room in dim gray light, and as he glanced at the letters—walking slowly clockwise around the room—he had the feeling he was in a cell.

It was Meridian's house—the old sweeper had pointed it out to him—and this was Meridian's room. But he felt as if he were in a cell. He looked about for some means of making himself comfortable, but there was nothing. She owned no furniture, beyond the sleeping bag, which, on inspection, did not appear to be very clean. However, from his student days, working in the Movement in the South, he knew how pleasant it could be to nap on a shaded front porch. With a sigh of nostalgia and anticipation, Truman bent down to remove his hot city shoes.

"How was I to know it was you?" he asked, lying, when her eyes opened. He could not have walked up to her in front of all those people. He was embarrassed for her.

"Why, Che Guevara," she said dreamily, then blinked her eyes. "Truman?" He had popped up too often in her life for her to be surprised. "You look like Che Guevara. Not," she began, and caught her breath, "not by accident I'm sure." She was referring to his olive-brown skin, his black eyes, and the neatly trimmed beard and moustache he'd grown since the last time she saw him. He was also wearing a tan cotton jacket of the type worn by Chairman Mao.

"You look like a revolutionary," she said. "Are you?"

"Only if all artists are. I'm still painting, yes." And he scrutinized her face, her bones, which he had painted many times.

"What are you continuing to do to yourself?" he asked, holding her bony, ice-cold hand in his. Her face alarmed him. It was wasted and rough, the skin a sallow, unhealthy brown, with pimples across her forehead and on her chin. Her eyes were glassy and yellow and did not seem to focus at once. Her breath, like her clothes, was sour.

Four men had brought her home, hoisted across their shoulders exactly as they would carry a coffin, her eyes closed, barely breathing, arms folded across her chest, legs straight. They had passed him without speaking as he lay, attempting to nap, on the porch, placed her on her sleeping bag, and left. They had not even removed her cap, and while she was still unconscious Truman had pushed back her cap as he wiped her face with his moistened handkerchief and saw she had practically no hair.

"Did they hurt you out there?" he asked.

"They didn't touch me," she said.

"You're just sick then?"

"Of course I'm sick," snapped Meridian. "Why else would I spend all this time trying to get well!"

"You have a strange way of trying to get well!"

But her voice became softer immediately, as she changed the subject.

"You look just *like* Che," she said, "while I must look like death eating a soda cracker." She reached up and pulled at the sides of her cap, bringing the visor lower over her eyes. Just before she woke up she had been dreaming about her father; they were running up and down steep green hills chasing each other. She'd been yelling "Wait!" and "Stop!" at the top of her lungs, but when she heard him call the same words to her she speeded up. Neither of them waited or stopped. She was exhausted and so she had woke up.

"I was waiting for you to come home—lying out on the proch—when I saw these people coming carrying a body"—Truman smiled—"which turned out to be you. They carried you

11

straight as a board across their shoulders. How'd they do that?"

Meridian shrugged. "They're used to carrying corpses."

"Ever since I've been here people have been bringing boxes and boxes of food. Your house is packed with stuff to eat. One man even brought a cow. The first thing that cow did was drop cowshit all over the front walk. Whew," said Truman, squeezing her hand, "folks sure are something down here."

"They're grateful people," said Meridian. "They *appreciate* it when someone volunteers to suffer."

"Well, you can't blame them for not wanting to go up against a tank. After all, everybody isn't bulletproof, like you."

"We have an understanding," she said.

"Which is?"

"That if somebody has to go it might as well be the person who's ready."

"And are you ready?"

"Now? No. What you see before you is a woman in the process of changing her mind."

"That's hard to believe."

"It's amazing how little that matters."

"You mean that kindly, of course."

"Yes."

"Tell me," said Truman, who did not want to show how sad he suddenly felt, "did you look inside the wagon yourself?"

"No."

"Why not?"

"I knew that whatever the man was selling was irrelevant to me, useless."

"The whole thing was useless, if you ask me," said Truman, with bitterness. "You make yourself a catatonic behind a lot of meaningless action that will never get anybody anywhere. What good did it do those kids to see that freak's freaky wife?"

"She was a fake. They discovered that. There was no salt, they said, left in the crevices of her eyesockets or in her hair. This

12

town is near the ocean, you know, the children have often seen dead things wash up from the sea. They said she was made of plastic and were glad they hadn't waited till Thursday when they would have to pay money to see her. Besides, it was a hot day. They were bored. There was nothing else to do."

"Did you fall down in front of them?"

"I try never to do that. I never have. Some of the men—the ones who brought me home—followed me away from the square; they always follow me home after I perform, in case I need them. I fell down only when I was out of the children's sight."

"And they folded your arms?"

"They folded my arms."

"And straightened your legs."

"They're very gentle and good at it."

"Do they know why you fall down?"

"It doesn't bother them. They have a saying for people who fall down as I do: If a person is hit hard enough, even if she stands, she falls. Don't you think that's perceptive?"

"I don't know what to think. I never have. Do you have a doctor?"

"I don't need one. I am getting much better by myself. . . ." Meridian moved her fingers, then lifted her arms slightly off the floor. "See, the paralysis is going away already." She continued to raise and lower her arms, flexing her fingers and toes as she did so. She rolled her shoulders forward and up and raised and twisted her ankles. Each small movement made her face look happier, even as the effort exhausted her.

Truman watched her struggle to regain the use of her body. "I grieve in a different way," he said.

"I know," Meridian panted.

"What do you know?"

"I know you grieve by running away. By pretending you were never there."

"When things are finished it is best to leave."

"And pretend they were never started?"

"Yes."

"But that's not possible."

Meridian had learned this in New York, nearly ten summers ago.

"You are a coward," one of the girls said then, though they knew she was not a coward.

"A masochist," sniffed another.

And Meridian had sat among them on the floor, her hands clasping the insides of her sneakers, her head down. To join this group she must make a declaration of her willingness to die for the Revolution, which she had done. She must also answer the question "Will you kill for the Revolution?" with a positive Yes. This, however, her tongue could not manage. Through her mind was running a small voice that screamed: "Something's missing in me. Something's *missing!*" And the voice made her heart pound and her ears roar. "Something the old folks with their hymns and proverbs forgot to put in! What is it? What? *What?*"

"Why don't you say something?" Anne-Marion's voice, angry and with the undisguised urgency of her contempt, attempted to suppress any tone of compassion. Anne-Marion had said, "Yes, I will kill for the Revolution" without a stammer; yet Meridian knew her tenderness, a vegetarian because she loved the eyes of cows.

Meridian alone was holding on to something the others had let go. If not completely, then partially—by their words today, their deeds tomorrow. But what none of them seemed to understand was that she felt herself to be, not holding on to something from the past, but *held* by something in the past: by the memory of old black men in the South who, caught by surprise in the eye of a camera, never shifted their position but looked directly back; by the sight of young girls singing in a country choir, their hair shining with brushings and grease, their voices the voices of angels. When she was transformed in church it was always by the purity of the singers' souls, which she could actually *hear*, the purity

14

that lifted their songs like a flight of doves above her music-drunken head. If they committed murder—and to her even revolutionary murder was murder—*what would the music be like?*

She had once jokingly asked Anne-Marion to imagine the Mafia as a singing group. The Mafia, Anne-Marion had hissed, is not a revolutionary cadre!

"You hate yourself instead of hating them," someone said.

"Why don't you say something?" said another, jabbing her in the ribs.

This group might or might not do something revolutionary. It was after all a group of students, of intellectuals, converted to a belief in violence only after witnessing the extreme violence, against black dissidents, of the federal government and police. Would they rob a bank? Bomb a landmark? Blow up a police station? Would they ever be face to face with the enemy, guns drawn? Perhaps. Perhaps not. "But that isn't the point!" the small voice screeched. The point was, she could not think lightly of shedding blood. And the question of killing did not impress her as rhetorical at all.

They were waiting for her to speak. But what could she say? Saying nothing, she remembered her mother and the day she lost her. She was thirteen, sitting next to her mother in church, drunk as usual with the wonderful music, the voices themselves almost making the words of songs meaningless; the girls, the women, the stalwart fathers singing

> The day is past and gone
> The evening shade appear
> Oh may we all remember well
> The night of death draw near

Sniffling, her heart breaking with love, it was her father's voice, discerned in clarity from all the others, that she heard. It enveloped her in an anguish for that part of him that was herself—how could he be so resigned to death, she thought. But how sweet his voice! It was her mother, however, whom she heeded, while trying not to: "Say it now, Meridian, and be saved. All He asks is that we acknowledge Him as our Master. Say you believe in Him." Looking at her daughter's tears: "Don't go against your heart!" But she had sat mute, watching her friends walking past her bench, accepting Christ, acknowledging God as their Master, Jesus their Savior, and her heart fluttered like that of a small bird about to be stoned. It was her father's voice that moved her, that voice that could come only from the life he lived. A life of withdrawal from the world, a life of constant awareness of death. It was the music that made her so tractable and willing she might have said anything, acknowledged anything, simply for peace from this pain that was rendered so exquisitely beautiful by the singers' voices.

But for all that her father sang beautifully, heartbreakingly, of God, she sensed he did not believe in Him in quite the same way her mother did. Her mind struck on a perennial conversation between her parents regarding the Indians:

"The Indians were living right here, in Georgia," said her father, "they had a town, an alphabet, a newspaper. They were going about their business, enjoying life . . . It was the same with them all over the country, and in Mexico, South America . . . doesn't this say anything to you?"

"No," her mother would say.

"And the women had babies and made pottery. And the men sewed moccasins and made drums out of hides and hollow logs."

"So?"

"It was a life, ruled by its own spirits."

"That's what you claim, anyway."

"And where is it now?"

Her mother sighed, fanning herself with a fan from the funeral home. "I never worry myself about those things. There's such a thing as progress. I didn't invent it, but I'm not going to argue with it either. As far as I'm concerned those people and how they kept off mosquitoes hasn't got a thing to do with me."

Meridian's mother would take up a fistful of wire clothes hangers, straighten them out, and red, yellow and white crepe paper and her shears, and begin to cut out rose petals. With a dull knife she scraped each petal against her thumb and then pressed both thumbs against the center of the petal to make a cup. Then she put smaller petals inside larger ones, made the bud of the rose by covering a small ball of aluminum foil with bright green paper, tied the completed flower head to the end of the clothes hanger, and stood the finished product in a churn already crowded with the artificial blooms. In winter she made small pillows, puckered and dainty, of many different colors. She stuck them in plastic bags that piled up in the closet. Prayer pillows, she called them. But they were too small for kneeling. They would only fit one knee, which Meridian's mother never seemed to notice.

Still, it is death not to love one's mother. Or so it seemed to Meridian, and so, understanding her mother as a willing know-nothing, a woman of ignorance and—in her ignorance—of cruelty, she loved her more than anything. But she respected even more her father's intelligence, though it seemed he sang, beautifully, only of death.

She struggled to retain her mother's hand, covering it with her own, and attempted to bring it to her lips. But her mother moved away, tears of anger and sadness coursing down her face. Her mother's love was gone, withdrawn, and there were conditions to be met before it would be returned. Conditions Meridian was never able to meet.

"Fallen asleep, have you?" It was a voice from the revolutionary group, calling her from a decidedly unrevolutionary past. They made her ashamed of that past, and yet all of them had shared it. The church, the music, the tolerance shown to different beliefs outside the community, the tolerance shown to strangers. She felt she loved them. But love was not what they wanted, it was not what they needed.

They needed her to kill. To say she would kill. She thought perhaps she could do it. Perhaps.

"I don't *know* if I can kill anyone . . ."

There was a relaxing of everyone. "Ah . . ."

"If I had to do it, perhaps I could. I would defend myself . . ."

"Sure you would . . ." sighed Anne-Marion, reining in the hatred about to run wild against her friend.

"Maybe I could sort of grow into the idea of killing other human beings . . ."

"Enemies . . ."

"Pigs . . ."

"But I'm not *sure* . . ."

"Oh, what a drag this girl is . . ."

"I know I want what is best for black people . . ."

"That's what we all want!"

"I know there must be a revolution . . ."

"Damn straight!"

"I know violence *is* as American as cherry pie!"

"Rap on!"

"I know nonviolence has failed . . ."

"Then you will kill for the Revolution, not just die for it?" Anne-Marion's once lovely voice, beloved voice. "Like a fool!" the voice added, bitterly and hard.

"I don't know."

"Shee-it . . . !"

"But can you *say* you probably will? That you *will*."

"No."

Everyone turned away.

"What will you do? Where will you go?" Only Anne-Marion still cared enough to ask, though her true eyes—with their bright twinkle—had been replaced with black marbles.

"I'll go back to the people, live among them, like Civil Rights workers used to do."

"You're not serious?"

"Yes," she had said, "I am serious."

And so she had left the North and come back South, moving

18

from one small town to another, finding jobs—some better or worse than others—to support herself; remaining close to the people—to see them, to be with them, to understand them and herself, the people who now fed her and tolerated her and also, in a fashion, cared about her.

Each time Truman visited Meridian he found her with less and less furniture, fewer and fewer pieces of clothing, less of a social position in the community—wherever it was—where she lived. From being a teacher who published small broadsides of poems, she had hired herself out as a gardener, as a waitress at middle-class black parties, and had occasionally worked as a dishwasher and cook.

"And now you're here," said Truman, indicating the bareness of the room.

"*Vraiment,*" said Meridian, and smiled at the startled look on Truman's face. "Why, you've forgotten your French!" she said. And then, soberly, "We really must let each other go, you know."

"You mean I really must let *you* go," said Truman. "You cut me loose a long time ago."

"And how is Lynne?"

"I haven't seen her in a long time. I've only seen her a few times since Camara died."

"I liked your daughter."

"She was beautiful." And then, because he did not want to talk about his daughter or his wife, he said, "I've never understood your illness, the paralysis, the breaking down . . . the way you can face a tank with absolute calm one minute and the next be unable to move. I always think of you as so strong, but look at you!"

"I *am* strong, actually," said Meridian, cockily, for someone who looked near death and had to do exercises before her body allowed her to crawl or stand. "I'm just not Superwoman."

"And why can't Anne-Marion leave you alone?" asked Truman, nodding at the letters on the wall. "Anyone who could write such hateful things is a real bitch."

"To tell the truth," said Meridian, "I keep the letters because they contain the bitch's handwriting."

"You're kidding?" asked Truman.

"No, I'm not," said Meridian.

MEDGAR EVERS/JOHN F. KENNEDY/MALCOLM X/
MARTIN LUTHER KING/ ROBERT KENNEDY/CHE
GUEVARA/PATRICE LAMUMBA/GEORGE JACKSON/
CYNTHIA WESLEY/ADDIE MAE COLLINS/DENISE
MCNAIR/CAROLE ROBERTSON/VIOLA LIUZZO

It was a decade marked by death. Violent and inevitable. Funerals became engraved on the brain, intensifying the ephemeral nature of life. For many in the South it was a decade reminiscent of earlier times, when oak trees sighed over their burdens in the wind; Spanish moss draggled bloody to the ground; amen corners creaked with grief; and the thrill of being able, once again, to endure unendurable loss produced so profound an ecstasy in mourners that they strutted, without noticing their feet, along the thin backs of benches: their piercing shouts of anguish and joy never interrupted by an inglorious fall. They shared rituals for the dead to be remembered.

But now television became the repository of memory, and each onlooker grieved alone.

It was during the first televised Kennedy funeral that Anne-Marion Coles became quite conscious of Meridian Hill. She had seen her around the campus before, but never really to speak to. Meridian appeared so aloof she could sit at a table for four in the dining room and never be asked to share it; or, if she were asked, the question would be put timidly, with deference. This barrier she erected seemed to astonish her, and when finally approached —whether in the dining room, the chapel, or under the campus trees—she was likely to seem too eager in her response, too generous, too friendly, her dark face whipped quickly into liveliness, and dark, rather sad eyes crinkled brightly into gladness.

Anne-Marion had the audacity of the self-confident person who, against whatever odds, intends to succeed. Hers was an exploitative rather than an altruistic nature, and she would never have attempted penetrating Meridian's reserve if she had not sensed behind it an intriguing and valuable inner life—an exploration of which would enrich her own existence. That she would learn to care for Meridian she did not foresee.

She sat across from Meridian as she and the other honor students watched the Kennedy family stride off toward Arlington National Cemetery behind the shattered body of their dead John. Jackie Kennedy, it was suggested by a newsman, had been given something that helped her not to cry. The students had been given nothing, and so they cried small floods. Meridian's face, grayish-blue from the television light, glistened with tears that dripped off her chin onto her blue cotton shirt. Slumped forward with grief, she did not bother to raise her hands from her lap, where they lay palms up, empty. She shivered as if she were cold.

Earlier that same year, when Medgar Evers was assassinated, Meridian had planted a wild sweet shrub bush among the plants in the formal garden in front of the honors house. Each day the jealous gardener had pulled a bit more of its delicate roots to the surface, so that it too soon died. Remembering this, seeing her shiver, Anne-Marion held out her sweater to Meridian. Scarcely looking at her, Meridian took it and wrapped herself up tight.

The Wild Child

The Wild Child was a young girl who had managed to live without parents, relatives or friends for all of her thirteen years. It was assumed she was thirteen, though no one knew for sure. She did not know herself, and even if she had known, she was not capable of telling. Wile Chile, as the people in the neighborhood called her (saying it slowly, musically, so that it became a kind of lewd, suggestive song), had appeared one day in the slum that surrounded Saxon College when she was already five or six years old. At that time, there were two of them, Wile Chile and a smaller boy. The boy soon disappeared. It was rumored that he was stolen by the local hospital for use in experiments, but this was never looked into. In any case, Wile Chile was seen going through garbage cans and dragging off pieces of discarded furniture, her ashy black arms straining at the task. When a neighbor came out of her house to speak to her, Wile Chile bolted, not to be seen again for several weeks. This was the pattern she followed for years. She would be seen scavenging for food in the garbage cans, and when called to, she would run.

In summer she wore whatever was available in castoff shorts and cotton tops. Or she would wear a pair of large rayon panties, pulled up under her arms, and nothing else. In winter she put together a collection of wearable junk and topped it with a mangy fur jacket that came nearly to the ground. By the age of eight (by the neighbors' reckoning) she had begun to smoke, and, as she dug about in the debris, kicking objects this way and that (and cursing, the only language she knew), she puffed on cigarette butts with a mature and practiced hand.

It was four or five winters after they first spotted her that the neighbors noticed Wile Chile was pregnant. They were critical of the anonymous "low-down dirty dog" who had done the impregnating, but could not imagine what to do. Wile Chile rummaged about as before, eating rancid food, dressing herself in castoffs, cursing and bolting, and smoking her brown cigarettes.

It was while she was canvassing voters in the neighborhood that Meridian first heard of The Wild Child. The neighbors had by then tried to capture her: A home for her lying-in had been offered. They failed to catch her, however. As one neighbor explained it, Wile Chile was slipperier than a greased pig, and unfortunately the comparison did not end there. Her odor was said to be formidable. The day Meridian saw The Wild Child she withdrew to her room in the honors house for a long time. When the other students looked into her room they were surprised to see her lying like a corpse on the floor beside her bed, eyes closed and hands limp at her sides. While lying there she did not respond to anything; not the call to lunch, not the phone, nothing. On the second morning the other students were anxious, but on that morning she was up.

With bits of cake and colored beads and unblemished cigarettes she tempted Wile Chile and finally captured her. She brought her onto the campus with a catgut string around her arm; when Wile Chile tried to run Meridian pulled her back. Into a tub went Wile Chile, whose body was caked with mud and rust, whose hair was matted with dust, and whose loud obscenities mocked Meridian's soothing voice. Wile Chile shouted words that were never uttered in the honors house. Meridian, splattered with soap and mud, broke down and laughed.

At dinner Wile Chile upset her tablemates with the uncouthness of her manners. Ignoring their horrified stares she drank from the tea pitcher and put cigarette ashes in her cup. She farted, as if to music, raising a thigh.

24

The house mother, called upon in desperation by the other honor students, attempted to persuade Meridian that The Wild Child was not her responsibility.

"She must not stay here," she said gravely. "Think of the influence. This is a school for young ladies." The house mother's marcel waves shone like real sea waves, and her light-brown skin was pearly under a mask of powder. Wile Chile trembled to see her and stood cowering in a corner.

The next morning, while Meridian phoned schools for special children and then homes for unwed mothers—only to find there were none that would accept Wile Chile—The Wild Child escaped. Running heavily across a street, her stomach the largest part of her, she was hit by a speeder and killed.

Sojourner

Meridian lived in a small corner room high under the eaves of the honors house and had decorated the ceiling, walls, backs of doors and the adjoining toilet with large photographs of trees and rocks and tall hills and floating clouds, which she claimed she *knew*.

While Meridian was thin and seemed to contain the essence of silence (so that hearing her laugh was always a surprise), her new friend, Anne-Marion, was rounded and lush, brash and eager to argue over the smallest issues. Her temper was easily lost. When she was attempting to be nonviolent and a policeman shoved her, she dug her nails into her arms to restrain herself, but could never resist sticking out, to its full extent, her energetic and expressive pink tongue.

"Meridian," she would whisper through clenched teeth, "tell me something sad or funny, *quick*, before I kick this bastard in the balls."

Anne-Marion was entirely unsympathetic to daily chapel, notoriously unresponsive to preachers—though she once declared she would follow King and "that handsome Andy Young" through the deepest dark swamp—and had no intention of singing or praying in public. If she bowed her head during protest demonstrations it was to see if her shoelace had come untied, and if she sang it was a song muttered through clenched teeth. She did not see why anyone should worry about her soul, even the people she marched with. "When it gives me trouble," she'd sneer, "I'll call y'all." In this, she and Meridian were exactly alike, except if some pathetic, distracted old marcher wished to bend Meridian's ear about his or her Jesus, Meridian would stand patiently and listen. She was constantly wanting to know about the songs: "Where did such and such a one come from?" or "How many years do you think black people have been singing this?"

Anne-Marion had also taken the first opportunity—once she had actually seen a natural on another woman's head—to cut off all her hair. For this she was called before the Dean of Women (whom she promptly christened "the Dead of Women")—whose own hair was long, processed and lavender—and reprimanded.

"First blue jeans before six o'clock and now this!" said the Dead of Women. "It is becoming clear you are some kind of oddity."

"Under the circumstances," Anne-Marion told Meridian later, "hearing this from her was a relief!"

Meridian agreed. A future of processed lavender hair didn't amount to much.

Like Meridian, Anne-Marion was a deviate in the honors house: there because of her brilliance but only tolerated because it was clear she was one, too, on whom true Ladyhood would never be conferred. Most of the students—timid, imitative, bright enough but never daring, were being ushered nearer to Ladyhood every day. It was for this that their parents had sent them to Saxon College. They learned to make French food, English tea and German music without once having the urge to slip off the heavily guarded campus at five in the morning to photograph a strange tree as the light hit it just the right way—as Meridian had—or to risk being raped in a rough neighborhood as they attempted to discover the economic causes of inner-city crime, as had Anne-Marion.

Meridian and Anne-Marion walked together, as they had many times before. Only now they moved slowly, carefully, their dark dresses down to the tops of their polished shoes, and their hands, underneath the narrow coffin, nearly touched. The mourners in front of them stopped, and a few stepped out of the line to stare at what appeared to be a commotion at the gate.

"I never would have guessed Wile Chile had so many friends," said Meridian dryly. Even in her heavy black dress and thick braided hair Meridian weighed less than a hundred pounds, and her deep-brown skin was filmed slightly with perspiration that reddened it. When she was thoughtful or when she was unaware of being observed, her face seemed deeply sad, as if she knew there was no hope, in the long run, for anyone in the world, and that whatever she was doing at the time was destined for a short, if perfect, life. When she smiled, as she did often when talking to her friends, this look of anticipated doom was almost wiped away, though traces of it always lingered in the depths of her eyes.

She was never thought of as a *pretty* girl. People might say she looked interesting, mysterious, older than her years and therefore intriguing, but she was considered *approaching beautiful* only when she looked sad. When she laughed, this beauty broke; and people, captivated by the sad quality of her face, seemed compelled to joke with her just long enough to cause her to laugh and lose it. Then, freed from their interest in her, they walked away. After these encounters, her mouth still quivering and contracting from her laughter of a moment before, she would curl her toes and stand on one foot, leaning like a crane into the space around her, rocked by the thump-thump of her bewildered—and, she felt then, rather stupid—heart.

Anne-Marion, seeing this happen too frequently to Meridian without anything being learned from it, always felt the urge, at the point where Meridian leaned on one foot, to rush forward and kick her.

Now Meridian strained upward on her toes in an effort to improve her view, but could see nothing beyond the milling about of the people at the gate.

"That flaky bastard," said Anne-Marion, her dark eyes flashing. "That mother's scum is going to turn us around."

"He wouldn't," said Meridian mildly.

"You wait and see. He's scared of us causing a commotion that could get in the cracker papers, just when he's fooled 'em that Saxon Knee-grows are *finally* your ideal improved type."

Anne-Marion wiped her brow and heaved the coffin more firmly against her cheek.

"He ain't nothing but a dishrag for those crackers downtown. He can't stand up to 'em no more than piss can fall upward. His mama should've drowned him in the commode the minute he was born."

"Leave folks' mamas alone," said Meridian, although Anne-Marion made her smile. She was relieved that the line had begun, slowly, to move again. Wile Chile was getting heavier with each pause. Soon they were abreast of the guards at the gate. "Hey, brother," she called to the good-looking one.

"Y'all gon' run into trouble," he called back nonchalantly.

It still surprised her to see a black man wearing a uniform and holstered gun. What was he protecting? she wondered. If he was protecting the campus, how silly that was, because nobody would ever dare harm the lovely old campus buildings; and he couldn't be protecting the students, because they were only just now coming onto the campus, following the six young women who sweated under the casket (which they had paid for) that held The Wild Child's body; and he couldn't be afraid of the crowd of Wile Chile's neighbors, whose odors and groans and hymns drifted up to them pungent with poverty and despair. Humbly, they were bringing up the rear.

Anne-Marion, having given up on winning over the guards long ago, refused now even to look at them. She could not see policemen, guards and such. "I have uniform blindness," she explained.

The street outside the gate was ordinary enough, with patched potholes and a new signal light just in front of the gate. The fence that surrounded the campus was hardly noticeable from the street and appeared, from the outside, to be more of an attempt at ornamentation than an effort to contain or exclude. Only the students who lived on campus learned, often painfully, that the beauty of a fence is no guarantee that it will not keep one penned in as securely as one that is ugly.

A dampness peculiar to the climate was turned lightly warm by the clear sunshine, and blossoms on apple and pear and cherry trees lifted the skeptical eye in wonder and peace. Running through so much green the road was as white as an egg, as if freshly scrubbed, and the red brick buildings, older than anyone still alive, sparkled in the sun.

"I'd like to wreck this place," Anne-Marion said, unmoved.

"You'd have to wreck me first," said Meridian. She needed this clean, if artificial, air to breathe.

There was, in the center of the campus, the largest magnolia tree in the country. It was called The Sojourner. Classes were sometimes held in it; a podium and platform had been built into its lower branches, with wooden steps leading up to them. The Sojourner had been planted by a slave on the Saxon plantation—later, of course, Saxon College. The slave's name was Louvinie. Louvinie was tall, thin, strong and not very pleasant to look at. She had a chin that stuck out farther than it should and she wore black headrags that made a shelf over her eyebrows. She became something of a local phenomenon in plantation society because it was believed she *could not* smile. In fact, throughout her long lifetime nothing even resembling a smile ever came to her poked-out lips.

In her own country in West Africa she had been raised in a family whose sole responsibility was the weaving of intricate tales with which to entrap people who hoped to get away with murder. This is how it worked: Her mother and father would be visited by the elders of the village, who walked the two miles to their hut singing the solemnest songs imaginable in order to move her parents' hearts, and to make it easier for the spirits who hung

31

around the hut to help them in their trouble. The elders would tell of some crime done in the village by a person or persons unknown. Louvinie's parents would ask a few questions: How was the person murdered? What was stolen, other than the life? Where were the other villagers at the time? etc., all the while making marks on the floor of the hut with two painted sticks. The sticks had no meaning except as a distraction: Louvinie's parents did not like to be stared at.

When the elders left, Louvinie's mother would change her face with paint and cover up her hair and put on a new dress and take up residence in the village proper. In a few days she would come back, and she and her husband would begin to make up a story to fit the activities of the criminal. When they completed it, they presented it to the villagers, who congregated in the dead of night to listen. Each person listening was required to hold a piece of treated fiber plant under his or her arm, snugly into the armpit. At the end of the story these balls of fiber were collected, and from them Louvinie's parents were able to identify the guilty party. How they were able to do this they had never had the chance to teach her.

On the Saxon plantation in America Louvinie had been placed in charge of the kitchen garden. She was considered too ugly to work in the house, and much too dour to be around the children. The children, however, adored her. When pressed, she would tell them stories of blood-curdling horror. They followed her wherever she went and begged her to tell them all the scary, horrible stories that she knew. She was pleased to do so, and would tell stories that made their hair stand on end. She made up new, American stories when the ones she remembered from Africa had begun to bore.

She might have continued telling stories had there not occurred a tragedy in the Saxon household that came about through no real fault of her own. It had never been explained to her that the youngest of the Saxon children, an only son, suffered from an abnormally small and flimsy heart. Encouraged by the children to become more and more extravagant in her description, more pitiless in her plot, Louvinie created a masterpiece of fright, and, bursting with the delight she always felt when creating (but never smiling at all—which seemed curious, even to the children), she sat under a tree at the back of the garden just as the sun was sinking slowly through a black cloud bank in the west, and told the children the intricate, chilling story of the old man whose hobby was catching and burying children up to their necks and then draping their heads—which stuck up in rows, like cabbages—with wriggly eels dipped in honey. Long before the culprit received his comeuppance, young Saxon had slumped dead to the ground of a heart attack. He was seven years old.

Many, many years ago, on the banks of the Lalocac River, in deepest Africa, there lived a man blacker than the night, whose occupation was catching little white children—those who had lost at least one tooth to the snags of time—and planting them in his garden. He buried everything except their heads: These he left above ground because he liked to hear them wail and scream and call for their mothers, who, of course, did not know where they were and never came.

He fed them honey and live eels still wriggling that slipped through their lips and down their throats while underneath their ears the eels' tails still struggled and slid. At night the children's heads were used as warming posts for the man's pet snakes, all of them healthy and fat and cold as ice, and loving to flick a keen, quick tail into a snuffling, defenseless nose. . . . The man used to laugh as he—

This portion of Louvinie's story was later discovered on a yellowed fragment of paper and was kept under glass in the Saxon library. It was in the childish handwriting of one of the older Saxon girls.

Louvinie's tongue was clipped out at the root. Choking on blood, she saw her tongue ground under the heel of Master Saxon. Mutely, she pleaded for it, because she knew the curse of her native land: Without one's tongue in one's mouth or in a special spot of one's own choosing, the singer in one's soul was lost forever, to grunt and snort through eternity like a pig.

Louvinie's tongue was kicked toward her in a hail of sand. It was like a thick pink rose petal, bloody at the root. In her own cabin she smoked it until it was as soft and pliable as leather. On a certain day, when the sun turned briefly black, she buried it under a scrawny magnolia tree on the Saxon plantation.

Even before her death forty years later the tree had outgrown all the others around it. Other slaves believed it possessed magic. They claimed the tree could talk, make music, was sacred to birds and possessed the power to obscure vision. Once in its branches, a hiding slave could not be seen.

In Meridian's second year at Saxon there was talk of cutting down the tree, and she had joined members of the Chamber Music Ensemble and their dotty Hungarian conductor when they chained themselves to its trunk. They had long ago dubbed The Sojourner "The Music Tree," and would not stand to have it cut down, not even for a spanking new music building that a Northern philanthropist—unmindful that his buildings had already eaten up most of Saxon's precious greenness—was eager to give. The tree was spared, but the platform and podium were dismantled, and the lower branches and steps—which had made access to the upper reaches of the tree so delightfully easy—were trimmed away. And why? Because students—believing the slaves of a hundred and fifty years ago—used the platform and who knows, even the podium, as places to make love. Meridian had made something approaching love there herself. And it was true, she had not been seen.

So many tales and legends had grown up around The Sojourner that students of every persuasion had a choice of which to accept. There was only one Sojourner ceremony, however, that united all the students at Saxon—the rich and the poor, the very black-skinned (few though they were) with the very fair, the stupid and the bright—and that was the Commemoration of Fast Mary of the Tower.

It was related that during the twenties a young girl named Mary had had a baby in the tower off one end of Tower Hall. She had concealed her pregnancy and muffled her cries (and of course was too ashamed to ask for help or tell anybody anything) as the child was being born. Then she had carefully chopped the infant into bits and fed it into the commode. The bits stuck and Fast Mary was caught. Caught, she was flogged before her instructors and her parents. At home she was locked in her room and denied the presence of a window. She hanged herself after three months.

Any girl who had ever prayed for her period to come was welcome to the commemoration, which was held in the guise of a slow May Day dance around the foot of The Sojourner (which had been, it was said, Fast Mary's only comfort and friend on Saxon campus). It was the only time in all the many social activities at Saxon that every girl was considered equal. On that day, they held each other's hands tightly.

The tree was visible from outside the campus walls, but its true magnificence was apparent only after one got near enough for a closer look, though then it was like staring into the side of a tall, rather lumpy building. From the road near the gate the mourners behind Wile Chile's body could see the top, and the massive body and foliage of the tree, in full bloom, was like a huge mountain lit with candles. Across from the square that held the tree, on both sides, stood the empty red brick dormitories. Some windows were bedecked with flowers. Others were crammed with symbols of the campus sororities: QEZ or ZEQ, or whatever they were. Still others had large handpainted signs addressed to The Wild Child. "God Will Bless You, W.C." "We Love You, 'Wile Chile.'" "Tell God We Ready, Wild One." Other windows were simply empty or from them floated crepe paper streamers of purple and gold. These were the school colors.

Now the commotion at the front of the line, which had been going on for some time, reached them. The girl in front of them, whose name was Charlene, turned around. She was tall, heavily made up, and wore a reddish wig. Her accent reflected the St.

Louis that she loved. She was a prisoner, temporarily, of the freshman class, a scholar under duress.

"They say the president say she can't have her funeral in you all's chapel." Charlene claimed nothing of the school except the men who walked over the grounds. She was chewing gum, popping it as she spoke.

Meridian laughed in spite of the occasion. She imagined the president—a tan, impeccably tailored patriarch with glinting, shifty gray eyes—coming up to The Wild Child's casket and saying, as if addressing a congregation: "We are sorry, young woman, but it is against the rules and regulations of this institution to allow you to conduct your funeral inside this chapel, which, as you may know, was donated to us by one of the finest robber baron families of New York. Besides, it is nearly time for Vespers, and you should have arranged for this affair *through the proper channels* much earlier."

And it seemed that, in fact, this was about what he did say, for there was a moiling about in front of the chapel (a stained-glass fortress made of stone, with gigantic circular columns supporting a jutting porch roof) as the mourners tried to plan what to do next.

When Meridian and Anne-Marion arrived at the chapel steps they found the two guards from the gate. The president, having issued his orders, had retired to his Victorian mansion on the hill, and they imagined him peering down at them from behind his Irish lace curtains on the second floor.

"I told y'all, y'all'd have trouble," said the guard. Only now he was not nonchalant. The mood of the students had changed from mournful to indignant. But they were nicely brought-up girls and their wrath was slow to rise. Still, it is the nature of wrath to rise, and the guard was no dope.

Anne-Marion, after the casket was lowered to the steps, examined the three-inch lock on the chapel door and looked about for a log or even a large rock to bash it in. But there was nothing. The people from the community, Wile Chile's neighbors, resplendent though they had felt themselves to be on entering Saxon gate—for they were in their Sunday-best outfits of red and yellow and peacock blue—now shrunk down inside their clothes and would not look the students in the eye. They appeared to melt away, slinking farther and farther back until they had vanished, like a snail that has salt poured on its tail. Holding out her arms and pleading, Meridian ran after them, but they would not come back.

The casket rested on the chapel steps, its color an orange to compete with the sunrise. There was a long moment of silence. Then the knowledge that The Wild Child was refused admittance to the chapel caused a cry to rise from the collective throats of the crowd in one long wail. For five minutes the air rang with shouts and the polite curses of young ladies whose home away from home the college was. They were so ashamed and angry they began to boo and stamp their feet and stick out their tongues through their tears. In the heat of their emotion they began to take off their jewelry and fling it to the ground—the heavy three-strand cultured pearl necklaces and the massive, circular gold-plated chastity pins, the globular, clustered earrings and their glittering bracelets of many-colored stones. They shook loose their straightened hair, and all the while they glared at the locked chapel door with a ferocity that was close to hatred.

Then, as if by mutual agreement—though no words were spoken—the pallbearers picked up the casket and carried it to the middle of the campus and put it down gently beneath The Sojourner, whose heavy, flower-lit leaves hovered over it like the inverted peaks of a mother's half-straightened kinky hair. Instead of flowers the students, as if they had planned it, quickly made wreaths from Sojourner's fallen leaves, and The Sojourner herself, ever generous to her children, dropped a leaf on the chest of The Wild Child, who wore for the first time, in her casket, a set of new clothes.

The students sang through tears that slipped like melting pellets of sleet down their grieved and angered cheeks:

"We shall overcome . . .
We shall overcome . . .
We shall overcome, someday . . .
Deep in my heart, I do believe . . .
We shall overcome, someday . . ."©

That night, after The Wild Child was buried in an overgrown corner of a local black cemetery, students, including Anne-Marion, rioted on Saxon campus for the first time in its long, placid, impeccable history, and the only thing they managed to destroy was The Sojourner. Though Meridian begged them to dismantle the president's house instead, in a fury of confusion and frustration they worked all night, and chopped and sawed down, level to the ground, that mighty, ancient, sheltering music tree.

"Have You Stolen Anything?"

Meridian was conscious always of a feeling of guilt, even as a child. Yet she did not know of what she might be guilty. When she tried to express her feelings to her mother, her mother would only ask: "Have you stolen anything?"

Her mother was not a woman who should have had children. She was capable of thought and growth and action only if unfettered by the needs of dependents, or the demands, requirements, of a husband. Her spirit was of such fragility that the slightest impact on it caused a shattering beyond restoration.

In the final days of her young adulthood she had known the luxury of lying in bed as late at nine or ten o'clock on Saturdays, and the joy of earning money as a schoolteacher. She had known the freedom of thinking out the possibilities of her life. They were actually two: She might stay in her home town and teach or she might move elsewhere and teach. She never tired of considering which she should do. This period of her life passed too quickly, so quickly she had not had time to properly value it. There had been a delight in her independence, an adventure in the fingering of her possibilities, but she wanted more of life to happen to her. More richness, more texture. She had begun to look about her for an increase in felicity over what she had. She noticed that other girls were falling in love, getting married. It seemed to produce a state of euphoria in them. She became unsure that her own way of living was as pleasant as she thought it was. It seemed to have an aimlessness to it that did not lead anywhere. Day followed day, and the calm level of her pleasures as a single woman remained constant. Certainly she never reached euphoria. And she wanted euphoria to add to the other good feelings she had.

Of course as a teacher she earned both money and respect. This mattered to her. But there grew in her a feeling that the mothers of her pupils, no matter that they envied her her clothes, her speech, her small black car, pitied her. And in their harried or passive but always overweight and hideously dressed figures she began to suspect a mysterious inner life, secret from her, that made them willing, even happy, to endure.

The man she married, Meridian's father, was also a schoolteacher. He taught history classes in the room next to hers. He was quiet and clean and sincere. They could talk together and were friends long before she felt a toleration for his personal habits that she identified as Love. He was a dreamy, unambitious person even then, who walked over the earth unhurriedly, as if conscious of every step and the print his footsteps would leave in the dirt. He cried as he broke into her body, as she was to cry later when their children broke out of it.

She could never forgive her community, her family, his family, the whole world, for not warning her against children. For a year she had seen some increase in her happiness: She enjoyed joining her body to her husband's in sex, and enjoyed having someone with whom to share the minute occurrences of her day. But in her first pregnancy she became distracted from who she was. As divided in her mind as her body was divided, between what part was herself and what part was not. Her frail independence gave way to the pressures of motherhood and she learned—much to her horror and amazement—that she was not even allowed to be resentful that she was "caught." That her personal life was over. There was no one she could cry out to and say "It's not fair!" And in understanding this, she understood a look she saw in the other women's eyes. The mysterious inner life that she had imagined gave them a secret joy was simply a full knowledge of the fact that they were dead, living just enough for their children. They, too, had found no one to whom to shout "It's not fair!" The women who now had eight, twelve, fifteen children: People made jokes about them, but she could feel now that such jokes were obscene; it was like laughing at a person who is being buried alive, walled away from her own life, brick by brick.

That was the beginning of her abstraction. When her children were older and not so burdensome—and they were burdens to her always—she wanted to teach again but could not pass the new exams and did not like the new generation of students. In fact, she discovered she had no interest in children, until they were adults; then she would pretend to those she met that she remembered them. She learned to make paper flowers and prayer pillows from tiny scraps of cloth, because she needed to feel something in her hands. She never learned to cook well, she never learned to braid hair prettily or to be in any other way creative in her home. She could have done so, if she had wanted to. Creativity was in her, but it was refused expression. It was all deliberate. A war against those to whom she could not express her anger or shout, "It's not fair!"

With her own daughter she certainly said things she herself did not believe. She refused help and seemed, to Meridian, never to understand. But all along she understood perfectly.

It was for stealing her mother's serenity, for shattering her mother's emerging self, that Meridian felt guilty from the very first, though she was unable to understand how this could possibly be her fault.

When her mother asked, without glancing at her, "Have you stolen anything?" a stillness fell over Meridian and for seconds she could not move. The question literally stopped her in her tracks.

Gold

One day when Meridian was seven she found a large chunk of heavy metal. It was so thickly encrusted with dirt that even when she had washed it the metal did not shine through. Yet she knew metal was there, because it was so heavy. Finally, when she had dried off the water, she took a large file and filed away some of the rust. To her amazement what she had found was a bar of yellow gold. Bullion they called it in the movies. She filed a spot an inch square and ran with it (heavy as it was) to her mother, who was sitting on the back porch shelling peas.

"I've found some gold!" she shouted. "Gold!" And she placed the large heavy gold bar in her mother's lap.

"Move that thing," her mother said sharply. "Don't you see I'm trying to get these peas ready for supper?"

"But it's gold!" she insisted. "Feel how heavy it is. Look how yellow it is. It's gold, and it could make us rich!"

But her mother was not impressed. Neither was her father or her brothers. She took her bar of gold and filed all the rust off it until it shone like a huge tooth. She put it in a shoe box and buried it under the magnolia tree that grew in the yard. About once a week she dug it up to look at it. Then she dug it up less and less . . . until finally she forgot to dig it up. Her mind turned to other things.

43

Indians and Ecstasy

Meridian's father had built for himself a small white room like a tool shed in the back yard, with two small windows, like the eyes of an owl, high up under the roof. One summer when the weather was very hot, she noticed the door open and had tiptoed inside. Her father sat at a tiny brown table poring over a map. It was an old map, yellowed and cracked with frayed edges, that showed the ancient settlements of Indians in North America. Meridian stared around the room in wonder. All over the walls were photographs of Indians: Sitting Bull, Crazy Horse, Geronimo, Little Bear, Yellow Flower, and even a drawing of Minnehaha and Hiawatha. There were actual photographs, perhaps priceless ones— which apparently her father had spent years collecting—of Indian women and children looking starved and glassy-eyed and doomed into the camera. There were also books on Indians, on their land rights, reservations, and their wars. As she tiptoed closer to the bookshelves and reached to touch a photograph of a frozen Indian child (whose mother lay beside her in a bloody heap) her father looked up from his map, his face wet with tears, which she mistook, for a moment, for sweat. Shocked and frightened, she ran away.

One day she overheard her parents talking. Her mother was filling fruit jars in the kitchen: "So you've gone and done it, have you?" said her mother, pouring apple slices into the jars with a sloshing noise.

"But the land already belonged to them," her father said, "I was just holding it. The rows of my cabbages and tomatoes run right up along the biggest coil of the Sacred Serpent. That mound is full of dead Indians. Our food is made healthy from the iron and calcium from their bones. Course, since it's a cemetery, we shouldn't own it anyhow."

Before the new road was cut it had not been possible to see the Serpent from the old one. It was news to most of the townspeople that an Indian mound existed there.

"That's disgusting," said her mother. "How can I enjoy my food if you're going to talk about dead Indians?"

"The mound is thousands of years old," said her father. "There's nothing but dust and minerals in there now."

"But to give our land to a naked Indian—"

"Naked? He ain't naked. You believe all that stuff they put on television. He wears a workshirt and blue jeans. His hair is the only thing that looks like Indians look on TV. It's cut off short though, blunt, right behind his jowls, like Johnny Cash's."

"How do you know he ain't a white man playing Indian?"

"Because I know. Grown-up white men don't want to pretend to be anything else. Not even for a minute."

"They'll become anything for as long as it takes to steal some land."

And once Meridian had actually seen the Indian. A tall, heavy man in cowboy boots, his face full of creases like a brown paper bag someone had oiled and pinched a lot of lines in with careless fingers. Squinty black eyes stared with steady intensity into space. He was a wanderer, a mourner, like her father; she could begin to recognize what her father was by looking at him. Only he wandered physically, with his body, not walking across maps with his fingers as her father did. And he mourned dry-eyed. She could not imagine that weathered dusky skin bathed in tears. She could not see his stout dirt-ringed wrists pressing against his silver temples, or flattening in despair the remainder of his still-black hair.

His name was Walter Longknife. Which caused Meridian to swallow her first hello when they were introduced, and he came from Oklahoma. He had started out in an old pickup truck that broke down in the shadow of Stone Mountain. He abandoned it, and was glad, he said—in a slurred voice, as if he were drunk, which he was not—to walk through the land of his ancestors, the Cherokees.

Her father gave Mr. Longknife the deed to the sixty acres his grandfather acquired after the Civil War. Land too rocky for plowing (until her father and brothers removed all the rocks by hand and wheelbarrow), and too hilly to be easy to sell (prospective buyers always thought the mounds were peculiar hills). Mr. Longknife had kept the paper in his shirt until he was ready to move on—he spent most of the summer camping out on the land—and then he had given it back to her father.

"Other men run away from their families outright," said her mother. "You stay, but give the land under our feet away. I guess that makes you a hero."

"We were part of it, you know," her father said.

"Part of what?"

"Their disappearance."

"Hah," said her mother. "You might have been, but I wasn't even born. Besides, you told me how surprised you were to find that some of them had the nerve to fight for the South in the Civil War. That ought to make up for those few black soldiers who rode against Indians in the Western cavalry."

Her father sighed. "I never said either side was innocent or guilty, just ignorant. They've been a part of it, we've been a part of it, everybody's been a part of it for a long time."

"I know," said her mother, scornfully, "and you would just fly away, if you could."

Meridian's father said that Mr. Longknife had killed a lot of people, mainly Italians, in the Second World War. The reasons he'd done this remained abstract. That was why he was a wanderer. He was looking for reasons, answers, anything to keep his historical vision of himself as a just person from falling apart.

47

"The answer to everything," said Meridian's mother, "is we live in America and we're not rich."

One day when she was helping her father tie up some running beans, three white men in government-issued trucks—army green with white lettering on the side—came out to the farm. They unloaded a large wire trash basket and two brown picnic tables. They said a bulldozer would be coming the next day. The Indian burial mounds of the Sacred Serpent and her father's garden of prize beans, corn and squash were to be turned into a tourist attraction, a public park.

When her father went to the county courthouse with his deed, the officials said they could offer only token payment; that, and the warning to stay away from Sacred Serpent Park which, now that it belonged to the public, was of course not open to Colored.

Each afternoon after school her father had gone out to the farm. It was beautiful land made more impressive by the five-hundred-yard Sacred Serpent that formed a curving, twisting hill beyond the corn. The garden itself was in rich, flat land that fitted into the curves of the Sacred Serpent like the waves of the ocean fit the shore. Across from the Serpent and the garden was a slow-moving creek that was brown and sluggish and thick, like a stream of liquid snuff. Meridian had always enjoyed being on the farm with him, though they rarely talked. Her brothers were not interested in farming, had no feeling for the land or for Indians or for crops. They ate the fresh produce their father provided while talking of cars and engines and tires and cut-rate hubcaps. They considered working at gas stations a step up. Anything but being farmers. To them the word "farm" was actually used as a curse word.

"Aw, go on back to the *farm*," they growled over delicious meals.

But Meridian grieved with her father about the loss of the farm, now Sacred Serpent Park. For she understood his gifts came too late and were refused, and his pleasures were stolen away.

———

Where the springing head of the Sacred Serpent crossed the barbed-wire fence of the adjoining farm, it had been flattened years before by a farmer who raised wheat. This was long before Meridian or her father was born. Her father's grandmother, a woman it was said of some slight and harmless madness, and whose name was Feather Mae, had fought with her husband to save the snake. He had wanted to flatten his part of the burial mound as well and scatter the fragmented bones of the Indians to the winds. "It may not mean anything to you to plant food over other folks' bones," Feather Mae had told her husband, "but if you do you needn't expect me to eat another mouthful in your house!"

It was whispered too that Feather Mae had been very hot, and so Meridian's great-grandfather had not liked to offend her, since he could not bear to suffer the lonely consequences.

She had liked to go there, Feather Mae had, and sit on the Serpent's back, her long legs dangling while she sucked on a weed stem. She was becoming a woman—this was before she married Meridian's insatiable great-grandfather—and would soon be married, soon be expecting, soon be like her own mother, a strong silent woman who seemed always to be washing or ironing or cooking or rousing her family from naps to go back to work in the fields. Meridian's great-grandmother dreamed, with the sun across her legs and her black, moon-bright face open to the view.

One day she watched some squirrels playing up and down the Serpent's sides. When they disappeared she rose and followed them to the center of the Serpent's coiled tail, a pit forty feet deep, with smooth green sides. When she stood in the center of the pit, with the sun blazing down directly over her, something extraordinary happened to her. She felt as if she had stepped into another world, into a different kind of air. The green walls began to spin, and her feeling rose to such a high pitch the next thing she knew she was getting up off the ground. She knew she had fainted but she felt neither weakened nor ill. She felt renewed, as from some strange spiritual intoxication. Her blood made warm explosions through her body, and her eyelids stung and tingled.

Later, Feather Mae renounced all religion that was not based on the experience of physical ecstasy—thereby shocking her Baptist church and its unsympathetic congregation—and near the end of her life she loved walking nude about her yard and worshiped only the sun.

This was the story that was passed down to Meridian.

It was to this spot, the pit, that Meridian went often. Seeking to understand her great-grandmother's ecstasy and her father's compassion for people dead centuries before he was born, she watched him enter the deep well of the Serpent's coiled tail and return to his cornfield with his whole frame radiating brightness like the space around a flame. For Meridian, there was at first a sense of vast isolation. When she raised her eyes to the pit's rim high above her head she saw the sky as completely round as the bottom of a bowl, and the clouds that drifted slowly over her were like a mass of smoke cupped in downward-slanting palms. She was a dot, a speck in creation, alone and hidden. She had contact with no other living thing; instead she was surrounded by the dead. At first this frightened her, being so utterly small, encircled by ancient silent walls filled with bones, alone in a place not meant for her. But she remembered Feather Mae and stood patiently, willing her fear away. And it had happened to her.

From a spot at the back of her left leg there began a stinging sensation, which, had she not been standing so purposely calm and waiting, she might have dismissed as a sign of anxiety or fatigue. Then her right palm, and her left, began to feel as if someone had slapped them. But it was in her head that the lightness started. It was as if the walls of earth that enclosed her rushed outward, leveling themselves at a dizzying rate, and then spinning wildly, lifting her out of her body and giving her the feeling of flying. And in this movement she saw the faces of her family, the branches of trees, the wings of birds, the corners of houses, blades of grass and petals of flowers rush toward a central point high above her and she was drawn with them, as whirling, as bright, as free, as they. Then the outward flow, the rush of images, returned to the center of the pit where she stood, and what had left her at its going was returned. When she came back to her body—and she felt sure she had left it—her eyes were stretched wide open, and they were dry, because she found herself staring directly into the sun.

Her father said the Indians had constructed the coil in the Serpent's tail in order to give the living a sensation similar to that of dying: The body seemed to drop away, and only the spirit lived, set free in the world. But she was not convinced. It seemed to her that it was a way the living sought to expand the consciousness of being alive, there where the ground about them was filled with the dead. It was a possibility they discussed, alone in the fields. Their secret: that they both shared the peculiar madness of her great-grandmother. It sent them brooding at times over the meaning of this. At other times they rejoiced over so tangible a connection to the past.

Later in her travels she would go to Mexico to a mountain that contained at its point only the remains of an ancient altar, the origin of which no one was certain. She would walk up a steep stair made of stones to the pinnacle of the altar and her face would disappear into the clouds, just as the faces of ancient priests had seemed to disappear into the heavens to the praying followers who knelt in reverence down below. There would again be a rushing out from her all that was surrounding, all that she might have touched, and again she would become a speck in the grand movement of time. When she stepped upon the earth again it would be to feel the bottoms of her feet curl over the grass, as if her feet were those of a leopard or a bear, with curving claws and bare rough pads made sensitive by long use.

In the Capital's museum of Indians she peered through plate glass at the bones of a warrior, shamelessly displayed, dug up in a crouched position and left that way, his front teeth missing, his arrows and clay pipes around him. At such sights she experienced nausea at being alive.

When blacks were finally allowed into Sacred Serpent Park, long after her father's crops had been trampled into dust, she returned one afternoon and tried in vain to relive her earlier ecstasy and exaltation. But there were people shouting and laughing as they slid down the sides of the great Serpent's coil. Others stood glumly by, attempting to study the meaning of what had already and forever been lost.

English Walnuts

"Why are you always so sourfaced about it?" some boy would breathe into her bosom in the back seat of his car during the fifties. "Can't you *smile* some? I mean, is it gon' kill you?"

Her answer was a shrug.

Later on she would frown even more when she realized that her mother, father, aunts, friends, passers-by—not to mention her laughing sister—had told her nothing about what to expect from men, from sex. Her mother never even used the word, and her lack of information on the subject of sex was accompanied by a seeming lack of concern about her daughter's morals. Having told her absolutely nothing, she had expected her to *do* nothing. When Meridian left the house in the evening with her "boy-friend"—her current eager, hot-breathing lover, who always drove straight to the nearest lovers' lane or its equivalent, which in her case was the clump of bushes behind the city dump—her mother only cautioned her to "be sweet." She did not realize this was a euphemism for "Keep your panties up and your dress down," an expression she *had* heard and been puzzled by.

And so, while not enjoying it at all, she had had sex as often as her lover wanted it, sometimes every single night. And, since she *had* been told by someone that one's hips become broader after sex, she looked carefully in her mirror each morning before she caught the bus to school. Her pregnancy came as a total shock.

They lived, she and the latest lover, in a small house not a mile from the school. He married her, as he had always promised he would "if things went wrong." She had listened to this promise for almost two years (while he milked the end of his Trojans for signs of moisture). It had meant nothing because she could not conceive of anything going more wrong than the wrong she was already in. She could not understand why she was doing something with such frequency that she did not enjoy.

His name was Eddie. She did not like the name and didn't know why. It seemed the name of a person who would never amount to much, though "Edward" would have suited her no better.

As her lover, Eddie had had certain lovable characteristics—some of which he retained. He was good-looking and of the high school hero type. He was tall, with broad shoulders, and even though his skin was dark brown (and delicious that way) there was something of the prevailing white cheerleader's delight about him; there was a square regularity about his features, a pugness to his nose. He was, of course, good at sports and excelled in basketball. And she had loved to watch him make baskets from the center of the gymnasium floor. When he scored he smiled across at her, and the envy of the other girls kept her attentive in her seat.

His hair was straight up, like a brush—neither kinky nor curly. A black version of the then popular crew cut. He wore brown loafers, too, with money in them. And turtlenecks—when they were popular—and the most gorgeous light-blue jeans. Which, she was to learn, required washing and starching and ironing every week, as his mother had done, for dirty jeans were not yet the fashion. His eyes were nice—black and warm; his teeth, perfect. She loved the way his breath remained sweet—like a cow's, she told him, smiling fondly.

Being with him did a number of things for her. Mainly, it saved her from the strain of responding to other boys or even noting the whole category of Men. This was worth a great deal, because she was afraid of men—and was always afraid until she was taken under the wing of whoever wandered across her defenses to become—in a remarkably quick time—her lover. This, then, was probably what sex meant to her; not pleasure, but a sanctuary in which her mind was freed of any consideration for all the other males in the universe who might want anything of her. It was resting from pursuit.

Once in her "sanctuary" she could, as it were, look out at the male world with something approaching equanimity, even charity; even friendship. For she could make male friends only when she was sexually involved with a lover who was always near—if only in the way the new male friends thought of her as "So-an-so's Girl."

Her mother was long-suffering, typically, about the marriage; What had she ever done? and so forth. Then dedicated to the well-being of the beginning small family. Eddie was a good boy, it was argued, it was agreed—in her family's estimation. And he was, by several of the prevailing standards: He was always clean—he bathed, in summer, two or three times a week. His pants, jeans and Sunday, were creased *always*. His shirts starched and not in loud colors. His white buckskin shoes were dirty only when it became the fashion for them to be dirty. When the fashion said otherwise, the buckskins absorbed one bottle of white polish a week. And Eddie was smart: He made B's and an A in Band. He might become a businessman like his father, who worked in his own lumber company. He did not drop out of school when he got married, but simply worked overtime at the restaurant where he had previously worked after school. He had absorbed the belief, prevalent in all their homes, that without at least a high school diploma, a person would never amount to anything. He was even sorry she was expelled from school because of the pregnancy.

"Do you forgive me?" he asked, burrowing his bristly head into her lap.

"Forgive you for what?" It had not occurred to her to blame *him*. She felt, being pregnant, almost as if she'd contracted a

55

communicable disease, that the germs had been in the air and that her catching the disease was no one's fault.

"You know I've always required a lot."

"Always?"

"I did it the first time when I was nine, standing on top of a washtub, under the girl's window."

They laughed. "Did you know what you were doing?"

"A balancing act. But it *felt* so good!"

When she was not nauseous or throwing up, they laughed a lot, though there was a dizziness about it for her, the laughter seemed muted, as if she did it underwater, and the echo of it whirled sluggishly through her head.

They lived simply. She became drawn into the life of his family. Became "another daughter" to his mother. Listened politely to his father's stories of his exploits during the days when black people were sure enough chicken-shit. *Considered* chicken-shit, he added. It was her mother-in-law—a plump, rosy-brown woman with one breast, the other lost to cancer—who told her the "mysteries" of life. Astonishing her with such facts as: It is not possible to become pregnant if love is made standing up. Together they bought cloth to make the baby's clothes. Shopped for secondhand furniture, bought quantities of seasonal foods the two households could share.

And through it all, she sat in the small house not a mile from the school and never thought about the baby at all—unless her mother-in-law called and mentioned it, or something to do with it. She knew she did not want it. But even this was blurred. How could she not want something she was not even sure she was having? Yet she *was* having it, of course. She grew and grew and grew, as pregnant women will. Her skin, always smooth as velvet, became blotchy, her features blunted; her face looked bloated, tight.

She did not, also, think of Eddie very much. She woke to his sweet breath on her face every morning—and wondered who, really, he was. What he was doing there in bed with her. Or she

56

lay with him quietly, after making love, and enjoyed the incredible warmth of his very beautiful young body. So nearly black, so glowing and healthy, so *slim* now, next to hers. She loved the warmth, would do anything for it, his gentleness. She was grateful that he was willing to work so hard for their future, while she could not even recognize it.

"One day," he said over lunch, "we'll have a house like Mr. Yateson's. It will have cactus plants around it and a sky-blue driveway and painted blue trim. In the dining room there'll be a chandelier like the ones in Joan Crawford movies. And there'll be carpeting wall to wall and all the rooms will be different colors."

Mr. Yateson was the principal of their school. His brand-new house, floating on the bright-blue driveway and concrete walks that encircled it, sat back from a dirt road that was impassable when it rained and made Meridian think of a fancy-dressed lady without shoes standing in a puddle of mud.

"Um *hum,*" she would nod vaguely at Eddie's dream.

At the restaurant he worked as a waiter and sometimes short-order cook—hard work, little pay. And yet he was always patient and gentle with her, protective. If he worried he kept it from her, justifying his silence by her "condition." The worries he was unable to hide were about small things that bothered him: the ironing of his clothes, and even her own, which she did not do nearly as well as his mother (who, finally, in the last stages of her daughter-in-law's pregnancy, began to collect their dirty clothes each Wednesday to bring them back on Friday stainless and pale from bleach); the cooking, which she was too queasy to do at all; and the sex, which she did not seem (he said) interested in.

One night as he climbed over her—because he could only make love to her by beginning his assault from her left side—he said:

"And tonight, please, open your legs all the way."

"What do you mean, open my legs?" she asked.

"I have to fight to get your legs open; you know that as well as I do. They're like somebody starched them shut."

She had not been aware that she locked her legs. Now that he had pointed it out to her, however, she found she closed them tighter than ever.

"You just don't care about it any more," he moaned, burying his head in the pillow next to hers.

In fact, this last worry surprised her. She did not see how he could feel she was less interested in sex, for she felt she had never shown anything approaching interest. Nor could she imagine why any woman *should*. She loved the warmth, the lying together, the peace. She endured the sex because it gave her these things. She would have been just as happy, happier, without it. But he did not understand this and would sometimes seem hurt and complain. She did not know what to do, so of course she put the blame on any handy thing: her big stomach, the queasiness, the coming baby, old wives' tales that forbade intercourse until three months after the baby was born (a fact she learned from his mother: that intercourse any earlier weakened one's brain).

By that time—and it did not surprise her—he had a woman who loved sex, and was able to get as much of it as he wanted every night.

But he was "good" to her, even then. He did not "cheat" and "beat" her both, which meant he was "good" to her, according to her mother, his mother, the other women in the neighborhood and in fact just about everyone she knew, who seemed always to expect the two occurrences together, like the twin faces of a single plague.

But had she lost interest in sex completely? She didn't know. It was simply that sex was now something that she knew and thought she understood. Before it had been curiosity about her body's power. Nor was her response to Eddie's lovemaking as uncomplicated as he appeared to think.

She had not been wandering exactly on those afternoons she had found herself in front of Daxter's funeral home—that huge, snowy, two-storied building that stood on a hill between a church and an all-night café. Daxter's was owned by George Daxter, an obese half-white man in his fifties. His mother, so the story went, was white. When her parents found she was pregnant by the black man who worked for them, they shut her up in the cellar and threw away the key. They fed her pig bran and a little watery milk. When Daxter was born he was thrown out into the street with the rest of the trash. He was raised by an old woman who later died of ptomaine poisoning. She had eaten some sour, rotten tomatoes Daxter gave her.

Daxter had been after Meridian since she was twelve years old. She would visit the funeral home on Saturday afternoons, as everybody did to see who was new in the viewing room. Daxter would entice her into the small back office where he kept a long sofa and two soft chairs. At first she thought Daxter generous: He gave her candy for a swift, exploratory feel. When she became older—fifteen or so—he would take out his wallet crammed with money, and leave it on the sofa between them while he felt her breasts and tried to pull her onto his lap. The only part she liked was when he sucked her nipples, and she liked to hear his breathing, like his throat was closing, when she let one chubby hand touch the bottom of her panties. She could sit, holding his head against her breasts—where he busily and noisily sucked—and feel the hot throbbing of his passion almost enter her. But his obesity, in the end, was distasteful to her. She had heard that fat men had short, stunted penises. She imagined Daxter's penis to look like an English walnut.

When Daxter was not around she allowed herself to be chased around the embalming table by his young assistant, an almost handsome man, but dissipated and with a face that—as the saying went—*begged* for pussy. He thought of nothing else. His tool of seduction (his description) was his voice, which he used to describe the act of intercourse. Holding her with her back tight against him so that his penis was like a hard, live bedpost against her hips, he would whisper in her ear: "Think of how it would feel," he would urge, grabbing one, then both, of her nipples, "to have this big, black, long, ummm . . ." and he would press the bedpost against her—"inside you. Slippin' in and slippin' out."

She hated him but was fascinated; she was also far from immune to the voice. The Assistant would manipulate her breasts and cram her between his legs and rub her so against him that her panties became flooded with the residue of her resistance. The Assistant was very clever and so never actually forced her beyond a certain point, but each time he left her with one of his little homilies: "Experience is the best, the *only,* teacher," and "Just looking at water will never teach you to swim."

One day The Assistant, who knew (he said) how much she wanted to, was *ready* to, be fucked—if not by him then by the Voice, the Bedpost—arranged for her to watch him while he seduced another schoolgirl (the same girl, in fact, who did baby-sitting for his wife). He did it in the small shed where the wicker baskets were stored. She watched because she was curious, wanted to learn without doing, if possible, and because she had nothing better to do on a hot Wednesday afternoon.

The Assistant began by standing with his bedpost against the back of the girl. She was about sixteen, and wore loafers and a red cardigan sweater turned backward with a neat little white collar. Her small brown hands kept checking the collar to be sure it had not become unfastened by the stripping quality of The Assistant's words. His hands were elsewhere. Already under the cardigan, kneading the nipples—then into her pants as her skirt fell to the floor. Then he hoisted her up onto the table and began to fuck her standing up. Then up on the table. The girl was bucking up and down as fast as she could, as if she feared to break a rhythm she had learned by heart. The Voice fucked more slowly, expertly, like a machine, and the Voice never stopped talking. At the end he watched her as if from a distance, his voice a monotone, his face greedy, obscene and ugly. When the girl tried to bury her face in his chest and force his arms around her, he pushed her away.

The Assistant said later that the girl was his now whenever he wanted her, because he had discovered a secret few men knew: how to make a woman come by using nothing but his penis and his beautiful voice. These were his gifts, The Assistant said, more skillful than the suppleness of wrist required to extract cold blood from a cadaver's vein. And what had she thought of his performance? She was willing to continue their meetings on one condition, she told him. What is that? he eagerly asked, sucking a lemon for his throat. If you hold me in your arms, she said casually, you must promise not to talk.

Of course she had given up Daxter and The Assistant when she became involved with Eddie—well, not just at first. She was guilty of having tried to use them to discover him, what he wanted from her; and yet their pawing over her and her refusal to do anything more than tease them had seemingly separated her from her young husband forever. For as much as she wanted to, she—her body, that is—never had any intention of *giving in*. She was suspicious of pleasure. She might approach it, might gaze on it with longing, but retreat was inevitable. Besides, Eddie did not seriously expect more than "interest" from her. She perceived there might be something more; but for him, it was enough that his pleasure should please her. Understanding this, they never discussed anything beyond her attitude.

The Happy Mother

She had been in hard labor for a day and a half. Then, when she brought the baby home, it had suffered through a month of colic, gasping and screaming and robbing her of sleep. She was so exhausted it was futile to attempt to think straight, or even to think at all. It took everything she had to tend to the child, and she had to do it, her body prompted not by her own desires, but by her son's cries. So this, she mumbled, lurching toward his crib in the middle of the night, is what slavery is like. Rebelling, she began to dream each night, just before her baby sent out his cries, of ways to murder him.

She sat in the rocker Eddie had bought and stroked her son's back, her fingers eager to scratch him out of her life. She realized he was even more helpless than herself, and yet she would diaper him roughly, yanking his fat brown legs in the air, because he looked like his father and because everyone who came to visit assumed she loved him, and because he did not feel like anything to her but a ball and chain.

The thought of murdering her own child eventually frightened her. To suppress it she conceived, quite consciously, methods of killing herself. She found it pleasantly distracting to imagine herself stiff and oblivious, her head stuck in an oven. Or coolly out of it, a hole through the roof of her mouth. It seemed to her that the peace of the dead was truly blessed, and each day she planned a new way of approaching it. Because of her growing reliance on suicide, the thought of it, she was able to function very well. She was told by everyone that she was an exemplary young mother, so mature, so calm. This pleased her because it was so amusing. She delighted in the praise. As her face grew warmer and warmer she began to giggle—to be praised some more for her good humor.

She felt as though something perched inside her brain was about to fly away. Eddie went to the restaurant, worked, came home (or did not come home), ate, slept, went off to school in the morning, as before. He loved his son, and was good to the child. He bought him the usual stupid presents, showed him off to his parents, took pictures every six weeks and even learned to change the baby's diaper—though he denied this expertise when his friends came to visit.

She wondered sometimes why she still did not love Eddie. It perplexed her. He was still good-looking, still sought after by women (several, by now, had caught him, at least for a time), and he treated her with gentleness and respect. But the longer they lived together the more she became obsessed with the horrible thought that Eddie, like his name, would never be grown up. She thought he would always be a boy. Not that she knew what a man should be; she did not know. She only knew that none of the boys she had dated or been friends with seemed capable of becoming men. She projected first one, then the other, of them into the future. They became older, but still boys. She could imagine them only in positions similar to—if on the surface vastly different from—the one Eddie held at the restaurant. Fetching and carrying and courteously awaiting orders from someone above. She could not imagine one of them becoming, for example, president of the local bank.

This affected her with a kind of lethargy. She could not become active again. She could not move about her own house purposefully. What was the use?

She could, however, criticize. And she began to find fault—with everything. Small things, at first. For starters: Why did his pants and shirts have to be starched and ironed after every second wearing? (By this time his mother had stopped doing the laundry for them.) It did not seem a reasonable answer to her that his mother "had *always* done this," or that he was "*used* to clean clothes." So what? she answered, so was she. But she had learned to wear her clothes longer than two days without changing them. Except for her underwear. And why, she wondered, must he shower for such a long time and fog up the bathroom so that if she came in, even to use the toilet, her hair was ruined by the steam? And did he still play basketball at school? And was there a point to staying fit? What damn good did he expect it to do?

More seriously: She hated the fact that although he was still in school and she was not, he did not seem to know anything about books—or about the world. She learned more than he knew from watching TV quiz programs.

He was not interested in "education," he said, but in finishing school. She despised this answer because she knew the truth of it. She knew also that it was the aim of everyone in the school, from the principal to the first-graders. In fact, "finishing school" was synonymous with "education." The point was, she did not believe it, now that she was no longer in school. School had been dreary, but only there had she occasionally experienced the quicksilver flash of learning that never came to her now.

She read *Sepia, Tan, True Confessions, Real Romances* and *Jet.* According to these magazines, Woman was a mindless body, a sex creature, something to hang false hair and nails on. Still, they helped her know for sure her marriage was breaking up. She lived with the awareness in her usual fog of unconcern. Yet the break, when it came, was not—as she had feared and sometimes hoped—cataclysmic. In fact, in a way she hardly noticed it. It did not come at once, with a heated argument, fighting, packing or slamming doors. It came in pieces, some larger or smaller than others. It came—on Eddie's part—with a night away here, three or four days absent there, and with a cooling off, slightly, of his usual affectionate attention to the baby. This was the only sign of calculation she could detect on his part. He assumed, naturally, that the baby would remain with her (this was, after all, how such arrangements had *always* gone), and he did not intend to see much more of either of them. On her side there was just—a continuation of her lethargy, an unwillingness to put forth effort for anything.

On the day he left, she had walked past a house, not far from theirs, where—since it was nearly summer—all the doors and windows were open. People, young people, were everywhere. They milled about inside, shouted out of windows to those outside, looked carefree (as childless young people, her own age, always now looked to her) and yet as if sensitive to some outside surveillance beyond her own staring. But she was the only person walking on that street. And she stopped to look only because it was a black family's house, in a black neighborhood, and there were several young white people. And all of the young people were strangely dressed and looked, really, funny and old-timey in the overalls and clodhoppers they wore. Even the girls (and she noticed especially a white girl with long brown hair) were dressed in overalls *with bibs!*

It was something to think about, the day Eddie moved out for good. She could not, somehow, concentrate on the fact of his leaving. She did not know deeply enough what it might mean. *Was* he gone for good? Did he actually take all his clothes—even the starched but unironed shirts balled up in the refrigerator? And who was to play with the baby when he woke up? Eddie usually did, if he had a few minutes between work and school.

Now she sat listlessly, staring at the TV. The house she had passed was on. There was to be a voter registration drive (she wondered what that was) that would begin in the city, at that house, and work its way out to the people in the country. Local blacks, volunteers, were needed. A group of young men made this announcement to a (white) newscaster who looked astonished and held his handkerchief over the mike when he presented it; when he talked into it himself, he removed the handkerchief. Black people were never shown in the news—unless of course they had shot their mothers or raped their bosses' grandparent—and a black person or persons giving a news conference was unheard of. But this concerned her, gathered her attention, only superficially, for all its surprise. It kept her mind somewhere else while she made her hands play with the baby, whom, even then, she had urges to kill. To strangle that soft, smooth, helpless neck, to push down that kinky head into a tub of water, to lock it in its room to starve. It looked at her with apprehension, looked about mournfully for its daddy. She forced herself to think only of the black faces on TV and about the house not far from her own.

The next morning as she lay in bed watching the early news, she was again shown pictures of the house—except now the house no longer existed anywhere but on film. During the night—between three and four A.M.—the house was demolished by firebombs. The bombs, exploding, set fire to—not just that house—the whole cluster of houses on that street. Three small children were injured—no, a flash at the bottom of the screen announced them dead; several grownups were injured. One adult, missing, was assumed dead. The others had somehow escaped. It seems they had posted a guard who was alerted by the sound of a pickup truck stopping several yards from the house and then, in a few minutes, racing off.

This struck her, that they had had a guard. Why did they need a guard? Then, a question more to the point: How had they *known* they would need a guard? Did they know something she did not know? She had lived in this town all her life, but could not have foreseen that the house would be bombed. Perhaps because nothing like this had ever happened before. Not in this town. Or *had* it? She recalled that the night before she had dreamed of Indians. She had thought she had forgotten about them.

And so it was that one day in the middle of April in 1960 Meridian Hill became aware of the past and present of the larger world.

Clouds

Each morning, after the bombing, she took the child—his name was Eddie Jr.—to spend the day with his uncle, his father's baby brother, who was only three years old. Eddie's mother, now forty-nine, had undoubtedly misinterpreted one of her sexual facts: Meridian could never quite believe her when she said she'd planned such a late baby. With Eddie Jr. gone, she returned to the house—now subsidized by her in-laws—and put her feet up against the windowsill in the back bedroom. The window looked out into a small enclosed back yard—usually green, except for the brief winter from December to March—and she attempted to meditate on her condition, unconscious, at first, of what she did. At first it was like falling back into a time that never was, a time of complete rest, like a faint. Her senses were stopped, while her body rested; only in her head did she feel something, and it was a sensation of lightness—a lightness like the inside of a drum. The air inside her head was pure of thought, at first. For hours she sat by the window looking out, but not seeing the pecan trees bending in the wind, or the blue cloudied sky, or the grass.

At three o'clock she moved to a side window and watched the children walk by on their way home from school. She watched the young girls, their bodies just forming into women's bodies. Watched how they bent against the wind or held their books in front of them in a gesture of defense, almost of shame. Certainly of fear. Then, in the slightly older ones, there was the beginning

69

pride in their bodies, so that they did not bend against the wind—wind real or wind imaginary—but stood with their breasts as obvious as possible so that the boys, galloping alongside and past them in herds—neighing, in their incoherent, aimless laughter and banter, like young ponies—looked boldly at them and grinned and teased and brought embarrassment and pleasure to the young girls. But, Meridian thought, for all their bodies' assertion, the girls moved protected in a dream. A dream that had little to do with the real boys galloping past them. For they did not perceive them clearly but as they might become in a different world from the one they lived in. Which might explain why she could herself recall nothing of those years, beyond the Saturday afternoons and evenings in the picture show. For it was the picture show that more than anything else filled those bantering, galloping years.

Movies: Rory Calhoun, Ava Gardner, Bette Davis, Slim Pickens. Blondes against brunettes and cowboys against Indians, good men against bad, darker men. This fantasy world made the other world of school—with its monotony and tedium—bearable. The young girls she watched were, for the most part, well brought up. They were polite, they were sweet, they were intelligent. They simply did not know they were living their own lives—between twelve and fifteen—but assumed they lived someone else's. They tried to live the lives of their movie idols; and those lives were fantasy. Not even the white people they watched and tried to become—the actors—lived them.

So they moved, did the young girls outside her window, in the dream of happy endings: of women who had everything, of men who ran the world. So had she.

But these thoughts, which were as random and fleeting as clouds, were simply the outside layer of skin on a very large onion.

She was still only seventeen. A drop-out from high school, a deserted wife, a mother, a daughter-in-law. This being so, in the late afternoons she went to her mother-in-law's house and picked up the child, who did not want to come home.

The Attainment of Good

Her mother's life was sacrifice. A blind, enduring, stumbling—though with dignity (as much as was possible under the circumstances)—through life. She did not appear to understand much beyond what happened in her own family, in the neighborhood and in her church. She did not take extreme positions on anything, unless unreasonably provoked over a long period. Then she spluttered out her rage in barely coherent complaints against—but what *had* her mother complained against? She did not complain against the church because she believed the church building—the mortar and bricks—to be holy; she believed that this holiness had rubbed off from years of scripture reading and impassioned prayers, so that now holiness covered the walls like paint. She thought the church was literally God's house, and believed she felt his presence there when she entered the door; when she stepped back outside there was a different feeling, she believed.

There were many things wrong with the church, of course. One was that the preacher was not usually understandable. That is, his words were not, his sentences were not. For years—thirty of them—she sat every Sunday convinced that this man—whoever was preaching at the time—was instilling in her the words and wisdom of God, when, in fact, every other sentence was incomprehensible. Preachers preached in a singsong voice that was rhythmic, often majestic and always passionate. They made elaborate modern examples from ancient texts. They were musicians. They were poets. She was aroused, her spirit enlarged by a desire to be good. (For that, she knew, was what all the words of God led to, whether she could hear them clearly or not.) To the attainment of Good. To a state of righteousness. She did not learn very much beyond a rudimentary knowledge of the birth and crucifixion of Christ (which seemed to have occurred so close together in History she often wondered if Christ had had a childhood), and of the miracle of Ezekiel's wheel (whose meaning was that even before the airplane man could get off the ground if he just had Faith), and of the Exodus, under the command of Moses, of the children of Israel (a race, unfortunately, no longer extant). The songs she understood. They allowed every sinner to sing of her sins to high heaven without the risk of being taken to task personally.

Mrs. Hill did not complain about anything political because she had no desire to understand politics. She had never voted in her life. Meridian grew up thinking voting days—with their strewn banners and long lines of people—were for celebration of some kind of weird festival especially for white people, who, grim and tight, disappeared into dreary, curtained boxes and emerged seconds later looking strongly relieved. Nor did Mrs. Hill complain about the education of her children. She believed the teachers to be eminently qualified (that is, more qualified than she herself) to teach them. If she felt contempt for them because she could no longer count herself among them and because they were poor housekeepers, she kept it very carefully to herself. She respected schoolteachers as a class but despised them as individuals. At the same time, she needed to believe in their infallibility. Otherwise she could not attempt to copy the clothes they wore, the way they fixed their hair or the way they spoke—or the authority with which they were able to confront and often dominate less well educated men.

In fact, she complained only about her husband, whose faults, she felt, more than made up for her ignorance of whatever faults might exist elsewhere.

In the ironing of her children's clothes she expended all the energy she might have put into openly loving them. Her children were spotless wherever they went. In their stiff, almost inflexible garments, they were enclosed in the starch of her anger, and had to keep their distance to avoid providing the soggy wrinkles of contact that would cause her distress.

Awakening

A month after the bombing Meridian walked through the gate of a house and knocked on the door.

"I've come to volunteer," she said to the dark young man staring at her there.

What was she volunteering into? She had no real idea. Something about the bombing had attracted her, the obliteration of the house, the knowledge that had foreseen this destruction. What would these minds, these people, be like?

"Swinburn," said the boy who opened the door, "look what the good Lord done gone and sent us." He was short and stout with puffy brown eyes behind his glasses. His smile was warm and welcoming, and when he preceded Meridian into the room she noticed he dipped and bobbed ever so slightly like a man pulling a dog on a leash.

Swinburn rose from a table in the back of the room near the window. "Thank God," he said. "Allah be praised and paid. Come on in here, lady, and let me ask you something. Can you type?"

"No," said Meridian, who had taken typing for three months before she'd started having morning sickness—all-day sickness, in her case.

"Can you learn quickly?" A young man, older than the other two, stood in the doorway. He was looking at her in a steady, cool, appraising way, and held some papers in his hands. She could not help staring at his nose, which was high-bridged and keen, and seemed to have come straight off the faces of Ethiopian warriors, whose photographs she had seen. It was wonderfully noble, she thought, and gave the young man an arrogant look. He was dressed in blue jeans and a polo shirt and his shirt front was covered with buttons. That he wore lots of buttons struck Meridian as odd, too playful, for such a cool, serious man. She wanted buttons like that, though. When he came closer she especially liked the large one that showed a black hand and a white hand shaking, although since the colors were flat the hands did not seem, on closer inspection, to be shaking at all; they seemed to be merely touching palms, or in the act of sliding away from each other.

"Yes," she said, "I guess I could learn."

The one called Swinburn was busy pecking out something on the typewriter in front of him, his thin back bent over, his ribs showing beneath his faded shirt. He was very dark brown, with full, neatly curved lips and large eyes behind wireless glasses that further magnified them. When he spoke, his deep voice coming up from the thin cavern of his chest was extraordinary. The timbre was so deep it seemed to make things rattle in the room. When he made an error typing he pulled at his short, rough hair. He was speeding up his pecking, now that he knew she was looking at him, but the number of errors he made soon caused him to jump up and offer his chair to her.

"Don't you want to know my name?"

"Oh," rumbled Swinburn, "I'm sorry. It's just that we've been so busy since the bombing. Getting another house, trying to raise money . . . My name is, uh, Swinburn, that's Chester Gray" (indicating one of the other young men).

"*Et je m'appelle* Truman Held," said the young man with the nose.

The other two men laughed at him: "It even rhymes!" they said. But Meridian was puzzled. Perhaps they were laughing at her, too, because she had not understood what had been said. She told them her name, they grunted and then turned away, except for Swinburn.

"This is just a petition," he said, standing over her. "You know about the bombing? We're trying to find out how many local people would be interested in marching downtown to protest. Just type out what I've written there, and I'll take it over to the school and see if I can have it mimeographed."

"You mean at *our* school?" she asked.

"Of course," said Swinburn.

"They won't do it over there."

"Why not?" asked Swinburn.

"I can't say why not," said Meridian, "all I know is they won't do it. They won't even let us wear shorts on the Easter egg hunt."

"Well, type it anyway," said Swinburn. "Some way or other we'll get enough copies made."

Meridian typed and typed, until her back seemed to be cracking and her eyes smarted. Her typing was horrible, and she felt ashamed of the amount of paper she was using. After an hour she was able to lay out a perfect copy of the petition, except that she'd put an "e" on Negro.

"It's all right," said Swinburn, crossing out the "e" with a thick, blunt pen, so that the beauty of the finished product was hopelessly marred, "all you need is practice."

Battle Fatigue

Truman Held was the first of the Civil Rights workers—for that's what they were called—who began to mean something to her, though it was months after their initial meeting that she knew. It was not until one night when first he, then she, was arrested for demonstrating outside the local jail, and then beaten.

There had been a Freedom march to the church, a prayer by the Reverend in charge, Freedom songs, several old women testifying (mainly about conditions inside the black section of the jail, which caused Meridian's body to twitch with dread) and finally, a plan of what their strategy was to be, and the singing of "Ain't Gonna Let Nobody Turn Me Round."

The strategy was for a midnight march, with candles, across the street from the jail by the people who had not been arrested earlier, of whom Truman was one. The strategy was, in fact, for everyone not formerly arrested to be so. This was in protest against the town's segregated hospital facilities. It was also an attempt to have the earlier demonstrators released from jail. But even as she marched, singing, to the courthouse square, which was across from the jail, Meridian could not figure out how it was supposed to work. The earlier demonstrators, she felt sure, would not be set free because a few singing people stood peacefully across from the jail. And the jail was too small to accommodate any more bodies. It must already be jammed.

They had been singing for only a few minutes when the town

became alive with flashing lights. Police cars came from everywhere. Dozens of state troopers surrounded them, forming a wall between them and the jail. She noticed they really *did* have crew cuts, they really *did* chew gum. Next, the jailhouse door was opened and the earlier demonstrators came wearily out, their faces misshapen from swellings and discolored from bruises. Truman limped along with the rest, moving in great pain and steadily muttering curses as the line of troopers hurried them relentlessly out of the square. It was a few seconds before Meridian understood that it was now their turn.

As soon as this line was out of sight, the troopers turned on them, beating and swinging with their bludgeons. One blow knocked Meridian to the ground, where she was trampled by people running back and forth over her. But there was nowhere to run. Only the jail door was open and unobstructed. Within minutes they had been beaten inside, where the sheriff and his deputies waited to finish them. And she realized why Truman was limping. When the sheriff grabbed her by the hair and someone else began punching her and kicking her in the back, she did not even scream, except very intensely in her own mind, and the scream was Truman's name. And what she meant by it was not even that she was in love with him: What she meant by it was that they were at a time and a place in History that forced the trivial to fall away—and they were absolutely together.

Later that summer, after another demonstration, she saw him going down a street that did not lead back to the black part of town. His eyes were swollen and red, his body trembling, and he did not recognize her or even see her. She knew his blankness was battle fatigue. They all had it. She was as weary as anyone, so that she spent a good part of her time in tears. At first she had burst into tears whenever something went wrong or someone spoke unkindly or even sometimes if they spoke, period. But now she was always in a state of constant tears, so that she could do whatever she was doing—canvassing, talking at rallies, tying her sneakers, laughing—while tears rolled slowly and ceaselessly down her cheeks. This might go on for days, or even weeks.

Then, suddenly, it would stop, and some other symptom would appear. The shaking of her hands, or the twitch in her left eye. Or the way she would sometimes be sure she'd heard a shot and feel the impact of the bullet against her back; then she stood absolutely still, waiting to feel herself fall.

She went up to à yard with an outdoor spigot and soaked the bottom of her blouse in water. When she came back down to the street to wipe the tear gas from Truman's eyes, he was gone. A police car was careening down the street. She stood in the street feeling the cool wet spot on her side, wondering what to do.

The majority of black townspeople were sympathetic to the Movement from the first, and told Meridian she was doing a good thing: typing, teaching illiterates to read and write, demonstrating against segregated facilities and keeping the Movement house open when the other workers returned to school. Her mother, however, was not sympathetic.

"As far as I'm concerned," said Mrs. Hill, "you've wasted a year of your life, fooling around with those people. The papers say they're crazy. God separated the sheeps from the goats and the black folks from the white. And me from anybody that acts as foolish as they do. It never bothered *me* to sit in the back of the bus, you get just as good a view and you don't have all those nasty white asses passing you."

Meridian attempted to ignore her, but her mother would continue. "If somebody thinks he'll have to pee when he gets to town, let him use his own toilet before he leaves home! That's what we did when I was coming up!" Eventually Mrs. Hill would talk herself out.

It had taken Meridian a long time to tell her mother she *was* in the Movement, and by the time she did, her mother already knew. Now she had news that was even more likely to infuriate her. To deliver it, she brought Delores Jones (another Movement worker) and Nelda Henderson, an old playmate, with her. It was cowardly of her, but Meridian could not face her mother alone.

While Meridian was still a student in high school she was tested and informed that, for her area and background, her IQ of 140 was unusually high. She was pregnant at the time, sick as a dog and about to be expelled from school; she had shrugged her shoulders at the news. But now, though she had not completed high school, she was to have—if she wanted it—a chance to go to college. Mr. Yateson told her this, explaining that a unique honor was being bestowed upon her—who might or might not be worthy; after all, nice girls did not become pregnant in high school—and that he expected her to set a high moral standard because she would be representing the kind of bright "product" his "plant" could produce.

He spoke so proprietarily she thought at first he intended to send her to college with his own money. But no. He explained that a generous (and wealthy) white family in Connecticut—who wished to help some of the poor, courageous blacks they saw marching and getting their heads whipped nightly on TV—had decided, as a gesture of their liberality and concern, to send a smart black girl to Saxon College in Atlanta, a school this family had endowed for three generations.

"You don't mean I'm the smartest one you've got!" said Meridian, humbly. But then the thought that this might be true simply because Mr. Yateson's "plant" generally produced nothing among its "products" but boredom tickled her and she smiled.

Mr. Yateson was annoyed. "In my day," he said, "we didn't reward bad behavior—nor did we think it was funny!"

So then Meridian felt she had to apologize for her smile, even though it had been such a pathetic one, and some of the joy of the experience went out of it for her.

It was Truman who put it back by telling her Saxon College was only two hours away, and just across the street from his own school, R. Baron College, which he attended when he was not working in the Movement out of town. Because of course there was an Atlanta Movement, in which he had already been involved. He and Meridian would see each other every day.

"Mais oui," Truman kept saying, as she looked shyly but happily up at him, "you will be just the Saxon type!"

But then, she had never told him she had a child.

"You have a right to go to college," said Delores. "You're lucky to have the chance." She was slender and brown, with a strong, big nose and eyebrows like black wings. She wore jeans and flowered shirts and was unafraid of everything. "Listen," she said, "it's not every day that somebody's going to care about your high IQ and offer you a scholarship. You ain't no dummy, girl, and don't you even consider acting like one now." They walked up to the front door, Nelda Henderson reaching out to squeeze Meridian's hand.

"No matter what your mother says," Delores continued, "just remember she spends all her time making prayer pillows."

Nelda said nothing about Meridian going to college because she wanted to save her words for Meridian's mother. Nelda cried easily and looked at Delores and Meridian with sad envy. She was pregnant again and it was just beginning to show. When Mrs. Hill came to the door there was a coolness in her response to Nelda's greeting, which brought the always close tears to the surface.

The Hills' house was white on the outside with turquoise shutters. It was cluttered with heavy brown furniture, white porcelain dolls, and churns filled with paper flowers. Dozens of snapshots of other people's children grinned down at them from the walls.

"Well, it can't be moral, that I know. It can't be right to give away your own child." They sat around the dining room table drinking tea. "If the good Lord gives you a child he means for *you* to take care of it."

"The good Lord didn't give it to her," muttered Delores. Delores was intrepid. Meridian loved her.

"But this is the only chance I have, Mama," she said.

"You should have thought about that before."

"I didn't *know* before," she said, looking into her glass. "How can I take care of Eddie Jr. anyway?" she asked. "I can't even take care of myself."

Mrs. Hill frowned. "Do you know how many women have thought that and had to have God make a way? You surprised me," she continued, sighing. "I always thought you were a *good* girl. And all the time, you were fast."

"I was something," said Meridian. "But I didn't even know what fast was. You always talked in riddles. 'Be sweet.' 'Don't be fast.' You never made a bit of sense."

"That's right," said Mrs. Hill. "Blame me for trusting you. But I know one thing: Everybody else that slips up like you did *bears* it. You're the only one that thinks you can just outright refuse . . ." Mrs. Hill stopped and wiped her eyes.

"Look at Nelda," she began, "I know *she'd* never . . ."

But Nelda interrupted. "Don't say that, Mrs. Hill," she said, her eyes tearing. "I'd do anything to have a chance to go to college like Meridian. I wish to God I could have made it to junior high."

For a moment, as she looked at Meridian's mother, there was hatred in her sad eyes. Hatred and comprehension of betrayal. She had lived across the street from the Hills all her life. She and Meridian played together in the Hills' back yard, they went to school together. Nelda knew that the information she had needed to get through her adolescence was information Mrs. Hill could have given her.

There had been about Nelda in those days a naïve and admirable sweetness, but there was also apparent, if one knew how to recognize such things (and Mrs. Hill might certainly have done so), a premonition of her fall, which grew out of her meek acceptance of her family's burdens. She had been left in charge of her five younger brothers and sisters every day while her mother worked. On Saturdays she struggled to town to do the shopping, the twins racing ahead of her down the street, the two toddlers holding to her arms and the baby strapped to her back. This was Nelda—as pretty, the boys used to say, as an Indian—at fourteen, just before she became pregnant herself.

On Sundays Nelda was free to do as she liked. Her mother did not work then, but spent most of the day—with all her other children neatly dressed and combed—in church. (She was a large, "bald-headed" woman, with massive breasts and a fine contralto singing voice. Her husband had been lost in France during the Second World War, and though only two of her children were his—Nelda and the next oldest child, a boy—they all carried his name. She had lost her hair, bit by bit, during each pregnancy.) Nelda was allowed to spend the day at home washing her hair, making dinner and doing her homework (she made it to school perhaps six times a month, and no truant officer ever knocked on her door), and in the late afternoons she went, with Meridian and Delores, to a movie in town, where the three of them sat in the gallery above the heads of the white movie goers and necked with their boyfriends of the moment.

Meridian knew the father of Nelda's first baby. He was an older boy, in high school, a gentle boy who treated Nelda as if he loved her more than life, which he might have. He bought her combs and blouses and Bermuda shorts, and her first pair of stockings—all from the three-dollar allowance his mother gave him each week plus his earnings from cutting lawns during the summer. While her mother was at work he often came by to cut their grass and stayed to help Nelda give the children supper, baths and put them to bed. Nelda was well into her third month before she realized something was wrong. It started, she confided to Meridian, by her noticing her pee smelled different.

"What do you mean, your *pee* smells different?" Meridian laughed.

"I don't know," Nelda giggled, "but this ain't its usual smell."

They sat on the toilets at school and laughed and laughed.

"You should *want* Eddie Jr.," said Mrs. Hill. "Unless you're some kind of monster. And no daughter of mine is a monster, surely."

Meridian closed her eyes as tight as she could.

Delores cleared her throat. "The only way Meridian can take

care of Eddie Jr. is if she moves in here with you and gets a job in somebody's kitchen while you take care of the kid."

"Of course I'll help out," said Mrs. Hill. "I wouldn't let either one of 'em starve, but—" she continued, speaking to Delores as if Meridian were not present, "this is a clean, upright, *Christian* home. We believe in God in this house."

"What's that got to do with anything?" asked Delores, whose face expressed belligerence and confusion. "The last time God had a baby he skipped, too."

Mrs. Hill pretended she wasn't angry and insulted. She smiled at this girl she wanted to hit. "You're not from around here," she said, "everybody knows people from up Atlanta have strange ideas. A lot of you young people have lost your respect for the church. Do you even believe in God?"

"I give it some thought," said Delores.

Mrs. Hill drew in her stomach and crossed her plump arms over it. "I just don't see how you could let another woman raise your child," she said. "It's just selfishness. You ought to hang your head in shame. I have six children," she continued self-righteously, "though I never wanted to have any, and I have raised every one myself."

"You probably could have done the same thing in slavery," said Delores.

"Let's all be monsters!" Delores joked as she and her friends left Mrs. Hill's house, but Meridian and Nelda did not laugh.

She might not have given him away to the people who wanted him. She might have murdered him instead. Then killed herself. They would all have understood this in time. She might have done it that way except for one thing: One day she really looked at her child and loved him with as much love as she loved the moon or a tree, which was a considerable amount of impersonal love. She wanted to know more about his perfect, if unplanned-for, existence.

"Who are you?" she asked him.

"Where were you when I was twelve?"

"Who *are* you?" she persisted, studying his face for signs of fire, watermarks, some scar that would intimate a previous life.

"Were there other people where you were? Did you come from a planet of babies?" She thought she could just imagine him there, on such a planet, pulling the blue grass up by the handfuls.

Now that she looked at him, the child was beautiful. She had thought him ugly, like a hump she must carry on her back.

"You will no longer be called Eddie Jr." she said. "I'll ask them to call you Rundi, after no person, I hope, who has ever lived."

When she gave him away she did so with a light heart. She did not look back, believing she had saved a small person's life.

But she had not anticipated the nightmares that began to trouble her sleep. Nightmares of the child, Rundi, calling to her, crying, suffering unbearable deprivations because she was not there, yet she knew it was just the opposite: Because she was not there he needn't worry, ever, about being deprived. Of his life, for instance. She felt deeply that what she'd done was the only thing, and was right, but that did not seem to matter. On some deeper level than she had anticipated or had even been aware of, she felt condemned, consigned to penitence, for life. The past pulled the present out of shape as she realized that what Delores Jones had said was *not*, in fact, true. If her mother had had children in slavery she would not, automatically, have been allowed to keep them, because they would not have belonged to her but to the white person who "owned" them all. Meridian knew that enslaved women had been made miserable by the sale of their children, that they had laid down their lives, gladly, for their children, that the daughters of these enslaved women had thought their greatest blessing from "Freedom" was that it meant they could keep their own children. And what had Meridian Hill done with *her* precious child? She had given him away. She thought of her mother as being worthy of this maternal history, and of herself as belonging to an unworthy minority, for which there was no

87

precedent and of which she was, as far as she knew, the only member.

After she had figuratively kissed the ground of the campus and walked about its lawns intent on bettering herself, she knew for certain she had broken something, for she began hearing a voice when she studied for exams, and when she walked about the academic halls, and when she looked from her third-floor dormitory window. A voice that cursed her existence—an existence that could not live up to the standard of motherhood that had gone before. It said, over and over, until she would literally reel in the streets, her head between her hands: Why don't you die? Why not kill yourself? Jump into the traffic! Lie down under the wheels of that big truck! Jump off the roof, as long as you're up there! Always, the voice. Mocking, making fun. It frightened her because the voice urging her on—the voice that said terrible things about her lack of value—was her own voice. It was talking to her, and it was full of hate.

Her teachers worked her hard, her first year at Saxon. She read night and day, making up for lost time. But no matter how hard she labored she was always willing to tackle more, because she knew almost no one there, and because Saxon was a peaceful but strange, still, place to her, and because she was grateful to be distracted. She was not to pause long enough to respond to this spiritual degeneration in herself until she was in her second year.

The Driven Snow

> *We are as chaste and pure as*
> *the driven snow.*
> *We watch our manners, speech*
> *and dress just so;*
> *And in our hearts we carry our*
> *greatest fame*
> *That we are blessed to perpetuate*
> *the Saxon name!*

She *had* felt blessed her first year at Saxon. It was so beautiful! The tall red brick towers, the old courtyards, the giant trees—especially the greatest tree of them all, The Sojourner. This tree filled her with the same sense of minuteness and hugeness, of past and present, of sorrow and ecstasy that she had known at the Sacred Serpent. It gave her a profound sense of peace (which was only possible when she could feel invisible) to know slaves had found shelter in its branches. When her spirits were low, as they were often enough that first year, she would sit underneath The Sojourner and draw comfort from her age, her endurance, the stories the years told of her, and her enormous size. When she sat beneath The Sojourner, she knew she was not alone.

She was happy to make friends with Anne-Marion Coles, who seemed to her as sharp and bright as a blade of sunlight. It was Anne-Marion who had balked at singing the school song as it was written and who created instead the "parallel song," the beginning of which was: "We are as choice and prime as the daily steak." Naturally, steak was a food they never had at Saxon. They sang it with gusto while their classmates sang tamely of being like driven snow.

Of course it was kept secret from everyone that Meridian had been married and divorced and had had a child. It was assumed that Saxon young ladies were, by definition, virgins. They were treated always as if they were thirteen years old. This included the imposition on the student body of a requirement that was particularly awkward for Meridian that had to do with religion: Each morning at eight all Saxon students were required to attend a chapel service at which one girl was expected to get up on the platform and tell—in a ten-minute speech—of some way in which she had resisted evil and come out on the right side of God. Meridian could not recall any temptation that she had resisted, and whether she had resisted temptation or not, she did not believe she now stood even in the vicinity of God. In fact, Meridian was not sure there was a God, and when her turn came, she said so. She was still a very naïve country girl who had expected an atmosphere in college that was different from that in her local church. She was wrong. When her fellow students found themselves near her afterward they would look about as if they expected lightning to strike, and her teachers let her know she was a willful, sinful girl.

She began to have headaches that were so severe they caused her to stutter when she spoke. She dreamed of such horrible things she would wake up shaking. Still, when she thought of the extraordinary opportunity she had in attending Saxon College, which had an excellent social and academic reputation, she knew herself to be extremely fortunate. She studied hard and made the dean's list, and during her second year she joined the Atlanta Movement. She found it impossible to study while others were being beaten and jailed. It was also, surprisingly, an escape for her. After her friendship with Anne-Marion, they marched often together and would go to jail with their toothbrushes and books and cigarettes under their arms. In jail they were allowed to smoke, which helped to calm their shrieking nerves. On Saxon campus itself, ironically, smoking led to explusion, as did any other form of "decadent" behavior.

The emphasis at Saxon was on form, and the preferred "form" was that of the finishing school girl whose goal, wherever she would later find herself in the world, was to be *accepted* as an equal because she knew and practiced all the proper social rules. The administration of the college neither condoned Saxon students' participation in the Atlanta Movement nor discouraged it. Once it was understood that the students could not be stopped, their involvement, as much as possible, was ignored. All of Saxon's rules, against smoking, drinking, speaking loudly, going off campus without an escort, remaining off campus after six, talking to boys before visiting hours, remained in effect. It was understood that a student who allowed herself to be arrested did so at her own academic risk. Fortunately, there were teachers who would lie for the students—a week in jail became a week on a field trip and was certainly as informative for the student as any field trip could ever be—though everyone knew this was a lie. Or a teacher might himself end up in jail. That too was ignored, though his name and photograph appeared in the papers.

A saying about Saxon was that you could do anything there, as long as you wore spotless white gloves. But because the gloves must remain clean and white, there was very little you could do. In fact, Meridian and the other students felt they had two enemies: Saxon, which wanted them to become something—ladies—that was already obsolete, and the larger, more deadly enemy, white racist society. It was not unusual for students to break down under the pressures caused by the two. One of Meridian's classmates, a gentle drama student from Ohio, had been dragged out of a picket line by four thugs and forced, on the main street in Atlanta, to drink a pint of ammonia. Later, after she had recovered physically, in the infirmary, though was obviously far from recovered mentally, she was severely chastised one evening for standing about in the bushes near her dorm with her boyfriend. Neither of them had noticed that calling hours had ended ten minutes earlier. The girl's nerves were wrecked, and she was forced to withdraw from school for the rest of the term.

Meridian, the former wife and mother, already felt herself to be flying under false colors as an "innocent" Saxon student. The scenes she personally witnessed in the Atlanta streets, combined with this, caused the majority of her waking moments to seem fragmented, surreal. She saw small black children, with short, flashing black legs, being chased by grown white men brandishing ax handles. She saw old women dragged out of stores and beaten on the sidewalk, their humility of a lifetime doing them no good. She saw young black men of great spiritual beauty changed overnight into men who valued nothing.

Things happened. One day, along with a group of demonstrators headed for downtown Atlanta, Meridian passed a young girl, nubile, pretty, with long brown pigtails, sitting on the steps of her house, waving. On impulse Meridian called to her: "Come join us," she cried. The girl, pigtails flying, came. Once downtown they sat in at a luncheon counter in Woolworth's and, after being doused with catsup, smeared with mustard and sprinkled with salt and pepper by white patrons of the store, they were arrested. Meridian had tried to keep the girl, whose name was Anne, with her, but in the confusion she disappeared. In the middle of the night there were screams from another cell, far down the row. Screams, according to the guards, of an alcoholic who thought she was being chased around her cell by giant spiders. But Meridian knew it was Anne, and though she never saw her again, she began to imagine she did, and the screams became an accompaniment to the guilt already weighing her down.

Meridian found, when she was not preoccupied with the Movement, that her thoughts turned with regularity and intensity to her mother, on whose account she endured wave after wave of an almost primeval guilt. She imagined her mother in church, in which she had invested all that was still energetic in her life, praying for her daughter's soul, and yet, having no concern, no understanding of her daughter's *life* whatsoever; but Meridian did not condemn her for this. Away from her mother, Meridian thought of her as Black Motherhood personified, and of that great institution she was in terrible awe, comprehending as she did the horror, the narrowing of perspective, for mother and for child, it had invariably meant.

Meridian felt as if her body, growing frailer every day under the stress of her daily life, stood in the way of a reconciliation between her mother and that part of her own soul her mother could, perhaps, love. She valued her body less, attended to it less, because she hated its obstruction.

Only during a crisis could she forget. While other students dreaded confrontation with police she welcomed it, and was capable of an inner gaiety, a sense of freedom, as she saw the clubs slashing down on her from above. Only once was she beaten into unconsciousness, and it was not the damage done to her body that she remembered when she woke up, but her feeling of yearning, of heartsick longing for forgiveness, as she saw the bright lights explode behind the red blood that curtained her face, and her feeling of hope as the harsh light of consciousness began to fade.

After The Wild Child's death she could not live on campus, although she continued to attend classes, and lived instead in the ghetto that surrounded it. It was a poor community but friendly and very clean. In order to pay her rent and to buy other items that one needed at a school like Saxon—tennis racket, bathing suit, ballet slippers and tights, etc.—she went to work as a typist for a professor who had recently retired and whose office was a few blocks from her door. He was a very old man who had, years ago, known her mother's family. It was her mother who encouraged her to take the job, reminding her that her father could not afford to send Meridian the two or three dollars a week she had asked him to send. His health was poor, and with the loss of the farm he was diminished in every way. He was no longer qualified to teach, now that integration was threatening the schools, and was doing odd jobs when and where he could find them.

It was her mother who first noticed that Meridian's thick, shoulder-length hair was beginning to thin. She even essayed a joke about how Meridian should be careful not to wind up bald, like Nelda's mother. It did not surprise Meridian that her hair came out as she combed it, any more than it surprised her that her vision sometimes blurred. She was too driven to notice· and it seemed essential to her then that whatever happened to her she should be prepared to accept. Besides, she was in love, with Truman.

The Conquering Prince

Truman stood on the other side of the screen door in a flowing Ethiopian robe of extravagantly embroidered white, his brown eyes aglow with excitement. Everyone thought him handsome because his nose was so keen and his skin was tan and not black; and Meridian, though disliking herself for it, thought him handsome for exactly those reasons, too. Or had, until, when she had known him for about a year, she began to look closely at him. With scrutiny, much of the handsomeness disappeared behind the vain, pretentious person Truman was. And his teeth were far from good.

But the sly, serious double takes were still in the future. Therefore, she threw open the door for him with such passionate force it banged like a shot against the wall. Truman strode in like a conquering prince returning to his lands.

"You look fantastic!" Meridian breathed, as she cuddled up in his arms.

"*Et toi aussi,*" he replied in French. "*Tu es très magnifique!*"

Truman loved all the foreign cultures of the world, but his favorite was French. He had spent a year in Avignon and Paris. He believed profoundly that anything said in French sounded better, and he also believed that people who spoke French were better than people (*les pauvres, les misérables!*) who did not.

Therefore, "*Bon!*" said Meridian—which was the only French expression with which she felt comfortable. Luckily, she under-

95

stood the language better than she spoke it, because Truman would continue to speak it throughout the evening. When he talked to her she had to translate every syllable into English before answering. Their conversation moved slowly. But it didn't matter. She loved being with Truman. She felt protected when she was with him. To her he was courageous and "new." He was, in any case, unlike any other black man she had known. He was a man who fought against obstacles, a man who could become anything, a man whose very words were unintelligible without considerable thought. She also wanted to make hot, quick, mindless love with him whenever he was near. When he touched her now, on the arms where they joined her shoulders, she trembled against him, faint with desire, as the description read in old novels. She had never felt faint with desire before and felt she had discovered a missing sense.

"I am so glad you came to Saxon," he whispered, *en français,* of course. "You were going to waste out there in the sticks. Speaking of which," he suddenly said, drawing back, but keeping his arms tight about her, "aren't you losing weight?"

She buried her nose in the center of his throat and sucked his collarbone. They were going to a party, but if he didn't stop caressing her shoulders, whispering in French (which did sound awfully sexy) and looking at her with his wild brown eyes, she knew they would never make it. So she said, "Let's go," abruptly, pushing him reluctantly but firmly from her, and preceded him out the door.

Driving through town Meridian told him of the three white exchange students who had come on the march with them that afternoon.

"From where?" Truman asked. "Swarthmore?"

"No, Smith and Carleton."

"What do they look like?"

"One is exactly like the little Dutch boy on Dutch Boy paints. A pale blonde with ear-length hair. She's the prettiest. The other two are kind of homely. Susan is short and mousy with thick legs.

Lynne is thin and dark, with bright black eyes that sort of stab at you. They've been here a week, and I've already been out canvassing voters with Lynne. I like her. She can't say 'saw,' she says, 'I *sarh* it.' And she starts her sentences with 'So.' Listen, let me tell you about this one lady's house we went to . . . way back in the sticks, on the edge of nowhere. This lady was sitting on her front porch, just as serene and untroubled as she could be. We should've seen that her Kingdom had already begun to approach, just by looking at her face. But we have to try everybody, right? She was one of these large, motherly types, with the tits, you know? Everybody's grandmother. Her food was cooking back somewhere on the stove. Butter beans, Lynne swore she could tell by the smell. Anyhow, we walked up and Lynne put one foot up on the lady's step. Her stomach was growling and she held her canvassing pad in front of it. The lady looked at her foot for a full minute.

"'How y'all durin'?' she asked, and started fanning herself real slow, with one of those fans that show Jesus walking on water.

"Lynne said, 'My name is Lynne Rabinowitz . . .'

"'LynnWizz,' the lady repeated.

"'Yes, ma'am,' said Lynne.

"'And who you down there uprootin' my collards with yo' eyes?'

"'Meridian Hill,' I said, starting to laugh, because I liked her and because I sure was eyeball deep in her greens. They were so healthy they flashed in the sun, like they'd been greased.

"'We came up here to ask you to register to vote.'

"'Did?' asked the woman.

"Lynne's stomach let out a massive growl. 'You're not already registered, are you?' she asked, clutching her pad.

"'Nome,' said the woman.

"'You are Mrs. Mabel Turner, aren't you?' asked Lynne. She knew she was but she had to work that 'Mrs.' in somewhere.

"The slow fanning stopped. The light of recognition beamed

from Mrs. Turner's eyes. 'Y'all must be them outside 'taters. Jooz an runnin' dogs. Y'all hongry?' She heaved herself up from her chair and started for the kitchen.

"We sat down at the table and had a big meal. Butter beans, collards, cornbread, the works. Mrs. Turner urged second helpings.

"'So isn't this terrific? I'm about to pop right open,' said Lynne.

"'If you did it wouldn't make much mess, skinny as you is,' said Mrs. Turner. 'I wants to feed y'all real good, 'cause I don't believe in votin'. The good Lord He take care of most of my problems. You know he heal the sick and race the dead. Comfort the uncomfortable and blesses the meek.'

"I said right then, 'We thank you for feeding us, Mrs. Turner,' and I got up to go, but Lynne wanted to argue.

"'So God fixes the road in front of your house, does he?' she asked, using her Northern logic.

"'Let's go,' I said. But no, she was just tuning up.

"'Jesus Christ must be pleased to let you live in a house like this. The good Lord must get his jollies every time you have to hop outside to that toilet in the rain. The Holy Ghost must rejoice when your children catch pneumonia every winter. . . .'

"'You sounds just like a blasphemer to me,' said Mrs. Turner. 'You sound like maybe you *is* kin to Judas Iscariot.' She frowned sadly and shook her head.

"Well, they argued and argued, until Mrs. Turner was afraid she had insulted her religion by feeding us. And Lynne refused to acknowledge the state of grace Mrs. Turner thought she was in.

"'If only we hadn't *eaten*,' she kept saying, 'if only we had refused the food, don't you think Mrs. Turner would have registered to vote?'

"Of course I said no. A blind man could have seen Mrs. Turner was just well beyond the boundaries of politics. . . ."

"*La fanatique,*" said Truman.

Meridian drew back as if to strike him. "Stop talking like that about your cousins and aunts!"

Truman laughed. "And grandmother and so forth. . . . What's the name of the Dutch Boy?"

"Jill."

"*C'est vrai?*"

"*Oui.*"

Meridian lit a cigarette and passed it to Truman. "I think they'll all be at the party tonight. They're eager to see how the natives make out after dark. Oka-mo-gah! Do you know what Charlene told me? She said that Jill was taking photographs of the girls straightening their hair and also of them coming out of the shower."

"*Et puis?*"

"Well, and then Charlene and the other girl whose pictures were being taken threatened to beat her up unless she destroyed the film. 'This here ain't New Guinea,' Charlene says she said."

"They were just curious about *les noirs*," said Truman. "When I was in Paris I was curious about the French. I'm sure I did strange things, too."

"Like photographing them while they styled their hair and when they emerged from the shower? Or is it true that the French never bathe?"

Truman laughed. "My little kitten has sharp claws. Still," he said, "it pays to have a little tolerance with other people's curiosity. It never bothers me any more when foreigners look at my hair and say, 'A leetle beet of zee tar brush, eh?' "

"Everyone is proud to acknowledge a tiny bit of a 'bad' thing," said Meridian. "They know how fascinating it makes them."

She looked out the car window and realized they had stopped a few houses down from where the party was. Truman reached for her and gathered her tightly into his arms. She felt his tongue licking the au de cologne off her earlobes. His hands were squeezing the nipples of her breasts. When she pulled her head away he buried his face in her lap, an action that briefly shocked her. She felt

99

warm tingling sensations creeping up from the bottom of her stomach.

"Let's not go to the party," he pleaded. "Let's go back to the apartment. Everybody else is here, we'll be alone. I want you."

"I love you," she said.

"And we're going to the party, right?" Truman sat up and ran his fingers through his hair.

"But do you understand?" Meridian asked. "I'm not a prude. Afraid, yes, but not a prude. One day soon we'll be together."

"You're so young," said Truman, getting out and adjusting his robe. "I wish I could make you feel how beautiful it would be with me."

"I feel it, I feel it!" cried Meridian, taking his hand and walking up the street.

At the party Meridian danced, as seemed to be her fate at most parties, with a plodding young man from Arkansas. His first name was Terence; she deliberately kept herself innocent of his last. They pushed along the floor until a white boy broke in. Terence, exhibiting his freedom from prejudice, practically shoved Meridian into his arms.

"You go to school around here?" the white boy asked.

"Yes," said Meridian, "more or less." He was a head taller than she and her chin, when she looked up at him, poked into his chest. He was not ugly, only plucked-looking, with short black hair, shaved down around the bottom of his hairline, and teeth that had tiny white spots in the enamel, as if tiny pieces of seashell had been embedded there.

"Where are you from?" she asked. She hated to think in clichés at a time like this, when she could see he was gazing at her admiringly, but his dance was *very* stiff.

"Connecticut," he said. "We came down from the University of Connecticut. Con U," he added, and laughed. Meridian did not get the joke. She almost asked, "What you want to con me for, already?"

Someone had put a fast record on and they plunged about the

room crazily. When they stopped to breathe Meridian looked about for Truman.

"I'm looking for my date," she explained to Con U, who was following the sweep her eyes made across the room, unable to conceal his anxiety that she might walk away.

"Isn't that him over there?" asked Con U, delight in his voice.

Truman was sitting on the stairs that led up from the basement. The Dutch Boy was sitting cross-legged on the floor beneath him, looking up at him with—admiration? curiosity? hunger? Meridian was not sure. That the girl's skirt was above her knees she could see.

Con U laughed. "Looks like he's doing all right for himself," and he sort of hunkered over her, his elbow against the wall. He seemed to her peculiarly rustic, and though now that she was in college she prided herself on having catholic tastes when it came to men, white farmers were not yet included.

"My name is Scott," he said, "after Scott Fitzgerald. My mother loves his books."

"Ummm . . ." said Meridian, grudgingly relinquishing her own name.

He was also going to be a talker.

Did she go to dances often? Did she like to dance? How far away was her home town? Did her mother like to dance? What kind of work did her father do? Did *he* like to dance? And what of the school—did she like it? Did they teach dancing there? And of the demonstrations—how many had she gone on? Did she believe, truly, that one ought to protest in this way? Wasn't there some other method that might work and prove less disastrous than marching in the street? Didn't our Constitution provide for just such emergencies as the present racial crisis? What did she think of the Constitution? the founding fathers? He wondered if they would like what was going on in the country? Did *they* believe in unlawful protest? He thought it was an interesting question. Wonder, come to think of it, how they passed their time when not drafting the Constitution? Did *they* dance?

"Terence," she called, clutching his shoulder as he plodded by, "I'm so glad you've come back. You know I promised you the last dance."

She looked about for Truman to rescue her but he was nowhere in sight.

Terence beamed with pride and joy. Off they moved to a dreary finish.

"I went out for cigarettes," said Truman, adjusting his robe. Meridian stood on the porch. Everyone else had left. Fearing the kindled gleam in Terence's eye and not feeling up to a struggle, she'd waited for Truman.

"God, you just don't know what a drag this evening was," said Meridian, who was too tired not to complain.

When they reached her house she invited him in, but he too was feeling tired and sleepy.

"Maybe tomorrow night," he said, stifling a yawn.

But she did not see Truman again, alone (except for one heart-breaking time), for several months, not until he had read *The Souls of Black Folk*, in fact. The exchange students, all three of them, had gone back North then, and he needed someone to discuss Du Bois with. "The man was a *genius!*" he cried, and he read passages from the book that he said were reflective of his and Meridian's souls. But Meridian was reading F. Scott Fitzgerald then, though she never gave up any of the Du Bois she already knew. It just seemed too deep for conversation with Truman, somehow. He was startled by the coolness with which she received his assertion that what he had decided, after reading "*le maître,*" was that if he dated white girls it must be, essentially, a matter of sex. She laughed when she saw he expected her to be pleased and reassured, a bitter laugh that sent him away again, his chin thrust forward against her misunderstanding.

The time she had seen Truman, after he began dating the exchange students, had been bitterly regretted. And for her part in what happened, Meridian paid dearly.

———

She had been walking down the street from her job at the old professor's and—walking with her head down—had not seen Truman coming toward her. They almost passed each other before he stopped and turned, his brown eyes very dark and hot against the green polo shirt he wore.

"Meridian?"

"Hi," she said, feeling embarrassed to see him now that he was busy dating the exchange students. It was strange and unfair, but the fact that he dated them—and so obviously because their color made them interesting—made *her* ashamed, as if she were less.

He came up to her and casually placed his arm around her shoulders. "You walk with your head down. It should be up. Proud and free." And he chucked her playfully under the chin.

She looked at him wondering if he had, as she had done, marched that day. As a rule, he said, he didn't march any more, "because what I believe cannot be placed on a placard." And she had teased him about that and said, "How about just the words 'Freedom, Liberty, Equality'? That would cover what you believe in, wouldn't it?" She was also tempted to add white exchange students. But how polite she was! How bewildered by his preference. It went against everything she had been taught to expect.

For she realized what she *had* been taught was that nobody wanted white girls except their empty-headed, effeminate counterparts—white boys—whom her mother assured her smelled (in the mouth) of boiled corn and (in the body) of thirty-nine-cent glue. As far back as she could remember it seemed something *understood*: that while white men would climb on black women old enough to be their mothers—"for the experience"—white women were considered sexless, contemptible and ridiculous by all. They did not even smell like glue or boiled corn; they smelled of nothing since they did not sweat. They were clear, dead water.

Her mother, though not a maid, had often worked for white families near Christmastime in order to earn extra money, and she told her family—in hushed, carefully controlled language, keeping her face set over her ironing board—about the lusty young sons home from school for the holidays, calling her by her first name, of course, and begging and pleading and even (and her mother scoffed) getting all blubbery the way white men get. "Gertrude pul-eze," her mother mocked the slow pull of the pseudocultivated Southern gentleman. "What are you talkin' 'bout, *Mr.* So-an-so?" (This to a twenty-one-year-old kid, her anger and her religion choking her.) "I'm old enough to be your grandma. I can remember when your mama was a girl. You wouldn't hang around any of your mama's friends like this. Why you botherin' me?"

This would lead Mrs. Hill directly into an exhortation on her religious as opposed to her human dignity. (Because she rightly assumed "Mr. So-an-so" would not be interested in the latter.) She was black, wasn't she? And a female. (Not lady, not even woman, since both these words conjured up something larger than sex; they spoke of a somebody as opposed to a something.) Yes, it was understood about white men. Some of them liked black women for sex and said so. For the others it was a matter of gaining experience, initiation into the adult world. The maid, the cook, a stray child, anything not too old or repulsive would do. In Mrs. Hill's voice there was a well, a reservoir, an ocean of disgust. And when she described white men it was with weary religion-restrained hatred. She could speak freely because the general opinion of white men, among blacks, was in her favor. She spoke of their faces as if they were the faces of moose, of oxen, of wet, slobbery walruses. Besides, she said, they were manipulated by their wives, which did not encourage respect.

But what had her mother said about white women? She could actually remember very little, but her impression had been that they were frivolous, helpless creatures, lazy and without ingenuity. Occasionally one would rise to the level of bitchery, and this one would be carefully set aside when the collective "others" were discussed. Her grandmother—an erect former maid who

104

was now a midwife—held strong opinions, which she expressed in this way: 1. She had never known a white woman she liked after the age of twelve. 2. White women were useless except as baby machines which would continue to produce little white people who would grow up to oppress her. 3. Without servants all of them would live in pigsties.

Who would dream, in her home town, of kissing a white girl? Who would want to? What were they good for? What did they do? They only seemed to hang about laughing, after school, until when they were sixteen or seventeen they got married. Their pictures appeared in the society column, you saw them pregnant a couple of times. Then you were no longer able to recognize them as girls you once "knew." They sank into a permanent oblivion. One never heard of them *doing* anything that was interesting. Oh, one might escape to join the WAC's. Quite a few—three or four a year, the homely ones—attended a college in the state (which kept the local library and English departments supplied) but there were positively no adventurers—unless you counted the alcoholics—among them. If one of them did manage to experiment with life to the extent that the process embarrassed her parents (or her parents' friends, the folks at home who filled the churches every Sunday) it was never found out by anyone in the black community.

On the other hand, black women were always imitating Harriet Tubman—escaping to become something unheard of. Outrageous. One of her sister's friends had become, somehow, a sergeant in the army and knew everything there was to know about enemy installations and radio equipment. A couple of girls her brothers knew had gone away broke and come back, years later, as a doctor and a schoolteacher. Two other girls went away married to men and returned home married to each other. This perked up the community. Tongues wagged. But in the end the couple enjoyed visiting their parents, old friends, and were enjoyed in turn. "How do you suppose they do it?" was a question which—though of course not printed in the newspaper—still made all the rounds. But even in more conventional things, black women struck out for the unknown. They left home scared, poor black girls and came back (some of them) successful secretaries and typists (this had seemed amazing to everyone, that there should be firms in Atlanta and other large cities that would *hire* black secretaries). They returned, their hair bleached auburn or streaked with silver, or perhaps they wore a wig. It would be bold, deathly straight or slightly curled, and remind everyone of the Italians—like Pier Angeli—one saw in the movies. Their pocketbooks, their shoes, would *shine*, and their faces (old remembered faces now completely reconstructed by Max Factor and Maybelline) perfected masks through which the voice of some person formerly known came through.

Then there were simply the good-time girls who came home full of bawdy stories of their exploits in the big city; one watched them seduce the local men with dazzling ease, some who used to be lovers and might be still. In their cheap, loud clothing, their newly repaired teeth, their flashy cars, their too-gold shimmering watches and pendants—they were still a success. They commanded attention. They deserved admiration. Only the rejects— not of men, but of experience, adventure—fell into the domestic morass that even the most intelligent white girls appeared to be destined for. There seemed nothing about white women that was enviable. Perhaps one might covet a length of hair, if it swung long and particularly fine. But that was all. And hair was dead matter that continued—only if oiled—to shine.

Of course Meridian appropriated all the good qualities of black women to herself, now that she was awake enough to be aware of them. In her life with Eddie she knew she had lacked courage, lacked initiative or a mind of her own. And yet, from somewhere, had come the *will* that had got her to Saxon College. At times she thought of herself as an adventurer. It thrilled her to think she belonged to the people who produced Harriet Tubman, the only American woman who'd led troops in battle.

But Truman, alas, did not want a general beside him. He did

not want a woman who tried, however encumbered by guilts and fears and remorse, to claim her own life. She knew Truman would have liked her better as she had been as Eddie's wife, for all that he admired the flash of her face across a picket line—an attractive woman, but asleep.

But now, as they walked under the trees along the campus paths and the chimes from the campus clock rang out their inappropriate eighteenth-century melodies, she needed his arm around her shoulders. The truth was, she had missed him and regretted every single time she had turned him down.

When they got to her apartment she was thankful that he walked in behind her.

"What did he give you this time?" Truman asked.

"Some raisins, Fig Newtons, a carton of Cokes," she said, swinging them up on the table, "and enough money to buy a *good* tennis racket."

"He sure must want a daughter," said Truman, opening a Coke and drinking it in long swallows. "Unless," he said, and grinned at her, "*unless* he's a sugar daddy." He burst out laughing at the thought. "Does he ever," he asked, his eyes twinkling, "hobble you around his desk?"

Meridian put the remainder of the Cokes into the refrigerator. She did not smile, until the silence caused her to consider what Truman said, then her lips briefly twitched. "Nope," she said quickly. "The thought of some live action would stew his old heart to death."

But of course that was not true. The truth was, she *was* chased around the desk by Mr. Raymonds. The truth was, her scholarship did not cover all her school expenses and her other needs, too. The truth *was* she depended on the extras Mr. Raymonds gave her. Every Coke, every cookie, every can of deviled ham, every tennis racket that he gave her meant one less that she had to buy.

Yes, Mr. Raymonds did *limp* her around his desk. And what

was more, and worse, he caught her. But she knew Truman would never understand. She had hardly understood or believed it herself, at first. The first time Mr. Raymonds accidentally brushed against her, she thought she'd imagined it. After all, he was somebody important, a university professor, covered with honors (his walls were, anyway). They fairly sagged with the plaques nailed there (and she was not sophisticated enough yet to find them tacky) saying he had been 1. Head of the Colored YMCA from 1919–1925; 2. An Elder in the Episcopalian Church; 3. The Masonic Temple's Man of the Year 1935–36; 4. Best Teacher of Farming Methods 1938–39. He had written books on various aspects of farming and was an expert. When he gave her copies of his books, autographed, she was as thrilled as anything, and quickly mailed them home to her father. He gave her the books her first day on the job.

He did not tell her anything about his wife, but she had seen a picture of her once, a sourfaced woman, very dark, as were the women often chosen by very light-skinned black men. She had noticed that it went either this way, with light-colored men, or the other. There didn't seem to be a middle ground. In Mr. Raymonds' case, he had probably chosen a dark-skinned wife because he was one of those old-fashioned "race men," the radical nationalists of his day—the 1920's. He loved to talk even now of The Race as if it were a lump of homogenized matter that could be placed this way or that way, at will, to effect change.

Mr. Raymonds stuck up for the race as a whole, although Meridian thought she detected a slightly defensive attitude around younger and darker-skinned men. It was as if he had to prove himself. He was also very emotional about protecting the virtue of black women from white men. Once he had seen her talking to a white divinity student on the corner before turning in to his building to work, and he had been red in the face from anger. Before she went home she had been told exactly how many black women had reported rape at the hands of white men in the years between 1896 and 1963. She assumed he made up the figure, but she gasped anyway. The divinity student, ironically, had been from South Africa, and she had spoken to him out of a kind of perverse curiosity. She thought because she was black she would notice some kind of strain come into his face, but there was nothing at all. She might have been as white and as near divinity as he.

This curiosity was the way she was, sometimes, with whites. Mostly they did not seem quite real to her. They seemed very stupid the way they attempted to beat down everybody in their path and then know nothing about it. She saw them sometimes as hordes of elephants, crushing everything underfoot, stolid and heavy and yet—unlike the elephant—forgetting.

Mr. Raymonds was tall and bony and the color of caramel candy that is being stretched, with short white hair and a drooping left eyelid. She hated his teeth; they were all false or mostly false, and held together with wires that would have glittered if he ever cleaned his mouth. He never did. Consequently his teeth seemed to be covered with yellowish flannel and the smell of his breath was nauseating, as if his whole mouth were a tunnel of sewerage. He had not always been thin. And even now he was more bony than thin. As a young man he had been heavily muscled. He grew gaunt with age. When he grabbed her as she stepped warily into his office and attempted to rub his old penis against her, she felt nothing but his hard pelvic bones poking her in the stomach.

He wanted her to sit on his lap, which she would sometimes do. Then he would open up his desk drawer and pull out the goodies he bought for her. Tins of tuna, bags of mints and Baby Ruths, dime-store combs and even, sometimes, typing paper. He nestled his long nose in her hair or as far under her chin as she would let him, all the while squirming under her so that some of the desperate delight he was experiencing would work its way up into his limp penis. He had no luck that she could ever tell.

Each day when she rose to go—having typed letters for him in a veritable swamp fog of bad breath—he clasped her in his arms, dragging her away from the door, the long bones of his thighs forcing her legs apart, attempting to force her to the floor. But she smiled and struggled and struggled and smiled, and pretended she knew nothing of his intentions—a thought which no doubt aroused him all the more. As she twisted and squirmed, keeping her face averted as much as possible from his lips and his breath, his face became gray with determination and sweat, his breathing became hoarse and labored, and when he looked at her the gleam in his eye was pathetic.

"What's the matter?" asked Truman.

"Nothing," she said quickly. "Tell me what's really been happening?"

"I've been working out at the country club again," he said, sighing and lying back on the sofa. "God, I hate those bastards. You just don't know how hard a time I have making a little bread." He reached out and caught her wrist, pulling her down to the couch. "Those crackers throw cigarettes in the pool for the express purpose of making me pick them out. And I can't wait until tomorrow either. Oh no. 'Trooo-munn,' some old shit calls, 'go git them butts out the pool buffore some more of our guests arrive.' And while I'm fishing for butts some of their old skinny broads saunter over to watch and of course to give advice. 'Trooo-munn,' they coo, 'I bleve you got to lean over more this way, don't you?' Or, 'You're just a very ajul boy, for a boy your size.' And I have to just stand there and grin and bear it. I despise them," he said vehemently, socking a pillow, his other hand tight around her arm. "You women sure are lucky not to have to be up against'em all the time."

The short muttering laugh that answered him was black with derision, and Truman looked at Meridian sharply.

"You're right," he said, "we don't have to talk about shit like that tonight. Come here, woman, I missed you."

She could not help remarking how his own sense of masculinity gratified him. The pressure around her wrist, like his crude order, was certainly not necessary, since she was already lying, like a beached fish, across his lap.

110

With his warm long fingers he stroked the insides of her arms, then kissed her on the lips. Her mind was still working perfectly. She had planned, because of the exchange students, to be unmoved, but something alive seemed to be moving, unfolding, spreading and reaching out in the bottom of her stomach. Indeed, she felt, and carefully noted it, as if the entire center of her body was beginning to melt. She decided to click her mind off, and her body seemed to move into his of its own accord. Deliberately though, when he began to suck her nipples through her blouse, she sat up and took it off. He fastened his mouth on one nipple and his fingers pinched and stroked the other.

The exchange students were banished to a corner of the world her thoughts did not need to follow. She chased them there with an imaginary broom, invented special for that purpose. It was a long black broom with a yellow ribbon around its handle. In her hands it scoured both heaven and earth until only the two of them were left. Truman hesitated when his hand touched her panties. She rose up, silently, and let her skirt, bra and panties drop to the floor. Her gaze fell on his penis. It seemed to her extremely large and oddly curving, as if distorted by its own arrogant weight. When she took it in her hand Truman shivered, his face contorted. His face moved her. She guided him into her and they fucked (she consciously thought of it as that), they fucked, it seemed, for hours, and over and over again she nearly reached a climax only to lose it. Finally, when she was weary enough to scream, Truman came and quickly fell asleep. He mumbled she was very sexy as he turned. It was only then that she remembered he had not worn a condom—the only means of contraception she knew.

Flinging his leg off her (he had slept with the curve of his foot locked about her ankle) she hurried to the bathroom and strained over the commode. She wished she had had a douche bag. Instead she took a glass of hot water and worked some of the water up her while lying in the tub. She had made up her mind before coming to Atlanta not to have sex. When she went back into the living room, Truman was gone.

111

He had gone back to the last of the exchange students, the one she had liked, Lynne Rabinowitz. It was for this reason, among others, that he never knew she was pregnant. On her way to have an abortion she saw them riding across campus in his father's new red car. From a distance, they both looked white to her, that day. Later, as the doctor tore into her body without giving her anesthesia (and while he lectured her on her morals) and she saw stars because of the pain, she was still seeing them laughing, carefree, together. It was not that she wanted him any more, she did not. It enraged her that she could be made to endure such pain, and that he was oblivious to it. She was also disgusted with the fecundity of her body that got pregnant on less screwing than anybody's she had ever heard of. It seemed doubly unfair that after all her sexual "experience" and after one baby and one abortion she had not once been completely fulfilled by sex.

Her doctor was the one from Saxon College, only now in private practice. "I could tie your tubes," he chopped out angrily, "if you'll let me in on some of all this extracurricular activity." His elbow somehow rested heavily on her navel and a whirling hot pain shot from her uterus to her toes. She felt sure she'd never walk again. She looked at him until his hard face began to blur. "Burn'em out by the roots for all I care." She had left his office wide-legged with blood soaking her super Kotex and cramps bending her double, but she was crying for other reasons.

Truman never knew. She thought about telling him, but when she considered he might have the nerve to pity her, she knew she would rather have bitten her tongue in half. After the exchange students left he strolled up to her one day as she emerged from one of her classes.

"You know," he said, squinting up his eyes as if seeing something clearly but with immense strain, "I don't know what was wrong with me. You're obviously a stone fox. I don't see why we had to break up."

"You're kidding?" She said this more to herself than to him. She felt nothing and was relieved. She wondered why, or rather how that term came to be so popular. Surely no one had bothered to analyze it as they said it. In her mind she carried a stone fox. It was heavy, gray and could not move.

"Aw, don't be like that," he said, stopping her on the walk and looking into her eyes. "I think I'm in love with you, African woman. Always have been. Since the first."

She laughed. It seemed only fair, and her mind was working perfectly after all. "You're kidding again?"

"We could be happy together. I *know* we could. I can make you come. I almost did it that time, didn't I?" He looked at her, waiting for her to stammer or blush. "All the time I thought you didn't like to fuck. You do, don't you? Anyway, your body is beautiful. So warm, so brown . . ."

She turned away, shame for him, for what he was revealing, making her sick.

"It's over. Let it stay."

But he looked at her with eyes of new discovery.

"You're *beautiful*," he whispered worshipfully. Then he said, urgently, *"Have* my beautiful black babies."

And she drew back her green book bag and began to hit him. She hit him three times before she even knew what was happening. Then she hit him again across the ear and a spiral from a tablet cut his cheek. Blood dripped onto his shirt. When she noticed the blood she turned and left him to the curiosity of the other students crowding there.

The Recurring Dream

She dreamed she was a character in a novel and that her existence presented an insoluble problem, one that would be solved only by her death at the end.

She dreamed she was a character in a novel and that her existence presented an insoluble problem, one that would be solved only by her death at the end.

She dreamed she was a character in a novel and that her existence presented an insoluble problem, one that would be solved only by her death at the end.

Even when she gave up reading novels that encouraged such a solution—and nearly all of them did—the dream did not cease.

She felt as if a small landslide had begun behind her brows, as if things there had started to slip. It was a physical feeling and she paid it no mind. She just began to take chances with her life. She would go alone to small towns where blacks were not welcome on the sidewalks after dark and she would stand waiting, watching the sun go down. She walked for miles up and down Atlanta streets until she was exhausted, without once paying any attention to the existence of cars. She began to forget to eat.

The day before her graduation from Saxon she suddenly noticed, as she looked at a rack of clean glasses in the dining room, that they were bathed in a bluish light. When she held up one hand in front of her face it seemed bluish also, as if washed in ink. Although Anne-Marion had moved in with her she did not mention the blue spells to her, and they would sit talking, eating the goodies she brought home from Mr. Raymonds and reading about Socialism.

Both girls had lived and studied enough to know they despised capitalism; they perceived it had done well in America because it had rested directly on their fathers' and mothers' backs. The difference between them was this: Anne-Marion did not know if she would be a success as a capitalist, while Meridian did not think she could enjoy owning things others could not have. Anne-Marion wanted black to have the same opportunity to make as much money as the richest white people. But Meridian wanted the destruction of the rich as a class and the eradication of all personal economic preserves. Her senior thesis was based on the notion that no one should be allowed to own more land than could be worked in a day, by hand. Anne-Marion thought this was quaint. When black people can own the seashore, she said, I want miles and miles of it. And I never want to see a face I didn't invite walking across my sand. Meridian reminded her of her professed admiration for Socialist and Communist theories. Yes, Anne-Marion replied. I have the deepest admiration for them, but since I haven't had a chance to have a capitalist fling yet, the practice of those theories will have to wait awhile.

But Anne-Marion, Meridian would say, that is probably exactly what Henry Ford said! Tell Henry I agree with him, said Anne-Marion.

These exchanges would be marked by laughter and the attempt to pretend they were not serious.

Fuck Democracy, Anne-Marion would say, biting into a cookie. Fuck the Free World. Let the Republicans and the Democrats-as-we-know-them fuck each other's grandmothers.

Meridian would laugh and laugh, until her arms grew tired from slapping the side of her bed.

But one day the blue became black and she temporarily—for two days—lost her sight. Until then she had not thought seriously of going to a doctor. For one thing, she had no money. For another, if she went to the campus doctor he would want payment for having tied her tubes. Still, when she awoke from a long faint several days after her eyesight returned and found him standing over her, she was not surprised. His presence seemed appropriate. Without waiting to hear her symptoms he had her lifted up on the examining table—using his best officious manner before his nurses—and she was given a thorough and painful pelvic examination. Her breasts were routinely and exhaustively felt. She was asked if she slept with boys. She was asked why she slept with boys. Didn't she know that boys nowadays were no good and could get her into trouble?

He thought she'd better come to his off-campus office for further consultation; there, he said, he had more elaborate equipment with which to test her.

She returned to the apartment sicker than when she left. Happily, two days later, neither the fainting nor the blue-black spells had returned. Then she found—on trying to get out of bed—that her legs no longer worked. Since she had experienced paralysis before, this worried her less than the losing of her sight. As the days passed—and she attempted to nibble at the dishes Anne-Marion brought—she discovered herself becoming more and more full, with no appetite whatsoever. And, to her complete surprise and astonished joy, she began to experience ecstasy.

Sometimes, lying on her bed, not hungry, not cold, not worried (because she realized the worry part of her brain had been the landslide behind her brows and that it had slid down and therefore no longer functioned), she felt as if a warm, strong light bore her up and that she was a beloved part of the universe; that she was innocent even as the rocks are innocent, and unpolluted as the first waters. And when Anne-Marion sat beside the bed and scolded her for not eating, she was amazed that Anne-Marion could not see how happy and content she was.

Anne-Marion was alarmed. Before her eyes, Meridian seemed to be slipping away. Still, the idea that Meridian might actually die, while smiling happily at a blank ceiling, seemed preposterous, and she did nothing about it. But one day, as she sat on her own bed across from Meridian's, reading a book of Marxist ideology that included *The Communist Manifesto*, which she considered a really thought-provoking piece of work, she glanced at Meridian's head in shock. For all around it was a full soft light, as if her head, the spikes of her natural, had learned to glow. The sight pricked an unconscious place in Anne-Marion's post-Baptist memory.

"Ah shit!" she said, stamping her foot, annoyed that she'd thought of Meridian in a religious context.

"What's the matter?" asked Meridian dreamily. She moved her head slightly and the soft bright light disappeared.

Anne-Marion hugged her book as if it were a lover going off on a long trip. "We've been raised wrong!" she said, "that's what's wrong." What she meant was, she no longer believed in God and did not like to think about Jesus (for whom she still felt a bitter, grudging admiration).

"How long has she been in bed?" asked Miss Winter.

"About a month," said Anne-Marion.

"You should have come to me sooner," said Miss Winter.

Miss Winter was also a misfit at Saxon College. Yellow, with bulging black eyes and an elaborate blue wig, she was the school's organist—one of only three black teachers on the faculty. The other two taught PE and French. It was she each morning who played the old English and German hymns the program required, and the music rose like marching souls toward the vaulted ceiling of the chapel. And yet, in her music class she deliberately rose against Saxon tradition to teach jazz (which she had learned somewhere in Europe to pronounce "jawhz") and spirituals and the blues (which she pronounced "blews"). It was thought each year that she would never survive to teach at Saxon the following one. But she endured. As aloof and ladylike as she appeared (and she never wore outfits the parts of which did not *precisely* match), her fights with the president and the college dean could be heard halfway across the campus.

Miss Winter was from Meridian's home town and had known Meridian's family all her life. She was a Saxon graduate herself, and when she learned Meridian had been accepted as a student she fought down her first feelings, which were base. She had enjoyed being the only person from her town to attend such a college; she did not wish to share this distinction. By the time Meridian arrived, however, she had successfully uprooted this feeling. She would not, even so, return the girl's timid greeting the first day they met.

She had once attended an oratorical competition at her old high school, where Meridian was well on her way to distinguishing herself. Meridian was reciting a speech that extolled the virtues of the Constitution and praised the superiority of The American Way of Life. The audience cared little for what she was saying, and of course they didn't believe any of it, but they were rapt, listening to her speak so passionately and with such sad valor in her eyes.

Then, in the middle of her speech, Meridian had seemed to forget. She stumbled and then was silent on the stage. The audience urged her on but she would not continue. Instead she covered her face with her hands and had to be led away.

Meridian's mother went out into the hallway where Meridian was and Miss Winter overheard them talking. Meridian was trying to explain to her mother that for the first time she really listened to what she was saying, knew she didn't believe it, and was so distracted by this revelation that she could not make the rest of her speech. Her mother, not listening to this explanation at all, or at least not attempting to understand it, was saying something else: She was reminding Meridian that whenever something went

119

wrong for *her* she simply trusted in God, raised her head a little higher than it already was, stared down whatever was in her path, never looked back, and so forth.

Meridian, who was seated and whose eyes were red from crying, was looking up at her mother hopelessly. Standing over her, her mother appeared huge, a giant, a woman who *could* trust in God, hold up her head, never look back, and get through everything, whether she believed in it or not. Meridian, on the other hand, appeared smaller than she actually was and looked as though she wanted to melt into her seat. She had doubled over, as if she might shrink into a ball and disappear.

Miss Winter had pushed back the cuff of her gray mink coat and put a perfumed arm around Meridian's shoulders. She told her not to worry about the speech. "It's the same one they made me learn when I was here," she told her, "and it's no more true now than it was then." She had never said anything of the sort to anyone before and was surprised at how good it felt. A blade of green grass blew briefly across her vision and a fresh breeze followed it. She realized the weather was too warm for mink and took off her coat.

But Meridian continued to huddle there, and her mother, her body as stately as the prow of a ship, moved off down the hall where she stood head and shoulders above all the girls—Meridian's classmates—who seemed an insubstantial mass of billowing crinolines and flashy dresses, gathered there.

To Meridian, her mother *was* a giant. She had never perceived her in any other way. Or, if she did have occasional thoughts that challenged this conception she swept them out of her mind as petty and ridiculous. Even on the day Miss Winter remembered, Meridian's sadness had been only that she had failed her mother. That her mother was deliberately obtuse about what had happened meant nothing beside her own feelings of inadequacy and guilt. Besides, she had already forgiven her mother for anything she had ever done to her or might do, because to her, Mrs. Hill had persisted in bringing them all (the children, the husband, the family, the race) to a point far beyond where she, in her mother's place, her grandmother's place, her great-grandmother's place, would have stopped.

This was her mother's history as Meridian knew it:

Her mother's great-great-grandmother had been a slave whose two children were sold away from her when they were toddlers. For days she had followed the man who bought them until she was able to steal them back. The third time—after her owner had exhausted one of his field hands whipping her, and glints of bone began to show through the muscles on her back—she was allowed to keep them on the condition that they would eat no food she did not provide herself.

During the summers their existence was not so hard. They learned to pick berries at night, after the day's work in the fields, and they gathered poke salad and in the autumn lived on nuts they found in the woods. They smoked fish they caught in streams and the wild game she learned to trap. They were able to exist this way until the children were in their teens. Then their mother died, the result of years of slow starvation. The children were sold the day of their mother's burial.

Mrs. Hill's great-grandmother had been famous for painting decorations on barns. She earned money for the man who owned her and was allowed to keep some for herself. With it she bought not only her own freedom, but that of her husband and children as well. In Meridian's grandmother's childhood, there were still barns scattered throughout the state that bloomed with figures her mother had painted. At the center of each tree or animal or bird she painted, there was somehow drawn in, so that it formed a part of the pattern, a small contorted face—whether of man or woman or child, no one could tell—that became her trademark.

Mrs. Hill's mother married a man of many admirable qualities. He was a person who kept his word, ran a prosperous farm and had a handsome face. But he also had no desire to raise children—though he enjoyed sex with any willing, good-looking woman who came his way—and he beat his wife and children with more pleasure than he beat his mules.

Mrs. Hill had spent the early part of her life scurrying out of her father's way. Later, when she was in her teens, she also learned to scurry out of the way of white men—because she was good-looking, defenseless and black. Her life, she told Meridian, was one of scurrying, and only one thing kept her going: her determination to be a schoolteacher.

The story of her pursuit of education was pitiful.

First, she had come up against her father, who said she did not need to go to school because if she only learned to cook collard greens, shortbread and fried okra, some poor soul of a man might have her, and second, she had to decide to accept the self-sacrifice of her mother, whom she had worshiped. Her mother, by that time, was pregnant with her twelfth child, and her hair had already turned white. But it was her mother who made the bargain with her father that allowed her to go to school. The agreement was wretched: School would cost twelve dollars a year, and her mother would have to earn every cent of it. Refusing to complain and, indeed, refusing even to discuss the hardship it would cause, her mother had gone out to do other people's laundry, and Meridian's mother remembered her trudging off—after doing her own washing and work in the fields—with her rub board under her arm.

Mrs. Hill had had only two pairs of cotton bloomers. She wore and washed, washed and wore. She had only one dress. She and her sister swapped dresses each day so they might have at least this much variety in their attire. They had gone without shoes much of the time. And yet, miraculously, Meridian's mother had finished school and, what was more, helped four of her sisters and brothers do the same. And she had become a schoolteacher, earning forty dollars a month, four months out of the year. (Her students were in the cotton fields the rest of the time.) She had bought her mother a coat and new pair of shoes with her first pay.

Hers had also been the honor, a short time later, of paying for her mother's pink coffin.

When her mother talked about her childhood Meridian wept and clung to her hands, wishing with all her heart she had not been born to this already overburdened woman. Whatever smugness crept into her mother's voice—as when she said "I never stole, I was always clean, I never did wrong by anyone, I was never *bad*; I simply trusted in the Lord"—was unnoticed by her. It seemed to Meridian that her legacy from her mother's endurance, her unerring knowledge of rightness and her pursuit of it through all distractions, was one she would never be able to match. It never occurred to her that her mother's and her grandmother's extreme purity of life was compelled by necessity. They had not lived in an age of choice.

None of these thoughts could she convey to Miss Winter. She merely smiled at her from the calm plateau in her illness she had happily reached. Now and again she saw clouds drift across Miss Winter's head and she amused herself picking out faces that she knew. When she slept she dreamed she was on a ship with her mother, and her mother was holding her over the railing about to drop her into the sea. Danger was all around and her mother refused to let her go.

"Mama, I *love* you. Let me go," she whispered, licking the salt from her mother's black arms.

Instinctively, as if Meridian were her own child, Miss Winter answered, close to her ear on the pillow, "I forgive you."

The next morning Meridian ate all her breakfast, though it would not all stay down. For the first time she asked for a mirror and tried to sit up in bed. Soon, her strength exhausted, she slept. Anne-Marion watched the sun climb again to illuminate the edges of her hair, and knew she could not endure a friendship that required such caring vigilance. Meridian, for all her good intentions, might never be ready for the future, and that would be too painful. Anne-Marion could not continue to care about a person she could not save. Nor could she end a close friendship without turning on the friend.

One morning, when Meridian was standing by the window, her face pensive, nearly beautiful and pathetically thin, Anne-Marion did something she had always wanted to do: It was the equivalent of a kick. She began telling jokes to make Meridian laugh—because she could not leave her while she looked this way—and when she succeeded, just at the point where Meridian's face lost its magically intriguing gloom, she said, with a very straight face herself, "Meridian, I can not afford to love you. Like the idea of suffering itself, you are obsolete."

Later, though they met again in New York and briefly shared a room, and Meridian had seemed not to remember this parting comment, Anne-Marion continued to think of it as her final word.

After Meridian had gone back South and Anne-Marion discovered herself writing letters to her, making inquiries month after month to find out which town she now lived in and to which address she should send her letters, no one could have been more surprised and confounded than she, who sat down to write each letter as if some heavy object had been attached to her knees, forcing them under her desk, as she wrote with the most galling ferocity, out of guilt and denial and rage.

Truman Held

THE LAST TOAST

I drink to our ruined house,
to the dolor of my life,
to our loneliness together;
and to you I raise my glass,
to lying lips that have betrayed us,
to dead-cold, pitiless eyes,
and to the hard realities:
that the world is brutal and coarse,
that God in fact has not saved us.

—Akhmatova

Truman and Lynne:
Time in the South

Lynne: She is sitting on the porch steps of a battered wooden house and black children are all around her. They look, from a distance, like a gigantic flower with revolving human petals. Lynne is the center. Nearer to them Truman notices the children are taking turns combing her hair. Her hair—to them lovely because it is easy to comb—shines, held up behind by black and brown hands as if it is a train. The children might be bridesmaids preparing Lynne for marriage. They do not see him. He frames a picture with his camera but something stops him before he presses the shutter. What stops him he will not, for the moment, have to acknowledge: It is a sinking, hopeless feeling about opposites, and what they do to each other. Suddenly he swings around, and bending on one knee takes a picture of the broken roofing and rusted tin on wood that makes up one wall of a shabby nearby house.

Truman and Lynne: They had a borrowed motorcycle. And on dusky evenings would go zooming down the back roads, the dust powdery and damp on their faces. She wore a helmet, her long hair caught up in back, wisps of it straying across her eyes, slinging itself across her mouth. She held him around the waist and felt his ribs strain against the wind. Through the puffy jacket his body felt fat and thin at the same time. Riding the motorcycle was dangerous because of the whiteness of her face, but at dusk they passed in a blur. At night they were more clear.

To Lynne, the black people of the South were Art. This she begged forgiveness for and tried to hide, but it was no use. To her eyes, used to Northern suburbs where every house looked sterile and identical even before it was completely built, where even the flowers were uniform and their nicknames were already in dictionaries, the shrubs incapable of strong odor or surprise of shape, and the people usually stamped with the seals of their professions; to her, nestled in a big chair made of white oak strips, under a quilt called The Turkey Walk, from Attapulsa, Georgia, in a little wooden Mississippi sharecropper bungalow that had never known paint, the South—and the black people living there—was Art. The songs, the dances, the food, the speech. Oh! She was such a romantic, so in love with the air she breathed, the honeysuckle that grew just beyond the door.

"I will pay for this," she often warned herself. "It is probably a sin to think of a people as Art." And yet, she would stand perfectly still and the sight of a fat black woman singing to herself in a tattered yellow dress, her voice rich and full of yearning, was always—God forgive her, black folks forgive her—the same weepy miracle that Art always was for her.

Truman had had enough of the Movement and the South. But not Lynne. Mississippi—after the disappearance of the three Civil Rights workers in 1964—began to beckon her. For two years she thought of nothing else: If Mississippi is the worst place in America for black people, it stood to reason, she thought, that the Art that was their lives would flourish best there. Truman, who had given up his earlier ambition to live permanently in France, wryly considered Mississippi a just alternative. And so a little over two years after the bodies—battered beyond recognition, except for the colors: two white, one black—of Cheney, Goodman and Schwerner were found hidden in a backwoods Neshoba County, Mississippi, dam, Lynne and Truman arrived.

Of Bitches and Wives

His feelings for Lynne had been undergoing subtle changes for some time. Yet it was not until the shooting of Tommy Odds in Mississippi that he noticed these changes. The shooting of Tommy Odds happened one evening just as he Truman, Tommy Odds and Trilling (a worker from Oklahoma since fled and never seen again) were coming out of the door of the Liberal Trinity Baptist Church. There had been the usual meeting with songs, prayers and strategy for the next day's picketing of downtown stores. They had assumed, also, that guards had been posted; not verifying was their mistake. As they stepped from the church and into the light from an overhanging bulb on the porch, a burst of machine-gun fire came from some bushes across the street. He and Trilling jumped off the sides of the steps. Tommy Odds, in the middle, was shot through the elbow.

When he went to visit Tommy Odds in the hospital he thought, as the elevator carried him to the fourth floor, of how funny it would be when the two of them talked about the frantic jump he and Trilling made. "You know one thing," he was going to say, laughing, to Tommy Odds, "you're just one *slow* nigger." Then they would wipe the tears of laughter from their eyes and open the bottle of Ripple he had brought. But it had not gone that way at all. First of all, Tommy Odds was not resting up after a flesh wound, as earlier reports had said; he had lost the lower half of his arm. He was propped up in bed now with a clear fluid dripping from a bottle into his other arm. But his horrible gray coloring, his cracked bloodless lips, his glazed eyes, were nothing compared to the utter lack of humor apparent in his face. Impossible to joke, to laugh, without tearing his insides to shreds.

Yet Truman had tried. "Hey, man!" he said, striding across the room with his bottle of Ripple under his arm. "Look what I brought you!" But Tommy Odds did not move his head or his eyes to follow him across the room. He lay looking at a spot slightly above the television, which was high in one corner of the room.

"Lynne says hurry up and get your ass out of here," he continued. "When you get out of here we gon' party for days."

"Don't mention that bitch to me, man," Tommy Odds said.

"What you say?"

"I said"—Tommy Odds turned his head and looked at him, moving his lips carefully so there would be no mistake—"don't mention that bitch to me. Don't mention that white bitch."

"Wait a minute, man," Truman stammered in surprise, "Lynne had nothing to do with this." And yet, while he was saying this, his tongue was slowed down by thoughts that began twisting like snakes through his brain. How could he say Lynne had nothing to do with the shooting of Tommy Odds, when there were so many levels at which she could be blamed?

"All white people are motherfuckers," said Tommy Odds, as listlessly but clearly as before. "I want to see them destroyed. I could watch their babies being torn limb from limb and I wouldn't lift a finger. The Bible says to dash out the brains of your enemy's children on the rocks. I understand that shit, now."

At this level, Truman thought, sinking into a chair beside his friend, is Lynne guilty? That she is white is true. That she is therefore a killer, evil, a motherfucker—how true? Not true at all! And yet—

"Man, all I do is think about what these crackers did with my motherfucking arm," said Tommy Odds.

"You want me to find out?"

"No, I guess not."

By being white Lynne was guilty of whiteness. He could not reduce the logic any further, in that direction. Then the question was, is it possible to be guilty of a color? Of course black people for years were "guilty" of being black. Slavery was punishment for their "crime." But even if he abandoned this search for Lynne's guilt, because it ended, logically enough, in racism, he was forced to search through other levels for it. For bad or worse, and regardless of what this said about himself as a person, he could not—after his friend's words—keep from thinking Lynne was, in fact, guilty. The thing was to find out how.

"I'm sorry, man," said Tommy Odds. "I shouldn't have come down on your old lady that way."

"It's okay, man, no sweat," Truman mumbled, while his thoughts continued to swirl up, hot and desperate. It was as if Tommy Odds had spoken the words that fit thoughts he had been too cowardly to entertain. On what other level might Lynne, his wife, be guilty?

"It's just that, you know, white folks are a bitch. If I didn't hate them on principle before, I hate them now for personal and concrete reasons. I've been thinking and thinking, lying here. And what I've thought is: Don't nobody offer me marching and preaching as a substitute for going after those jokers' *balls*."

Was it because she was a white woman that Lynne was guilty? Ah, yes. That was it. Of course. And Truman remembered one night when he and Tommy Odds and Trilling and Lynne had gone to the Moonflower café for a sandwich. They shouldn't have done it, of course. They had been warned against it. They knew better. But there are times in a person's life when to risk everything is the only *affirmation* of life. That night was such a time. What had they been celebrating? Oh, yes. Tommy Odds's niggers-on-the-corner.

For months Tommy Odds had hung out every Saturday evening at the pool hall on Carver Street, talking and shooting pool. He had been playing with the niggers-on-the-corner for almost a month before he ever opened his mouth about the liberating effects of voting. At first he had been hooted down with shouts of "Man, I don't wanna hear that shit!" and "Man, let's keep this a clean game!" But the good thing about Tommy Odds was his patience. At first he just shut up and worked out with his cue. But in a few days, he'd bring it up again. By the end of the first month his niggers-on-the-corner liked him too much not to listen to him. At the end of three months they'd formed a brigade called "The Niggers-on-the-Corner-Voter-Machine." It was through them that all the derelicts, old grandmamas and grandpas and tough young hustlers and studs, the prostitutes and even the boozy old guy who ran the pool hall registered to vote in the next election. And on this particular Saturday night they decided to celebrate at the Moonflower, a greasy hole-in-the-wall that still had "Whites Only" on its door.

The food was so bad they had not been able to eat it. But they left in high spirits, Lynne giggling about the waitress's hair that was like a helmet made of blonde foil. But as they walked down the street a car slowly followed them until, turning down Carver Street, they were met by some of Tommy Odds's NOTC, who walked them to safety in front of the pool hall. After that night he and Lynne were careful not to be seen together. But since Lynne was the only white woman in town regularly seen only with black people, she was easily identified. He had not thought they would be, too.

So for that night, perhaps Lynne was guilty. But why had she been with them? Had she invited herself? No. Tommy Odds had invited them both to his little party. Even so, it was Lynne's presence that had caused the car to follow them. So she *was* guilty. Guilty of whiteness, as well as stupidity for having agreed to come.

Yet, Lynne loved Tommy Odds, she admired his NOTC. It was Lynne who designed and sewed together those silly badges that they wore, that gave them so much pride.

"What do NOTC mean?" asked the old grandmamas who were escorted like queens down the street to the courthouse.

132

"Oh, it mean 'Not Only True, but Colored,'" the hustlers replied smoothly. Or, "Not on Time, but Current," said the prostitutes to the old grandpas, letting the old men dig on their cleavage. Or, "Notice of Trinity, with Chirst," the pool sharks said to the religious fanatics, who frowned, otherwise, on pool sharks.

So Lynne was guilty on at least two counts; of being with them, and of being, period. At least that was how Tommy Odds saw it. And who was he to argue, guilty as he was of loving the white bitch who caused his friend to lose his arm?

Thinking this, he shot up from his chair by the bed as if from an electric shock. The bottle of Ripple slipped from his fingers and crashed to the floor.

"Just don't tell me you done wasted the wine," said Tommy Odds, groaning. "I was just working myself up for a taste."

"I'll bring another bottle," Truman said, getting towels from the bathroom and mopping up. He cut his finger on a piece of glass and realized he was trembling. When he'd put the wastebasket outside the door for the janitor he looked back at Tommy Odds. Some small resemblance of his friend remained on the bed. But he could feel the distance that already separated them. When he went out that door they would both be different. He could read the message that Tommy Odds would not, as his former friend, put into words. "Get rid of your bitch, man." That was all.

Getting rid of a bitch is simple, for bitches are dispensable. But getting rid of a wife?

He had read in a magazine just the day before that Lamumba Katurim had gotten rid of his. She was his wife, true, but apparently she was even in that disguise perceived as evil, a castoff. And people admired Lamumba for his perception. It proved his love of his own people, they said. But he was not sure. Perhaps it proved only that Lamumba was fickle. That he'd married his bitch in the first place for shallow reasons. Perhaps he was considering marrying a black woman (as the article said he was) for reasons just as shallow. For how could he state so assuredly that he would marry a black woman next when he did not appear to have any *specific* black woman in mind?

133

If his own sister told him of her upcoming marriage to Lamumba he would have to know some answers before the nuptial celebration. Like, how many times would Lamumba require her to appear on television with him, or how many times would he parade her before his friends as proof of his blackness.

He thought of Randolph Kay, the Movie Star, who also shucked his white bitch wife, to black applause. But now Randolph Kay *and* his shiny new black wife had moved into the white world completely, to the extent of endorsing the American bombing of civilian targets in Vietnam. Randolph Kay, in fact, now sang love songs to the President! But perhaps it was perverse of him to be so suspicious. Perhaps, after all, he was just trying to cover up his own inability to act as decisively and to the public order as these men had done. No doubt these *were* great men, who perceived, as he could not, that to love the wrong person is an error. If only he could believe it *possible* to love the wrong person he would be home free. As it was, how difficult hating his wife was going to be. He would not even try.

But of course he had.

There was a man he despised, whose name was Tom Johnson. Tom had lived with a white woman for years, only most people didn't know about it. He shuttled her back and forth from his house to a friend's house down the street. Whenever he had important guests, Margaret was nowhere to be found. She was waiting át their friend's house. She was a fleshy blonde, with big tits and a hearty laugh. Once he asked Tom—who was thinking of running for political office—why he didn't marry her. Tom laughed and said, "Boy, you don't understand anything yet. Margaret is a sweet ol' thing. We been living together in harmony for five years. But she's white. Or hadn't you noticed?" Tom had reached out a chubby hand to bring Truman's head closer to his own and his small eyes danced. "It's just a matter of pussy. That's all. Just a matter of my *personal* taste in pussy." And then he had pulled Truman's head even closer and said with conspiratorial glee, "It's *good* stuff. Want some?"

"I used to believe that—" he had begun, but Tom cut him off.

"This is war, man, *war!* And all's fair that fucks with the suckers' minds!"

Then he had begun to see them together. Not in public, but with small groups of men, in the back rooms of bars. Margaret could play poker and he liked to see her when she won. She jumped up, squealing, in her small-girl voice, her big tits bouncing at the top of her low-cut blouse, and all the men looked at her tolerantly, in amusement, their curiosity about her big body already at rest. After what Tom had told him this did not surprise him: the exhibition of her delight in winning, the men's amused solidarity, their willingness to share her in this position of secrecy. And Margaret? Those squeals of delight—what did she feel? Or was it unmanly, unblack now, even to care, to ask?

When the community center was built, he began painting a mural of the struggle along one wall. The young men who would use the center for dances, Ping-Pong, card games, etc., were building tables and chairs. They were a shy, sweet bunch, country boys and naïve as possible, who were literally afraid of white women. Their first meeting with Lynne had been comic. Nobody wanted to be seen talking to her alone, and even as a group they would only talk to her from a distance. She could, just by speaking to them and walking up to them as she spoke, force them back twenty yards. This shamed him now as he thought of Tommy Odds.

Why should they be afraid of her? She was just a woman. Only they could not see her that way. To them she was a route to Death, pure and simple. They felt her power over them in their bones; their mothers had feared her even before they were born. Watching their fear of her, though, he saw a strange thing: They did not even see her as a human being, but as some kind of large, mysterious doll. A thing of movies and television, of billboards and car and soap commercials. They liked her hair, not because it was especially pretty, but because it was long. To them, *length* was beauty. They loved the tails of horses.

Against this fear, Lynne used her considerable charm. She baked cookies for them, allowed them to drink wine in her house, and played basketball with them at the center. Jumping about in her shorts, tossing her long hair, she laughed and sweated and shouted and cursed. She forced them to like her.

But while this building of trust and mutual liking was coming into being, the Movement itself was changing. Lynne was no longer welcome at any of the meetings. She was excluded from the marches. She was no longer allowed to write articles for the paper. She spent most of her time in the center or at home. The boys, unsure now what their position as young black men should be, remained inexplicably loyal. They came to visit her, bringing news she otherwise would not have heard. For Truman too was under pressure of ostracism from the group, and though he remained a member of all Movement discussions it was understood he would say nothing to his wife.

The New York Times

He had gone to Meridian three years after he married Lynne, driving across from Mississippi to a small town in Alabama where Meridian, at that time, lived. She had still owned a few possessions then, and was teaching in a Freedom school and keeping rather than burning her poems. He had begged her, or tried to beg her (because she did not seem to understand what begging constituted), to give him another chance. She loved him, he rashly assumed—as she smiled at him—and he did not see why she should deny herself.

"For Lynne's sake alone, I couldn't do it," she had said languidly, rocking slowly in her yellow chair. "What does she have now besides you?"

"Everything," he said sarcastically. "She's still an American white woman."

"Is that so easy?" asked Meridian, stopping her rocking, turning away from him toward the window. The light exposed small petal-shaped flecks of black in her brown eyes. "She was that when she decided she'd rather have you than everything. True? Or not?"

"How can you take her side?"

"Her side? I'm sure she's already taken it. I'm trying to make the acquaintance of my side in all this. What side *is* mine?" She was not uptight. Nothing trembled. She thought. Rocked. "Don't you think you owe something to Camara?" She looked him square in the eye.

"I owe more to all the little black kids being blown away by whitey's racism."

"Of which your daughter is one, surely?" She steadied the rocker, listened.

"Besides," he continued, "I don't love Lynne the way I do you. You notice I don't lie and say I don't love her *at all*. She's meant a great deal to me. But you're different. *Loving* you is different—"

"Because I'm black?"

"You make me feel healthy, purposeful—"

"Because I'm black?"

"Because you're *you*, damn it! The woman I should have married and didn't!"

"Should have *loved*, and didn't," she murmured.

And Truman sank back staring, as if at a lifeboat receding in the distance.

Truman had felt hemmed in and pressed down by Lynne's intelligence. Her inability to curb herself, her imagination, her wishes and dreams. It came to her, this lack of restraint, which he so admired at first and had been so refreshed by, because she had never been refused the exercise of it. She assumed that nothing she could discover was capable of destroying her. He was charmed by her presumption; still, he was not prepared to love her over a long period, but for a short one.

How marvelous it was at first to find that she read everything. That she thought, deeply. That she longed to put her body on the line for his freedom. How her idealism had warmed him, brought him into the world, made him eager to tuck her under his wing, under himself, sheltering her from her own illusions. Her awareness of wrong, her indignant political response to whatever caused him to suffer, was a definite part of her charm, and yet he preferred it as a part of her rarely glimpsed, commented upon in passing, as one might speak of the fact that Lenin wore a beard. And as she annoyed him with her irrepressible questions that kept bursting out and bubbling up into their lives, like spring water rising beside a reservoir and undermining the concrete of the dam, he had thought of Meridian, whom he imagined as more calm, predictable. Her shy, thin grace, her relative inarticulateness (Lynne, by comparison, never seemed to stop talking, and her accent was unpleasant), her brown strength that he imagined would not mind being a resource for someone else. . . . In Meridian, all the things lacking in Lynne seemed apparent. Here was a woman to rest in, as a ship must have a port. As a train must have a shed.

He was stunned to learn that she had long ago dismissed him. In fact, when he looked into her eyes, he knew he was remembering someone else, someone he had made up. Why, he had not known this woman at all! For the first time he detected a quality in Meridian that Lynne—who had known her only briefly—had insisted anyone could see. Meridian, no matter what she was saying to you, and no matter what you were saying to her, seemed to be thinking of something else, another conversation perhaps, an earlier one, that continued on a parallel track. Or of a future one that was running an identical course. This was always true.

There was also something dark, Truman thought, a shadow, that seemed to swing, like the pendulum of a clock, or like a blade, behind her open, candid eyes, that made one feel condemned. That made one think of the guillotine. That made one suspect she was unbalanced. When he noticed it he felt a shrinking, a retreating of his balls: He wanted her still, but would not have wanted (or been able) to make love to her.

And in front of this restlessness behind her eyes, this obvious mental activity, she placed a deceptive outer calm. He knew that in this woman who never seemed to hurry, and whom he was destined to pursue, the future might be short, but memory was very long.

He groaned. Mightily, and at length.

"Oh no," Meridian said pleasantly. "You wanted a virgin, don't you remember?" (He could remember nothing of the kind.) "You wanted a woman who was not 'sexually promiscuous.'"

(When had he said he wanted that?) "But on the other hand, you wanted a woman who had had worldly experiences . . . to match your own. Now, since I already had a son, whose existence you frightened me into denying, and since you also wanted to make love to me, and since I had no worldly experience to speak of, marriage between us never reached the point of discussion. In Lynne you captured your ideal: a virgin who was eager for sex and well-to-do enough to have had 'worldly experiences.'" She explained this in the voice of instruction.

What she said was absolutely true. Though he was positive he had never told her any of these things. He *had* wanted a virgin, had been raised to expect and *demand* a virgin; and never once had he questioned this. He had been as predatory as the other young men he ran with, as eager to seduce and devirginize as they. Where had he expected his virgin to come from? Heaven?

When he made love to Meridian it had been almost impossible to penetrate her; it was as if her vagina were sealed shut by a taut muscle that fought him. Afterward there was no blood and although she had not said she was a virgin, he had assumed it. It was only later that he could begin to understand why her vagina had been clenched so tightly against him. She had been spasmodic with fear. Fear because sex was always fraught with ugly consequences for her, and fear because if she did not make love with him she might lose him, and if she did make love with him he might lose interest. As he must have seemed, to her, to have done.

But the truth was different. After they had made love, he learned she had been married and had had a child. How could he have a wife who already had a child? And that she had given that child away. What repugnance there arose in him for her. For her eyes which, he thought, burned unnaturally bright. For her thin body on which her breasts (which he much admired) hung much too heavily: When he knew about the child he thought of her breasts as used jugs. They had belonged to some other man.

He had wanted a woman perfect in all the eyes of the world,

140

not a savage who bore her offspring and hid it. *And yet,* had she approached him on the street, dragging her child with her by the hand, he would never have glanced at her. For him she would not even have existed as a woman he might love.

Ironically, it was this awareness of his own limitation, which grew keener year by year, that caused Meridian to remain, a constant reproach, in his thoughts. Wherever he was he would think of her face, her body, the way her hands had fluttered over his back when she kissed him. He thought of the times she had seemed embarrassed for him and he did not know why. He thought of how frequently he had felt superior to her. There was one memory in particular that pained him: Years ago when he was dating the white exchange students she had asked him, the words blurted out in so thick a shame he knew she intended to forget she'd ever asked—"But what do you *see* in them?"

And he had replied cruelly, thoughtlessly, in a way designed to make her despise the confines of her own provincial mind:

"They read *The New York Times.*"

Truman felt that that exchange, too, rested somewhere behind Meridian's eyes. It would have been joy to him to forget her, as it would have been joy never to have been his former self. But running away from Lynne, at every opportunity, and existing a few days in Meridian's presence, was the best that he could do.

Visits

The summer before Meridian arrived in Chicokema, which was near the Georgia coast, Lynne visited her. They had not seen each other since the death of Lynne and Truman's daughter, Camara, a year earlier. Meridian was living in an adequately furnished house that the black community—having witnessed one of her performances and the paralysis that followed it—provided. The house was in an obscure farming village on the Georgia-Alabama line, and how Lynne tracked her there Meridian was at first unable to imagine. The simple answer was that Truman, who was also visiting her at that time, and whose visits had become so commonplace she hardly noticed them, had apparently phoned her.

There were periods in Meridian's life when it could not be perceived that she was ill. It was true that she'd lost so much of her hair that finally she had shaved her head and begun wearing a striped white and black railroad worker's cap: the cotton was durable and light and the visor shaded her eyes from the sun. And it was also true that she was frail and sickly-looking. But among the impoverished, badly nourished black villagers—who attempted to thrive on a diet of salt meat and potatoes during the winter, and fresh vegetables without meat during the summer—she did not look out of place. In fact, she looked as if she belonged.

Like them, she could summon whatever energy a task that had to be performed required, and like them, this ability seemed to her something her ancestors had passed on from the days of slavery when there had been no such thing as a sick slave, only a "malingering" one. Like the luckless small farmers around her who tended their crops "around the weather"—sitting out the days of rain, rushing out to plant or chop or harvest when the sun came out—she lived "around" her illness. Like them, it seemed pointless to her to complain.

Meridian wondered who the stout white woman could be, knocking at her door as if her fist were made of iron. Then she saw that it was Lynne, a great deal changed.

"I'll make us some tea," she said, inviting her in.

"Thanks, Meridian," said Lynne, unburdening herself of her satchel bag and flopping heavily onto the couch. "I'm exhausted!"

She wore a long Indian bedspread skirt—yellow, with brown and black elephants—and a loose black blouse embroidered with flowers and small mirrors around the neck. Intricately worked gold earrings dangled against her neck. Her olive complexion, which tanned golden in a day of sun, was now chalk-white, her eyes were red-veined and her eyelids drooped. Her dark hair was tangled and dull.

"I haven't slept for three motherfuckin' *days*," said Lynne.

"You should have stopped at one of those new Scottish Inns. They're cheap."

"Not cheap if you're broke," Lynne said flatly, looking about the room, her eyes resting for a moment on one of Meridian's broadside poems which she had stapled to the wall. It was the last object of personal value Meridian owned, and she intended, when she vacated the house, to leave it there.

"Truman's here, you know," Meridian said, bringing in the tea. She had added bologna and light bread, the two foods people donated to her upkeep wherever she went, and a peanut butter and jelly sandwich. Lynne began eating the bologna without the bread, which was white and spongy, rolled up like a wiener. Then she licked the jelly from the peanut butter, poking at it delicately but never missing, like a cat.

144

"I thought he might be," she said, all attention focused on her food.

"Really, Lynne, there's not the slightest thing between us. We're as innocent as brother and sister." Meridian stopped. Perhaps that was not as innocent as it might sound. "There's nothing between us."

"I know there's nothing between you." Lynne laughed, a short bark that ended in a cough. Her voice was hoarse from smoking and her top lip curled back in a way Meridian did not remember. "That's why he flies to you like a goddamn homing pigeon. Nothing between you, my ass." She had almost said "but my ass."

"Lynne . . ."

"There'll *always* be something between you." Lynne laughed again, and pulled out a cigarette. "Maybe you *don't* know what it is," she said with some surprise, but with more undisguised cynicism. "What's between you is everything that could have happened and didn't, because you were both scared to death of each other. Black men and women *are* scared to death of each other, you know. Not your *average* black men and women, of course, who accept each other as only natural, but people like you and Truman who have to keep analyzing each other's problems. People like you and Truman ought to lock yourselves up in a room somewhere and smoke yourselves silly, fall into each other's black arms and fuck your brains out." She frowned. "Of course, you all do have that super-long line of failure in y'all's personal relationships. That must be hard to go against. Or maybe it's just too many blonde white women selling foot powder and Noxzema shaving cream. Did you know that Truman prefers blondes? I think he does. . . ." She inhaled deeply and slowly let out the smoke.

"It must be deep," she said after a pause. "He married me, and keeps trying to screw himself to death all over the place, and you—well, who knows what you do with yourself. . . . I don't blame you though, for not getting married. That was real smart. *Real* smart. I wish somebody'd let me turn in my oaths. It was a shitty arrangement, after we had the kid." She lifted her teacup and put it down without tasting.

"I've gained weight, haven't I?" she asked.

"We've all gained," said Meridian, "or lost."

"Well, you sure haven't gained," said Lynne, glancing sharply at her, "in fact, you—"

"You just can't see it," said Meridian, deliberately cutting her off. She knew what she looked like; it didn't bother her; but she did not wish to hear Lynne comment on it.

"And my hair is turning gray," said Lynne. "I have gray strands all across the top. I started to dye it once. You know, it is so hard to live with myself, looking old so quick." She reached up to touch the almost invisible strands of gray at her temples.

"You've had a hard life," said Meridian.

"The only people who ever loved me," Lynne continued absently, looking about for a mirror, "were the po' folks down in the woods, the swamps. They never looked down on me. Never despised me. After I had Camara I brought her back down here one time to show her off and they loved us both. Didn't despise us. Didn't try to make us feel we had stolen one of y'all's scarce few men. Made us feel like family. Of course they were the old type of black people, like that old religious lady who fed us that time. Remember her? They just came out on the porch and said: 'Y'all *come* in. Here, girl, let me *see* this big old fine baby. What you name her? Camara. Now that's *real* cute. Lord, ain't she got a head of *hair*. And will you *look* at them big eyes. Just as *brown*. Naw, I think they's *green*. Naw, I believe they *is* brown. Well, just come on to your kinfolk. Come on here. That's right.'"

Lynne was beginning to weep. Tears slid off her chin.

"It looks more like it was bleached in the sun," said Meridian.

"Never made us feel like there was nobody on earth so low as to want us. Me and my brown sugar baby. 'Hair,' she said, coming back, 'looks like it was bleached in the sun'—my ass. Kind, polite, courteous—that's that Southern charm folks down here have. It's such shit."

146

"Truman is out with his camera. He really should be back any minute."

"With his camera! Probably taking pictures of all the poor little girls he'd like to fuck. That's his only interest in the poor. Not to mention the black." She wiped her eyes and lifted her cup in a salute.

"I forgot sugar," said Meridian, rising and going into the kitchen.

"Mustn't forget *sugar*," said Lynne. "*Oy vey*, you're a regular Betty Crocker. How do y'all do it, I wonder? Always gracious and calm. Perfect little ladies; whether you lived in the big house as Big Missy or as slave. It must've been all that corn bread. Made y'all mealy-mouthed."

"I didn't invite Truman," said Meridian. "I never have."

"I don't care about Truman," said Lynne, lighting up a reefer and taking a deep drag. "I don't care about the son of a bitch any more."

Meridian watched them meet in her back yard. They did not smile or touch. Truman was frowning, Lynne's face was tense. Meridian stood in the center of the living room and began doing exercises. First she pretended she was slowly jumping rope, bouncing lightly off the floor and springing into the air. Then she touched her toes. Then she lay down and began raising first one leg and then the other, holding them suspended to the count of ten.

"What the fuck do you mean, nigger?" Lynne's voice, harsh and wild, came from the back yard. It dropped into the quietness of the neighborhood like a stone.

"Will you shut the fuck up, *beast*."

"Not until you tell me why I can't ever find you unless I look in Meridian's back yard."

"I don't live with you. I don't have to explain myself to you. Not any more, I don't."

"Look at me!" she said, foolishly, since he *was* looking at her. "You think you can step over me and just keep going . . . ruin my life."

147

"Don't bring up your lousy dancing career," he snarled. "If you people could dance you wouldn't have to copy us all the time."

"You asshole," she said. "You're a fine one to talk. You're the only nigger in the Free World who can't dance a lick. Every time you get out there shaking your ass you look like a faggot with cramps."

His voice was suddenly menacing: "Cut out the 'nigger' shit."

"I could have made it," she said. "At least I could have stayed healthy."

"You always needed a shrink," he said. "It's symptomatic of your race."

Lynne had begun to cry, wiping her nose on the edge of her skirt. Truman watched with disgust.

"My race? My *race*?" Lynne turned her face up as if imploring the trees. She laughed in spite of herself.

He had never hated, aesthetically, the whiteness of Lynne so much. It shocked him. Her nose was red and peeling, her hair was stringy and—he scrutinized it quickly—there was some gray! And she was so stout! Stouter even than the last time he'd seen her, after Camara died. He could not stop himself from thinking she looked very much like a pig. Her eyes seemed tinier than he'd ever seen them and her white ears needed only to grow longer and flop over a bit.

But what was happening (had happened) to him, that he should have these thoughts? There was a large pecan tree beside him. He leaned against it.

"Lynne," he said finally, "why don't you go on back home? There's nothing between me and Meridian. Not like you think. She doesn't understand why I keep bothering her any more than I do."

"Bull."

"Meridian is my past, my *sister* . . ." Truman began, but Lynne cut him off.

"I've heard all that shit before," she said. "But it doesn't speak to what you did to me and Camara. Running off as soon as black became beautiful . . ."

It was his turn to laugh. "You don't *believe* that?" he asked.

"You bet your stinking life I do. You must think I'm stupid. You only married me because you were too much of a coward to throw a bomb at all the crackers who make you sick. You're like the rest of those nigger zombies. No life of your own at all unless it's something against white folks. You can't even enjoy a good fuck without hoping some cracker is somewhere grinding his teeth."

"I married you because I loved you."

"Yeah, and you wanted something *strange* around the house to entertain your friends."

"Shut up, Lynne," said Truman, as he saw Meridian coming out of the house.

"I'm going for a walk," said Meridian to Lynne. "But if you're sleepy or tired you can take a nap on the couch in the living room. I'll leave the door open."

"Doesn't True look well?" Lynne asked, as Meridian stood watching them. She had not been able to ignore their loud voices and was annoyed with them.

"He looks divine," she said.

"So *mature*," said Lynne, "yet so young . . . don't you think? You're thirty-four now, aren't you, darlin'?" she asked, turning briefly to Truman, who scowled at her. "Would you believe he's heading for middle age? I wouldn't. It comes from easy living and of course he's a vampire. Sucks the blood of young white virgins to keep him vigorous. Did you know that?" She turned a bright, tight face to Truman. "Tell her about this thing you have, darlin' (and of course he's not the only one), for young white virgins. And don't lie and say I wasn't one."

"Shut *up*!"

"You Southern girls lead such sheltered lives," Lynne said, affecting a Southern belle accent and twirling a lock of her unwashed, rather oily hair around her finger, "I declare I'd be just bored to death. That's why your men come North, sugah, looking for that young white meat that proves they have arrived. You know? Tell me, how does it feel to be a complete *flop*" (this said with a Bette Davis turn of her wrist) "at keeping your men?

"You know, I could—yes, fat ass 'n' all, walk up the street anywhere around here and Hey Presto! I'd have all y'all's men following after me, their little black tongues hanging out."

Truman felt as if his soul, hanging precariously for a lifetime, had fallen off the shelf.

"It would take a sick mind to be pleased with that old racist chestnut, you silly heifer." He would have liked the power to wither her, literally, with a glance.

Lynne took out her sunglasses and put them on, smiling and nodding, as if her audience were large.

"Bra*vo!*" she said. "Underneath that old-fashioned cullud exterior beats the heart of a murderer. I knew it."

"Forgive me, both of you," said Meridian, "but I'm locking the house."

"A locked house, a locked pussy," said Lynne, giggling.

"I didn't mean anything by it, Meridian," said Lynne, later, crying into the pillows of the couch. "It's just that you have everything. I mean, you're so strong, your people love you, and you can cope. I don't have anything. I gave up everything for True, and he just shit on me."

She had stayed in the yard arguing with Truman until he walked away. Then she had gotten into Meridian's house through an open window. Just like these country bumpkins, she thought, to lock the door and leave the window wide open.

Meridian had walked until she wore herself out, and one thought had preoccupied her mind: "The only new thing now," she had said to herself, mumbling it aloud, so that people turned to stare at her, "would be the refusal of Christ to accept crucifixion. King," she had said, turning down a muddy lane, "should have refused. Malcolm, too, should have refused. All those characters in all those novels that require death to end the book should refuse. All saints should walk away. Do their bit, then—just walk away. See Europe, visit Hawaii, become agronomists or raise Dalmatians." She didn't care what they did, but they should do it.

She looked at Lynne, who was definitely not yet a saint. She did not know what Lynne should do. She was too tired, at the moment, to care.

"Listen," said Lynne, "when Camara and I lived in the East Village—oh hell, Lower East Side, on 12th Street—I couldn't walk down the street to take her to kindergarten without niggers wanting to jump me. What could I do? I'm a woman, right? They never let up until they got me in bed. Then the crying and the pleading when I didn't feel like giving'em any. So usually I just said Fuck it! I've got to get some sleep. So get on up on me, nigger. Just don't take all night. Sometimes I'd go to sleep with'em still at it."

"*Must* you say nigger?" Meridian asked wearily. She realized that among many hip people the use of the word was not considered offensive but rather a matter of style. That she would hate it till the dirt was thrown over her face she knew mattered not at all to people who would eventually appropriate anything they could laugh at, or talk about, or wear. "Why did you let these people in, if you didn't want to be bothered?"

"Aw, I don't know. I got so tired. Begging, listening to people begging, is tiring. Besides, you don't know what's going on in the cities. There are all these white girls that are so fucked up with guilt they're willing and happy to keep a black guy, even if he's obviously a junkie bum. Not like me, at least I try for the classier bums—like the old poets and jazz stars of yesteryear. Like—"

"Don't give me any names," said Meridian. "Believe me when I say I don't want to know."

"I don't freak myself out, analyzing everything I do. What's a screw between friends, anyhow?"

"Between friends would be different."

"You can't understand. Your life is so .. . . there's something wrong with your life, you know. It's so, so, pro*scribed*. Like you drew a circle around it and only walk as far as the edge. Why did you come back down here? What are you looking for? These people will always be the same. You can't change them. Nothing will."

"But I can change," said Meridian. "I hope I will."

"I live for the moment, no looking back for me. Take what life offers . . . ah shit! It's just that my life is so fucked up. Truman was the only stable thing in it. I don't even have a photograph of my folks." Lynne's eyes narrowed. "Not that I need one to remember them. All I have to do is close my eyes and I see them all too well.

"My father was, actually, my father was wonderful—at least I thought he was wonderful. He wasn't your dashing prince, but in his dull, careful, Jewish way, he was terrific. He never spoke more than a dozen words to me in anger, all the time I was growing up. Always so gentle, so fair. I couldn't believe it when I called to tell them Camara had been attacked and died. You know what he said? My mother wouldn't even speak to me, although she could tell I was crying. My father took the phone and asked me to repeat. I told him my daughter was dead and he said, 'So's our daughter,' meaning me! And when I stopped breathing, because I thought I'd heard wrong, he said—as calmly as anything—'*Nu?* So what else?' " Lynne was eating grapes, she spat out a grape seed. "The heartless bastard, the least he could have done was prepare me for the creep he turned out to be. Fathers suck," she added, frowning. "When my old Tata is dead, then I'll remember his kindness. I refuse to do so until then.

"Mothers are beasts, too," continued Lynne. "All my mother thinks about is herself as perceived by the neighbors."

Meridian sat deep in her chair, her legs had fallen asleep. "It's all behind you," she said.

"You don't know the half," said Lynne, darting a glance at her. "Really you don't."

152

Sleepy, puzzled, off-guard, Meridian stared at her.

"Truman said one of my fantasies was being raped by a black man. That was what he reduced everything to. But it *wasn't!*" Her eyes, pleading, were filled with tears. She sat up on the couch and wiped her eyes. "You're the only one I can talk to about it. The only one who would believe it wasn't my fault that it happened. True let one of his friends . . ."

"I can't listen to this," said Meridian, rising abruptly and throwing up her hands. "I'm sorry, I just can't."

"Wait a minute," cried Lynne. "I know you're thinking about lynchings and the way white women have always lied about black men raping them. Maybe this wasn't rape. I don't know. I think it was. It *felt* like it was."

Meridian sat down again and looked at Lynne through her fingers, which were spread, like claws, over her face.

"Can't you understand I can't listen to you? Can't you understand there are some things I don't want to know?"

"You wouldn't believe me *either*?" Lynne asked.

"No," Meridian said, coldly.

"Well fuck you."

"Go to bed, Lynne. Why don't you go to bed?"

But Lynne did not intend to leave the room. Perhaps Meridian wouldn't listen to her, but she could sit there herself and try to remember what had happened to her and Truman's life.

Lynne

She remembered it was spring, and she had left her parents' house, she hoped, for good. And if this hope was not to become reality she did not intend to struggle over it or care. They headed south over the Interstate, their old car, a venerable black ruin, loaded down with her books, his paints, rolls of canvas, two cameras, and filled with music from a black radio station in Newark that, miraculously, they held until they reached the vicinity of the Maryland border.

For six months they'd met secretly in his mother's house. His room at the top of the stairs, the paintings—by Romare Bearden, Charles White, Jacob Lawrence—on the walls, as familiar to her as her own room across town. More familiar, because her room seemed still to be the hideout of a sixteen-year-old kid—with dancing shoes, tights, paper flowers from some forgotten high school decoration, and the faces of movie stars her mother encouraged her to like. No black faces, of course (though she had once had a picture of Sammy Davis, Jr., and Mai), which was not unusual. Not even any really Jewish faces, for that matter. No faces as dark, ripening, lean and high-nosed as her own. A *young* room, fresh, tacky, that wore innocence like the wrong shade of face powder, youth beneath the pink canopied bed like a bright rose preserved under glass. And she—entering her room—felt now a superiority to it, as if she now knew more (since her relationship with Truman) than the room was capable of containing.

For although it was her room, it was in her mother's house. Vulnerable to search and seizure, and the contemplative scrutiny of her mother's always uneasy mind.

When her mother tracked her to Truman's house they heard her screaming from three blocks away, because it was then that her mother noticed she had tracked her only daughter—who had slipped out of the house as furtively as a rabbi from a pogrom—to a black neighborhood. And she had screamed without ceasing, without, seemingly, even stopping to inhale, all the way to the Helds' steps. Where she had paused long enough to press the bell, the ringing of the bell itself like a blunter bellowing of her anguish. That harsh buzz, followed by the continuation of her mother's, by then, howl, rested in the back of Lynne's brain like a spinning record on which the sound was turned down. It would never leave her, even when she was most happy. Like the birth cry to a lucid mother it existed simultaneously with the growth of herself away from and apart from her mother. When she died she knew it would still be spinning soundlessly there.

Tommy Odds

"Altuna *Jones?*" Tommy Odds laughed. "*Hedge* Phillips, and what was that other guy's name?" He stood over her while she sewed, his usually sad black eyes brightly twinkling.

"I bet them guys never saw nobody like you. And if they did they never would let on. I bet you're scaring them niggers to death in them shorts."

He was only half-playful because he disliked what whites in the Movement chose to wear in black communities. A girl who had volunteered to take notes at church meetings had liked to sit with her dress pulled up so high you could see her drawers. This she did in the amen corner. The pious old women and hacked-down prayerful old men had hardly been able to express their grievances. And she, a blonde with a blank, German face—had placidly chewed gum and scratched her thighs, oblivious to what was hanging the people up. And of course nobody dared tell her. It wasn't fear. They were simply too polite to tell a guest in their community that she was behaving like a tramp.

Tommy Odds looked at Lynne carefully. She had tanned since coming South. She seemed relaxed and happy. He thought of her life with Truman—how they could never ride on the same seat of their car, but must always sit as if one of them were chauffeuring the other. And there was no entertainment for them at night. They were too poor to own a television set. But they seemed content. Truman with his sculpting and building the recreation cen-

157

ter. Lynne writing poems occasionally, reading them to her friends, then tearing them up. Sometimes she would paste an especially good one—one she liked—in front of the commode, at eye level. You had no choice but to read it. These were usually love poems to Truman, or poems about the need for gentleness in the heart of the Revolution. Her favorite book was Jane Stembridge's plea for love and community, *I Play Flute*. It was clear also in her poetry and in the things she said that to her black people had a unique beauty, a kind of last-gasp loveliness, which, in other races, had already become extinct.

He had wanted to make love to her. Because she was white, first of all, which meant she would assume she was in control, and because he wanted—at first—to force her to have him in ways that would disgust and thrill her. He thought of hanging her from a tree by her long hair and letting her weight gradually pull the hair from her scalp. He wondered if that would eventually happen to a person hung up in that way.

But Lynne grew on him, as she did on everyone. And she was a good worker. Better—to be honest—than the black women who always wanted to argue a point instead of doing what they were told. And she liked doing things for him; it was almost as if she knew he must be placated, obeyed. She had sewed the armbands willingly, and listened to his teasing enthusiastically, and tried to be carefree and not too Northern or hip. And she had worn her hair—for some strange reason that amounted almost to a premonition—in tight braids that she pinned securely to the top of her head.

Lynne

For of course it was Tommy Odds who raped her. As he said, it wasn't really rape. She had not screamed once, or even struggled very much. To her, it was worse than rape because she felt circumstances had not permitted her to scream. As Tommy Odds said, he was just a lonely one-arm nigger down on his luck that nobody had time for any more. But she would have time—wouldn't she? Because she was not like those rough black women who refused to be sympathetic and sleep with him—was she? She would be kind and not like those women or any other women who turned him down because they were repulsed and prejudiced and the maroon stump of his arm made them sick. She would be a true woman and save him—wouldn't she?

"But Tommy *Odds*," she pleaded, pushing against his chest, "I'm married to your friend. You can't *do* this."

"You don't have to tell him," he said, undoing her braids and wrapping his hand twice in her hair. "Kiss me," he said, pulling her against him. Water stood in her eyes as she felt her hair being tugged out at the roots.

"Please don't do this," she whimpered softly.

"You *knows* I cain't hep mysef," he said in loose-lipped mockery, looking at her red cheeks where tiny red capillaries ran swollen and broken. His eyes were sly, half-closed, filled with a sensuousness that was ice-cold. "You're so white and red, like a pretty little ol' pig." He lifted her briefly by her hair, pulled her closer to him.

159

"Tommy Odds—"

"Put your arms around me," he said, "and tell me you love me."

"Tommy Odds *please.*" She was crying aloud now and when she flailed her arms she bumped against his stump. Her throat worked.

"It makes you sick?" asked Tommy Odds. "You think I'm a cripple? Or is it just that you really don't dig niggers? Ones darker than your old man?"

"You know that's not true," she groaned.

He had tripped her back onto the bed and was pulling up her skirt with his teeth. His hand came out of her hair and was quickly inside her blouse. He pinched her nipples until they stung.

" *Please,*" she begged.

"I didn't really mean that," he said. "I know your heart is in the right place" (sucking her left nipple). "You're not like the others."

"God—" she said.

There was a moment when she knew she could force him from her. But it was a flash. She lay instead thinking of his feelings, his hardships, of the way he was black and belonged to people who lived without hope; she thought about the loss of his arm. She felt her own guilt. And he entered her and she did not any longer resist but tried instead to think of Tommy Odds as he was when he was her friend—and near the end her arms stole around his neck, and before he left she told him she forgave him and she kissed his slick rounded stump that was the color of baked liver, and he smiled at her from far away, and she did not know him. "Be seein' you," he said.

The next day Tommy Odds appeared with Raymond, Altuna and Hedge.

"Lynne," he said, pushing the three boys in front of him into the room, "I'm going to show you what you are."

She thought, helplessly, as if it were waiting for just this moment to emerge from her memory, of a racist painting she had

160

once seen in *Esquire* of a nude white woman spread-eagled on a rooftop surrounded by black men. She thought: *gang rape.* Her anal muscles tightened, her throat closed with an audible choking sound.

"What do you want?" she asked, looking—for the first time—downward toward the genitals of Hedge and Altuna and Raymond. They were looking sideways at her, as if embarrassed. All of them had been smoking grass, she smelled it on them.

Pointing to her body as if it were conquered territory, Tommy Odds attempted to interest the boys in exploring it: "Tits," he said, flicking them with his fingers, "ass."

"What do you want?" demanded Lynne, furious because seeing the faces of Altuna, Hedge and Raymond through the front window had reassured her, and she had not locked her door.

"What did we do yesterday afternoon?" Tommy asked lazily, idly, holding the back of her neck. "What did I do?"

Lynne gathered her courage. "You raped me."

"Um hum," he said, smiling at the boys who were attentive, curious and silent, as if holding their breath. "And what did you do when I was getting ready to get out of you?"

She did not reply. He squeezed her neck.

"I—" she began.

"A little nine-year-old black girl was raped by a white animal last week in Tchula," said Tommy Odds, "they pulled her out of the river, dead, with a stick shoved up her. Now that was rape. Not like us." He tightened his grip. "Tell us, bitch, what did you do when it started getting good to you?"

"It was never good," said Lynne. Then, "I kissed your arm."

"My stub," he corrected her. "You hugged me and you kissed my stub. And what else did you do?"

He was holding her neck in the crook of his elbow, her chin was pointed at the ceiling. He squeezed.

"I forgave you," said Lynne.

Tommy Odds laughed. "Forgave *me*," he said.

"Yes," said Lynne.

He loosened his grip. They stood together now, his arm around her shoulders, his fingers lightly stroking her breast. From the reflection in the windowpane they appeared to be a couple. Lynne looked into the horrified faces of Altuna, Hedge and Raymond. But perhaps, she thought, they are not horrified. Perhaps that is not a true reading of what I see on their faces (for the first time it seemed to her that black features were grossly different—more sullen and cruel—than white). Though none of them smiled, she could have sworn they were grinning. She imagined their gleaming teeth, with sharp, pointed edges. Oh, God, she thought, what a racist cliché.

"You want it?" Tommy Odds asked the boys.

Lynne closed her eyes. She could not imagine they would say no. The whole scene flashed before her. She was in the center of the racist *Esquire* painting, her white body offered up as a sacrifice to black despair. She thought of the force, the humiliation, the black power. These boys were no longer her friends; the sight of her naked would turn them into savages.

"Go on," said Tommy Odds. "Have some of it."

Altuna Jones—whose head was shaped exactly like a person's head would be shaped with such a name, like a melon, long, and with close-cut hair—cleared his throat.

"It? *It?* " he said. "What *it* you talking about? That ain't no *it*, that's Lynne."

Hedge Phillips spoke. Like his name there was evasion in his looks. He was short and fat and so oily black his features were hard to distinguish until he smiled. When he talked one foot stroked the ground experimentally, as if eager to move off down the street.

"We not gon' hurt you," he said to Lynne. "Us thought it was a party here this evening."

Raymond, shyer even than the other two, but grasping somehow that a masculine line, no matter how weak, must be taken, said, plaintively as it turned out, to Tommy Odds, "You *know*, Tommy, that I have a girlfriend."

"Look," said Odds, with contempt, "she's nothing particular. You guys are afraid of her, that's all. Shit. Crackers been raping your mamas and sisters for generations and here's your chance to get off on a piece of their goods."

"Man, you crazy," said Altuna Jones, and he looked at Lynne with pity, for she had obviously not been—in his opinion—raped. All his life he had heard it was not possible to rape a woman without killing her. To him, in fact, rape meant that you fucked a corpse. That Lynne would actually stoop to sleeping with Tommy Odds meant something terrible was wrong with her, and he was sorry.

The three boys left.

"They're not like you," said Lynne, though she had barely finished thinking they would be exactly like Tommy Odds. "They don't need to rape white women to prove they're somebody."

"Rape," said Tommy Odds. "I fucked you. *We* fucked."

Again he pressed her down on the bed and fumbled with her clothes. Even before she began to fight him off she knew she would not have to. Tommy Odds was impotent. He spat in her face, urinated on the floor, and left her lying there.

When Truman came home again, Lynne could not talk about it. She could hardly talk at all. She was packed and ready to leave. She wished she could go to the police, but she was more afraid of them than she was of Tommy Odds, because they would attack young black men in the community indiscriminately, and the people she wanted most to see protected would suffer. Besides, she thought as long as she didn't tell, Truman would never know. It would hurt him, she thought, to know how much his friend hated her. To know how low was her value. It was as if Tommy Odds thought she was not a human being, as if her whiteness, the mystique of it, the *danger* of it, the historically *verboten* nature of it, encouraged him to attempt to destroy her without any feelings of guilt. It was so frightening a thought that she shook with it.

She had insisted on viewing them all as people who suffered

without hatred; this was what intrigued her, made her like a child in awe of them. But she had not been thinking of individual lives, of young men like Tommy Odds whose thin defense against hatred broke down under personal assault. Revenge was his only comfort. And, she thought, on whom was such a man likely to take this revenge? Not on white men at large; certainly not. Not on the sheriff or the judge or the businessman sitting home over his drink. Not on the businessman's wife, because she *would* scream and put him away for good. He—Tommy Odds—had actually reached (and she understood this too well for her own comfort) an *improvement* in his choice of whom to punish, when he chose her. For, look at this: He had not, as black men had done foolishly for years, gotten drunk on the weekend and stabbed another black man to death. Nor had he married a black woman in order to possess, again erroneously, his own whipping post. Surely this was proof of a weird personal growth on Tommy's part. There were no longer any white boys, either, in the Movement, so that they could no longer be beaten up or turned, with guilty contempt, out into the street. That left her: a white woman without friends. A woman the white community already assumed was fucking every nigger in sight. Yes, Tommy Odds's logic—convoluted though it might be—was perfect.

But Truman didn't want her to leave. He would not give her money to leave even after she told him, hysterical finally, what had happened. He chose not to believe her.

Ask Tommy, she had cried. Just ask him! But if he did, she never knew.

"Why did you do it, man," Truman asked Tommy Odds.

"Because your woman ain't shit. She didn't even fight. She was just laying back waiting to give it up."

Lynne cried every night in her sleep. Truman could not bear it, so he did not usually come home. He slept on a couch in the center. His hand shot out and caught Odds at the base of the throat, which was black and scrawny, like the neck of a hen.

164

"She's better than you," he said, as Tommy Odds stretched his eyes wide, feigning fear. "You creep," said Truman, with a sneer. "you motherfucker. She felt sorry for you, because you lost your fucking arm."

He raised his clenched fist underneath Odds's chin and, holding the collar of his shirt, rocked him back and forth, his feet nearly off the floor. It was like lifting a bag of loose, dirty laundry. "She felt sorry for you and look what you did."

Odds did not raise his hand to defend himself. He looked into Truman's eyes, and his own eyes were laughing. The laughter in them was like two melting ice cubes gleaming in a dish.

"You wish it was my fucking arm she felt sorry for."

"What do you mean, you son of a bitch?"

But Tommy Odds, tired now of being held in an awkward position, yanked himself out of Truman's grasp. He straightened his collar, tucked his shirt into his pants, extended his stub out from his side, like a turkey flapping a wing, and ran his fingers through his hair.

"Why don't you wise up," he said. "She didn't get involved with you because of anything you lost."

"Why don't you say what you mean!"

"I mean," said Tommy Odds mockingly, "it is true that you speaks French when you wants to impress folks, and it is true that you went to college, and it is true that you can draw and stuff and one time lived overseas for six months without pig feet or greens. But that ain't what won you Miss Lady Fair. Oh nooooo . . . you're like a book she hadn't read; like a town she wanted to pass through; like a mango she wanted to taste because mangoes don't grow in her own yard. Boy, if you'd had an arm missing she probably would have kidnaped you a lot sooner than she did."

Truman wanted very much to destroy Tommy Odds. The impulse was overwhelming.

"Black men get preferential treatment, man, to make up for all we been denied. She ain't been fucking you, she's been atoning for her sins."

"That's not true," said Truman, sounding weak, even to himself.

"She felt sorry for me because I'm black, man," said Tommy Odds, and for the first time there was dejection in his voice. *"The one thing that gives me some consolation in this stupid world, and she thinks she has to make up for it out of the bountifulness of her pussy."* His voice hardened. *"I should have killed her."*

"No," said Truman, *"no—"*

Tommy Odds stood facing him. He looked terrible. Puny and exhausted and filthy. Dead. *"Listen, man, you want to defend her. It's all right with me. I don't care, man. You want to beat me up,"* he said, *"I'm ready, man. You want to kill me. Look, I won't even complain. You want me to go find you a gun? Or do you want to do it with your fists? Come on, man. Hit me. We'll feel better."*

But Truman had already turned away.

And so Lynne sat alone, at home always now because she was afraid to go over to the center she had helped create. Afraid and ashamed and not even conscious enough of her own worth to be angry that she was ashamed. She counted the days until she was sure she was not pregnant. When she sold one of her poems—to an anthologist who wanted to document the Movement in poetry, and who wanted the white woman's point of view—she bought birth control pills. Enough for two months.

Because of what Tommy Odds had done Lynne locked her door, even to her friends Hedge and Altuna and Raymond.

They came back again and again. At first she looked at them from behind a window shade, ashamed and resentful of her fear. Eventually—from loneliness only—she opened the door and soon everything was, seemingly, back to normal. The boys were as courteous and shy as ever. Truman was not at home very much and when he was home he didn't speak to her. Some nights when she became lonely to the point of suicide, she played checkers with Alonzo, Altuna's brother, who worked at the scrap yard. A man who appeared completely unaware of the Movement and who never had any interest in voting, marching or anything else, he treated her with the stiff, sober courtesy of old-time Negroes. For his kindness, she invited him to sleep with her. In his gratitude, he licked her from her earlobes to her toes.

On Saturday nights her house became a place of music. She was protected now because she had a special friend in Alonzo. (Everyone seemed to understand that Truman no longer cared.) Men and women came to the house because they heard you could listen to records and dance and smoke reefers. But if she thought being Alonzo's friend was going to save her from other men she was wrong. They pleaded, they cajoled, they begged. And always, in refusing them, she saw their softening, earnest faces go rigid with hatred and she shivered, and began, over the months, to capitulate. She tried in vain to make them her friends, as Alonzo was. But they began to drive up, take her to bed (or on the floor, upside the wall), as if she were a prostitute, get up and leave. In public they did not speak to her.

Still, the women found out. They began to curse her and to threaten her, attacking her physically, some of them. And she began perversely to enjoy their misguided rage, to use it as acknowledgment of her irresistible qualities. It was during this time that whenever she found herself among black women, she found some excuse for taking down and combing her hair. As she swung it and felt it sweep the back of her waist, she imagined she possessed treasures they could never have.

She began to believe the men fucked her from love, not from hatred. For as long as they did not hate her she felt she could live. She could bear the hatred of her own father and mother, but not the hatred of black men. And when they no longer came to her— and she did not know why they did not—she realized she needed them. And then there were only Lynne and Truman and when her pills gave out she became pregnant with Camara, and finally took a bus to New York, where Welfare placed her in a one-room apartment near Avenue C.

Truman she had magnanimously sent back to Meridian, at his insistence.

On Giving Him Back
to His Own

The subway train rushed through the tunnel screeching and sending out sparks like a meteor. And Lynne would not sit down while
it flew. Ninety-sixth Street flashed by, then 125th, then there was
a screaming halt, a jolt as the car resisted the sudden stop, and
the doors slid back with a rubbery thump. The graffiti, streaked
on the walls in glowing reds and glaring yellows, did not brighten
at all the dark damp cavern of the station.

"Legs, man," a boy whispered to his comrade, pausing on the
oily stairs as she passed.

"Right on," he was answered.

She darted up and around people as she rushed upward to the
air, thinking, with a part of her brain, that fresh air was certainly
what she needed. Nor did she notice any longer that nowhere in
the city was the air fresh. Only sometimes, when she took Camara to the park, and even then . . . She turned left as she
emerged from the subway, trotting now on her dancer's legs,
thinking of herself already in the apartment, the neat space of
quiet light and white walls where Truman worked night and day
on the century's definitive African-American masterpieces.

They would not fight, she warned herself. She would be ladylike and precise and he would respond to her cry of help for their
child.

"Our daughter has been hurt," she would say, with the sweet
desperation of Loretta Young. Or, "I mean," slouching with her

hands in her pockets like Mia Farrow looking for a tacos stand, "the kid's been beat *up*." Or, looking as if about to choke on her own vomit, like Sandy Dennis, but *cool*, "There's been. . . . an accident. Our child. Attacked. Oh, can't you hurry?" And Truman would respond with all the old tenderness that she knew.

She took the stairs two at a time, her hair streaming and unwashed, her face feeling sooty, until she stood in front of his door. Apartment 3-C. Truman Held, Artist.

It was only then that she thought to rest, to compose herself, to suck in her stomach, which felt flabby and at the same time inflated. She was no longer a size seven. This mattered, the longer she huddled there.

Even when Truman was leaving her she had been conscious of her size, her body, from years of knowing how he compared it to the bodies of black women. "Black women let themselves go," he said, even as he painted them as magnificent giants, breeding forth the warriors of the new universe. "They are so *fat*," he would say, even as he sculpted a "Big Bessie Smith" in solid marble, caressing her monstrous and lovely flanks with an admiring hand.

Her figure then, supple from dancing, was like a straw in the wind, he said, her long hair a song of lightness—untangled, glistening and free. And yet, in the end, he had stopped saying those things, at least out loud. It was as if the voluptuous black bodies, with breasts like melons and hair like a crown of thorns, reached out—creatures of his own creation—and silenced his tongue. They began to claim him. When she walked into a room where he painted a black woman and her heaving, pulsating, fecund body, he turned his work from her, or covered it up, or ordered her out of the room.

She had loved the figures at first—especially the paintings of women in the South—the sculptures, enduring and triumphant in spite of everything. But when Truman changed, she had, too. Until she did not want to look at the women, although many of them she knew, and loved. And by then she was willing to let him go.

Almost. So worthless did the painted and sculptured women make her feel, so sure was she that Truman, having fought through his art to the reality of his own mother, aunts, sisters, lovers, to their beauty, their greatness, would naturally seek them again in the flesh.

He would always be Camara's father, he said, repeatedly. He would never forsake *her*. White-looking though she was.

She rang the bell, long and insistently.

"Why the fuck don't he answer," she muttered. She pulled her jacket close around her body and pressed her arms against her sides. She heard the crunch and crackle of a bag of fried plantains being crushed in her pocket. Her other pocket contained a small rubber ball, some string, a sliver of cheese Camara had slipped in when she wasn't looking. Pennies that she'd collected from Camara's clothing at the hospital rattled in her purse.

A light across her toes preceded the opening of the door. Truman, his hair in two dozen small braids, looked out at her.

"It's me," she said, trying to smile. Smiling, in fact.

He did not throw open the door.

"Who is it, True?" a voice from the bedroom beyond wafted out. Lynne felt a tingling at the base of her neck, like a rash trying to break through the skin.

"Just a minute," he called back. Warily he loosened the chain. But when Lynne moved forward she bumped into him. He was moving out, pulling the door closed behind him.

"Shit," she said, stepping back. "Why don't you just tell Meridian it's me. We don't have any secrets, do we?"

"What do you want, Lynne?"

"Really," she said, still smiling a silly too-bright smile, "I thought I would have a chance to come in and tell you in style, if not exactly in comfort. I'm thirsty, got any sodas?" She knew she was acting like a silly bitch—one of his favorite, most benign descriptions of her, but she couldn't help it. How could she tell him that his six-year-old daughter—whom he insisted on nicknaming Princess (tacky, *tacky*, she'd told him)—had been attacked by a grown man and was now lying nearly dead in the hospital. How could she tell him she just needed his fucking support, standing on a stairwell in the dark?

"It's not Meridian," Truman said. He reached into his jeans and brought out his little cigars. She had leaned against the wall, thinking—like the silly bitch she was—but I gave you up for Meridian. For black, brown-skinned Meridian, with her sweet colored-folks' mouth, and her heroic nigger-woman hair.

"I am *not* going to make a scene," she mumbled warningly to herself. "We're not going to fight like we usually do."

"Of course we're not going to fight," said Truman, his artist's eye taking her in from white parched face and cracked lips to the thick unstylish bulges she thought she was hiding under her coat.

"Anybody I know?" she sang, with a laugh, as faked as her smile.

"No."

"I am not going to make a scene," she began again. "We're not going to fight. . . ." But before he could stop her she had pushed the door open and stood halfway across the room staring into the eyes of a tiny blonde girl in a tiny, tiny slip that was so sheer she had time to notice—before Truman swung her around—that the girl's pubic hair was as blonde as the hair on her head.

"Will you tell me why you come up here bothering me? Or is this just some more of your shit?"

Just some more, she wanted to assure him. But she couldn't speak. She stood between Truman and the girl and looked from one to the other. The girl said "I—" and Truman cut her off.

"Go back in there," he ordered, twisting his head.

"But I—" the girl began again.

And Lynne began to laugh. She laughed and laughed and laughed. She laughed so hard she got stitches in her side. Then she stopped. She felt that tingle again at the base of her throat.

"Why is it I don't ever learn *nothing*?" she asked. "Why is it that everybody in the fucking *world* learns what makes it go round before I do? Am I just dumb, or what? What do you reckon, Miss?" She turned to the girl and reached out her hand.

"Don't shut up, sugah," she said. "Talk. I wants to hear Miz Scarlet talk." Truman moved close to her and she waved him away.

"Troo-*mun*?" the girl said, stepping around Lynne as if she had lice. But Truman had turned his back. He stood by the window smoking, looking down into the street.

"Shoot," said Lynne, and she noticed her voice was now completely changed; she did not sound at all like herself. "Don't pay that ol' sucker no mind. Talk. You silly bitch yourself!"

And then the girl's words, melodious as song, southerly as trade winds, came softly out, like the bewildered mewling of a cat.

"Why, what's *wrong*?" drawled the girl, and the pine scents of Alabama, the magnolia smell of Georgia and Mississippi floated out of her mouth. "We've been livin' together for two months. Soon as—Truman says soon as he sells some more of his paintings we're goin' to be married. I don't need to tell you how I expect my folks to take it. . . . " A gleam of conspiracy had the nerve to be observed in her eye. She raised a delicate hand to point to all of Lynne's lost and grieved old friends gazing down serenely from the walls. "Aren't they *great*?" she innocently asked.

Two Women

And then there was the part Meridian knew, because she had been the first person Truman sent for when Camara died. Lynne didn't know what had happened to Scarlet O'Hara. It was Meridian they both needed, and it was Meridian who was, miraculously, there.

"Help me through this shit," Truman had said when Meridian walked off the bus into his arms. And she had, but she had also tried to help Lynne.

She had spent a month shuttling between his lovely bright studio uptown (where a painting of her own face surprised her on every wall) to Lynne's tiny hovel downtown. Between them they had drained her dry. She could not even think of that miserable month, later, without seeing it as a story told about someone else. She remembered the last days especially as one of those silent movies with Meridian Hill the poor star, dashing in and out of subways, cooking meals, listening to monologues thickened with grief, being pulled into bed—by Lynne, who held on to her like a child afraid of the dark—and by Truman, who almost drowned his body with her own, stuffing her flesh into his mouth as if he literally starved for her. It was then that her feeling for Truman returned, but it was not sexual. It was love totally free of possessiveness or contempt. It was love that purged all thought of blame from her too accurate memory. It was forgiveness.

Lynne remembered Meridian's last evening with her.

175

"What time is Truman coming?" she had asked, because she did not want to be there when he arrived.

"He ought to be here any minute," said Lynne, beginning to rock, and feeling herself, in the rocking, growing old.

As they sat they watched a television program. One of those Southern epics about the relationship of the Southern white man to madness, and the closeness of the Southern black man to the land. It did not delve into the women's problems, black or white. They sat, companionable and still in their bathrobes, watching the green fields of the South and the indestructible (their word) faces of black people much more than they watched the madness. For them, the madness was like a puzzle they had temporarily solved (Meridian would sometimes, in the afternoons, read poems to Lynne by Margaret Walker, and Lynne, in return, would attempt to cornrow Meridian's patchy short hair), they hungered after more intricate and enduring patterns. Sometimes they talked, intimately, like sisters, and when they did not they allowed the television to fill the silences.

There was a scene on the television of a long, shady river bank and people—mothers and fathers, children, grandparents— almost elegantly fishing, and then the face, close up, of a beautiful young black man with eyes as deceptively bright as dying stars. Now that he had just about won the vote, he was saying, where was he to get the money to pay for his food? Looks like this whole Movement for the vote and to get into motels was just to teach him that everything in this country, from the vote to motels, had to be changed. In fact, he said, looks like what he needed was a gun.

To them both this was obvious. That the country was owned by the rich and that the rich must be relieved of this ownership before "Freedom" meant anything was something so basic to their understanding of America they felt naïve even discussing it. Still, the face got to them. It was the kind of face they had seen only in the South. A face in which the fever of suffering had left an immense warmth, and the heat of pain had lighted a candle behind the eyes. It sought to understand, to encompass everything, and the struggle to live honorably and understand everything at the same time, to allow for every inconsistency in nature, every weird possibility and personality, had given it a weary serenity that was so entrenched and stable it could be mistaken for stupidity. It made them want to love. It made them want to weep. It made them want to cry out to the young man to run away, or at least warn him about how deeply he would be hurt. It made them homesick.

"We got any peaches?"

"I'd settle for a pine tree limb."

And Meridian and Lynne got up, rummaged around the apartment, looking for some traces of their former Southern home. Lynne found her Turkey Walk quilt and spread it over her knees.

In the small, shabby apartment there were mementos of other places, other things. There was, for example, a child's day bed folded up in a corner of the living room. Toys—if you opened the closet door too quickly—fell on your head. Tiny scuffed white shoes were still hiding—one of them, anyhow—under the headboard of the bed. Small worn dresses, ripped, faded or in good repair, hung on nails in a small back room.

The absence of the child herself was what had finally brought them together. Together they had sustained a loss not unlike the loss of Martin Luther King or Malcolm X or George Jackson. They grieved more because the child, Camara (after Camara Laye, the African novelist who, of course, did not know of her existence, but whose book *The Radiance of the King* had struck a responsive chord in Lynne), had been personally known, had been small—six years old—and had died after horrible things were done to her. They knew her suffering did not make her unique; but knowing that crimes of passion or hatred against children are not considered unique in a society where children are not particularly valued, failed to comfort them.

They waited for the pain of Camara's death to lessen. They waited to ask forgiveness of each other. They waited until they could talk again. And they waited for Truman, Camara's father, to come to his wife who had faced her tragedy as many a welfare mother before her had done: She had turned to pills, excesses of sex (or excesses of abstinence; Meridian wasn't sure which), and she had wandered back to the South, where she and Truman—she seemed fuzzily to remember—had for a short time been happy. And she had had a public mental breakdown. The first that many of the people there had seen. (For when their own relatives regularly freaked out a breakdown was not what it was called. Breakdown was, after all, different from *broke down*—as in "So-and-so just broke *down*." Usually at a funeral.)

"I want to tell you something," said Meridian. "I tried very hard not to hate you. And I think I always succeeded."

"It ain't easy not to hate the omnipresent honky woman," said Lynne.

"I agree."

Meridian's bags had not actually been unpacked. She collected her tights and toothbrush from the bathroom.

"Thanks, Meridian, for everything. I honestly don't know what I would have done without you."

"You would have had Truman," said Meridian.

"Ah, Truman," said Lynne. "The last thing that held us together is safely buried." And she bit her lip in an effort not to cry. "I guess I should be glad," she said. "I guess I should be thankful it's over. 'You can go home now,' is what Truman said to me. Like, this little flirtation of yours to find out how the other half lives is over now, so you can just take your sorry white ass home. Can't you just see me walking in on my folks: 'Hi, y'all, that black nigger I run off with done left me, my *mu*latto kid done died. I reckon I'm ready to go to graduate school.' Meridian," she said, looking up at her, "do you realize how fucked up everything *is?*"

"Yep," said Meridian.

"I can't go back home. I don't even have a home. I wouldn't go back if I could. I know white folks are evil and fucked up, I *know*

178

they're doomed. But where does that leave me? I *know* I have feelings, like any other human being. Camara wasn't just some little black kid that got ripped off on the street. She was my *child*. I'd have to walk over my child's *grave* to go back, and I won't.''

"I know," said Meridian.

Meridian had hugged her, she had hugged Meridian, and they had parted. Lynne had soon drifted into a kind of sleep, while thinking of the South.

Lynne

Yes, she had gone back to the South. Back to the small unpainted house. It was deserted, forlorn, an abandoned friend.

She did not stop to wonder if someone would charge breaking and entering. She pulled herself up on the porch, feeling glass beneath her feet, and tried first to look into a window. She could reach her hand right through, because some of the panes were gone. Then she tried the door. It was not locked: She had not wondered whether it would or would not be. She entered the house as she used to, stepping quickly over the raised doorjamb, stepping down, then reached out to flick on the light. It was not working, whether because the power had been shut off or not she did not care. It was dark. She felt, with her fingers sliding through cobwebs, over dust, for some familiar objects on a windowsill. Soon she lit the remains of a multicolored candle. The dust burned with a keen dry smell. The cot was there. She threw herself upon it, raising still more dust. She spread her scarf under her head, her cheek. She was more tired than hungry. She kicked off her shoes. Drew her coat over her. And fell asleep.

She slept the clock around, so that when she awoke it was still quite dark. She rose unsteadily, feeling in the moment of rising refreshed, not in need yet of the blue and orange pills in clear plastic phials in her bag. She put on her shoes easily in the darkness, her feet were cold, and moved over to the window. It was a night with clouds, gray and luminous clouds because the moon was behind them. Through the trees just off the porch she could almost see it. The yard was quiet, even the trees did not bow and whisper as she had remembered them doing. But maybe that was because it was not yet summer. It was not yet even spring, though here it seemed spring. After the long winter in the North, where winter winds still raged and snow had followed the bus as far as northern Tennessee, the air here was light and warm on her skin, a trifle moist; with something kissing, she thought, with that easy poetical association she did not admire in herself.

In that yard they had sat in July and August and other hot days, eating countless watermelons, sticky, cool, good, running juice making tracks down her arms. He had photographed her once eating watermelon, and the lines on her arms ruined the picture; they came through like inverted veins, as if some slimy thing had left a whitish scar that dug into the skin. In spite of this she had liked the picture. Her hair, as usual, was loose, coming to below her waist, black, without curl. Her eyes bright (also black, in the photograph, without their brown subtlety), bold, searching for the thumb that would press the camera button. No surprise. Waiting. So that now when she looked out at the steps she thought she might still be sitting there, unmoved by all that had happened over the years. Sitting there, slender still, her white face happily covered by a fake sheet of brown, glowing, she thought, with health; and in any case, hiding the sickness.

The outhouse was not exactly out, but on the back porch. A dingy door-scratched room. Small, with only the essentials. She had lit another stub of a candle; no one seemed to have lived here since she left. There was still a shard of glass over the washbasin, like a triangle of flawed silver, the dust wiped off in a roll. The toilet gurgled and boiled before it worked. The posters had fallen away from the walls or rotted, but when she held her candle up to one she saw the grayed outline of hundreds of marching forms, though underneath this faded picture the words had been completely eroded away. It was as if the marchers moved through some ghostly, unreal place, specters themselves and not in the least afraid, apprehensive about what would happen when they floated off the picture, off the wall, into a place even more dead, more final.

She was moved to peel and eat an orange. Slowly. Sitting with her feet tucked under her, the candle on the floor, flickering with the small breezes that blew through the paneless window. In her sack she carried oranges, three apples, a triangle of cheese from the delicatessen: where the owners had recognized her and frozen up. She had stood smiling in the irritating way she had (the smile was even irritating to her, but she still used it) when she confronted bigots who also thought they owned her. They did not quite fling the food at her, across the counter, as they had done in the early days, when she would come in with one, maybe two, black men, or women. Or when she was beginning to show her pregnancy.

In the beginning she had actually been able to hear the intake of their breaths: the matronly woman who stood at the cash register, the younger woman who stood over the black cooks in the kitchen, the youngish man who, in the end (by the time Camara was ready to be born), spoke kindly to her, but with a kind of fear of her, like a fear for his own life, his precarious safety. She snatched her money up, looking steadily at all three of them, letting her eyes judge them. They made her conscious, heavily, of her Jewishness, when, in fact, they wanted to make her feel her whiteness. And, beyond her whiteness, the whiteness that now engulfed this family (originally, she heard, from New York) like a shroud.

In the early days she would drop in for German beer with her black friends and the eye exchanges, a struggle of which her friends were completely unaware, would go on furiously between her and the three shopkeepers. The youngish man, already balding, his skin sallow from hanging there slicing salami week after week, could, by and by, speak quite plainly with his eyes. He said: We do not want you. Still, come back to us. It is not yet too late. (This was before she became pregnant.) They said: Have you found? Have you found? Her own eyes said to the women with their Southern-style, contrived, hornet-nest hair: You are wasted.

Wasted. Surrounded by exotic foods! To the youngish balding man her eyes said: Yes! Yes! I have found. I am happy. Why do you think I glow this way? Idiot. Weakling. Slicer of salami. No-sex. Come back to you? Worm. You are crazy. And what would you do if I did come back? Set me to wrapping pastrami? To fishing for pickles? Shithead. Unliving creature. Maker of money. Slicer of Salami. Baker of Challah!

Never once did they ask her what she was. And to them she spoke good finishing school English. It was just that they knew, as she knew about them. That they were transplanted, as they had always been, to a place where they fit like extra toes on a foot. Where they were trusted by no one, exploited, when possible, by anyone with political ambitions. Where they lived in a delicatessen, making money hand over fist because they could think of nothing more exciting to do with their lives. Making money to buy houses—garish, large, separate—outside the city. Making money to send their Elaines and Davids to law and medical school, without a word of official Hebrew, except when they visited in synagogues in the North where they also felt like strangers.

Goyim flitted in and out of the delicatessen, reeking of Southern tolerance and charm, like knife edges the forced smiles, the appreciation (genuine) of the food. Unusual, exotic, excellent. A change from pecan pie and gumbo eaten with a tall glass of ginger ale or Tom Collins.

She watched them over the years she lived in the town (because she would shop there, even though it was expensive and she had little money), and even watched the outside of the delicatessen when they closed it after the local synagogue was bombed. They were shocked, the papers said. Aghast at the bombing! She laughed at their naïveté. Laughed at their precarious "safety." Laughed with such bitter contempt that she could not speak to a Southern Jew without wanting to hit him or her.

The cheese, a tin of Danish camembert, melted like butter on her tongue. . . .

The taste of the cheese brought her back, though she kept her head against the back of her chair, her eyes closed. She sat up, opened her eyes, looked at Meridian who had fallen asleep, and sprang to her feet, yawning loudly.

"Black folks aren't so special," she said. "I hate to admit it. But they're not."

"Maybe," said Meridian, as if she had been wide awake all along, "the time for being special has passed. Jews are fighting for Israel with one hand stuck in a crack in the Wailing Wall. Look at it this way, black folks and Jews held out as long as they could." Meridian rubbed her eyes.

"Good God, this is depressing," said Lynne. "It's even more depressing than knowing I want Truman back."

"That *is* depressing," said Meridian.

"Oh, I know he's not much," she said. "But he saved me from a fate worse than death. Because of him, I can never be as dumb as my mother was. Even if I practiced not knowing what the world is like, even if I lived in Scarsdale or some other weird place, and never had to eat welfare food in my life, I'd still *know*. By nature I'm not cut out to be a member of the oppressors. I don't like them; they make me feel guilty all the time. They're ugly and don't know poor people laugh at them and are just waiting to drag them out. No, Truman isn't much, but he's *instructional*," said Lynne. "Besides," she continued, "nobody's perfect."

"Except white women," said Meridian, and winked.

"Yes," said Lynne, "but their time will come."

Ending

No foreign sky protected me,
no stranger's wing shielded my face.
I stand as witness to the common lot,
survivor of that time, that place.
                    —Akhmatova: "Requiem"

Free at Last

A DAY IN APRIL, 1968

Long before downtown Atlanta was awake, she was there beside the church, her back against the stone. Like the poor around her, with their meager fires in braziers against the April chill, she had brought fried chicken wrapped in foil and now ate it slowly as she waited for the sun. The nearby families told their children stories about the old days before black people marched, before black people voted, before they could allow their anger or even their exhaustion to show. There were stories, too, of Southern hunts for coons and 'possums among the red Georgia hills, and myths of strong women and men, Indian and black, who knew the secret places of the land and refused to be pried from them. As always they were dressed in their very Sunday best, and were resigned; on their arms the black bands of crepe might have been made of iron.

They were there when the crowd began to swell, early in the morning. Making room, giving up their spots around the entrance to the church, yet still pressing somehow forward, with their tired necks extended, to see, just for a moment, just for a glimpse, the filled coffin.

They were there when the limousines began to arrive, and there when the family, wounded, crept up the steps, and there when the senators running for President flashed by, and there when the horde of clergy in their outdone rage stomped by, and there when the movie stars glided, as if slowly blown, into the church, and

189

there when all these pretended not to see the pitiable crowd of no-bodies who hungered to be nearer, who stood outside throughout the funeral service (piped out to them like scratchy Muzak) and shuffled their feet in their too tight shoes, and cleared their throats repeatedly against their tears and all the same helplessly cried.

Later, following the casket on its mule-drawn cart, they began to sing a song the dead man had loved. "I come to the gar-den *a-lone* . . . . While the dew is still on the *ro*-ses. . . ." Such an old favorite! And neutral. The dignitaries who had not already slipped away—and now cursed the four-mile walk behind the great dead man—opened their mouths eagerly in genial mime. Ahead of Meridian a man paraded a small white poodle on a leash. The man was black, and a smiler. As he looked about him a tooth encased in patterned gold sparkled in his mouth. On the dog's back a purple placard with white lettering proclaimed "I have a dream."

Then she noticed it: As they walked, people began to engage each other in loud, even ringing, conversation. They inquired about each other's jobs. They asked after members of each other's families. They conversed about the weather. And every-where the call for Coca-Colas, for food, rang out. Popcorn ap-peared, and along their route hot-dog stands sprouted their broad, multicolored umbrellas. The sun came from behind the clouds, and the mourners removed their coats and loosened girdles and ties. Those who had never known it anyway dropped the favorite song, and there was a feeling of relief in the air, of liberation, that was repulsive.

Meridian turned, in shame, as if to the dead man himself.

"It's a black characteristic, man," a skinny black boy tapping on an imaginary drum was saying. "We don't go on over death the way whiteys do." He was speaking to a white couple who hung on guiltily to every word.

Behind her a black woman was laughing, laughing, as if all her cares, at last, had flown away.

Questions

"I'm afraid I won't be able to live up to what is required of me—by history, by economics. . . ."

"But there's so much you can give, other than being able to kill. That should be self-evident."

"It isn't though."

"I used to raise my arm and shout, 'Death to honkies,' too," said Truman, "but I understood I didn't really mean it. Not *really*. Not like the men who attacked the police during the riots. I thought of what it would be like to kill, when I thought I was going to be drafted. In the army, killing would be all right, I supposed. Since I wasn't drafted, it seemed useless to think about it.

"In the army you would simply kill to keep yourself alive. Revolutionary killing is systematic. You line people up who have abused you, as a group, and you simply eradicate them, like you would eradicate a disease."

"A disease with faces, with children . . . human voices."

"Yes, but a disease nonetheless." To Truman the discussion was academic, so he could state his points neatly. "By the way," he now said, "do you think you *could* kill anyone, lined up before you like so much diphtheria or smallpox? Or cancer?" Although, to Truman, the rich were a cancer on the world, he would not mind being rich himself.

Meridian laughed, the stubborn ambivalence of her nature at last amusing her. "Sometimes I'm positive I could. Other times I'm just as sure I could not. And even if I felt sure I could do it all

191

the time I still couldn't *know*, could I, until the occasion for killing someone presented itself? Besides," she said, "I don't trust revolutionaries enough to let them choose who should be killed. *I* would probably end up on the wrong side of the firing squad, myself."

"No one would ask killing of *you*," said Truman.

"Because I'm a woman?"

"Oh, Christ," said Truman, "because you're obviously not cut out for it. You're too sensitive. One shot and even though you missed you'd end up a basket case."

"That's true," said Meridian, "but do you think that has anything to do with it? I don't. I mean, I think that all of us who want the black and poor to have equal opportunities and goods in life will have to ask ourselves how we stand on killing, even if no one else ever does. Otherwise we will never know—in advance of our fighting—how much we are willing to give up."

"Suppose you found out, without a doubt, that you could murder other people in a just cause, what would you do? Would you set about murdering them?"

"Never alone," said Meridian. "Besides, revolution would not begin, do you think, with an act of murder—wars might begin in that way—but with teaching."

"Oh yes, *teach*ing," said Truman, scornfully.

"I would like to teach again," said Meridian. "I respect it, when it's done right. After all, people want to be taught how to live. . . ."

"And do you think you could teach them?"

"I don't know. I imagine good teaching as a circle of earnest people sitting down to ask each other meaningful questions. I don't see it as a handing down of answers. So much of what passes for teaching is merely a pointing out of what items to want."

"Meridian," Truman said. "Do you realize no one is thinking about these things any more? Revolution was the theme of the sixties: Medgar, Malcolm, Martin, George, Angela Davis, the

192

Panthers, people blowing up buildings and each other. But all that is gone now. I am, myself, making a statue of Crispus Attucks for the Bicentennial. We're here to stay: the black and the poor, the Indian, and now all those illegal immigrants from the West Indies who adore America just the way it is."

"Then you think revolution, like everything else in America, was reduced to a fad?"

"Of course," said Truman. "The leaders were killed, the restless young were bought off with anti-poverty jobs, and the clothing styles of the poor were copied by Seventh Avenue. And you *know* how many middle-class white girls from Brooklyn started wearing kinky hair."

"But don't you think the basic questions raised by King and Malcolm and the rest still exist? Don't you think people, somewhere deep inside, are still attempting to deal with them?"

"No," said Truman.

"Is there no place in a revolution for a person who *cannot* kill?" asked Meridian, obviously not believing him.

"Why do you drive yourself crazy over these questions?" asked Truman, leaning over her. "When the time comes, trust yourself to do the right thing."

"The 'right' thing? Or merely the thing that will save my life?"

"Don't nitpick."

"No. Don't you see, what you mean is that I should trust myself to do the 'correct' thing. But I've always had trouble telling the 'correct' thing from the 'right' thing. The right thing is never to kill. I will always believe that. The correct thing is to kill when killing is necessary. And it sometimes is, I *know* that."

She could not help struggling with these questions. Just as Truman could not help thinking such struggle useless. In the end people did what they had to do to survive. They acquiesced, they rebelled, they sold out, they shot it out, or they simply drifted with the current of the time, whatever it was. And they didn't endanger life and limb agonizing over what they would lose, which was what separated them from Meridian.

———

It was a small white house, freshly painted by the black community, with green shutters and a green door. It sat on a bank over a dirt street as did all the other houses. The "street" was a road filled with ruts, and on each side were shallow gullies thick with weeds and straggly yellow flowers. From the road the house was almost entirely hidden by a fence made of hog wire that had slowly, over the years, become covered with running vines which revealed themselves each summer to be blue and purple morning glories and orange and yellow honeysuckle, and in the winter there was a green and leafy ivy. The gate, too, was vine-covered and opened with a rusty iron clasp. From the road, only the chimney could be seen, and a ribbon of black roof. The yard sloped down in back to a large ditch that ran the length of the street, which the residents of the area called, with impotent bitterness, "the pool." When it rained, children were forbidden to play outside because the water in the pool could rise silently as a thief until it covered the head of a three-year-old.

But the children loved to play in the pool when the weather was hot and would sneak behind their houses to wade in it. The public white swimming pool, having been ordered, by the federal government, opened to blacks, was closed by city officials who were all rich and white and who had, moreover, their own private swimming pools in their own back yards. There had never been a public swimming pool for blacks, few of whom, consequently, knew how to swim.

Flooding was especially bad in the spring and fall because the heaviest rains came then. But in addition to this, the same city officials who had closed the public swimming pool had erected a huge reservoir very near the lower-lying black neighborhood. When the waters of the reservoir rose from the incessant rains, the excess was allowed to drain off in any direction it would. Since this was done without warning, the disobedient children caught wading in the pool were knocked off their feet and drowned.

Whenever this happened, as it did every year, the people of the community habitually cried and took gifts of fruit and fried chicken to the bereaved family. The men stood about in groups, cursing the mayor and the city commissioner and the board of aldermen, whom they, ironically, never failed to refer to as "the city fathers." The women would sit with the mother of the lost child, recall their own lost children, stare at their cursing husbands—who could not look back at them—and shake their heads.

It was Meridian who had led them to the mayor's office, bearing in her arms the bloated figure of a five-year-old boy who had been stuck in the sewer for two days before he was raked out with a grappling hook. The child's body was so ravaged, so grotesque, so disgusting to behold, his own mother had taken one look and refused to touch him. To the people who followed Meridian it was as if she carried a large bouquet of long-stemmed roses. The body might have smelled just that sweet, from the serene, set expression on her face. They had followed her into a town meeting over which the white-haired, bespectacled mayor presided, and she had placed the child, whose body was beginning to decompose, beside his gavel. The people had turned with her and followed her out. They had been behind her when, at some distance from the center of town, she had suddenly buckled and fallen to the ground.

When she was up again they came to her and offered her everything, including the promise that they would name the next girl child they had after her. Instead she made them promise they would learn, as their smallest resistance to the murder of their children, to use the vote.

At first the people laughed nervously. "But that's nothing," these people said, who had done nothing before beyond complaining among themselves and continually weeping. "People will laugh at us because that is not radical," they said, choosing to believe radicalism would grow over their souls, like a bright armor, overnight.

There were two rooms. In one, a hot plate, a table and a battered chair (brought by the neighbors when they brought the food and the cow), and in the other, where Meridian slept, only her sleeping bag on the floor, some toilet articles on a windowsill (which Truman had overlooked before) and a jar of dried wildflowers in a green wine bottle placed in a corner. And, of course, the letters.

Truman was always looking for Meridian, even when he didn't know it. He was always finding her, as if she pulled him by an invisible string. But though he always found her, she was never what he expected. This time would not be different.

She would not ride in his new green car. "That's a pretty car," she said, "but I prefer to walk."

"Ten years ago," said Truman, "when your kind of protest was new and still fashionable, we *had* to walk. Now we can ride. Or is riding in new cars part of what you are protesting?"

"I suppose it is something like that," she said.

"Then why not go all out," he said, "and put rocks in your shoes?"

Camara

Sometime after the spring of '68, Meridian began going, irregular-ly, to church. The first time, a hot Sunday in June, she had stood in the doorway of a store across the street, watching the people arrive. They drove up in shiny cars of green and brown and black, and emerged well dressed, powdered and brushed, hair glisten-ing, handbags of patent leather, the men formal and cool in dark brown, gray or black suits, the women colorful in dresses of bright pink, yellow and pastel blue, with flowers.

She felt a certain panic, watching them. They seemed so un-changed by everything that had happened to them. True, the church was not like the ones of her childhood; it was not shabby or small. It was large, of brick, with stained-glass windows of yel-low and brown squares, and no red or blue. An imposing struc-ture; and yet it did not reach for the sky, as cathedrals did, but settled firmly on the ground. She was aware of the intense heat that closed around the church and the people moving slowly, al-most grandly up the steps, as if into an ageless photograph. And she, standing across the street, was not part of it. Rather, she sensed herself an outsider, as a single eye behind a camera that was aimed from a corner of her youth, attached now only be-cause she watched. If she were not there watching, the scene would be exactly the same, the "picture" itself never noticing that the camera was missing.

Each Sunday, for several weeks, she chose a different church.

Finally, for no reason she was sure of, she found herself in front of a large white church, Baptist (with blue and red in its stained windows, perhaps that was what drew her), and she sucked in her breath and went up the steps and inside. The church was nearly full and an usher—a quiet young boy, strong-limbed but *contained* in his somber blue suit—showed her to a seat near the entrance. It was unreal to her that people still *came*, actually got out of bed on Sunday morning and came, to church; and she stared up at them as they passed, her mouth slightly open.

A dark, heavy man with bulging red eyes—eyes sad or mean she could not tell—shuffled by her bench and went up to the pulpit, which drew her attention to the small group of people assembled there. A humble-looking creature in a snuff brown suit brought from behind the altar a large photograph of a slain martyr in the Civil Rights struggle. Two tiny black girls promptly rose and placed tall vases of lilies—white and unblemished (their green stalks waxy and succulent)—on either side.

She stood as the people began to sing a once quite familiar song. But now she could not remember the words; they seemed stuck in some pinched-over groove in her memory. She stared at the people behind the altar, distractedly clutching the back of the bench in front of her. She did not want to find right then whatever it was she was looking for. She had no idea, really, what it was. And yet, she was *there*. She opened her mouth and attempted to sing, but soon realized it was the melody of the song she remembered, not the words, because these words sounded quite new to her.

The man with the red eyes whispered to the people around him, mopping his face and neck with a handkerchief that showed snowy against his glistening skin. One of the men rose and asked someone to lead them in prayer. The man who came forward did not kneel. He stood straight, his shoulders back, his face stern before the congregation. He said they were glad to have this opportunity to be with one another again. He said they were thankful to be alive and to be, for the most part, healthy, and holding together as a community and as families. He said he was thankful they could count on each other in times of trouble. He said he would not pray any longer because there was a lot of work for the community to do. He sat down.

This prayer was followed by another song that was completely foreign to Meridian, whose words were completely hidden from her by the quite martial melody. It seemed to Meridian that this was done deliberately; in any case, her consciousness was no longer led off after a vain search for words she could not recall, but began instead to slowly merge itself with the triumphant forcefulness of the oddly death-defying music.

"Let the martial songs be written," she found herself quoting Margaret Walker's famous poem; "let the dirges disappear!" She started and looked quickly around her. The people looked exactly as they had ever since she had known black churchgoing people, which was all her life, but they had changed the music! She was shocked.

The minister—in his thirties, dressed in a neat black suit and striped tie of an earlier fashion—spoke in a voice so dramatically like that of Martin Luther King's that at first Meridian thought his intention was to dupe or to mock. She glanced about to see if anyone else showed signs of astonishment or derision. But every face on her bench looked forward stoically, and even the chattering young men across the aisle from her did not seem perturbed. Her first impulse had been to laugh bitterly at the pompous, imitative preacher. But she began, instead, to listen. David and Goliath were briefly mentioned, to illustrate a point. Then the preacher launched into an attack on President Nixon, whom he called "Tricky Dick"! He looked down on the young men in the audience and forbade them to participate in the Vietnam war. He told the young women to stop looking for husbands and try to get something useful in their heads. He told the older congregants that they should be ashamed of the way they let their young children fight their battles for them. He told them they were cowardly and pathetic when they sent their small children alone into white neighborhoods to go to school. He abused the black teachers present who did not, he said, work hard enough to teach black youth because they obviously had no faith in them.

It struck Meridian that he was deliberately imitating King, that he and all his congregation *knew* he was consciously keeping that voice alive. It was like a *play*. This startled Meridian; and the preacher's voice—not his own voice at all, but rather the voice of millions who could no longer speak—wound on and on along its now heated, now cool, track. God was not mentioned, except as a reference.

She was suddenly aware that the sound of the "ah-mens" was different. Not muttered in resignation, not shouted in despair. No one bounced in his seat. No one even perspired. Just the "ah-mens" rose clearly, unsentimentally, and with a firm tone of "We are fed up."

When the red-eyed man rose there was a buzzing throughout the church. The preacher introduced him as the father of the slain man whose picture was flanked by the white lilies. Yes, now that he was introduced, Meridian remembered him. When his son was killed he had gone temporarily insane. Meridian had read about it in the paper. He had wrecked his own house with an ax, swinging until, absolutely, profoundly silent and blank, he had been carried out of the state and placed in a sanitarium. He had returned red-eyed and heavier and deadly calm—still taking tranquilizers, it was said, and thinking (the people whispered, hoped) of running for office. But this had not materialized.

He lived peacefully in the ruins of his wrecked house, his sanity coming back—unwelcomed—for days at a time. Then he bellowed out his loss. At other times he talked, in his normally reserved, rather ironic voice, to his wife and other children who were already dead (lost previously in a fire). His martyred son was all the family he had. He had boasted when the boy was younger, that his son—slender, black, as gentle and graceful as his mother had been, with her precious small hands—would be his bulwark, his refuge, when he grew old. He had not understood when his son chose struggle. He had understood even less when his son began to actually fight, to talk of bullets, of bombs, of revolution. For his talk alone (as far as his father knew, or believed, or wanted to know) they had killed him. And to his father—on sane days, doped to the gills with tranquilizers (because it was true, he ate them by the handfuls)—it still made no sense. He had thought that somehow, the power of his love alone (and how rare even he knew it was!) would save his son. But his love—selfless, open, a kissing, touching love—had only made his son strong enough to resist everything that was not love. Strong, beloved, knowing through his father's eyes his own great value, he had set out to change the ways of the world his father feared. And they had murdered him.

His father knew the beauty of his son's soul, as a jeweler knows the brilliance of the jewel beneath the stone, the gentleness at the heart of the warrior. And it was for this loss he wept and detested life as capricious and unreasonable. And felt his life empty, and his heart deprived.

The people tried to be kind, as he had felt confident, even in his madness, they would be. It was a feeling he had shared with his son. For no matter how distrustful his son was of white people, rich people, or people who waged wars to destroy others, he had had absolute faith in the people among whom he had grown up. People like his father—who had been a simple mechanic, who owned his own small cluttered shop in which he did fine, proud, honest work—who could bear the weight of any oppression or any revolution as long as they knew they were together and believed the pain they suffered would come to a *righteous* end. The people would open themselves totally to someone else's personal loss, if it was allowed them to do so. But the father, insane half the time, and gladly so, did not allow closeness. He was, after a while, left alone with his memories and his ghosts.

It was only on occasions such as this, only on anniversaries of his son's death, that his presence was specifically requested, and he came out to the various schools and churches. He never looked at his son's picture, but would come and stand before the people because they, needing reminders, requested it of him. They accepted him then in whatever form he presented himself and knew him to be unpredictable. Today he stood for several minutes, his throat working, his eyes redder than ever, without tears. The congregation was quiet with reverence and an expectation that was already grateful, whatever he would give them. The words came from a throat that seemed stoppered with anxiety, memory, grief and dope. And the words, the beginning of a speech he had laboriously learned years ago for just such occasions as this when so much was asked of him, were the same that he gave every year. The same, exact, three. "My son died."

He stood there for several minutes more, on display. Sunk in his own memories, in confusion, in loss, then was led back gently to his seat, his large body falling heavily into his chair, his arms hanging limply, showing ashen palms to the crowd. And then there rose the sweet music, that received its inimitable *soul* from just such inarticulate grief as this, and a passing of the collection plate with the money going to the church's prison fund, and the preacher urged all those within his hearing to vote for black candidates on the twenty-third. And the service was over.

For a while, the congregation did not move. Meridian sat thinking of how much she had always disliked church. Whenever she was in a church, she felt claustrophobic, as if the walls were closing in. She had, even as a child, felt pity for the people who sat through the long and boring sermons listlessly fanning in the summer heat and hoping, vainly, she felt, for the best. The music she loved. Next to the music, she had liked only the stained-glass windows, when there were any, because the colored glass changed ordinary light into something richer, of gold and rose and mauve. It was restful and beautiful and inspired the reverence the sermons had failed to rouse. Thinking of the glass now she raised her head to look at the large stained-glass window across from her.

Instead of the traditional pale Christ with stray lamb there was a tall, broad-shouldered black man. He was wearing a brilliant blue suit through which the light swam as if in a lake, and a bright red tie that looked as if someone were pouring cherries down his chest. His face was thrown back, contorted in song, and sweat, like glowing diamonds, fell from his head. In one hand he held a guitar that was attached to a golden strap that ran over his shoulder. It was maroon, much narrower at one end than at the other, with amber buttons, like butterscotch kisses, on the narrow end. The other arm was raised above his head and it held a long shiny object the end of which was dripping with blood.

"What's that?" she asked the placid woman sitting next to her, who was humming and swatting flies and bopping her restless children, intermittently, on the head.

"What?" she turned kindly to Meridian and smiled in a charming and easygoing way. "Oh, *that*. One of our young artists did that. It's called "B.B., With Sword.""

And what was Meridian, who had always thought of the black church as mainly a reactionary power, to make of this? What was anyone? She was puzzled that the music had changed. Puzzled that everyone in the congregation had anticipated the play. Puzzled that young people in church nowadays did not fall asleep. Perhaps it was, after all, the only place left for black people to congregate, where the problems of life were not discussed fraudulently and the approach to the future was considered communally, and moral questions were taken seriously.

She considered the face of the young man in the photograph as she was walking away. A face destroyed by clubs held by men. Now it would be nothing but the cracked bones, falling free as the skin rotted away, coming apart into the bottom of the casket; and the gentle fingers, all broken and crushed under the wheels of cars, would point directions no more. She would always love this young man who had died before she had a chance to know him. But how, she wondered, could she show her love for someone who was already dead?

There was a reason for the ceremony she had witnessed in the church. And, as she pursued this reason in her thoughts, it came to her. The people in the church were saying to the red-eyed man that his son had not died for nothing, and that if his son should come again they would protect his life with their own. "Look," they were saying, "we are slow to awaken to the notion that we are only as other women and men, and even slower to move in anger, but we are gathering ourselves to fight for and protect what your son fought for on behalf of us. If you will let us weave your story and your son's life and death into what we already know— into the songs, the sermons, the 'brother and sister'—we will soon be so angry we cannot help but move. Understand this," they were saying, "the church" (and Meridian knew they did not mean simply "church," as in Baptist, Methodist or whatnot, but rather communal spirit, togetherness, righteous convergence), "the music, the form of worship that has always sustained us, the kind of ritual you share with us, these are the ways to transformation that we know. We want to take this with us as far as we can."

In comprehending this, there was in Meridian's chest a breaking as if a tight string binding her lungs had given way, allowing her to breathe freely. For she understood, finally, that the respect she owed her life was to continue, against whatever obstacles, to live it, and not to give up any particle of it without a fight to the death, preferably *not* her own. And that this existence extended beyond herself to those around her because, in fact, the years in America had created them One Life. She had stopped, considering this, in the middle of the road. Under a large tree beside the road, crowded now with the cars returning from church, she made a promise to the red-eyed man herself: that yes, indeed she *would* kill, before she allowed anyone to murder his son again.

Her heart was beating as if it would burst, sweat poured down her skin. Meridian did not dare to make promises as a rule for fear some unforeseen event would cause her to break them. Even a promise to herself caused her to tremble with good faith. It was not a vain promise; and yet, if anyone had asked her to explain what it meant exactly she could not have told them. And certainly to boast about this new capacity to kill—which she did not, after all, admire—would be to destroy the understanding she had acquired with it. Namely, this: that even the contemplation of murder required incredible delicacy as it required incredible spiritual work, and the historical background and present setting must be right. Only in a church surrounded by the righteous guardians of the people's memories could she even approach the concept of retaliatory murder. Only among the pious could this idea both comfort and uplift.

Meridian's dedication to her promise did not remain constant. Sometimes she lost it altogether. Then she thought: I have been allowed to see how the new capacity to do anything, including kill, for our freedom—beyond sporadic acts of violence—is to emerge, and flower, but I am not yet at the point of being able to kill anyone myself, nor—except for the false urgings that come to me in periods of grief and rage—will I ever be. I am a failure then, as the kind of revolutionary Anne-Marion and her acquaintances were. (Though in fact she had heard of nothing revolutionary this group had done, since she left them ten summers ago. Anne-Marion, she knew, had become a well-known poet whose poems were about her two children, and the quality of the light that fell across a lake she owned.)

It was this, Meridian thought, I have not wanted to face, this that has caused me to suffer: I am not to belong to the future. I am to be left, listening to the old music, beside the highway. But then, she thought, perhaps it will be my part to walk behind the real revolutionaries—those who know they must spill blood in order to help the poor and the black and therefore go right ahead—and when they stop to wash off the blood and find their throats too choked with the smell of murdered flesh to sing, I will come forward and sing from memory songs they will need once more to hear. For it is the song of the people, transformed by the experience of each generation, that holds them together, and if any part of it is lost the people suffer and are without soul. If I can only do that, my role will not have been a useless one after all.

But at other times her dedication to her promise came back strongly. She needed only to see a starving child or attempt to register to vote a grown person who could neither read nor write. On those occasions such was her rage that she actually felt as if the rich and racist of the world should stand in fear of her, because she—though apparently weak and penniless, a little crazy and without power—was yet of a resolute and relatively fearless character, which, sufficient in its calm acceptance of its own purpose, could bring the mightiest country to its knees.

Travels

"Mama," a half-naked little boy called as they walked up to the porch, "it's some people out here, and one of 'em is that woman in the cap."

The wooden steps were broken and the porch sagged. In the front room a thin young man worked silently in a corner. In front of him was a giant pile of newspapers that looked as though they'd been salvaged from the hands of children who ate dinner over the funnies. Meridian and Truman watched the man carefully smooth out the paper, gather ten sheets, then twenty, and roll them into a log around which he placed a red rubber band. When he finished the "log" he stacked it, like a piece of wood, on top of the long pile of such "logs" that ran across one side of the poorly furnished, rather damp and smelly room.

Through the inner door he had a view of his wife—when he turned around to put the paper on the pile—lying on the bed. He nodded to them that they should enter his wife's room.

"How're you?" asked Meridian, as she and Truman looked about for chairs.

"Don't sit there," the woman said to Truman, who sat in a straight chair the young son brought. "You blocks my view of my husband."

"I'm sorry," said Truman, quickly moving.

"I'm feelin' a little better today," said the woman, "a little better." Her small black face was childlike, all bony points and big brown eyes that never left her husband's back.

"My husband Johnny went out and got me some venison and made me up a little stew. I think that's helping me to git my strength up some." She laughed, for no reason that her visitors could fathom. It was a soft, intimate chuckle, weak but as if she wanted them to understand she could endure whatever was wrong.

"Where did he get deer this time of year?" asked Truman.

"Don't tell anybody," the sick woman chuckled again, slyly, "but he went hunting out at one of those places where the sign says 'Deer Crossin'.' If we had a refrigerator we wouldn't need any more meat for the rest of the year. Johnny—" she began, showing all her teeth as one hand clutched the bedspread with the same intensity as her rather ghastly smile.

"Did you say somethin', Agnes?" asked Johnny, getting up from his chore with the newspapers and coming to stand at the foot of the bed. "You hongry again?"

"I gets full just lookin' at you, sugah," said the sick woman co-quettishly. "That's about the only reason I hate to die," she said, looking at her visitors for a split second, "I won't be able to see my ol' good-lookin' man."

"Shoot," said Johnny, going back to the other room.

"He used to be a worker at the copper plant, used to make wire. They fired him 'cause he wouldn't let the glass in front of his table stay covered up. You know in the plant they don't want the working folks to look at nothing but what's right on the table in front of them. But my Johnny said he wasn't no mule to be wearing blinders. He wanted to see a little bit of grass, a little bit of sky. It was bad enough being buried in the basement over there, but they wanted to even keep out the sun." She looked at her husband's back as if she could send her fingers through her eyes.

"What does he do with the newspapers?" asked Truman.

"Did you see how many he has?" asked the woman. "You should see the room behind this one. Rolled newspapers up to the ceiling. Half the kitchen is rolled newspapers." She chuckled hoarsely. "So much industry in him. Why, in the wintertime he and little Johnny will take them logs around to folks with fireplaces and sell'em for a nickel apiece and to colored for only three pennies."

"Hummm—" said Meridian. "Maybe we could help him roll a few while we're here. We just came by to ask if you all want to register to vote, but I think we could roll a few newspapers while you think about it."

"Vote?" asked the woman, attempting to raise her voice to send the question to her husband. Then she lay back. "Go on in there and git a few pages," she said.

As soon as she touched the newspapers Meridian realized Johnny must have combed the city's garbage cans, trash heaps, and department store alleys for them. Many were damp and even slimy, as if fish or worse had been wrapped in them. She began slowly pressing the papers flat, then rolling them into logs.

The sick woman was saying, "I have this dream that if the Father blesses me I'll die the week before the second Sunday in May because I want to be buried on Mother's Day. I don't know why I want that, but I do. The pain I have is like my kidneys was wrapped in that straining gauze they use in dairies to strain milk, and something is squeezing and squeezing them. But when I die, the squeezing will stop. Round Mother's Day, if the merciful Father say so."

"Mama's goin' to heaven," said Johnny Jr., who came to roll the papers Meridian had smoothed.

"She's already sweet like an angel," said Meridian impulsively, rubbing his hair and picking away the lint, "like you."

"What good is the vote, if we don't own nothing?" asked the husband as Truman and Meridian were leaving. The wife, her eyes steadily caressing her husband's back, had fallen asleep, Johnny Jr. cuddled next to her on the faded chenille bedspread. In winter the house must be freezing, thought Truman, looking at the cracks in the walls; and now, in spring, it was full of flies.

"Do you want free medicine for your wife? A hospital that'll take black people through the front door? A good school for Johnny Jr. and a job no one can take away?"

"You know I do," said the husband sullenly.

"Well, voting probably won't get it for you, not in your life-time," Truman said, not knowing whether Meridian intended to lie and claim it would.

"What *will* it get me but a lot of trouble," grumbled the husband.

"I don't know," said Meridian. "It may be useless. Or maybe it can be the beginning of the use of your voice. You have to get used to using your voice, you know. You start on simple things and move on. . . ."

"No," said the husband, "I don't have time for foolishness. My wife is dying. My boy don't have shoes. Go somewhere else and find somebody that ain't got to work all the time for pennies, like I do."

"Okay," said Meridian. Surprised, Truman followed as she calmly walked away.

"What's this here?" asked the husband ten minutes later as they came through his front door with two bags of food.

"To go with the venison." Meridian grinned.

"I ain't changed my mind," said the husband, with a suspicious peek into the bags.

And they did not see him again until the Monday after Mother's Day, when he brought them six rabbits already skinned and ten newspaper logs; and under the words WILL YOU BE BRAVE ENOUGH TO VOTE in Meridian's yellow pad, he wrote his name in large black letters.

Treasure

They first saw the home of Miss Margaret Treasure through a landscape of smoke, while walking down a flat dirt road looking for people the census takers always missed. It was the middle of summer, hot as an oven, and sweat fell from their skin and evaporated before it hit the ground. On both sides of the road last year's cornstalks rustled in dry, lonely talk, and as the chimneys of the house wavered through the haze they saw a large black woman in a tight red dress hobbling toward them, a gasoline can in her hand. She was setting fire to the field.

Truman and Meridian stopped to watch her, and when the woman reached them she too stood still. She was obviously surprised to see them and dropped her gasoline can at Meridian's feet.

On the wide front porch of Miss Treasure's neat white house there was a gigantic mahogany bed with head and footboards towering over their heads. Meridian held the fat left hand of Miss Treasure and helped her down on it. Miss Treasure's tears dripped onto the snowy covering and had already washed pink grooves into the blackness of her skin.

"I got to burn this bed," said Miss Treasure, slamming her head against the footboard.

"Wait awhile," said Meridian, looking out at the burning cornfield, "and Truman and I will help you."

"You *will?*" asked Miss Treasure. Her tears, for the moment, subsided, and she smiled quite happily. Because she was so fat they had not realized how old she was, but now they could see that, indeed, she was an old woman. Her hands were ropey with veins and knotted from arthritis, her moist eyes were rimmed with cataracts. As Meridian and Truman sat with Miss Treasure on the bed, a younger woman, perhaps in her middle sixties, came to the door and leaned outward against the screen.

"Git away, Lucille!" croaked the old woman, Miss Treasure, whose voice was hoarse from crying.

"Shame," said the other woman primly, turning away. "Shame. Shame. Shame. Upon our father's name."

Miss Treasure rose from the bed and went inside the house, emerging a few minutes later with a pitcher of lemonade and a tall glossy black wig on her head. Under the wig her face was ravaged and wrinkled.

"In the first place," said Miss Treasure, sipping her lemonade, "I'm only burning what is my own. All this land you see belongs to yours truly. I can burn it up if I want to, ain't that right?"

"Sure," said Truman.

"Yes, ma'am," said Meridian.

"You hear that, sister!" called Miss Treasure.

"Humph!" came from behind the screen.

"What you say y'all name was?"

"Meridian and Truman," said Meridian.

"I'm Miss Margaret Treasure, and that's Little Sister Lucille."

"*Miss* Lucille Treasure," said the voice behind the screen. "I'm a Miss same as you."

"Y'all children want some lemonade?" asked Miss Treasure, pouring it.

Miss Lucille Treasure came out on the porch. Thin and the color of wet sand, she carried herself with the rigid arrogance of a walking stick held in the hand of a prince. There was cruelty in her eyes when she looked at her sister.

"What mind she got left," she sniffed, "is gone wandering."

"It ain't," protested Miss Margaret Treasure. And she began

to tell her story: They had lived on the Treasure plantation—not as tenants but as owners—all their lives. How their father had managed to own a plantation in that part of Georgia they had been as children forbidden to ask. In any case, Miss Margaret Treasure—at Little Sister Lucille's prompting—had been selling bits and pieces of the place until now all that was left could be seen from the front and back porches. They had lived for years without seeing anyone, except when Little Sister Lucille went into town for staples she bought, as her father had done, twice a year. Everything else they needed the farm provided. They had chickens, a few cows, a pig. The only time they saw people for any length of time was when Little Sister Lucille contracted with painters to come and paint the house every five years. It was at the last painting of the house that Miss Margaret Treasure's troubles started. She had fallen in love with one of the painters.

Well, Miss Margaret continued, now she was down to the last few acres and the house, which she wanted to keep. But she had to sell them in order to keep her good name and her self-respect. Because six months ago she had looked out of her bedroom window and seen a face hanging there above a ladder. It was the face of her fate. His name was Rims Mott. A dog's name, she added, bursting into fresh tears.

Little Sister Lucille stood with her hands on her hips, scowling at the quivering shoulders of her fat sister.

"They was keeping company," she said sourly, spitting over the porch rail, her brown spittle falling between two blue hydrangea bushes. "At her age! All night long I'd hear 'em at it. Yowlin' and goin' on like alley cats."

"Git back!" said the crying woman. "I don't need you to stand over me and gloat. Just because he never looked at you!"

"What do I want with a forty-five-year-old man?" asked Little Sister Lucille. "I knowed better than to let *my*self get messed up. At least," she sniffed, "I'm going to meet my maker a *clean* woman, just as pure on that day as the day I was born."

Miss Margaret's wet face was twisted in agony. From a compact which she held in trembling fingers she dabbed on more face powder, even as her tears continued to wash it away. "They say I got to marry him," she sobbed, "but I don't want to *now.*"

"Then don't marry him," said Truman and Meridian in the same breath.

"Because if I marry him," Miss Margaret continued, "he'll be sure to outlive me, and then his name will be on this house. He'll own it, and I don't trust him enough to raise no child."

Meridian's face at last showed surprise, and at the same time, the reason for Miss Margaret's tears came to Truman.

"Yes," said Little Sister Lucille smugly, watching their changed faces, "she's fat and black and seventy-two years old, and the first man she opened her legs to made her pregnant."

"Sixty-nine," said Miss Margaret.

Laughter, like a wicked silver snake, wriggled up Truman's spine. It knocked him out to hear Meridian ask, *conversationally,* "How far along *are* you?" He glanced at her expecting to see a face fighting to control itself, but there was only a slight blush already fading into her brown skin.

"Ahhh!" Miss Margaret screamed and jumped to her feet, pulling at the heavy bed. "Help me burn it up now, y'all," she cried, and yanked with such force her wig fell off at their feet. Little Sister Lucille grabbed it up and began to laugh, forgetting, apparently, that her own hair was severely marcelled and dyed a foolish orange.

Truman and Meridian took hold of the bed and pushed with all their strength. It hung over the edge of the porch like an ancient ship hovering over the edge of the sea. Miss Margaret pulled and the bed crashed down the steps and into the yard, Miss Margaret's leg caught under it. She did not seem to feel the pain but tugged relentlessly at the bed trying to pull it over her and out to the edge of the cornfields where the fire, by this time, had gone out.

"You're out of gasoline," said Meridian, holding up the can.

Meridian and Truman sat in the yard under a hot midsummer sun, binding Miss Margaret's leg in cold-water wraps.

"Miss Margaret," said Meridian, holding the leg on her lap and giving it an affectionate pat every now and then, "from the way you handle yourself, I don't think you're pregnant. Do you think she looks pregnant?" she asked Truman. "Truman's wife had a little girl," she explained to Miss Treasure, "so he'd be a good person to ask because he'd know."

Truman shook his head slowly, "You don't look a bit pregnant to me," he choked out.

Miss Margaret's face lit up, but quickly went dark again. "Rims said it, too," she said. "Him and Little Sister Lucille *both* said it."

"Well," said Meridian, "when we take you in to the doctor for your leg we can ask him."

Miss Margaret looked at them in fear. It had been years since she was off the plantation, and from the magazines she read the world beyond her property was not safe. She grieved over her life and moaned from the pain coming into her wounded leg. She had been a virgin until Rims came into her life, filling it with fluttery anticipation and making her body so changed, so full of hurting brightness she had known it was a sin for which she would be punished. She lay on the hot ground like a lost child, or like a dog kicked so severely it has lost its sense of smell and wanders about and leans on the tree it otherwise would have soiled.

Truman and Meridian supported her every step of the way, holding her fat arms firmly, up to the very door of the doctor's examination room. Her face, when she emerged an hour later, held a vacancy of grief that made it appear blank and smooth, as if all her wrinkles had been, by kisses, erased. The next day she came to place her name in Meridian's yellow pad.

"Ask me to do anything, young peoples," said Miss Treasure. "I'm y'all's!"

Pilgrimage

And so they must go to the prison. And so they must. And so they must see the child who murdered her child, nothing new. But the prison was. Only two stories high, it was set back from the road in a sea of green, the black trees around it like battlements around a castle. The grate of the key, the lock, the creaking door opening inward, sucking in the light into the gloom. Signing in. Hearing the harsh music of women's voices, women confined to sit and buzz like insects, whine, wait in line. Who was that person? That man/woman person with a shaved part in close-cut hair? A man's blunt face and thighs, a woman's breasts? But they had not come to stare or feel the cold security of being who they were, unconfined.

She was in a cell as small, as tidy, as a nearly empty closet. Meridian had brought magazine pictures of green fields, a blue river, a single red apple on a white page, large, containing in itself all the mystery there ever was or will be in the world. It was the apple (not the river or the green fields) the girl liked. She liked red, liked roundness, liked a clean shine on things she ate.

Yes. She had bitten her baby's cheek, bitten out a plug, before she strangled it with a piece of curtain ruffle. So round and clean it had been, too. But not red, alas, before she bit. And wasn't it right to seek to devour a perishable? That, though sweet to the nose, soft to the touch, yummy, is yet impossible to keep? It was as if (she said, dreamily) I had taken out my heart (red and round,

217

fine, a glistening valentine!) and held it in my hands (my heart was sweet, sweet, smelled sweet, like apple blossoms) and took a bite out of it. It was my heart I bit, I strangled till it died. I hid beside the river. My heart the roaming dog dug up, barking for the owner of that field. My heart. Where I am (she continues) no one is. And why am I alive, without my heart? And how is this? And who, in the hell, are you?

"People who ask people to vote." (To struggle away, beyond, all in the world they have ever known.)

(She laughs, heartily and young.) Well, you don't think there's anybody here to vote? Peals of laughter washing them down to the absurdity of worms after a rain wrigglingly constructing ridges of sand to sink between before the crushing boot that's raised above comes crushing down.

"Your mother and sister told us where you were."

A mother and sister oddly smug about this child who killed her child. Thirteen (her mother said) and *too* damn grown, since before she was even ten. Doomed, I told her. Get out of my house. Walk the streets for all I care. She never was (turning to look) like Carrie Mae, the one that pained me most being born. Must have been because all my pain from Carrie Mae come then, and was got over with. Now (lifting her chin) this 'un in the prison was *too* easy coming. Like grease.

Spare me (says the girl). Across her face the sun has burned squares between the lighter color protected by the bars. I look out of my window every evening (she says) until it goes down, warming my chest. If you all can't give me back my heart (she says suddenly, with venom), go the fuck away.

It is too much for them. Outside again they are strangers to the green land, the ground they walk on, have known forever. It is so close to Meridian she takes to her sleeping bag, there to weep underneath Truman's trembling arm, there to rouse her own heart to compassion for her son. But her heart refuses to beat faster, to warm, except for the girl, the child who killed her child. Doomed, she thought, doomed. A fucking heart of stone.

Truman lay as if slaughtered, feeling a warmth, as of hot blood, wash over him. *Shame.* But for what? For whom? What had he done?

Meridian sat, watching the workmen from the city begin to clear the debris from the ditch, preparatory to filling it in (yes, the voters had won this small, vital service), and she wrote with such intensity and passion the pen dug holes in the paper—

> i want to put an end to guilt
> i want to put an end to shame
> whatever you have done my sister
> (my brother)
> know i wish to forgive you
> love you
> it is not the crystal stone
> of our innocence
> that circles us
> not the tooth of our purity
> that bites bloody our hearts.

She slept that night with Truman's arms around her, while Truman's dreams escaped from his lips to make a moaning, crying song.

One day, after Truman—who was beginning to experience moments with Meridian when he felt intensely maternal—had wiped her forehead with a cloth soaked in cold water, Meridian wrote:

> there is water in the world for us
> brought by our friends
> though the rock of mother and god
> vanishes into sand
> and we, cast out alone
> to heal
> and re-create
> ourselves.

These poems she did not burn. She placed them just above Anne-Marion's letters, after which she did not look at the letters, the poems, or even the walls, again.

(Atonement: Later, in the Same Life)

Truman held her hands away from his shoulders. "I have something to tell you, Lynne. Try not to be upset."

"You're going to divorce me," said Lynne bravely, sillily.

"No. I don't think so. The truth is, I still love you."

"Still?"

"I always did. I love you. You irritate me sometimes . . . "

"You irritate me, often."

". . . but. But I don't desire you any more."

Lynne sank back into her rocker. Truman knelt on the floor.

"Is it because I'm fat?" she asked. "Is it because I smell, maybe? Is it because my hair is messy? Or is it because—" and she laughed a strangled laugh—"is it because I have now become Art?"

"No, no," he said, wondering about her. "I do love you. It's just that—I don't want to do anything but provide for you and be your friend. Your brother. Can you accept that?"

Lynne chuckled, thinking of the South, the green fields . . .

"Maybe we can start over again," she said. "Let's go back South."

"What for?" he asked.

Settling Accounts

"But do you know what I want from you?" Truman asked Meridian, leaning over her sleeping bag. "Promise me you won't laugh at me. . . ." He hesitated. "I want you to love me."

"But I *do* love you," said Meridian.

"You pity me. I want your love the way I had it a long time ago. I used to feel it springing out to me whenever you looked into my eyes. It flowed over me like a special sun, like grace."

"My love for you changed. . . ."

"You withdrew it."

"No, I set you free. . . ."

"Hah," he said bitterly, "why don't you admit you learned to hate me, to disrespect me, to wish I were dead. It was your contempt for me that made it impossible for me to forget."

"I meant it when I said it sets you free. You are free to be whichever way you like, to be with whoever, of whatever color or sex you like—and what you risk in being truly yourself, the way you want to be, is not the loss of me. You are *not* free, however, to think I am a fool."

He noticed, above their heads, an addition to the line of letters. A blank sheet of paper and, next to it, forming the end of the line, a photograph of an enormous bull's-eye. When he stood up close to it he discovered—after much twisting of his head and neck—that it was not a bull's-eye at all but a gigantic tree stump. A tiny branch, no larger than his finger, was growing out of one side.

The piece of paper next to it was not blank, though the handwriting was grotesquely small. Even so, he recognized it as Anne-Marion's. It contained one line: "Who would be happier than you that The Sojourner did not die?" She had written, also in a minute script, "perhaps me," but then had half-erased it.

Behind him on the floor Meridian was bending forward again and again to touch her toes, her flushed face tense with determination; a rush of gratitude that she was alive flooded Truman's body. When she stopped for breath he dropped to the floor beside her and gathered her into his arms. But Meridian leaned against him for only a moment, then she continued to flex and stretch her muscles.

"Truman," Meridian said, when she lay back, exhausted, on the floor. "Do you remember what happened the last time we went out? Remember how that woman attacked me and then slammed the door in our faces?"

He remembered.

"I never explained to you why she did that. She did it because I know something about her life that she told me, but now she wishes I didn't know it because she's afraid of what people will think about her if they know. That woman left her husband because he was infatuated with his dog."

Truman laughed.

"No, no, I mean it. He was in love with a dog. He bought the best of everything for the dog to eat. He brushed its coat a dozen times a day. He talked to it constantly, ignoring his children and his wife. He let it sleep on the best bed in the guest room. Some nights he would stay with it. When his wife finally screamed and asked him why, he explained that the dog had better qualities than she had. The wife left him. Took all their five children and went to live with her mother. But her mother didn't want her because the children gave her a headache, and so she convinced the daughter that even if the story she told was true, it would be better to go back to him. Because, after all, he owned his own house and was not stingy or mean. They ate well and he did not come home drunk on the weekends and beat her. The wife had no choice; she went back to her husband because alone she could not feed her children. Of course she made her husband promise to kill the dog."

"And did he kill the dog?"

Meridian shrugged.

"I suspect that is not the point." she said.

Release

She was strong enough to go and owned nothing to pack. She had discarded her cap, and the soft wool of her newly grown hair framed her thin, resolute face. His first thought was of Lazarus, but then he tried to recall someone less passive, who had raised himself without help. Meridian would return to the world cleansed of sickness. That was what he knew.

What he *felt* was that something in her was exactly the same as she had always been and as he had, finally, succeeded in knowing her. That was the part he might now sense but could not see. He would never see "his" Meridian again. The new part had grown out of the old, though, and that was reassuring. This part of her, new, sure and ready, even eager, for the world, he knew he must meet again and recognize for its true value at some future time.

"Your ambivalence will always be deplored by people who consider themselves revolutionists, and your unorthodox behavior will cause traditionalists to gnash their teeth," said Truman, who was not, himself, concerned about either group. To him, they were practically imaginary. It was still amazing to him how deeply Meridian allowed an idea—no matter where it came from—to penetrate her life.

"I hate to think of you always alone."

"But that is my value," said Meridian. "Besides, all the people who are as alone as I am will one day gather at the river. We will watch the evening sun go down. And in the darkness maybe we will know the truth."

She hugged him, long, lingeringly (her nose and lips rooting about at his neck, causing him to laugh), and then she went, walking as if hurrying to catch up with someone.

Truman turned, tears burning his face, and began, almost blindly, to read the poems she had left on the walls. He could not bring himself to read the letters yet. It was his house now, after all. His cell. Tomorrow the people would come and bring him food. Someone would come and milk his cow. They would wait patiently for him to perform, to take them along the next guideless step. Perhaps he would.

"whatever you have done, my brother . . . know i wish to forgive you . . . love you   it is not the crystal stone of our innocence   that circles us   not the tooth of our purity   that bites bloody our hearts."

Truman felt the room begin to turn and fell to the floor. A moment later, dizzy, he climbed shakily into Meridian's sleeping bag. Underneath his cheek he felt the hard edge of her cap's visor, he pulled it out and put it on his head. He had a vision of Anne-Marion herself arriving, lost, someday, at the door, which would remain open, and wondered if Meridian knew that the sentence of bearing the conflict in her own soul which she had imposed on herself—and lived through—must now be borne in terror by all the rest of them.

The Color Purple

To the Spirit:

Without whose assistance
Neither this book
Nor I
Would have been
Written.

Show me how to do like you
Show me how to do it.

—Stevie Wonder

The Color Purple

You better not never tell nobody but God. It'd kill your mammy.

Dear God,

I am fourteen years old. ~~I am~~ I have always been a good girl. Maybe you can give me a sign letting me know what is happening to me.

Last spring after little Lucious come I heard them fussing. He was pulling on her arm. She say It too soon, Fonso, I ain't well. Finally he leave her alone. A week go by, he pulling on her arm again. She say Naw, I ain't gonna. Can't you see I'm already half dead, an all of these chilren.

She went to visit her sister doctor over Macon. Left me to see after the others. He never had a kine word to say to me. Just say You gonna do what your mammy wouldn't. First he put his thing up gainst my hip and sort of wiggle it around. Then he grab hold my titties. Then he push his thing inside my pussy. When that hurt, I cry. He start to choke me, saying You better shut up and git used to it.

But I don't never git used to it. And now I feels sick every time I be the one to cook. My mama she fuss at me an look at me. She happy, cause he good to her now. But too sick to last long.

Dear God,

My mama dead. She die screaming and cussing. She scream at me. She cuss at me. I'm big. I can't move fast enough. By time I git back from the well, the water be warm. By time I git the tray ready the food be cold. By time I git all the children ready for school it be dinner time. He don't say nothing. He set there by the bed holding her hand an cryin, talking bout don't leave me, don't go.

She ast me bout the first one Whose it is? I say God's. I don't know no other man or what else to say. When I start to hurt and then my stomach start moving and then that little baby come out my pussy chewing on it fist you could have knock me over with a feather.

Don't nobody come see us.

She got sicker an sicker.

Finally she ast Where it is?

I say God took it.

He took it. He took it while I was sleeping. Kilt it out there in the woods. Kill this one too, if he can.

Dear God,

He act like he can't stand me no more. Say I'm evil an always up to no good. He took my other little baby, a boy this time. But I don't think he kilt it. I think he sold it to a man an his wife over Monticello. I got breasts full of milk running down myself. He say Why don't you look decent? Put on something. But what I'm sposed to put on? I don't have nothing.

I keep hoping he fine somebody to marry. I see him looking at my little sister. She scared. But I say I'll take care of you. With God help.

Dear God,

He come home with a girl from round Gray. She be my age but they married. He be on her all the time. She walk round like she don't know what hit her. I think she thought she love him. But he got so many of us. All needing somethin.

My little sister Nettie is got a boyfriend in the same shape almost as Pa. His wife died. She was kilt by her boyfriend coming home from church. He got only three children though. He seen Nettie in church and now every Sunday evening here come Mr. _____. I tell Nettie to keep at her books. It be more then a notion taking care of children ain't even yourn. And look what happen to Ma.

Dear God,

He beat me today cause he say I winked at a boy in church. I may have got somethin in my eye but I didn't wink. I don't even look at mens. That's the truth. I look at women, tho, cause I'm not scared of them. Maybe cause my mama cuss me you think I kept mad at her. But I ain't. I felt sorry for mama. Trying to believe his story kilt her.

Sometime he still be looking at Nettie, but I always git in his light. Now I tell her to marry Mr. _____. I don't tell her why.

I say Marry him, Nettie, an try to have one good year out your life. After that, I know she be big.

But me, never again. A girl at church say you git big if you bleed every month. I don't bleed no more.

Dear God,

Mr. _____ finally come right out an ast for Nettie hand in marriage. But He won't let her go. He say she too young, no experience. Say Mr. _____ got too many children already. Plus What about the scandal his wife cause when somebody kill her? And what about all this stuff he hear bout Shug Avery? What bout that?

I ast our new mammy bout Shug Avery. What it is? I ast. She don't know but she say she gon fine out.

She do more then that. She git a picture. The first one of a real person I ever seen. She say Mr. _____ was taking somethin out his billfold to show Pa an it fell out an slid under the table. Shug Avery was a woman. The most beautiful woman I ever saw. She more pretty then my mama. She bout ten thousand times more prettier then me. I see her there in furs. Her face rouge. Her hair like somethin tail. She grinning with her foot up on somebody motocar. Her eyes serious tho. Sad some.

I ast her to give me the picture. An all night long I stare at it. An now when I dream, I dream of Shug Avery. She be dress to kill, whirling an laughing.

Dear God,

I ast him to take me instead of Nettie while our new mammy sick. But he just ast me what I'm talking bout. I tell him I can fix myself up for him. I duck into my room and come out wearing horsehair, feathers, and a pair of our new mammy high heel shoes. He beat me for dressing trampy but he do it to me anyway.

Mr. _____ come that evening. I'm in the bed crying. Nettie she finally see the light of day, clear. Our new mammy she see it too. She in her room crying. Nettie tend to first one, then the other. She so scared she go out doors and vomit. But not out front where the two mens is.

Mr. _____ say, Well Sir, I sure hope you done change your mind.

He say, Naw, Can't say I is.

Mr. _____ say, Well, you know, my poor little ones sure could use a mother.

Well, He say, real slow, I can't let you have Nettie. She too young. Don't know nothing but what you tell her. Sides, I want her to git some more schooling. Make a schoolteacher out of her. But I can let you have Celie. She the oldest anyway. She ought to marry first. She ain't fresh tho, but I spect you know that. She spoiled. Twice. But you don't need a fresh woman no how. I got a fresh one in there myself and she sick all the time. He spit, over the railing. The children git on her nerve, she not much of a cook. And she big already.

Mr. _____ he don't say nothing. I stop crying I'm so surprise.

She ugly. He say. But she ain't no stranger to hard work.

And she clean. And God done fixed her. You can do everything just like you want to and she ain't gonna make you feed it or clothe it.

Mr. _____ still don't say nothing. I take out the picture of Shug Avery. I look into her eyes. Her eyes say Yeah, it *bees* that way sometime.

Fact is, he say, I got to git rid of her. She too old to be living here at home. And she a bad influence on my other girls. She'd come with her own linen. She can take that cow she raise down there back of the crib. But Nettie you flat out can't have. Not now. Not never.

Mr. _____ finally speak. Clearing his throat. I ain't never really look at that one, he say.

Well, next time you come you can look at her. She ugly. Don't even look like she kin to Nettie. But she'll make the better wife. She ain't smart either, and I'll just be fair, you have to watch her or she'll give away everything you own. But she can work like a man.

Mr. _____ say How old she is?

He say, She near twenty. And another thing—She tell lies.

Dear God,

It took him the whole spring, from March to June, to make up his mind to take me. All I thought about was Nettie. How she could come to me if I marry him and he be so love struck with her I could figure out a way for us to run away. Us both be hitting Nettie's schoolbooks pretty hard, cause us know we got to be smart to git away. I know I'm not as pretty or as smart as Nettie, but *she* say I ain't dumb.

The way you know who discover America, Nettie say, is think bout cucumbers. That what Columbus sound like. I learned all about Columbus in first grade, but look like he the first thing I forgot. She say Columbus come here in boats call the Neater, the Peter, and the Santomareater. Indians so nice to him he force a bunch of 'em back home with him to wait on the queen.

But it hard to think with gitting married to Mr. _____ hanging over my head.

The first time I got big Pa took me out of school. He never care that I love it. Nettie stood there at the gate holding tight to my hand. I was all dress for first day. You too dumb to keep going to school, Pa say. Nettie the clever one in this bunch.

But Pa, Nettie say, crying, Celie smart too. Even Miss Beasley say so. Nettie dote on Miss Beasley. Think nobody like her in the world.

Pa say, Whoever listen to anything Addie Beasley have to say. She run off at the mouth so much no man would have her. That how come she have to teach school. He never look up from cleaning his gun. Pretty soon a bunch of white mens come walking cross the yard. They have guns too.

Pa git up and follow 'em. The rest of the week I vomit and dress wild game.

But Nettie never give up. Next thing I know Miss Beasley at our house trying to talk to Pa. She say long as she been a teacher she never know nobody want to learn bad as Nettie and me. But when Pa call me out and she see how tight my dress is, she stop talking and go.

Nettie still don't understand. I don't neither. All us notice is I'm all the time sick and fat.

I feel bad sometime Nettie done pass me in learnin. But look like nothing she say can git in my brain and stay. She try to tell me something bout the ground not being flat. I just say, Yeah, like I know it. I never tell her how flat it look to me.

Mr. _____ come finally one day looking all drug out. The woman he had helping him done quit. His mammy done said No More.

He say, Let me see her again.

Pa call me. *Celie*, he say. Like it wasn't nothing. Mr. _____ want another look at you.

I go stand in the door. The sun shine in my eyes. He's still up on his horse. He look me up and down.

Pa rattle his newspaper. Move up, he won't bite, he say.

I go closer to the steps, but not too close cause I'm a little scared of his horse.

Turn round, Pa say.

I turn round. One of my little brothers come up. I think it was Lucious. He fat and playful, all the time munching on something.

He say, What you doing that for?

Pa say, Your sister thinking bout marriage.

Didn't mean nothing to him. He pull my dresstail and ast can he have some blackberry jam out the safe.

I say, Yeah.

She good with children, Pa say, rattling his paper open more. Never heard her say a hard word to nary one of them. Just give 'em everything they ast for, is the only problem.

Mr. _____ say, That cow still coming?

He say, Her cow.

Dear God,

I spend my wedding day running from the oldest boy. He twelve. His mama died in his arms and he don't want to hear nothing bout no new one. He pick up a rock and laid my head open. The blood run all down tween my breasts. His daddy say Don't *do* that! But that's all he say. He got four children, instead of three, two boys and two girls. The girls hair ain't been comb since their mammy died. I tell him I'll just have to shave it off. Start fresh. He say bad luck to cut a woman hair. So after I bandage my head best I can and cook dinner—they have a spring, not a well, and a wood stove look like a truck—I start trying to untangle hair. They only six and eight and they cry. They scream. They cuse me of murder. By ten o'clock I'm done. They cry theirselves to sleep. But I don't cry. I lay there thinking bout Nettie while he on top of me, wonder if she safe. And then I think bout Shug Avery. I know what he doing to me he done to Shug Avery and maybe she like it. I put my arm around him.

Dear God,

I was in town sitting on the wagon while Mr. _____ was in the dry good store. I seen my baby girl. I knowed it was her. She look just like me and my daddy. Like more us then us is ourself. She be tagging long hind a lady and they be dress just alike. They pass the wagon and I speak. The lady speak pleasant. My little girl she look up and sort of frown. She fretting over something. She got my eyes just like they is today. Like everything I seen, she seen, and she pondering it.

I think she mine. My heart say she mine. But I don't know she mine. If she mine, her name Olivia. I embroder Olivia in the seat of all her daidies. I embrody lot of little stars and flowers too. He took the daidies when he took her. She was bout two month old. Now she bout six.

I clam down from the wagon and I follow Olivia and her new mammy into a store. I watch her run her hand long side the counter, like she ain't interested in nothing. Her ma is buying cloth. She say Don't touch nothing. Olivia yawn.

That real pretty, I say, and help her mama drape a piece of cloth close to her face.

She smile. Gonna make me an my girl some new dresses, she say. Her daddy be so proud.

Who her daddy, I blurt out. It like *at last* somebody know.

She say Mr. _____. But that ain't my daddy name.

Mr. _____? I say. Who he?

She look like I ast something none of my bidniss.

The *Reverend* Mr. _____, she say, then turn her face to the clerk. He say, Girl you want that cloth or not? We got other customers sides you.

14

She say, Yes sir. I want five yards, please sir.

He snatch the cloth and thump down the bolt. He don't measure. When he think he got five yard he tare it off. That be a dollar and thirty cent, he say. You need thread?

She say, Naw suh.

He say, You can't sew thout thread. He pick up a spool and hold it gainst the cloth. That look like it bout the right color. Don't you think.

She say, Yessuh.

He start to whistle. Take two dollars. Give her a quarter back. He look at me. You want something gal? I say, Naw Suh.

I trail long behind them on the street.

I don't have nothing to offer and I feels poor.

She look up and down the street. He ain't here. He ain't here. She say like she gon cry.

Who ain't? I ast.

The Reverend Mr. _____, she say. He took the wagon.

My husband wagon right here, I say.

She clam up. I thank you kindly, she say. Us sit looking at all the folks that's come to town. I never seen so many even at church. Some be dress too. Some don't hit on much. Dust git all up the ladies dress.

She ast me Who is my husband, now I know all bout hers. She laugh a little. I say Mr. _____. She say, Sure nuff? Like she know all about him. Just didn't know he was married. He a fine looking man, she say. Not a finer looking one in the county. White or black, she say.

He do look all right, I say. But I don't think about it while I say it. Most times mens look pretty much alike to me.

How long you had your little girl? I ast.

Oh, she be seven her next birthday.

When that? I ast.

She think back. Then she say, December.

I think, November.

I say, real easy, What you call her?

She say, oh, we calls her Pauline.

My heart knock.

Then she frown. But *I* calls her Olivia.

Why you call her Olivia if it ain't her name? I ast.

Well, just look at her, she say sort of impish, turning to look at the child, don't she look like a Olivia to you? Look at her eyes, for god's sake. Somebody ole would have eyes like that. So I call her *ole* Livia. She chuckle. Naw. Olivia, she say, patting the child hair. Well, here come the Reverend Mr. _____, she say. I see a wagon and a great big man in black holding a whip. We sure do thank you for your hospitality. She laugh again, look at the horses flicking flies off they rump. *Horse*pitality, she say. And I git it and laugh. It feel like to split my face.

Mr. _____, come out the store. Clam up in the wagon. Set down. Say real slow. What you setting here laughing like a fool fer?

Dear God,

Nettie here with us. She run way from home. She say she hate to leave our stepma, but she had to git out, maybe fine help for the other little ones. The boys be alright, she say. They can stay out his way. When they git big they gon fight him.

Maybe kill, I say.

How is it with you and Mr. _____? she ast. But she got eyes. He still like her. In the evening he come out on the porch in his Sunday best. She be sitting there with me shelling peas or helping the children with they spelling. Helping me with spelling and everything else she think I need to know. No matter what happen, Nettie steady try to teach me what go on in the world. And she a good teacher too. It nearly kill me to think she might marry somebody like Mr. _____ or wind up in some white lady kitchen. All day she read, she study, she practice her handwriting, and try to git us to think. Most days I feel too tired to think. But Patient her middle name.

Mr. _____ children all bright but they mean. They say Celie, I want dis. Celie, I want dat. Our Mama let us have it. He don't say nothing. They try to get his tention, he hide hind a puff of smoke.

Don't let them run over you, Nettie say. You got to let them know who got the upper hand.

They got it, I say.

But she keep on. You got to fight. You got to fight.

But I don't know how to fight. All I know how to do is stay alive.

That's a real pretty dress you got on, he say to Nettie.
She say, Thank you.

Them shoes look just right.

She say, Thank you.

Your skin. Your hair. Your teefs. Everyday it something else to make miration over.

First she smile a little. Then she frown. Then she don't look no special way at all. She just stick close to me. She tell me, Your skin. Your hair. Your teefs. He try to give her a compliment, she pass it on to me. After while I git to feeling pretty cute.

Soon he stop. He say one night in bed, Well, us done help Nettie all we can. Now she got to go.

Where she gon go? I ast.

I don't care, he say.

I tell Nettie the next morning. Stead of being mad, she glad to go. Say she hate to leave me is all. Us fall on each other neck when she say that.

I sure hate to leave you here with these rotten children, she say. Not to mention with Mr. _____. It's like seeing you buried, she say.

It's worse than that, I think. If I was buried, I wouldn't have to work. But I just say, Never mine, never mine, long as I can spell G-o-d I got somebody along.

But I only got one thing to give her, the name of Reverend Mr. _____. I tell her to ast for his wife. That maybe she would help. She the only woman I even seen with money.

I say, Write.

She say, What?

I say, Write.

She say, Nothing but death can keep me from it.

She never write.

G-o-d,

Two of his sister come to visit. They dress all up. Celie, they say. One thing is for sure. You keep a clean house. It not nice to speak ill of the dead, one say, but the truth never can *be* ill. Annie Julia was a nasty 'oman bout the house.

She never want to be here in the first place, say the other.

Where she want to be? I ast.

At home. She say.

Well that's no excuse, say the first one, Her name Carrie, other one name Kate. When a woman marry she spose to keep a decent house and a clean family. Why, wasn't nothing to come here in the winter time and all these children have colds, they have flue, they have direar, they have newmonya, they have worms, they have the chill and fever. They hungry. They hair ain't comb. They too nasty to touch.

I touch 'em. Say Kate.

And cook. She wouldn't cook. She act like she never seen a kitchen.

She hadn't never seen his.

Was a scandal, say Carrie.

He sure was, say Kate.

What you mean? say Carrie.

I mean he just brought her here, dropped her, and kept right on running after Shug Avery. That what I mean. Nobody to talk to, nobody to visit. He be gone for days. Then she start having babies. And she young and pretty.

Not so pretty, say Carrie, looking in the looking glass. Just that head of hair. She too black.

Well, brother must like black. Shug Avery black as my shoe.

Shug Avery, Shug Avery, Carrie say. I'm sick of her.

Somebody say she going round trying to sing. Umph, what she got to sing about. Say she wearing dresses all up her leg and headpieces with little balls and tassles hanging down, look like window dressing.

My ears perk up when they mention Shug Avery. I feel like I want to talk about her my own self. They hush.

I'm sick of her too, say Kate, letting out her breath. And you right about Celie, here. Good housekeeper, good with children, good cook. Brother couldn't have done better if he tried.

I think about how he tried.

This time Kate come by herself. She maybe twenty-five. Old maid. She look younger than me. Healthy. Eyes bright. Tongue sharp.

Buy Celie some clothes. She say to Mr. _____.

She need clothes? he ast.

Well look at her.

He look at me. It like he looking at the earth. It need somethin? his eyes say.

She go with me in the store. I think what color Shug Avery would wear. She like a queen to me so I say to Kate, Somethin purple, maybe little red in it too. But us look an look and no purple. Plenty red but she say, Naw, he won't want to pay for red. Too happy lookin. We got choice of brown, maroon or navy blue. I say blue.

I can't remember being the first one in my own dress. Now to have one made just for me. I try to tell Kate what it mean. I git hot in the face and stutter.

She say. It's all right, Celie. You deserve more than this.

Maybe so. I think.

Harpo, she say. Harpo the oldest boy. Harpo, don't let Celie be the one bring in all the water. You a big boy now. Time for you to help out some.

Women work, he say.

What? she say.

Women work. I'm a man.

You're a trifling nigger, she say. You git that bucket and bring it back full.

He cut his eye at me. Stumble out. I hear him mutter somethin to Mr. _____ sitting on the porch. Mr. _____ call his sister. She stay out on the porch talking a little while, then she come back in, shaking.

Got to go, Celie, she say.

She so mad tears be flying every which way while she pack.

You got to fight them, Celie, she say. I can't do it for you. You got to fight them for yourself.

I don't say nothing. I think bout Nettie, dead. She fight, she run away. What good it do? I don't fight, I stay where I'm told. But I'm alive.

Dear God,

Harpo ast his daddy why he beat me. Mr. _____ say,
Cause she my wife. Plus, she stubborn. All women good for—
he don't finish. He just tuck his chin over the paper like he do.
Remind me of Pa.

Harpo ast me, How come you stubborn? He don't ast How
come you his wife? Nobody ast that.

I say, Just born that way, I reckon.

He beat me like he beat the children. Cept he don't never
hardly beat them. He say, Celie, git the belt. The children be
outside the room peeking through the cracks. It all I can do not
to cry. I make myself wood. I say to myself, Celie, you a tree.
That's how come I know trees fear man.

Harpo say, I love Somebody.

I say, Huh?

He say, A Girl.

I say, You do?

He say, Yeah. Us plan to marry.

Marry, I say. You not old enough to marry.

I is, he say. I'm seventeen. She fifteen. Old enough.

What her mama say, I ast.

Ain't talk to her mama.

What her daddy say?

Ain't talk to him neither.

Well, what *she* say?

Us ain't never spoke. He duck his head. He ain't so bad
looking. Tall and skinny, black like his mama, with great big bug
eyes.

Where yall see each other? I ast. I see her in church, he say. She see me outdoors.

She like you?

I don't know. I wink at her. She act like she scared to look.

Where her daddy at while all this going on?

Amen corner, he say.

Dear God,

Shug Avery is coming to town! She coming with her orkestra. She going to sing in the Lucky Star out on Coalman road. Mr. _____ going to hear her. He dress all up in front the glass, look at himself, then undress and dress all over again. He slick back his hair with pomade, then wash it out again. He been spitting on his shoes and hitting it with a quick rag.

He tell me, Wash this. Iron that. Look for this. Look for that. Find this. Find that. He groan over holes in his sock.

I move round darning and ironing, finding hanskers. Anything happening? I ast.

What you mean? he say, like he mad. Just trying to git some of the hick farmer off myself. Any other woman be glad.

I'm is glad, I say.

What you mean? he ast

You looks nice, I say. Any woman be proud.

You think so? he say.

First time he ast me. I'm so surprise, by time I say Yeah, he out on the porch, trying to shave where the light better.

I walk round all day with the announcement burning a hole in my pocket. It pink. The trees tween the turn off to our road and the store is lit up with them. He got bout five dozen in his trunk.

Shug Avery standing upside a piano, elbow crook, hand on her hip. She wearing a hat like Indian Chiefs. Her mouth open showing all her teef and don't nothing seem to be troubling her mind. Come one, come all, it say. The Queen Honeybee is back in town.

Lord, I wants to go so bad. Not to dance. Not to drink. Not to play card. Not even to hear Shug Avery sing. I just be thankful to lay eyes on her.

Dear God,

Mr. _____ be gone all night Saturday, all night Sunday and most all day Monday. Shug Avery in town for the week-end. He stagger in, throw himself on the bed. He tired. He sad. He weak. He cry. Then he sleep the rest of the day and all night.

He wake up while I'm in the field. I been chopping cotton three hours by time he come. Us don't say nothing to each other.

But I got a million question to ast. What she wear? Is she still the same old Shug, like in my picture? How her hair is? What kind lipstick? Wig? She stout? She skinny? She sound well? Tired? Sick? Where you all children at while she singing all over the place? Do she miss 'em? Questions be running back and forth through my mind. Feel like snakes. I pray for strength, bite the insides of my jaws.

Mr. _____ pick up a hoe and start to chop. He chop bout three chops then he don't chop again. He drop the hoe in the furrow, turn right back on his heel, walk back to the house, go git him a cool drink of water, git his pipe, sit on the porch and stare. I follow cause I think he sick. Then he say, You better git on back to the field. Don't wait for me.

Dear God,

Harpo no better at fighting his daddy back than me. Every day his daddy git up, sit on the porch, look out at nothing. Sometime look at the trees out front the house. Look at a butterfly if it light on the rail. Drink a little water in the day. A little wine in the evening. But mostly never move.

Harpo complain bout all the plowing he have to do.

His daddy say, You gonna do it.

Harpo nearly big as his daddy. He strong in body but weak in will. He scared.

Me and him out in the field all day. Us sweat, chopping and plowing. I'm roasted coffee bean color now. He black as the inside of a chimney. His eyes be sad and thoughtful. His face begin to look like a woman face.

Why you don't work no more? he ast his daddy.

No reason for me to. His daddy say. You here, ain't you? He say this nasty. Harpos feeling be hurt.

Plus, he still in love.

Dear God,

Harpo girl daddy say Harpo not good enough for her. Harpo been courting the girl a while. He say he sit in the parlor with her, the daddy sit right there in the corner till everybody feel terrible. Then he go sit on the porch in front the open door where he can hear everything. Nine o'clock come, he bring Harpo his hat.

Why I'm not good enough? Harpo ast Mr. _____. Mr. _____ say, Your mammy.

Harpo say, What wrong with my mammy?

Mr. _____ say, Somebody kill her.

Harpo be trouble with nightmares. He see his mama running cross the pasture trying to git home. Mr. _____, the man they say her boyfriend, catch up with her. She got Harpo by the hand. They both running and running. He grab hold of her shoulder, say, You can't quit me now. You mine. She say, No I ain't. My place is with my children. He say, Whore, you ain't got no place. He shoot her in the stomach. She fall down. The man run. Harpo grab her in his arms, put her head in his lap.

He start to call, Mama, Mama. It wake me up. The other children too. They cry like they mama just die. Harpo come to, shaking.

I light the lamp and stand over him, patting his back.

It not her fault somebody kill her, he say. It not! It not!

Naw, I say. It not.

Everybody say how good I is to Mr. _____ children. I be good to them. But I don't feel nothing for them. Patting Harpo back not even like patting a dog. It more like patting another piece of wood. Not a living tree, but a table, a chifferobe. Anyhow, they don't love me neither, no matter how good I is.

They don't mind. Cept for Harpo they won't work. The girls face always to the road. Bub be out all times of night drinking with boys twice his age. They daddy puff on his pipe.

Harpo tell me all his love business now. His mind on Sofia Butler day and night.

She pretty, he tell me. Bright.

Smart?

Naw. Bright *skin*. She smart too though, I think. Sometime us can git her away from her daddy.

I know right then the next thing I hear, she be big.

If she so smart how come she big? I ast.

Harpo shrug. She can't git out the house no other way, he say. Mr. _____ won't let us marry. Say I'm not good enough to come in his parlor. But if she big I got a right to be with her, good enough or no.

Where yall gon stay?

They got a big place, he say. When us marry I'll be just like one of the family.

Humph, I say. Mr. _____ didn't like you before she big, he ain't gonna like you *cause* she big.

Harpo look trouble.

Talk to Mr. _____, I say. He your daddy. Maybe he got some good advice.

Maybe not. I think.

Harpo bring her over to meet his daddy. Mr. _____ say he want to have a look at her. I see 'em coming way off up the road. They be just marching, hand in hand, like going to war. She in front a little. They come up on the porch, I speak and move some chairs closer to the railing. She sit down and start to fan herself with a hansker. It sure is hot, she say. Mr. _____ don't say nothing. He just look her up and down. She bout seven or eight months pregnant, bout to bust out her dress. Harpo so black he think she bright, but she ain't that bright. Clear medium brown skin, gleam on it like on good furniture. Hair notty but a lot of it, tied up on her head in a mass of plaits. She not quite as tall as Harpo but much bigger, and strong and ruddy looking, like her mama brought her up on pork.

She say, How you, Mr. _____?

He don't answer the question. He say, Look like you done got yourself in trouble.

Naw suh, she say. I ain't in no trouble. Big, though.

She smooth the wrinkles over her stomach with the flats of her hands.

Who the father? he ast.

She look surprise. Harpo, she say.

How he know that?

He know. She say.

Young womens no good these days, he say. Got they legs open to every Tom, Dick and Harry.

Harpo look at his daddy like he never seen him before. But he don't say nothing.

Mr. _____ say, No need to think I'm gon let my boy marry you just cause you in the family way. He young and limited. Pretty gal like you could put anything over on him.

Harpo still don't say nothing.

Sofia face git more ruddy. The skin move back on her forehead. Her ears raise.

But she laugh. She glance at Harpo sitting there with his head down and his hands tween his knees.

She say, What I need to marry Harpo for? He still living here with you. What food and clothes he git, you buy.

He say, Your daddy done throwed you out. Ready to live in the street I guess.

She say, Naw. I ain't living in the street. I'm living with my sister and her husband. They say I can live with them for the rest of my life. She stand up, big, strong, healthy girl, and she say, Well, nice visiting. I'm going home.

Harpo get up to come too. She say, Naw, Harpo, you stay here. When you free, me and the baby be waiting.

He sort of hang there between them a while, then he sit down again. I look at her face real quick then, and seem like a shadow go cross it. Then she say to me, Mrs. _____, I'd thank you for a glass of water before I go, if you don't mind.

The bucket on the shelf right there on the porch. I git a clean glass out the safe and dip her up some water. She drink it down, almost in one swallow. Then she run her hands over her belly again and she take off. Look like the army change direction, and she heading off to catch up.

Harpo never git up from his chair. Him and his daddy sit there and sit there and sit there. They never talk. They never move. Finally I have supper and go to bed. I git up in the morning it feel like they still sitting there. But Harpo be in the outhouse, Mr. _____ be shaving.

Dear God,

Harpo went and brought Sofia and the baby home. They got married in Sofia sister house. Sister's husband stand up with Harpo. Other sister sneak way from home to stand up with Sofia. Another sister come to hold the baby. Say he cry right through the service, his mama stop everything to nurse him. Finish saying I do with a big ole nursing boy in her arms.

Harpo fix up the little creek house for him and his family. Mr. _____ daddy used it for a shed. But it sound. Got windows now, a porch, back door. Plus it cool and green down by the creek.

He ast me to make some curtains and I make some out of flower sack. It not big, but it homey. Got a bed, a dresser, a looking glass, and some chairs. Cookstove for cooking and heating, too. Harpo daddy give him wages for working now. He say Harpo wasn't working hard like he should. Maybe little money goose his interest.

Harpo told me, Miss Celie, I'm going on strike.

On what?

I ain't going to work.

And he don't. He come to the field, pull two ears of corn, let the birds and weevil eat two hundred. Us don't make nothing much this year.

But now Sofia coming, he always busy. He chop, he hammer, he plow. He sing and whistle.

Sofia look half her size. But she still a big strong girl. Arms got muscle. Legs, too. She swing that baby about like it nothing. She got a little pot on her now and give you the feeling she all there. Solid. Like if she sit down on something, it be mash.

She tell Harpo, Hold the baby, while she come back in the house with me to git some thread. She making some sheets. He take the baby, give it a kiss, chuck it under it chin. Grin, look up on the porch at his daddy.

Mr. _____ blow smoke, look down at him, and say, Yeah, I see now she going to switch the traces on you.

Dear God,

Harpo want to know what to do to make Sofia mind. He sit out on the porch with Mr. _____. He say, I tell her one thing, she do another. Never do what I say. Always backtalk.

To tell the truth, he sound a little proud of this to me.

Mr. _____ don't say nothing. Blow smoke.

I tell her she can't be all the time going to visit her sister. Us married now, I tell her. Your place is here with the children. She say, I'll take the children with me. I say, Your place is with me. She say, You want to come? She keep primping in front the glass, getting the children ready at the same time.

You ever hit her? Mr. _____ ast.

Harpo look down at his hands. Naw suh, he say low, embarrass.

Well how you spect to make her mind? Wives is like children. You have to let 'em know who got the upper hand. Nothing can do that better than a good sound beating.

He puff on his pipe.

Sofia think too much of herself anyway, he say. She need to be taken down a peg.

I like Sofia, but she don't act like me at all. If she talking when Harpo and Mr. _____ come in the room, she keep right on. If they ast her where something at, she say she don't know. Keep talking.

I think bout this when Harpo ast me what he ought to do to her to make her mind. I don't mention how happy he is now. How three years pass and he still whistle and sing. I think bout how every time I jump when Mr. _____ call me, she look surprise. And like she pity me.

Beat her. I say.

Next time us see Harpo his face a mess of bruises. His lip cut. One of his eyes shut like a fist. He walk stiff and say his teef ache.

I say, What happen to you, Harpo?

He say, Oh, me and that mule. She fractious, you know. She went crazy in the field the other day. By time I got her to head for home I was all banged up. Then when I got home, I walked smack dab into the crib door. Hit my eye and scratch my chin. Then when that storm come up last night I shet the window down on my hand.

Well, I say, After all that, I don't spect you had a chance to see if you could make Sofia mind.

Nome, he say.

But he keep trying.

Dear God,

Just when I was bout to call out that I was coming in the yard, I hear something crash. It come from inside the house, so I run up on the porch. The two children be making mud pies on the edge of the creek, they don't even look up.

I open the door cautious, thinking bout robbers and murderers. Horsethieves and hants. But it Harpo and Sofia. They fighting like two mens. Every piece of furniture they got is turned over. Every plate look like it broke. The looking glass hang crooked, the curtains torn. The bed look like the stuffing pulled out. They don't notice. They fight. He try to slap her. What he do that for? She reach down and grab a piece of stove wood and whack him cross the eyes. He punch her in the stomach, she double over groaning but come up with both hands lock right under his privates. He roll on the floor. He grab her dress tail and pull. She stand there in her slip. She never blink a eye. He jump up to put a hammer lock under her chin, she throw him over her back. He fall *bam* up gainst the stove.

I don't know how long this been going on. I don't know when they spect to conclude. I ease on back out, wave to the children by the creek, walk back on up home.

Saturday morning early, us hear the wagon. Harpo, Sofia, the two babies be going off for the week-end, to visit Sofia sister.

Dear God,

For over a month I have trouble sleeping. I stay up late as I can before Mr. _____ start complaining bout the price of kerosene, then I soak myself in a warm bath with milk and epsom salts, then sprinkle little witch hazel on my pillow and curtain out all the moonlight. Sometimes I git a few hours sleep. Then just when it look like it ought to be gitting good, I wakes up.

At first I'd git up quick and drink some milk. Then I'd think bout counting fence post. Then I'd think bout reading the Bible.

What it is? I ast myself.

A little voice say, Something you done wrong. Somebody spirit you sin against. Maybe

Way late one night it come to me. Sofia. I sin against Sofia spirit.

I pray she don't find out, but she do.

Harpo told.

The minute she hear it she come marching up the path, toting a sack. Little cut all blue and red under her eye.

She say, Just want you to know I looked to you for help.

Ain't I been helpful? I ast.

She open up her sack. Here your curtains, she say. Here your thread. Here a dollar for letting me use 'em.

They yourn, I say, trying to push them back. I'm glad to help out. Do what I can.

You told Harpo to beat me, she said.

No I didn't, I said.

Don't lie, she said.

I didn't mean it, I said.

Then what you say it for? she ast.

She standing there looking me straight in the eye. She look tired and her jaws full of air.

I say it cause I'm a fool, I say. I say it cause I'm jealous of you. I say it cause you do what I can't.

What that? she say.

Fight. I say.

She stand there a long time, like what I said took the wind out her jaws. She mad before, sad now.

She say, All my life I had to fight. I had to fight my daddy. I had to fight my brothers. I had to fight my cousins and my uncles. A girl child ain't safe in a family of men. But I never thought I'd have to fight in my own house. She let out her breath. I loves Harpo, she say. God knows I do. But I'll kill him dead before I let him beat me. Now if you want a dead son-in-law you just keep on advising him like you doing. She put her hand on her hip. I used to hunt game with a bow and arrow, she say.

I stop the little trembling that started when I saw her coming. I'm *so* shame of myself, I say. And the Lord he done whip me little bit too.

The Lord don't like ugly, she say.

And he ain't stuck on pretty.

This open the way for our talk to turn another way.

I say, You feels sorry for me, don't you?

She think a minute. Yes ma'am, she say slow, I do.

I think I know how come, but I ast her anyhow.

She say, To tell the truth, you remind me of my mama. She under my daddy thumb. Naw, she under my daddy foot. Anything he say, goes. She never say nothing back. She never stand up for herself. Try to make a little half stand sometime for the children but that always backfire. More she stand up for us, the harder time he give her. He hate children and he hate where they come from. Tho from all the children he got, you'd never know it.

I never know nothing bout her family. I thought, looking at her, nobody in her family could be scared.

How many he got? I ast.

Twelve. She say.

Whew, I say. My daddy got six by my mama before she die, I say. He got four more by the wife he got now. I don't mention the two he got by me.

How many girls? she ast.

Five, I say. How bout in your family?

Six boys, six girls. All the girls big and strong like me. Boys big and strong too, but all the girls stick together. Two brothers stick with us too, sometime. Us git in a fight, it's a sight to see.

I ain't never struck a living thing, I say. Oh, when I was at home I tap the little ones on the behind to make 'em behave, but not hard enough to hurt.

What you do when you git mad? she ast.

I think. I can't even remember the last time I felt mad, I say. I used to git mad at my mammy cause she put a lot of work on me. Then I see how sick she is. Couldn't stay mad at her. Couldn't be mad at my daddy cause he my daddy. Bible say, Honor father and mother no matter what. Then after while every time I got mad, or start to feel mad, I got sick. Felt like throwing up. Terrible feeling. Then I start to feel nothing at all.

Sofia frown. Nothing at all?

Well, sometime Mr. _____ git on me pretty hard. I have to talk to Old Maker. But he my husband. I shrug my shoulders. This life soon be over, I say. Heaven last all ways.

You ought to bash Mr. _____ head open, she say. Think bout heaven later.

Not much funny to me. That funny. I laugh. She laugh. Then us both laugh so hard us flop down on the step.

Let's make quilt pieces out of these messed up curtains, she say. And I run git my pattern book.

I sleeps like a baby now.

Dear God,

Shug Avery sick and nobody in this town want to take the
Queen Honeybee in. Her mammy say She told her so. Her
pappy say, Tramp. A woman at church say she dying—maybe
two berkulosis or some kind of nasty woman disease. What? I
want to ast, but don't. The women at church sometime nice to
me. Sometime not. They look at me there struggling with Mr.
_____ children. Trying to drag 'em to the church, trying to keep
'em quiet after us get there. They some of the same ones used to
be here both times I was big. Sometimes they think I don't
notice, they stare at me. Puzzle.

I keep my head up, best I can. I do a right smart for the
preacher. Clean the floor and windows, make the wine, wash
the altar linen. Make sure there's wood for the stove in wintertime. He call me Sister Celie. Sister Celie, he say, You faithful as
the day is long. Then he talk to the other ladies and they mens. I
scurry bout, doing this, doing that. Mr. _____ sit back by the
door gazing here and there. The womens smile in his direction
every chance they git. He never look at me or even notice.

Even the preacher got his mouth on Shug Avery, now she
down. He take her condition for his text. He don't call no name,
but he don't have to. Everybody know who he mean. He talk
bout a strumpet in short skirts, smoking cigarettes, drinking
gin. Singing for money and taking other women mens. Talk
bout slut, hussy, heifer and streetcleaner.

I cut my eyes back at Mr. _____ when he say that.
Streetcleaner. Somebody got to stand up for Shug, I think. But
he don't say nothing. He cross his legs first to one side, then to

the other. He gaze out the window. The same women smile at him, say amen gainst Shug.

But once us home he never stop to take off his clothes. He call down to Harpo and Sofia house. Harpo come running.

Hitch up the wagon, he say.

Where us going? say Harpo.

Hitch up the wagon, he say again.

Harpo hitch up the wagon. They stand there and talk a few minutes out by the barn. Then Mr. _____ drive off.

One good thing bout the way he never do any work round the place, us never miss him when he gone.

Five days later I look way off up the road and see the wagon coming back. It got sort of a canopy over it now, made out of old blankets or something. My heart begin to beat like furry, and the first thing I try to do is change my dress.

But too late for that. By time I git my head and arm out the old dress, I see the wagon pull up in the yard. Plus a new dress won't help none with my notty head and dusty headrag, my old everyday shoes and the way I smell.

I don't know what to do, I'm so beside myself. I stand there in the middle of the kitchen. Mind whirling. I feels like Who Would Have Thought.

Celie, I hear Mr. _____ call. *Harpo.*

I stick my head and my arm back in my old dress and wipe the sweat and dirt off my face as best I can. I come to the door. Yessir? I ast, and trip over the broom I was sweeping with when I first notice the wagon.

Harpo and Sofia in the yard now, looking inside the wagon. They faces grim.

Who this? Harpo ast.

The woman should have been your mammy, he say.

Shug Avery? Harpo ast. He look up at me.

Help me git her in the house, Mr. _____ say.

I think my heart gon fly out my mouth when I see one of her foots come poking out.

She not lying down. She climbing down tween Harpo and Mr. _____. And she dress to kill. She got on a red wool dress and chestful of black beads. A shiny black hat with what look like chickinhawk feathers curve down side one cheek, and she carrying a little snakeskin bag, match her shoes.

She look so stylish it like the trees all round the house draw themself up tall for a better look. Now I see she stumble, tween the two men. She don't seem that well acquainted with her feets.

Close up I see all this yellow powder caked up on her face. Red rouge. She look like she ain't long for this world but dressed well for the next. But I know better.

Come on in, I want to cry. To shout. Come on in. With God help, Celie going to make you well. But I don't say nothing. It not my house. Also I ain't been told nothing.

They git halfway up the step, Mr. _____ look up at me. Celie, he say. This here Shug Avery. Old friend of the family. Fix up the spare room. Then he look down at her, hold her in one arm, hold on to the rail with the other. Harpo on the other side, looking sad. Sofia and the children in the yard, watching.

I don't move at once, cause I can't. I need to see her eyes. I feel like once I see her eyes my feets can let go the spot where they stuck.

Git moving, he say, sharp.

And then she look up.

Under all that powder her face black as Harpo. She got a long pointed nose and big fleshy mouth. Lips look like black plum. Eyes big, glossy. Feverish. And mean. Like, sick as she is, if a snake cross her path, she kill it.

She look me over from head to foot. Then she cackle. Sound like a death rattle. You sure *is* ugly, she say, like she ain't believed it.

Dear God,

Ain't nothing wrong with Shug Avery. She just sick. Sicker than anybody I ever seen. She sicker than my mama was when she die. But she more evil than my mama and that keep her alive.

Mr. _____ be in the room with her all time of the night or day. He don't hold her hand though. She too evil for that. Turn loose my goddam hand, she say to Mr. _____. What the matter with you, you crazy? I don't need no weak little boy can't say no to his daddy hanging on me. I need me a man, she say. A man. She look at him and roll her eyes and laugh. It not much of a laugh but it keep him away from the bed. He sit over in the corner away from the lamp. Sometime she wake up in the night and don't even see. But he there. Sitting in the shadows chewing on his pipe. No tobacco in it. First thing she said, I don't want to smell no stinking blankety-blank pipe, you hear me, Albert?

Who Albert, I wonder. Then I remember Albert Mr. _____ first name.

Mr. _____ don't smoke. Don't drink. Don't even hardly eat. He just got her in that little room, watching every breath.

What happen to her I ast?

You don't want her here, just say so, he say. Won't do no good. But if that the way you feel . . . He don't finish.

I want her here, I say, too quick. He look at me like maybe I'm planning something bad.

I just want to know what happen, I say.

I look at his face. It tired and sad and I notice his chin weak.

Not much chin there at all. I have more chin, I think. And his clothes dirty, dirty. When he pull them off, dust rise.

Nobody fight for Shug, he say. And a little water come to his eyes.

Dear God,

They have made three babies together but he squeamish bout giving her a bath. Maybe he figure he start thinking bout things he shouldn't. But what bout me? First time I got the full sight of Shug Avery long black body with it black plum nipples, look like her mouth, I thought I had turned into a man.

What you staring at? she ast. Hateful. She weak as a kitten. But her mouth just pack with claws. You never seen a naked woman before?

No ma'am, I said. I never did. Cept for Sofia, and she so plump and ruddy and crazy she feel like my sister.

She say, Well take a good look. Even if I is just a bag of bones now. She have the nerve to put one hand on her naked hip and bat her eyes at me. Then she suck her teef and roll her eyes at the ceiling while I wash her.

I wash her body, it feel like I'm praying. My hands tremble and my breath short.

She say, You ever have any kids?

I say, Yes ma'am.

She say, How many and don't you yes ma'am me, I ain't that old.

I say, two.

She ast me Where they is?

I say, I don't know.

She look at me funny.

My kids with they grandma, she say. She could stand the kids, I had to go.

You miss 'em? I ast.

Naw, she say. I don't miss nothing.

Dear God,

I ast Shug Avery what she want for breakfast. She say,
What yall got? I say ham, grits, eggs, biscuits, coffee, sweet milk
or butter milk, flapjacks. Jelly and jam.

She say, Is that all? What about orange juice, grapefruit,
strawberries and cream. Tea. Then she laugh.

I don't want none of your damn food, she say. Just gimme a
cup of coffee and hand me my cigarettes.

I don't argue. I git the coffee and light her cigarette. She
wearing a long white gown and her thin black hand stretching
out of it to hold the white cigarette looks just right. Something
bout it, maybe the little tender veins I see and the big ones I try
not to, make me scared. I feel like something pushing me
forward. If I don't watch out I'll have hold of her hand, tasting
her fingers in my mouth.

Can I sit in here and eat with you? I ast.

She shrug. She busy looking at a magazine. White women
in it laughing, holding they beads out on one finger, dancing on
top of motocars. Jumping into fountains. She flip the pages.
Look dissatisfied. Remind me of a child trying to git something
out a toy it can't work yet.

She drink her coffee, puff on her cigarette. I bite into a big
juicy piece of home cured ham. You can smell this ham for a mile
when you cooking it, it perfume up her little room with no
trouble at all.

I lavish butter on a hot biscuit, sort of wave it about. I sop
up ham gravey and splosh my eggs in with my grits.

She blow more and more smoke. Look down in her coffee
like maybe its something solid at the bottom.

46

Finally she say, Celie, I believe I could drink a glass of water. And this here by the bed ain't fresh.

She hold out her glass.

I put my plate down on the card table by the bed. I go dip her up some water. I come back, pick up my plate. Look like a little mouse been nibbling the biscuit, a rat run off with the ham.

She act like nothing happen. Begin to complain bout being tired. Doze on off to sleep.

Mr. _____ ast me how I git her to eat.

I say, Nobody living can stand to smell home cured ham without tasting it. If they dead they got a chance. Maybe.

Mr. _____ laugh.

I notice something crazy in his eyes.

I been scared, he say. Scared. And he cover up his eyes with his hands.

Dear God,

Shug Avery sit up in bed a little today. I wash and comb out her hair. She got the nottiest, shortest, kinkiest hair I ever saw, and I loves every strand of it. The hair that come out in my comb I kept. Maybe one day I'll get a net, make me a rat to pomp up my own hair.

I work on her like she a doll or like she Olivia—or like she mama. I comb and pat, comb and pat. First she say, hurry up and git finish. Then she melt down a little and lean back gainst my knees. That feel just right, she say. That feel like mama used to do. Or maybe not mama. Maybe grandma. She reach for another cigarette. Start hum a little tune.

What that song? I ast. Sound low down dirty to me. Like what the preacher tell you its sin to hear. Not to mention sing.

She hum a little more. Something come to me, she say. Something I made up. Something you help scratch out my head.

Dear God,

Mr. _____ daddy show up this evening. He a little short shrunk up man with a bald head and gold spectacles. He clear his throat a lot, like everything he say need announcement. Talk with his head leant to the side.

He come right to the point.

Just couldn't rest till you got her in your house, could you? he say, coming up the step.

Mr. _____ don't say nothing. Look out cross the railing at the trees, over the top of the well. Eyes rest on the top of Harpo and Sofia house.

Won't you have a seat? I ast, pushing him up a chair. How bout a cool drink of water?

Through the window I hear Shug humming and humming, practicing her little song. I sneak back to her room and shet the window.

Old Mr. _____ say to Mr. _____, Just what is it bout this Shug Avery anyway, he say. She black as tar, she nappy headed. She got legs like baseball bats.

Mr. _____ don't say nothing. I drop little spit in Old Mr. _____ water.

Why, say Old Mr. _____, she ain't even clean. I hear she got the nasty woman disease.

I twirl the spit round with my finger. I think bout ground glass, wonder how you grind it. But I don't feel mad at all. Just interest.

Mr. _____ turn his head slow, watch his daddy drink. Then say, real sad, You ain't got it in you to understand, he say. I love Shug Avery. Always have, always will. I should have married her when I had the chance.

49

Yeah, say Old Mr. _____. And throwed your life away. (Mr. _____ grunt right there.) And a right smart of my money with it. Old Mr. _____ clear his throat. Nobody even sure exactly who her daddy is.

I never care who her daddy is, say Mr. _____.

And her mammy take in white people dirty clothes to this day. Plus all her children got different daddys. It all just too trifling and confuse.

Well, say Mr. _____ and turn full face on his daddy, All Shug Avery children got the same daddy. I vouch for that.

Old Mr. _____ clear his throat. Well, this my house. This my land. Your boy Harpo in one of my houses, on my land. Weeds come up on my land, I chop 'em up. Trash blow over it I burn it. He rise to go. Hand me his glass. Next time he come I put a little Shug Avery pee in his glass. See how he like that.

Celie, he say, you have my sympathy. Not many women let they husband whore lay up in they house.

But he not saying this to me, he saying it to Mr. _____.

Mr. _____ look up at me, our eyes meet. This the closest us ever felt.

He say, Hand Pa his hat, Celie.

And I do. Mr. _____ don't move from his chair by the railing. I stand in the door. Us watch Old Mr. _____ begin harrumping and harrumping down the road home.

Next one come visit, his brother Tobias. He real fat and tall, look like a big yellow bear. Mr. _____ small like his daddy, his brother stand way taller.

Where she at? he ast, grinning. Where the Queen Honeybee? Got something for her, he say. He put little box of chocolate on the railing.

She sleeping, I say. Didn't sleep much last night.

How you doing there, Albert, he say, dragging up a chair. He run his hand over his slicked back hair and try to feel if there's a bugga in his nose. Wipe his hand on his pants. Shake out the crease.

I just heard Shug Avery was here, he say. How long you had her?

Oh, say Mr. _____, couple of months.

Hell, say Tobias, I heard she was dying. That goes to show, don't it, that you can't believe everything you hear. He smooth down his mustache, run his tongue out the corners of his lips.

What you know good, Miss Celie? he say.

Not much, I say.

Me and Sofia piecing another quilt together. I got bout five squares pieced, spread out on the table by my knee. My basket full of scraps on the floor.

Always busy, always busy, he say. I wish Margaret was more like you. Save me a bundle of money.

Tobias and his daddy always talk bout money like they still got a lot. Old Mr. _____ been selling off the place so that nothing much left but the houses and the fields. My and Harpo fields bring in more than anybody.

I piece on my square. Look at the colors of the cloth.

Then I hear Tobias chair fall back and he say, *Shug*.

Shug halfway tween sick and well. Halfway tween good and evil, too. Most days now she show me and Mr. _____ her good side. But evil all over her today. She smile, like a razor opening. Say, Well, well, look who's here to*day*.

She wearing a little flowery shift I made for her and nothing else. She look bout ten with her hair all cornrowed. She skinny as a bean, and her face full of eyes.

Me and Mr. _____ both look up at her. Both move to help her sit down. She don't look at him. She pull up a chair next to me.

She pick up a random piece of cloth out the basket. Hold it up to the light. Frown. How you sew this damn thing? she say.

I hand her the square I'm working on, start another one. She sew long crooked stiches, remind me of that little crooked tune she sing.

That real good, for first try, I say. That just fine and dandy. She look at me and snort. Everything I do is fine and dandy to you, Miss Celie, she say. But that's cause you ain't got good sense. She laugh. I duck my head.

She got a heap more than Margaret, say Tobias. Margaret take that needle and sew your nostrils together.

All womens not alike, Tobias, she say. Believe it or not.

Oh, I believe it, he say. Just can't prove it to the world.

First time I think about the world.

What the world got to do with anything, I think. Then I see myself sitting there quilting tween Shug Avery and Mr. _____. Us three set together gainst Tobias and his fly speck box of chocolate. For the first time in my life, I feel just right.

Dear God,

Me and Sofia work on the quilt. Got it frame up on the porch. Shug Avery donate her old yellow dress for scrap, and I work in a piece every chance I get. It a nice pattern call Sister's Choice. If the quilt turn out perfect, maybe I give it to her, if it not perfect, maybe I keep. I want it for myself, just for the little yellow pieces, look like stars, but not. Mr. _____ and Shug walk up the road to the mailbox. The house quiet, cept for the flies. They swing through every now and then, drunk from eating and enjoying the heat, buzz enough to make me drowsy.

Sofia look like something on her mind, she just not sure what. She bend over the frame, sew a little while, then rear back in her chair and look out cross the yard. Finally she rest her needle, say, Why do people eat, Miss Celie, tell me that.

To stay alive, I say. What else? Course some folks eat cause food taste good to 'em. Then some is gluttons. They love to feel they mouth work.

Them the only reasons you can think of? she ast.

Well, sometime it might be a case of being undernourish, I say.

She muse. He not undernourish, she say.

Who ain't? I ast.

Harpo. She say.

Harpo?

He eating more and more every day.

Maybe he got a tape worm?

She frown. Naw, she say. I don't think it a tape worm. Tape worm make you hungry. Harpo eat when he ain't even hungry.

What, force it down? This hard to believe, but sometime

you hear new things everyday. Not me, you understand, but some folk do say that.

Last night for supper he ate a whole pan of biscuits by himself.

Naw. I say.

He sure did. And had two big glasses of butter milk along with it. This was after supper was over, too. I was giving the children they baths, getting 'em ready for bed. He sposed to be washing the dishes. Stead of washing plates, he cleaning 'em with his mouth.

Well maybe he was extra hungry. Yall is been working hard.

Not that hard, she say. And this morning, for breakfast, darn if he didn't have six eggs. After all that food he look too sick to walk. When us got to the field I thought he was going to faint.

If Sofia say DARN something wrong. Maybe he don't want to wash dishes, I say. His daddy never wash a dish in his life.

You reckon? she say. He seem so much to love it. To tell the truth, he love that part of housekeeping a heap more 'en me. I rather be out in the fields or fooling with the animals. Even chopping wood. But he love cooking and cleaning and doing little things round the house.

He sure is a good cook, I say. Big surprise to me that he knew anything about it. He never cooked so much as a egg when he lived at home.

I bet he wanted to, she said. It seem so natural to him. But Mr. _____. You know how he is.

Oh, he all right, I say.

You feeling yourself, Miss Celie? Sofia ast.

I mean, he all right in some things, not in others.

Oh, she say. Anyway, next time he come here, notice if he eat anything.

I notice what he eat all right. First thing, coming up the steps, I give him a close look. He still skinny, bout half Sofia size, but I see a little pot beginning under his overalls.

What you got to eat, Miss Celie? he say, going straight to the warmer and a piece of fried chicken, then on to the safe for a slice of blackberry pie. He stand by the table and munch, munch. You got any sweet milk? he ast.

Got clabber, I say.

He say, Well, I love clabber. And dip him out some.

Sofia must not be feeding you, I say.

Why you say that? he ast with his mouth full.

Well, it not that long after dinner and here you is hungry again.

He don't say nothing. Eat.

Course, I say, suppertime not too far off either. Bout three four hours.

He rummage through the drawer for a spoon to eat the clabber with. He see a slice of cornbread on the shelf back of the stove, he grab it and crumble it into the glass.

Us go back out on the porch and he put his foots up on the railing. Eat his clabber and cornbread with the glass near bout to his nose. Remind me of a hog at the troth.

Food tasting like food to you these days huh, I say, listening to him chew.

He don't say nothing. Eat.

I look out cross the yard. I see Sofia dragging a ladder and then lean it up gainst the house. She wearing a old pair of Harpo pants. Got her head tied up in a headrag. She clam up the ladder to the roof, begin to hammer in nails. Sound echo cross the yard like shots.

Harpo eat, watch her.

Then he belch. Say, Scuse me, Miss Celie. Take the glass and spoon back in the kitchen. Come out and say Bye.

No matter what happening now. No matter who come. No matter what they say or do, Harpo eat through it. Food on his mind morning, noon and night. His belly grow and grow, but the rest of him don't. He begin to look like he big.

When it due? us ast.

Harpo don't say nothing. Reach for another piece of pie.

Dear God,

Harpo staying with us this week-end. Friday night after Mr.
———— and Shug and me done gone to bed, I heard this
somebody crying. Harpo sitting out on the steps, crying like his
heart gon break. Oh, boo-hoo, and boo-hoo. He got his head in
his hands, tears and snot running down his chin. I give him a
hansker. He blow his nose, look up at me out of two eyes close
like fists.

What happen to your eyes? I ast.

He clam round in his mind for a story to tell, then fall back
on the truth.

Sofia, he say.

You still bothering Sofia? I ast.

She my wife, he say.

That don't mean you got to keep on bothering her, I say.
Sofia love you, she a good wife. Good to the children and good
looking. Hardworking. Godfearing and *clean*. I don't know what
more you want.

Harpo sniffle.

I want her to do what I say, like you do for Pa.

Oh, Lord, I say.

When Pa tell you to do something, you do it, he say. When
he say not to, you don't. You don't do what he say, he beat
you.

Sometime beat me anyhow, I say, whether I do what he say
or not.

That's right, say Harpo. But not Sofia. She do what she
want, don't pay me no mind at all. I try to beat her, she black my
eyes. Oh, boo-hoo, he cry. Boo-hoo-hoo.

I start to take back my hansker. Maybe push him and his

black eyes off the step. I think bout Sofia. She tickle me. I used to hunt game with a bow and arrow, she say.

Some womens can't be beat, I say. Sofia one of them. Besides, Sofia love you. She probably be happy to do most of what you say if you ast her right. She not mean, she not spiteful. She don't hold a grudge.

He sit there hanging his head, looking retard.

Harpo, I say, giving him a shake, Sofia *love* you. You *love* Sofia.

He look up at me best he can out his fat little eyes. Yes ma'am? he say.

Mr. _____ marry me to take care of his children. I marry him cause my daddy made me. I don't love Mr. _____ and he don't love me.

But you his wife, he say, just like Sofia mine. The wife spose to mind.

Do Shug Avery mind Mr. _____? I ast. She the woman he wanted to marry. She call him Albert, tell him his drawers stink in a minute. Little as he is, when she git her weight back she can sit on him if he try to bother her.

Why I mention weight. Harpo start to cry again. Then he start to be sick. He lean over the edge of the step and vomit and vomit. Look like every piece of pie for the last year come up. When he empty I put him in the bed next to Shug's little room. He fall right off to sleep.

Dear God,

I go visit Sofia, she still working on the roof.

The darn thing leak, she say.

She out to the woodpile making shingles. She put a big square piece of wood on the chopping block and chop, chop, she make big flat shingles. She put the ax down and ast me do I want some lemonade.

I look at her good. Except for a bruise on her wrist, she don't look like she got a scratch on her.

How it going with you and Harpo? I ast.

Well, she say, he stop eating so much. But maybe this just a spell.

He trying to git as big as you, I say.

She suck in her breath. I kinda thought so, she say, and let out her breath real slow.

All the children come running up, Mama, Mama, us want lemonade. She pour out five glasses for them, two for us. Us sit in a wooden swing she made last summer and hung on the shady end of the porch.

I'm gitting tired of Harpo, she say. All he think about since us married is how to make me mind. He don't want a wife, he want a dog.

He your husband, I say. Got to stay with him. Else, what you gon do?

My sister husband caught in the draft, she say. They don't have no children, Odessa love children. He left her on a little farm. Maybe I go stay with them a while. Me and my children.

I think bout my sister Nettie. Thought so sharp it go through me like a pain. Somebody to run to. It seem too sweet to bear.

Sofia go on, frowning at her glass.

I don't like to go to bed with him no more, she say. Used to be when he touch me I'd go all out my head. Now when he touch me I just don't want to be bothered. Once he git on top of me I think bout how that's where he always want to be. She sip her lemonade. I use to love that part of it, she say. I use to chase him home from the field. Git all hot just watching him put the children to bed. But no more. Now I feels tired all the time. No interest.

Now, now, I say. Sleep on it some, maybe it come back. But I say this just to be saying something. I don't know nothing bout it. Mr. _____ clam on top of me, do his business, in ten minutes us both sleep. Only time I feel something stirring down there is when I think bout Shug. And that like running to the end of the road and it turn back on itself.

You know the worst part? she say. The worst part is I don't think he notice. He git up there and enjoy himself just the same. No matter what I'm thinking. No matter what I feel. It just him. Heartfeeling don't even seem to enter into it. She snort. The fact he can do it like that make me want to kill him.

Us look up the path to the house, see Shug and Mr. _____ sitting on the steps. He reach over and pick something out her hair.

I don't know, say Sofia. Maybe I won't go. Deep down I still love Harpo, but—he just makes me *real* tired. She yawn. Laugh. I need a vacation, she say. Then she go back to the woodpile, start making some more shingles for the roof.

Dear God,

Sofia right about her sisters. They all big strong healthy girls, look like amazons. They come early one morning in two wagons to pick Sofia up. She don't have much to take, her and the children clothes, a mattress she made last winter, a looking glass and a rocking chair. The children.

Harpo sit on the steps acting like he don't care. He making a net for seining fish. He look out toward the creek every once in a while and whistle a little tune. But it nothing compared to the way he usually whistle. His little whistle sound like it lost way down in a jar, and the jar in the bottom of the creek.

At the last minute I decide to give Sofia the quilt. I don't know what her sister place be like, but we been having right smart cold weather long in now. For all I know, she and the children have to sleep on the floor.

You gon let her go? I ast Harpo.

He look like only a fool could ast the question. He puff back, She made up her mind to go, he say. How I'm gon stop her? Let her go on, he say, cutting his eyes at her sister wagons.

Us sit on the steps together. All us hear from inside is the thump, thump, thump of plump and stout feet. All Sofia sisters moving round together at one time make the house shake.

Where us going? ast the oldest girl.

Going to visit Aunt Odessa, say Sofia.

Daddy coming? she ast.

Naw, say Sofia.

How come daddy ain't coming? another one ast.

Daddy need to stay here and take care of the house. Look after Dilsey, Coco and Boo.

The child come stand in front of his daddy and just look at him real good.

You not coming? he say.

Harpo say, Naw.

Child go whisper to the baby crawling round on the floor, Daddy not coming with us, what you think of that.

Baby sit real still, strain real hard, fart.

Us all laugh, but it sad too. Harpo pick it up, finger the daidie, and get her ready for a change.

I don't think she wet, say Sofia. Just gas.

But he change her anyway. Him and the baby over in a corner of the little porch out of the way of traffic. He use the old dry daidie to wipe his eyes.

At the last, he hand Sofia the baby and she sling it up side her hip, sling a sack of daidies and food over her shoulder, corral all the little ones together, tell 'em to Say Good-bye to Daddy. Then she hug me best she can what with the baby and all, and she clam up on the wagon. Every sister just about got a child tween her knees, cept the two driving the mules, and they all quiet as they leave Sofia and Harpo yard and drive on up past the house.

Dear God,

Sofia gone six months, Harpo act like a different man. Used to be a homebody, now all the time in the road.

I ast him what going on. He say, Miss Celie, I done learned a few things.

One thing he learned is that he cute. Another that he smart. Plus, he can make money. He don't say who the teacher is.

I hadn't heard so much hammering since before Sofia left, but every evening after he leave the field, he knocking down and nailing up. Sometime his friend Swain come by to help. The two of them work all into the night. Mr. _____ have to call down to tell them to shut up the racket.

What you building? I ast.

Jukejoint, he say.

Way back here?

No further back than any of the others.

I don't know nothing bout no others, only bout the Lucky Star.

Jukejoint sposed to be back in the woods, say Harpo. Nobody be bothered by the loud music. The dancing. The fights.

Swain say, the killings.

Harpo say, and the polices don't know where to look.

What Sofia gon say bout what you doing to her house? I ast. Spose she and the children come back. Where they gon sleep.

They ain't coming back, say Harpo, nailing together planks for a counter.

How you know? I ast.

He don't answer. He keep working, doing every thing with Swain.

Dear God,

The first week, nobody come. Second week, three or four. Third week, one. Harpo sit behind his little counter listening to Swain pick his box.

He got cold drinks, he got barbecue, he got chitlins, got store bought bread. He got a sign saying Harpo's tacked up on the side of the house and another one out on the road. But he ain't got no customers.

I go down the path to the yard, stand outside, look in. Harpo look out and wave.

Come on in, Miss Celie, he say.

I say, Naw thank you.

Mr. _____ sometime walk down, have a cold drink, listen to Swain. Miss Shug walk down too, every once in a while. She still wearing her little shifts, and I still cornrow her hair, but it getting long now and she say soon she want it press.

Harpo puzzle by Shug. One reason is she say whatever come to mind, forgit about polite. Sometime I see him staring at her real hard when he don't think I'm looking.

One day he say, Nobody coming way out here just to hear Swain. Wonder could I get the Queen Honeybee?

I don't know, I said. She a lot better now, always humming or singing something. She probably be glad to git back to work. Why don't you ask her?

Shug say his place not much compared to what she used to, but she think maybe she might grace it with a song.

Harpo and Swain got Mr. _____ to give 'em some of Shug old announcements from out the trunk. Crossed out The Lucky Star of Coalman Road, put in Harpo's of _____ plantation.

Stuck 'em on trees tween the turn off to our road and town. The first Saturday night so many folks come they couldn't git in.

Shug, Shug baby, us thought you was dead.

Five out of a dozen say hello to Shug like that.

And come to find out it was you, Shug say with a big grin.

At last I git to see Shug Avery work. I git to watch her. I git to hear her.

Mr. _____ didn't want me to come. Wives don't go to places like that, he say.

Yeah, but Celie going, say Shug, while I press her hair. Spose I git sick while I'm singing, she say. Spose my dress come undone? She wearing a skintight red dress look like the straps made out of two pieces of thread.

Mr. _____ mutter, putting on his clothes. My wife can't do this. My wife can't do that. No wife of mines . . . He go on and on.

Shug Avery finally say, Good thing I ain't your damn wife.

He hush then. All three of us go down to Harpo's. Mr. _____ and me sit at the same table. Mr. _____ drink whiskey. I have a cold drink.

First Shug sing a song by somebody name Bessie Smith. She say Bessie somebody she know. Old friend. It call A Good Man Is Hard to Find. She look over at Mr. _____ a little when she sing that. I look over at him too. For such a little man, he all puff up. Look like all he can do to stay in his chair. I look at Shug and I feel my heart begin to cramp. It hurt me so, I cover it with my hand. I think I might as well be under the table, for all they care. I hate the way I look, I hate the way I'm dress. Nothing but churchgoing clothes in my chifferobe. And Mr. _____ looking at Shug's bright black skin in her tight red dress, her feet in little sassy red shoes. Her hair shining in waves.

Before I know it, tears meet under my chin.

And I'm confuse.

He love looking at Shug. I love looking at Shug.

But Shug don't love looking at but one of us. Him.

But that the way it spose to be. I know that. But if that so, why my heart hurt me so?

My head droop so it near bout in my glass.

Then I hear my name.

Shug saying Celie. Miss Celie. And I look up where she at.

She say my name again. She say this song I'm bout to sing is call Miss Celie's song. Cause she scratched it out of my head when I was sick.

First she hum it a little, like she do at home. Then she sing the words.

It all about some no count man doing her wrong, again. But I don't listen to that part. I look at her and I hum along a little with the tune.

First time somebody made something and name it after me.

Dear God,

Pretty soon it be time for Shug to go. She sing every week-end now at Harpo's. He make right smart money off of her, and she make some too. Plus she gitting strong again and stout. First night or two her songs come out good but a little weak, now she belt them out. Folks out in the yard hear her with no trouble. She and Swain sound real good together. She sing, he pick his box. It nice at Harpo's. Little tables all round the room with candles on them that I made, lot of little tables outside too, by the creek. Sometime I look down the path from our house and it look like a swarm of lightening bugs all in and through Sofia house. In the evening Shug can't wait to go down there.

One day she say to me, Well, Miss Celie, I believe it time for me to go.

When? I ast.

Early next month, she say. June. June a good time to go off into the world.

I don't say nothing. Feel like I felt when Nettie left.

She come over and put her hand on my shoulder.

He beat me when you not here, I say.

Who do, she say, Albert?

Mr. _____, I say.

I can't believe it, she say. She sit down on the bench next to me real hard, like she drop.

What he beat you for? she ast.

For being me and not you.

Oh, Miss Celie, she say, and put her arms around me.

Us sit like that for maybe half a hour. Then she kiss me on the fleshy part of my shoulder and stand up.

I won't leave, she say, until I know Albert won't even think about beating you.

Dear God,

Now we all know she going sometime soon, they sleep together at night. Not every night, but almost every night, from Friday to Monday.

He go down to Harpo's to watch her sing. And just to look at her. Then way late they come home. They giggle and they talk and they rassle until morning. Then they go to bed until it time for her to get ready to go back to work.

First time it happen, it was a accident. Feeling just carried them away. That what Shug say. He don't say nothing.

She ast me, Tell me the truth, she say, do you mind if Albert sleep with me?

I think, I don't care who Albert sleep with. But I don't say that.

I say, You might git big again.

She say, Naw, not with my sponge and all.

You still love him, I ast.

She say, I got what you call a passion for him. If I was ever going to have a husband he'd a been it. But he weak, she say. Can't make up his mind what he want. And from what you tell me he a bully. Some things I love about him though, she say. He smell right to me. He so little. He make me laugh.

You like to sleep with him? I ast.

Yeah, Celie, she say, I have to confess, I just *love* it. Don't you?

Naw, I say. Mr. _____ can tell you, I don't like it at all. What is it to like? He git up on you, heist your nightgown round your waist, plunge in. Most times I pretend I ain't there. He never know the difference. Never ast me how I feel, nothing. Just do his business, get off, go to sleep.

She start to laugh. Do his business, she say. Do his business. Why, Miss Celie. You make it sound like he going to the toilet on you.

That what it feel like, I say.

She stop laughing.

You never enjoy it at all? she ast, puzzle. Not even with your children daddy?

Never, I say.

Why Miss Celie, she say, you still a virgin.

What? I ast.

Listen, she say, right down there in your pussy is a little button that gits real hot when you do you know what with somebody. It git hotter and hotter and then it melt. That the good part. But other parts good too, she say. Lot of sucking go on, here and there, she say. Lot of finger and tongue work.

Button? Finger and *tongue*? My face hot enough to melt itself.

She say, Here, take this mirror and go look at yourself down there, I bet you never seen it, have you?

Naw.

And I bet you never seen Albert down there either.

I felt him, I say.

I stand there with the mirror.

She say, What, too shame even to go off and look at yourself? And you look so cute too, she say, laughing. All dressed up for Harpo's, smelling good and everything, but scared to look at your own pussy.

You come with me while I look, I say.

And us run off to my room like two little prankish girls.

You guard the door, I say.

She giggle. Okay, she say. Nobody coming. Coast clear.

I lie back on the bed and haul up my dress. Yank down my bloomers. Stick the looking glass tween my legs. Ugh. All that hair. Then my pussy lips be black. Then inside look like a wet rose.

It a lot prettier than you thought, ain't it? she say from the door.

It mine, I say. Where the button?

Right up near the top, she say. The part that stick out a little.

I look at her and touch it with my finger. A little shiver go through me. Nothing much. But just enough to tell me this the right button to mash. Maybe.

She say, While you looking, look at your titties too. I haul up my dress and look at my titties. Think bout my babies sucking them. Remember the little shiver I felt then too. Sometimes a big shiver. Best part about having the babies was feeding 'em.

Albert and Harpo coming, she say. And I yank up my drawers and yank down my dress. I feel like us been doing something wrong.

I don't care if you sleep with him, I say.

And she take me at my word.

I take me at my word too.

But when I hear them together all I can do is pull the quilt over my head and finger my little button and titties and cry.

Dear God,

One night while Shug singing a hot one, who should come prancing through the door of Harpo's but Sofia.

She with a big tall hefty man look like a prize fighter.

She her usual stout and bouncy self.

Oh, Miss Celie, she cry. It so good to see you again. It even good to see Mr. _____, she say. She take one of his hands. Even if his handshake is a little weak, she say.

He act real glad to see her.

Here, pull up a chair, he say. Have a cold drink.

Gimme a shot of white lightening, she say.

Prizefighter pull up a chair, straddle it backwards, hug on Sofia like they at home.

I see Harpo cross the room with his little yellowskin girlfriend. He look at Sofia like she a hant.

This Henry Broadnax, Sofia say. Everybody call him Buster. Good friend of the family.

How you all? he say. He smile pleasant and us keep listening to the music. Shug wearing a gold dress that show her titties near bout to the nipple. Everybody sorta hoping something break. But that dress strong.

Man oh man, say Buster. Fire department won't do. Somebody call the Law.

Mr. _____ whisper to Sofia. Where your children at?

She whisper back, My children at home, where yours?

He don't say nothing.

Both the girls bigged and gone. Bub in and out of jail. If his granddaddy wasn't the colored uncle of the sheriff who look just like Bub, Bub be lynch by now.

I can't git over how good Sofia look.

Most women with five children look a little peaked, I say to her cross the table when Shug finish her song. You look like you ready for five more.

Oh, she say, I got six children now, Miss Celie.

Six. I am shock.

She toss her head, look over at Harpo. Life don't stop just cause you leave home, Miss Celie. You know that.

My life stop when I left home, I think. But then I think again. It stop with Mr. _____ maybe, but start up again with Shug.

Shug come over and she and Sofia hug.

Shug say, Girl, you look like a good time, you do.

That when I notice how Shug talk and act sometimes like a man. Men say stuff like that to women, Girl, you look like a good time. Women always talk bout hair and health. How many babies living or dead, or got teef. Not bout how some woman they hugging on look like a good time.

All the men got they eyes glued to Shug's bosom. I got my eyes glued there too. I feel my nipples harden under my dress. My little button sort of perk up too. Shug, I say to her in my mind, Girl, you looks like a real good time, the Good Lord knows you do.

What you doing here? ast Harpo.

Sofia say, Come to hear Miss Shug. You got a nice place here Harpo. She look around. This and that her eyes admire.

Harpo say, It just a scandless, a woman with five children hanging out in a jukejoint at night.

Sofia eye go cool. She look him up and down.

Since he quit stuffing himself, he gained a bunch of weight, face, head and all, mostly from drinking home brew and eating left-over barbecue. By now he just about her size.

A woman need a little fun, once in a while, she say.

A woman need to be at home, he say.

She say, This is my home. Though I do think it go better as a jukejoint.

Harpo look at the prize fighter. Prizefighter push back his chair a little, pick up his drink.

I don't fight Sofia battle, he say. My job to love her and take her where she want to go.

Harpo breathe some relief.

Let's dance, he say.

Sofia laugh, git up. Put both arms round his neck. They slow drag out cross the floor.

Harpo little yellowskin girlfriend sulk, hanging over the bar. She a nice girl, friendly and everything, but she like me. She do anything Harpo say.

He give her a little nickname, too, call her Squeak.

Pretty soon Squeak git up her nerve to try to cut in.

Harpo try to turn Sofia so she can't see. But Squeak keep on tapping and tapping on his shoulder.

Finally he and Sofia stop dancing. They bout two feet from our table.

Shug say, uh-oh, and point with her chin, something bout to blow right there.

Who dis woman, say Squeak, in this little teenouncy voice.

You know who she is, say Harpo.

Squeak turn to Sofia. Say, You better leave him alone.

Sofia say, Fine with me. She turn round to leave.

Harpo grab her by the arm. Say, You don't have to go no where. Hell, this your house.

Squeak say, What you mean, Dis her house? She walk out on you. Walk away from the house. It over now, she say to Sofia.

Sofia say, Fine with me. Try to pull away from Harpo grip. He hold her tight.

Listen Squeak, say Harpo, Can't a man dance with his own wife?

Squeak say, Not if he my man he can't. You hear that, bitch, she say to Sofia.

Sofia gitting a little tired of Squeak, I can tell by her ears. They sort of push back. But she say again, sorta end of argument like, Hey, fine with me.

Squeak slap her up cross the head.

What she do that for. Sofia don't even deal in little ladyish things such as slaps. She ball up her fist, draw back, and knock two of Squeak's side teef out. Squeak hit the floor. One toof hanging on her lip, the other one upside my cold drink glass.

Then Squeak start banging on Harpo leg with her shoe.

You git that bitch out a here, she cry, blood and slobber running down her chin.

Harpo and Sofia stand side by side looking down at Squeak, but I don't think they hear her. Harpo still holding Sofia arm. Maybe half a minute go by. Finally he turn loose her arm, reach down and cradle poor little Squeak in his arms. He coo and coo at her like she a baby.

Sofia come over and git the prizefighter. They go out the door and don't look back. Then us hear a car motor start.

Dear God,

Harpo mope. Wipe the counter, light a cigarette, look outdoors, walk up and down. Little Squeak run long all up under him trying to git his tension. Baby this, she say, Baby that. Harpo look through her head, blow smoke.

Squeak come over to the corner where me and Mr. _____ at. She got two bright gold teef in the side of her mouth, generally grin all the time. Now she cry. Miss Celie, she say, What the matter with Harpo?

Sofia in jail, I say.

In jail? She look like I say Sofia on the moon.

What she in jail for? she ast.

Sassing the mayor's wife, I say.

Squeak pull up a chair. Look down my throat.

What your real name? I ast her. She say, Mary Agnes.

Make Harpo call you by your real name, I say. Then maybe he see you even when he trouble.

She look at me puzzle. I let it go. I tell her what one of Sofia sister tell me and Mr. _____.

Sofia and the prizefighter and all the children got in the prizefighter car and went to town. Clam out on the street looking like somebody. Just then the mayor and his wife come by.

All these children, say the mayor's wife, digging in her pocketbook. Cute as little buttons though, she say. She stop, put her hand on one of the children head. Say, and such strong white teef.

Sofia and the prizefighter don't say nothing. Wait for her to pass. Mayor wait too, stand back and tap his foot, watch her with a little smile. Now Millie, he say. Always going on over colored. Miss Millie finger the children some more, finally look at Sofia and the prizefighter. She look at the prizefighter car. She eye Sofia wristwatch. She say to Sofia, All your children so clean, she say, would you like to work for me, be my maid?

Sofia say, Hell no.

She say, What you say?

Sofia say, Hell no.

Mayor look at Sofia, push his wife out the way. Stick out his chest. Girl, what you say to Miss Millie?

Sofia say, I say, Hell no.

He slap her.

I stop telling it right there.

Squeak on the edge of her seat. She wait. Look down my throat some more.

No need to say no more, Mr. _____ say. You know what happen if somebody slap Sofia.

Squeak go white as a sheet. *Naw*, she say.

Naw nothing, I say. Sofia knock the man down.

The polices come, start slinging the children off the mayor, bang they heads together. Sofia really start to fight. They drag her to the ground.

This far as I can go with it, look like. My eyes git full of water and my throat close.

Poor Squeak all scrunch down in her chair, trembling.

They beat Sofia, Mr. _____ say.

Squeak fly up like she sprung, run over hind the counter to Harpo, put her arms round him. They hang together a long time, cry.

What the prizefighter do in all this? I ast Sofia sister, Odessa.

He want to jump in, she say. Sofia say No, take the children home.

Polices have they guns on him anyway. One move, he dead. Six of them, you know.

Mr. _____ go plead with the sheriff to let us see Sofia. Bub be in so much trouble, look so much like the sheriff, he and Mr.

_____ almost on family terms. Just long as Mr. _____ know he colored.

Sheriff say, She a crazy woman, your boy's wife. You know that?

Mr. _____ say, Yassur, us do know it. Been trying to tell Harpo she crazy for twelve years. Since way before they marry. Sofia come from crazy peoples, Mr. _____ say, it not all her fault. And then again, the sheriff know how womens is, anyhow.

Sheriff think bout the women he know, say, Yep, you right there.

Mr. _____ say, We gon tell her she crazy too, if us ever do git in to see her.

Sheriff say, Well make sure you do. And tell her she lucky she alive.

When I see Sofia I don't know why she still alive. They crack her skull, they crack her ribs. They tear her nose loose on one side. They blind her in one eye. She swole from head to foot. Her tongue the size of my arm, it stick out tween her teef like a piece of rubber. She can't talk. And she just about the color of a eggplant.

Scare me so bad I near bout drop my grip. But I don't. I put it on the floor of the cell, take out comb and brush, nightgown, witch hazel and alcohol and I start to work on her. The colored tendant bring me water to wash her with, and I start at her two little slits for eyes.

Dear God,

They put Sofia to work in the prison laundry. All day long from five to eight she washing clothes. Dirty convict uniforms, nasty sheets and blankets piled way over her head. Us see her twice a month for half a hour. Her face yellow and sickly, her fingers look like fatty sausage.

Everything nasty here, she say, even the air. Food bad enough to kill you with it. Roaches here, mice, flies, lice and even a snake or two. If you say anything they strip you, make you sleep on a cement floor without a light.

How you manage? us ast.

Every time they ast me to do something, Miss Celie, I act like I'm you. I jump right up and do just what they say.

She look wild when she say that, and her bad eye wander round the room.

Mr. _____ suck in his breath. Harpo groan. Miss Shug cuss. She come from Memphis special to see Sofia.

I can't fix my mouth to say how I feel.

I'm a good prisoner, she say. Best convict they ever see. They can't believe I'm the one sass the mayor's wife, knock the mayor down. She laugh. It sound like something from a song. The part where everybody done gone home but you.

Twelve years a long time to be good though, she say.

Maybe you git out on good behavior, say Harpo.

Good behavior ain't good enough for them, say Sofia. Nothing less than sliding on your belly with your tongue on they boots can even git they attention. I dream of murder, she say, I dream of murder sleep or wake.

Us don't say nothing.

How the children? she ast.

They all fine, say Harpo. Tween Odessa and Squeak, they git by.

Say thank you to Squeak, she say. Tell Odessa I think about her.

Dear God,

Us all sit round the table after supper. Me, Shug, Mr.
———, Squeak, the prizefighter, Odessa and two more of Sofia
sisters.

Sofia not gon last, say Mr. ———.

Yeah, say Harpo, she look little crazy to me.

And what she had to say, say Shug. My God.

Us got to do something, say Mr. ——— and be right quick
about it.

What can us do? ast Squeak. She look a little haggard with
all Sofia and Harpo children sprung on her at once, but she
carry on. Hair a little stringy, slip show, but she carry on.

Bust her out, say Harpo. Git some dynamite off the gang
that's building that big bridge down the road, blow the whole
prison to kingdom come.

Shut up, Harpo, say Mr. ———, us trying to think.

I got it, say the prizefighter, smuggle in a gun. Well, he rub
his chin, maybe smuggle in a file.

Naw, say Odessa. They just come after her if she leave that
way.

Me and Squeak don't say nothing. I don't know what she
think, but I think bout angels, God coming down by chariot,
swinging down real low and carrying ole Sofia home. I see 'em
all as clear as day. Angels all in white, white hair and white
eyes, look like albinos. God all white too, looking like some
stout white man work at the bank. Angels strike they cymbals,
one of them blow his horn, God blow out a big breath of fire and
suddenly Sofia free.

Who the warden's black kinfolks? say Mr. ———.

Nobody say nothing.

Finally the prizefighter speak. What his name? he ast.

Hodges, say Harpo. Bubber Hodges.

Old man Henry Hodges' boy, say Mr. _____. Used to live out on the old Hodges' place.

Got a brother name Jimmy? ast Squeak.

Yeah, say Mr. _____. Brother name Jimmy. Married to that Quitman girl. Daddy own the hardware. You know them?

Squeak duck her head. Mumble something.

Say what? ast Mr. _____.

Squeak cheek turn red. She mumble again.

He your what? Mr. _____ ast.

Cousin, she say.

Mr. _____ look at her.

Daddy, she say. She cut her eye at Harpo. Look at the floor.

He know anything bout it? ast Mr. _____.

Yeah, she say. He got three children by my mama. Two younger than me.

His brother know anything bout it? ast Mr. _____.

One time he come by the house with Mr. Jimmy, he give us all quarters, say we sure do look like Hodges.

Mr. _____ rear back in his chair, give Squeak a good look from head to foot. Squeak push her greasy brown hair back from her face.

Yeah, say Mr. _____. I see the resemblance. He bring his chair down on the floor.

Well, look like you the one to go.

Go where, ast Squeak.

Go see the warden. He your uncle.

Dear God,

Us dress Squeak like she a white woman, only her clothes patch. She got on a starch and iron dress, high heel shoes with scuffs, and a old hat somebody give Shug. Us give her a old pocketbook look like a quilt and a little black bible. Us wash her hair and git all the grease out, then I put it up in two plaits that cross over her head. Us bathe her so clean she smell like a good clean floor.

What I'm gon say? she ast.

Say you living with Sofia husband and her husband say Sofia not being punish enough. Say she laugh at the fool she make of the guards. Say she gitting along just fine where she at. Happy even, long as she don't have to be no white woman maid.

Gracious God, say Squeak, how I'm gonna tune up my mouth to say all that?

He ast you who you is, make him remember. Tell him how much that quarter he give you meant to you.

That was fifteen years ago, say Squeak, he ain't gonna remember that.

Make him see the Hodges in you, say Odessa. He'll remember.

Tell him you just think justice ought to be done, yourself. But make sure he know you living with Sofia husband, say Shug. Make sure you git in the part bout being happy where she at, worse thing could happen to her is to be some white lady maid.

I don't know, say the prizefighter. This sound mighty much like some ole uncle Tomming to me.

Shug snort, Well, she say, Uncle Tom wasn't call Uncle for nothing.

Dear God,

Poor little Squeak come home with a limp. Her dress rip. Her hat missing and one of the heels come off her shoe.

What happen? us ast.

He saw the Hodges in me, she say. And he didn't like it one bit.

Harpo come up the steps from the car. My wife beat up, my woman rape, he say. I ought to go back out there with guns, maybe set fire to the place, burn the crackers up.

Shut up, Harpo, say Squeak. I'm telling it.

And she do.

Say, the minute I walk through the door, he remembered me.

What he say? us ast.

Say, What you want? I say, I come out of the interest I haves in seeing justice is done. What you say you want? he ast again.

I say what yall told me to say. Bout Sofia not being punish enough. Say she happy in prison, strong girl like her. Her main worry is just the thought of ever being some white woman maid. That what start the fight, you know, I say. Mayor's wife ask Sofia to be her maid. Sofia say she never going to be no white woman's nothing, let alone maid.

That so? he ast, all the time looking me over real good.

Yessir, I say. Say, prison suit her just fine. Shoot, washing and ironing all day is all she do at home. She got six children, you know.

That a fact? he say.

He come from behind his desk, lean over my chair.

Who your folks? he ast.

I tell him my mama's name, grandmama's name. Grandpa's name.

Who your daddy? he ast. Where you git them eyes?

Ain't got no daddy, I say.

Come on now, he say. Ain't I seen you before?

I say, Yessir. And one time bout ten years ago, when I was a little girl, you give me a quarter. I sure did preshate it, I say.

I don't remember that, he say.

You come by the house with my mama friend, Mr. Jimmy, I say.

Squeak look round at all of us. Then take a deep breath. Mumble.

Say what? ast Odessa.

Yeah, say Shug, if you can't tell us, who you gon tell, God?

He took my hat off, say Squeak. Told me to undo my dress. She drop her head, put her face in her hands.

My God, say Odessa, and he your uncle.

He say if he was my uncle he wouldn't do it to me. That be a sin. But this just little fornication. Everybody guilty of that.

She turn her face up to Harpo. Harpo, she say, do you really love me, or just my color?

Harpo say, I love you, Squeak. He kneel down and try to put his arms round her waist.

She stand up. My name Mary Agnes, she say.

Dear God,

6 months after Mary Agnes went to git Sofia out of prison, she begin to sing. First she sing Shug's songs, then she begin to make up songs her own self.

She got the kind of voice you never think of trying to sing a song. It little, it high, it sort of meowing. But Mary Agnes don't care.

Pretty soon, us git used to it. Then us like it a whole lot.

Harpo don't know what to make of it.

It seem funny to me, he say to me and Mr. _____. So sudden. It put me in the mind of a gramaphone. Sit in the corner a year silent as the grave. Then you put a record on, it come to life.

Wonder if she still mad Sofia knock her teef out? I ast.

Yeah, she mad. But what good being mad gon do? She not evil, she know Sofia life hard to bear right now.

How she git long with the children? ast Mr. _____.

They love her, say Harpo. She let 'em do anything they want.

Oh-oh, I say.

Besides, he say, Odessa and Sofia other sisters always on hand to take up the slack. They bring up children like military.

Squeak sing,

> They calls me yellow
> like yellow be my name
>
> They calls me yellow
> like yellow be my name

But if yellow is a name
Why ain't black the same

Well, if I say Hey black girl
Lord, she try to ruin my game

Dear God

Sofia say to me today, I just can't understand it.

What that? I ast.

Why we ain't already kill them off.

Three years after she beat she out of the wash house, got her color and her weight back, look like her old self, just all time think bout killing somebody.

Too many to kill off, I say. Us outnumbered from the start. I speck we knock over one or two, though, here and there, through the years, I say.

We sit on a piece of old crate out near the edge of Miss Millie's yard. Rusty nails stick out long the bottom and when us move they creak gainst the wood.

Sofia job to watch the children play ball. The little boy throw the ball to the little girl, she try to catch it with her eyes shut. It roll up under Sofia foot.

Throw me the ball, say the little boy, with his hands on his hip. Throw me the ball.

Sofia mutter to herself, half to me. I'm here to watch, not to throw, she say. She don't make a move toward the ball.

Don't you hear me talking to you, he shout. He maybe six years old, brown hair, ice blue eyes. He come steaming up to where us sit, haul off and kick Sofia leg. She swing her foot to one side and he scream.

What the trouble? I ast.

Done stab his foot with a rusty nail, Sofia say.

Sure enough, blood come leaking through his shoe.

His little sister come watch him cry. He turn redder and redder. Call his mama.

Miss Millie come running. She scared of Sofia. Everytime she talk to her it like she expect the worst. She don't stand close to her either. When she git a few yards from where us sit, she motion for Billy to come there.

My foot, he say to her.

Sofia do it? she ast.

Little girl pipe up. Billy do it his own self, she say. Trying to kick Sofia leg. The little girl dote on Sofia, always stick up for her. Sofia never notice, she as deef to the little girl as she is to her brother.

Miss Millie cut her eyes at her, put one arm round Billy shoulder and they limp into the back of the house. Little girl follow, wave bye-bye to us.

She seem like a right sweet little thing, I say to Sofia.

Who is? She frown.

The little girl, I say. What they call her, Eleanor Jane?

Yeah, say Sofia, with a real puzzle look on her face, I wonder why she was ever born.

Well, I say, us don't have to wonder that bout darkies.

She giggle. Miss Celie, she say, you just as crazy as you can be.

This the first giggle I heard in three years.

Dear God,

Sofia would make a dog laugh, talking about those people she work for. They have the nerve to try to make us think slavery fell through because of us, say Sofia. Like us didn't have sense enough to handle it. All the time breaking hoe handles and letting the mules loose in the wheat. But how anything they build can last a day is a wonder to me. They backward, she say. Clumsy, and unlucky.

Mayor _____ bought Miz Millie a new car, cause she said if colored could have cars then one for her was past due. So he bought her a car, only he refuse to show her how to drive it. Every day he come home from town he look at her, look out the window at her car, say, How you enjoying 'er Miz Millie. She fly off the sofa in a huff, slam the door going in the bathroom.

She ain't got no friends.

So one day she say to me, car been sitting out in the yard two months, Sofia, do you know how to drive? I guess she remembered first seeing me up gainst Buster Broadnax car.

Yes ma'am, I say. I'm slaving away cleaning that big post they got down at the bottom of the stair. They act real funny bout that post. No finger prints is sposed to be on it, ever.

Do you think you could teach me? she says.

One of Sofia children break in, the oldest boy. He tall and handsome, all the time serious. And mad a lot.

He say, Don't say slaving, Mama.

Sofia say, Why not? They got me in a little storeroom up under the house, hardly bigger than Odessa's porch, and just about as warm in the winter time. I'm at they beck and call all night and all day. They won't let me see my children. They won't let me see no mens. Well, after five years they let me see you once a year. I'm a slave, she say. What would you call it?

A captive, he say.

Sofia go on with her story, only look at him like she glad he hers.

So I say, Yes ma'am. I can teach you, if it the same kind of car I learned on.

Next thing you know there go me and Miz Millie all up and down the road. First I drive and she watch, then she start to try to drive and I watch her. Up and down the road. Soon as I finish cooking breakfast, putting it on the table, washing dishes and sweeping the floor—and just before I go git the mail out of the box down by the road—we go give Miz Millie her driving lesson.

Well, after while she got the hang of it, more or less. Then she really git it. Then one day when we come home from riding, she say to me, I'm gonna drive you home. Just like that.

Home? I ast.

Yes, she say. Home. You ain't been home or seen your children in a while, she say. Ain't that right?

I say, Yes ma'am. It been five years.

She say, That's a shame. You just go git your things right now. Here it is, Christmas. Go get your things. You can stay all day.

For all day I don't need nothing but what I got on, I say.

Fine, she say. Fine. Well git in.

Well, say Sofia, I was so use to sitting up there next to her teaching her how to drive, that I just naturally clammed into the front seat.

She stood outside on her side the car clearing her throat.

Finally she say, Sofia, with a little laugh, This *is* the South.

Yes ma'am, I say.

She clear her throat, laugh some more. Look where you sitting, she say.

I'm sitting where I always sit, I say.

That's the problem, she say. Have you ever seen a white person and a colored sitting side by side in a car, when one of 'em wasn't showing the other one how to drive it or clean it?

I got out the car, opened the back door and clammed in. She

sat down up front. Off us traveled down the road, Miz Millie hair blowing all out the window.

It's real pretty country out this way, she say, when we hit the Marshall county road, coming toward Odessa's house.

Yes ma'am, I say.

Then us pull into the yard and all the children come crowding round the car. Nobody told them I was coming, so they don't know who I is. Except the oldest two. They fall on me, and hug me. And then all the little ones start to hug me too. I don't think they even notice I was sitting in the back of the car. Odessa and Jack come out after I was out, so they didn't see it.

Us all stand round kissing and hugging each other, Miz Millie just watching. Finally, she lean out the window and say, Sofia, you only got the rest of the day. I'll be back to pick you up at five o'clock. The children was all pulling me into the house, so sort of over my shoulder I say, Yes ma'am, and I thought I heard her drive off.

But fifteen minutes later, Marion says, That white lady still out there.

Maybe she going to wait to take you back, say Jack.

Maybe she sick, say Odessa. You always say how sickly they is.

I go out to the car, say Sofia, and guess what the matter is? The matter is, she don't know how to do nothing but go forward, and Jack and Odessa's yard too full of trees for that.

Sofia, she say, How you back this thing up?

I lean over the car window and try to show her which way to move the gears. But she flustered and all the children and Odessa and Jack all standing round the porch watching her.

I go round on the other side. Try to explain with my head poked through that window. She stripping gears aplenty by now. Plus her nose red and she look mad and frustrate both.

I clam in the back seat, lean over the back of the front, steady trying to show her how to operate the gears. Nothing happen. Finally the car stop making any sound. Engine dead.

Don't worry, I say, Odessa's husband Jack will drive you home. That's his pick-up right there.

Oh, she say, I couldn't ride in a pick-up with a strange colored man.

I'll ask Odessa to squeeze in too, I say. That would give me a chance to spend a little time with the children, I thought. But she say, No, I don't know her neither.

So it end up with me and Jack driving her back home in the pick-up, then Jack driving me to town to git a mechanic, and at five o'clock I was driving Miz Millie's car back to her house.

I spent fifteen minutes with my children.

And she been going on for months bout how ungrateful I is.

White folks is a miracle of affliction, say Sofia.

Dear God,

Shug write she got a big surprise, and she intend to bring it home for Christmas.

What it is? us wonder.

Mr. _____ think it a car for him. Shug making big money now, dress in furs all the time. Silk and satin too, and hats made out of gold.

Christmas morning us hear this motor outside the door. Us look out.

Hot diggidy dog, say Mr. _____ throwing on his pants. He rush to the door. I stand in front the glass trying to make something out my hair. It too short to be long, too long to be short. Too nappy to be kinky, too kinky to be nappy. No set color to it either. I give up, tie on a headrag.

I hear Shug cry, Oh, Albert. He say, *Shug*. I know they hugging. Then I don't hear nothing.

I run out the door. *Shug*, I say, and put out my arms. But before I know anything a skinny big toof man wearing red suspenders is all up in my face. Fore I can wonder whose dog he is, he hugging me.

Miss Celie, he say. Aw, Miss Celie. I heard so much about you. Feel like we old friends.

Shug standing back with a big grin.

This Grady, she say. This my husband.

The minute she say it I know I don't like Grady. I don't like his shape, I don't like his teef, I don't like his clothes. Seem like to me he smell.

Us been driving all night, she say. Nowhere to stop, you know. But here us is. She come over to Grady and put her arms round him, look up at him like he cute and he lean down and give her a kiss.

I glance round at Mr. _____. He look like the end of the world. I know I don't look no better.

And this my wedding present to us, say Shug. The car big and dark blue and say Packard on the front. Brand new, she say. She look at Mr. _____, take his arm, give it a little squeeze. While we here, Albert, she say, I want you to learn how to drive. She laugh. Grady drive like a fool, she say. I thought the polices was gonna catch us for sure.

Finally Shug really seem to notice me. She come over and hug me a long time. Us two married ladies now, she say. Two married ladies. And hungry, she say. What us got to eat?

Dear God,

Mr. _____ drink all through Christmas. Him and Grady. Me and Shug cook, talk, clean the house, talk, fix up the tree, talk, wake up in the morning, talk.

She singing all over the country these days. Everybody know her name. She know everybody, too. Know Sophie Tucker, know Duke Ellington, know folks I ain't never heard of. And money. She make so much money she don't know what to do with it. She got a fine house in Memphis, another car. She got one hundred pretty dresses. A room full of shoes. She buy Grady anything he think he want.

Where you find him at? I ast.

Up under my car, she say. The one at home. I drove it after the oil give out, kilt the engine. He the man fixed it. Us took one look at one nother, that was it.

Mr. _____ feelings hurt, I say. I don't mention mine.

Aw, she say. That old stuff finally over with. You and Albert feel just like family now. Anyhow, once you told me he beat you, and won't work, I felt different about him. If you was my wife, she say, I'd cover you up with kisses stead of licks, and work hard for you too.

He ain't beat me much since you made him quit, I say. Just a slap now and then when he ain't got nothing else to do.

Yall make love any better? she ast.

Us try, I say. He try to play with the button but feel like his fingers dry. Us don't git nowhere much.

You still a virgin? she ast.

I reckon. I say.

Dear God,

Mr. _____ and Grady gone off in the car together. Shug ast me could she sleep with me. She cold in her and Grady bed all alone. Us talk bout this and that. Soon talk bout making love. Shug don't actually say making love. She say something nasty. She say fuck.

She ast me, How was it with your children daddy?

The girls had a little separate room, I say, off to itself, connected to the house by a little plank walk. Nobody ever come in there but Mama. But one time when mama not at home, he come. Told me he want me to trim his hair. He bring the scissors and comb and brush and a stool. While I trim his hair he look at me funny. He a little nervous too, but I don't know why, till he grab hold of me and cram me up tween his legs.

I lay there quiet, listening to Shug breathe.

It hurt me, you know, I say. I was just going on fourteen. I never even thought bout men having nothing down there so big. It scare me just to see it. And the way it poke itself and grow.

Shug so quiet I think she sleep.

After he through, I say, he make me finish trimming his hair.

I sneak a look at Shug.

Oh, Miss Celie, she say. And put her arms round me. They black and smooth and kind of glowy from the lamplight.

I start to cry too. I cry and cry and cry. Seem like it all come back to me, laying there in Shug arms. How it hurt and how much I was surprise. How it stung while I finish trimming his hair. How the blood drip down my leg and mess up my stocking. How he don't never look at me straight after that. And Nettie.

Don't cry, Celie, Shug say. Don't cry. She start kissing the water as it come down side my face.

After while I say, Mama finally ast how come she find his hair in the girls room if he don't never go in there like he say. That when he told her I had a boyfriend. Some boy he say he seen sneaking out the back door. It the boy's hair, he say, not his. You know how she love to cut anybody hair, he say.

I did love to cut hair, I say to Shug, since I was a little bitty thing. I'd run go git the scissors if I saw hair coming, and I'd cut and cut, long as I could. That how come I was the one cut his hair. But always before I cut it on the front porch. It got to the place where everytime I saw him coming with the scissors and the comb and the stool, I start to cry.

Shug say, Wellsah, and I thought it was only whitefolks do freakish things like that.

My mama die, I tell Shug. My sister Nettie run away. Mr. _____ come git me to take care his rotten children. He never ast me nothing bout myself. He clam on top of me and fuck and fuck, even when my head bandaged. Nobody ever love me, I say.

She say, I love you, Miss Celie. And then she haul off and kiss me on the mouth.

Um, she say, like she surprise. I kiss her back, say, *um,* too. Us kiss and kiss till us can't hardly kiss no more. Then us touch each other.

I don't know nothing bout it, I say to Shug.

I don't know much, she say.

Then I feels something real soft and wet on my breast, feel like one of my little lost babies mouth.

Way after while, I act like a little lost baby too.

Dear God,

Grady and Mr. _____ come staggering in round daybreak.
Me and Shug sound asleep. Her back to me, my arms round her
waist. What it like? Little like sleeping with mama, only I can't
hardly remember ever sleeping with her. Little like sleeping
with Nettie, only sleeping with Nettie never feel this good. It
warm and cushiony, and I feel Shug's big tits sorta flop over my
arms like suds. It feel like heaven is what it feel like, not like
sleeping with Mr. _____ at all.

Wake up Sugar, I say. They back. And Shug roll over, hug
me, and git out of the bed. She stagger into the other room and
fall on the bed with Grady. Mr. _____ fall into bed next to me,
drunk, and snoring before he hit the quilts.

I try my best to like Grady, even if he do wear red
suspenders and bow ties. Even if he do spend Shug's money
like he made it himself. Even if he do try to talk like somebody
from the North. Memphis, Tennessee ain't North, even I know
that. But one thing I sure nuff can't stand, the way he call Shug
Mama.

I ain't your fucking mama, Shug say. But he don't pay her
no mind.

Like when he be making goo-goo eyes at Squeak and Shug
sorta tease him about it, he say, Aw, Mama, you know I don't
mean no harm.

Shug like Squeak too, try to help her sing. They sit in
Odessa's front room with all the children crowded round them
singing and singing. Sometime Swain come with his box, Harpo
cook dinner, and me and Mr. _____ and the prizefighter bring
our preshation.

It nice.

Shug say to Squeak, I mean, Mary Agnes, You ought to sing in public.

Mary Agnes say, *Naw*. She think cause she don't sing big and broad like Shug nobody want to hear her. But Shug say she wrong.

What about all them funny voices you hear singing in church? Shug say. What about all them sounds that sound good but they not the sounds you thought folks could make? What bout that? Then she start moaning. Sound like death approaching, angels can't prevent it. It raise the hair on the back of your neck. But it really sound sort of like panthers would sound if they could sing.

I tell you something else, Shug say to Mary Agnes, listening to you sing, folks git to thinking bout a good screw.

Aw, *Miss Shug*, say Mary Agnes, changing color.

Shug say, What, too shamefaced to put singing and dancing and fucking together? She laugh. That's the reason they call what us sing the devil's music. Devils love to fuck. Listen, she say, Let's go sing one night at Harpo place. Be like old times for me. And if I bring you before the crowd, they better listen with respect. Niggers don't know how to act, but if you git through the first half of one song, you got 'em.

You reckon that's the truth? say Mary Agnes. She all big eyed and delight.

I don't know if I want her to sing, say Harpo.

How come? ast Shug. That woman you got singing now can't git her ass *out* the church. Folks don't know whether to dance or creep to the mourner's bench. Plus, you dress Mary Agnes up the right way and you'll make piss pots of money. Yellow like she is, stringy hair and cloudy eyes, the men'll be crazy bout her. Ain't that right, Grady, she say.

Grady look little sheepish. Grin. Mama you don't miss a thing, he say.

And don't you forget it, say Shug.

Dear God,

This the letter I been holding in my hand.

Dear Celie,

I know you think I am dead. But I am not. I been writing to you too, over the years, but Albert said you'd never hear from me again and since I never heard from you all this time, I guess he was right. Now I only write at Christmas and Easter hoping my letter get lost among the Christmas and Easter greetings, or that Albert get the holiday spirit and have pity on us.

There is so much to tell you that I don't know, hardly, where to begin—and anyway, you probably won't get this letter, either. I'm sure Albert is still the only one to take mail out of the box.

But if this do get through, one thing I want you to know, I love you, and I am not dead. And Olivia is fine and so is your son.

We are all coming home before the end of another year.

Your loving sister,

Nettie

One night in bed Shug ast me to tell her bout Nettie. What she like? Where she at?

I tell her how Mr. _____ try to turn her head. How Nettie refuse him, and how he say Nettie have to go.

Where she go? she ast.

I don't know, I say. She leave here.

And no word from her yet? she ast.

Naw, I say. Every day when Mr. _____ come from the

mailbox I hope for news. But nothing come. She dead, I say.

Shug say, She wouldn't be someplace with funny stamps, you don't reckon? She look like she studying. Say, Sometimes when Albert and me walk up to the mailbox there be a letter with a lot of funny looking stamps. He never say nothing bout it, just put it in his inside pocket. One time I ast him could I look at the stamps but he said he'd take it out later. But he never did.

She was just on her way to town, I say. Stamps look like stamps round here. White men with long hair.

Hm, she say, look like a little fat white woman was on one. What your sister Nettie like? she ast. Smart?

Yes, Lord, I say. Smart as anything. Read the newspapers when she was little more than talking. Did figures like they was nothing. Talked real well too. And sweet. There never was a sweeter girl, I say. Eyes just brimming over with it. She love me too, I say to Shug.

She tall or short? Shug ast. What kind of dress she like to wear? What her birthday? What her favorite color? Can she cook? Sew? What about hair?

Everything bout Nettie she want to know.

I talk so much my voice start to go. Why you want to know so much bout Nettie? I ast.

Cause she the only one you ever love, she say, sides me.

Dear God,

All of a sudden Shug buddy-buddy again with Mr. _____.
They sit on the steps, go down Harpo's. Walk to the mailbox.

Shug laugh and laugh when he got anything to say. Show
teef and tits aplenty.

Me and Grady try to carry on like us civilize. But it hard.
When I hear Shug laugh I want to choke her, slap Mr. _____
face.

All this week I suffer. Grady and me feel so down he turn to
reefer, I turn to prayer.

Saturday morning Shug put Nettie letter in my lap. Little fat
queen of England stamps on it, plus stamps that got peanuts,
coconuts, rubber trees and say Africa. I don't know where
England at. Don't know where Africa at either. So I still don't
know where Nettie at.

He been keeping your letters, say Shug.

Naw, I say. Mr. _____ mean sometimes, but he not that
mean.

She say, Humpf, he that mean.

But how come he to do it? I ast. He know Nettie mean
everything in the world to me.

Shug say she don't know, but us gon find out.

Us seal the letter up again and put it back in Mr. _____
pocket.

He walk round with it in his coat all day. He never mention
it. Just talk and laugh with Grady, Harpo and Swain, and try to
learn how to drive Shug car.

I watch him so close, I begin to feel a lightening in the head.
Fore I know anything I'm standing hind his chair with his razor
open.

Then I hear Shug laugh, like something just too funny. She say to me, I know I told you I need something to cut this hangnail with, but Albert git real niggerish bout his razor.

Mr. _____ look behind him. Put that down, he say. Women, always needing to cut this and shave that, and always gumming up the razor.

Shug got her hand on the razor now. She say, Oh it look dull anyway. She take and sling it back in the shaving box.

All day long I act just like Sofia. I stutter. I mutter to myself. I stumble bout the house crazy for Mr. _____ blood. In my mind, he falling dead every which a way. By time night come, I can't speak. Every time I open my mouth nothing come come out but a little burp.

Shug tell everybody I got a fever and she put me to bed. It probably catching, she say to Mr. _____. Maybe you better sleep somewhere else. But she stay with me all night long. I don't sleep. I don't cry. I don't do nothing. I'm cold too. Pretty soon I think maybe I'm dead.

Shug hold me close to her and sometimes talk.

One thing my mama hated me for was how much I love to fuck, she say. She never love to do nothing had anything to do with touching nobody, she say. I try to kiss her, she turn her mouth away. Say, Cut that out Lillie, she say. Lillie Shug's real name. She just so sweet they call her Shug.

My daddy love me to kiss and hug him, but she didn't like the looks of that. So when I met Albert, and once I got in his arms, nothing could git me out. It was good, too, she say. You know for me to have three babies by Albert and Albert weak as he is, it had to be good.

I had every one of my babies at home, too. Midwife come, preacher come, a bunch of the good ladies from the church. Just when I hurt so much I don't know my own name, they think a good time to talk bout repent.

She laugh. I was too big a fool to repent. Then she say, I loved me some Albert _____.

I don't even want to say nothing. Where I'm at it peaceful. It calm. No Albert there. No Shug. Nothing.

Shug say, the last baby did it. They turned me out. I went to stay with my mama wild sister in Memphis. She just like me, Mama say. She drink, she fight, she love mens to death. She work in a roadhouse. Cook. Feed fifty men, screw fifty-five.

Shug talk and talk.

And dance, she say. Nobody dance like Albert when he was young. Sometime us did the moochie for a hour. After that, nothing to do but go somewhere and lay down. And funny. Albert was so *funny*. He kept me laughing. How come he ain't funny no more? she ast. How come he never hardly laugh? How come he don't dance? she say. Good God, Celie, she say, What happen to the man I love?

She quiet a little while. Then she say, I was so surprise when I heard he was going to marry Annie Julia, she say. Too surprise to be hurt. I didn't believe it. After all, Albert knew as well as me that love would have to go some to be better than ours. Us had the kind of love couldn't be improve. That's what I thought.

But, he weak, she say. His daddy told him I'm trash, my mama trash before me. His brother say the same. Albert try to stand up for us, git knock down. One reason they give him for not marrying me is cause I have children.

But they *his*, I told old Mr. _____.

How us know? He ast.

Poor Annie Julia, Shug say. She never had a chance. I was so mean, and so wild, Lord. I used to go round saying, I don't care who he married to, I'm gonna fuck him. She stop talking a minute. Then she say, And I did, too. Us fuck so much in the open us give fucking a bad name.

But he fuck Annie Julia too, she say, and she didn't have nothing, not even a liking for him. Her family forgot about her once she married. And then Harpo and all the children start to come. Finally she start to sleep with that man that shot her down. Albert beat her. The children dragged on her. Sometimes I wonder what she thought about while she died.

I know what I'm thinking bout, I think. Nothing. And as much of it as I can.

I went to school with Annie Julia, Shug say. She was pretty, man. Black as anything, and skin just as smooth. Big black eyes look like moons. And sweet too. Hell, say Shug, I liked her myself. Why I hurt her so? I used to keep Albert away from home for a week at the time. She'd come and beg him for money to buy groceries for the children.

I feel a few drops of water on my hand.

And when I come here, say Shug. I treated you so mean. Like you was a servant. And all because Albert married you. And I didn't even want him for a husband, she say. I never really wanted Albert for a husband. But just to choose me, you know, cause nature had already done it. Nature said, You two folks, hook up, cause you a good example of how it sposed to go. I didn't want nothing to be able to go against that. But what was good tween us must have been nothing but bodies, she say. Cause I don't know the Albert that don't dance, can't hardly laugh, never talk bout nothing, beat you and hid your sister Nettie's letters. Who he?

I don't know nothing, I think. And glad of it.

Dear God,

Now that I know Albert hiding Nettie's letters, I know exactly where they is. They in his trunk. Everything that mean something to Albert go in his trunk. He keep it locked up tight, but Shug can git the key.

One night when Mr. _____ and Grady gone, us open the trunk. Us find a lot of Shug's underclothes, some nasty picture postcards, and way down under his tobacco, Nettie's letters. Bunches and bunches of them. Some fat, some thin. Some open, some not.

How us gon do this? I ast Shug.

She say, Simple. We take the letters out of the envelopes, leave the envelopes just like they is. I don't think he look in this corner of the trunk much, she say.

I heated the stove, put on the kettle. Us steam and steam the envelopes until we had all the letters laying on the table. Then us put the envelopes back inside the trunk.

I'm gonna put them in some kind of order for you, say Shug.

Yeah, I say, but don't let's do it in here, let's go in you and Grady room.

So she got up and us went into they little room. Shug sat in a chair by the bed with all Nettie letters spread round her, I got on the bed with the pillows behind my back.

These the first ones, say Shug. They postmark right here.

Dear Celie, *the first letter say,*

You've got to fight and get away from Albert. He ain't no good.

When I left you all's house, walking, he followed me on his horse. When we was well out of sight of the house he caught up with me and started trying to talk. You know how he do, You sure is looking fine, Miss Nettie, and stuff like that. I tried to ignore him and walk faster, but my bundles was heavy and the sun was hot. After while I had to rest, and that's when he got down from his horse and started to try to kiss me, and drag me back in the woods.

Well, I started to fight him, and with God's help, I hurt him bad enough to make him let me alone. But he was some mad. He said because of what I'd done I'd never hear from you again, and you would never hear from me.

I was so mad myself I was shaking.

Anyhow, I got a ride into town on somebody's wagon. And that same somebody pointed me in the direction of the Reverend Mr. _____'s place. And what was my surprise when a little girl opened the door and she had your eyes set in your face.

love,
Nettie

Next one said,

Dear Celie,

I keep thinking it's too soon to look for a letter from you. And I know how busy you is with all Mr. _____'s children. But I miss you *so* much. Please write to me, soon as you have a chance. Every day I think about you. Every minute.

The lady you met in town is name Corrine. The little girl's name is Olivia. The husband's name is Samuel. The little boy's name is Adam. They are sanctified religious and very good to me. They live in a nice house next to the church where Samuel preaches, and we spend a lot of time on church business. I say "we" because they always try to include me in everything they do, so I don't feel so left out and alone.

But God, I miss you, Celie. I think about the time you laid yourself down for me. I love you with all my heart,

Your sister,

Nettie

Next one say,

Dearest Celie,

By now I am almost crazy. I think Albert told me the truth, and that he is not giving you my letters. The only person I can think of who could help us out is Pa, but I don't want him to know where I am.

I asked Samuel if he would visit you and Mr. _____, just to see how you are. But he says he can't risk putting himself between man and wife, especially when he don't know them. And I felt bad for having to ask him, he and Corrine have been so nice to me. But my heart is breaking. It is breaking because I can not find any work in this town, and I will have to leave. After I leave, what will happen to us? How will we ever know what is going on?

Corrine and Samuel and the children are part of a group of people called Missionaries, of the American and African Missionary Society. They have ministered to the Indians out west and are ministering to the poor of this town. All in preparation for the work they feel they were born for, missionary work in Africa.

I dread parting from them because in the short time we've been together they've been like family to me. Like family might have been, I mean.

Write if you can. Here are some stamps.

love, Nettie

Next one, fat, dated two months later, say,

Dear Celie,

I wrote a letter to you almost every day on the ship coming to Africa. But by the time we docked I was so down, I tore them into little pieces and dropped them into the water. Albert is not going to let you have my letters and so what use is there in writing them. That's the way I felt when I tore them up and sent them to you on the waves. But now I feel different.

I remember one time you said your life made you feel so ashamed you couldn't even talk about it to God, you had to write it, bad as you thought your writing was. Well, now I know what you meant. And whether God will read letters or no, I know you will go on writing them; which is guidance enough for me. Anyway, when I don't write to you I feel as bad as I do when I don't pray, locked up in myself and choking on my own heart. I am so *lonely*, Celie.

The reason I am in Africa is because one of the missionaries that was supposed to go with Corrine and Samuel to help with the children and with setting up a school suddenly married a man who was afraid to let her go, and refused to come to Africa with her. So there they were, all set to go, with a ticket suddenly available and no missionary to give it to. At the same time, I wasn't able to find a job anywhere around town. But I never dreamed of going to Africa! I never even thought about it as a real place, though Samuel and Corrine and even the children talked about it all the time.

Miss Beasley used to say it was a place overrun with savages who didn't wear clothes. Even Corrine and Samuel thought like this at times. But they know a lot more about it than Miss Beasley or any of our other teachers, and besides, they spoke of all the good things they could do for the downtrodden people from whom they sprang. People who need Christ and good medical advice.

One day I was in town with Corrine and we saw the mayor's wife and her maid. The mayor's wife was shopping —going in and out of stores—and her maid was waiting for her on the street and taking the packages. I don't know if you have ever seen the mayor's wife. She looks like a wet cat. And there was her maid looking like the very last person in the world you'd expect to see waiting on anybody, and in particular not on anybody that looked like that.

I spoke. But just speaking to me seemed to make her embarrassed and she suddenly sort of erased herself. It was the strangest thing, Celie! One minute I was saying howdy to a living woman. The next minute nothing living was there. Only its shape.

All that night I thought about it. Then Samuel and Corrine told me what they'd heard about how she got to be the mayor's maid. That she attacked the mayor, and then the mayor and his wife took her from the prison to work in their home.

In the morning I started asking questions about Africa and started reading all the books Samuel and Corrine have on the subject.

Did you know there were great cities in Africa, greater than Milledgeville or even Atlanta, thousands of years ago? That the Egyptians who built the pyramids and enslaved the Israelites were colored? That Egypt is in Africa? That the Ethiopia we read about in the bible meant all of Africa?

Well, I read and I read until I thought my eyes would fall out. I read where the Africans sold us because they loved money more than their own sisters and brothers. How we came to America in ships. How we were made to work.

I hadn't realized I was so *ignorant*, Celie! The little I knew about my own self wouldn't have filled a thimble! And to think

Miss Beasley always said I was the smartest child she ever taught! But one thing I do thank her for, for teaching me to learn for myself, by reading and studying and writing a clear hand. And for keeping alive in me somehow the desire to *know*. So when Corrine and Samuel asked me if I would come with them and help them build a school in the middle of Africa, I said yes. But only if they would teach me everything they knew to make me useful as a missionary and someone they would not be ashamed to call a friend. They agreed to this condition, and my real education began at that time.

They have been as good as their word. And I study everything night and day.

Oh, Celie, there are colored people in the world who want us to know! Want us to grow and see the light! They are not all mean like Pa and Albert, or beaten down like ma was. Corrine and Samuel have a wonderful marriage. Their only sorrow in the beginning was that they could not have children. And then, they say, "God" sent them Olivia and Adam.

I wanted to say, "God" has sent you their sister and aunt, but I didn't. Yes, their children, sent by "God" are your children, Celie. And they are being brought up in love, Christian charity and awareness of God. And now "God" has sent me to watch over them, to protect and cherish them. To lavish all the love I feel for you on them. It is a miracle, isn't it? And no doubt impossible for you to believe.

But on the other hand, if you can believe I am in Africa, and I am, you can believe anything.

Your sister, Nettie

The next letter after that one say,

Dear Celie,

While we were in town Corrine bought cloth to make me two sets of traveling outfits. One olive green and the other gray. Long gored skirts and suit jackets to be worn with white cotton blouses and lace-up boots. She also bought me a woman's boater with a checkered band.

Although I work for Corrine and Samuel and look after the children, I don't feel like a maid. I guess this is because they teach me, and I teach the children and there's no beginning or end to teaching and learning and working—it all runs together.

Saying good-bye to our church group was hard. But happy, too. Everyone has such high hopes for what can be done in Africa. Over the pulpit there is a saying: *Ethiopia Shall Stretch Forth Her Hands to God.* Think what it means that Ethiopia is Africa! All the Ethiopians in the bible were colored. It had never occurred to me, though when you read the bible it is perfectly plain if you pay attention only to the words. It is the pictures in the bible that fool you. The pictures that illustrate the words. All of the people are white and so you just think all the people from the bible were white too. But really *white* white people lived somewhere else during those times. That's why the bible says that Jesus Christ had hair like lamb's wool. Lamb's wool is not straight, Celie. It isn't even curly.

What can I tell you about New York—or even about the train that took us there! We had to ride in the sit-down section of the train, but Celie, there are beds on trains! And a restaurant! And toilets! The beds come down out of the walls, over the tops of the seats, and are called berths. Only white people can ride in the beds and use the restaurant. And they have different toilets from colored.

One white man on the platform in South Carolina asked us where we were going—we had got off the train to get some fresh air and to dust the grit and dust out of our clothes. When we said Africa he looked offended and tickled too. Niggers going to Africa, he said to his wife. Now I *have* seen everything.

When we got to New York we were tired and dirty. But so excited! Listen, Celie, New York is a *beautiful* city. And colored own a whole section of it, called Harlem. There are colored people in more fancy motor cars than I thought existed, and living in houses that are finer than any white person's house down home. There are more than a hundred churches! And we went to every one of them. And I stood before each congregation with Samuel and Corrine and the children and sometimes our mouths just dropped open from the generosity and goodness of those Harlem people's hearts. They live in such beauty and dignity, Celie. And they give and give and then reach down and give some more, when the name "Africa" is mentioned.

They *love* Africa. They defend it at the drop of a hat. And speaking of hats, if we had passed our hats alone they would not have been enough to hold all the donations to our enterprise. Even the children dredged up their pennies. Please give these to the children of Africa, they said. They were all dressed so beautifully, too, Celie. I wish you could have seen them. There is a fashion in Harlem now for boys to wear something called knickers—sort of baggy pants, fitted tight just below the knee, and for girls to wear garlands of flowers in their hair. They must be the most beautiful children alive, and Adam and Olivia couldn't take their eyes off them.

Then there were the dinners we were invited to, the breakfasts, lunches, and suppers. I gained five pounds just from tasting. I was too excited to really eat.

And all the people have indoor toilets, Celie. And gas or electric lights!

Well, we had two weeks of study in the Olinka dialect, which the people in this region speak. Then we were examined by a doctor (colored!) and given medical supplies for ourselves and for our host village by the Missionary Society of New York. It is run by white people and they didn't say anything about caring about Africa, but only about duty. There is already a white woman missionary not far from our village who has lived in Africa for the past twenty years. She is said to be much loved by the natives even though she thinks they are an entirely different species from what she calls Europeans. Europeans are white people who live in a place called Europe. That is where the white people down home came from. She says an African daisy and an English daisy are both flowers, but totally different kinds. The man at the Society says she is successful because she doesn't "coddle" her charges. She also speaks their language. He is a white man who looks at us as if we cannot possibly be as good with the Africans as this woman is.

My spirits sort of drooped after being at the Society. On every wall there was a picture of a white man. Somebody called Speke, somebody called Livingstone. Somebody called Daly. Or was it Stanley? I looked for a picture of the white woman but didn't see one. Samuel looked a little sad too, but then he perked up and reminded us that there is one big advantage we have. We are not white. We are not Europeans. We are black like the Africans themselves. And that we and the Africans will be working for a common goal: the uplift of black people everywhere.

Your sister, Nettie

Dear Celie,

Samuel is a big man. He dresses in black almost all the time, except for his white clerical collar. And *he* is black. Until you see his eyes you think he's somber, even mean, but he has the most thoughtful and gentle brown eyes. When he says something it settles you, because he never says anything off the top of his head and he's never out to dampen your spirit or to hurt. Corrine is a lucky woman to have him as her husband.

But let me tell you about the ship! The ship, called The Malaga, was three stories high! And we had rooms (called cabins) with beds. Oh, Celie, to lie in a bed in the middle of the ocean! And the ocean! Celie, more water than you can imagine in one place. It took us two weeks to cross it! And then we were in England, which is a country full of white people and some of them very nice and with their own Anti-Slavery & Missionary Society. The churches in England were also very eager to help us and white men and women, who looked just like the ones at home, invited us to their gatherings and into their homes for tea, and to talk about our work. "Tea" to the English is really a picnic indoors. Plenty of sandwiches and cookies and of course hot tea. We all used the same cups and plates.

Everyone said I seemed very young to be a missionary, but Samuel said that I was very willing, and that, anyway, my primary duties would be helping with the children and teaching a kindergarten class or two.

Our work began to seem somewhat clearer in England because the English have been sending missionaries to Africa and India and China and God knows where all, for over a hundred years. And the things they have brought back! We spent a morning in one of their museums and it was packed with jewels, furniture, fur carpets, swords, clothing, even *tombs* from all the countries they have been. From Africa they have *thousands* of vases, jars, masks, bowls, baskets, statues—and they are all so beautiful it is hard to imagine that the people who made them don't still exist. And yet the English assure us they do not. Although Africans once had a better civilization than the European (though of course even the English do not say this: I get this from reading a man named J. A. Rogers) for several centuries they have fallen on hard times. "Hard times" is a phrase the English love to use, when speaking of Africa. And it is easy to forget that Africa's "hard times" were made harder by them. Millions and millions of Africans were captured and sold into slavery—you and me, Celie! And whole cities were destroyed by slave catching wars. Today the people of Africa—having murdered or sold into slavery their strongest folks—are riddled by disease and sunk in spiritual and physical confusion. They believe in the devil and worship the dead. Nor can they read or write.

Why did they sell us? How could they have done it? And why do we still love them? These were the thoughts I had as we tramped through the chilly streets of London. I studied England on a map, so neat and serene, and I became hopeful in spite of myself that much good for Africa is possible, given hard work and the right frame of mind. And then we sailed for Africa. Leaving Southampton, England on the 24th of July and arriving in Monrovia, Liberia on the 12th of September. On the way we stopped in Lisbon, Portugal and Dakar, Senegal.

Monrovia was the last place we were among people we were somewhat used to, since it is an African country that was "founded" by ex-slaves from America who came back to Africa to live. Had any of their parents or grandparents been sold *from* Monrovia, I wondered, and what was their feeling, once sold as slaves, now coming back, with close ties to the country that bought them, to rule.

Celie, I must stop now. The sun is not so hot now and I must prepare for the afternoon classes and vesper service.

I wish you were with me, or I with you.

My love,

Your sister, Nettie

Dearest Celie,

It was the funniest thing to stop over in Monrovia after my first glimpse of Africa, which was Senegal. The capital of Senegal is Dakar and the people speak their own language, Senegalese I guess they would call it, and French. They are the blackest people I have ever seen, Celie. They are black like the people we are talking about when we say, "So and so is blacker than black, he's *blue*black." They are so black, Celie, they shine. Which is something else folks down home like to say about real black folks. But Celie, try to imagine a city full of these shining, blueblack people wearing brilliant blue robes with designs like fancy quilt patterns. Tall, thin, with long necks and straight backs. Can you picture it at all, Celie? Because I felt like I was seeing black for the first time. And Celie, there is something magical about it. Because the black is so black the eye is simply dazzled, and then there is the shining that seems to come, really, from moonlight, it is so luminous, but their skin glows even in the sun.

But I did not really like the Senegalese I met in the market. They were concerned only with their sale of produce. If we did not buy, they looked through us as quickly as they looked through the white French people who live there. Somehow I had not expected to see any white people in Africa, but they are here in droves. And not all are missionaries.

There are bunches of them in Monrovia, too. And the president, whose last name is Tubman, has some in his cabinet. He also has a lot of white-looking colored men in his cabinet. On our second evening in Monrovia we had tea at the presidential palace. It looks very much like the American white house (where our president lives) Samuel says. The president talked a good bit about his efforts trying to develop the country and about his problems with the natives, who don't want to work to help build the country up. It was the first time I'd heard a black man use that word. I knew that to white people all colored people are natives. But he cleared his throat and said he only meant "native" to Liberia. I did not see any of these "natives" in his cabinet. And none of the cabinet members' wives could pass for natives. Compared to them in their silks and pearls, Corrine and I were barely dressed, let alone dressed for the occasion. But I think the women we saw at the palace spend a lot of their time dressing. Still, they look dissatisfied. Not like the cheery school-teachers we saw only by chance, as they herded their classes down to the beach for a swim.

Before we left we visited one of the large cacoa plantations they have. Nothing but cacoa trees as far as the eye can see. And whole villages built right in the middle of the fields. We watched the weary families come home from work, still carrying their cacoa seed buckets in their hands (these double as lunch buckets next day), and sometimes—if they are women—their children on their backs. As tired as they are, they sing! Celie. Just like we do at home. Why do tired people sing? I asked Corrine. Too tired to do anything else, she said. Besides, they don't own the cacoa fields, Celie, even president Tubman doesn't own them. People in a place called Holland do. The people who make Dutch chocolate. And there are overseers who make sure the people work hard, who live in stone houses in the corners of the fields.

Again I must go. Everyone is in bed and I am writing by lamplight. But the light is attracting so many bugs I am being eaten alive. I have bites everywhere, including my scalp and the bottoms of my feet.

But—

Did I mention my first sight of the African coast? Something struck in me, in my soul, Celie, like a large bell, and I just vibrated. Corrine and Samuel felt the same. And we kneeled down right on deck and gave thanks to God for letting us see the land for which our mothers and fathers cried—and lived and died—to see again.

Oh, Celie! Will I ever be able to tell you all?

I dare not ask, I know. But leave it all to God.

Your everloving sister, Nettie

Dear God,

What with being shock, crying and blowing my nose, and trying to puzzle out words us don't know, it took a long time to read just the first two or three letters. By the time us got up to where she good and settled in Africa, Mr. _____ and Grady come home.

Can you handle it? ast Shug.

How I'm gon keep from killing him, I say.

Don't kill, she say. Nettie be coming home before long. Don't make her have to look at you like us look at Sofia.

But it so hard, I say, while Shug empty her suitcase and put the letters inside.

Hard to be Christ too, say Shug. But he manage. Remember that. Thou Shalt Not Kill, He said. And probably wanted to add on to that, Starting with me. He knowed the fools he was dealing with.

But Mr. _____ not Christ. I'm not Christ, I say.

You somebody to Nettie, she say. And she be pissed if you change on her while she on her way home.

Us hear Grady and Mr. _____ in the kitchen. Dishes rattling, safe door open and shut.

Naw, I think I feel better if I kill him, I say. I feels sickish. Numb, now.

Naw you won't. Nobody feel better for killing nothing. They feel *something* is all.

That better than nothing.

Celie, she say, Nettie not the only one you got to worry bout.

Say what? I ast.

Me, Celie, think about me a little bit. Miss Celie, if you kill Albert, Grady be all I got left. I can't even stand the thought of that.

I laugh, thinking bout Grady's big toofs.

Make Albert let me sleep with you from now on, while you here, I say.

And somehow or other, she do.

Dear God,

Us sleep like sisters, me and Shug. Much as I still want to be with her, much as I love to look, my titties stay soft, my little button never rise. Now I know I'm dead. But she say, Naw, just being mad, grief, wanting to kill somebody will make you feel this way. Nothing to worry about. Titties gonna perk up, button gonna rise again.

I loves to hug up, period, she say. Snuggle. Don't need nothing else right now.

Yeah, I say. Hugging is good. Snuggle. All of it's good.

She say, Times like this, lulls, us ought to do something different.

Like what? I ast.

Well, she say, looking me up and down, let's make you some pants.

What I need pants for? I say. I ain't no man.

Don't git uppity, she say. But you don't have a dress do nothing for you. You not made like no dress pattern, neither.

I don't know, I say. Mr. _____ not going to let his wife wear pants.

Why not? say Shug. You do all the work around here. It's a scandless, the way you look out there plowing in a dress. How you keep from falling over it or getting the plow caught in it is beyond me.

Yeah? I say.

Yeah. And another thing, I used to put on Albert's pants when we was courting. And he one time put on my dress.

No he didn't.

Yes he did. He use to be a lot of fun. Not like now. But he loved to see me in pants. It was like a red flag to a bull.

Ugh, I say. I could just picture it, and I didn't like it one bit.

Well, you know how they is, say Shug.

What us gon make 'em out of, I say.

We have to git our hands on somebody's army uniform, say Shug. For practice. That good strong material and free.

Jack, I say. Odessa's husband.

Okay, she say. And every day we going to read Nettie's letters and sew.

A needle and not a razor in my hand, I think.

She don't say nothing else, just come over to me and hug.

Dear God,

Now I know Nettie alive I begin to strut a little bit. Think, When she come home us leave here. Her and me and our two children. What they look like, I wonder. But it hard to think bout them. I feels shame. More than love, to tell the truth. Anyway, is they all right here? Got good sense and all? Shug say children got by incest turn into dunces. Incest part of the devil's plan.

But I think bout Nettie.

It's hot, here, Celie, she write. Hotter than July. Hotter than August *and* July. Hot like cooking dinner on a big stove in a little kitchen in August and July. Hot.

Dear Celie,

We were met at the ship by an African from the village we are settling in. His Christian name is Joseph. He is short and fat, with hands that seem not to have any bones in them. When he shook my hand it felt like something soft and damp was falling and I almost caught it. He speaks a little English, what they call pidgin English. It is very different from the way we speak English, but somehow familiar. He helped us unload our things from the ship into the boats that came out to get us. These boats are really dug-out canoes, like the Indians had, the ones you see in pictures. With all our belongings we filled three of them, and a fourth one carried our medical and teaching supplies.

Once in the boat we were entertained by the songs of our boatmen as they tried to outpaddle each other to the shore. They paid very little attention to us or our cargo. When we reached the shore they didn't bother to help us alight from the boat and actually set some of our supplies right down in the water. As soon as they had browbeat poor Samuel out of a tip that Joseph said was too big, they were off hallooing another group of people who were waiting at the edge of the water to be taken to the ship.

The port is pretty, but too shallow for large ships to use. So there is a good business for the boatmen, during the season the ships come by. These boatmen were all considerably larger and more muscular than Joseph, though all of them, including Joseph, are a deep chocolate brown. Not black, like the Senegalese. And Celie, they all have the strongest, cleanest, whitest teeth! I was thinking about teeth a lot on the voyage over, because I had toothache nearly the entire time. You know how rotten my back teeth are. And in England I was struck by the English people's teeth. So crooked, usually, and blackish with decay. I wondered if it was the English water. But the Africans' teeth remind me of horses' teeth, they are so fully formed, straight and strong.

The port's "town" is the size of the hardware store in town. Inside there are stalls filled with cloth, hurricane lamps and oil, mosquito netting, camp bedding, hammocks, axes and hoes and machetes and other tools. The whole place is run by a white man, but some of the stalls that sell produce are rented out to Africans. Joseph showed us things we needed to buy. A large iron pot for boiling water and our clothes, a zinc basin. Mosquito netting. Nails. Hammer and saw and pick-ax. Oil and lamps.

Since there was nowhere to sleep in the port, Joseph hired some porters from among the young men loafing around the trading post and we left right away for Olinka, some four days march through the bush. Jungle, to you. Or maybe not. Do you know what a jungle is? Well. Trees and trees and then more trees on top of that. And big. They are so big they look like they were built. And vines. And ferns. And little animals. Frogs. Snakes too, according to Joseph. But thank God we did not see any of these, only humpbacked lizards as big as your arm which the people here catch and eat.

They love meat. All the people in this village. Sometimes if you can't get them to do anything any other way, you start to mention meat, either a little piece extra you just happen to have or maybe, if you want them to do something big, you talk about a barbecue. Yes, a barbecue. They remind me of folks at home!

Well, we got here. And I thought I would never get the kinks out of my hips from being carried in a hammock the whole way. Everybody in the village crowded round us. Coming out of little round huts with something that I thought was straw on top of them but is really a kind of leaf that grows everywhere. They pick it and dry it and lay it so it overlaps to make the roof rainproof. This part is women's work. Menfolks drive the stakes for the hut and sometimes help build the walls with mud and rock from the streams.

You never saw such curious faces as the village folks surrounded us with. At first they just looked. Then one or two of the women touched my and Corrine's dresses. My dress was so dirty round the hem from dragging on the ground for three nights of cooking round a campfire that I was ashamed of myself. But then I took a look at the dresses they were wearing. Most looked like they'd been drug across the yard by the pigs. And they don't fit. So then they moved up a little bit—nobody saying a word yet—and touched our hair. Then looked down at our shoes. We looked at Joseph. Then he told us they were acting this way because the missionaries before us were all white. And they naturally thought all missionaries were white people, and vice versa. The men had been to the port, some of them, and had seen the white merchant, so they knew white men could be something else too. But the women had never been to the port and the only white person they'd seen was the missionary they had buried a year ago.

Samuel asked if they'd ever seen the white woman missionary twenty miles farther on, and he said no. Twenty miles through the jungle is a very long trip. The men might hunt up to ten miles around the village, but the women stayed close to their huts and fields.

Then one of the women asked a question. We looked at Joseph. He said the woman wanted to know if the children belonged to me or to Corrine or to both of us. Joseph said they belonged to Corrine. The woman looked us both over, and said something else. We looked at Joseph. He said the woman said they both looked like me. We all laughed politely.

Then another woman had a question. She wanted to know if I was also Samuel's wife.

Joseph said no, that I was a missionary just like Samuel and Corrine. Then someone said they never suspected missionaries could have children. Then another said he never dreamed missionaries could be black.

Then someone said, That the new missionaries would be black and two of them women was exactly what he *had* dreamed, and just last night, too.

By now there was a lot of commotion. Little heads began to pop from behind mothers' skirts and over big sisters' shoulders. And we were sort of swept along among the villagers, about three hundred of them, to a place without walls but with a leaf roof, where we all sat down on the ground, men in front, women and children behind. Then there was loud whispering among some very old men who looked like the church elders back home—with their baggy trousers and shiny, ill-fitting coats—Did black missionaries drink palm wine?

Corrine looked at Samuel and Samuel looked at Corrine. But me and the children were already drinking it, because someone had already put the little brown clay glasses in our hands and we were too nervous not to start sipping.

We got there around four o'clock, and sat under the leaf canopy until nine. We had our first meal there, a chicken and groundnut (peanut) stew which we ate with our fingers. But mostly we listened to songs and watched dances that raised lots of dust.

The biggest part of the welcoming ceremony was about the roofleaf, which Joseph interpreted for us as one of the villagers recited the story that it is based upon. The people of this village think they have always lived on the exact spot where their village now stands. And this spot has been good to them. They plant cassava fields that yield huge crops. They plant groundnuts that do the same. They plant yam and cotton and millet. All kinds of things. But once, a long time ago, one man in the village wanted more than his share of land to plant. He wanted to make more crops so as to use his surplus for trade with the white men on the coast. Because he was chief at the time, he gradually took more and more of the common land, and took more and more wives to work it. As his greed increased he also began to cultivate the land on which the roofleaf grew. Even his wives were upset by this and tried to complain, but they were lazy women and no one paid any attention to them. Nobody could remember a time when roofleaf did not exist in overabundant amounts. But eventually, the greedy chief took so much of this land that even the elders were disturbed. So he simply bought them off—with axes and cloth and cooking pots that he got from the coast traders.

But then there came a great storm during the rainy season that destroyed all the roofs on all the huts in the village, and the people discovered to their dismay that there was no longer any roofleaf to be found. Where roofleaf had flourished from time's beginning, there was cassava. Millet. Groundnuts.

For six months the heavens and the winds abused the people of Olinka. Rain came down in spears, stabbing away the mud of their walls. The wind was so fierce it blew the rocks out of the walls and into the people's cooking pots. Then cold rocks, shaped like millet balls, fell from the sky, striking everyone, men and women and children alike, and giving them fevers. The children fell ill first, then their parents. Soon the village began to die. By the end of the rainy season, half the village was gone.

The people prayed to their gods and waited impatiently for the seasons to change. As soon as the rain stopped they rushed to the old roofleaf beds and tried to find the old roots. But of the endless numbers that had always grown there, only a few dozen remained. It was five years before the roofleaf became plentiful again. During those five years many more in the village died. Many left, never to return. Many were eaten by animals. Many, many were sick. The chief was given all his storebought utensils and forced to walk away from the village forever. His wives were given to other men.

On the day when all the huts had roofs again from the roofleaf, the villagers celebrated by singing and dancing and telling the story of the roofleaf. The roofleaf became the thing they worship.

Looking over the heads of the children at the end of this tale, I saw coming slowly towards us, a large brown spiky thing as big as a room, with a dozen legs walking slowly and carefully under it. When it reached our canopy, it was presented to us. It was our roof.

As it approached, the people bowed down.

The white missionary before you would not let us have this ceremony, said Joseph. But the Olinka like it very much. We know a roofleaf is not Jesus Christ, but in its own humble way, is it not God?

So there we sat, Celie, face to face with the Olinka God. And Celie, I was so tired and sleepy and full of chicken and groundnut stew, my ears ringing with song, that all that Joseph said made perfect sense to me.

I wonder what you will make of all this?

I send my love,

Your sister,
Nettie

Dear Celie,

It has been a long time since I had time to write. But always, no matter what I'm doing, I am writing to you. Dear Celie, I say in my head in the middle of Vespers, the middle of the night, while cooking, Dear, dear Celie. And I imagine that you really do get my letters and that you are writing me back: Dear Nettie, this is what life is like for me.

We are up at five o'clock for a light breakfast of millet porridge and fruit, and the morning classes. We teach the children English, reading, writing, history, geography, arithmetic and the stories of the bible. At eleven o'clock we break for lunch and household duties. From one until four it is too hot to move, though some of the mothers sit behind their huts and sew. At four o'clock we teach the older children and at night we are available for adults. Some of the older children are used to coming to the mission school, but the smaller ones are not. Their mothers sometimes drag them here, screaming and kicking. They are all boys. Olivia is the only girl.

The Olinka do not believe girls should be educated. When I asked a mother why she thought this, she said: A girl is nothing to herself; only to her husband can she become something.

What can she become? I asked.

Why, she said, the mother of his children.

But I am not the mother of anybody's children, I said, and I am something.

You are not much, she said. The missionary's drudge.

It is true that I work harder here than I ever dreamed I could work, and that I sweep out the school and tidy up after service, but I don't feel like a drudge. I was surprised that this woman, whose Christian name is Catherine, saw me in this light.

She has a little girl, Tashi, who plays with Olivia after school. Adam is the only boy who will speak to Olivia at school. They are not mean to her, it is just—what is it? Because she is where they are doing "boys' things" they do not see her. But never fear, Celie, Olivia has your stubbornness and clearsightedness, and she is smarter than all of them, including Adam, put together.

Why can't Tashi come to school? she asked me. When I told her the Olinka don't believe in educating girls she said, quick as a flash, They're like white people at home who don't want colored people to learn.

Oh, she's sharp, Celie. At the end of the day, when Tashi can get away from all the chores her mother assigns her, she and Olivia secret themselves in my hut and everything Olivia has learned she shares with Tashi. To Olivia right now Tashi alone is Africa. The Africa she came beaming across the ocean hoping to find. Everything else is difficult for her.

The insects, for instance. For some reason, all of her bites turn into deep, runny sores, and she has a lot of trouble sleeping at night because the noises from the forest frighten her. It is taking a long time for her to become used to the food, which is nourishing but, for the most part, indifferently prepared. The women of the village take turns cooking for us, and some are cleaner and more conscientious than others. Olivia gets sick from the food prepared by any of the chief's wives. Samuel thinks it may be the water they use, which comes from a separate spring that runs clear even in the dry season. But the rest of us have no ill effects. It is as if Olivia fears the food from these wives because they all look so unhappy and work so hard. Whenever they see her they talk about the day when she will become their littlest sister/wife. It is just a joke, and they like her, but I wish they wouldn't say it. Even though they are unhappy and work like donkeys they still think it is an honor to be the chief's wife. He walks around all day holding his belly up and talking and drinking palm wine with the healer.

Why do they say I will be a wife of the chief? asks Olivia.

That is as high as they can think, I tell her.

He is fat and shiny with huge perfect teeth. She thinks she has nightmares about him.

You will grow up to be a strong Christian woman, I tell her. Someone who helps her people to advance. You will be a teacher or a nurse. You will travel. You will know many people greater than the chief.

Will Tashi? she wants to know.

Yes, I tell her, Tashi too.

Corrine said to me this morning, Nettie, to stop any kind of confusion in the minds of these people, I think we should call one another brother and sister, all the time. Some of them can't seem to get it through their thick skulls that you are not Samuel's other wife. I don't like it, she said.

Almost since the day we arrived I've noticed a change in Corrine. She isn't sick. She works as hard as ever. She is still sweet and good-natured. But sometimes I sense her spirit is being tested and that something in her is not at rest.

That's fine, I said. I'm glad you brought it up.

And don't let the children call you Mama Nettie, she said, even in play.

This bothered me a little, but I didn't say anything. The children do call me Mama Nettie sometimes because I do a good bit of fussing over them. But I never try to take Corrine's place.

And another thing, she said. I think we ought to try not to borrow each other's clothes.

Well, she never borrowed anything of mine because I don't have much. But I'm all the time borrowing something of hers.

You feeling yourself? I asked her.

She said yes.

I wish you could see my hut, Celie. I *love* it. Unlike our school, which is square, and unlike our church, which doesn't have walls—at least during the dry season—my hut is round, walled, with a round roofleaf roof. It is twenty steps across the middle and fits me to a T. Over the mud walls I have hung Olinka platters and mats and pieces of tribal cloth. The Olinka are known for their beautiful cotton fabric which they hand-weave and dye with berries, clay, indigo and tree bark. Then there is my paraffin camp stove in the center, and my camp bed to one side, covered with mosquito netting so that it almost looks like the bed of a bride. Then I have a small writing table where I write to you, a lamp, and a stool. Some wonderful rush mats on the floor. It is all colorful and warm and homey. My only desire for it now is a window! None of the village huts have windows, and when I spoke of a window to the women they laughed heartily. The rainy season makes the thought of a window ridiculous, apparently. But I am determined to have one, even if a flood collects daily on my floor.

I would give anything for a picture of you, Celie. In my trunk I have pictures donated to us by the missionary societies in England and America. Pictures of Christ, the Apostles, Mary, the Crucifixion. Speke, Livingstone. Stanley. Schweitzer. Maybe one day I'll put them up, but once, when I held them up to my fabric and mat covered walls they made me feel very small and unhappy, so I took them down. Even the picture of Christ which generally looks good anywhere looks peculiar here. We of course have all of these pictures hung in the school and many of Christ behind the altar at the church. That is enough, I think, though Samuel and Corrine have pictures and relics (crosses) in their hut as well.

Your sister,
Nettie

Dear Celie,

Tashi's mother and father were just here. They are upset because she spends so much time with Olivia. She is changing, becoming quiet and too thoughtful, they say. She is becoming someone else; her face is beginning to show the spirit of one of her aunts who was sold to the trader because she no longer fit into village life. This aunt refused to marry the man chosen for her. Refused to bow to the chief. Did nothing but lay up, crack cola nuts between her teeth and giggle.

They want to know what Olivia and Tashi do in my hut when all the other little girls are busy helping their mothers.

Is Tashi lazy at home? I asked.

The father looked at the mother. She said, No, on the contrary, Tashi works harder than most girls her age. And is quicker to finish her work. But it is only because she wishes to spend her afternoons with Olivia. She learns everything I teach her as if she already knows it, said the mother, but this knowledge does not really enter her soul.

The mother seemed puzzled and afraid.

The father, angry.

I thought: Aha. Tashi knows she is learning a way of life she will never live. But I did not say this.

The world is changing, I said. It is no longer a world just for boys and men.

Our women are respected here, said the father. We would never let them tramp the world as American women do. There is always someone to look after the Olinka woman. A father. An uncle. A brother or nephew. Do not be offended, Sister Nettie, but our people pity women such as you who are cast out, we know not from where, into a world unknown to you, where you must struggle all alone, for yourself.

So I am an object of pity and contempt, I thought, to men and women alike.

Furthermore, said Tashi's father, we are not simpletons. We understand that there are places in the world where women live differently from the way our women do, but we do not approve of this different way for our children.

But life is changing, even in Olinka, I said. We are here.

He spat on the ground. What are you? Three grownups and two children. In the rainy season some of you will probably die. You people do not last long in our climate. If you do not die, you will be weakened by illness. Oh, yes. We have seen it all before. You Christians come here, try hard to change us, get sick and go back to England, or wherever you come from. Only the trader on the coast remains, and even he is not the same white man, year in and year out. We know because we send him women.

Tashi is very intelligent, I said. She could be a teacher. A nurse. She could help the people in the village.

There is no place here for a woman to do those things, he said.

Then we should leave, I said. Sister Corrine and I.

No, no, he said.

Teach only the boys? I asked.

Yes, he said, as if my question was agreement.

There is a way that the men speak to women that reminds me too much of Pa. They listen just long enough to issue instructions. They don't even look at women when women are speaking. They look at the ground and bend their heads toward the ground. The women also do not "look in a man's face" as they say. To "look in a man's face" is a brazen thing to do. They look instead at his feet or his knees. And what can I say to this? Again, it is our own behavior around Pa.

Next time Tashi appears at your gate, you will send her straight home, her father said. Then he smiled. Your Olivia can visit her, and learn what women are for.

I smiled also. Olivia must learn to take her education about life where she can find it, I thought. His offer will make a splendid opportunity.

Good-bye until the next time, dear Celie, from a pitiful, cast-out woman who may perish during the rainy season.

Your loving sister,

Nettie

Dear Celie,

At first there was the faintest sound of movement in the forest. A kind of low humming. Then there was chopping and the sound of dragging. Then a scent, some days, of smoke. But now, after two months, during which I or the children or Corrine has been sick, all we hear is chopping and scraping and dragging. And every day we smell smoke.

Today one of the boys in my afternoon class burst out, as he entered, The road approaches! The road approaches! He had been hunting in the forest with his father and seen it.

Every day now the villagers gather at the edge of the village near the cassava fields, and watch the building of the road. And watching them, some on their stools and some squatted down on their haunches, all chewing cola nuts and making patterns in the dirt, I feel a great surge of love for them. For they do not approach the roadbuilders empty-handedly. Oh, no. Each day since they saw the road's approach they have been stuffing the roadbuilders with goat meat, millet mush, baked yam and cassava, cola nuts and palm wine. Each day is like a picnic, and I believe many friendships have been made, although the roadbuilders are from a different tribe some distance to the North and nearer the coast, and their language is somewhat different. I don't understand it, anyway, though the people of Olinka seem to. But they are clever people about most things, and understand new things very quickly.

It is hard to believe we've been here five years. Time moves slowly, but passes quickly. Adam and Olivia are nearly as tall as me and doing very well in all their studies. Adam has a special aptitude for figures and it worries Samuel that soon he will have nothing more to teach him in this field, having exhausted his own knowledge.

When we were in England we met missionaries who sent their children back home when it was no longer possible to teach them in the bush. But it is hard to imagine life here without the children. They love the open feeling of the village, and love living in huts. They are excited by the hunting expertise of the men and the self-sufficiency of the women in raising their crops. No matter how down I may be, and sometimes I get very down indeed, a hug from Olivia or Adam completely restores me to the level of functioning, if nothing else. Their mother and I are not as close as we once were, but I feel more like their aunt than ever. And the three of us look more and more alike every day.

About a month ago, Corrine asked me not to invite Samuel to my hut unless she were present. She said it gave the villagers the wrong idea. This was a real blow to me because I treasure his company. Since Corrine almost never visits me herself I will have hardly anybody to talk to, just in friendship. But the children still come and sometimes spend the night when their parents want to be alone. I love those times. We roast ground-nuts on my stove, sit on the floor and study maps of all the countries in the world. Sometimes Tashi comes over and tells stories that are popular among the Olinka children. I am encouraging her and Olivia to write them down in Olinka and English. It will be good practice for them. Olivia feels that, compared to Tashi, she has no good stories to tell. One day she started in on an "Uncle Remus" tale only to discover Tashi had the original version of it! Her little face just fell. But then we got into a discussion of how Tashi's people's stories got to America, which fascinated Tashi. She cried when Olivia told how her grandmother had been treated as a slave.

No one else in this village wants to hear about slavery, however. They acknowledge no responsibility whatsoever. This is one thing about them that I definitely do not like.

We lost Tashi's father during the last rainy season. He fell ill with malaria and nothing the healer concocted saved him. He refused to take the medicine we use for it, or to let Samuel visit him at all. It was my first Olinka funeral. The women paint their faces white and wear white shroudlike garments and cry in a high keening voice. They wrapped the body in barkcloth and buried it under a big tree in the forest. Tashi was heartbroken. All her young life she has tried to please her father, never quite realizing that, as a girl, she never could. But the death brought her and her mother closer together, and now Catherine feels like one of us. By one of us I mean me and the children and sometimes Samuel. She is still in mourning and sticking close to her hut, but she says she will not marry again (since she already has five boy children she can now do whatever she wants. She has become an honorary man) and when I went to visit her she made it very clear that Tashi must continue to learn. She is the most industrious of all Tashi's father's widows, and her fields are praised for their cleanliness, productivity and general attractiveness. Perhaps I can help her with her work. It is in work that the women get to know and care about each other. It was through work that Catherine became friends with her husband's other wives.

This friendship among women is something Samuel often talks about. Because the women share a husband but the husband does not share their friendships, it makes Samuel uneasy. It *is* confusing, I suppose. And it *is* Samuel's duty as a Christian minister to preach the bible's directive of one husband and one wife. Samuel is confused because to him, since the women are friends and will do anything for one another—not always, but more often than anyone from America would expect—and since they giggle and gossip and nurse each other's children, then they must be happy with things as they are. But many of the women rarely spend time with their husbands. Some of them were promised to old or middle-aged men at birth. Their lives always center around work and their children and other women (since a woman cannot really have a man for a friend without the worst kind of ostracism and gossip). They indulge their husbands, if anything. You should just see how they make admiration over them. Praise their smallest accomplishments. Stuff them with palm wine and sweets. No wonder the men are often childish. And a grown child is a dangerous thing, especially since, among the Olinka, the husband has life and death power over the wife. If he accuses one of his wives of witchcraft or infidelity, she can be killed.

Thank God (and sometimes Samuel's intervention) this has not happened since we've been here. But the stories Tashi tells are often about such gruesome events that happened in the recent past. And God forbid that the child of a favorite wife should fall ill! That is the point at which even the women's friendships break down, as each woman fears the accusation of sorcery from the other, or from the husband.

Merry Christmas to you and yours, dear Celie. We celebrate it here on the "dark" continent with prayer and song and a large picnic complete with watermelon, fresh fruit punch, and barbecue!

God bless you,
Nettie

Dearest Celie,

I meant to write you in time for Easter, but it was not a good time for me and I did not want to burden you with any distressing news. So a whole year has gone by. The first thing I should tell you about is the road. The road finally reached the cassava fields about nine months ago and the Olinka, who love nothing better than a celebration, outdid themselves preparing a feast for the roadbuilders who talked and laughed and cut their eyes at the Olinka women the whole day. In the evening many were invited into the village itself and there was merrymaking far into the night.

I think Africans are very much like white people back home, in that they think they are the center of the universe and that everything that is done is done for them. The Olinka definitely hold this view. And so they naturally thought the road being built was for them. And, in fact, the roadbuilders talked much of how quickly the Olinka will now be able to get to the coast. With a tarmac road it is only a three-day journey. By bicycle it will be even less. Of course no one in Olinka owns a bicycle, but one of the roadbuilders has one, and all the Olinka men covet it and talk of someday soon purchasing their own.

Well, the morning after the road was "finished" as far as the Olinka were concerned (after all, it had reached their village), what should we discover but that the roadbuilders were back at work. They have instructions to continue the road for another thirty miles! And to continue it on its present course right through the village of Olinka. By the time we were out of bed, the road was already being dug through Catherine's newly planted yam field. Of course the Olinka were up in arms. But the roadbuilders were literally up in arms. They had guns, Celie, with orders to shoot!

It was pitiful, Celie. The people felt so betrayed! They stood by helplessly—they really don't know how to fight, and rarely think of it since the old days of tribal wars—as their crops and then their very homes were destroyed. Yes. The roadbuilders didn't deviate an inch from the plan the headman was following. Every hut that lay in the proposed roadpath was leveled. And, Celie, our church, our school, my hut, all went down in a matter of hours. Fortunately, we were able to save all of our things, but with a tarmac road running straight through the middle of it, the village itself seems gutted.

Immediately after understanding the roadbuilders' intentions, the chief set off toward the coast, seeking explanations and reparations. Two weeks later he returned with even more disturbing news. The whole territory, including the Olinkas' village, now belongs to a rubber manufacturer in England. As he neared the coast, he was stunned to see hundreds and hundreds of villagers much like the Olinka clearing the forests on each side of the road, and planting rubber trees. The ancient, giant mahogany trees, all the trees, the game, everything of the forest was being destroyed, and the land was forced to lie flat, he said, and bare as the palm of his hand.

At first he thought the people who told him about the English rubber company were mistaken, if only about its territory including the Olinka village. But eventually he was directed to the governor's mansion, a huge white building, with flags flying in its yard, and there had an audience with the white man in charge. It was this man who gave the roadbuilders their orders, this man who knew about the Olinka only from a map. He spoke in English, which our chief tried to speak also.

It must have been a pathetic exchange. Our chief never learned English beyond an occasional odd phrase he picked up from Joseph, who pronounces "English" "Yanglush."

But the worst was yet to be told. Since the Olinka no longer own their village, they must pay rent for it, and in order to use the water, which also no longer belongs to them, they must pay a water tax.

At first the people laughed. It really did seem crazy. They've been here forever. But the chief did not laugh.

We will fight the white man, they said.

But the white man is not alone, said the chief. He has brought his army.

That was several months ago, and so far nothing has happened. The people live like ostriches, never setting foot on the new road if they can help it, and never, ever, looking towards the coast. We have built another church and school. I have another hut. And so we wait.

Meanwhile, Corrine has been very ill with African fever. Many missionaries in the past have died from it.

But the children are fine. The boys now accept Olivia and Tashi in class and more mothers are sending their daughters to school. The men do not like it: who wants a wife who knows everything her husband knows? they fume. But the women have their ways, and they love their children, even their girls.

I will write more when things start looking up. I trust God they will.

Your sister,
Nettie

Dearest Celie,

This whole year, after Easter, has been difficult. Since Corrine's illness, all her work has fallen on me, and I must nurse her as well, which she resents.

One day when I was changing her as she lay in bed, she gave me a long, mean, but somehow pitiful look. Why do my children look like you? she asked.

Do you really think they look so much like me? I said.

You could have spit them out, she said.

Maybe just living together, loving people makes them look like you, I said. You know how much some old married people look alike.

Even these women saw the resemblance the first day we came, she said.

And that's worried you all this time? I tried to laugh it off. But she just looked at me.

When did you first meet my husband? she wanted to know.

And that was when I knew what she thought. She thinks Adam and Olivia are my children, and that Samuel is their father!

Oh, Celie, this thing has been gnawing away at her all these years!

I met Samuel the same day I met you, Corrine, I said. (I still haven't got the hang of saying "Sister" all the time.) As God is my witness, that's the truth.

Bring the bible, she said.

I brought the bible, and placed my hand on it, and swore.

You've never known me to lie, Corrine, I said. Please believe I am not lying now.

Then she called Samuel, and made him swear that the day she met me was the day he met me also.

He said: I apologize for this, Sister Nettie, please forgive us.

As soon as Samuel left the room she made me raise my dress and she sat up in her sickbed to examine my stomach.

I felt so sorry for her, and so humiliated, Celie. And the way she treats the children is the hardest part. She doesn't want them near her, which they don't understand. How could they? They don't even know they were adopted.

The village is due to be planted in rubber trees this coming season. The Olinka hunting territory has already been destroyed, and the men must go farther and farther away to find game. The women spend all their time in the fields, tending their crops and praying. They sing to the earth and to the sky and to their cassava and groundnuts. Songs of love and farewell.

We are all sad, here, Celie. I hope life is happier for you.

Your sister,
Nettie

Dear Celie,

Guess what? Samuel thought the children were mine too! That is why he urged me to come to Africa with them. When I showed up at their house he thought I was following my children, and, soft-hearted as he is, didn't have the heart to turn me away.

If they are not yours, he said, whose are they?

But I had some questions for him, first.

Where did you get them? I asked. And Celie, he told me a story that made my hair stand on end. I hope you, poor thing, are ready for it.

Once upon a time, there was a well-to-do farmer who owned his own property near town. Our town, Celie. And as he did so well farming and everything he turned his hand to prospered, he decided to open a store, and try his luck selling dry goods as well. Well, his store did so well that he talked two of his brothers into helping him run it, and, as the months went by, they were doing better and better. Then the white merchants began to get together and complain that this store was taking all the black business away from them, and the man's blacksmith shop that he set up behind the store, was taking some of the white. This would not do. And so, one night, the man's store was burned down, his smithy destroyed, and the man and his two brothers dragged out of their homes in the middle of the night and hanged.

The man had a wife whom he adored, and they had a little girl, barely two years old. She was also pregnant with another child. When the neighbors brought her husband's body home, it had been mutilated and burnt. The sight of it nearly killed her, and her second baby, also a girl, was born at this time. Although the widow's body recovered, her mind was never the same. She continued to fix her husband's plate at mealtimes just as she'd always done and was always full of talk about the plans she and her husband had made. The neighbors, though not always intending to, shunned her more and more, partly because the plans she talked about were grander than anything they could even conceive of for colored people, and partly because her attachment to the past was so pitiful. She was a good-looking woman, though, and still owned land, but there was no one to work it for her, and she didn't know how herself; besides she kept waiting for her husband to finish the meal she'd cooked for him and go to the fields himself. Soon there was nothing to eat that the neighbors did not bring, and she and her small children grubbed around in the yard as best they could.

While the second child was still a baby, a stranger appeared in the community, and lavished all his attention on the widow and her children; in a short while, they were married. Almost at once she was pregnant a third time, though her mental health was no better. Every year thereafter, she was pregnant, every year she became weaker and more mentally unstable, until, many years after she married the stranger, she died.

Two years before she died she had a baby girl that she was too sick to keep. Then a baby boy. These children were named Olivia and Adam.

This is Samuel's story, almost word for word.

The stranger who married the widow was someone Samuel had run with long before he found Christ. When the man showed up at Samuel's house with first Olivia and then Adam, Samuel felt not only unable to refuse the children, but as if God had answered his and Corrine's prayers.

He never told Corrine about the man or about the children's "mother" because he hadn't wanted any sadness to cloud her happiness.

But then, out of nowhere, I appeared. He put two and two together, remembered that his old running buddy had always been a scamp, and took me in without any questions. Which, to tell the truth, had always puzzled me, but I put it down to

Christian charity. Corrine had asked me once whether I was running away from home. But I explained I was a big girl now, my family back home very large and poor, and it was time for me to get out and earn my own living.

Tears had soaked my blouse when Samuel finished telling me all this. I couldn't begin, then, to tell him the truth. But Celie, I can tell you. And I pray with all my heart that you will get this letter, if none of the others.

Pa is not our pa!

Your devoted Sister,
Nettie

Dear God,

That's it, say Shug. Pack your stuff. You coming back to Tennessee with me.

But I feels daze.

My daddy lynch. My mama crazy. All my little half-brothers and sisters no kin to me. My children not my sister and brother. Pa not pa.

You must be sleep.

Dear Nettie,

For the first time in my life I wanted to see Pa. So me and Shug dress up in our new blue flower pants that match and big floppy Easter hats that match too, cept her roses red, mine yellow, and us clam in the Packard and glide over there. They put in paved roads all up and down the county now and twenty miles go like nothing.

I saw Pa once since I left home. One day me and Mr. _____ was loading up the wagon at the feed store. Pa was with May Ellen and she was trying to fix her stocking. She was bent down over her leg and twisting the stocking into a knot above her knee, and he was standing over her tap-tap-tapping on the gravel with his cane. Look like he was thinking bout hitting her with it.

Mr. _____ went up to them all friendly, with his hand stuck out, but I kept loading the wagon and looking at the patterns on the sacks. I never thought I'd ever want to see him again.

Well, it was a bright Spring day, sort of chill at first, like it be round Easter, and the first thing us notice soon as we turn into the lane is how green everything is, like even though the ground everywhere else not warmed up good, Pa's land is warm and ready to go. Then all along the road there's Easter lilies and jonquils and daffodils and all kinds of little early wildflowers. Then us notice all the birds singing they little cans off, all up and down the hedge, that itself is putting out little yellow flowers smell like Virginia creeper. It all so different from the rest of the country us drive through, it make us real quiet. I know this sound funny, Nettie, but even the sun seem to stand a little longer over our heads.

Well, say Shug, all this is pretty enough. You never said how pretty it was.

It wasn't this pretty, I say. Every Easter time it used to flood, and all us children had colds. Anyhow, I say, us stuck close to the house, and it sure ain't so hot.

That ain't so hot? she ast, as we swung up a long curving hill I didn't remember, right up to a big yellow two story house with green shutters and a steep green shingle roof.

I laughed. Us must have took the wrong turn, I say. This some white person's house.

It was so pretty though that us stop the car and just set looking at it.

What kind of trees all them flowering? ast Shug.

I don't know, I say. Look like peach, plum, apple, maybe cherry. But whatever they is, they sure pretty.

All round the house, all in back of it, nothing but blooming trees. Then more lilies and jonquils and roses clamming over everything. And all the time the little birds from all over the rest of the county sit up in these trees just going to town.

Finally, after us look at it awhile, I say, It so quiet, nobody home, I guess.

Naw, say Shug, probably in church. A nice bright Sunday like this.

Us better leave then, I say, before whoever it is lives here gits back. But just as I say that I notice my eye is staying on a fig tree it recognize, and us hear a car turning up the drive. Who should be in the car but Pa and some young girl look like his child.

He git out on his side, then go round to open the door for her. She dress to kill in a pink suit, big pink hat and pink shoes, a little pink purse hanging on her arm. They look at our license tag and then come up to the car. She put her hand through his arm.

Morning, he says, when he gits up to Shug's window.

Morning, she says slow, and I can tell he not what she expect.

Anything I can do for you? He ain't notice me and probably wouldn't even if he looked at me.

Shug say, under her breath, Is this him?

I say, Yeah.

What shock Shug and shock me too is how young he look. He look older than the child he with, even if she is dress up like a woman, but he look young for somebody to be anybody that got grown children and nearly grown grandchildren. But then I remember, he not my daddy, just my children daddy.

What your mama do, ast Shug, rob the cradle?

But he not so young.

I brought Celie, say Shug. Your daughter Celie. She wanted to visit you. Got some questions to ast.

He seem to think back a second. *Celie?* he say. Like, Who Celie? Then he say, Yall git out and come up on the porch. Daisy, he say to the little woman with him, go tell Hetty to hold dinner. She squeeze his arm, reach up and kiss him on the jaw. He turn his head and watch her go up the walk, up the steps, and through the front door. He follow us up the steps, up on the porch, help us pull out rocking chairs, then say, Now, what yall want?

The children here? I ast.

What children? he say. Then he laugh. Oh, they gone with they mama. She up and left me, you know. Went back to her folks. Yeah, he say, you would remember May Ellen.

Why she leave? I ast.

He laugh some more. Got too old for me, I reckon.

Then the little woman come back out and sit on the armrest of his chair. He talk to us and fondle her arm.

This Daisy, he say. My new wife.

Why, say Shug, you don't look more than fifteen.

I ain't, say Daisy.

I'm surprise your people let you marry.

She shrug, look at Pa. They work for him, she say. Live on his land.

I'm her people now, he say.

I feels so sick I almost gag. Nettie in Africa, I say. A missionary. She wrote me that you ain't our real Pa.

Well, he say. So now you know.

Daisy look at me with pity all over her face. It just like him to keep that from you, she say. He told me how he brought up two little girls that wasn't even his, she say. I don't think I really believed it, till now.

Naw, he never told them, say Shug.

What a old sweetie pie, say Daisy, kissing him on top the head. He fondle and fondle her arm. Look at me and grin.

Your daddy didn't know how to git along, he say. Whitefolks lynch him. Too sad a story to tell pitiful little growing girls, he say. Any man would have done what I done.

Maybe not, say Shug.

He look at her, then look at me. He can tell she know. But what do he care?

Take me, he say, I know how they is. The key to all of 'em is money. The trouble with our people is as soon as they got out of slavery they didn't want to give the white man nothing else. But the fact is, you got to give 'em something. Either your money, your land, your woman or your ass. So what I did was just right off offer to give 'em money. Before I planted a seed, I made sure this one and that one knowed one seed out of three was planted for *him*. Before I ground a grain of wheat, the same thing. And when I opened up your daddy's old store in town, I bought me my own white boy to run it. And what make it so good, he say, I bought him with whitefolks' money.

Ask the busy man your questions, Celie, say Shug. I think his dinner getting cold.

Where my daddy buried, I ast. That all I really want to know.

Next to your mammy, he say.

Any marker, I ast.

He look at me like I'm crazy. Lynched people don't git no marker, he say. Like this something everybody know.

Mama got one? I ast.

He say, Naw.

The birds sing just as sweet when us leave as when us come. Then, look like as soon as us turn back on the main road, they stop. By the time us got to the cemetery, the sky gray.

Us look and look for Ma and Pa. Hope for some scrap of wood that say something. But us don't find nothing but weeds and cockleburrs and paper flowers fading on some of the graves. Shug pick up a old horseshoe somebody horse lose. Us took that old horseshoe and us turned round and round together until we was dizzy enough to fall out, and where us would have fell us stuck the horseshoe in the ground.

Shug say, Us each other's peoples now, and kiss me.

Dear Celie,

I woke up this morning bound to tell Corrine and Samuel everything. I went over to their hut and pulled up a stool next to Corrine's bed. She's so weak by now that all she can do is look unfriendly—and I could tell I wasn't welcome.

I said, Corrine, I'm here to tell you and Samuel the truth.

She said, Samuel already told me. If the children yours, why didn't you just say so?

Samuel said, Now, honey.

She said, Don't Now Honey me. Nettie swore on the bible to tell me the truth. To tell God the truth, and she lied.

Corrine, I said, I didn't lie. I sort of turned my back more on Samuel and whispered: You saw my stomach, I said.

What do I know about pregnancy, she said. I never experienced it myself. For all I know, women may be able to rub out all the signs.

They can't rub out stretch marks, I said. Stretch marks go right into the skin, and a woman's stomach stretches enough so that it keeps a little pot, like all the women have here.

She turned her face to the wall.

Corrine, I said, I'm the children's aunt. Their mother is my older sister, Celie.

Then I told them the whole story. Only Corrine was still not convinced.

You and Samuel telling so many lies, who can believe anything you say? she asked.

You've got to believe Nettie, said Samuel. Though the part about you and Pa was a real shock to him.

Then I remembered what you told me about seeing Corrine and Samuel and Olivia in town, when she was buying cloth to make her and Olivia dresses, and how you sent me to her because she was the only woman you'd ever seen with money. I tried to make Corrine remember that day, but she couldn't.

She gets weaker and weaker, and unless she can believe us and start to feel something for her children, I fear we will lose her.

Oh, Celie, unbelief is a terrible thing. And so is the hurt we cause others unknowingly.

Pray for us,

Nettie

Dearest Celie,

Every day for the past week I've been trying to get Corrine to remember meeting you in town. I know if she can just recall your face, she will believe Olivia (if not Adam) is your child. They think Olivia looks like me, but that is only because I look like you. Olivia has your face and eyes, exactly. It amazes me that Corrine didn't see the resemblance.

Remember the main street of town? I asked. Remember the hitching post in front of Finley's dry goods store? Remember how the store smelled like peanut shells?

She says she remembers all this, but no men speaking to her.

Then I remember her quilts. The Olinka men make beautiful quilts which are full of animals and birds and people. And as soon as Corrine saw them, she began to make a quilt that alternated one square of appliqued figures with one nine-patch block, using the clothes the children had outgrown, and some of her old dresses.

I went to her trunk and started hauling out quilts.

Don't touch my things, said Corrine. I'm not gone yet.

I held up first one and then another to the light, trying to find the first one I remembered her making. And trying to remember, at the same time, the dresses she and Olivia were wearing the first months I lived with them.

Aha, I said, when I found what I was looking for, and laid the quilt across the bed.

Do you remember buying this cloth? I asked, pointing to a flowered square. And what about this checkered bird?

She traced the patterns with her finger, and slowly her eyes filled with tears.

She was so much like Olivia! she said. I was afraid she'd want her back. So I forgot her as soon as I could. All I let myself think about was how the clerk treated me! I was acting like somebody because I was Samuel's wife, and a Spelman Seminary graduate, and he treated me like any ordinary nigger. Oh, my feelings were hurt! And I was mad! And that's what I thought about, even told Samuel about, on the way home. Not about your sister—what was her name?—Celie? Nothing about her.

She began to cry in earnest. Me and Samuel holding her hands.

Don't cry. Don't cry, I said. My sister was glad to see Olivia with you. Glad to see her alive. She thought both her children were dead.

Poor thing! said Samuel. And we sat there talking a little and holding on to each other until Corrine fell off to sleep.

But, Celie, in the middle of the night she woke up, turned to Samuel and said: I believe. And died anyway.

Your Sister in Sorrow,
Nettie

Dearest Celie,

Just when I think I've learned to live with the heat, the constant dampness, even steaminess of my clothes, the swampiness under my arms and between my legs, my friend comes. And cramps and aches and pains—but I must still keep going as if nothing is happening, or be an embarrassment to Samuel, the children and myself. Not to mention the villagers, who think women who have their friends should not even be seen.

Right after her mother's death, Olivia got *her* friend; she and Tashi tend to each other is my guess. Nothing is said to me, in any event, and I don't know how to bring the subject up. Which feels wrong to me; but if you talk to an Olinka girl about her private parts, her mother and father will be annoyed, and it is very important to Olivia not to be looked upon as an outsider. Although the one ritual they do have to celebrate womanhood is so bloody and painful, I forbid Olivia to even think about it.

Do you remember how scared I was when it first happened to me? I thought I had cut myself. But thank God you were there to tell me I was all right.

We buried Corrine in the Olinka way, wrapped in barkcloth under a large tree. All of her sweet ways went with her. All of her education and a heart intent on doing good. She taught me so much! I know I will miss her always. The children were stunned by their mother's death. They knew she was very sick, but death is not something they think about in relation to their parents or themselves. It was a strange little procession. All of us in our white robes and with our faces painted white. Samuel is like someone lost. I don't believe they've spent a night apart since their marriage.

And how are you? dear Sister. The years have come and gone without a single word from you. Only the sky above us do we hold in common. I look at it often as if, somehow, reflected from its immensities, I will one day find myself gazing into your eyes. Your dear, large, clean and beautiful eyes. Oh, Celie! My life here is nothing but work, work, work, and worry. What girlhood I might have had passed me by. And I have nothing of my own. No man, no children, no close friend, except for Samuel. But I *do* have children, Adam and Olivia. And I *do* have friends, Tashi and Catherine. I even have a family—this village, which has fallen on such hard times.

Now the engineers have come to inspect the territory. Two white men came yesterday and spent a couple of hours strolling about the village, mainly looking at the wells. Such is the innate politeness of the Olinka that they rushed about preparing food for them, though precious little is left, since many of the gardens that flourish at this time of the year have been destroyed. And the white men sat eating as if the food was beneath notice.

It is understood by the Olinka that nothing good is likely to come from the same persons who destroyed their houses, but custom dies hard. I did not speak to the men myself, but Samuel did. He said their talk was all of workers, kilometers of land, rainfall, seedlings, machinery, and whatnot. One seemed totally indifferent to the people around him—simply eating and then smoking and staring off into the distance—and the other, somewhat younger, appeared to be enthusiastic about learning the language. Before, he says, it dies out.

I did not enjoy watching Samuel speaking to either of them. The one who hung on every word, or the one who looked through Samuel's head.

Samuel gave me all of Corrine's clothes, and I need them, though none of our clothing is suitable in this climate. This is true even of the clothing the Africans wear. They used to wear very little, but the ladies of England introduced the Mother Hubbard, a long, cumbersome, ill-fitting dress, completely shapeless, that inevitably gets dragged in the fire, causing burns aplenty. I have never been able to bring myself to wear one of these dresses, which all seem to have been made with giants in mind, so I was glad to have Corrine's things. At the same time, I dreaded putting them on. I remembered her saying we should stop wearing each other's clothes. And the memory pained me.

Are you sure Sister Corrine would want this? I asked Samuel.

Yes, Sister Nettie, he said. Try not to hold her fears against her. At the end she understood, and believed. And forgave —whatever there was to forgive.

I should have said something sooner, I said.

He asked me to tell him about you, and the words poured out like water. I was dying to tell someone about us. I told him about my letters to you every Christmas and Easter, and about how much it would have meant to us if he had gone to see you after I left. He was sorry he hesitated to become involved.

If only I'd understood then what I know now! he said.

But how could he? There is so much we don't understand. And so much unhappiness comes because of that.

    love and Merry Christmas to you,

Your sister Nettie

Dear Nettie,

I don't write to God no more, I write to you.

What happen to God? ast Shug.

Who that? I say.

She look at me serious.

Big a devil as you is, I say, you not worried bout no God, surely.

She say, Wait a minute. Hold on just a minute here. Just because I don't harass it like some peoples us know don't mean I ain't got religion.

What God do for me? I ast.

She say, Celie! Like she shock. He gave you life, good health, and a good woman that love you to death.

Yeah, I say, and he give me a lynched daddy, a crazy mama, a lowdown dog of a step pa and a sister I probably won't ever see again. Anyhow, I say, the God I been praying and writing to is a man. And act just like all the other mens I know. Trifling, forgitful and lowdown.

She say, Miss Celie. You better hush. God might hear you.

Let 'im hear me, I say. If he ever listened to poor colored women the world would be a different place, I can tell you.

She talk and she talk, trying to budge me way from blasphemy. But I blaspheme much as I want to.

All my life I never care what people thought bout nothing I did, I say. But deep in my heart I care about God. What he going to think. And come to find out, he don't think. Just sit up there glorying in being deef, I reckon. But it ain't easy, trying to do without God. Even if you know he ain't there, trying to do without him is a strain.

I is a sinner, say Shug. Cause I was born. I don't deny it. But once you find out what's out there waiting for us, what else can you be?

Sinners have more good times, I say.

You know why? she ast.

Cause you ain't all the time worrying bout God, I say.

Naw, that ain't it, she say. Us worry bout God a lot. But once us feel loved by God, us do the best us can to please him with what us like.

You telling me God love you, and you ain't never done nothing for him? I mean, not go to church, sing in the choir, feed the preacher and all like that?

But if God love me, Celie, I don't have to do all that. Unless I want to. There's a lot of other things I can do that I speck God likes.

Like what? I ast.

Oh, she say. I can lay back and just admire stuff. Be happy. Have a good time.

Well, this sound like blasphemy sure nuff.

She say, Celie, tell the truth, have you ever found God in church? I never did. I just found a bunch of folks hoping for him to show. Any God I ever felt in church I brought in with me. And I think all the other folks did too. They come to church to *share* God, not find God.

Some folks didn't have him to share, I said. They the ones didn't speak to me while I was there struggling with my big belly and Mr. _____ children.

Right, she say.

Then she say: Tell me what your God look like, Celie.

Aw naw, I say. I'm too shame. Nobody ever ast me this before, so I'm sort of took by surprise. Besides, when I think about it, it don't seem quite right. But it all I got. I decide to stick up for him, just to see what Shug say.

Okay, I say. He big and old and tall and graybearded and white. He wear white robes and go barefooted.

Blue eyes? she ast.

Sort of bluish-gray. Cool. Big though. White lashes, I say.

She laugh.

Why you laugh? I ast. I don't think it so funny. What you expect him to look like, Mr. _____ ?

That wouldn't be no improvement, she say. Then she tell me this old white man is the same God she used to see when she prayed. If you wait to find God in church, Celie, she say, that's who is bound to show up, cause that's where he live.

How come? I ast.

Cause that's the one that's in the white folks' white bible.

Shug! I say. God wrote the bible, white folks had nothing to do with it.

How come he look just like them, then? she say. Only bigger? And a heap more hair. How come the bible just like everything else they make, all about them doing one thing and another, and all the colored folks doing is gitting cursed?

I never thought bout that.

Nettie say somewhere in the bible it say Jesus' hair was like lamb's wool, I say.

Well, say Shug, if he came to any of these churches we talking bout he'd have to have it conked before anybody paid him any attention. The last thing niggers want to think about they God is that his hair kinky.

That's the truth, I say.

Ain't no way to read the bible and not think God white, she say. Then she sigh. When I found out I thought God was white, and a man, I lost interest. You mad cause he don't seem to listen to your prayers. Humph! Do the mayor listen to anything colored say? Ask Sofia, she say.

But I don't have to ast Sofia. I know white people never listen to colored, period. If they do, they only listen long enough to be able to tell you what to do.

Here's the thing, say Shug. The thing I believe. God is inside you and inside everybody else. You come into the world with God. But only them that search for it inside find it. And sometimes it just manifest itself even if you not looking, or don't know what you looking for. Trouble do it for most folks, I think. Sorrow, lord. Feeling like shit.

It? I ast.

Yeah, It. God ain't a he or a she, but a It.

But what do it look like? I ast.

Don't look like nothing, she say. It ain't a picture show. It ain't something you can look at apart from anything else, including yourself. I believe God is everything, say Shug. Everything that is or ever was or ever will be. And when you can feel that, and be happy to feel that, you've found It.

Shug a beautiful something, let me tell you. She frown a little, look out cross the yard, lean back in her chair, look like a big rose.

She say, My first step from the old white man was trees. Then air. Then birds. Then other people. But one day when I was sitting quiet and feeling like a motherless child, which I was, it come to me: that feeling of being part of everything, not separate at all. I knew that if I cut a tree, my arm would bleed. And I laughed and I cried and I run all round the house. I knew just what it was. In fact, when it happen, you can't miss it. It sort of like you know what, she say, grinning and rubbing high up on my thigh.

Shug! I say.

Oh, she say. God love all them feelings. That's some of the best stuff God did. And when you know God loves 'em you enjoys 'em a lot more. You can just relax, go with everything that's going, and praise God by liking what you like.

God don't think it dirty? I ast.

Naw, she say. God made it. Listen, God love everything you love—and a mess of stuff you don't. But more than anything else, God love admiration.

You saying God vain? I ast.

Naw, she say. Not vain, just wanting to share a good thing. I think it pisses God off if you walk by the color purple in a field somewhere and don't notice it.

What it do when it pissed off? I ast.

Oh, it make something else. People think pleasing God is all God care about. But any fool living in the world can see it always trying to please us back.

Yeah? I say.

Yeah, she say. It always making little surprises and springing them on us when us least expect.

You mean it want to be loved, just like the bible say.

Yes, Celie, she say. Everything want to be loved. Us sing and dance, make faces and give flower bouquets, trying to be loved. You ever notice that trees do everything to git attention we do, except walk?

Well, us talk and talk bout God, but I'm still adrift. Trying to chase that old white man out of my head. I been so busy thinking bout him I never truly notice nothing God make. Not a blade of corn (how it do that?) not the color purple (where it come from?). Not the little wildflowers. Nothing.

Now that my eyes opening, I feels like a fool. Next to any little scrub of a bush in my yard, Mr. _____'s evil sort of shrink. But not altogether. Still, it is like Shug say, You have to git man off your eyeball, before you can see anything a'tall.

Man corrupt everything, say Shug. He on your box of grits, in your head, and all over the radio. He try to make you think he everywhere. Soon as you think he everywhere, you think he God. But he ain't. Whenever you trying to pray, and man plop himself on the other end of it, tell him to git lost, say Shug. Conjure up flowers, wind, water, a big rock.

But this hard work, let me tell you. He been there so long, he don't want to budge. He threaten lightening, floods and earthquakes. Us fight. I hardly pray at all. Every time I conjure up a rock, I throw it.

Amen

Dear Nettie,

When I told Shug I'm writing to you instead of to God, she laugh. Nettie don't know these people, she say. Considering who I been writing to, this strike me funny.

It was Sofia you saw working as the mayor's maid. The woman you saw carrying the white woman's packages that day in town. Sofia Mr. _____'s son Harpo's wife. Polices lock her up for sassing the mayor's wife and hitting the mayor back. First she was in prison working in the laundry and dying fast. Then us got her move to the mayor's house. She had to sleep in a little room up under the house, but it was better than prison. Flies, maybe, but no rats.

Anyhow, they kept her eleven and a half years, give her six months off for good behavior so she could come home early to her family. Her bigger children married and gone, and her littlest children mad at her, don't know who she is. Think she act funny, look old and dote on that little white gal she raise.

Yesterday us all had dinner at Odessa's house. Odessa Sofia's sister. She raise the kids. Her and her husband Jack. Harpo's woman Squeak, and Harpo himself.

Sofia sit down at the big table like there's no room for her. Children reach cross her like she not there. Harpo and Squeak act like a old married couple. Children call Odessa mama. Call Squeak little mama. Call Sofia "Miss." The only one seem to pay her any tention at all is Harpo and Squeak's little girl, Suzie Q. She sit cross from Sofia and squinch up her eyes at her.

As soon as dinner over, Shug push back her chair and light a cigarette. Now is come the time to tell yall, she say.

Tell us what? Harpo ast.

Us leaving, she say.

Yeah? say Harpo, looking round for the coffee. And then looking over at Grady.

Us leaving, Shug say again. Mr. _____ look struck, like he always look when Shug say she going anywhere. He reach down and rub his stomach, look off side her head like nothing been said.

Grady say, Such good peoples, that's the truth. The salt of the earth. But—time to move on.

Squeak not saying nothing. She got her chin glued to her plate. I'm not saying nothing either. I'm waiting for the feathers to fly.

Celie is coming with us, say Shug.

Mr. _____'s head swivel back straight. Say what? he ast.

Celie is coming to Memphis with me.

Over my dead body, Mr. _____ say.

You satisfied that what you want, Shug say, cool as clabber.

Mr. _____ start up from his seat, look at Shug, plop back down again. He look over at me. I thought you was finally happy, he say. What wrong now?

You a lowdown dog is what's wrong, I say. It's time to leave you and enter into the Creation. And your dead body just the welcome mat I need.

Say what? he ast. Shock.

All round the table folkses mouths be dropping open.

You took my sister Nettie away from me, I say. And she was the only person love me in the world.

Mr. _____ start to sputter. ButButButButBut. Sound like some kind of motor.

But Nettie and my children coming home soon, I say. And when she do, all us together gon whup your ass.

Nettie and your children! say Mr. _____. You talking crazy.

I got children, I say. Being brought up in Africa. Good schools, lots of fresh air and exercise. Turning out a heap better than the fools you didn't even try to raise.

Hold on, say Harpo.

Oh, hold on hell, I say. If you hadn't tried to rule over Sofia the white folks never would have caught her.

Sofia so surprise to hear me speak up she ain't chewed for ten minutes.

That's a lie, say Harpo.

A little truth in it, say Sofia.

Everybody look at her like they surprise she there. It like a voice speaking from the grave.

You was all rotten children, I say. You made my life a hell on earth. And your daddy here ain't dead horse's shit.

Mr. _____ reach over to slap me. I jab my case knife in his hand.

You bitch, he say. What will people say, you running off to Memphis like you don't have a house to look after?

Shug say, Albert. Try to think like you got some sense. Why any woman give a shit what people think is a mystery to me.

Well, say Grady, trying to bring light. A woman can't git a man if peoples talk.

Shug look at me and us giggle. Then us laugh sure nuff. Then Squeak start to laugh. Then Sofia. All us laugh and laugh.

Shug say, Ain't they something? Us say um *hum*, and slap the table, wipe the water from our eyes.

Harpo look at Squeak. Shut up Squeak, he say. It bad luck for women to laugh at men.

She say, Okay. She sit up straight, suck in her breath, try to press her face together.

He look at Sofia. She look at him and laugh in his face. I already had my bad luck, she say. I had enough to keep me laughing the rest of my life.

Harpo look at her like he did the night she knock Mary Agnes down. A little spark fly cross the table.

I got six children by this crazy woman, he mutter.

Five, she say.

He so outdone he can't even say, Say what?

He look over at the youngest child. She sullen, mean, mischeevous and too stubborn to live in this world. But he love her best of all. Her name Henrietta.

Henrietta, he say.

She say, Yesssss . . . like they say it on the radio.

Everything she say confuse him. Nothing, he say. Then he say, Go git me a cool glass of water.

She don't move.

Please, he say.

She go git the water, put it by his plate, give him a peck on the cheek. Say, Poor Daddy. Sit back down.

You not gitting a penny of my money, Mr. _____ say to me. Not one thin dime.

Did I ever ast you for money? I say. I never ast you for nothing. Not even for your sorry hand in marriage.

Shug break in right there. Wait, she say. Hold it. Somebody else going with us too. No use in Celie being the only one taking the weight.

Everybody sort of cut they eyes at Sofia. She the one they can't quite find a place for. She the stranger.

It ain't me, she say, and her look say, Fuck you for entertaining the thought. She reach for a biscuit and sort of root her behind deeper into her seat. One look at this big stout graying, wildeyed woman and you know not even to ast. Nothing.

But just to clear this up neat and quick, she say, I'm home. Period.

Her sister Odessa come and put her arms round her. Jack move up close.

Course you is, Jack say.

Mama crying? ast one of Sofia children.

Miss Sofia too, another one say.

But Sofia cry quick, like she do most things.

Who going? she ast.

Nobody say nothing. It so quiet you can hear the embers dying back in the stove. Sound like they falling in on each other.

Finally, Squeak look at everybody from under her bangs. Me, she say. I'm going North.

You going What? say Harpo. He so surprise. He begin to sputter, sputter, just like his daddy. Sound like I don't know what.

I want to sing, say Squeak.

Sing! say Harpo.

Yeah, say Squeak. Sing. I ain't sung in public since Jolentha was born. Her name Jolentha. They call her Suzie Q.

You ain't had to sing in public since Jolentha was born. Everything you need I done provided for.

I need to sing, say Squeak.

Listen Squeak, say Harpo. You can't go to Memphis. That's all there is to it.

Mary Agnes, say Squeak.

Squeak, Mary Agnes, what difference do it make?

It make a lot, say Squeak. When I was Mary Agnes I could sing in public.

Just then a little knock come on the door.

Odessa and Jack look at each other. Come in, say Jack.

A skinny little white woman stick most of herself through the door.

Oh, you all are eating dinner, she say. Excuse me.

That's all right, say Odessa. Us just finishing up. But there's plenty left. Why don't you sit down and join us. Or I could fix you something to eat on the porch.

Oh lord, say Shug.

It Eleanor Jane, the white girl Sofia used to work for.

She look round till she spot Sofia, then she seem to let her breath out. No thank you, Odessa, she say. I ain't hungry. I just come to see Sofia.

Sofia, she say. Can I see you on the porch for a minute.

All right, Miss Eleanor, she say. Sofia push back from the table and they go out on the porch. A few minutes later us hear Miss Eleanor sniffling. Then she really boo-hoo.

What the matter with her? Mr. _____ ast.

Henrietta say, Prob-limbszzzz . . . like somebody on the radio.

Odessa shrug. She always underfoot, she say.

A lot of drinking in that family, say Jack. Plus, they can't keep that boy of theirs in college. He get drunk, aggravate his sister, chase women, hunt niggers, and that ain't all.

That enough, say Shug. Poor Sofia.

Pretty soon Sofia come back in and sit down.

What the matter? ast Odessa.

A lot of mess back at the house, say Sofia.

You got to go back up there? Odessa ast.

Yeah, say Sofia. In a few minutes. But I'll try to be back before the children go to bed.

Henrietta ast to be excuse, say she got a stomach ache.

Squeak and Harpo's little girl come over, look up at Sofia, say, You gotta go Misofia?

Sofia say, Yeah, pull her up on her lap. Sofia on parole, she say. Got to act nice.

Suzie Q lay her head on Sofia chest. Poor Sofia, she say, just like she heard Shug. Poor Sofia.

Mary Agnes, darling, say Harpo, look how Suzie Q take to Sofia.

Yeah, say Squeak, children know good when they see it. She and Sofia smile at one nother.

Go on sing, say Sofia, I'll look after this one till you come back.

You will? say Squeak.

Yeah, say Sofia.

And look after Harpo, too, say Squeak. Please ma'am.

                                                                Amen

Dear Nettie,

Well, you know wherever there's a man, there's trouble. And it seem like, going to Memphis, Grady was all over the car. No matter which way us change up, he want to sit next to Squeak.

While me and Shug sleeping and he driving, he tell Squeak all about life in North Memphis, Tennessee. I can't half sleep for him raving bout clubs and clothes and forty-nine brands of beer. Talking so much bout stuff to drink make me have to pee. Then us have to find a road going off into the bushes to relieve ourselves.

Mr. _____ try to act like he don't care I'm going.

You'll be back, he say. Nothing up North for nobody like you. Shug got talent, he say. She can sing. She got spunk, he say. She can talk to anybody. Shug got looks, he say. She can stand up and be notice. But what you got? You ugly. You skinny. You shape funny. You too scared to open your mouth to people. All you fit to do in Memphis is be Shug's maid. Take out her slop-jar and maybe cook her food. You not that good a cook either. And this house ain't been clean good since my first wife died. And nobody crazy or backward enough to want to marry you, neither. What you gon do? Hire yourself out to farm? He laugh. Maybe somebody let you work on they railroad.

Any more letters come? I ast.

He say, What?

You heard me, I say. Any more letters from Nettie come?

If they did, he say, I wouldn't give 'em to you. You two of a kind, he say. A man try to be nice to you, you fly in his face.

I curse you, I say.

What that mean? he say.

I say, Until you do right by me, everything you touch will crumble.

He laugh. Who you think you is? he say. You can't curse nobody. Look at you. You black, you pore, you ugly, you a woman. Goddam, he say, you nothing at all.

Until you do right by me, I say, everything you even dream about will fail. I give it to him straight, just like it come to me. And it seem to come to me from the trees.

Whoever heard of such a thing, say Mr. _____. I probably didn't whup your ass enough.

Every lick you hit me you will suffer twice, I say. Then I say, You better stop talking because all I'm telling you ain't coming just from me. Look like when I open my mouth the air rush in and shape words.

Shit, he say. I should have lock you up. Just let you out to work.

The jail you plan for me is the one in which you will rot, I say.

Shug come over to where us talking. She take one look at my face and say Celie! Then she turn to Mr. _____. Stop Albert, she say. Don't say no more. You just going to make it harder on yourself.

I'll fix her wagon! say Mr. _____, and spring toward me.

A dust devil flew up on the porch between us, fill my mouth with dirt. The dirt say, Anything you do to me, already done to you.

Then I feel Shug shake me. Celie, she say. And I come to myself.

I'm pore, I'm black, I may be ugly and can't cook, a voice say to everything listening. But I'm here.

Amen, say Shug. Amen, amen.

Dear Nettie,

So what is it like in Memphis? Shug's house is big and pink and look sort of like a barn. Cept where you would put hay, she got bedrooms and toilets and a big ballroom where she and her band sometime work. She got plenty grounds round the house and a bunch of monuments and a fountain out front. She got statues of folks I never heard of and never hope to see. She got a whole bunch of elephants and turtles everywhere. Some big, some little, some in the fountain, some up under the trees. Turtles and elephants. And all over her house. Curtains got elephants, bedspreads got turtles.

Shug give me a big back bedroom overlook the backyard and the bushes down by the creek.

I know you use to morning sun, she say.

Her room right cross from mine, in the shade. She work late, sleep late, git up late. No turtles or elephants on her bedroom furniture, but a few statues spread out round the room. She sleep in silks and satins, even her sheets. And her bed round!

I wanted to build me a round house, say Shug, but everybody act like that's backward. You can't put windows in a round house, they say. But I made me up some plans, anyway. One of these days . . . she say, showing me the papers.

It a big round pink house, look sort of like some kind of fruit. It got windows and doors and a lot of trees round it.

What it made of? I ast.

Mud, she say. But I wouldn't mind concrete. I figure you could make the molds for each section, pour the concrete in, let it get hard, knock off the mold, glue the parts together somehow and you'd have your house.

Well, I like this one you got, I say. That one look a little small.

It ain't bad, say Shug. But I just feel funny living in a square. If I was square, then I could take it better, she say.

Us talk bout houses a lot. How they built, what kind of wood people use. Talk about how to make the outside around your house something you can use. I sit down on the bed and start to draw a kind of wood skirt around her concrete house. You can sit on this, I say, when you get tired of being in the house.

Yeah, she say, and let's put awning over it. She took the pencil and put the wood skirt in the shade.

Flower boxes go here, she say, drawing some.

And geraniums in them, I say, drawing some.

And a few stone elephants right here, she say.

And a turtle or two right here.

And how us know you live here too? she ast.

Ducks! I say.

By the time us finish our house look like it can swim or fly.

Nobody cook like Shug when she cook.

She get up early in the morning and go to market. Buy only stuff that's fresh. Then she come home and sit on the back step humming and shelling peas or cleaning collards or fish or whatever she bought. Then she git all her pots going at once and turn on the radio. By one o'clock everything ready and she call us to the table. Ham and greens and chicken and cornbread. Chitlins and blackeyed peas and souse. Pickled okra and watermelon rind. Caramel cake and blackberry pie.

Us eat and eat, and drink a little sweet wine and beer too.

Then Shug and me go fall out in her room to listen to music till all that food have a chance to settle. It cool and dark in her room. Her bed soft and nice. Us lay with our arms round each other. Sometimes Shug read the paper out loud. The news always sound crazy. People fussing and fighting and pointing fingers at other people, and never even looking for no peace.

People insane, say Shug. Crazy as betsy bugs. Nothing built this crazy can last. Listen, she say. Here they building a dam so they can flood out a Indian tribe that been there since time. And look at this, they making a picture bout that man that kilt all them women. The same man that play the killer is playing the priest. And look at these shoes they making now, she say. Try to walk a mile in a pair of them, she say. You be limping all the way home. And you see what they trying to do with that man that beat the Chinese couple to death. Nothing whatsoever.

Yeah, I say, but some things pleasant.

Right, say Shug, turning the page. Mr. and Mrs. Hamilton Hufflemeyer are pleased to announce the wedding of their daughter June Sue. The Morrises of Endover Road are spearheading a social for the Episcopal church. Mrs. Herbert Edenfail was on a visit last week to the Adirondacks to see her ailing mother, the former Mrs. Geoffrey Hood.

All these faces look happy enough, say Shug. Big and beefy. Eyes clear and innocent, like they don't know them other crooks on the front page. But they the same folks, she say.

But pretty soon, after cooking a big dinner and making a to-do about cleaning the house, Shug go back to work. That mean she never give a thought to what she eat. Never give a thought to where she sleep. She on the road somewhere for weeks at a time, come home with bleary eyes, rotten breath, overweight and sort of greasy. No place hardly to stop and really wash herself, especially her hair, on the road.

Let me go with you, I say. I can press your clothes, do your hair. It would be like old times, when you was singing at Harpo's.

She say, Naw. She can act like she not bored in front of a audience of strangers, a lot of them white, but she wouldn't have the nerve to try to act in front of me.

Besides, she say. You not my maid. I didn't bring you to Memphis to be that. I brought you here to love you and help you get on your feet.

And now she off on the road for two weeks, and me and Grady and Squeak rattle round the house trying to get our stuff together. Squeak been going round to a lot of clubs and Grady been taking her. Plus he seem to be doing a little farming out back the house.

I sit in the dining room making pants after pants. I got pants now in every color and size under the sun. Since us started making pants down home, I ain't been able to stop. I change the cloth, I change the print, I change the waist, I change the pocket. I change the hem, I change the fullness of the leg. I make so many pants Shug tease me. I didn't know what I was starting, she say, laughing. Pants all over her chairs, hanging all in front of the china closet. Newspaper patterns and cloth all over the table and the floor. She come home, kiss me, step over all the mess. Say, before she leave again, How much money you think you need *this* week?

Then finally one day I made the perfect pair of pants. For my sugar, naturally. They soft dark blue jersey with teeny patches of red. But what make them so good is, they totally comfortable. Cause Shug eat a lot of junk on the road, and drink, her stomach bloat. So the pants can be let out without messing up the shape. Because she have to pack her stuff and fight wrinkles, these pants are soft, hardly wrinkle at all, and the little figures in the cloth always look perky and bright. And they full round the ankle so if she want to sing in 'em and wear 'em sort of like a long dress, she can. Plus, once Shug put them on, she knock your eyes out.

Miss Celie, she say. You is a wonder to behold.

I duck my head. She run round the house looking at herself in mirrors. No matter how she look, she look good.

You know how it is when you don't have nothing to do, I say, when she brag to Grady and Squeak bout her pants. I sit here thinking bout how to make a living and before I know it I'm off on another pair pants.

By now Squeak see a pair *she* like. Oh, Miss Celie, she say. Can I try on those?

She put on a pair the color of sunset. Orangish with a little grayish fleck. She come back out looking just fine. Grady look at her like he could eat her up.

Shug finger the pieces of cloth I got hanging on everything. It all soft, flowing, rich and catch the light. This a far cry from that stiff army shit us started with, she say. You ought to make up a special pair to thank and show Jack.

What she say that for. The next week I'm in and out of stores spending more of Shug's money. I sit looking out cross the yard trying to see in my mind what a pair of pants for Jack would look like. Jack is tall and kind and don't hardly say anything. Love children. Respect his wife, Odessa, and all Odessa amazon sisters. Anything she want to take on, he right there. Never talking much, though. That's the main thing. And then I remember one time he touch me. And it felt like his fingers had eyes. Felt like he knew me all over, but he just touch my arm up near the shoulder.

I start to make pants for Jack. They have to be camel. And soft and strong. And they have to have big pockets so he can keep a lot of children's things. Marbles and string and pennies and rocks. And they have to be washable and they have to fit closer round the leg than Shug's so he can run if he need to snatch a child out the way of something. And they have to be something he can lay back in when he hold Odessa in front of the fire. And . . .

I dream and dream and dream over Jack's pants. And cut and sew. And finish them. And send them off.

Next thing I hear, Odessa want a pair.

Then Shug want two more pair just like the first. Then everybody in her band want some. Then orders start to come in from everywhere Shug sing. Pretty soon I'm swamp.

One day when Shug come home, I say, You know, I love doing this, but I got to git out and make a living pretty soon. Look like this just holding me back.

She laugh. Let's us put a few advertisements in the paper, she say. And let's us raise your prices a hefty notch. And let's us just go ahead and give you this diningroom for your factory and git you some more women in here to cut and sew, while you sit back and design. You making your living, Celie, she say. Girl, you on your way.

Nettie, I am making some pants for you to beat the heat in Africa. Soft, white, thin. Drawstring waist. You won't ever have to feel too hot and overdress again. I plan to make them by hand. Every stitch I sew will be a kiss.

Amen,

Your Sister, Celie
Folkspants, Unlimited.
Sugar Avery Drive
Memphis, Tennessee

Dear Nettie,

I am so happy. I got love, I got work, I got money, friends and time. And you alive and be home soon. With our children.

Jerene and Darlene come help me with the business. They twins. Never married. Love to sew. Plus, Darlene trying to teach me how to talk. She say US not so hot. A dead country give-away. You say US where most folks say WE, she say, and peoples think you dumb. Colored peoples think you a hick and white folks be amuse.

What I care? I ast. I'm happy.

But she say I feel more happier talking like she talk. Can't nothing make me happier than seeing you again, I think, but I don't say nothing. Every time I say something the way I say it, she correct me until I say it some other way. Pretty soon it feel like I can't think. My mind run up on a thought, git confuse, run back and sort of lay down.

You sure this worth it? I ast.

She she say Yeah. Bring me a bunch of books. Whitefolks all over them, talking bout apples and dogs.

What I care bout dogs? I think.

Darlene keep trying. Think how much better Shug feel with you educated, she say. She won't be shame to take you anywhere.

Shug not shame no how, I say. But she don't believe this the truth. Sugar, she say one day when Shug home, don't you think it be nice if Celie could talk proper?

Shug say, She can talk in sign language for all I care. She make herself a nice cup of herb tea and start talking bout hot oiling her hair.

But I let Darlene worry on. Sometimes I think bout the

apples and the dogs, sometimes I don't. Look like to me only a fool would want you to talk in a way that feel peculiar to your mind. But she sweet and she sew good and us need something to haggle over while us work.

I'm busy making pants for Sofia now. One leg be purple, one leg be red. I dream Sofia wearing these pants, one day she was jumping over the moon.

Amen,

Your sister, Celie

Dear Nettie,

Walking down to Harpo and Sofia house it feel just like old times. Cept the house new, down below the juke-joint, and it a lot bigger than it was before. Then too I feels different. Look different. Got on some dark blue pants and a white silk shirt that look righteous. Little red flat-heel slippers, and a flower in my hair. I pass Mr. _____ house and him sitting up on the porch and he didn't even know who I was.

Just when I raise my hand to knock, I hear a crash. Sound like a chair falling over. Then I hear arguing.

Harpo say, Whoever heard of women pallbearers. That all I'm trying to say.

Well, say Sofia, you said it. Now you can hush.

I know she your mother, say Harpo. But still.

You gon help us or not? say Sofia.

What it gon look like? say Harpo. Three big stout women pallbearers look like they ought to be home frying chicken.

Three of our brothers be with us, on the other side, say Sofia. I guess they look like field hands.

But peoples use to men doing this sort of thing. Women weaker, he say. People think they weaker, say they weaker, anyhow. Women spose to take it easy. Cry if you want to. Not try to take over.

Try to take over, say Sofia. The woman dead. I can cry and take it easy and lift the coffin too. And whether you help us or not with the food and the chairs and the get-together afterward, that's exactly what I plan to do.

It git real quiet. After while Harpo say, real soft to Sofia, Why you like this, huh? Why you always think you have to do things your own way? I ast your mama bout it one time, while you was in jail.

What she say? ast Sofia.

She say you think your way as good as anybody else's. Plus, it yours.

Sofia laugh.

I know my timing bad, but I knock anyhow.

Oh, Miss Celie, say Sofia, flinging open the screen. How good you look. Don't she look good, Harpo? Harpo stare at me like he never seen me before.

Sofia give me a big hug and kiss me on the jaw. Where Miss Shug? she ast.

She on the road, I say. But she was real sorry to hear your mama pass.

Well, say Sofia, Mama fight the good fight. If there's a glory anywhere she right in the middle of it.

How you, Harpo? I ast. Still eating?

He and Sofia laugh.

I don't reckon Mary Agnes could come back this time, say Sofia. She was just here bout a month ago. You just ought to see her and Suzie Q.

Naw, I say. She finally working steady, singing at two or three clubs round town. Folks love her a lot.

Suzie Q so proud of her, she say. Love her singing. Love her perfume. Love her dresses. Love to wear her hats and shoes.

How she doing in school? I ast.

Oh, she fine, say Sofia. Smart as a little whip. Once she got over being mad her mama left her and found out I was Henrietta's real mama, she was all right. She dote on Henrietta.

How Henrietta?

Evil, say Sofia. Little face always look like stormy weather. But maybe she'll grow out of it. It took her daddy forty years to learn to be pleasant. He used to be nasty to his own ma.

Yall see much of him? I ast.

Bout as much as us see of Mary Agnes, say Sofia.

Mary Agnes not the same, say Harpo.

What you mean? I ast.

I don't know, he say. Her mind wander. She talk like she

drunk. And every time she turn round look like she want to see Grady.

They both smoke a lot of reefer, I say.

Reefer, say Harpo. What kind of a thing is that?

Something make you feel good, I say. Something make you see visions. Something make your love come down. But if you smoke it too much it make you feebleminded. Confuse. Always need to clutch hold of somebody. Grady grow it in the backyard, I say.

I never heard of such a thing, say Sofia. It grow in the ground?

Like a weed, I say. Grady got half a acre if he got a row.

How big it git? ast Harpo.

Big, I say. Way up over my head. And bushy.

And what part they smoke?

The leaf, I say.

And they smoke up all that? he ast.

I laugh. Naw, he sell most of it.

You ever taste it? he ast.

Yeah, I say. He make it up in cigarettes, sell 'em for a dime. It rot your breath, I say, but yall want to try one?

Not if it make us crazy, say Sofia. It hard enough to git by without being a fool.

It just like whiskey, I say. You got to stay ahead of it. You know a little drink now and then never hurt nobody, but when you can't git started without asking the bottle, you in trouble.

You smoke it much, Miss Celie? Harpo ast.

Do I look like a fool? I ast. I smoke when I want to talk to God. I smoke when I want to make love. Lately I feel like me and God make love just fine anyhow. Whether I smoke reefer or not.

Miss Celie! say Sofia. Shock.

Girl, I'm bless, I say to Sofia. God know what I mean.

Us sit round the kitchen table and light up. I show 'em how to suck in they wind. Harpo git strangle. Sofia choke.

Pretty soon Sofia say, That funny, I never heard that humming before.

What humming? Harpo ast.

Listen, she say.

Us git real quiet and listen. Sure enough, us hear ummmmmmmmm.

What it coming from? ast Sofia. She git up and go look out the door. Nothing there. Sound git louder. Ummmmmmmm.

Harpo go look out the window. Nothing out there, he say. Humming say UMMMMMMMM.

I think I know what it is, I say.

They say, What?

I say, Everything.

Yeah, they say. That make a lots of sense.

Well, say Harpo at the funeral, here come the amazons.

Her brothers there too, I whisper back. What you call them?

I don't know, he say. Them three always stood by they crazy sisters. Nothing yet could get 'em to budge. I wonder what they wives have to put up with.

They all march stoutly in, shaking the church, and place Sofia mother in front the pulpit.

Folks crying and fanning and trying to keep a stray eye on they children, but they don't stare at Sofia and her sisters. They act like this the way it always done. I love folks.

Amen

Dear Nettie,

The first thing I notice bout Mr. _____ is how clean he is. His skin shine. His hair brush back.

When he walk by the casket to review Sofia mother's body he stop, whisper something to her. Pat her shoulder. On his way back to his seat he look over at me. I raise my fan and look off the other way.

Us went back to Harpo's after the funeral.

I know you won't believe this, Miss Celie, say Sofia, but Mr. _____ act like he trying to git religion.

Big a devil as he is, I say, trying is bout all he can do.

He don't go to church or nothing, but he not so quick to judge. He work real hard too.

What? I say. Mr. _____ work!

He sure do. He out there in the field from sunup to sundown. And clean that house just like a woman.

Even cook, say Harpo. And what more, wash the dishes when he finish.

Naw, I say. Yall must still be dope.

But he don't talk much or be round people, Sofia say.

Sound like craziness closing in to me, I say.

Just then, Mr. _____ walk up.

How you Celie, he say.

Fine, I say. I look in his eyes and I see he feeling scared of me. Well, good, I think. Let him feel what I felt.

Shug didn't come with you this time? he say.

Naw, I say. She have to work. Sorry bout Sofia mama though.

Anybody be sorry, he say. The woman that brought Sofia in the world brought something.

I don't say nothing.

They put her away nice, he say.

They sure did, I say.

And so many grandchildren, he say. Well. Twelve children, all busy multiplying. Just the family enough to fill the church.

Yeah, I say. That's the truth.

How long you here for? he say.

Maybe a week, I say.

You know Harpo and Sofia baby girl real sick? he say.

Naw, I didn't, I say. I point to Henrietta in the crowd. There she is over there, I say. She look just fine.

Yeah, she look fine, he say, but she got some kind of blood disease. Blood sort of clot up in her veins every once in a while, make her sick as a dog. I don't think she gon make it, he say.

Great goodness of life, I say.

Yeah, he say. It hard for Sofia. She still have to try to prop up that white gal she raise. Now her mama dead. Her health not that good either. Plus, Henrietta a hard row to hoe whether she sick or well.

Oh, she a little mess, I say. Then I think back to one of Nettie's letters bout the sicknesses children have where she at in Africa. Seem like to me she mention something bout blood clots. I try to remember what she say African peoples do, but I can't. Talking to Mr. _____ such a surprise I can't think of nothing. Not even nothing else to say.

Mr. _____ stand waiting for me to say something, looking off up to his house. Finally he say, Good evening, and walk away.

Sofia say after I left, Mr. _____ live like a pig. Shut up in the house so much it stunk. Wouldn't let nobody in until finally Harpo force his way in. Clean the house, got food. Give his daddy a bath. Mr. _____ too weak to fight back. Plus, too far gone to care.

He couldn't sleep, she say. At night he thought he heard bats outside the door. Other things rattling in the chimney. But the worse part was having to listen to his own heart. It did pretty well as long as there was daylight, but soon as night come, it went crazy. Beating so loud it shook the room. Sound like drums.

Harpo went up there plenty nights to sleep with him, say Sofia. Mr. _____would be all cram up in a corner of the bed. Eyes clamp on different pieces of furniture, see if they move in his direction. You know how little he is, say Sofia. And how big and stout Harpo is. Well, one night I walked up to tell Harpo something—and the two of them was just laying there on the bed fast asleep. Harpo holding his daddy in his arms.

After that, I start to feel again for Harpo, Sofia say. And pretty soon us start work on our new house. She laugh. But did I say it been easy? If I did, God would make me cut my own switch.

What make him pull through? I ast.

Oh, she say, Harpo made him send you the rest of your sister's letters. Right after that he start to improve. You know meanness kill, she say.

Amen

Dearest Celie,

By now I expected to be home. Looking into your face and saying Celie, is it really you? I try to picture what the years have brought you in the way of weight and wrinkles—or how you fix your hair. From a skinny, hard little something I've become quite plump. And some of my hair is gray!

But Samuel tells me he loves me plump and graying.

Does this surprise you?

We were married last Fall in England where we tried to get relief for the Olinka from the churches and the Missionary Society.

As long as they could, the Olinka ignored the road and the white builders who came. But eventually they had to notice them because one of the first things the builders did was tell the people they must be moved elsewhere. The builders wanted the village site as headquarters for the rubber plantation. It is the only spot for miles that has a steady supply of fresh water.

Protesting and driven, the Olinka, along with their missionaries, were placed on a barren stretch of land that has no water at all for six months of the year. During that time, they must buy water from the planters. During the rainy season there is a river and they are trying to dig holes in the nearby rocks to make cisterns. So far they collect water in discarded oil drums, which the builders brought.

But the most horrible thing to happen had to do with the roofleaf, which, as I must have written you, the people worship as a God and which they use to cover their huts. Well, on this barren strip of ground the planters erected workers' barracks. One for men and one for women and children. But, because the Olinka swore they would never live in a dwelling not covered by their God, Roofleaf, the builders left these barracks uncovered. Then they proceeded to plow under the Olinka village and everything else for miles around. Including every last stalk of roofleaf.

After nearly unbearable weeks in the hot sun, we were awakened one morning by the sound of a large truck pulling into the compound. It was loaded with sheets of corrugated tin.

Celie, we had to *pay* for the tin. Which exhausted what meager savings the Olinka had, and nearly wiped out the money Samuel and I had managed to put by for the education of the children once we return home. Which we have planned to do each year since Corrine died, only to find ourselves more and more involved in the Olinka's problems. Nothing could be uglier than corrugated tin, Celie. And as they struggled to put up roofs of this cold, hard, glittery, ugly metal the women raised a deafening ululation of sorrow that echoed off the cavern walls for miles around. It was on this day that the Olinka acknowledged at least temporary defeat.

Though the Olinka no longer ask anything of us, beyond teaching their children—because they can see how powerless we and our God are—Samuel and I decided we must do something about this latest outrage, even as many of the people to whom we felt close ran away to join the *mbeles* or forest people, who live deep in the jungle, refusing to work for whites or be ruled by them.

So off we went, with the children, to England.

It was an incredible voyage, Celie, not only because we had almost forgot about the rest of the world, and such things as ships and coal fires and streetlights and oatmeal, but because on the ship with us was the white woman missionary whom we'd heard about years ago. She was now retired from missionary work and going back to England to live. She was traveling with a little African boy whom she introduced as her grandchild!

Of course it is impossible to ignore the presence of an aging white woman accompanied by a small black child. The ship was in a tither. Each day she and the child walked about the deck alone, groups of white people falling into silence as they passed.

She is a jaunty, stringy, blue-eyed woman, with hair the

color of silver and dry grass. A short chin, and when she speaks she seems to be gargling.

I'm pushing on for sixty-five, she told us, when we found ourselves sharing a table for dinner one night. Been in the tropics most of my life. But, she said, a big war is coming. Bigger than the one they were starting when I left. It'll go hard on England, but I expect we'll survive. I missed the other war, she said. I mean to be present for this one.

Samuel and I had never really thought about war.

Why, she said, the signs are all over Africa. India too, I expect. First there's a road built to where you keep your goods. Then your trees are hauled off to make ships and captain's furniture. Then your land is planted with something you can't eat. Then you're forced to work it. That's happening all over Africa, she said. Burma too, I expect.

But Harold here and I decided to get out. Didn't we Harry? she said, giving the little boy a biscuit. The child said nothing, just chewed his biscuit thoughtfully. Adam and Olivia soon took him off to explore the lifeboats.

Doris' story—the woman's name is Doris Baines—is an interesting one. But I won't bore you with it as we eventually became bored.

She was born to great wealth in England. Her father was Lord Somebody or Other. They were forever giving or attending parties that were no fun. Besides, she wanted to write books. Her family were against it. Totally. They hoped she'd marry.

Me *marry*! she hooted. (Really, she has the oddest ideas.)

They did everything to convince me, she said. You can't imagine. I never saw so many milkfed young men in all my life as when I was nineteen and twenty. Each one more boring than the last. Can anything *be* more boring than an upper-class Englishman? she said. They remind one of bloody mushrooms.

Well, she rattled on, through endless dinners, because the captain assigned us permanently to the same table. It seems the notion of becoming a missionary struck her one evening she was getting ready for yet another tedious date, and lay in the tub thinking a convent would be better than the castle in which she lived. She could think, she could write. She could be her own boss. But wait. As a nun she would not be her own boss. God would be boss. The virgin mother. The mother superior. Etc. Etc. Ah, but a missionary! Far off in the wilds of India, alone! It seemed like bliss.

And so she cultivated a pious interest in heathens. Fooled her parents. Fooled the Missionary Society, who were so taken with her quick command of languages they sent her to Africa (worst luck!) where she began writing novels about everything under the sun.

My pen name is Jared Hunt, she said. In England and even in America, I'm a run-away success. Rich, famous. An eccentric recluse who spends most of his time shooting wild game.

Well now, she continued, several evenings later, you don't think I paid much attention to the heathen? I saw nothing wrong with them as they were. And they seemed to like *me* well enough. I was actually able to help them a good deal. I was a writer, after all, and I wrote reams of paper in their behalf: about their culture, their behavior, their needs, that sort of thing. You'd be surprised how good writing matters when you're going after money. I learned to speak their language faultlessly, and to throw off the missionary snoopers back at headquarters I wrote entire reports in it. I tapped the family vaults for close on to a million pounds before I got anything from the missionary societies or rich old family friends. I built a hospital, a grammar school. A college. A swimming pool—the one luxury I permitted myself, since swimming in the river one is subject to attack by leeches.

You wouldn't believe the peace! she said, at breakfast, halfway to England. Within a year everything as far as me and the heathen were concerned ran like clockwork. I told them right off that their souls were no concern of mine, that I wanted to write books and not be disturbed. For this pleasure I was prepared to pay. Rather handsomely.

In a burst of appreciation one day, I'm afraid the chief—not knowing what else to do, no doubt—presented me with a couple of wives. I don't think it was commonly believed I was a woman. There seemed some question in their minds just what I was. Anyhow. I educated the two young girls as best I could.

Sent them to England, of course, to learn medicine and agriculture. Welcomed them home when they returned, gave them away in marriage to two young chaps who were always about the place, and began the happiest period of my life as the grandmother of their children. I must say, she beamed, I've turned out to be fab-o as a grand*mama*. I learned it from the Akweans. They never spank their children. Never lock them away in another part of the hut. They do a bit of bloody cutting around puberty. But Harry's mother the doctor is going to change all that. Isn't she Harold?

Anyway, she said. When I get to England I'll put a stop to their bloody encroachments. I'll tell them what to do with their bloody road and their bloody rubber plantations and their bloody sunburned but still bloody boring English planters and engineers. I am a very wealthy woman, and I *own* the village of Akwee.

We listened to most of this in more or less respectful silence. The children were very taken with young Harold, though he never said a word in our presence. He seemed fond of his grandmother and used to her, but her verbosity produced in him a kind of soberly observant speechlessness.

He's quite different with us though, said Adam, who is really a great lover of children, and could get through to any child given half an hour. Adam makes jokes, he sings, he clowns and knows games. And he has the sunniest smile, most of the time—and great healthy African teeth.

As I write about his sunny smile I realize he's been unusually glum during this trip. Interested and excited, but not really *sunny*, except when he's with young Harold.

I will have to ask Olivia what's wrong. She is thrilled at the thought of going back to England. Her mother used to tell her about the thatched cottages of the English and how they reminded her of the roofleaf huts of the Olinka. They are square, though, she'd say. More like our church and school than like our homes, which Olivia thought very strange.

When we reached England, Samuel and I presented the Olinka's grievances to the bishop of the English branch of our church, a youngish man wearing spectacles who sat thumbing through a stack of Samuel's yearly reports. Instead of even mentioning the Olinka the bishop wanted to know how long it had been since Corrine's death, and why, as soon as she died, I had not returned to America.

I really did not understand what he was driving at.

Appearances, Miss _____, he said. Appearances. What must the natives think?

About what? I asked.

Come, come, he said.

We behave as brother and sister to each other, said Samuel.

The bishop smirked. Yes, he did.

I felt my face go hot.

Well, there was more of this, but why burden you with it? You know what some people are, and the bishop was one of them. Samuel and I left without even a word about the Olinka's problems.

Samuel was so angry, I was frightened. He said the only thing for us to do, if we wanted to remain in Africa, was join the *mbeles* and encourage all the Olinka to do the same.

But suppose they do not want to go? I asked. Many of them are too old to move back into the forest. Many are sick. The women have small babies. And then there are the youngsters who want bicycles and British clothes. Mirrors and shiny cooking pots. They want to work for the white people in order to have these things.

Things! he said, in disgust. Bloody *things!*

Well, we have a month here anyway, I said, let's make the most of it.

Because we had spent so much of our money on tin roofs and the voyage over, it had to be a poor man's month in England. But it was a very good time for us. We began to feel ourselves a family, without Corrine. And people meeting us on the street never failed (if they spoke to us at all) to express the sentiment that the children looked just like the two of us. The children began to accept this as natural, and began going out to view the sights that interested them, alone. Leaving their father and me to our quieter, more sedate pleasures, one of which was simple conversation.

Samuel, of course, was born in the North, in New York, and grew up and was educated there. He met Corrine through his aunt who had been a missionary, along with Corrine's aunt, in the Belgian Congo. Samuel frequently accompanied his aunt Althea to Atlanta, where Corrine's aunt Theodosia lived.

These two ladies had been through marvelous things together, said Samuel, laughing. They'd been attacked by lions, stampeded by elephants, flooded out by rains, made war on by "natives." The tales they told were simply incredible. There they sat on a heavily antimacassared horsehair sofa, two prim and proper ladies in ruffles and lace, telling these stupendous stories over tea.

Corrine and I as teenagers used to attempt to stylize these tales into comics. We called them such things as THREE MONTHS IN A HAMMOCK, or SORE HIPS OF THE DARK CONTINENT. Or, A MAP OF AFRICA: A GUIDE TO NATIVE INDIFFERENCE TO THE HOLY WORD.

We made fun of them, but we were riveted on their adventures, and on the ladies' telling of them. They were so staid looking. So proper. You really couldn't imagine them actually building—with their own hands—a school in the bush. Or battling reptiles. Or unfriendly Africans who thought, since they were wearing dresses with things that looked like wings behind, they should be able to fly.

Bush? Corrine would snicker to me or me to her. And just the sound of the word would send us off into quiet hysteria, while we calmly sipped our tea. Because of course they didn't realize they were being funny, and to us they were, very. And of course the prevailing popular view of Africans at that time contributed to our feeling of amusement. Not only were Africans savages, they were bumbling, inept savages, rather like their bumbling, inept brethren at home. But we carefully, not to say studiously, avoided this very apparent connection.

Corrine's mother was a dedicated housewife and mother who disliked her more adventurous sister. But she never prevented Corrine from visiting. And when Corrine was old enough, she sent her to Spelman Seminary where Aunt Theodosia had gone. This was a very interesting place. It was started by two white missionaries from New England who used to wear identical dresses. Started in a church basement, it soon moved up to Army barracks. Eventually these two ladies were able to get large sums of money from some of the richest men in America, and so the place grew. Buildings, trees. Girls were taught everything: Reading, Writing, Arithmetic, sewing, cleaning, cooking. But more than anything else, they were taught to serve God and the colored community. Their official motto was OUR WHOLE SCHOOL FOR CHRIST. But I always thought their unofficial motto should have been OUR COMMUNITY COVERS THE WORLD, because no sooner had a young woman got through Spelman Seminary than she began to put her hand to whatever work she could do for her people, anywhere in the world. It was truly astonishing. These very polite and proper young women, some of them never having set foot outside their own small country towns, except to come to the Seminary, thought nothing of packing up for India, Africa, the Orient. Or for Philadelphia or New York.

Sixty years or so before the founding of the school, the Cherokee Indians who lived in Georgia were forced to leave their homes and walk, through the snow, to resettlement camps in Oklahoma. A third of them died on the way. But many of them refused to leave Georgia. They hid out as colored people and eventually blended with us. Many of these mixed-race people were at Spelman. Some remembered who they actually were, but most did not. If they thought about it at all (and it became harder to think about Indians because there were none around) they thought they were yellow or reddish brown and wavy haired because of white ancestors, not Indian.

Even Corrine thought this, he said. And yet, I always felt her Indianness. She was so quiet. So reflective. And she could erase herself, her spirit, with a swiftness that truly startled, when she knew the people around her could not respect it.

It did not seem hard for Samuel to talk about Corrine while we were in England. It wasn't hard for me to listen.

It all seems so improbable, he said. Here I am, an aging man whose dreams of helping people have been just that, dreams. How Corrine and I as children would have laughed at ourselves.

TWENTY YEARS A FOOL OF THE WEST, OR MOUTH AND ROOFLEAF DISEASE: A TREATISE ON FUTILITY IN THE TROPICS. Etc. Etc. We failed so utterly, he said. We became as comical as Althea and Theodosia. I think her awareness of this fueled Corrine's sickness. She was far more intuitive than I. Her gift for understanding people much greater. She used to say the Olinka resented us, but I wouldn't see it. But they do, you know.

No, I said, it isn't resentment, exactly. It really is indifference. Sometimes I feel our position is like that of flies on an elephant's hide.

I remember once, before Corrine and I were married, Samuel continued, Aunt Theodosia had one of her at-homes. She had them every Thursday. She'd invited a lot of "serious young people" as she called them, and one of them was a young Harvard scholar named Edward. DuBoyce was his last name, I think. Anyhow, Aunt Theodosia was going on about her African adventures, leading up to the time King Leopold of Belgium presented her with a medal. Well Edward, or perhaps his name was Bill, was a very impatient sort. You saw it in his eyes, you could see it in the way he moved his body. He was never still. As Aunt Theodosia got closer to the part about her surprise and joy over receiving this medal—which validated her service as an exemplary missionary in the King's colony—DuBoyce's foot began to pat the floor rapidly and uncontrollably. Corrine and I looked at each other in alarm. Clearly this man had heard this tale before and was not prepared to endure it a second time.

Madame, he said, when Aunt Theodosia finished her story and flashed her famous medal around the room, do you realize King Leopold cut the hands off workers who, in the opinion of his plantation overseers, did not fulfill their rubber quota? Rather than cherish that medal, Madame, you should regard it as a symbol of your unwitting complicity with this despot who worked to death and brutalized and eventually exterminated thousands and thousands of African peoples.

Well, said Samuel, silence struck the gathering like a blight. Poor Aunt Theodosia! There's something in all of us that wants a medal for what we have done. That wants to be appreciated.

And Africans certainly don't deal in medals. They hardly seem to care whether missionaries exist.

Don't be bitter, I said.

How can I not? he said.

The Africans never asked us to come, you know. There's no use blaming them if we feel unwelcome.

It's worse than unwelcome, said Samuel. The Africans don't even *see* us. They don't even recognize us as the brothers and sisters they sold.

Oh, Samuel, I said. Don't.

But you know, he had started to cry. Oh Nettie, he said. That's the heart of it, don't you see. We love them. We try every way we can to show that love. But they reject us. They never even listen to how we've suffered. And if they listen they say stupid things. Why don't you speak our language? they ask. Why can't you remember the old ways? Why aren't you happy in America, if everyone there drives motorcars?

Celie, it seemed as good a time as any to put my arms around him. Which I did. And words long buried in my heart crept to my lips. I stroked his dear head and face and I called him darling and dear. And I'm afraid, dear, dear Celie, that concern and passion soon ran away with us.

I hope when you receive this news of your sister's forward behavior you will not be shocked or inclined to judge me harshly. Especially when I tell you what a total joy it was. I was transported by ecstasy in Samuel's arms.

You may have guessed that I loved him all along; but I did not know it. Oh, I loved him as a brother and respected him as a friend, but Celie, I love him bodily, *as a man!* I love his walk, his size, his shape, his smell, the kinkiness of his hair. I love the very texture of his palms. The pink of his inner lip. I love his big nose. I love his brows. I love his feet. And I love his dear eyes in which the vulnerability and beauty of his soul can be plainly read.

The children saw the change in us immediately. I'm afraid, my dear, we were radiant.

We love each other dearly, Samuel told them, with his arm around me. We intend to marry.

But before we do, I said, I must tell you something about my life and about Corrine and about someone else. And it was then I told them about you, Celie. And about their mother Corrine's love of them. And about being their aunt.

But where is this other woman, your sister? asked Olivia.

I explained your marriage to Mr. _____ as best I could.

Adam was instantly alarmed. He is a very sensitive soul who hears what isn't said as clearly as what is.

We will go back to America soon, said Samuel to reassure him, and see about her.

The children stood up with us in a simple church ceremony in London. And it was that night, after the wedding dinner, when we were all getting ready for bed, that Olivia told me what has been troubling her brother. He is missing Tashi.

But he's also very angry with her, she said, because when we left, she was planning to scar her face.

I didn't know this. One of the things we thought we'd helped stop was the scarring or cutting of tribal marks on the faces of young women.

It is a way the Olinka can show they still have their own ways, said Olivia, even though the white man has taken everything else. Tashi didn't want to do it, but to make her people feel better, she's resigned. She's going to have the female initiation ceremony too, she said.

Oh, no, I said. That's so dangerous. Suppose she becomes infected?

I know, said Olivia. I told her nobody in America or Europe cuts off pieces of themselves. And anyway, she should have had it when she was eleven, if she was going to have it. She's too old for it now.

Well, some men are circumcized, I said, but that's just the removal of a bit of skin.

Tashi was happy that the initiation ceremony isn't done in Europe or America, said Olivia. That makes it even more valuable to her.

I see, I said.

She and Adam had an awful fight. Not like any they've had before. He wasn't teasing her or chasing her around the village or trying to tie roofleaf twigs in her hair. He was mad enough to strike her.

Well, it's a good thing he didn't, I said. Tashi would have jammed his head through her rug loom.

I'll be glad when we get back home, said Olivia. Adam isn't the only one who misses Tashi.

She kissed me and her father good night. Adam soon came in to do the same.

Mama Nettie, he said, sitting on the bed next to me, how do you know when you really love someone?

Sometimes you don't know, I said.

He is a beautiful young man, Celie. Tall and broad-shouldered, with a deep, thoughtful voice. Did I tell you he writes verses? And loves to sing? He's a son to make you proud.

Your loving sister,

Nettie

P.S. Your brother Samuel sends his love as well.

Dearest Celie,

When we returned home everyone seemed happy to see us. When we told them our appeal to the church and the Missionary Society failed, they were disappointed. They literally wiped the smiles off their faces along with the sweat, and returned, dejected, to their barracks. We went on to our building, a combination church, house and school, and began to unpack our things.

The children . . . I realize I shouldn't call them children, they're grown, went in search of Tashi; an hour later they returned dumbfounded. They discovered no sign of her. Catherine, her mother, is planting rubber trees some distance from the compound, they were told. But no one had seen Tashi all day.

Olivia was very disappointed. Adam was trying to appear unconcerned, but I noticed he was absentmindedly biting the skin around his nails.

After two days it became clear that Tashi was deliberately hiding. Her friends said while we were away she'd undergone both the facial scarification ceremony and the rite of female initiation. Adam went quite gray at this news. Olivia merely stricken and more concerned than ever to find her.

It was not until Sunday that we saw Tashi. She'd lost a considerable amount of weight, and seemed listless, dull-eyed and tired. Her face was still swollen from half a dozen small, neat incisions high on each cheek. When she put out her hand to Adam he refused to take it. He just looked at her scars, turned on his heel and left.

She and Olivia hugged. But it was a quiet, heavy embrace.

Nothing like the boisterous, giggling behavior I expect from them.

Tashi is, unfortunately, ashamed of these scars on her face, and now hardly ever raises her head. They must be painful too because they look irritated and red.

But this is what the villagers are doing to the young women and even the men. Carving their identification as a people into their children's faces. But the children think of scarification as backward, something from their grandparents' generation, and often resist. So the carving is done by force, under the most appalling conditions. We provide antiseptics and cotton and a place for the children to cry and nurse their wounds.

Each day Adam presses us to leave for home. He can no longer bear living as we do. There aren't even any trees near us, just giant boulders and smaller rocks. And more and more of his companions are running away. The real reason, of course, is he can no longer bear his conflicting feelings about Tashi, who is beginning, I think, to appreciate the magnitude of her mistake.

Samuel and I are truly happy, Celie. And so grateful to God that we are! We still keep a school for the littlest children; those eight and over are already workers in the fields. In order to pay rent for the barracks, taxes on the land, and to buy water and wood and food, everyone must work. So, we teach the young ones, babysit the babies, look after the old and sick, and attend birthing mothers. Our days are fuller than ever, our sojourn in England already a dream. But all things look brighter because I have a loving soul to share them with.

Your sister,
Nettie

Dearest Nettie,

The man us knowed as Pa is dead.

How come you still call him Pa? Shug ast me the other day.

But, too late to call him Alphonso. I never even remember Ma calling him by his name. She always said, Your Pa. I reckon to make us believe it better. Anyhow, his little wife, Daisy, call me up on the telephone in the middle of the night.

Miss Celie, she say, I got bad news. Alphonso dead.

Who? I ast.

Alphonso, she say. Your stepdaddy.

How he die? I ast. I think of killing, being hit by a truck, struck by lightening, lingering disease. But she say, Naw, he died in his sleep. Well, not quite in his sleep, she say. Us was spending a little time in bed together, you know, before us drop off.

Well, I say, you have my sympathy.

Yes ma'am, she say, and I thought I had this house too, but look like it belong to your sister Nettie and you.

Say what? I ast.

Your stepdaddy been dead over a week, she say. When us went to town to hear the will read yesterday, you could have knock me over with a feather. Your real daddy owned the land and the house and the store. He left it to your mama. When your mama died, it passed on to you and your sister Nettie. I don't know why Alphonso never told you that.

Well, I say, anything coming from him, I don't want it.

I hear Daisy suck in her breath. How about your sister Nettie, she say. You think she feel the same way?

I wake up a little bit then. By the time Shug roll over and ast me who it is, I'm beginning to see the light.

Don't be a fool, Shug say, nudging me with her foot. You got your own house now. Your daddy and mama left it for you. That dog of a stepdaddy just a bad odor passing through.

But I never had no house, I say. Just to think about having my own house enough to scare me. Plus, this house I'm gitting is bigger than Shug's, got more land around it. And, it come with a store.

My God, I say to Shug. Me and Nettie own a drygood store. What us gon sell?

How bout pants? she say.

So us hung up the phone and rush down home again to look at the property.

About a mile before us got to town us come up on the entrance to the colored cemetery. Shug was sound asleep, but something told me I ought to drive in. Pretty soon I see something look like a short skyscraper and I stop the car and go up to it. Sure enough it's got Alphonso's name on it. Got a lot of other stuff on it too. Member of this and that. Leading business-man and farmer. Upright husband and father. Kind to the poor and helpless. He been dead two weeks but fresh flowers still blooming on his grave.

Shug git out the car and come stand by me.

Finally she yawn loud and stretch herself. The son of a bitch still dead, she say.

Daisy try to act like she glad to see us, but she not. She got two children and look pregnant with one more. But she got nice clothes, a car, and Alphonso left her all his money. Plus, I think she manage to set her folks up while she live with him.

She say, Celie, the old house you remember was torn down so Alphonso could build this one. He got an Atlanta architect to design it, and these tiles come all the way from New York. We was standing in the kitchen at the time. But he put tiles everywhere. Kitchen, toilet, back porch. All around the fireplac-es in back and front parlour. But this the house go with the place, right on, she say. Of course I did take the furniture, because Alphonso bought it special for me.

Fine with me, I say. I can't get over having a house. Soon as Daisy leave me with the keys I run from one room to another like I'm crazy. Look at this, I say to Shug. Look at that! She look, she grin. She hug me whenever she git the chance and I stand still.

You doin' all right, Miss Celie, she say. God know where you live.

Then she took some cedar sticks out of her bag and lit them and gave one of them to me. Us started at the very top of the house in the attic, and us smoked it all the way down to the basement, chasing out all the evil and making a place for good.

Oh, Nettie, us have a house! A house big enough for us and our children, for your husband and Shug. Now you can come home cause you have a home to come to!

Your loving sister,
Celie

Dear Nettie,

My heart broke.

Shug love somebody else.

Maybe if I had stayed in Memphis last summer it never would have happen. But I spent the summer fixing up the house. I thought if you come anytime soon, I want it to be ready. And it is real pretty, now, and comfortable. And I found me a nice lady to live in it and look after it. Then I come home to Shug.

Miss Celie, she say, how would you like some Chinese food to celebrate your coming home?

I loves Chinese food. So off us go to the restaurant. I'm so excited bout being home again I don't even notice how nervous Shug is. She a big graceful woman most of the time, even when she mad. But I notice she can't git her chopsticks to work right. She knock over her glass of water. Somehow or nother her eggroll come unravel.

But I think she just so glad to see me. So I preen and pose for her and stuff myself with wonton soup and fried rice.

Finally the fortune cookies come. I love fortune cookies. They so cute. And I read my fortune right away. It say, because you are who you are, the future look happy and bright.

I laugh. Pass it on to Shug. She look at it and smile. I feel at peace with the world.

Shug pull her slip of paper out real slow, like she scared of what might be on it.

Well? I say, watching her read it. What it say?

She look down at it, look up at me. Say, It say I got the hots for a boy of nineteen.

Let me see, I say, laughing. And I read it out loud. A burnt finger remember the fire, it say.

I'm trying to tell you, Shug say.

Trying to tell me what? I'm so dense it still don't penetrate. For one thing, it been a long time since I thought about boys and I ain't never thought about men.

Last year, say Shug, I hired a new man to work in the band. I almost didn't because he can't play nothing but flute. And who ever heard of blues flute? I hadn't. The very notion sound crazy. But it was just my luck that blues flute is the one thing blues music been lacking and the minute I heard Germaine play I knew this for a fact.

Germaine? I ast.

Yeah, she say, Germaine. I don't know who give him that flittish name, but it suit him.

Then she start right in to rave about this boy. Like all his good points have to be stuff I'm dying to hear.

Oh, she say. He little. He cute. Got nice buns. You know, real bantu. She so used to telling me everything she rattle on and on, gitting more excited and in-love looking by the minute. By the time she finish talking bout his neat little dancing feet and git back up to his honey brown curly hair, I feel like shit.

Hold it, I say. Stop. Shug, you killing me.

She halt in mid-praise. Her eyes fill with tears and her face crumple. Oh God, Celie, she say. I'm sorry. I just been dying to tell somebody, and you the somebody I usually tell.

Well, I say, if words could kill, I'd be in the ambulance.

She put her face in her hands and start to cry. Celie, she say, through her fingers, I still love you.

But I just sit there and watch her. Seem like all my wonton soup turn to ice.

Why you so upset? she ast, when us got back home. You never seem to git upset bout Grady. And he was my husband.

Grady never bring no sparkle to your eye, I think. But I don't say nothing. I'm too far away.

Course, she say, Grady so dull, Jesus. And when you finish talking bout women and reefer you finish Grady. But still, she say.

I don't say nothing.

She try to laugh. I was so glad he lit out after Mary Agnes I didn't know what to do, she say. I don't know who tried to teach him what to do in the bedroom, but it must have been a furniture salesman.

I don't say nothing. Stillness, coolness. Nothingness. Coming fast.

You notice when they left here together going to Panama I didn't shed a tear? But now really, she say, what they gon look like in Panama?

Poor Mary Agnes, I think. How could anybody guess old dull Grady would end up running a reefer plantation in Panama?

Course they making boocoos of money, say Shug. And Mary Agnes outdress everybody down there, the way she tell it in her letters. And at least Grady let her sing. What little snatches of her songs she can still remember. But really, she say, Panama? Where is it at, anyhow? Is it down there round Cuba? Us ought to go to Cuba, Miss Celie, you know? Lots of gambling there and good times. A lots of colored folks look like Mary Agnes. Some real black, like us. All in the same family though. Try to pass for white, somebody mention your grandma.

I don't say nothing. I pray to die, just so I don't never have to speak.

All right, say Shug. It started when you was down home. I missed you, Celie. And you know I'm a high natured woman.

I went and got a piece of paper that I was using for cutting patterns. I wrote her a note. It said, Shut up.

But Celie, she say. I have to make you understand. Look, she say. I'm gitting old. I'm fat. Nobody think I'm good looking no more, but you. Or so I thought. He's nineteen. A baby. How long can it last?

He's a man. I write on the paper.

Yeah, she say. He is. And I know how you feel about men. But I don't feel that way. I would never be fool enough to take any of them seriously, she say, but some mens can be a lots of fun.

Spare me, I write.

Celie, she say. All I ast is six months. Just six months to have my last fling. I got to have it Celie. I'm too weak a woman not to. But if you just give me six months, Celie, I will try to make our life together like it was.

Not hardly. I write.

Celie, she say, Do you love me? She down on her knees by now, tears falling all over the place. My heart hurt so much I can't believe it. How can it keep beating, feeling like this? But I'm a woman. I love you, I say. Whatever happen, whatever you do, I love you.

She whimper a little, lean her head against my chair. Thank you, she say.

But I can't stay here, I say.

But Celie, she say, how can you leave me? You're my friend. I love this child and I'm scared to death. He's a third of my age. A third of my size. Even a third of my color. She try to laugh again. You know he gon hurt me worse than I'm hurting you. Don't leave me, please.

Just then the door bell ring. Shug wiped her face and went to answer it, saw who it was and kept on out the door. Soon I heard a car drive off. I went on up to bed. But sleep remain a stranger to this night.

Pray for me,

Your sister, Celie

Dear Nettie,

The only thing keep me alive is watching Henrietta fight for her life. And boy can she fight. Every time she have an attack she scream enough to wake the dead. Us do what you say the peoples do in Africa. Us feed her yams every single day. Just our luck she hate yams and she not too polite to let us know. Everybody for miles around try to come up with yam dishes that don't taste like yams. Us git plates of yam eggs, yam chitlins, yam goat. And soup. My God, folks be making soup out of everything but shoe leather trying to kill off the yam taste. But Henrietta claim she still taste it, and is likely to throw whatever it is out the window. Us tell her in a little while she'll have three months not to eat yams, but she say that day don't seem like it ever want to come. Meanwhile, her joints all swole, she hot enough to burn, she say her head feel like its full of little white men with hammers.

Sometime I meet up with Mr. _____ visiting Henrietta. He dream up his own little sneaky recipes. For instance, one time he hid the yams in peanut butter. Us sit by the fire with Harpo and Sofia and play a hand or two of bid whist, while Suzie Q and Henrietta listen to the radio. Sometime he drive me home in his car. He still live in the same little house. He been there so long, it look just like him. Two straight chairs always on the porch, turned against the wall. Porch railings with flower cans on them. He keep it painted now though. Fresh and white. And guess what he collect just cause he like them? He collect shells. All kinds of shells. Tarrapin, snail and all kinds of shells from the sea.

Matter of fact, that's how he got me up to the house again. He was telling Sofia bout some new shell he had that made a loud sea sound when you put it to your ear. Us went up to see it. It was big and heavy and speckled like a chicken and sure enough, seem like you could hear the waves or something crashing against your ear. None of us ever seen the ocean, but Mr. _____ learn about it from books. He order shells from books too, and they all over the place.

He don't say that much about them while you looking, but he hold each one like it just arrive.

Shug one time had a seashell, he say. Long time ago, when us first met. Big white thing look like a fan. She still love shells? he ast.

Naw, I say. She love elephants now.

He wait a little while, put all the shells back in place. Then he ast me, You like any special thing?

I love birds, I say.

You know, he say, you use to remind me of a bird. Way back when you first come to live with me. You was so skinny, Lord, he say. And the least little thing happen, you looked about to fly away.

You saw that, I say.

I saw it, he said, just too big a fool to let myself care.

Well, I say, us lived through it.

We still man and wife, you know, he say.

Naw, I say, we never was.

You know, he say, you look real good since you been up in Memphis.

Yeah, I say, Shug took good care of me.

How you make your living up there? he say.

Making pants, I say.

He say, I notice everybody in the family just about wearing pants you made. But you mean you turned it into a business?

That's right, I say. But I really started it right here in your house to keep from killing you.

He look down at the floor.

Shug help me make the first pair I ever did, I say. And then, like a fool, I start to cry.

He say, Celie, tell me the truth. You don't like me cause I'm a man?

I blow my nose. Take off they pants, I say, and men look like frogs to me. No matter how you kiss 'em, as far as I'm concern, frogs is what they stay.

I see, he say.

By the time I got back home I was feeling so bad I couldn't do nothing but sleep. I tried to work on some new pants I'm trying to make for pregnant women, but just the thought of anybody gitting pregnant make me want to cry.

Your sister,
Celie

Dear Nettie,

The only piece of mail Mr. ———— ever put directly in my hand is a telegram that come from the United States Department of Defense. It say the ship you and the children and your husband left Africa in was sunk by German mines off the coast of someplace call Gibralta. They think you all drowned. Plus, the same day, all the letters I wrote to you over the years come back unopen.

I sit here in this big house by myself trying to sew, but what good is sewing gon do? What good is anything? Being alive begin to seem like a awful strain.

Your sister,
Celie

Dearest Celie,

Tashi and her mother have run away. They have gone to join the *mbeles*. Samuel and the children and I were discussing it just yesterday, and we realized we do not even know for sure the *mbeles* exist. All we know is that they are said to live deep in the forest, that they welcome runaways, and that they harass the white man's plantations and plan his destruction—or at least for his removal from their continent.

Adam and Olivia are heartbroken because they love Tashi and miss her, and because no one who has gone to join the *mbeles* ever returned. We try to keep them busy around the compound and because there is so much sickness from malaria this season there is plenty for them to do. In plowing under the Olinka's yam crop and substituting canned and powdered goods, the planters destroyed what makes them resistant to malaria. Of course they did not know this, they only wanted to take the land for rubber, but the Olinka have been eating yams to prevent malaria and to control chronic blood disease for thousands and thousands of years. Left without a sufficient supply of yams, the people—what's left of them—are sickening and dying at an alarming rate.

To tell you the truth, I fear for our own health, and especially for the children. But Samuel feels we will probably be all right, having had bouts with malaria during the first years we were here.

And how are you, dearest sister? Nearly thirty years have passed without a word between us. For all I know you may be dead. As the time nears for us to come home, Adam and Olivia ask endless questions about you, few of which I can answer. Sometimes I tell them Tashi reminds me of you. And, because there is no one finer to them than Tashi, they glow with delight. But will you still have Tashi's honest and open spirit, I wonder, when we see you again? Or will years of childbearing and abuse from Mr. _____ have destroyed it? These are thoughts I don't pursue with the children, only with my beloved companion, Samuel, who advises me not to worry, to trust in God, and to have faith in the sturdiness of my sister's soul.

God is different to us now, after all these years in Africa. More spirit than ever before, and more internal. Most people think he has to look like something or someone—a roofleaf or Christ—but we don't. And not being tied to what God looks like, frees us.

When we return to America we must have long talks about this, Celie. And perhaps Samuel and I will found a new church in our community that has no idols in it whatsoever, in which each person's spirit is encouraged to seek God directly, his belief that this is possible strengthened by us as people who also believe.

There is little to do here for entertainment, as you can imagine. We read the papers and magazines from home, play any number of African games with the children. Rehearse the African children in parts of Shakespeare's plays—Adam was always very good as Hamlet giving his To Be or Not to Be soliloquy. Corrine had firm notions of what the children should be taught and saw to it that every good book advertised in the papers became part of their library. They know many things, and I think will not find American society such a shock, except for the hatred of black people, which is also very clear in all the news. But I worry about their very African independence of opinion and outspokenness, also extreme self-centeredness. And we will be poor, Celie, and it will be years no doubt before we even own a home. How will they manage the hostility towards them, having grown up here? When I think of them in America I see them as much younger than they appear here. Much more naive. The worst we have had to endure here is indifference and a certain understandable shallowness in our personal relationships—excluding our relationship with Catherine and Tashi. After all, the Olinka know we can leave, they must stay. And, of course, none of this has to do with color. And—

Dearest Celie,

Last night I stopped writing because Olivia came in to tell me Adam is missing. He can only have gone after Tashi.

Pray for his safety,

Your sister, Nettie

Dearest Nettie,

Sometimes I think Shug never love me. I stand looking at my naked self in the looking glass. What would she love? I ast myself. My hair is short and kinky because I don't straighten it anymore. Once Shug say she love it no need to. My skin dark. My nose just a nose. My lips just lips. My body just any woman's body going through the changes of age. Nothing special here for nobody to love. No honey colored curly hair, no cuteness. Nothing young and fresh. My heart must be young and fresh though, it feel like it blooming blood.

I talk to myself a lot, standing in front the mirror. Celie, I say, happiness was just a trick in your case. Just cause you never had any before Shug, you thought it was time to have some, and that it was gon last. Even thought you had the trees with you. The whole earth. The stars. But look at you. When Shug left, happiness desert.

Every once in a while I git a postcard from Shug. Her and Germaine in New York, in California. Gone to see Mary Agnes and Grady in Panama.

Mr. _____ seem to be the only one understand my feeling.

I know you hate me for keeping you from Nettie, he say. And now she dead.

But I don't hate him, Nettie. And I don't believe you dead. How can you be dead if I still feel you? Maybe, like God, you changed into something different that I'll have to speak to in a different way, but you not dead to me Nettie. And never will be. Sometime when I git tired of talking to myself I talk to you. I even try to reach our children.

Mr. _____ still can't believe I have children. Where you git children from? he ast.

My stepdaddy, I say.

You mean he knowed he was the one damage you all along? he ast.

I say, Yeah.

Mr. _____ shake his head.

After all the evil he done I know you wonder why I don't hate him. I don't hate him for two reasons. One, he love Shug. And two, Shug use to love him. Plus, look like he trying to make something out himself. I don't mean just that he work and he clean up after himself and he appreciate some of the things God was playful enough to make. I mean when you talk to him now he really listen, and one time, out of nowhere in the conversation us was having, he said Celie, I'm satisfied this the first time I ever lived on Earth as a natural man. It feel like a new experience.

Sofia and Harpo always try to set me up with some man. They know I love Shug but they think womens love just by accident, anybody handy likely to do. Everytime I go to Harpo's some little policy salesman git all up in my face. Mr. _____ have to come to the rescue. He tell the man, This lady my wife. The man vanish out the door.

Us sit, have a cold drink. Talk about our days together with Shug. Talk about the time she come home sick. The little crooked song she use to sing. All our fine evenings down at Harpo's.

You was even sewing good way back then, he say. I remember the nice little dresses Shug always wear.

Yeah, I say. Shug could wear a dress.

Remember the night Sofia knock Mary Agnes' toofs out? he ast.

Who could forget it? I say.

Us don't say nothing bout Sofia's troubles. Us still can't laugh at that. Plus, Sofia still have trouble with that family. Well, trouble with Miss Eleanor Jane.

You just don't know, say Sofia, what that girl done put me through. You know how she use to bother me all the time when she had problems at home? Well finally she start bothering me when anything good happen. Soon as she snag that man she married she come running to me. Oh, Sofia, she say, you just have to meet Stanley Earl. And before I can say anything, Stanley Earl is in the middle of my front room.

How you, Sofia, he say, grinning and sticking out his hand. Miss Eleanor Jane done told me so much about you.

I wonder if she told him they made me sleep up under their house, say Sofia. But I don't ask. I try to be polite, act pleasant. Henrietta turn the radio up loud in the back room. I have to almost holler to make myself understood. They stand round looking at the children's pictures on the wall and saying how good my boys look in they army uniforms.

Where they fighting? Stanley Earl want to know.

They in the service right here in Georgia, I say. But pretty soon they be bound for overseas.

He ast me do I know which part they be station in? France, Germany or the Pacific.

I don't know where none of that is so I say, Naw. He say he want to fight but got to stay home and run his daddy's cotton gin.

Army got to wear clothes, he say, if they fighting in Europe. Too bad they not fighting in Africa. He laugh. Miss Eleanor Jane smile. Henrietta turn the dial high as it can go. Got on some real sorry whitefolks music sound like I don't know what. Stanley Earl snap his fingers and try to tap one of his good size foots. He got a long head go straight up and hair cut so short it look fuzzy. His eyes real bright blue and never hardly blink. Good God, I think.

Sofia raise me, practically, say Miss Eleanor Jane. Don't know what we would have done without her.

Well, say Stanley Earl, everybody round here raise by colored. That's how come we turn out so well. He wink at me, say, Well Sugar Pie, to Miss Eleanor Jane, time for us to mosey along.

She leap up like somebody stuck her with a pin. How Henrietta doing? she ast. Then she whisper, I brought her something with yams so well hid she won't never suspect. She run out to the car and come back with a tuna casserole.

Well, say Sofia, one thing you have to say for Miss Eleanor

Jane, her dishes almost always fool Henrietta. And that mean a lots to me. Of course I never tell Henrietta where they come from. If I did, out the window they would go. Else she'd vomit, like it made her sick.

But finally, the end come to Sofia and Miss Eleanor Jane, I think. And it wasn't nothing to do with Henrietta, who hate Miss Eleanor Jane's guts. It was Miss Eleanor Jane herself and that baby she went and had. Every time Sofia turned round Miss Eleanor Jane was shoving Reynolds Stanley Earl in her face. He a little fat white something without much hair, look like he headed for the Navy.

Ain't little Reynolds sweet? say Miss Eleanor Jane, to Sofia. Daddy just love him, she say. Love having a grandchild name for him and look so much like him, too.

Sofia don't say nothing, stand there ironing some of Susie Q and Henrietta's clothes.

And so smart, say Eleanor Jane. Daddy say he never saw a smarter baby. Stanley Earl's mama say he smarter than Stanley Earl was when he was this age.

Sofia still don't say nothing.

Finally Eleanor Jane notice. And you know how some white-folks is, won't let well enough alone. If they want to bad enough, they gon harass a blessing from you if it kill.

Sofia mighty quiet this morning, Miss Eleanor Jane say, like she just talking to Reynolds Stanley. He stare back at her out of his big stuck open eyes.

Don't you think he sweet? she ast again.

He sure fat, say Sofia, turning over the dress she ironing.

And he sweet, too, say Miss Eleanor Jane.

Just as plump as he can be, say Sofia. And tall.

But he sweet, too, say Eleanor Jane. And he smart. She haul off and kiss him up side the head. He rub his head, say Yee.

Ain't he the smartest baby you ever saw? she ast Sofia.

He got a nice size head on him, say Sofia. You know some peoples place a lot of weight on head size. Not a whole lot of hair on it either. He gon be cool this summer, for sure. She fold the piece she iron and put it on a chair.

Just a sweet, smart, cute, *innocent* little baby boy, say Miss

Eleanor Jane. Don't you just love him? she ast Sofia point blank.

Sofia sigh. Put down her iron. Stare at Miss Eleanor Jane and Reynolds Stanley. All the time me and Henrietta over in the corner playing pitty pat. Henrietta act like Miss Eleanor Jane ain't alive, but both of us hear the way the iron sound when Sofia put it down. The sound have a lot of old and new stuff in it.

No ma'am, say Sofia. I do not love Reynolds Stanley Earl. Now. That's what you been trying to find out ever since he was born. And now you know.

Me and Henrietta look up. Miss Eleanor Jane just that quick done put Reynolds Stanley on the floor where he crawling round knocking stuff over. Head straight for Sofia's stack of ironed clothes and pull it down on his head. Sofia take up the clothes, straighten them out, stand by the ironing board with her hand on the iron. Sofia the kind of woman no matter what she have in her hand it look like a weapon.

Eleanor Jane start to cry. She always have felt something for Sofia. If not for her, Sofia never would have survive living in her daddy's house. But so what? Sofia never wanted to be there in the first place. Never wanted to leave her own children.

Too late to cry, Miss Eleanor Jane, say Sofia. All us can do now is laugh. Look at him, she say. And she do laugh. He can't even walk and already he in my house messing it up. Did I ast him to come? Do I care whether he sweet or not? Will it make any difference in the way he grow up to treat me what I think?

You just don't like him cause he look like daddy, say Miss Eleanor Jane.

You don't like him cause he look like daddy, say Sofia. I don't feel nothing about him at all. I don't love him, I don't hate him. I just wish he couldn't run loose all the time messing up folks stuff.

All the time! All the time! say Miss Eleanor Jane. Sofia, he just a baby. Not even a year old. He only been here five or six times.

I feel like he been here forever, say Sofia.

I just don't understand, say Miss Eleanor Jane. All the other colored women I know love children. The way you feel is something unnatural.

I love children, say Sofia. But all the colored women that say they love yours is lying. They don't love Reynolds Stanley any more than I do. But if you so badly raise as to ast 'em, what you expect them to say? Some colored people so scared of white-folks they claim to love the cotton gin.

But he just a little baby! say Miss Eleanor Jane, like saying this is spose to clear up everything.

What you want from me? say Sofia. I feel something for you because out of all the people in your daddy's house you showed me some human kindness. But on the other hand, out of all the people in your daddy's house, I showed you some. Kind feeling is all I have to offer you. I don't have nothing to offer your relatives but just what they offer me. I don't have nothing to offer him.

Reynolds Stanley by this time is over on Henrietta pallet look like trying to rape her foot. Finally he start to chew her leg and Henrietta reach up on the windowsill and hand him a cracker.

I feel like you the only person love me, say Miss Eleanor Jane. Mama only love Junior, she say. Cause that's who daddy really love.

Well, say Sofia. You got your own husband to love you now.

Look like he don't love nothing but that cotton gin, she say. Ten o'clock at night and he still down there working. When he not working, he playing poker with the boys. My brother see a lot more of Stanley Earl than I do.

Maybe you ought to leave him, say Sofia. You got kin in Atlanta, go stay with some of them. Git a job.

Miss Eleanor Jane toss her hair back, act like she don't even hear this, it such a wild notion.

I got my own troubles, say Sofia, and when Reynolds Stanley grow up, he's gon be one of them.

But he won't, say Miss Eleanor Jane. I'm his mama and I won't let him be mean to colored.

You and whose army? say Sofia. The first word he likely to speak won't be nothing he learn from you.

You telling me I won't even be able to love my own son, say Miss Eleanor Jane.

No, say Sofia. That not what I'm telling you. I'm telling you *I* won't be able to love your own son. You can love him just as much as you want to. But be ready to suffer the consequences. That's how the colored live.

Little Reynolds Stanley all up on top Henrietta's face by now, just slobbering and sucking. Trying to kiss. Any second I think she gon knock him silly. But she lay real still while he zamine her. Every once in a while he act like he peeking into her eyeball. Then he sit down with a bounce on top her chest and grin. He take one of her playing cards and try to give her a bite of it.

Sofia come over and lift him off.

He not bothering me, say Henrietta. He make me tickle.

He bother me, say Sofia.

Well, Miss Eleanor Jane say to the baby, picking him up, we not wanted here. She say it real sad, like she done run out of places to go.

Thank you for all you done for us, say Sofia. She don't look so good herself, and a little water stand in her eyes. After Miss Eleanor Jane and Reynolds Stanley leave, she say, It's times like this make me know us didn't make this world. And all the colored folks talking bout loving everybody just ain't looked hard at what they thought they said.

So what else new?

Well, your sister too crazy to kill herself. Most times I feels like shit but I felt like shit before in my life and what happen? I had me a fine sister name Nettie. I had me another fine woman friend name Shug. I had me some fine children growing up in Africa, singing and writing verses. The first two months was hell though, I tell the world. But now Shug's six months is come and gone and she ain't come back. And I try to teach my heart not to want nothing it can't have.

Besides, she give me so many good years. Plus, she

learning new things in her new life. Now she and Germaine staying with one of her children.

Dear Celie, she wrote me, Me and Germaine ended up in Tucson, Arizona where one of my children live. The other two alive and turned out well but they didn't want to see me. Somebody told them I lives a evil life. This one say he want to see his mama no matter what. He live in a little mud looking house like they have out here, call adobe, so you know I feels right at home (smile). He a schoolteacher too and work on the Indian reservation. They call him the black white man. They have a word that mean that, too, and it really bother him. But even if he try to tell them how he feel, they don't seem to care. They so far gone nothing strangers say mean nothing. Everybody not a Indian they got no use for. I hate to see his feelings hurt, but that's life.

It was Germaine who had the idea to look up my children. He notice how I always love dressing him up and playing with his hair. He didn't make it like a mean suggestion. He just said if I knowed how my children was doing I would probably feel better in my life.

This son we staying with is name James. His wife is name Cora Mae. They have two kids name Davis and Cantrell. He say he thought something was funny bout his mama (my mama) cause she and big daddy was so old and strict and set in they ways. But still, he felt a lot of love from them, he say.

Yeah son, I tell him. They had a lot of love to give. But I needed love plus understanding. They run a little short of that.

They *been* dead now, he say. Nine or ten years. Sent us all to school as far as they could.

You know I never think bout mama and daddy. You know how tough I think I is. But now that they dead and I see my children doing well, I like to think about them. Maybe when I come back I can put some flowers on they graves.

Oh, she write me now near bout every week. Long newsy letters full of stuff she thought she had forgot. Plus stuff bout the desert and the Indians and the rocky mountains. I wish I could be traveling with her, but thank God she able to do it.

Sometimes I feel mad at her. Feel like I could scratch her hair right off her head. But then I think, Shug got a right to live too. She got a right to look over the world in whatever company she choose. Just cause I love her don't take away none of her rights.

The only thing bother me is she don't never say nothing bout coming back. And I miss her. I miss her friendship so much that if she want to come back here dragging Germaine I'd make them both welcome, or die trying. Who am I to tell her who to love? My job just to love her good and true myself.

Mr. _____ ast me the other day what it is I love so much bout Shug. He say he love her style. He say to tell the truth, Shug act more manly than most men. I mean she upright, honest. Speak her mind and the devil take the hindmost, he say. You know Shug will fight, he say. Just like Sofia. She bound to live her life and be herself no matter what.

Mr. _____ think all this is stuff men do. But Harpo not like this, I tell him. You not like this. What Shug got is womanly it seem like to me. Specially since she and Sofia the ones got it.

Sofia and Shug not like men, he say, but they not like women either.

You mean they not like you or me.

They hold they own, he say. And it's different.

What I love best bout Shug is what she been through, I say. When you look in Shug's eyes you know she been where she been, seen what she seen, did what she did. And now she know.

That's the truth, say Mr. _____.

And if you don't git out the way, she'll tell you about it.

Amen, he say. Then he say something that really surprise me cause it so thoughtful and common sense. When it come to what folks do together with they bodies, he say, anybody's guess is as good as mine. But when you talk bout love I don't have to guess. I have love and I have been love. And I thank God he let me gain understanding enough to know love can't be halted just cause some peoples moan and groan. It don't surprise me you love Shug Avery, he say. I have love Shug Avery all my life.

What load of bricks fell on you? I ast.

228

No bricks, he say. Just experience. You know, everybody bound to git some of that sooner or later. All they have to do is stay alive. And I start to git mine real heavy long about the time I told Shug it was true that I beat you cause you was you and not her.

I told her, I say.

I know it, he say, and I don't blame you. If a mule could tell folks how it's treated, it would. But you know some womens would have just love to hear they man say he beat his wife cause she wasn't them. Shug one time was like that bout Annie Julia. Both of us messed over my first wife a scanless. And she never told nobody. Plus, she didn't have nobody to tell. After they married her off to me her folks behave like they'd throwed her down a well. Or off the face of the earth. I didn't want her. I wanted Shug. But my daddy was the boss. He give me the wife he wanted me to have.

But Shug spoke right up for you, Celie, he say. She say Albert, you been mistreating somebody I love. So as far as you concern, I'm gone. I couldn't believe it, he say. All along in there we was as hot for each other as two pistols. Excuse me, he say. But we was. I tried to laugh it off. But she meant what she said.

I tried to tease her. You don't love old dumb Celie, I said. She ugly and skinny and can't hold a candle to you. She can't even screw.

What I want to say that for. From what she tell me, Shug said, she don't have no reason to screw. You on and off like a jackrabbit. Plus, she say, Celie say you not always clean. And she turn up her nose.

I wanted to kill you, said Mr. _____ and I did slap you around a couple of times. I never understood how you and Shug got along so well together and it bothered the hell out of me. When she was mean and nasty to you, I understood. But when I looked around and the two of you was always doing each other's hair, I start to worry.

She still feel for you, I say.

Yeah, he say. She feel like I'm her brother.

What so bad about that, I ast. Don't her brothers love her?

Them clowns, he say. They still act the fool I use to be.

Well, I say, we all have to start somewhere if us want to do better, and our own self is what us have to hand.

I'm real sorry she left you, Celie. I remember how I felt when she left me.

Then the old devil put his arms around me and just stood there on the porch with me real quiet. Way after while I bent my stiff neck onto his shoulder. Here us is, I thought, two old fools left over from love, keeping each other company under the stars.

Other times he want to know bout my children.

I told him you say they both wear long robes, sort of like dresses. That was the day he come to visit me while I was sewing and ast me what was so special bout my pants.

Anybody can wear them, I said.

Men and women not suppose to wear the same thing, he said. Men spose to wear the pants.

So I said, You ought to tell that to the mens in Africa.

Say what? he ast. First time he ever thought bout what Africans do.

People in Africa try to wear what feel comfortable in the heat, I say. Of course, missionaries have they own ideas bout dress. But left to themself, Africans wear a little sometimes, or a lot, according to Nettie. But men and women both preshate a nice dress.

Robe you said before, he say.

Robe, dress. Not pants, anyhow.

Well, he say. I'll be dog.

And men sew in Africa, too, I say.

They do? he ast.

Yeah, I say. They not so backward as mens here.

When I was growing up, he said, I use to try to sew along with mama cause that's what she was always doing. But everybody laughed at me. But you know, I liked it.

Well, nobody gon laugh at you now, I said. Here, help me stitch in these pockets.

But I don't know how, he say.

I'll show you, I said. And I did.

Now us sit sewing and talking and smoking our pipes.

Guess what, I say to him, folks in Africa where Nettie and the children is believe white people is black peoples children.

Naw, he say, like this interesting but his mind really on the slant of his next stitch.

They named Adam some other name soon as he arrive. They say the white missionaries before Nettie and them come told them all about Adam from the white folks point of view and what the white folks know. But they know who Adam is from they own point of view. And for a whole lot longer time ago.

And who that? Mr. _____ ast.

The first man that was white. Not the first man. They say nobody so crazy they think they can say who was the first man. But everybody notice the first white man cause he was white.

Mr. _____ frown, look at the different color thread us got. Thread his needle, lick his finger, tie a knot.

They say everybody before Adam was black. Then one day some woman they just right away kill, come out with this colorless baby. They thought at first it was something she ate. But then another one had one and also the women start to have twins. So the people start to put the white babies and the twins to death. So really Adam wasn't even the first white man. He was just the first one the people didn't kill.

Mr. _____ look at me real thoughtful. He not such a bad looking man, you know, when you come right down to it. And now it do begin to look like he got a lot of feeling hind his face.

Well, I say, you know black folks have what you call albinos to this day. But you never hear of white folks having nothing black unless some black man been messing with 'em. And no white folks been in Africa back yonder when all this happen.

So these Olinka people heard about Adam and Eve from the white missionaries and they heard about how the serpent tricked Eve and how God chased them out of the garden of Eden. And they was real curious to hear this, cause after they had chased the white Olinka children out of the village they hadn't hardly thought no more about it. Nettie say one thing about Africans, Out of sight, out of mind. And another thing, they don't like nothing around them that look or act different. They want everybody to be just alike. So you know somebody white wouldn't last long. She say seem like to her the Africans throwed out the white Olinka peoples for how they look. They throwed out the rest of us, all us who become slaves, for how us act. Seem like us just wouldn't do right no matter how us try. Well, you know how niggers is. Can't nobody tell 'em nothing even today. Can't be rule. Every nigger you see got a kingdom in his head.

But guess what else, I say to Mr. _____. When the missionaries got to the part bout Adam and Eve being naked, the Olinka peoples nearly bust out laughing. Especially when the missionaries tried to make them put on clothes because of this. They tried to explain to the missionaries that it was *they* who put Adam and Eve out of the village because they *was* naked. Their word for naked is white. But since they are covered by color they are not naked. They said anybody looking at a white person can tell they naked, but black people can not be naked because they can not be white.

Yeah, say Mr. _____. But they was wrong.

Right, I said. Adam and Eve prove it. What they did, these Olinka peoples, was throw out they own children, just cause they was a little different.

I bet they do that same kind of stuff today, Mr. _____ say.

Oh, from what Nettie say, them Africans is a mess. And you know what the bible say, the fruit don't fall too far from the tree. And something else, I say. Guess who they say the snake is?

Us, no doubt, say Mr. _____.

Right, I say. Whitefolks sign for they parents. They was so mad to git throwed out and told they was naked they made up they minds to crush us wherever they find us, same as they would a snake.

You reckon? Mr. _____ ast.

That's what these Olinka peoples say. But they say just like they know history before the white children start to come, they know the future after the biggest of 'em leave. They say they know these particular children and they gon kill each other off, they still so mad bout being unwanted. Gon kill off a lot of other folk too who got some color. In fact, they gon kill off so much of the earth and the colored that everybody gon hate them just like they hate us today. Then they will become the new serpent. And wherever a white person is found he'll be crush by somebody not white, just like they do us today. And some of the Olinka peoples believe life will just go on and on like this forever. And every million years or so something will happen to the earth and folks will change the way they look. Folks might start growing two heads one of these days, for all us know, and then the folks with one head will send 'em all someplace else. But some of 'em don't think like this. They think, after the biggest of the white folks no longer on the earth, the only way to stop making somebody the serpent is for everybody to accept everybody else as a child of God, or one mother's children, no matter what they look like or how they act. And guess what else about the snake?

What? he ast.

These Olinka peoples worship it. They say who knows, maybe it is kinfolks, but for sure it's the smartest, cleanest, slickest thing they ever seen.

These folks sure must have a heap of time just to sit and think, say Mr. _____.

Nettie say they real good at thinking, I say. But they think so much in terms of thousands of years they have a hard time gitting themself through one.

So what they name Adam?

Something sound like Omatangu, I say. It mean a un-naked man somewhere near the first one God made that knowed what he was. A whole lot of the men that come before the first man was men, but none of 'em didn't know it. You know how long it take some mens to notice anything, I say.

Took me long enough to notice you such good company, he say. And he laugh.

He ain't Shug, but he begin to be somebody I can talk to.

And no matter how much the telegram said you must be drown, I still git letters from you.

Your sister,

Celie

Dear Celie,

After two and a half months Adam and Tashi returned!
Adam overtook Tashi and her mother and some other members
of our compound as they were nearing the village where the
white woman missionary had lived, but Tashi would not hear of
turning back, nor would Catherine, and so Adam accompanied
them to the *mbeles* encampment.

Oh, he says, it is the most extraordinary place!

You know, Celie, in Africa there is a huge depression in the
earth called the great rift valley, but it is on the other side of the
continent from where we are. However, according to Adam,
there is a "small" rift on our side, several thousand acres large
and even deeper than the great rift, which covers millions of
acres. It is a place set so deep into the earth that it can only really
be seen, Adam thinks, from the air, and then it would seem just
an overgrown canyon. Well, in this overgrown canyon are a
thousand people from dozens of African tribes, and even one
colored man—Adam swears—from Alabama! There are farms.
There is a school. An infirmary. A temple. And there are male
and female warriors who do indeed go on missions of sabotage
against the white plantations.

But all this seemed more a marvel in the recounting than in
the actual experiencing of it, if I am any judge of Adam and
Tashi. Their minds seem to have been completely riveted on
each other.

I wish you could have seen them as they staggered into the
compound. Filthy as hogs, hair as wild as could be. Sleepy.
Exhausted. Smelly. God knows. But still arguing.

Just because I came back with you, don't think I am saying
yes to marriage, says Tashi.

Oh yes you are, says Adam, heatedly, but through a yawn. You promised your mother. *I* promised your mother.

Nobody in America will like me, says Tashi.

I will like you, says Adam.

Olivia ran and enfolded Tashi in her arms. Ran about preparing food and a bath.

Last night, after Tashi and Adam had slept most of the day, we had a family conference. We informed them that because so many of our people had gone to join the *mbeles* and the planters were beginning to bring in Moslem workers from the North, and because it was time for us to do so, we would be leaving for home in a matter of weeks.

Adam announced his desire to marry Tashi.

Tashi announced her refusal to be married.

And then, in that honest, forthright way of hers, she gave her reasons. Paramount among them that, because of the scarification marks on her cheeks Americans would look down on her as a savage and shun her, and whatever children she and Adam might have. That she had seen the magazines we receive from home and that it was very clear to her that black people did not truly admire blackskinned black people like herself, and especially did not admire blackskinned black women. They bleach their faces, she said. They fry their hair. They try to look naked.

Also, she continued, I fear Adam will be distracted by one of these naked looking women and desert me. Then I would have no country, no people, no mother and no husband and brother.

You'd have a sister, said Olivia.

Then Adam spoke. He asked Tashi to forgive his initial stupid response to the scarification. And to forgive the repugnance he'd felt about the female initiation ceremony. He assured Tashi that it was she he loved and that in America she would have country, people, parents, sister, husband, brother and lover, and that whatever befell her in America would also be his own choice and his own lot.

Oh, Celie.

So, the next day, our boy came to us with scars identical to Tashi's on his cheeks.

And they are so happy. So happy, Celie. Tashi and Adam Omatangu.

Samuel married them, of course, and all the people left in the compound came to wish them happiness and an abundance of roofleaf forever. Olivia stood up with the bride and a friend of Adam's—a man too old to have joined the *mbeles*—stood up with him. Immediately after the wedding we left the compound, riding in a lorry that took us to a boat at the coast inlet that flows out to sea.

In a few weeks, we will all be home.

Your loving sister,

Nettie

Dear Nettie,

Mr. _____ talk to Shug a lot lately by telephone. He say as soon as he told her my sister and her family was missing, she and Germaine made a beeline for the State department trying to find out what happen. He say Shug say it just kill her to think I'm down here suffering from not knowing. But nothing happen at the State department. Nothing at the department of defense. It's a big war. So much going on. One ship lost feel like nothing, I guess. Plus, colored don't count to those people.

Well, they just don't know, and never did. Never will. And so what? I know you on your way home and you may not git here till I'm ninety, but one of these days I do expect to see your face.

Meanwhile, I hired Sofia to clerk in our store. Kept the white man Alphonso got to run it, but put Sofia in there to wait on colored cause they never had nobody in a store to wait on 'em before and nobody in a store to treat 'em nice. Sofia real good at selling stuff too cause she act like she don't care if you buy or not. No skin off her nose. And then if you do decide to buy anyhow, well, she might exchange a few pleasant words with you. Plus, she scare that white man. Anybody else colored he try to call 'em auntie or something. First time he try that with Sofia she ast him which colored man his mama sister marry.

I ast Harpo do he mind if Sofia work.

What I'm gon mind for? he say. It seem to make her happy. And I can take care of anything come up at home. Anyhow, he say, Sofia got me a little help for when Henrietta need anything special to eat or git sick.

Yeah, say Sofia. Miss Eleanor Jane gon look in on Henrietta

and every other day promise to cook her something she'll eat. You know white people have a look of machinery in they kitchen. She whip up stuff with yams you'd never believe. Last week she went and made yam ice cream.

How this happen? I ast. I thought the two of you was through.

Oh, say Sofia. It finally dawn on her to ast her mama why I come to work for them.

I don't expect it to last, though, say Harpo. You know how they is.

Do her peoples know? I ast.

They know, say Sofia. They carrying on just like you know they would. Whoever heard of a white woman working for niggers, they rave. She tell them, Whoever heard of somebody like Sofia working for trash.

She bring Reynolds Stanley with her? I ast.

Henrietta say she don't mind him.

Well, say Harpo, I'm satisfied if her menfolks against her helping you, she gon quit.

Let her quit, say Sofia. It not my salvation she working for. And if she don't learn she got to face judgment for herself, she won't even have live.

Well, you got me behind you, anyway, say Harpo. And I loves every judgment you ever made. He move up and kiss her where her nose was stitch.

Sofia toss her head. Everybody learn something in life, she say. And they laugh.

Speaking of learning. Mr. _____ say one day us was sewing out on the porch, I first start to learn all them days ago I use to sit up there on my porch, staring out cross the railing.

Just miserable. That's what I was. And I couldn't understand why us have life at all if all it can do most times is make us feel bad. All I ever wanted in life was Shug Avery, he say. And one while, all she wanted in life was me. Well, us couldn't have each other, he say. I got Annie Julia. Then you. All them rotten children. She got Grady and who know who all. But still, look like she come out better than me. A lot of people love Shug, but nobody but Shug love me.

Hard not to love Shug, I say. She know how to love somebody back.

I tried to do something bout my children after you left me. But by that time it was too late. Bub come with me for two weeks, stole all my money, laid up on the porch drunk. My girls so far off into mens and religion they can't hardly talk. Everytime they open they mouth some kind of plea come out. Near bout to broke my sorry heart.

If you know your heart sorry, I say, that mean it not quite as spoilt as you think.

Anyhow, he say, you know how it is. You ast yourself one question, it lead to fifteen. I start to wonder why us need love. Why us suffer. Why us black. Why us men and women. Where do children really come from. It didn't take long to realize I didn't hardly know nothing. And that if you ast yourself why you black or a man or a woman or a bush it don't mean nothing if you don't ast why you here, period.

So what you think? I ast.

I think us here to wonder, myself. To wonder. To ast. And that in wondering bout the big things and asting bout the big things, you learn about the little ones, almost by accident. But you never know nothing more about the big things than you start out with. The more I wonder, he say, the more I love.

And people start to love you back, I bet, I say.

They do, he say, surprise. Harpo seem to love me. Sofia and the children. I think even ole evil Henrietta love me a little bit, but that's cause she know she just as big a mystery to me as the man in the moon.

Mr. _____ is busy patterning a shirt for folks to wear with my pants.

Got to have pockets, he say. Got to have loose sleeves. And definitely you not spose to wear it with no tie. Folks wearing ties look like they being lynch.

And then, just when I know I can live content without Shug, just when Mr. _____ done ast me to marry him again,

this time in the spirit as well as in the flesh, and just after I say
Naw, I still don't like frogs, but let's us be friends, Shug write
me she coming home.

Now. Is this life or not?

I be so calm.

If she come, I be happy. If she don't, I be content.

And then I figure this the lesson I was suppose to learn.

Oh Celie, she say, stepping out of the car, dress like a
moving star, I missed you more than I missed my own mama.

Us hug.

Come on in, I say.

Oh, the house look so nice, she say, when us git to her
room. You know I love pink.

Got you some elephants and turtles coming, too, I say.

Where your room? she ast.

Down the hall, I say.

Let's go see it, she say.

Well, here it is, I say, standing in the door. Everything in
my room purple and red cept the floor, that painted bright
yellow. She go right to the little purple frog perch on my
mantlepiece.

What this? she ast.

Oh, I say, a little something Albert carve for me.

She look at me funny for a minute, I look at her. Then us
laugh.

Where Germaine at? I ast.

In college, she say. Wilberforce. Can't let all that talent go to
waste. Us through, though, she say. He feel just like family
now. Like a son. Maybe a grandson. What you and Albert been
up to? she ast.

Nothing much, I say.

She say, I know Albert and I bet he been up to *some*thing,
with you looking as fine as you look.

Us sew, I say. Make idle conversation.

How idle? she ast.

What do you know, I think. Shug jealous. I have a good
mind to make up a story just to make her feel bad. But I don't.

Us talk bout you, I say. How much us love you.

She smile, come put her head on my breast. Let out a long breath.

Your sister,
Celie

Dear God. Dear stars, dear trees, dear sky, dear peoples. Dear Everything. Dear God.

Thank you for bringing my sister Nettie and our children home.

Wonder who that coming yonder? ast Albert, looking up the road. Us can see the dust just aflying.

Me and him and Shug sitting out on the porch after dinner. Talking. Not talking. Rocking and fanning flies. Shug mention she don't want to sing in public no more—well, maybe a night or two at Harpo's. Think maybe she retire. Albert say he want her to try on his new shirt. I talk bout Henrietta. Sofia. My garden and the store. How things doing generally. So much in the habit of sewing something I stitch up a bunch of scraps, try to see what I can make. The weather cool for the last of June, and sitting on the porch with Albert and Shug feel real pleasant. Next week be the fourth of July and us plan a big family reunion outdoors here at my house. Just hope the cool weather hold.

Could be the mailman, I say. Cept he driving a little fast.

Could be Sofia, say Shug. You know she drive like a maniac.

Could be Harpo, say Albert. But it not.

By now the car stop under the trees in the yard and all these peoples dress like old folks git out.

A big tall whitehaired man with a backward turn white collar, a little dumpty woman with her gray hair in plaits cross on top her head. A tall youngish man and two robust looking youngish women. The whitehaired man say something to the driver of the car and the car leave. They all stand down there at the edge of the drive surrounded by boxes and bags and all kinds of stuff.

By now my heart is in my mouth and I can't move.

It's Nettie, Albert say, gitting up.

All the people down by the drive look up at us. They look at the house. The yard. Shug and Albert's cars. They look round at the fields. Then they commence to walk real slow up the walk to the house.

I'm so scared I don't know what to do. Feel like my mind stuck. I try to speak, nothing come. Try to git up, almost fall. Shug reach down and give me a helping hand. Albert press me on the arm.

When Nettie's foot come down on the porch I almost die. I stand swaying, tween Albert and Shug. Nettie stand swaying tween Samuel and I reckon it must be Adam. Then us both start to moan and cry. Us totter toward one nother like us use to do when us was babies. Then us feel so weak when us touch, us knock each other down. But what us care? Us sit and lay there on the porch inside each other's arms.

After while, she say *Celie*.

I say *Nettie*.

Little bit more time pass. Us look round at a lot of peoples knees. Nettie never let go my waist. This my husband Samuel, she say, pointing up. These our children Olivia and Adam and this Adam's wife Tashi, she say.

I point up at my peoples. This Shug and Albert, I say.

Everybody say Pleased to Meetcha. Then Shug and Albert start to hug everybody one after the other.

Me and Nettie finally git up off the porch and I hug my children. And I hug Tashi. Then I hug Samuel.

Why us always have family reunion on July 4th, say Henrietta, mouth poke out, full of complaint. It so hot.

White people busy celebrating they independence from England July 4th, say Harpo, so most black folks don't have to work. Us can spend the day celebrating each other.

Ah, Harpo, say Mary Agnes, sipping some lemonade, I didn't know you knowed history. She and Sofia working together on the potato salad. Mary Agnes come back home to pick up Suzie Q. She done left Grady, move back to Memphis and live with her sister and her ma. They gon look after Suzie Q while she work. She got a lot of new songs, she say, and not too knocked out to sing 'em.

After while, being with Grady, I couldn't think, she say. Plus, he not a good influence for no child. Course, I wasn't either, she say. Smoking so much reefer.

Everybody make a lot of miration over Tashi. People look at her and Adam's scars like that's they business. Say they never suspect African ladies could look so *good*. They make a fine couple. Speak a little funny, but us gitting use to it.

What your people love best to eat over there in Africa? us ast.

She sort of blush and say *barbecue*.

Everybody laugh and stuff her with one more piece.

I feel a little peculiar round the children. For one thing, they grown. And I see they think me and Nettie and Shug and Albert and Samuel and Harpo and Sofia and Jack and Odessa real old and don't know much what going on. But I don't think us feel old at all. And us so happy. Matter of fact, I think this the youngest us ever felt.

Amen

I thank everybody in this book for coming.
A.W., author and medium